THE SPINWARD FRINGE SERIES

For other books by Randolph Lalonde visit:
www.RandolphLalonde.com

Spinward Fringe Broadcast 7

FRAMEWORK

Book 3 of the Rogue Element Trilogy

Randolph Lalonde

Print ISBN: 978-0-9865942-8-1
EBook ISBN: 978-0-9865942-9-8

To science fiction fans around the world, especially the few who have been waiting for this book.
I hope you find an ending. I hope you find a beginning.

CHAPTER 1
BEAST OF BURDEN

The glare of the sun streaming through the window to Roman's left was so bright it was almost blinding. The golden rays were a welcome sight even though they carried no warmth with them. He and his hostess were on one side of a rectangular room with rounded corners. He sat across from her at a small wrought iron table. A piping hot pot of black tea, two cups, and a plate of blueberry biscuits had been placed on the transparent top.

His finger traced the edge of the fine porcelain cup in front of him as he muttered, "I can't believe the new configuration of events brought me here. Since I took guardianship of the Victory Machine and began seeing, I've noticed you from afar. But not once was there an indication that you were anything but a secondary influence on the future. I've watched you help the main influencers since Pandem, alter the course of lives without realizing it, and I've seen you die five times after Ayan the First sighed her last. None of that made a lasting difference to humanity's collective fate."

"You've seen me die?" an older Ayan the Second said with an upraised eyebrow. Her manner was lighter in her current iteration, and her British accent thicker.

"Your worst fate came as you were about to leave Pandem." He only allowed himself to glance at her, but it was enough to take in the image of the woman she'd become. The first dozen times he'd seen her in the future she appeared wildly different, but that started to change. In the last few versions of the future, he couldn't help noticing that Ayan the Second's appearance and demeanour were becoming more and more consistent.

He allowed himself to take in the image of her as she existed in the future he was visiting. Long curly red hair trickled down the front of a long overcoat of thin synthetic material. It was marked with a skull on the left and a many-pointed star on the right. Her clothing wasn't the style he'd expected, either. Her vacsuit was layered, with loosened sleeves and a skirted waist. "Valance saved you with framework regeneration after you were shot in the back. He still doesn't know how, but he was able to take direct control of the technology. I should have known you would be his inspiration for becoming a true model two. The future you create by surviving is the most unlikely one, but it's the one I'm living in."

"I was supposed to stay dead, then," she said.

"The likelihood of Valance discovering that the limitations on his framework body were all in his mind were small. He was supposed to fail and retreat into darkness until the beginning of the Fifth Era," Roman said.

"And then?"

"Go on a rampage across the stars. His name was to be listed with Attila, Cortez, Napoleon, and Riz-Tain in history."

1

"He's not far from that now," Ayan said.

"But your existence, your actions since your arrival on Tamber in this new timeline, have changed him. What you have watched come to pass over the past nine years is vastly different from the timeline I've been watching all this time." Roman tried to pick up the teacup with a trembling hand, but gave up as it rattled against the saucer.

"The Machine is nearly critical, your vision is fading. What is it you're here to ask me? How can I help you understand the situation in this future?" Ayan the Second asked quietly. There was great sympathy in her manner.

It gave him pause and he stared at her openly. "I've been dealing with the last rogue element, Valance, for so long that I had forgotten these visions can be a refuge."

"Only of the mind," she said.

"Yes, and I think that is why I've dreamed you up using the Machine and all the history it remembers. If I approach you in this timeline to try to stop the destruction of Pandem, will it change everything I've seen here? Will Haven Shore still exist? Will the darkness still stop at the gate?"

Ayan the Second paused a moment, staring at him with kind blue eyes.

Roman knew the pause was a result of the Victory Machine calculating. It was considering the actions of billions of individuals over the nine years that were yet to pass. A violent tremor seized him and he wrapped his arms around himself tightly to try and suppress it.

As the calculations completed, Ayan the Second smiled. "The likelihood of anyone saving the new populace of Pandem is minimal, in the thousandths of a percent. The key to causing a brighter future is in another place. You came here, to this time, to this version of Ayan because showing her what she can become early in the Fifth Era will only affect positive change. As far as the darkness you used to whisper to Hampon about, well, your efforts to set him on a path to save what's important have borne too much fruit. His course, and that of Pandem, are irreversible – but that could be for the best."

"What about Valance? What if I approach him instead of Ayan the Second? If I approach him on his ship to warn him about the days ahead, will he still kill Hampon and Eve then save Pandem?"

"That was always a precarious future, Roman. Unlikely. Besides, you could ruin everyone surrounding him if you force him in an unnatural direction. He was made for desperate times, you'll see."

"But it was more certain when he was the rogue element, when Hampon, Meunez, and Wheeler were watching him from afar."

"I am the primary rogue element now. The path on which you see Valance is as certain as any part of the shifting future can be. Consider carefully which prescient instant you show Ayan the Second. She is at a crossroads. One set of choices will ensure the destruction of everything around her. It would be the kind of wildfire that could make way for a period of growth. Another will lead to a war that could last a century, but there would be recovery in some areas while it rages on. The third and riskiest path will cut the Fifth Era War short. Few lives lost, much higher risks taken, and great sacrifices that will leave jagged scars on the future."

"What information will she need the most? How can I assure she takes the right path?" Roman asked.

Ayan the Second fixed him with a knowing smile. "You already know the answer. Every version of Ayan has a need to improve her environment and protect the people she cares for. You only have to convince her to continue to apply those instincts on a large scale. The burden you place on her is not only something she is capable of carrying, but it's the only way she'll have a truly fulfilling life. It's what she's waiting for and what she resists at the same time."

It was difficult for Roman to collect his thoughts through his increasing tremors and the pressure building in his chest. The Victory Machine's wormhole originating from the future generated temporal radiation, and it could only store so much as energy before it had to be released. It was almost at capacity. "Then it's as simple as providing her with the right purpose."

Roman looked directly into the golden sunlight, still marveling at the simplicity and elegance of his realization. For the first time, the light warmed him and he had a moment of peace as he watched the new future reconfigure itself towards a more positive balance. A tremor shook him hard enough to rattle the tea set on the table, reminding him that what he was only a directed dream informed by his companion, the Victory Machine.

"It was good meeting you," Ayan said with a wink.

It was the last thing he saw before abruptly waking in the wasted alley he'd taken refuge in the night before. No one bothered to so much as glance at a man in a filthy old hazard suit, especially when he was lying in a pile of garbage. The readings from the Victory Machine indicated that it couldn't contain any more of the byproduct energy from the microscopic high compression wormhole at its centre. The cables attaching him to it were getting warm, the temperature in his suit was rising, there wasn't much time left.

He struggled to his feet and shambled down the alley into the busy walkway of Caine, a Regent Galactic sponsored city just outside the edge of their conquered space. The people going about their daily lives gave him plenty of room. To them, he was an emaciated man in a dirty old hazard suit carrying a battered case. A group of people dressed in business attire - colourful blouses, pressed square-cut suits and clean casual wear - stared at him from across the street.

Roman stared back as he pictured the interior of the Triton, concentrating on it as his only desired destination. There was more than enough power collected for the Victory Machine to open a secondary wormhole that would take him there in one-one-hundredth the time it would for the most highly powered generator. He only had to direct it properly.

He felt the Victory Machine confirm his destination through the neural link and the case opened. Roman closed his eyes and raised the device up in front of him.

"What's that? Some kinda old camping lantern?" he heard one passerby ask.

"Someone should tell him to turn it down," another winced.

Before anyone could get too close, Roman felt the familiar crushing force embrace him. The instant before he lost consciousness, he found himself growing eager. It felt like he was once again on the right path. All the previous choices he'd made while influencing events seemed to fall neatly in place behind the new direction he was taking. Seeking out Ayan the Second and gifting her with purpose, setting her up in the centre of the human struggle would be a fitting final act.

Chapter 2
Gabriel Meunez

To the surprise of the hundreds of people on Aegis Street that morning, a surge of light brought about the disappearance of the man in the old hazard suit. Some thought he was vaporized by some kind of localized explosion, others assumed he was some kind of street performer, while even more still forgot about the incident by noon.

One onlooker knew exactly what it was. Gabriel Meunez watched playback of the incident minutes later from the Regent Galactic central control room. His mind was flooded with energy readings and his wasted mouth stretched in a broad grin. The Victory Machine was hiding on one of our own worlds, he thought to himself. Citadel was right to entrust Roman with guardianship over it all this time. He must be near death if he's exposing himself now, though. Hampon had been frantically searching for him ever since the transmission frequency changed. If I hurry, I might be able to obtain the Victory Machine for myself.

An irrational lust rose in Meunez as he considered the thought of being connected to a machine that could not only see into the future, but calculate how to change it. Ever since they discovered the Machine's frequency when they were working with Vindyne, it had been an obsession of Hampon's, and Meunez never had to ask why. The power that came with such a device was obvious.

If he hadn't been distracted by his brush with Alice on the Overlord II, he suspected he would have shared Hampon's obsession. As he sat in the control chair, connected to the entire Regent Galactic network through numerous cables affixed to the cybernetic portion of his brain, he weighed the advantages and disadvantages of going after the device personally.

All the while, he focused the computing power at his command, entire planets worth of networked processors, on discovering the destination of the crush gate style wormhole Roman had taken. Even with all that power, he was unable to determine the wasted man's destination with a great deal of accuracy, but the general directionality determined without a doubt that Roman was headed in Pandem's general direction.

"So he goes to see either Hampon, Eve, or the enemy settling in the Rega Gain system. I'm going to find you, Roman. I'm going to find you myself, so no one can get between me and the Victory Machine." He took a deep, painful, shuddering breath in preparation for what would come next.

One hundred and five worlds were within the scope of his vision, with all their recruitment centres, shopping complexes, temples, concourses, and trillions of points of access. The nirvana of direct contact, instant access to information was coming to an end. He would have access, but without the nest of cables surrounding him, it wouldn't be certain or as quick. He would have to settle for limited, wireless contact, but he vowed to make the most of it.

His work in Regent Galactic space was complete. Eve would be more than satisfied. He had even managed to tame the virus she'd implanted in his mind. Gabriel Meunez re-tasked the thing and sent it out into the Regent Galactic network with a pure purpose, one that it served brilliantly.

It assisted him in directing the general policies of over a hundred worlds, driving trillions of people to embrace the Order of Eden and invest their currency and themselves in the advancement towards Eden itself. The Holocaust Virus had struck every world under Meunez's control, only this time he orchestrated the destruction with the help of Eve's version of the virus.

A halftime machine-versus-machine derby at a Crush League Rugby tournament turned into a blood bath when every mechanised being turned on the audience. Thousands were killed, none of whom had purchased their membership with the Order of Eden. In Yimporo Square, automated vendors and security androids suddenly began an all out assault on the crowd during the Morrison Music Festival. Only one Order of Eden believer was superficially injured, but thousands who hadn't paid their hundred thousand credits were slain.

His most recent demonstration of Eve's updated Holocaust Virus was seen across all of his worlds, as sky transports carrying non-Eden registrants simply fell out of the sky, killing most of their passengers when they hurtled towards other unregistered civilians like guided missiles. It was clear to those who didn't ponder the reasons behind the attacks for too long that you had to raise the funds required to register with the Order of Eden and join the Enlightenment Program or be killed by the Holocaust Virus.

In Eden the people found protection, peace, and enlightenment while they travelled the path to paradise. Actors were promised great advancement to appear and publicly offer testimony. Several citizens actually recorded a journey to Eden Prime for all to see. They were perfect examples of good followers who spent incredible amounts of time and currency on progressing down the path to paradise. Each was sure evidence that it was possible to reach paradise during their lifetime using the tools provided. The world they were delivered to was a terraformed jewel in the Axet solar system. No one would ever know that their entire Ascension to Eden experience was an elaborate show.

The protesters made it interesting. They gathered in places they thought machines couldn't go or see. There was no such place. They claimed to use electrical tools that couldn't contain an artificial intelligence, but they were moronic to think that even simple tools were out of reach. Either he, or Eve's Holocaust Virus, would reach out and orchestrate their destruction by finding ways to assume control. While the bulk of the resistance tried to live out of his sight, others endeavoured to get their message out to the people. He'd twist their words, turning one well-known expression - Hate Fate - into Fate Hates and place it on wanted posters. The rewards for turning in those individuals who fought the Order would go towards a follower's Ascension, a valuable step forward for anyone who yearned to enter paradise. The protestors were foolish to remain on Regent Galactic worlds; anywhere else would have been safer, but they believed that Regent Galactic had to be convinced as well. Little did they know that the board of directors were dead, that one man and the virus itself had complete control. The Order of Eden had infected the Regent Galactic worlds, and there was no curing them.

Over thirty percent of the population endeavoured to ascend to Eden, while over forty-two had paid their registration fee. Those were numbers he could live with and he knew that, in his absence, the mass slavery would continue. The ultimate quest to own what no one could hold in their hands, a place in paradise, would be undertaken by billions more.

People who couldn't afford to register robbed until they could and then worked themselves to the bone for penance. The ones with nothing worked the hardest, sacrificed the most, and he hated them more than anything he'd ever seen. They were useless as anything but workers, and he made sure they were pressed the hardest.

Yes, he had fulfilled his mission. Yes, Eve would be proud. He surveyed the worlds under his control for a lingering moment, and allowed himself a moment of pride. Regardless of all his work, the changes he'd made, and the power he'd come to enjoy, to remain in that chair at the centre of Regent Galactic space was to be put aside. He was where Hampon and Eve could watch him, neatly out of the way.

He had lost track of Alice completely, and after weeks of hoping that he'd glance some sign of her as he reconfigured the core Regent Galactic worlds, he found nothing. With the new Holocaust Virus trained to work in his stead, and the Victory Machine in the open, he would be a fool not to reach for a new destiny. Perhaps if he could not find Alice in the ever-expanding digital universe, he could find her in time. A person could not go swiftly backwards in a timeline, but it was possible to look, communicate, and to transport data both ways. If he could not find her using the means he had, he would bring her forward in time from where he last saw her.

That pang in his heart was what drove him to finally let go of all the power he'd become attached to. His new understanding of the universe and sense of what must be would be concentrated on locating the Victory Machine and taking it for himself. "I will take it and reconnect with the networks of the universe, conduct existence like a symphony. Alice, whether as an AI or in person, will be at my side."

In the weeks of existing attached to the vast Regent Galactic network, Gabriel Meunez had forgotten to watch over his physical wellbeing. When he finally did, he saw nothing but a wasted thing in a state of slow decay. His cybernetic mind had expanded outside of his skull, and pain wracked his joints from nanobot contamination. Blood toxicity overworked his biological maintenance implants, and he didn't have long left. He could either move entirely into a computer system, or transfer as much of himself as possible into a form made specifically for his needs.

He chose the latter, knowing that most of his personality had moved out of his biological mind, and into the mechanical. He sent a signal to a darkened gallery in the Kraken and watched as his new body was swiftly constructed. After only a few moments, the new framework, with cybernetic assistant nodes to increase his pace and depth of thought and several backup modules to preserve his being, was ready.

The Kraken descended towards the city of New Versailles, its nine kilometre width casting a shadow over the forest of sky scrapers. In a quarter of a second all that was Gabriel Meunez was transmitted up to the gargantuan ship's new Genesis Hall.

Gabriel felt hollow at first, as if he were missing a critical element that made him who he was. All the information was there, he'd made the transfer to the bare framework that awaited him, but there was still something missing.

He watched from inside as the materializer and nanobot systems initiated, creating flesh, supplemental bone, and sinew from raw energy. The second phase of his data transfer began as soon as his human brain was constructed, and the compressed image of his old human mind was transplanted. The connection between active cybernetics and living brain was made, and Gabriel opened his eyes. It was like taking a deep breath after nearly suffocating.

The Lauren Star's white light bathed the massive octagonal Genesis chamber and cast long shadows to his left. There were technicians waiting for him, and they helped him dress. In the polished deck he could see his reborn face, youthful and smiling. Straight white hair framed that comely visage and was long enough to tickle the back of his neck. His body had come out fit, sculpted to match the current style of taught muscle, and health. He would have to eat and exercise, do all the things that humans did. He would be as Alice was, dedicated to being connected with their environment in both ways, through the physical and digital.

His servants helped him into simple leggings with a hidden emergency vacuum suit built in, a long tailed, loosely fit dark green shirt that tended to open at the front, and a green jacket that had no sleeves or sides. Two panels hung down to his shins in the front and it flared out into a wide tailed back. It was adorned with silver thread, like something the monarchs of old wore. When they had him dressed, one white suited servant stepped in front of him and unrolled a full-length mirror.

"That will do," he managed to say, though the words felt strange. It had only been weeks since he'd used a mouth to speak, but it felt like years and it would take some getting used to.

He glanced around the room and smiled even more brightly at seeing all the identical faces. There were three identical men and four identical women, all of them version one framework constructs made to serve his every personal need. Looking past them, he looked to the stadium sized Genesis Deck, where twenty thousand framework cubicles housed silver skeletons, all ready to be born, all ready to serve in whatever capacity he desired.

"Inform Command: we are to set course for Thamba, meet our new Caran Enterprises fleet, and then proceed to Pandem. We will make an appearance and begin tracking my target." He passed his own orders to the Command level several decks down, but it felt good to announce his intentions. There was something particularly robust about filling the air with words that would change the universe.

Chapter 3
The More You Know...

"Break's over in fifteen minutes," said Technical Crewman Sitte over Ashley's work band. She was easy to work for, an issyrian who preferred to remain in the form of a human woman. Ashley had half a day with her crew of workers, or knuckle draggers as they had come to be called. They were moving components and high tolerance metal beams from the tall pile of salvage from the command ship they'd captured, the Enforcer 1109.

The pieces were too small for the loader suits to bother with, but too big for most people outside of a vacsuit with muscle augmentation to budge. The work detail was all part of the Samson crew's effort to mix in. The worst thing was, they all had to keep their suits sealed, showing no identifying features. Even though Ashley knew the air would be rich with the fragrances of grease, cheap burnt fuel, and garbage, she wanted nothing more than to retract her head piece and experience the open air.

The sunlight gleaming down between the swiftly moving air traffic overhead made that freedom even more enticing. Stephanie and Captain Valance had a plan, however, and Ashley wouldn't be the first to violate it. Hiding in plain sight had kept them safe from bounty hunters for weeks. There had been several breaches in their perimeter by people who snuck in to steal what they could carry, or to bag themselves a Samson crewmember.

Ashley looked through the crack between the three metre by three metre storage crates she hid behind. The landing site Ayan had bargained for weeks before had become a city. Over two thousand people from the Triton remained, including most of the slaves they rescued. Staying in the Triton settlement was safer than wandering out into the dangerous shanty port. After being there for a few weeks, Ashley started hearing about other safe havens, however. Drifton was rough, a gutter by most standards, but she knew she could find work there, possibly get on with another crew, and it was a social hub. That was the kind of place where she could endear herself to people who would want her for themselves, new protectors.

The thought of leaving the Triton crew made her heart ache, but as time drew on and she continued to fail at contacting the Trition's main computer, it became more evident that her crime against them would get her kicked from the crew. *As soon as they find out I've been holding master control codes without telling them for weeks, they'll just put me off. Don't blame them though, I should have told Captain right away, but there's no knowing where Larry is. If he found out I blabbed about him and Citadel, he'd kill me in my sleep.*

Ashley used her head's up display as an interface, gesturing with glances until she managed to open a secure channel to the Triton through the General Solar System Network. It was something she tried to do several times a day. She waited for the ship to reply.

SPECIFIED RECIPIENT IS UNAVAILABLE, came the reply she had

grown accustomed to. Ashley tried Larry.

CREWMEMBER IS OUT OF RANGE, replied Crewcast after searching for several seconds.

Ashley sighed and shook her head. Just as she was about to creep out from behind the crates, something in the corner of her eye drew her attention. A glance through the crack revealed someone in a black vacsuit looking straight at her. Without thinking she jerked to the side, hiding completely behind one of the storage blocks. *Well, that's not suspicious at all,* Ashley scolded herself.

She walked out of the narrow lane between the crates, struggling with the exit because her vacsuit had been inflated a little in some places to disguise her body shape, but managed to squeak out without looking too ridiculous. She looked around and didn't see Jason. A hand on her shoulder made her jump.

"It's me, Steph," the unmarked worker said. They were all in bright green suits. "You okay?"

"Fine. Well, really sore, but okay," Ashley said, relaxing a little. "Just hard to tell who's who with all of us dressed the same."

"I know, but I don't mind the work. This 'different job every day' stuff is clearing my head and getting me back in shape," Stephanie replied. "What hurts? Anything serious?"

"Everything hurts," Ashley said, stretching. "I thought the muscles in the suit were s'posed to take care of all the work. I didn't think this would be such a workout."

They started walking down a street that ran between five shipping containers that had become home to hundreds. Workers dressed in green were a common sight, and Triton security forces in black patrolled leisurely, holding rifles across their chests. Other numerous workers in grey or blue made their way around carrying tools and chatting in groups. Along the roadside, people on their days off and civilians went about their business taking care of children, chatting their time away, or playing games some of the former slaves brought with them. Dominos and dice were favourites.

"Welcome to the world of the labour ranks," Stephanie said. "Just moving those muscles of yours is enough to get you back into shape. Did you hear that Ayan started drilling with Oz and his troops?"

"No, why would she have to do that?" Ashley asked.

"I think she's trying to slim down the hard way and training muscle memory," Stephanie said. "Rumour is that that new body of hers has never jogged or marched in its life, so she's trying to get it back up to her standards."

"That's gotta suck," Ashley said.

"Sure, but I'd pay real GC to see her sweat for a while," Stephanie chuckled. "I tried to catch them training outside the main hangar yesterday but just missed them."

"Do you miss it?" Ashley asked.

"What?"

"The military stuff, training, security and being in charge."

"In the mood for poking at open wounds today?" Stephanie asked.

"Ohmigosh, I'm sorry. I was just askin', I mean, I miss flying around, I thought-"

"I'm just buggin' ya," Stephanie said, resting a calming hand on Ashley's arm. "Are you really okay? You seem really high strung."

"It's just," Ashley scrambled for the best, easiest, most believable excuse, glad that Stephanie couldn't scan her for signs of deceit. "Since we left the Triton things have been," she hesitated, "wrong."

"We'll get back up," Stephanie said. "Don't worry. Just take this duty rotation as time to think and learn about what's going into that," she said, gesturing towards the hangar doors ahead.

They came through the side door of the main hangar. Ashley looked upon the Samson, where it rested in scaffolding. The frame of the upper hull was being rebuilt while crewmembers on the rest of the hull were getting it ready for its new skin. Uninsulated cables were being anchored to the finished frame down the length of the ship, while other crewmen welded plates of activated ergranian steel intermittently across the ship's exterior.

Two gutted ships brought down from the Enforcer 1109 were piled just outside the hangar. They had become the source of so many of their components since they were flown down, including new rotary engines for the Samson. They lay at the rear of the older ship, waiting to be lifted into place and wired in. Ground crews were pairing them up, welding them together with heavy bars and wiring them up so the power of two captured ships would become half the thrust available to the Samson.

"Captain says they're a week away from her first flight," Stephanie said.

"He said that last week," Ashley sighed.

"This time Laura and Frost are saying it too," Stephanie replied. "With all this manpower, I think they're right. She's going to be better than ever."

"I hope I get to fly her," Ashley said.

"Who else would?" Stephanie asked, laughing lightly.

"Break's over," announced their boss for the day.

CHAPTER 4
LIMITED EVE

One metre by one metre doors lined the walls of the seemingly endless labyrinth of the Rasa Vin Hotel. Few of the doors to the tiny rooms were open. She was looking for one door in particular: 3570b. Someone was chasing her. She swore she could feel their eyes on her bare back right before she rounded the corner.

The few transients who hung out of their holes to get some air turned their heads as she ran passed, half dressed and struggling to hold her jacket as she shoved her arms into her suit. The door she was looking at wasn't far off. Reaching it meant escape, and she'd be among friends again.

An explosion of sparks beside her urged her around the next corner faster than the last, and she cursed the freshly washed, slick floor as she slid into a ladder.

The dreamt impact jerked Eve awake. Her body was being held aloft by an antigravity field in a containment chamber, and she could immediately tell she wasn't connected to any of the systems around her. The chamber door opened and the field moved her out of the small cylindrical space where a pair of women in faded orange technician uniforms waited.

The lighting was subdued but it still took her a moment to adjust. There were several rows of upright, cylindrical suspension chambers marked with red, green, and blue on the top. She remembered what the colour scheme meant from browsing through the ship's systems. A red designation meant that the occupant was suspended in liquid for long term, green was for shorter-term antigravity suspension, and blue meant the occupant was in accelerated recovery from a medical procedure. She looked over her shoulder as her capsule closed and was shocked to see blue markings. As it re-sealed and began self-sterilisation procedures, the markings faded.

The absence of connectivity put Eve on edge. The two people that greeted her were a mystery. There was no way to look them up in a computer system, find out their service history or glean some sense of their personalities from personal data. "Where am I?" she asked quietly, as though it was the ultimate expression of ignorance. Eve felt like she was in the middle of a tug of war between fear and frustration.

"You're in the Overlord Two's secure containment facility," one of the female technicians answered as she helped Eve into a white, fitted short-legged bodysuit made of a material she didn't recognise. "General Hampon's inner cloister."

"What is this?" The frustration at having to ask was maddening.

"It's a personal management suit. It'll change shape, colour, and temperature depending on your needs. It also includes all the computing devices you might need; it's standard on the Overlord. I'm Lina, by the way. General Hampon has put me in charge of your personal needs," she said as she helped Eve into a dark green jacket with long tails that reached so far forward that it was more like a skirt.

"What has he done to me?"

"He saved you. If you'll follow me, you'll be able to ask him yourself. This room doesn't allow communications with the outside so everyone in these capsules is protected," she answered as she helped her put low-topped boots on.

Eve followed Lina down an aisle and when she saw the door they were headed towards she picked up the pace, passing the woman. The door opened to a room with a transparent wall opposite. The green and blue globe of Pandem dominated the view. A group of Regent Galactic destroyers passed between them and the atmosphere. She instinctively reached out to identify what she was seeing and find out more about her own location on the ship but found nothing to connect with. Her frustration began to grow into anger.

The room was furnished with comfortable seating and tables. Some kind of waiting or observation room, she guessed. Eve called up an interface on the table and tried to locate herself, to find out why she was in stasis. She only had access to the older data archive. There was an incredible amount of knowledge stored there, but she had no way to see scanners, recent security records, or anything else she wanted at that moment. "Hampon!" she cried as she whirled about. Her mind worked to find a way to communicate with any system wirelessly by reflex.

At long last a hologram of his face appeared in front of her. "I'm here, Eve."

"What did you do to me? Why have you put me in this prison?"

"I had to isolate you in my section of the ship for your own safety. Your connection to the Overlord Two woke something that was buried deep in her systems and there was no other way of isolating you from it."

"What are you talking about? How could that help me when I was fighting for control of my body with Gloria? I'd think the solution would be in sanitising my framework backup systems or-"

"Let me put it this way; Gloria Parker is dead. Her mind was scanned years ago to see if she had the potential to become a candidate for the Jonas program, but she fell short, so the scans were deleted. When her brain was removed from the body you occupy, Gloria Parker was killed."

"Then how was she still present?"

"She wasn't. Somehow trace elements of the DLG virus that infected this ship years ago was interfacing with you without your knowledge using your neural communications systems."

"Impossible, I would have sensed it," Eve replied.

"Oh? So it's more likely that the ghost of Gloria Parker was taking control of you whenever you were at rest or mentally exhausted? No, our theory makes more sense, especially since we've managed to find evidence that all of Gloria Parker's records were accessed several times by a program that looks much like the DLG virus. It wanted you to think a memory imprint from Gloria Parker was trying to take possession of you while it was committing sabotage through you."

"Some of the DLG program features were base components for the Holocaust Virus, but they were so integrated that it couldn't have acted on its own."

"You're right, that's why I'm of the mind that the DLG virus was in a dormant system you must have activated while you were exploring the ship's computers. It infected your limiter chip and used it to take over whenever it could. It may have even been watching while you were in control. We were able to subdue you, place you in a dormant state and then remove your direct neural computing systems," Hampon explained.

"Why don't I remember any of this?"

"We had to purge your framework backup systems completely, deleting several minutes of memory. You attempted to kill me moments after we met. It took several guards to subdue you. The only way to render you unconscious was to shoot you with several electromagnetic rifles. Apparently, whatever was left of the DLG virus was out for revenge, but that's just an assumption based on my experience with it and the Jonas program."

"You didn't contain the virus?" Eve asked, outraged.

"It used your neural communications system to escape. I'm sorry," Hampon replied casually.

"Wait, if the cloistered section of the ship suppresses wireless communications, how did she transmit herself?"

"The answer will lead to more questions, but you deserve to know. Watch." A holographic image of Hampon in his life extension chair appeared in front of them. The hideous display was enough to cause Lina to flinch. She looked away from the scrap of a human being with its blood cleansing tubes, emergency materialisation nodes crawling across his sores and lesions. The playback started and Eve watched an image of herself leap atop the rotting man, savagely tearing at two red tubes in Hampon's neck. Blood sprayed, Hampon panicked, trapped in place. His working arm tried to fend her off as she dug her hand into a soft, pink span of flesh on his stomach. "You won't kill these people! I should have stayed on the Overlord the first time and murdered you when I had the chance!"

Guards finally got their hands on her, and she ripped a data cable from the base of Hampon's skull. Without hesitation she jammed it into her mouth and gripped the back of the seat. One guard tried to rip it out but she held it firmly between clenched teeth. Blood seeped from one eye as her face twisted in agony. Two guards managed to pull her off, and she was shot several times, the electromag rounds made her twitch and writhe.

"I was almost killed," Hampon said as the image faded. "I assumed that whatever was taking control of you was doing so wirelessly, and I was wrong."

"Evidently," Eve said quietly.

"It could be anywhere in the fleet by now, but we're running scans. We've verified that your system has been purged, however. You are yourself."

"No, I'm a shadow of myself, unable to control anything remotely. What's worse, there are whole segments of this ship's memory that I can't access anymore. I can't even look up this Jonas program you keep bringing up."

"It's a failed initiative. We're more interested in developing the framework system into a full-fledged foundation for a new life form."

"I don't care about your programs or initiatives! Return me to full functionality!"

"You could not deal with the DLG virus if it comes out of hiding again. Remember what it accomplished using the guise of Gloria last time? It hijacked your project and sent it after me with a small army of framework soldiers."

"I'll know what to look for this time. I suspected that there was something else behind my... episodes before."

"Nonsense. You were completely fooled, terrified. Once we've found and eradicated the DLG virus and any backups, I'll consider modifying your limiter chip so you can regenerate your neural communication systems."

"I can help you find it if you-" Eve pleaded.

"No. The best thing you can do is join me in completing the New Genesis program. We need to increase the regeneration speed of framework systems by over nine hundred percent to accomplish my goal."

Even knowing what she was looking for, it took Eve several seconds to locate the data on the New Genesis program and several minutes to review it on the computer screen. "If I complete this project for you, then you'll find a way to re-enable my neural communications systems?"

"Complete this project? You think it's that easy? We've been working on it for years, in fact, you're in the body of the first test subject that showed any measure of promise."

"I know," Eve said as she walked to a table. With a hurried hand she brought up the fleet interface and began scanning nearby space. "Where are the primary elements of my fleet?"

"A sizeable portion of the Eden Fleet took their place three light years from here to begin construction on armed platforms so we can enforce our new frontier. They began work a little over two weeks ago."

Eve checked for data referring to what he was saying and discovered the Eden Frontier. She activated the long range sensors of the nearest hypertransmitter and focused in on a three hundred meter long ship with several small hangars. Broad solar collectors extended from its sides, and large arrays of dark intake cones splayed out from the bottom and front.

"It looks like a silver butterfly, beautiful," Lina commented from behind her.

"It is a manufacturing ship. Given the right conditions, it can fabricate hundreds of drones in a standard day, and those enable it to create much more. I cannot command it without a neural interface. Hampon, order this ship to join us here."

"It is needed in that section," Hampon said stoically. "We must create a manageable perimeter. Enemy forces are already scanning our Frontier."

"If you want me to improve the framework technology I need the systems on that ship. I'll also need to understand how limiter chips work."

"So you can modify your own when you're ready to connect to the network before we've taken care of the DLG virus? You'd be at its mercy if it saw your presence on the network again. You need to learn to protect yourself first, to focus."

"Then teach me, but without knowing what the limiter chip does and how, I will only be able to improve framework technology so much."

"I will give you access to the Jonas project. You'll be able to find everything you need there," Hampon said.

"And my construction vessel?" Eve asked.

"We can fabricate anything it can on this ship. The Overlord Two is fully equipped."

"Yes, but it cannot fabricate in the same way, or at the same resolution or speed," Eve retorted as she brought up a decryption interface and began to enter an equation.

"Tell me what Eden technology you need and why so we can work together on this problem."

"Never mind," she said as she finished entering the numerical sequence and sent it to the fabrication ship. "I've just ordered it to come to me. It would take me months to teach your people how to construct the equipment I need. That ship will arrive tomorrow with everything I require to solve your problem. Eden technology has been capable of what you propose with machines for well over a century. Combining Eden and framework technology properly will solve your problem."

"You know the technology," Hampon said. "You don't need the fabrication ship, you only need to run simulations. I am not asking you for a prototype next-generation framework, only a computer model for simulation and eventual production."

"I have always used practical testing. I prove my own theories. Besides, computer simulations will take days to program without an interface. You're trying my hands and demanding miracles."

"You know I only limited your capabilities for your own protection," Hampon said to her, half pleadingly.

"If you want me to fix your problem - increase the regeneration rate of the framework technology so it can rebuild you cell by cell fast enough to heal your temporal radiation sickness - then you're going to have to trust me. You're going to have to let me take control of the development."

"That is not the only reason why I want to perfect the technology."

"I know that's your primary reason, survival. Having been nearly killed several times, I can relate. But regardless of your reasoning, I cannot accept being disabled as I am."

"We are doing everything we can to locate and eradicate the DLG virus. Seeing that you were unable to defend yourself before, I can't have you vulnerable. You are too important," Hampon told her.

"I know, you need Eden technology."

"I also need you to take the place of the Child Prophet. The Order of Eden needs someone to follow, and instead of putting some grinning figurehead in front of them, I'd like you to take the position. A large part of the Order's philosophy was built on a foundation you laid down on Eden Two long ago. Moving into the next phase of faith building is essential, and I want you to be the messenger and icon."

"To continue the farce of preaching purity and balance? Everything I've seen on Pandem so far is pointing towards a trend of overpopulation and irresponsible socialisation. The frivolity of your tribute to Eden is insulting."

"You don't know all the facts. When you present me with your improvements to the framework technology, I promise to tell you everything about my plans. Pandem, what the Jonas Project was supposed to prove, I'll fill in all the gaps. For now, I need you to begin delivering the message of immortality made real for the followers of the highest order."

Eve couldn't imagine giving such a gift to any of the humans she observed on Pandem. Machines could be immortal, but they didn't have to destroy or corrupt their environment, they could even be programmed to repair the damage done by organics. Immortal humans would corrupt without end. "I'll do it on one condition," she said, trying to hide her disgust at the idea, but failing.

"What I can give you is limited," Hampon warned.

"Give me a basic connection, wetware only," Eve said.

"No connection to the framework technology," Hampon replied. He thought for a moment. "I'll allow you to install a Simex surface jack."

"Not even an implant?" Eve replied. "I could find one myself, that's not much of an upgrade."

"But the Order will not allow you to wear one without my permission. This is the compromise I can offer. No direct internal connection can be made with your mind or the framework."

"You want me to represent the Order," Eve said. "In exchange for this?"

"Not only will you represent the Order, but you'll do so well. This will be the second time we've saved you, after all."

CHAPTER 5
PATROL FOR PAY

"Some way to earn," Quiz said from the seat of his Uriel fighter. "Not much better than patrolling empty space then coming back to a neat pile of GC and a pat on the back from the Carthans."

Minh could hear him suppressing a yawn and momentarily considered dosing him with a mild stim but retreated from the medical command interface. "You'd rather the sector was crawling with Order fighters? Maybe some Eden drones?" Minh checked the course their Uriel fighters followed once more. In a way, the younger pilot was right; the sector was dead. "We're out here because our Uriels have better sensors than the Carthan custom patrol ships."

"Oh, why wasn't that in the brief?" Fringer asked.

Minh liked Quiz, but he'd been asking a lot of questions that he could have answered himself just by thinking the situation through. He took a deep breath then reactivated his communicator. "Mostly because the morning brief was already two hours long, and Slick has been mentioning it every time he does the mission brief."

"Oh," Quiz said. "Well, it's pretty sad when their customs ships don't have great sensors."

"They're used to having a network of satellites as support. They're too new to this system to have that set up," Minh explained. "It's your turn to do a deep scan." Minh took an opportunity to stretch, and couldn't help but notice the empty seat behind him. He missed flying with Slick, but he was busy commanding his half of the fighter wing. Flying alone in a Uriel wasn't difficult, but it was much busier. Picking up the duties of pilot and copilot was sometimes too much for some.

Minh watched the readout on Quiz's fighter as he generated a millimetre wide wormhole that stretched out into deep space. "That's a little wide for a long range scan," Minh said. "You're using extra power."

"Right, sorry," Quiz said as he focused his scanners on the tiny wormhole aperture and activated them.

"No worries, that's why we're off in pairs," Minh replied. "I'll have plenty of power built up for a transit wormhole just in case we have to get out of here."

"Nine patrols so far, and we haven't seen anything," Quiz said. "I doubt we'll have any reason to bug out."

The scan results started coming in from Quiz's fighter and Minh started calculations for a transit wormhole. "Quiz, are you looking at your scan results?" he asked.

"Oh, there's something to see this time?" he asked.

"Shut down the wormhole and look at the results," Minh ordered. "And get ready to manoeuvre for home. We have work to do."

"Holy shit! There's a whole fleet headed for home!" Quiz said.

Minh confirmed the scan results to verify he was seeing the same thing. It was actually a large oval ship measuring just under a kilometre in length and three hundred small drones. He didn't bother addressing Quiz's overreaction, there were more important things to think about. "Stop charging up weapons, we can't intercept while they're moving that fast." He opened several small wormholes that were pre-set to point at the other patrol sectors and sent a burst transmission containing the scan data. The message would give Skydock, the main defence for Kambis, a little over two minutes' warning, and the rest of Minh's fighter patrol group would be able to do scans of their own. After they were finished they'd retreat to assist with the defence, the next thing on Minh's list of things to do.

"Why are those ships moving -"

"-so fast? Because they're decelerating after faster than light travel!" Minh replied, letting his frustration get the better of him as he finished the calculations for a transit wormhole back to Kambis. "You know this stuff already, you just have to use your head to interpret the basic information in front of you." He flipped his fighter end over end and began generating a wormhole. "This'll be open in four seconds, begin manoeuvring now," he ordered.

"Aye," Quiz replied.

"We have to help Skydock."

The wormhole opened, and to Minh's relief, Quiz manoeuvred inside and began accelerating hard, perfectly. He followed suit and started his systems check. It was something no one had to do, but it was better than staring at the sensor displays in the cockpit of his Uriel and the heads up display in his vacsuit visor.

"That's the real deal," Quiz said quietly. "Eden ships."

Minh brought up a small window inside his visor so he could see what Quiz was looking at. It was a digital model of one of the drones headed for Skydock, Kambis, and possibly the moon they called home – Tamber. "Absolutely," Minh replied. "You got a good scan, almost better than the ones from the Triton."

"The ones taken from the attack that cost Chief Frost his leg," Quiz said.

Minh finished checking his mini-missile load-out and checked the transit timer. They would have to begin decelerating in twenty-eight seconds. The enemy force would reach Kambis orbit in one hundred five seconds.

"These drones are different," Minh said. "They're the small, fighter model. Make sure your ship checks out, we'll be in for a fight until orbital defence can engage."

"Almost done," Quiz replied. "I have a question for you, though."

"I hope it's a short one," Minh replied.

"Yeah, why are we rushing to the defence? I thought we were just being paid to patrol?"

"You didn't read the entire contract, did you?" Minh asked with a sigh.

"Who reads those things? I mean, they go on forever."

"Well, since we've got about forty one seconds, I'll explain it. We get paid a flat rate if we're helping with patrols. If we catch something on scanners, we're expected to assist with the defence. We get damage, trauma, and danger pay if there's a firefight."

"Oh."

Minh watched as the engine pods of their Uriel fighters rotated one hundred eighty degrees and fired as hard as they did during the acceleration phase of their transit. It wouldn't be long before they were in immediate range of Skydock. "Right now, I'm just looking forward to shooting something." He used the counting clock as a focal point as he breathed deeply, releasing frustration, tension, and doubt with every exhale. "A frenzied mind sees, a tranquil mind comprehends."

"So this means a big pile of cash," Quiz said.

"Yes, but try to forget about everything but surviving the next few minutes," Minh replied during a long exhale. "Get ready, we're coming out."

They emerged from the wormhole to see Skydock. The traffic around it was dissipating as civilian ships followed navnet directions to the opposite side of Kambis, the massive, canyon-ridden planet ahead.

Skydock was a many-segmented station that had been built on for centuries. The outer segments of its fifty six kilometre length and forty eight kilometre girth were more gracefully designed with smooth curves and complimentary angles. The interior was a mix of square, utilitarian sections with hundreds of docking bays and thousands of large transparesteel windows. Minh had heard the view on the opposite side, facing the planet, was incredible. Tamber, the moon Minh and the remaining Triton crewmembers had come to call home, was on the opposite side of Kambis, far from where the fighting would begin.

"This is Skydock to Ronin," a port officer addressed through Minh's communicator.

"Ronin here," Minh-Chu Buu replied. "Did you receive our alert?"

"Yes, fighters are scrambling now, and we have four destroyers ready to intercept. Advise on best position of pulse barrier, please."

Minh was surprised, the pulse barrier was the most powerful weapon the station had at their disposal. "If you're asking me where to point that thing, I'd say right behind us, just give us ten seconds to get out of the way," Minh replied.

"That's in line with our thinking, you have fourteen seconds to leave the target area."

Minh plotted a course before navnet could send him a similar route and he set his thrusters to maximum. Quiz was less than a second behind.

"Are we about to see a light show, Ronin?" Quiz asked. He sounded almost giddy.

"I think so, I didn't think they had that thing working, but I guess we get lucky today." As soon as they were clear, Minh turned his attention to the station and the area of space the Eden ships would arrive in. Seventy metre long emitters running along the oldest part of the station, at its centre, began to glow red then flashed to white.

The Eden vessels emerged from the wormhole, their engines flaring brightly as they decelerated. Several missiles launched from the main, shining oval ship at the centre.

Minh targeted the missiles with six of his own mini-rockets and fired six at each. After a brief moment they were moving too fast to see with the naked eye. His computer registered five hits less than four seconds later. He'd destroyed their missiles.

"Are they going to fire that thing or what?" Quiz asked.

"That pulse weapon is a little old," Minh replied. "It might have a pretty short range." He watched the enemy fleet approach the base, closing to ten thousand kilometres.

"A few drones are heading for us," Quiz said.

"Go evasive," Minh ordered. "Split right." He locked on to the nearest drone with mini-missiles and rapid-fired half a pod, twenty eight shots. Several beams swept across his shields as he strafed. As the first drone was struck and destroyed by his barrage of missiles, a second crossed in front of him, and he fired his pulse guns. The little machine's shields shrugged the damage off, then it changed direction so quickly Minh lost sight of it for a moment.

Minh-Chu set his guns to autofire; they would react faster than he could to the drone if it crossed into his firing arc. He spun his fighter around and tried to get a missile lock, but the drone was too close, and closing quickly. He barely had time to begin thrusting in reverse before the drone struck him hard enough to completely deplete his forward shields and pepper his fighter with shrapnel as it exploded.

The drone was gone. He'd taken minor damage, but there was a bigger problem. The three remaining drones turned on Quiz, and he was firing at one with his guns, letting himself be guided into a slow figure eight. Two Uriel fighters emerged from their wormholes - it was Slick and Joyboy.

"Holy hell!" shouted Slick. "You're being lured! Break and evade!"

"You're gonna get slagged, man!" Joyboy added. "Get outta there!"

In the time it took for them to comment on the situation and start closing, Minh was able to get a missile lock on the two drones that were positioning themselves out of Quiz's sight. Their cutting beams began focusing on his shields, and if Minh's guess was right, Quiz only had a few seconds.

Minh engaged all his thrusters, pushing them to the limit and, when he was sure of his missile lock, he fired, hoping the added speed from his craft's thrust would help close the gap faster. He changed direction to get a better angle on the drones for guns and they autofired solid rounds as well as energy pulses. Something under his seat started rattling, resonating with the rattling of his solid round gun pod. "Analyze that, please," he told the computer as he guided his ship closer to Quiz and his pursuers.

"Interior sensors are disabled," replied the passive computer voice.

The cockpit began to heat up, and Minh shut down his guns. He'd have to make do with missiles. A collision alarm went off, and he looked up in time to see the drone Quiz was following had turned so his fighter was thrusting directly at Minh.

Minh-Chu barely avoided a lethal collision with Quiz, but one of the other drones following him slammed into his ship from the port side. His shields began recharging from reserve power immediately, and Minh adjusted for the damage to a port side engine pod as he tried to get his fighter under control.

"Sorry!" Quiz offered lamely. "I've almost got this guy!"

To Minh's relief, one of the drones Minh targeted with his missiles exploded in a fury of shrapnel. The other was struck by a couple of his missiles, but kept after Quiz, staying behind him, away from his main guns.

Slick and Joyboy entered combat range and began firing on the target Quiz chased as well as the one that sought to pierce his shields using an intense beam.

Minh stopped his fighter from spinning just in time to see Skydock station's pulse weapon activate. The Eden ship and hundreds of drones were slammed by a barrier of light and force that struck at half the speed of light. Most of the drones were unrecognisable, while the main ship had split into several sections that lazily drifted and rotated away from the station.

Quiz finished off the drone he'd been chasing for almost two minutes as Slick obliterated the one that had been drilling into his shields.

"Not a bad day's work, huh guys?" Quiz asked.

Minh took a deep breath and let it out slowly. "Let's get back to patrolling, we have three hours left on the shift and I'll be stopping in to see an old friend when we've finished our sweeps."

Chapter 6
The Burden Of Command

The ancient transparent steel windows stretching across the quiet boardroom provided Ayan with an expansive view of the city atop Greydock. They were in one of the upper towers, reserved for affairs of government. A Carthan representative was behind her, reading the terms of the latest draft of their privateering and compensation agreement. He droned on, as drones were known to do. Jason and his wife, Laura, sat at the table, listening quietly. Liam Grady was only an arm's length away, watching the city below as well.

Ayan had stopped being surprised when he came along for the negotiations weeks before. He didn't miss one session, was always the last to speak, and didn't say anything if he didn't have something to add. His council, and their growing friendship, were becoming something she hoped wouldn't end when the negotiations ended.

She idly took in the view. The city was still being rebuilt, but the largest of the structures atop the Greydock tower showed no real damage. Corrosion was the enemy, and whatever metal was used centuries before had oxidised and turned a rich rust red.

A high wind picked up rust and concrete dust from the street twenty stories below. A cloud of the stuff swept down a long avenue only to split and dissipate as it collided with the city's high outer wall. It reminded her of the ashes she'd poured into the wind the day before. Instead of listening to the ongoing reading behind her, she allowed her thoughts to drift.

Everyone who could attend the funeral the day before did so. It was held on an old stone and bioplast boardwalk. The brown biological plastic material mixed with large dirty purple quartz gave the weathered structure an earthly quality. The waters were calm, the sun was rising and it would be for hours, bathing them in a warm, golden light. Waiting for the long dawn was an idea from Ugo Dallego, an Axionist from the Samaritan Order who occasionally visited her, and she was glad she'd taken his advice.

"Where is the dawn?" recited Axiologist Liam Grady. He stood at the edge of the dock looking back at all the crewmembers who had turned out, over nine hundred in number. The breeze didn't stir Liam's heavy cotton robes. People gathered to stare at the Triton crew. All in uniform, they lined up along the structure and the beach where it dipped and been reclaimed by the sand. Every one of them held an urn, some held two.

Liam continued; "Timothy looked to his brother and replied, 'It will be late today. All our fears were justified. The leaders in the East committed to one last war. All the great cities have been reduced to rubble, and their ashes will fall on us in a matter of hours.'

Samuel did not believe him and said; 'No, they were the last chance we had to stop the civil war in the West. Someone with power must have survived.'

'Anyone left alive with the means to help have left for Centauri Station in hopes of finding their way to one of the new colonies.' He considered the horizon before he spoke again. 'The British were right to leave when we made them unwelcome. Now they rule the stars.'

'There will be opposition. War will spread. Too many leaders have left from this side of the world as well. Without them, all the stability in the West is gone, and they'll make an attempt to wrest power from the new colonists.'

Timothy looked to his brother, with the love he'd known in his heart since they were children. Samuel was well moneyed and a patron of many frivolous pursuits, but he was not without wisdom. 'Your face is known to most powerful men and women, Samuel. You must join those that have ventured out into the stars and lead who you can. Lead them to peace.'

'You'll come with me. If we're going to start over somewhere else, then I'll need your help,' said Samuel.

'This is my place. Make sure you pass on my message; that the meek inherited the Earth, but only after the strong thought there was nothing left to fight over.'

'What do you think you can salvage here? Your love of God has kept your feet on the ground your entire life, but not even He would want you to try to resurrect his garden on a world covered in ashes.'

'In a Kingdom of ashes the cinder is both destroyer and king. It's time for the faithful to come together and begin the long process of rebuilding. From death and destruction will come the lesson, and from the lesson: hope."' Liam Grady cleared his throat and looked over the massive gathering. His voice was carried to everyone on the crew through their communications system. "That was a reading from The Book Of The Departure, as recorded by Samuel himself on the first day of the Stellar Calendar. He and his brother were forever separated after the destruction of the majority of the upper Eastern continent on Earth. Countries that we watch videos about, like Germany, Russia, China, Korea, and England were almost completely destroyed on the day that conversation took place, and a nuclear winter was about to envelop the entire globe. We know that time now as the First Fall Of Man. Axiologists know it as The Departure, when our race divided. Some interpret that division as the materialistic-minded leaving a ruined earth behind, so they could plunder the virgin galaxy.

"I prefer to look at it another way. Both sides of humanity still had hope. The majority hoped they could find or make a place that was like the one they left, much like this." Liam gestured broadly, taking in the ocean and beach. The sound of the waves lapping up against the shore was all anyone could hear until he went on. "Those that remained on Earth to rebuild had a special kind of hope. That is the hope that leads us through the darkness even after we have lost friends, loved ones, have seen terrible violence and waste. In reflection, I couldn't help but compare our situation to The Departure. So many have fled, much like Samuel. After leaving the Triton behind, our old crewmates either sought new opportunities or could not stay because the memories would not rest while they were surrounded by the people who shared their experiences. We must not blame them for their departures. Everyone within the reach of my voice has decided to remain because you see hope where your fellows did not. Whether that hope is perceived as security in numbers, the power of camaraderie, or the warmth of love and friendship, it is hope nonetheless. We do ourselves and those that could not survive to see this dawn credit by holding on to that hope. We honour them by building a place in the galaxy for ourselves. It is thanks to their sacrifice that we stand here, and we should celebrate as though they stand right beside us. We commit their remains to the waters, and celebrate the dawn in their presence."

Hundreds of crewmembers tilted their urns. The quiet hiss of ashes pouring from hundreds of vessels was a sound Ayan would never forget. It was unlike anything she'd ever heard, and with all her heart she hoped she'd never hear it again. Beside her, Oz poured the remains of one of the enemy leaders, Major Harold Cumberland. No one claimed his body, so the Carthan Government gave them the option of letting them dispose of it, or giving the ashes to the Triton crew. Oz claimed them.

Beside him was Paula, who poured the ashes of Deck Chief Angelo Vercelli. Liam Grady was on Ayan's right, and he poured Alice Valent's ashes since Jacob, the rest of the Samson crew, and many others couldn't attend. The urns themselves turned to sand when they were empty, leaving them with a small metal placard as a memento.

Liam Grady broke the mournful silence that followed. "In a well known transmission to Samuel, long after the departure, long after he'd made his home in New Udalpur, he tells his brother, 'Earth is remembered. You are remembered. Hope is remembered.' As their bond could not be broken, your bond with those who have gone cannot be broken. Now let us watch this fresh dawn for a moment before we take some time to be with each other."

It was the perfect service. Ayan wouldn't say it aloud, but she felt lucky. She lent her shoulder to many people she didn't know, heard stories about crewmembers she didn't have a chance to know well, or at all. She didn't carry the burden that everyone else did. The urn she carried through the service contained the ashes of three people who couldn't be identified. Everyone suspected they were liberated slaves who made it aboard, but were never properly registered. They were probably right. Their deaths were sad, but she couldn't help but feel fortunate that she wasn't committing the remains of someone near and dear to her. That luck came with its own measure of guilt. She tried her best to put it aside.

The service was overdue, and it was a great help to everyone in attendance. She wished Jacob could have been there. It had been a week since she'd seen him. Since they were forced away from the Triton, it was difficult to find time alone together. She suspected that many of the mourners, especially the ones who had been aboard the longest, were also lamenting the loss of that ship. When she let herself think of the Triton, she lamented the loss of opportunity, freedom, security, and organisation.

That was the last time she wore a Triton uniform. She went back to the loose skirted, scoop necked maxi dress design she'd discovered in the vacsuit shape database during her early days on the Triton. The texture was what convinced people it was a normal garment, made to imitate high thread count stretch cotton, an expensive fabric on most worlds. During negotiations, she dressed in pastel blue, green and white – the most disarming colours. It provided the same protection a basic combat vacsuit did, but it looked nothing like one.

Laura dressed in the same fashion, only opting for a tighter fitting version. Jason had taken to wearing a white long coat over his uniform, while Liam Grady opted for his long robes. The old-fashioned blue cloth robes almost hid his black vacsuit.

As Ayan stood at that window, recalling the service, the irritation at it taking so long for the Carthans to turn over the remains of the crewmembers killed aboard the Triton must have resurfaced. She was equally galled by the Carthans' release of their accumulated captives aboard the Triton. The news that the slave master, Doctor Thurge, Burke, and a few malcontents were sent into the wild was delivered as a sidenote with the delivery of their cremated dead. Ayan felt she and her people had been tread on; it was impossible to shake.

Liam Grady's warm hand rested on her bare skin, where the cutout in the back of her dress left her skin exposed. It was generous comfort, but she made an effort not to take solace in it. "Six weeks," she muttered as she wiped a tear away.

The droning of Percy the negotiator behind her stopped. "Pardon?" He asked politely.

"It's been six weeks and one day since we left our ship," Ayan said. She patted Liam's arm and he withdrew it gracefully. It was easier to find her anger and impatience without his touch. "You conducted a full forensic investigation, presented us with whatever personal items were left and a cargo container filled with urns."

Percy, the negotiator drone, regarded her with earnest surprise. He straightened in his seat. "I'm sorry, Commander. I didn't have anything to do with how that was handled."

"That's just it. We're being handled. We keep dancing back and forth in negotiations. I keep asking for what my people think they deserve while you keep short-changing us and citing provisions of galactic laws that only marginally apply here."

"Might I remind you that part of our negotiations are for a ship you technically don't own. The Triton is a stolen-"

"Right," Ayan cut him short. "Screw the Triton. Screw the claim that was legitimised by the Aucharians."

"That claim can't be verified, their government has collapsed and is still in a state of cris-"

"I know!" Ayan burst. "For the hundredth bloody time, I know!" She took a breath and went on.

"Port law," the negotiator said, red faced, "states simply, 'If her rightful owner doesn't claim her in five years, the first claimant can pay her docking and repair fees then the ship defaults to the most suitable claimant' and that's Lucius Wheeler, then you, Commander. You should take comfort in that, it's a generous ruling because we don't see any command codes, and the Carthan War Act gives us the option of using the ship ourselves for those five years. That is, unless you provide command codes."

Ayan felt like her blood was boiling; his repetition of the law was making her angrier by the second. "Fine," she spat through clenched teeth. Ayan took a breath and continued. "Since we're the second claimants in line we'll deal with that when the time comes. For the time being, let's move these negotiations to their logical conclusion, shall we?" Ayan stated bitterly. She brought up the boardwalk they'd had the funeral service on and sent the image to the map on the table. "I want that land, I'll pass on your offer for the weaponry aboard Enforcer

Eleven Oh Nine, take fourty three million Galactic Currency for what's left of it, and you'll give us a five percent increase on any captured food, essential technology or building materials we bring you."

"Ayan, are you sure about this?" Jason asked urgently. "We've gained a lot of ground over the last six weeks. The contract we've negotiated so far is worth more than currency and land: a say in politics for this hemisphere, orbital dock privileges, departure arrangements for anyone leaving the crew, not to mention rights to emergency aid."

"Land ownership will get us the rights we need to influence what goes on nearby, and we won't need emergency aid if we can afford to feed ourselves. They're buying time because they don't want to, or have the cash to pay us fairly. Everyone in this room knows that," Ayan retorted. "To put faith in this negotiation process is to let them set the time table, and we can't afford that."

"Your colleague brings up a few good points. What will you do with departing crewmembers and workers if there are no arrangements for them to join the Carthan work force or leave the solar system?" Percy asked.

"If they're so hot to leave, they can pay their own way off-world with what they earn while they're working for us. Let me finish giving you my demands," Ayan said forcefully, clearly. "The land you give us will be a full grant of property and sovereignty. I know you've given parcels of land away to other settling crews, so that shouldn't be a problem. Aside from that, you'll provide us with an unregulated communications band to operate on in your space, permanent passes for Navnet, clearance to make our own recognised local idents and the Carthan government will pardon everyone under my command of all crimes, no questions asked." Ayan brought up the legal documents that Jason had prepared over the past six weeks. They were a comprehensive defence of Jacob Valance and a petition to rescind the order to detain his crew for questioning. There was also a land grant application with as many useful options selected as possible, and their claim as an independent government. "The Carthan government will ratify this document without amending it. You'll also extend your legal protection to the Samson crew, so they cannot be captured in your space or allied territory."

Percy began to skim through the document's preamble.

"It hasn't changed since we presented it to your team four days ago," Jason said wearily.

The negotiator inhaled sharply and started to shake his head. "Sovereignty isn't on the table. Neither is signing a document that backs a terrorist."

"You lend Jake Valance your support or the entire Carthan government looks like a pack of idiots when the petition for dismissal my legal people transmitted last week hits."

"Petition for dismissal?" asked Percy. "Something like this has been transmitted outside of these negotiations?"

Ayan flicked her finger across her transparent blue bracelet and another petition appeared above the table. "It states that Jonas Valent and Jacob Valance are two separate entities, citing years worth of evidence including a death record from the Triton that your government just certified when they wrapped up their forensic analysis of her logs. The Galactic courts, Order of Eden, and Regent Galactic have no case against Jacob, and in a few days' time, it'll be interstellar news. Now, how is it going to look if the Carthan government didn't back him while he was in their space? Everyone is watching this solar system. Even Hart News has a ship here, and I'm sure they'd love to cover every end of our falling out with the Carthan government."

"If we pardon him, the land grant gets pushed off the table completely, never mind sovereignty."

Ayan's short laughter came almost as a bark. She strode for the door. Her feet were moving in that direction before she realised it, but by the time she was half way out of the room she was fully committed to leaving for good.

"Where are you going?" Percy asked, alarmed.

"To open up talks with another government and get my people ready to leave. The British Union already has laws that will protect Jacob Valance and I hear they're on their way here. When the charges against Valance are dismissed, everyone who has suffered damage from the Order of Eden will want him. Unlike you lot, I'm smart enough to make sure that I'm standing right beside him when that happens." Jason, Laura, and Liam all started to leave as well.

"All right! But I can only give you the dockside, not the adjacent land. There's an island offshore with a moderate tropical climate, your people can build a settlement there." Percy replied hurriedly. "A sizeable settlement. We were going to start a new batch of land grants on Tamber next month, and those are the premium lots."

Ayan stopped and made eye contact with Liam, who wore a slightly surprised smile. That expression slowly changed into a look of approval. She looked back to Percy, who was hurriedly bringing up a holographic image of an island with a cliff face on one side, dense jungle in the higher, central regions, and gently sloped white dunes on the other side. She knew it well. When Jason put it on the list of requested parcels on their land grant application, she argued with him about reaching too far. It would be large enough to build permanent settlements for many times their number. "No one has a claim to this island?" she asked with an upturned eyebrow as she read the details listed on the tabletop.

"No one, but we won't allow anything but zero emissions craft and power provisioning near it for the time being. You're going to have to build your own infrastructure and obey all environmental laws," Percy explained. It looked as though he was fighting to keep his job. Something about her party leaving the room without a resolution had rattled him.

"Who owned it before?" Liam Grady asked.

"It was a wilderness development project, only scientists and agricultural experts lived there and most of them are dead or gone. It belongs to the government, and we're willing to give it to you in trade for forty two percent of the value of the Enforcer eleven-oh-nine and mechanical fixtures. That leaves a little over eighteen million in Galactic Currency, which we can deliver in two days."

"You're not serious," Ayan said. "The land grant will be in addition to what you owe us for the Enforcer. You should consider yourselves lucky that we've loaned you the use of our fighter squadrons and helped you monitor our sector for defence and navnet."

"We pay you fairly for that on a flight by flight basis," Percy countered.

"Everyone else is offering more. We could have made triple your rate if we ran security for shipments coming into the system," Jason said. "She's right, you've had us for a bargain."

"Do you have the power to make this decision?" asked Liam quietly. "You know we will be a positive influence on the political landscape of this moon, it will serve your career well in the long run."

Percy looked surprised by the statement, as though his authority had been questioned one moment, then he was given the justification he needed to agree to their terms the next. "I'll approve this on the condition that I write three things in," he said in a calmer tone.

"I'm listening," Ayan said, sitting down at the opposite end of the table.

"You'll get a launching area on that beach instead of a full-on section. Acquiring adjacent land is up to you. Secondly, you'll be responsible for defending the island, and proportionally defending our orbital space. Lastly, Jacob Valance will appear and accept a Carthan statement of support in person."

"And you're paying us the full price of our captured ship? Granting us full sovereignty? Agreeing to the rest of our terms?" Ayan asked.

"With the amendments I just put forward, yes."

Ayan looked to Jason, who looked relieved, then to Liam, who nodded calmly, and to Laura, who whispered, "just approve it before he thinks of something else."

Relief washed over Ayan as she brought the amended contract up on the table, brought up an ident entry box and put her hand down on it. "Your turn," she told Percy.

Three people entered from a door behind Percy. Two were witnesses from his office, wearing squared suit coats, and the third was a colonel. His uniform wasn't like the ornate type she'd been seeing for weeks. The armour he wore was pockmarked, its dark surface discoloured from heat damage. Symbols signifying combat medals scrolled across a small section of his left breastplate. He spared Ayan and her party only a momentary glance before focusing on the blinking approval square on the table. "On with it, I have work to do," he muttered at Percy.

Percy pressed his hand to the designated part of the table. The military representative was next, and he was out the door before the other two witnesses did their part.

Laura, Jason, and Liam all submitted their approval by pressing their hands on the identity verification box and the contract blinked green. It was as good as law.

Percy stood and straightened his black suit jacket. He started down the length of the table, and Ayan met him half way. "I know it's been a long process, so you may not believe me, but it's been a pleasure negotiating with you," he said.

"I think everyone will be happy in the end," Ayan replied, offering a smile. "Thank you, Percy."

He nodded, seemingly more at ease, and said, "you're welcome," before heading for the door. "The room is yours for as long as you need."

As soon as the door closed behind him, Jason activated a small cylindrical surveillance scrambler and set it on the table. "An island and sovereignty. I knew he had a lot of negotiating power to play with, but that's way past what I would have pushed for."

"You and I both. I didn't expect him to offer anything like this," Ayan agreed.

"When I said we'd probably be walking away from the table today, I expected the worst. I didn't think they'd offer us anything like this. It's got to be half quicksand and half man-eating jungle," Laura chuckled as she started looking at reports from numerous scientists who had worked there.

"Not at all," Liam said. "Where quicksand is concerned, at least. As far as man-eaters, the biological record doesn't show anything big enough, but they're four years old, so we can't know for sure."

"I wasn't serious," Laura said.

"I know," Liam said with a wink. "They are desperate for privateers, and this moon is more than they can govern," Liam said quietly. "Kambis is many, many times the size of Tamber, and it's their priority. Their presence on Tamber can't be beneficial yet, especially since they can't spare the men or equipment to provide law enforcement outside of Grey Dock. It's a good idea for them to give land to people who need it, especially when it's likely that whoever they grant the land to will give up once they realise how much work it will take to build an environmentally-friendly landing structure." He brought up the geological scans of the island and studied them.

"Only, we won't be privateering," Jason said. He brought up a specific article and enlarged it. "This is more of a treaty, giving a new government guidelines for formation on their world. We can form our own military, and we agreed to this before they could put any restrictions on size, that's the real win here."

"Good thing they brought in someone from the military who has better things to do," Laura said.

"We lucked out," Jason said. "Poor guy was probably just passing by when his comm beeped with orders to put a military stamp on a civilian negotiation."

"Or," Liam said, bringing up the identity of their Carthan Military approver. Colonel Jarod Ironmonger was his name, and he had served for eight years as the tail end of a penal term, then continued to serve in the Carthan military for another twenty-seven. "He's been following this and supports us. Like you said, they need fighters, allies."

"I'll do some research," Jason said. "If you're right, I want to know for sure."

Jason was looking through the negotiation logs for the day, ensuring that everything they discussed and agreed on was reflected in the document. They only had twenty hours to do so, and at the rate he was working, he'd be finished in minutes. "I don't see any surprises here, but there is a clause that states that if the island is under-utilised for more then three years, it becomes Carthan property again. What they term as under-utilised isn't a problem for us. If we settle there, half of the people we have will be plenty to demonstrate occupation. What you're saying about them being stretched thin is true too. They're contracting out most of the law enforcement on Kambis, and I've been seeing reports on the Stellarnet of Confederate rebels in every big city in the solar system. If there's one thing the Carthans know for sure, it's that we're not Confederates who refuse to leave, and we'll defend whatever they give us."

"So Tamber is home now," Laura said quietly.

"Are you all right with that?" Ayan asked.

"Yeah, it just happened so fast at the end that it's like a surprise, even though

I knew a land grant was something we were looking for," Laura replied. "National Sovereignty though, that's something I never thought we'd get. I mean, I understood why we kept putting it on the table, you need to ask big so the lower option is still good, but getting it... Wow. It's just starting to settle in."

"The Carthans don't have time to govern us," Jason said. "I think it's that simple. I wonder how happy Jake will be with this. He doesn't seem like the 'land and settle' type."

Ayan had been avoiding the thought. "We need a base of operations. We'll be able to operate from a stable base. It won't be privateering, but better. I only wish we didn't still have to pay for slips in Port Rush, but it's going to take us months to build a proper spaceport." She shook her head at the realisation.

Liam's hand landed gently on her shoulder as he asked, "are you all right?"

"It's just a lot to think on," Ayan answered. "You ask for something for so long not thinking you'll get it, then it's yours and you have to deliver."

"You're not alone," Liam said.

She patted his hand and looked into his brown eyes, smiling. "I know." A long moment passed as she shared a gaze with him. Her bracelet sent a sense that there was an incoming message. She shook herself free of the moment with a long inhale.

Ayan looked at the short text message and raised an eyebrow. "It's Jake, he's in Gray Dock."

"He's supposed to be blending in with the salvage workers aboard the Enforcer," Jason said.

"Well, he's here, has a surprise for me," Ayan said. "Are you all right reviewing the rest of this yourself?"

"Go ahead, you two have barely seen each other in weeks," Laura said, interrupting an objection from Jason.

"Can you hold off on sending the news of this out for a few minutes? I'd like to surprise Jake," Ayan asked Jason.

"Sure," he said, not looking away from the scrolling documents in front of him. "You go have fun."

CHAPTER 7
REPORTING IN

The debrief on Skydock was thorough and boring. Minh's entire squadron was held after their ten hour patrol was concluded. Even though the core of the orbital station looked ancient from the outside, the condition of the interior was remarkable. The surfaces were clean, but not reflective, as he would have thought they were. The matte finish had the strange characteristic of looking like it wanted to shine, but the reflections were somehow impeded by the surface coat of metallic green and silver.

He and Slick were the last to leave the briefing room, a half-circle space with blue padded seats surrounding a small stage in the centre. He'd said everything he had to, filled in all the blanks, and the rest of his wing had done the same.

"Hold one moment," called Lieutenant Commander Moda.

Slick and Ronin stopped and turned. The twelve pilots under their command, all formerly from the Triton, waited expectantly in the hall. The tall, wiry Lieutenant Commander in charge of patrol outsourcing for that sector smiled at them a little nervously. She seemed new in her command. "I have a couple more questions for you two," she said, closing the distance between them.

"Fire away," Minh replied.

"First, for the record, what is the name of your fighter wing? Does it have one yet?"

They were still tossing around ideas, and Minh was still undecided, so he hesitated. It seemed that Slick had already made up his mind, judging from his answer. "Samurai Squadron," he said.

Minh regarded Slick with an upraised eyebrow for a moment, but his former copilot didn't react, so he nodded. "That's us. Samurai Squadron, under the direction of Ronin." He was a little surprised when no one caught the issue with the terms 'Samurai' and 'Ronin' mingling.

"All right, it is so recorded," replied the Lieutenant Commander. "I have an elective question for you: Did you think the Carthan military responded appropriately to the threat?"

"Elective, meaning we don't have to answer," Slick said.

"I'll answer," Minh said before Lieutenant Commander Moda could reply. "No, I don't think they used the appropriate countermeasures. That barrier weapon was heavy-handed for the threat, and I'll bet half my pay that those Eden ships had an uplink to a hypertransmitter somewhere that sent readings to the nearest Order ship. Your commanders should have sent the destroyers they had on standby in to flank while your station's missile batteries tore everything else to shreds."

Slick regarded Minh-Chu with mild surprise. "Don't hold back, now."

"She asked," Minh said with a shrug. "That was the Eden fleet checking defences. I'd be surprised if those ships were anything more than antiques."

"Thank you very much, Wing Commander," replied Lieutenant Commander Moda. "You'll find your payment with your lead fighters in lock boxes secured with the agreed upon combinations."

They were nearly outside of the room when Minh-Chu gave into an impulse to say something that seemed to be hovering overhead for the entire briefing. "You're going to need to hire more pilots."

Lieutenant Commander Moda stopped and said, "Pardon me, Sir?"

"If your government has friends in higher places, they should start making calls and bringing help in. The war is almost here, and you won't be able to fight it with the ships you have in this solar system, even if you spend everything you have on outsourcing."

"Do you have information you haven't shared?" Lieutenant Commander Moda asked.

"No, but I've seen two wars start in my lifetime, and this will be number three," Minh replied. He turned back towards the doorway, through which he could see the faces of his pilots. Some were ashen white, others were concerned, while Joyboy seemed unbothered by anything he'd overheard.

"Which wars?" asked Lieutenant Commander Moda. "Sir! Which wars?"

Minh didn't bother turning around but answered. "The All-Con conflict, and the Vindyne liberation."

"Why isn't that in the record?"

"Because I'd rather tell stories that have a happy ending, and both left millions in the cold."

The door closed behind them, and Slick stopped Minh-Chu. "What's going on?" he asked in a whisper. "You've been in a bad mood for days and now I know it has nothing to do with Paula dogging you whenever you make landfall."

"Let's start with the pilots that shouldn't be here," Minh said levelly. "A third of our wing would make passable transit pilots, but they're not ready for combat. You and I both know they're only here because we're trying to earn as much as we can, running extra patrols using filler. We have to cut back on our patrols so we can use our best pilots every time."

"Pardon me, Sir," interjected Quiz, a thin young man who was a little shorter than Ronin and nothing but skin and bones. "I bagged one of those 'bots, I know, but I could still use experience. How am I supposed to get that if I'm grounded?"

"I give you credit for knowing you're one of the pilots I was talking about," Minh-Chu said. "We'll rig a computer to host simulations for you and the other greens. You're going to spend some time in sims, and you'll spend as much time with the physical training group."

"What?" Quiz replied. "Physical training?"

Ronin sighed and looked at Slick.

"If you want to fly," Slick said. "You're going to have to train our way. It's our fault for putting you up here too early. Enjoy flying your ship back to Tamber, it could be the last time you see the inside of a cockpit for a while."

"Hell, no!" Quiz shouted. "I get my first kill and you pull me? Is this your way of telling us you want all the kill pay for yourselves? We're just goddamn decoys?"

"Don't get me started on what's wrong with your kill," Ronin replied. "If we keep you in the pilot's seat, you're going to get yourself or others killed. I'll prevent that however I can, so you're grounded. If you can't live with that, then maybe you can qualify for transit, I hear we're low on shuttle pilots," Minh-Chu finished with an upraised eyebrow.

Slick stepped in just as Quiz was about to forcefully retort. "Cool off on your way to the launch bay," he said. "You're dismissed."

"Let's make that trip," Joyboy said to the pilots. "Come on."

Ronin and Slick waited for the group to leave via the elevator. "I hope that's the last pilot we take in from Patrizia Salustri. That's one thing checked off your list," Slick said. "What else is bothering you?"

"I think what we have to do next won't help our popularity with the Carthans, Nathan," Minh-Chu replied. "We can't come back to Skydock."

"You're thinking this is a target now," Slick said.

Minh-Chu nodded. They started walking to the elevator and pushed the call button. "The next time Skydock comes under attack, it'll be from long range. There won't be anything we can do about it except get killed in the crossfire."

"That's what I'd do if I were the Order," Slick said. "Or they'll avoid the base until they could come at it from planet side, from behind. Either way, we won't be any use to them patrolling these sectors."

"Exactly," Minh-Chu said. "So, we launch and return to our own slips, take the lower rate of pay."

"Commander McPatrick won't like it, that's a big hit and a lot of busy work on the ground."

"Don't worry about Oz, I'll talk to him," Minh-Chu said. The elevator arrived and they stepped inside. There were two maintenance workers within. They looked and smelled like they had just finished crawling through a sewer line.

Minh-Chu did his best not to retch as the fragrance made itself at home in his mouth and nose before he had a chance to seal the hood of his vacsuit.

"I'm just finding it hard to swallow that we're going to war on a galactic scale," Slick said.

"Knowing much of the history myself, I can't see how it can be prevented. I only hope it's short," Minh-Chu said.

"Any words of comfort, Confucius?" asked Slick.

Minh-Chu chuckled then sighed. "About war? Nothing comforting."

"But something," Slick pressed.

"Something."

"So?"

"You don't want to hear it," Minh-Chu said.

Slick nodded and let the silence grow as thick as the smell. The man knew Minh-Chu too well. He couldn't keep the thought he tried to keep from airing to himself after being called to share. Not for more than a few minutes, anyway. "War calls many, and rewards few."

The doors opened, and Slick said, "You're right, that's no comfort at all."

Chapter 8
Enforcer 1109

There was no supervision by the Carthan government aboard Enforcer 1109 as the ship was pillaged for essential components. There was no need. The second most frustrating thing to Jake about the operation was that they were incapable of taking many of the larger, more important systems from the ship and installing them into their settlement below.

The most frustrating thing was that he had to spend several days as a normal worker, unable to issue commands or directions to other crewmembers while he was mixing in aboard. The effort to hide amongst the crew was working; no one had been attacked in all the weeks since they landed on Tamber, but it was getting harder by the day.

The half-lit, hundreds of meters long main hangar was busy. Over half of the available manpower from their settlement was working there, and Jake had been watching, making sure that there were no surveillance devices or crewmembers he couldn't account for. Someone was dragging half a self-contained shield generator, trailing cables behind and letting one end scrape along the deck. Before he could jump to their aid, another crewmember picked up the rear end.

"Going to chance it today, Captain?" Frost asked over a secure proximity radio channel.

Jake finished loading a crate aboard one of the Enforcer's nine armoured shuttles and descended the embarkation ramp. "The crew's slowing down, getting sloppier - it might be a good time."

"Ayan will have your head if she finds out, though," Frost replied. "And she will find out."

Frost was in a loader suit, undistinguishable from the other suits they had operating on the massive hangar. The software in the machine was set to correct for his limp so it was the only way he could reasonably hide.

They managed to get two emergency generators running aboard the Command Enforcer 1109, but it wasn't enough to make it useful. However, it was more than they needed for the five weeks they would spend stripping the vessel of much needed machinery, essential comforts, personal weaponry, and housing. There was enough portable living space for three thousand.

There were also intact ships – fighters, two forty two meter long patrol craft, nine heavy shuttles, and several smaller repair and personnel shuttles that the old Enforcer crew called 'Mice' that could carry six people.

The eighteen meter long armoured transport behind Jake lifted off, on its way down to their settlement on Tamber. "I'm getting tired of hiding," he told Frost. "But I'm not so pissed at this situation that I'm ready to kill the plan. We're hidden because we're protecting the people who might get caught in the crossfire if someone tries to make a capture."

"Yeah," Frost replied with a sigh. "So you've said more times n' I can count, lad. It doesn't bother you at all that the Samson's hull is getting her finishing touches tomorrow? Whole new hull on a redesign you and your old crew hammered out."

Jake picked up a crate ready to be loaded into a small shuttle behind him and began walking it up the rear ramp. The standard muscle augmentation in his suit creaked. He'd used that suit so much that the enhancement systems were showing real wear and tear. "You had a hand in it too," Jake told Frost. The sealed hood and darkened faceplate kept anyone from overhearing what he was saying. "Ever see a hybrid-organic hull grown onto a ship before?"

"Can't say I have."

"Then maybe we should both take a day and work down there instead of up here," Jake said. "This scavenger duty is busy work, Leland March could probably do it. I want to get back down there today if I can. Besides, your old gunnery deck crew has this all set."

"I hear ya," Frost replied. "Not like there's any complicated work left to do aboard this gutted beast. Your old friend Everin is going to have a problem with us shirking his big plan to keep us scattered and hidden."

Jake bristled at the mention of Jason Everin - the man had changed, and it wasn't to his liking. "Between you and me, Jason's head is too big. Ayan's given him too much control."

"Can't disagree," Frost replied. "I'm waiting for him to screw up, because it'll be in grand fashion, and we'll have to pick up the pieces." He paused a moment before adding, "Between you and me."

"How do you think that'll go down?" Jake asked. "His big screw up."

"Not sure, but he's moving us around like we're pieces on an old game board, drawing up new petitions for the Carthans every couple days, and trying to run this operation too clean," Frost said. "If he doesn't screw one of us over by mistake, or get the Carthans irritated enough to kick us off their rock, or insult a crime lord by being snobbish, then I'll be surprised."

"You're thinking you'd do better?" Jake asked.

"No, I think *you'd* do better," Frost replied. "That's why I keep askin' when you're going to go bare-faced and start running the show again. Ayan's fine, got all the right training, but her team's got holes. Seems to me, she's the only one with the stones to go nose to nose with a Carthan Fleet Warden and not flinch. Everyone else in her little diplomatic party are just thinkers. You have to get something she doesn't have to watch over running, maybe get a couple crews organised so we can start pirating and earning, like you were saying the other night."

"We'll see," Jake replied. He watched the loading crew on the expansive, dimly lit hangar going about the business of moving the bundled and crated salvage to the shuttles. It looked like a leisurely pace to him, and it wasn't what he wanted to see. "We've got six hours to finish flying everything we want from this boat down to Tamber before the Carthans take possession. Pass the word to your old gunnery crew; there's extra liberty for them if they finish on time. If they don't, I'll make sure they lose a week's pay."

"Aye, aye," Frost said. "I still think things would move along faster if they saw your lovely face, Captain."

"Frost…" Jake said, a warning in his tone.

"Hail, mighty Captain Valance," Minh announced over a private channel as his fighter was lifted into the hangar by an elevation pad.

"It's more like knuckle-dragger number twenty eight, right now," Jake replied. "What brings you to vulture-town?"

"Ah, Ronin's here," Frost discerned from Jake's side of the conversation. He couldn't hear Minh, thanks to the private channel communication protocol instated by Jason. They were only able to speak to one person at a time unless they were using their disguiser. "He's probably bearing another message from your lady below. Ask him if he's got anything from Steph."

"I will, but he won't," Jake replied. He didn't understand Frost and Stephanie Vega's relationship, but he didn't think about it much. It was as if they were taking a vacation from each other, especially over the last two weeks when Frost and Jake were living aboard the Enforcer.

"What's that, Jake?" Minh asked, unable to hear Frost's side of the conversation.

"Just Frost, asking if you've got something for him from Steph," Jake replied.

"I do!" Minh declared. "She says; 'hurry up.'"

"He's got a message from her," Jake told Frost.

"Oh-ho!" he replied.

"She says, 'hurry up.'" Jake relayed.

"Ah, she misses me, just the right time to wrap this up and head home," Frost said.

"You old softie," Jake teased. "I'm going to talk to Minh here, catch up with you later."

"Aye," Frost said, closing his private channel.

"So, he's happy," Jake told Minh-Chu.

"I bet," Minh said with a chuckle. "As far as I can tell, Steph's itching to get social. She's feeling a bit isolated. So are Finn, Agameg, and probably everyone else, except for Ashley."

"Really?" Jake said. It was strange; he'd think that Ashley would be the most eager to stop hiding and start socialising again.

"Steph says she's been really quiet," Minh said. He sounded worried. "Like, depressed quiet."

"Any idea what the problem is?"

"Stephanie figures that between the isolation and not being able to see Zoe, that orphan she rescued, it's getting to her."

"Another reason why Jason's plan isn't working out," Jake said. "I'm going a little crazy myself."

"Well, Ayan says 'hi.' She says she's cleared her schedule tonight," Minh said. "And if that's code, I want details later."

"I think it is," Jake said. "But I won't be over-sharing on the details." He was eager to see Ayan again. They had just started getting to know each other, and they were becoming closer in all respects when Jason Everin came up with his plan for the Samson crew to go into hiding.

"But my vicarious life will be missing a chapter," Minh replied.

"I thought I was living vicariously through *you*," Jake replied. "If you think what I'm doing right now is more exciting, then you're in real trouble. Besides, don't you have someone waiting on your every landing?"

"Funny thing, I just broke it off with Paula," Minh said.

"How did that go?" Jake asked. "God, I must be bored, I'm becoming a gossip."

"Welcome to the human race," Minh teased. "We're all gossips here, even if we deny it."

"So, what happened with Paula?" Jake asked with a resigning sigh.

"Oh, yeah. I told her we had to break things off and she said; 'I don't believe you,' gave me a kiss on the cheek and walked away."

Jake laughed. "So you're making a stop here to avoid her. You could have bounced that off our receiver as you did your usual flyby."

"I wish that were the only reason," Minh-Chu said. "The armour plate under my seat is cracked and I have to fix so I can go atmospheric."

"I'll give you a hand," Jake said as he started heading towards Minh's fighter. "I'm surprised there's no backup for that."

"That is the backup," Minh replied. "The energy and hard shielding is all right, so I should be fine to enter atmo - and even our vacsuits can take the heat - but I'd rather have all systems go for reentry. Just call me paranoid. Safe, but paranoid."

Jake walked onto the elevation platform and noticed a pigment-shift painting on the side of his aircraft. An image of Paula lounging under Minh-Chu's callsign: RONIN, her modesty maintained only by smoke trailing from a recently fired gun in her hand. Jake stared at it a moment, stunned, then burst into a debilitating bout of laughter.

"What?" Minh asked, alarmed. He looked at the side of the fighter and hung his head. "Yeah, she bonded that on yesterday."

"Well, she looks pretty good," Jake said, taking a breath. "I hope you'll be happy together!" He managed to say before he burst anew.

"But I-" Minh began to offer lamely as he finished stepping down from the fighter.

Jake put his hand on his friend's shoulder and looked him in the eye. "If she's so mad for you that she's done this, there'll be no shaking her off. I hope she's got some redeeming traits we haven't seen."

"She can be nice in quiet moments, and she's ambitious," Minh said. "Doesn't think people take her very seriously, though."

Jake straightened up and recovered. "Well, this isn't going to help. I'll get a scrubber and we'll get this off."

"Yeah," Minh said. "I'm sticking to my guns though, we're split. She's getting harder and harder to keep at arm's length. I still can't believe she didn't believe me."

"Just stop," Jake said. "Or I'll get started up again."

"It's not that funny!" Minh retorted. "It's actually pretty scary!"

Jake was just starting to snicker again when a bold message appeared on his head's up display:

NOW! DO IT NOW!

The elevation pad dropped two metres in half a second. The side Jake stood on lowered more, and before he could move the Uriel skidded in his direction, trapping him against the side of the elevation shaft.

Minh tripped over one of the thruster pods, the emergency hood of his vacsuit activated before he struck his head soundly against the side. "We've got a malfunction with lift six!" He announced to the deck crew.

"This isn't a malfunction," Jake said. He tried to push the rear thruster pod of the fighter away from him, but the left arm of his suit's strength augmentation failed. "I'm pinned." Just as he said it, a man wearing a grey worker's vacsuit leaned over the opening of the short elevator shaft and dropped a roughly rewired compact battery right on top of him.

"EMP grenade!" Jake warned.

It went off, effecting the fighter through its open cockpit, and the systems on Jake's lower quality vacsuit. He could feel the little artificial muscle there was layered into it stiffen. Without power, the material would be more hindrance to movement than assistance.

"I'm pinned," Jake said again, struggling under the weight of the fighter and the panic rising in his mind. "My suit's keeping me from getting crushed, but it's not doing anything else."

"Hold on, my suit's okay," Minh said. "I might be able to get you out."

"You've barely got augmentation, that's a pilot's suit," Jake said. He opened a channel to Frost. "Get over here, we need your loader to pick up this fighter."

"Is this an accident?" Frost asked.

"You know it isn't," Jake replied.

Three grey suited workers dropped into the elevation pit, one falling on top of Minh as he was balanced on an engine pod pylon. The pair went crashing down, and that's when Jake saw a makeshift restraint in the attacker's hand. "Watch it, Minh!" Jake said. "He's trying to get a restraint on you!"

One end of the modified metal cargo tie clapped closed around Minh's arm before he could turn over and react. He flipped from his stomach onto his back and punched his attacker in the throat. The blow would have been devastating if the worker wasn't protected by a labour suit.

One of the other workers moved to stand over Jake, who looked up to him and said; "I promise you'll suffer the worst." Panic intermingled with hate as he blindly struggled under the fighter's engine. He took note of a green stain pattern on that worker's legs. It made his suit unique, and Jake promised himself it would be the man's undoing.

The man above him didn't reply, only pressed a button on a makeshift control box. The pressure doors above started to close just as Frost's loader suit came into view. "I got ya, lad," Frost said as he caught the doors in the hands of the suit. The pair of heavy doors clamped shut on its hands and severed several fingers.

Frost would be fine, fingers intact, but no help at all. "I was sure that'd work," he said with a chuckle. "I'll get the hatch open from up here, you just threaten and sneer, might frighten them into givin' up."

"Not funny, you sonofabitch!" Jake shot back as he watched a second worker drop down and help his mate with Minh, who had gotten the upper hand and clobbered his first attacker with his half-fastened restraint. He drew his sidearm with the other hand and was just about to take aim as it was knocked out of his hand from behind.

"How did you let hunters onto your crew?" Minh asked. He tried to scramble after his weapon but was equally preoccupied by a new set of hands trying to grab the half-affixed restraint.

The entire scene was thrown into chaos as the elevator's base dropped suddenly. The gravity deactivated and the air rushed out of the space, drawing Minh, Jake, and their three attackers out with it.

Jake was free, but didn't have so much as an emergency manoeuvring jet. He was turned away from the action. "Did you get your sidearm back, Minh?" Jake asked as he let himself turn.

"Not so much," Minh replied. When he came into view, his hands were up. One of the workers must have gotten hold of Minh's sidearm right before the elevator decompressed, and it was pointed at the pilot's head.

"Now, you're going to be cooperative or I'm going to start shooting at your friend here," said the worker. "Aren't these Violator sidearms designed to cut through suits just like this?"

Jake had nothing to say. He drifted slowly, helplessly, as he spotted a point of light in the distance. They knew too much about them, their plan was too good. There was a knowledgeable informant involved who probably even knew about Jake's regenerative abilities, otherwise they'd be pointing the gun at him.

"Lad, bad news," Frost said. "There's a shuttle going in your directions. I'm headed for an emergency hatch. I've contacted our flyboys, but I don't think either of us are going to make it in time."

"I know," Jake replied. "Get to a gun emplacement on the Enforcer and contact the Carthan authorities. If they can't intercept, I want you to get a cannon working and disable the shuttle."

CHAPTER 9
REACHING OUT

It had been weeks since Ayan had seen Jake. Jason's plan to keep the Samson crew, Jake especially, mixed in with the rest of their workers was only effective if they visited people they cared about as little as possible. According to Jason, if Jake or any of the crewmembers visited known associates often, then someone could track them over time and discern with fair certainty who was who, or at least who was important.

Ayan didn't like it, neither did the Samson crew, but Jason was right. As a result, Jake hadn't set foot on the Clever Dream, or gone near Ayan, for weeks. He couldn't even check his personal messages more than once every few days in case someone found a way to watch network activity.

When Ayan realised she was actually nervous, she attributed it to that separation. As she made her way through Greydock, the strange guilt at feeling perhaps a little closer than she should to Liam Grady was pressed away by memories of Jake. He was a great communicator too, when there was time to sit and talk, and they'd done so for hours.

If anything, she was sure her guilt with regards to Liam Grady came from the thought that she might be leading him on, by being open to his supportive presence that was made so much warmer, so much more intimate by his gentle hands. Touching someone's bare skin on Freeground was more personal than it was in many other cultures, as they spent so much time covered up under the skin of a vacsuit. Liam might not have known, but he made her skin tingle when his warm hands made contact with the bare skin her dress afforded her. There was nothing indecent or unwelcome about his attention. In fact, he wouldn't make her think twice if he behaved that way with other people. For all she knew, his caring hands paid attention to other people just the same.

"But he doesn't touch Laura that way," Ayan muttered to herself, drawing a glance from a young man passing her in the quiet, lush, carpeted hallway. She flashed him a smile, which he returned shyly. The walls were adorned with dark hardwood planking and flickering sconces. She'd only seen anything like it in old movies and period interactives, never in person.

It reminded her of Liam more than anything. The earth tones, dim yellow light and air of luxury were all things that she associated with him. A brief, unintentional recollection of his comforting hand on her back became a daydream. She was standing at the window in that boardroom and the negotiator was reading aloud, but he may as well of been in a different room for all the attention she afforded him.

Instead of embracing her anger and turning on him the moment after Liam Grady's reassuring hand touched her back, she turned towards him, his arms and his robes wrapped around her. She imagined his embrace would be warm, firm, and that she'd have all his attention in that moment.

Ayan brought herself back to reality, clearing her throat and shaking her head. The door to the room Jake had rented for their rendezvous was right up ahead, and she was blushing because of a daydream that brought more guilt than she thought she deserved. "Fickle, stupid girl," she cursed under her breath to the empty hallway.

She checked the lines of her dress, and straightened it a little before touching the entry pad. It recognised her and the door slipped open silently. There, looking out a window overlooking the other side of Greydock, was Jacob Valance. His long coat and dark gloved hands contrasted against the buildings around the hospitality tower. Long ago they had been painted green and blue, plated in silver and gold, but time had worn down their tones, their sheens. The metal beneath was red in most cases, white in others. It was old construction, still useful and sturdy, but not as appealing as it once was.

He turned and practically grinned at her as he crossed the room. It was rare of him to be so openly happy, and her heart skipped a beat as she met him in the middle. Jake picked her up off her feet and whirled her, nearly knocking a serving tray off a table with her heels. "I couldn't stay away," he whispered against her ear.

Thoughts of Liam fled from her mind at the sound of those words. The thought that the need to see her could break the discipline in a man like Jacob Valance was thrilling. To her, Jake was more stalwart and honour-driven than even Oz. "I missed you," she said, a tear squeezing through her clenched eyelids.

He put her down and held her more loosely, kissing her briefly before looking her in the eye. There was an eagerness in everything he did that was surprising, refreshing. "You're supposed to be on the Enforcer, there are only a few hours left," she scolded playfully.

"You're supposed to be in negotiations," he retorted, imitating her.

"We just came to an agreement. They've agreed to a land grant, a low but significant price for what remains of the Enforcer, most of the other things we were after, including a lift on the local warrant for you and the rest of your crew. Oh, and we've secured sovereignty."

"All that in a few weeks," Jake said. "It felt like forever, mind you, but you reached high and I'm impressed," he told her.

She smiled at him because of the uncharacteristic praise, not in the fact that it came, but in how it was said. Somehow it didn't sound like him, even in the burst messages they'd shared through Jason, the way Jacob was speaking was somehow – off. "Thank you," she replied. "Is everything-"

Before she could finish the question, his lips were on hers, and she knew that whoever was kissing her was not Jacob. This man's eager manipulations were nothing like the man she knew, and she tried to pull away.

He caught her arm and yanked her to him. "Wheeler sends his regards," he whispered against her temple.

***

Minh closed the canopy on his Uriel fighter and it began to come to life. He kept his eye on Jacob the entire time; they were adrift outside the Enforcer, and that ship was almost in range. "I've got ya, Jake," Minh said. "I'm coming to get you."

"Don't use real names on comms!" erupted Lowell, the second in command for the salvage operation.

"It doesn't much matter now, lad," Frost replied over the channel. "Seems like whoever's behind this knows who's who."

"Any luck getting the doors open so you can give me a hand?" Minh asked as he signalled his fighter wing. They'd be there in six minutes, maybe more. Not fast enough.

"We're cutting now," Frost replied. "They burned up all the door mechanisms we've checked."

"The emergency cranks don't work?" Jacob asked.

"Aye, they planted burners on timers, destroyed the shafts," Frost replied. "Must've taken a week or two to plant 'em."

The heavy transport shuttle came around the port side of the Enforcer and into sight. It's side loading doors were open and Minh could see three crewmen ready with weapons. He locked weapons on it right away, but held his fire. "Shuttle to my three o'clock, at one two seven by nine zero zero five three, by two zero five, you will power down immediately or be destroyed," Minh warned. It was less than two hundred meters away from Jake, with a side loading door open.

"God dammit! I'm never hiding again," Jake said. "I'd be able to take care of this myself if I were properly geared!"

"Power down, Ronin. This will be your only warning," replied an unfamiliar voice. The passengers on the shuttle fired at Jake, who barely had time to flinch before several shots struck him in the legs and chest.

"You all right?" Minh asked, checking the reading he had on him. Two of the shots punctured his suit, burning his leg to the bone and obliterating his shoulder, damaging his left lung severely. To Minh's astonishment, the wounds healed in seconds, regenerating back to a perfect state. He'd heard about the framework technology, seen the results, but he'd never been watching a status readout on Jake as it did its job. The miracle of the technology didn't make up for one thing, however: the holes in his vacsuit.

Minh cringed at the sound of Jake struggling with the pain, releasing grunts and suppressed cries for the first few seconds that his bare flesh was exposed to the freezing vacuum of space. "Let them take me!" he shouted.

Jake's framework kicked in, repairing the freezing and pressure damage, but he didn't suffer gracefully for long. Jacob's screams filled the comm frequency, setting Minh's teeth on edge and testing his will. There was nothing he wanted more than to rush to his friend's aid and catch him in his Uriel's small but pressurisable cargo compartment.

"Warning shot, Ronin," said the calm captor. "We'll get just as much money for him if he's a smouldering heap."

"I've got to do something," Minh said on a private channel to Frost.

"Stand down, lad. Captain says he wants to be taken. We leave him to this, they'll get more than they bargain for."

"Can he survive this?"

"Ignore him and look at the scans," Frost said. "He's keeping up with the damage."

"Understood." He started a focused scan of the shuttle and everything inside as he spectated on Jake's capture. The screams stopped, and, with a glance at his medical scanner, he could see that Jake had passed out but he was healing faster than before.

The shuttle slowly closed the distance between it and his friend, then the crew dragged him inside. One of them shot Jake several times, and Minh watched him twitch as the door to the shuttle closed. It began to accelerate towards Kambis.

Minh switched to a new channel. "Tamber Navnet, I have a bogey."

"We see you, Ronin," replied the non-automated operator on the other end. "A bogey on this side of the system?"

"Aye, mark the Enforcer Heavy Transport I'm transmitting to you now. It just captured Captain Jacob Valance."

"Captain Valance?" the operator replied, surprised.

"Please, keep it professional," Minh said.

"Yes, Sir. I see it moving from your position," replied the operator. "Why aren't you pursuing?"

"They'll kill him if they see me in the rear."

"What would you like Tamber support to do, Wing Commander?" asked the operator, sounding more than a little confused.

"Just track him," Minh said. He turned his fighter and hit the thrusters; it took less than three seconds to accelerate past the Enforcer. "I have birds on the way, but I'll need your eyes."

"My supervisor just authorised the resources," the Operator said. "Good hunting."

***

Ayan's dress went into emergency mode the moment it detected she was in a physical altercation, and it snapped back to vacsuit form. Her head was completely covered with a faceplate and a hood, her body lightly armoured. The imitation Jacob hurled her across the room in frustration.

While it wasn't an enjoyable tumble, it didn't cause her any harm. The suit prevented even the slightest bruise. She was on her feet, furious, and looking forward to beating the imitator when a side door opened. "Easy, Commander," said the blonde woman she knew as Doctor Tamera Thurge. "We have a message for you."

"They told me they released you," Ayan said, looking her up and down. She was wearing an armoured red coat with a fitted shield suit beneath. The fabric shifted colour as the surface tilted in the light. The man with her had dispensed with overclothes and simply wore a shield suit, a weapon holster, and a pack on his back. "I don't like the idea of slavers roaming free, but I took comfort in the thought that you'd be far from here by now."

The imitation of Jake walked more leisurely towards Ayan, and she stepped back. She cursed herself inwardly for letting her guard down, for growing lax in protecting herself. She didn't even carry a weapon during the negotiations. There was nothing she'd like more than to slag the leering imitation of Jacob that stopped less than a meter from her.

"I planned to move along," Doctor Thurge said. "But Lucius was waiting for me when I was released. He knows how to court a lady, I'll tell you."

"I'm sure," Ayan said, not shifting her gaze from the Jacob imitation.

"Not just ladies, mum. With the cash he flashed, he could charm me off a core world prostitute," said Thurge's companion.

"Classy," Ayan said.

"He offered money and an opportunity to get a shot at Frost, your captain, and the whole bloody crew."

"Well said, Burke," said Thurge. "But you're missing the best part. Lucius has a plan, one that even has a place for people like you, clone."

"I don't want anything Wheeler's selling," Ayan replied. "And I'm not a clone."

"I don't care what you are, all you have to do is tell us which one of your crew has the primary command codes for the Triton. We'll find him and take care of the rest."

Ayan was surprised at the request but did her best to hide it. If there was someone with the command codes, then they could bypass the whole mess they were in with the Carthans. They'd have their own land as well as the Triton back in their possession, more than she could have dreamt.

"Don't try to lie, we know someone's been trying to reactivate the main computer core several times a day since you landed on Tamber," Thurge pressed.

"What's stopping the transmission?" Ayan asked, playing along just in case they actually did have someone with the codes. Turning the situation to her advantage was something she couldn't pass up.

"The Carthans disconnected the core form the ship then wrapped it in shielding. I thought you'd know, having spent so much time in the negotiation room."

"Never occurred," Ayan replied. "It doesn't matter, I don't know who has the codes."

"Bullshit!" Burke shouted. "A prissy bitch like you wouldn't let something like that wander around outside of her control."

"Why the Triton? Isn't what Wheeler's trading earning him enough for a ship he can manage?" Ayan asked. "The Triton is a half broken ship and he never got her running at her full potential in the first place."

"Not your concern, sweetheart," replied Burke. "Just tell us who has the codes, and we'll know you're worthy of the cash and prizes."

Ayan noticed the butt of a handgun poking out from the fake Jake's coat. "I'll think about it," she said the instant before she snatched at it and pushed away.

The false Jacob caught her by the throat with inhuman speed. He flicked the sidearm out of her hand with his free hand and grinned.

"Give her a reason to reconsider," Doctor Thurge said. "Time to go, Burke."

"Yes, mum," Burke said.

"I love you, Ayan," the imitation Jacob said earnestly. "So you know this will hurt me as much as it'll hurt you."

Ayan's suit kept her throat from being crushed, but her attempts at fighting him off were completely ineffective. Her fists struck his face, his throat, and when he pulled her up off the floor, Ayan kicked him frantically. She knew her suit signalled an alert the moment it changed from its dress shape to protective mode, but there was no telling how long it would take for help to arrive.

"I love you, Ayan," he said again, holding his free hand up.

"Whoever programmed you must be a real charmer with the ladies. What are you, anyway?" she asked as she pressed both her feet against his chest and pushed as hard as she could. Nothing budged.

He pointed his hand at the belly of her suit and a particle beam so fine she could barely see it began testing the vacsuit. She writhed with renewed vigour, and found herself pinned on the floor a moment later, one of her hands caught in his grip. He knelt on her legs.

It didn't take more than a few seconds for him to catch her other arm and clasp both her wrists in one hand. He smiled at her, a warm, loving expression that made her want to retch.

"Don't kill her. Do anything else Wheeler programmed you for, but don't kill her," said Tamera Thurge.

"You're going to want to give up that name sooner, rather than later," Burke said as the door closed behind them.

The imitation Jake's beam cut across her chest, leaving scars across her vacsuit and raising alarms on her visor. She kept struggling as her eye movements directed her communications and command bracelet to begin materialising compound 35B. Before it complied, it warned her that it was a highly illegal substance on Tamber.

Her assailant swept his cutting tool down her belly, and celebrated a small opening over her belly button with a lecherously gleeful expression. "Don't resist, Love," it said. He shoved his fingers into the hole and tried to tear it open.

Ayan hurriedly signalled her command and control unit to bypass the safeties and begin manufacturing the compound. She gnashed her teeth and fought harder at the sound of the false Jacob ripping her vacsuit enough to get a grip on the tear in her suit's belly with his other hand.

His leering, excited eyes were focused on that opening, his expression filling her with rage and disgust. She wailed on him with her fists, and when her comm unit announced that it had finished manufacturing an eighth of a gram of compound thirty-five, she held her bracelet up to his eyes and ordered the miniature materialiser within to apply an electric charge.

With a flash of heat and incredible pain, the explosive went off.

CHAPTER 10
THE SHADE

The lights went out on most of the Triton's decks two weeks earlier. The army of investigators and repair personnel took their turn with the ship for four weeks solid. There wasn't a minute where a portion of the ship wasn't being examined or serviced for storage. It took their best over a week to ensure that all systems were powered down, and three more to secure everything aboard for a long storage period. Considering how different the Earth technology was compared to their own, it didn't take them long.

The Carthan Engineering Corps couldn't take all the credit, however. Larry made sure they found instructions and repair schematics for the entire ship. If they wanted to waste their time and resources preserving the Triton, he was more than happy to make sure they did it right. There were no secrets to betray. Most of the technology aboard was between fifty and seventy years old; Sol Defence had since moved on to even better technology, so the fact that the Carthans learned a few things while they were rebuilding wouldn't displease Larry's superiors - much. He stayed out of their way. It was like dodging a herd of glowing elephants. Even when the repair people were dead quiet, they had no concern for stealth. Everyone believed that the old Triton crew was gone, that they were servicing an empty ship.

An hour after the repair people left, the cleaning crew started to arrive. They were even easier to avoid. He even pretended to be one of them for two days, cleaning several crew quarters himself so he could get access to the safe in Captain Valance's old quarters, where he found exactly what he was looking for. He sunk back into the shadows that night, watching as the cleaning crews used special equipment to scour the blood and other evidence of carnage from the decks. The repair crews were efficient and came in force, but they didn't work on damaged portions of the ship, only made sure its condition wouldn't degrade if it was left in port. At one time, the ship's passive security sensors reported over twelve hundred crew armed with little helper drones scouring the ship. Two hundred experts and support staff accompanied them.

The Carthans sent a testing team aboard on the last day of cleaning. They ran the Triton's built-in diagnostic tools and decided the ship was ready for long-term storage. It was then that Larry began to formulate a plan to dissuade the Carthans from taking possession of the ship. He wouldn't let an unknown captain take command, not when he knew exactly who he and Sol Defence would want sitting in that chair. To his surprise, they simply shut all but the life support systems down and left. They didn't enter a senior officer into the ship record, try to hack into the computer's cold backups, or even post a scanning patrol aboard. The airlocks were sealed with Carthan sensor tape. The lights went out, and they moored the Triton somewhere inside an orbital dock around Kambis.

For the first time in his life, Larry was completely isolated. For several days, he didn't dare to deactivate his cloaksuit. Not even to use the privy, even though he despised what the Freegrounders called 'built-in plumbing,' which took care of human waste. He recalled Ashley talking about it in the galley, when she managed to explain the mystery of the built-in plumbing perfectly to a newer crewmember. "No, no," she said. "You don't figure the private bits of your vacsuit out. They figure YOU out. You shoulda seen my face the first time I put on a - how did Captain put it? Right, a fully equipped suit." He laughed along then, but as he wandered the ship, he couldn't help but miss using a toilet.

When he thought of Ashley or Oz – and he thought of them often – it was with some regret. He never let Oz know his role aboard; it would have gone against his orders, but Larry was sure it would have been to his benefit. When he let Ashley in on his secret, he mismanaged the whole thing. He could have had her trust, selectively let other important crewmembers know his real position, and a diplomatic solution would have been found when the Carthans took possession. The Triton would be crewed. Unfortunately, his hands were still tied. He was an observer, and he'd broken enough rules by killing several West Keepers. Even if the ship was stuck in port for five years, his duty was to watch human behaviour and chronicle the story of the ship.

Even still, he wished he could just engage the computer core and reveal to the galaxy that he was the true master of the Triton. He missed the crew, especially members like Agameg and Finn, though he was starting to like Jason, who reminded him of his brother. Even if he wanted to turn the lights on, it took two command level codes to bring the primary computer core online, a fact that he'd kept from Ashley, and the main reason why it hadn't been active since the ship was allowed to be stolen from Kuiper Drydock. If another officer were assigned to the Triton and made the journey from Earth, then they would bring the main computer core online, and they'd begin a new mission.

It was something Larry sometimes caught himself dreaming of. The chances of that were slim. He fully expected to be aboard or near the Triton for the next thirty years before being summoned home. The fantasy he let himself indulge in sometimes was of the crew who had adopted and honoured her returning to take the Triton back. With Terry Ozark McPatrick in the lead, they'd break through the Carthan seals, start the ship up again, and to everyone's surprise, he and Ashley would bring the Triton back to full functionality for the first time in decades.

It was nothing more than a fantasy. Any attempt would be a brash display of heroism and stupidity, but it didn't stop him from wishing something would happen. The fantasy didn't hold boredom off for long. Sometimes he'd retract the headpiece of his vacsuit and come out of stealth just to see if the Carthan guards would come running, or even step out of the shadows in stealth suits of their own. No one was watching. They had the ship locked down tight, sealed along every hatch and seam.

No one would scold him for not leaving the ship and send him down to Tamber, where he could reunite with the Triton crew and offer the good news. If he did so on purpose, it would be a severe breach of orders with Citadel Command. Leaving was not an option. He'd have to wait and hope that Ashley found her way back to him. He'd apologise and find a way to tell her how to issue a command code to someone he trusted. That way he could be indirectly responsible for the revival of the Triton, and perhaps avoid a harsh sentence from Citadel.

No matter how he planned, or how he fantasised, he was still stuck aboard. The ship began to take on an entirely new character after the lights went out. The slightest sound echoed down the darkened halls. Thick bulkhead doors sounded like rolling thunder, bringing on a fresh wave of hyper-vigilance. Every time he thought he'd made enough noise to trip a passive port sensor, he was wrong. The ship wasn't meant to be empty. She had been built to house thousands of working men and women.

After a week in the utter stillness, Larry realised he wouldn't last much longer. He didn't even blame Ashley for her rash act, or for leaving him fully exposed. He was conscious and free before the Carthans found him, and his place was with the Triton anyway.

It was time for him to sit and watch quietly, to wait. He tapped into the Triton's passive sensors, and didn't attract notice from the port. They didn't need enough power to register, since they were designed to operate while the ship was cloaked.

His direct connection to the sensors was made in one of the officers' quarters, and he found the days he spent there more comfortable. Avoiding the halls, the vault-like central areas. and the all too silent concourses seemed to be the key to maintaining sanity. After he was sure everyone was gone for the long term, he tried sleeping in a bed. It was a fitful sleep, and he woke with a start in the middle of the night, not knowing why. When he replayed the recording taken by his comm unit, he burst out laughing as he watched the slumbering image of himself wake suddenly after a particularly deep snore. For reasons he couldn't understand, the laughter became weeping. It had been seven weeks since the crew of the Triton left the ship.

"You're trained for this. Citadel agents must thrive in isolation and civilisation alike," he told himself. "Contemplative and watchful while at peace. Cunning and swift in war. We are Citadel - defenders of balance and enablers of the righteous," he recited through tears. He buried his face in his hands, noticing how rough his stubble was against his palms. "When did I stop shaving? Was it last week? Two weeks ago?" he idly asked himself.

Larry leapt to his feet at the sound of his command and control unit vibrating a warning signal against his skin. He hurriedly activated the holoprojector, which transmitted its images directly into his eyes. "A crush gate? Tainted with temporal radiation? Why would the Victory Machine be coming here?"

His self-pity and loneliness lifted from him as quickly as a flock of startled birds. In seconds he strapped on his weapons and pack, and had his stealth suit sealed. He knew that port control would pick up the stirrings of strange energy. He only had a few minutes before the exit of the wormhole fully manifested, and he ran as hard as he could towards the botanical gallery, where the Sol Defence software he'd installed on his comm unit predicted it would appear. He made surprisingly good time, but by the time he ran through the heavy protective doors of the botanical gallery his lungs and his leg muscles were burning.

He ran across the long grass, down paths that had already begun to become overgrown and finally into a clearing near one of the large ponds. A spike in ambient energy gave him just enough warning to cover his eyes and turn away from the exit of the wormhole only metres away. A violent flash of light announced the arrival of the crush gate traveller.

Larry braced himself before turning around. Crush gates were highly compressed wormholes that were severely directional, forcing the traveller through it at speeds many people failed to survive. It was still experimental when he left Mars years before, and was being hailed as the future of travel. One could travel dozens of light years in the space of a few days. To the traveller it would seem like only seconds had passed. The Victory Machine dumped most of its waste energy into a crush gate generator the creators had built in, and there was a limit to how much it could contain before the bearer had to create a gate and travel.

To Larry's relief, no temporal radiation was leaking from the bearer's suit or the small box containing the Victory Machine, and he turned around. "You, you're not supposed to be here," rasped the man in the old, heavy containment suit. He was face down, struggling to push himself upright.

"You mean, on the Triton?" Larry asked, hopefully. He loved the ship, but freedom would be a sudden and joyous blessing.

"No, with me. You'll get caught. You have to run, keep hiding."

Larry crossed the space between them and helped the man by propping him up against a tree. His face was ashen, and there was no strength left in his frame, which looked like it was once sturdy, even powerful. "My control unit has a basic medical treatment component. I can try and get you on your feet before the Carthans get here," Larry said.

"Don't bother. There's something wrong with the containment suit. Been dosing me with temporal rads since I gated from Mount Elbrus. At least now I know why I've been sick these ten years," replied the traveller.

It was an awful, mysterious truth of temporal radiation. One dose in the future would make you ill in the past, a paradox even the brightest minds on Earth couldn't fully puzzle out. The Victory Machine had a nine year reach by default, so it only made sense that this man was ill for nine years before he was exposed, inasmuch as anyone could make sense of temporal radiation. "What am I supposed to do? Where am I supposed to be?" asked Larry, desperate for direction. "Am I the next bearer in line?"

The man began to laugh but coughed violently instead. Once it passed, he shook his head. "No, the bearer who's been passing me information from the future is here somewhere. They never let on who they were, but I think I know where they want me to be. At least I'm sure the rogue element is nearby. I don't know much about you though, except you're not supposed to get caught with me."

"There's nothing I can do to help you?"

"No. We're working a bigger picture, the next and me. You get to wander around doing what you're doing until you get a better idea. Just don't try too hard," replied the traveller.

"How is the next bearer going to get his hands on this thing if the Carthans are busy studying it?"

"Who says the next bearer will be a man? Besides, with the suit serving as secondary containment, there's no way anyone but the bearer will pick this thing up. It's not like the Carthans, or anyone out here, for that matter, know how to repair this thing. No one's built one for a few centuries."

Larry looked at the weary man for a moment. "How long am I going to be here?"

"What, alone? Don't worry, you'll come out fine. Just think of me next time you're feeling you got an unfair hand, that'll set you straight," the bearer chuckled ruefully. "Now get going. You have a place, Larry Nevil. You'll see where you're needed when the time comes. For now, it's time for you to forget your birth name and embrace the one you chose when you left the Sol System. That's all I can tell you."

The tip wasn't as satisfying as he'd like, but it was better than nothing. "Thank you for your service, I'll remember you," Larry hesitated a moment. "I never got your name."

"Roman. Just call me Roman. I gave up my birth name over twenty years ago."

"Thank you, Roman," Larry said as he activated his stealth suit. The Carthan port guards were close, he could hear them in the garden. "I'll wait," he said, knowing no one could hear him. "I'll be ready when the time comes." It was a resolution he didn't need anyone else to hear.

CHAPTER 11
POTENTIAL

Jonas was still trying to process the idea of boarding the ship that would take him and his engineering team to All-Con Prime. Academy training was supposed to prepare you for it - the departure, the adjustment - but it didn't do the whole job.

Everyone knew the war raged on there, and that he was a very small part of Freeground's final, all-or-nothing push to win a war that had cost too much in lives and resources. That ship, the Courser, was going to be his home for a long time if the war continued to draw on. Past the boarding ramp, he could see the thick, battered hull. There were signs of repair all across its three-quarter kilometre length, and seeing some of that up close was as daunting as it was amazing.

He'd seen big ships up close before, but this was a war ship, with rail cannons so big he could walk through one of their barrels without crouching. His father noticed him staring open-mouthed and Jonas caught him smiling.

"Sorry, first time I've seen it this close up," Jonas said.

His father waved his comment off mildly with a calloused hand. "This trip will change you."

Other recruits in tan and grey moved up the boarding ramp past them, all carrying everything they would depend on in a backpack and a case. He hid his long coat in the bottom of his backpack, refusing to leave it at home. The excitement of embarking on a long journey to another world was almost overwhelming. Though he wanted to skip the awkward goodbye his father would initiate, Jonas owed him that much.

His father was a great engineer, a man who respected a solid day's work, and something built much more than something bought. He turned towards him and, to his surprise, found his father's steady hand on his shoulder.

He offered his hand and Jonas shook it, trying to match his father's grip. "I'm proud of you," he said, his voice steady and thick with emotion.

They remained there, frozen for a couple of seconds before his father nodded as if sure he'd said all he needed to then let go of his son's hand and turned away.

The academy had been hard, but he'd graduated with high marks. He was a terrible shot, but got through boot camp and the physical training all through his mandatory period of conditioning, though there was never much indication that his father cared enough to track his progress. They didn't talk about it, and Jonas even suspected that his father didn't approve of him joining the Freeground Fleet.

But what his father said changed everything. He didn't only have his father's approval, but he felt he'd proven himself. He was ready to board the Courser, to do something important in the galaxy.

The perfect memory faded, and a flood of information assaulted him. He lived every moment as Jonas right until he saved the First Light by surrendering to Vindyne. His memories as Jacob began then, starting with his rough birth aboard the Samson.

They weren't just memories, they were the ultimate recollection of being. He *was* Jonas. Suddenly, that entire set of experiences fit with who he had been for years, Jacob Valance. He hadn't felt like he was one man, living one life since he'd discovered the hidden mental storehouse of Jonas' memories, but something had drastically changed, and he felt integrated.

He regained consciousness slowly, discovering pulsing pain coming from three parts of his body: his hip, his leg, and his arm. He could see them as though sensing with his framework systems, which were partially disabled every time the mini electromagnetic pulse rounds his captors shot him with while he was unconscious went off.

Jake was also keenly aware of the fact that he'd just recovered from death. The people who took him damaged his brain badly enough for his backup systems to load all of his memories back into a freshly constructed one, and from what he could tell, they got it right for the first time.

He'd never been aware of his framework systems before, never had control, but he could feel everything. After a particularly painful pulse, he concentrated on forcing his working framework systems to draw power from the devices. It took more effort than he'd ever put into anything to think through the pulsating rounds, through the convulsions, but after a few seconds the shocks began to diminish.

They were down to almost nothing when he started to pretend that he was still convulsing, faking a twitch fit every three seconds.

He opened his eyes to slits and observed. One man was sitting right next to him, holding an automatic rifle across his lap. Two more were in the front of the shuttle, and another was in the rear. Jake was on the floor in the middle. The dim shuttle was crowded with supplies from the Enforcer.

The framework had finished absorbing all the energy from the rounds, and it offered him a new option: to use the remaining material to build something. As soon as he thought about a high-range sub-dermal communicator, his body began generating thousands of nanobots internally.

He faked one more twitch, and satisfied that his captors didn't notice anything strange, he decided on his next action. Jacob waited three seconds, then, instead of faking a twitch, he jerked towards the man sitting beside him and yanked his rifle out of his hands.

He fired five rounds at the guard in the rear, scoring three hits to his face. The faceplate of the less durable crew vacsuit broke, but he was still alive when Jake shot him twice more.

Stronger, Jake thought as he brought the butt of the rifle around and smashed the rifleman in the head. Framework materialisers began working, and Jake could feel something changing. A second later he had the answer – they were causing a shift in his muscle density and size, suppressing pain as the work began.

Jake grabbed the struggling rifleman by the back of his hood and hauled him out of his seat, tripping him to the floor between him and the cockpit. "Do you want to live?" Jake asked through his teeth as he pointed the rifle at the man's head.

"God dammit!" shouted one of the men up front as he turned around, drawing his sidearm. It was another slug thrower, possibly loaded with the same disabling shells that Jacob had been shot with before.

Jake opened fire on the copilot, raking him with rounds from his hand to his shoulder. He was alive, saved by his vacsuit, but he'd dropped his sidearm. The rifleman on the deck between them tried to sweep Jake's feet out from under him, but he recovered at the last moment.

Jacob had enough, and stepped on the rifleman's neck, feeling more physically powerful than he could ever remember. Muscles tightened like thick cords drawn on heavy winches. Jake braced his hand against the low ceiling of the craft and looked at the man underfoot.

The rifleman stared back in horror, trying to push Jake's foot off his throat as it was forced down. "You'll remember how this feels for the rest of your life, just like I remember how it feels to die."

The hardened vacsuit protected the man's neck, but only to a point. The framework system finished augmenting and improving Jake's body, and with new strength he crushed through the vacsuit with a loud pop, then the man's neck and spine with a wet crunch. Emergency stasis might save him, but it was never a sure thing.

Jacob turned his hateful glare towards the copilot with a twitch that made the man flinch. "You can take your punishment now, or in front of witnesses," Jake told him.

The copilot raised his hands and nodded. He was joined by the pilot, who quickly took in the scene in the cabin before saying: "with witnesses."

CHAPTER 12
GHOSTS

Eve had eaten, washed, and completed other human tasks. Lina insisted, getting in the way until Eve gave in. The little woman was insufferable, and always close at hand.

"What else is there to know?" Eve asked herself as she entered a media room, something she didn't need before. It was a circular space with seating for about eight in the middle.

"About what?" Lina asked.

"I was talking to myself," Eve snapped. Using her uplink to the database of the Overlord II didn't feel right somehow. She could read detailed reports at an incredible pace, but when it came to viewing visual recordings, she was limited by what her primitive eyes could process. Lina suggested they adjourn to the media room so they could watch the collection of holographic records in comfort. Eve relented out of fear that the woman would make an issue of it until she complied anyway.

Eve sighed and sat down beside Lina on the circular centre seat. "I've already developed a framework copy of someone using the same formula that was utilised when Jacob Valance was created. His name was Beaudric, and because I played on his emotions using the personal history we implanted in him, it worked perfectly."

"What happened to him?"

"Someone hijacked my body and convinced him that he should assassinate the Child Prophet."

"But nothing's happened to the Child Prophet. He was preaching just yesterday."

Eve couldn't believe that she had momentarily forgotten that there was an android walking around pretending to be the Child Prophet. She reminded herself to ask Hampon why they couldn't just replace the clone, and why he made one for himself in the first place. It would have been much easier to create a framework instead.

Lina's clearance level didn't allow her to discover that Hampon was a fake, even though it was almost as high as it could be. His last sermon addressed the enemies of the Order of Eden, and how they threatened their quest for purity. "I see," was all Eve offered in response. "Then Beaudric was not successful. I'm glad," she reinforced the lie mechanically.

"So, you were able to make your own Jonas and you're wondering why General Hampon doesn't see it as finished work?"

"Exactly," Eve replied, surprised that Lina had caught on. She called up the recordings she wanted. "It has something to do with this limiter chip, I think. I couldn't see these records before, they were isolated from available storage. Since this section of the ship blocks all wireless signals and isn't connected to the rest of the Overlord, I couldn't get access."

"We see a great deal within the inner chambers of the Order. It is one of the gifts a Senior West Watcher enjoys. Our discipline and respect is demonstrated by our silence."

"I see," Eve muttered. "I should learn more about your discipline."

"I'd be happy to show you," Lina offered enthusiastically.

"It would be faster if I read it myself." Eve summoned the record most viewed by Hampon, Collins, and Meunez. It was seven years old. She was mystified at the image that appeared around them. Two identical Jonas Valents sat across a simple metal table from each other in a small room.

Her deception with Beaudric, ensuring that he thought he was the only one, was key to recreating someone as a framework being. Why they would expose a framework to his original was beyond her. The record stated it was the fourteenth time the copy of Jonas Valent had been imprinted. It was the fifth time Jonas had met his double.

Eve started the playback and watched as the figures came to life.

"I'm not the original," the one on the right said. "Pretty good copy, though. I was really convinced for a minute there."

"It's been the same every time. They hit the reset switch, re-scan me, burn whatever they're looking for into your head and bring you back," replied the one on the left. The pair seemed more amused than anything. Their heart rates were reading as calm.

"What's the point?"

"I'm convinced it's the most expensive form of torture ever invented. Then again, I don't mind your company. The repetition might get to me after a while, though. What was it that Minh used to say?"

"If variety is the spice of life," started the copy.

"Then redundancy is a kitchen filled with endlessly boiling pots of noodles."

The pair laughed. She felt she was watching an out of sync mirror. There was something unsettling about seeing Jonas - the most well known terrorist in the galaxy - doubled.

"Why are you still here? No chance to escape?"

"I've had a few chances," said Jonas to his doppelgänger slyly.

"You're protecting Freeground."

He nodded. "Break the deal and Vindyne starts pointing the big guns towards home."

"So we're down to what, passive resistance? I've only been awake a few minutes and I'm already pissed we're still here. You've gotta be about ready to rip your hair out."

"Freeground doesn't need Vindyne's full attention. If I can slow them down by taking my meds and sitting here, then that's what I'll do."

"Well, I don't have to sit here like a lab stooge," the copy declared. "I have an idea."

"That's new."

"Maybe I'm a little smarter than the others," the copy said with a shrug. "Anyway, I know if I were sitting where you're sitting, I would only want there to be one of me. Nothing feels right anyway, so..." The copy closed his eyes.

"What's the idea?"

"I can feel..." The duplicate paused a moment, searching for the right words, "how my flesh is connected. It's like a name on the tip of my tongue. If I can only remember it, I'll be able to take complete control."

"Seriously?"

"There it is. I can feel where the memories were burned in. Nice knowing you, Jonas," said the copy as he began to concentrate harder.

"Remember the last thing my father said to me?"

"Don't get all sappy on me, now. I'm just another Vindyne product."

"Well, if there's one thing you should remember, it's what he said."

"Thanks, now that's the first thing I'll forget." He gripped the edge of the table, white-knuckled and gnashing his teeth. "Here we go."

The door burst open and men in Vindyne uniforms grabbed the copy, injecting him with a sedative. The copy's heart rate spiked instead. It only lasted a moment, but apparently it gave him enough time to accomplish his goal. Moments later - after the copy fell into unconsciousness - Hampon entered the room with a high resolution scanning tool in his hand. He still looked healthy, just beginning his decline.

After a moment of scanning the copy's head, Hampon dropped the scanner. "He did it himself. He wiped his own memory clean. There's nothing but trace fragments left and they're degrading," he said to one of the walls. Collins was watching from behind it.

The recording ended and Eve sat back. "He took complete control," she concluded aloud. "But how can he remain in the condition he's in for so long when he can just start modifying himself? No one can remain intact with that kind of self-access. You could dream that your heart stops beating, and the connection could make it happen. A bout of paranoia or fear could bring on a physical attack, which would be lethal if it wasn't caught in time."

Hampon's younger self reappeared in front of them. Eve knew Hampon was controlling the hologram from his central chamber. She didn't blame him for using a younger, healthier image to communicate. "That is why the Jonas project was so important. Something in his subconscious mind was keeping the framework stable, helping him direct the control he had and release it when it could cause harm. We theorised that it was a strong self-image, perhaps a level of mental health that was rare, or any number of other factors, but we never found out for certain. Our trials with Wheeler discounted the theory that there was something in their early Freeground training that instilled what they required at a young age. After another year of probing, we still had nothing."

"So you allowed him to be rescued by Alice," Eve replied. "To see how long he would remain stable in the wild?"

"No. We could have done that in a controlled environment. We wanted him to evolve. It was impossible for us to re-imprint Jonas' memories, so we installed knowledge of medicine, engineering, combat, and other modules and let Meunez leak his whereabouts. For reasons of his own, he needed a way to find out where Alice was, and he would be allowed to pursue her after the copy of Jonas was rescued."

"Has he evolved since?"

"The only record of him exhibiting direct control over his framework body is from Pandem, when a long time associate, Ayan Rice, was mortally wounded. The backup chip in his neck had already managed to bypass whatever was preventing the framework from being implanted with memories. It was installing Jonas Valent's memories, so we assume it was an emotional response, instinctive."

"I can't find any record of you creating frameworks with psychological modifications that were made to match subject four. Did you ever try?"

"Yes. The results were unpleasant."

"Show me."

The image of Hampon was replaced with a coffin-like box featuring a framework skeleton. The empty sockets of its shiny silver skull seemed to stare at them until it was activated. The materialiser system built into the framework built the flesh from the bone outward, inspiring a gasp from Lina. She cringed and uttered, "oh my God," from behind a hand covering her mouth.

In less than a minute, the nondescript male framework construct drew breath. It was an advanced model, not only able to materialise flesh and bone while collecting energy from its surroundings, but capable of materialising a lightly armoured uniform. It knelt down and picked up its rifle. It stepped into its boots and put on its helmet.

A shot came from behind them, sizzling against the framework's box. He took aim and fired at something that was out of sight, not part of the recording. His grip and posture was perfect, something common to the basic male soldier framework model.

A bolt of energy struck its arm, leaving a burn mark on the light armour. The construct barely flinched. Before their eyes the damage to his armour was repaired as he continued to fire. His face began to change colour to match his uniform. Over the next few seconds, Eve and Lina watched as the construct's skin turned into the same armoured plating as his armour and blood began to seep through the cracks.

The construct stopped firing after a moment, no longer able to see, and fell to his knees. The spectacle became worse, as the armour softened, shifted, but didn't become proper skin.

"What's happening to him?" asked Lina, flinching her gaze away as a low moan escaped the construct's lips.

"He's trying to re-stabilise his form. I assume his first instinct was to improvise a better way to protect himself. His second was to improve his modifications and survive."

An agonised scream filled the room as the construct fell forward and his right arm split apart so violently that something that looked like bone matter erupted from the inside. It only took Eve a second of closer inspection to realise he had materialised the front half of a weapon. "It's the way his body is communicating. It's implementing momentary thoughts as though they were commands. The system can't filter his second to second impulses."

The image disappeared, replaced by Hampon's younger self. "I'll spare you the rest. That was one of the most advanced models, with a cybernetic governor device that tried to rule out all but final decisions. We even tried to replicate the custom framework that the Jonas project was built on. For some reason, framework constructs would not stabilise after their subconscious directives were modified."

"Except for Jacob Valance."

"Yes. So, now you understand why he has been allowed to run rampant, and why you need to build a framework that does not try to go past specification. It must have a limiter chip as well, to reduce the chance of self-destruction or unnatural levels of self control," said Hampon.

"While generating flesh in a tenth the time of the current model and implanting or preserving a set of memories. The limiter chip will have to be modified," noted Eve.

"Feel free to do so, but ensure that stability issues do not arise."

"Don't worry. When you are implanted with framework technology that works quickly enough to replace all your cells fast enough to beat temporal radiation without killing you, the technology will be perfect. I already have workable theories. This file has given me a few ideas," Eve said.

CHAPTER 13
RECKONING

Jake had to pilot the shuttle around Kambis to get back to the Enforcer, but he didn't mind. The passenger compartment was filled with the ration meal packs he'd commanded his former captors to empty from a crate before he forced them inside. It was a tight squeeze, but the crates were still large enough to fit one man each, and they sealed from the outside.

As the shuttle crossed one of the main navnet lanes leading out of the system, the shuttle lurched. "Ronin to shuttle pilot," announced Minh through the communicator. "This extended model Uriel fighter has eight engines that can each out thrust everything your little boat's got, and I'm latched on." Jake leaned back in the pilot's seat and decided to let Minh finish. "There's also an entire wing hiding in orbital traffic," Minh continued. "If any further harm comes to Jacob Valance, I'll drag your asses back to the Enforcer and we'll use you for target practice. It's been a long, boring salvage, I'm sure they could use the distraction."

"Good speech," Jake said. "I'm terrified."

There was an unexpected hesitation before Minh replied. "You could have stopped me earlier," Minh said with a chuckle.

"No, really, it was very good. I especially like the target practice bit," Jake replied. "Now that you're latched on, let's get back to the Enforcer at fighter speed. This shuttle's a brick strapped to a thruster."

"You have something in mind," Minh said, more of a conclusion than a question.

"I do, it'll be a surprise."

"Are you all right?" Minh asked.

"Better than ever," Jake replied. "Better than I've been for a very long time. How did you sneak up on me, by the way?"

"Ah, Tamber navnet has been tracking you. I got under a big freighter hauling hot cargo and waited for you to pass."

"I saw that one, you didn't even come up on scanners."

"Well, I was between the main engines," Minh replied. "You wouldn't expect a ship there."

"I know I didn't," Jake replied.

A new navnet route was assigned, and Minh rolled into a thrusting dive, accelerating to maximum pattern speed in seconds. Within minutes, the Enforcer 1109 was in sight.

"Welcome back," Frost said once they were in proximity radio range. "Still in one piece?"

"New and improved, actually," Jake said. He could feel full control of his framework systems come flooding back, a sensation that made him feel excitable and powerful. He took a deep, shuddering breath and consciously let it go. The sensations faded, and he felt normal again.

The subdermal communicator he'd constructed on a whim worked better than any he'd used before. The tiny mechanism was nested in his jaw, requiring no more power than his body could naturally provide. He'd seen a design for one like it once, and remembered shaking his head at how expensive the miniaturised stealth technology was. It was tempting to try more, to push the framework to create other enhancements. He looked at his hand, squeezed it open and shut, marvelling at how much stronger he was, at how strange it felt. He could feel the muscles flexing under his skin, as though they were bands that begged to be stretched and stressed.

They landed on an elevation pad and emerged in the main hold. "Time for some discipline," he said as much to himself as to anyone listening in.

He opened the side door of the shuttle and hurled the first crate containing a captor out so hard it bounced and rolled. The second was right behind it. The outrage at being captured returned as he grabbed the belt of the captor he'd crushed under foot and carried him out into the main hold. There was a crowd gathering, many of them looking at the man he dragged along. His head was hanging at an awkward, unnatural angle.

Jake dropped him at his feet and retracted the hood of his own vacsuit. "Get those crates open and bring the men inside here," he ordered. He turned to Minh, who was half out of his fighter. "I'll need your sidearm for this."

"We can't do that, Jake," Minh whispered back. "If you execute someone here, then this becomes a crime scene."

"And that'll slow down the sale of the ship," Jake finished. "I have another idea, get some sealant foam."

"Sealant foam?" Minh asked, cocking his head.

"It's good to twenty eight hundred degrees, right?" Jake asked.

"I know what he's thinkin', lad," Frost said, grabbing a can of sealant foam from a box nearby. "It so happens we needed some while we repaired this lift, so there's some ready at hand."

A few crewmen dragged one of the captors, while the other was dragged by a grinning, broad shouldered crewman Jake recognised – David, a former slave, then defender of the Triton under Agameg's command. "Your luggage, Sir," he announced as he pushed the man to his knees. "Crewcast says he's Regan Diri."

Three crewmen forced the other to kneel in front of Jake. The captors turned captives eyed the crowd warily and avoided their commander's eyes.

Jake knelt down. "Who organized this?" he asked Regan.

He hesitated, glancing at his companion before Jake caught his forehead in his hand and looked him in the eye. "This took a long time to put together and you must have had a plan to get out of the solar system. Who was helping you?"

"We planned it ourselves," Regan replied. "The five of us."

"I killed one of you, put another in stasis, and there's you two," Jake paused a moment, staring at the man, who was growing more nervous by the second. "That makes four! Who's number five!"

"Four!" Regan cried. "I meant four!"

Jake let him go and stepped back. He took a can of foam sealant from Frost and tossed it to David. "Paste this guy to the front of my shuttle," he ordered, gesturing towards the shuttle behind him, "and use the whole can. I don't want him falling off when I enter the atmosphere."

Some of the people in the crowd surrounding them were shocked, but most laughed or cheered, including Frost, whose belly laughter rose above even the hundreds that gathered.

Regan tried to fight David as he was drawn up to his feet, but David clutched the man's suit between the shoulder blades and shook hard. A few helping hands held Regan's arms while they tied his wrists with binding straps.

"Now, what's your name?" Jake asked the other one.

"Fullerton, Bernard Fullerton," replied the remaining captor. His attention was noticeably split between Jake and the front of the shuttle, where David and a couple of other crewmen were spraying sealant beneath the front viewport.

"All right, Fullerton, who was waiting in a ship with a faster than light drive?" Jake asked him.

"It was a guy named Edward, left the group a while ago," Fullerton replied.

"I remember that bastard, Edward Sherman, set fire to crew quarters in the green section of the Triton," Frost said. "Never thought a man of science could be such a pain in the ass."

"Where were you going to take me?" Jake asked, smiling a little.

Fullerton relaxed a little. "Port Sullivan, in UCW territory; they could pay the full bounty there."

"How long have you been planning this?"

"Ever since we got aboard the Enforcer, Sir," replied Fullerton. "I, I apologise," he stammered. "This wasn't my idea. They needed a good pilot and I didn't think they'd hurt you."

"Well," Jake said, grinning a little too much. "It's good to hear that you weren't interested in slagging me or stunning me, just passing me off to my worst enemies for cash." He looked to Frost and sighed. "Put him beside his friend there, I want to ride these morons through the atmosphere and see if the vacsuits hold up."

The laughter and excitement filling that huge hold made Jake feel like things were falling in order again. "We make the final trip in twenty minutes, load up!" he ordered.

"Good to have you back, Captain," Frost said as he came to stand beside Jake. "Just wondering, what are you going to do with the broken neck fellow and the corpse?"

"Put them in one of those combat gurneys we planned to leave behind. We're going to have to take them with us so the Carthans don't have something new to bitch about when they take possession of the ship."

Minh took his place on the opposite side of Jake, shaking his head at the sight of Regan getting pasted to the front of the shuttle. The crew were behaving as if it was a party game. "A crew that plays together..." Minh said.

"Stays together," Frost finished with a satisfied grin.

CHAPTER 14
DETERMINATION

"I actually felt guilty for a while after they gave me my new body. It was so easy when I spent most of my time with the Child Prophet," Eve said as they strode towards the airlock nearest to her quarters. The hallways in that section of the Overlord II were older, the shiny black decks slightly worn down from being polished thousands of times over the years. It seemed most of the ship was scrubbed, if not once a day, several times a week by mindless bots that went out of their way not to be seen. "They used to call me Nora."

"That was your name before your father-" Lina started to ask quietly.

"That's in the past now. Hampon hasn't called me that once since his toy clone was killed."

"Another one is almost finished. He's being implanted today."

"Why would Hampon create another Child Prophet? His Victory Machine stopped sending him information weeks ago."

"I don't know about that, but I think he wants a live clone so he can properly introduce you to the Order Of Eden flock."

"Flock. I hate that word. It makes them all sound so helpless and mindless."

"Hampon said it was apt, especially from your point of view."

Eve thought for a moment and nodded. "He's right. The people below are mindless. They follow their stomachs and baser needs. I cannot believe that there are nineteen million of them already. Pregnancy rates are over twenty percent."

"Twenty one point seven percent, actually. They seem to be embracing the goal of repopulating the galaxy wholeheartedly," said Lina.

"If there's one thing I've learned, humans don't have to be told to breed. As far as I'm concerned, the only reason the pregnancy rate is so high is because we disable contraception as part of the intake process when someone arrives on Pandem. Directive or not, that world is about to be awash with humanity and everything they've rebuilt or are building will look used and stained within a year," Eve said.

"I think that's why some ships carrying new followers are being sent to another system now, closer to the New Frontier. There is a greater purpose to Pandem, though. I'm sure Hampon will enlighten-"

"I'm not interested in Pandem. There is one thing I want from this solar system, and it's something I already own anyway." She stopped in front of a large airlock door and regarded Lina. "You've been sent to make sure I behave, and that extends well past making sure I eat and sleep regularly. Who are you, really, Lina?"

"I'm your loyal servant," Lina said, warily.

A flash of silver metal moved past the transparent door of the airlock, and Lina flinched. She stared through it a moment before her eyes widened. "That's a construction ship," she said. "You've summoned it here against the wishes of our

Master."

A surge of rage seized Eve, and she slapped Lina so hard she was almost pulled off-balance herself. "Hampon will never be my master!" she shouted. "He's a deluded, diseased waste of a being, and he won't keep me from taking what's mine."

Lina's cheek was already turning red. As Eve moved towards the airlock, Lina rushed into her path, punching the disengage key as the construction ship tried to dock outside.

Eve tried to pull the shorter woman aside. Lina turned towards her and pushed Eve's hands away, preventing her from getting a grip on her robes. "I can't let you do this," Lina said. "The Virus!"

With a lunge, Eve caught Lina's throat in her hands and started to squeeze. "It's a lie, he's only trying to keep me helpless. I won't be in his thrall."

"It's true," Lina croaked.

"You're blind," Eve said as she squeezed harder and looked into the woman's dull brown eyes. "You're useless to me."

A harsh blow caught her behind the knees, and Eve caught sight of a pair of armoured guards as she fell to the ground. They'd come up behind her while she was focused on Lina, something that would never have happened if she'd been in direct communication with the system.

A flash of light from a high-powered stunner blocked her vision and made her numb. Another flash rendered Eve unconscious.

CHAPTER 15
AN ENTRANCE

Agameg and Finn always found a way to connect when their shift started in the morning, despite the nondescript grey worker vacsuits everyone were sealed up in. They were assigned to work on the Samson after a long argument with their new head of intelligence, Jason. At first, Jason had them running around from one random job to another, something different every day, but on day six Jason's system had Agameg and Finn working on the same trash removal detail.

Finn recognised Agameg when he saw him shift between the two forms he spent the most time in while hiding amongst the workers. There were other issyrians on the detail, but there was something about the way he shifted that suggested it was him. When Finn caught him shifting into the shape of a portly man behind a crate one afternoon, he couldn't stop laughing.

"Apparently, you find fat people very funny," Agameg said.

Finn shook his head, then pointed at Agameg's knees. "I don't think-" he took a breath, "-don't think they're supposed to waddle below the middle so much," he managed before another bout of laughter.

With a little help, Agameg shifted into a more convincing portly human. No one seemed to notice that Agameg could shift some of the bulk out of the way when necessary, so it didn't impede his work.

Separately, they may have never complained openly about being kept away from the Samson, but together they felt fortified enough to approach Jason Everin directly, and tell him they wouldn't go along unless they were allowed to participate in the Samson project. Finn and Agameg, being two of the new designers for the ship, were given a way to give orders and instructions to other workers using proxies, so no one could tell who the orders came from; all they knew was that they came from someone with more authority.

In the weeks since, Finn and Agameg watched morale plummet. Sealed vacsuits with blacked out faceplates and instructions to keep your identity to yourself made for brutal conditions. Hundreds of people worked on the Samson, and they needed visible leaders who could be present. They also needed each other for support and camaraderie, and to feel like a proper crew. Finn hated Jason's plan, couldn't believe it had gone on for so long, but he had to admit he was learning a lot about leadership. He and Agameg used the proxy band not only to issue commands, but after a few weeks they used it to cheer people up with comments like, 'Your Secret Overlords are highly impressed with worker 1128. Please dance with them for one minute if you see them today. Vigorously.' One worker on ground duty, or 'move and pile objects' duty, was not only surprised but entertained all day, and Agameg never stopped laughing when he saw someone stop and follow instructions upon seeing that worker.

There were others, like making a few kiddie pools out of scrap outside the hangar that were eventually used for their intended purpose, but initially used by the more lighthearted crewmembers. They didn't use them to cool down, but to take funny holoimages during breaks in their sealed vacsuits. Oz first noticed them when one of the larger wading pools had as many people sitting along the inside as possible. "I think the pretence of so many humans who cannot feel the water relaxing in once place has broken, Oz," Agameg said as the Commander laughed so hard he had to sit down. They waved, and beckoned for him to join them, making it much worse.

Most of the 'Overlord Gags' as they came to be called weren't as elaborate. Though they did become a daily thing, they could only do so much for morale. Agameg and Finn were careful not to suggest anything that got in the way of the work or put anyone in danger, and Finn was sure that's why they were allowed to keep it up for as long as they had.

Over several weeks, Finn had the pleasure of watching the Samson get torn down to her skeleton then rebuilt. The design was a collaborative effort between all their qualified people: Ayan, Liam Grady, Laura Everin, Frost, Agameg, Captain Valance, Finn himself, and others. They focused on a design that would be quick to build, and it changed depending on the materials available. The ship was going to be something very different, thanks to her original, multipurpose frame design and the heavy building girders they used to reinforce her.

All kinds of scrap metal was available, thanks to a junk yard that encroached on the nearby forest. Alaka's team were incredible salvagers. Finn wished he could have gone on more than one ride with them, but after a firefight broke out between them and two other groups of scavengers, someone above Finn's head removed that option.

"I wonder how Ashley and Stephanie are doing with their rotation?" Agameg asked over a private channel. "I haven't spoken to either of them in twelve days."

"I know, this limited communication thing is a pain in the ass," Finn said, checking the connections on a wormhole generator. It was originally intended for an extended model Uriel fighter, but the Samson borrowed four. "Stephanie said it wasn't that bad when I got in touch with her last week. Ashley's learning a lot, but she doesn't seem to like it much."

"You spoke to her?" Agameg asked.

"No, she hasn't spoken to me since this started, but Steph gave me an update." Finn sighed before going on. "I guess there's some residual weirdness after our last date."

"I wish you humans had better senses," Agameg said. "You'd know if you were compatible right away."

"That would make dating simpler," Finn replied. "Can you tell if people are a match?"

"Sometimes," Agameg said. "I try not to let people know I can smell their mood. I told Bella once, and she said it 'creeped her out' so I keep that to myself."

"Who's Bella?"

"Oh, I suppose she left the Samson before you came aboard. Very kind human, she enjoyed watching people, so we were a natural pair," Agameg replied, closing the casing of the wormhole module. They walked down the hallway to a junction and opened it. Hundreds of wires ran into and through the box.

"So, can you do it through a vacsuit?" Finn asked.

"No, not if it's sealed. Some humans are difficult to read if they have only retracted their head gear, too."

"How easy am I to read?"

"You are," Agameg considered his wording for a moment. "More complex than many humans."

"What about Stephanie? Or Frost?" Finn asked, holding a band of metal up to a cable and punching a bolt through it with a multitool so the power line was secured to the inner bulkhead.

"Frost is almost always very relaxed, but there is a bite to his fragrance that speaks of the warrior within. Of all the humans I've ever met, he carries the least guilt. Stephanie reads very differently when she's on duty. Calm, controlled, confident. When she's off duty, she's more like Ashley than I would like to tell her."

Finn wished he'd had that conversation weeks before, and took the opportunity to ask about the one person he wanted to learn of most. "What about Ashley?"

"She's very smelly," Agameg replied.

Finn doubled over with laughter.

Agameg stopped checking the cables running from the junction and looked at Finn. "Smelly is the right word," he explained. "I just checked."

"I know," Finn replied, recovering. "It's just not the word I expected."

"Oh," Agameg replied. "Would 'pungent' be better?"

Finn shook his head, "I get what you mean, but she might not like the word. 'Fragrant', maybe?" He waited as Agameg looked it up.

"I suppose, it is pleasant once you get over the shock," Agameg replied. "It's difficult to put into words, she's like," he hesitated, rubbing his hand up and down one arm, something he'd started doing when looking for the right word or phrase. "Like those long meal tables with different foods?"

"A buffet?" Finn offered.

"Yes! Her moods mix and change until she seems to settle on one, then you can't help but know what mood she's in. Her influence is greater than she thinks," Agameg said.

"So it's a good smell," Finn said.

"Yes," Agameg replied. "That wasn't clear?"

"When you say 'smelly' or 'pungent' we think about things like trash cleanup."

"Ah," Agameg replied, recoiling slightly. "I am understanding why there are so many misunderstandings in your language more all the time."

Finn began scanning the wiring and nodded down the hallway. "Check the one at frame nine, I can handle this one."

"You don't want to know how you and Ashley are together?" Agameg asked as he walked down the hall at a good pace. Checking junctions and cable runs were necessary, but boring. They both wanted to get it over with.

"I'm surprised you remember, we haven't met up in a while," Finn replied.

"I'd never forget," Agameg said. "When you are together, and there is no one else near, there is a calming fragrance. You have that affect on many people, but more so on her."

Finn thought for a moment, reassured by Agameg's interpretation. "Thank you, that explains a lot, I think."

A Stellarnet news alert popped up in the corner of Finn's visor. He froze at the sight of a shuttle with two people in vacsuits affixed to the front burning through the atmosphere. One was holding his arms up in front of his face, the other struggled to break free of the sealant foam that held him fast to the hull – not a good plan, Finn thought, but the man was obviously panicking. The caption at the bottom of the alert read: JACOB VALANCE RETURNS!

Finn checked the local air traffic and found the shuttle, flanked by a wing of fighters and the rest of the shuttles from the Enforcer. "Agameg!"

"I can hear you perfectly clearly over comms," Agameg replied. "There's no need to yell."

"Captain's back, and it looks like he's changing the plan," Finn said, making sure his scan was complete and the wiring was correct before slamming a panel door and running for the nearest exit.

"Oh?"

"He's landing now, link up with the main crew channel." Finn nearly bumped into a crewman as he came around a corner to one of the main debarkation ramps. "Sorry," he said as he pushed past. He followed his own advice and connected to the main and command channels using his real ident. He wasn't the only one; he saw Stephanie, Frost, March, and a moment later, Agameg and Ashley popped in.

"- won't be happy about this," Oz said over the command channel. "Uh, hey guys, your idents are showing."

"That's over," Captain Valance said. "If they want to operate in the open, like I do, then they're welcome to. The plan worked for a while, I'll give Jason credit for that, but the idiots riding on the front of my shuttle found cracks, so I'm calling it."

Finn came out from under the Samson and looked to the opening in the tall hangar doors. He was treated to the sight of an entire wing of Uriel fighters, and over a dozen shuttles landing all at once. The first to touch down was Jacob's shuttle.

He stepped outside a moment later, in a grey vacsuit with burn holes at the shoulder, leg, and torso. Finn joined the crowd that gathered around. Someone was broadcasting his landing to the Stellarnet, and the video window on his visor showed that viewership was going up by the thousands per second.

Jacob walked to the front of his shuttle and faced the crowd with the two hanging men behind him. "These two tried to kidnap me and claim the bounty on my head," Captain Valance announced. "The rest of the bounty hunters that came with them didn't survive."

Minh-Chu Buu joined Captain Valance, with crossed arms and a stern expression that made him look much older than Finn would have ever guessed. Finn noticed a new emblem on his chest: a skull with crossed samurai swords on its forehead and lettered teeth that read: SAMURAI SQUADRON. Along the contour of the upper half of the skull was written: FIRST STRIKE FIGHTER SQUADRON.

With a quick check, Finn saw that the emblem change was performed by the other squadron leader, Nathan Kipp, also known as Slick. "Big change coming," Finn said under his breath.

"I agree," Agameg said.

"By hunting me, these men put my crew at risk," Captain Valance said. He only had to put his hand out and Minh-Chu knew to unholster his firearm, a heavy, armour piercing weapon known as the Spectral Dynamics Violator Handgun, and hand it to Captain Valance. He deftly adjusted the settings on the weapon, turned, and without a second's hesitation, shot one of the hanging men in the head until the rounds burst through the worker's vacsuit. It took less than a second. The sight and sound of the act was so sudden, so violent, that Finn and many other onlookers flinched. The man's head was gone in a mist of red, the hull of the shuttle behind sparked and smouldered fitfully.

He returned his attention to the crowd, lowering the smoking sidearm. "I hunted the trash of the galaxy for years, you cannot surprise me. You may be able to catch me, but you'll regret it every time," Captain Valance said. His expression was enough to force Finn to unconsciously take a step back.

"Come after me and I'll make everything you own mine, kill you and your crew, then leave your carcass in the open so everyone knows where I tore you to pieces. That includes every military organisation that seems to be confused about who I am, and what I'm responsible for."

The viewer counter on the Stellarnet feed had jumped into the millions, and it was climbing faster. Finn had never seen anything like it, and couldn't help but get excited.

"So there is no confusion, I'll tell you my story, and what I intend to do next. I was created in a Vindyne lab less than a decade ago, stolen by a woman who is part of a great legacy. Vindyne gave me the name Jacob Valance. For some reason, they didn't come to take me back after Regent Galactic bought Vindyne, so I continued on, took on a crew, started hunting, and then I found another man's memories in my head. Jonas Valent. I have all his memories, they feel like my own, but I'm a different man, a more severe man, a killer and a pirate. The Order of Eden likes to call me a terrorist.

"The charges submitted to the courts by Regent Galactic, that Jonas Valent is responsible for the Holocaust Virus that cost so many lives, are misdirected at me. The man they're looking for is dead. He was also innocent. I'm the last living part of his legacy, and in honour of him, I'm taking his last name. I'm also answering to a calling that I think he'd be proud of.

"My ship, the Samson, may have been destroyed, but I have a new vessel, one that has been built on a promise I made after assisting Holocaust victims in the Enreega system. I cannot imagine that anyone but the Eden Cult are responsible for the Holocaust Virus, and the deaths of billions, yet no one is willing to declare war.

"So let me be the first. You've cost me my ship, beloved crewmembers, and the daughter of the Valent legacy: Alice. I will hunt Eden ships, Order of Eden allies, Regent Galactic assets, and disrupt, capture or destroy them whenever and wherever I can. You want to see a terrorist? I'll show you one."

Captain Jacob Valent turned and took aim at the last hanging man, who struggled to get free of the sealant that held him fast to the shuttle's hull. "And my message to the hunters out there is simple: don't get in my way." He pulled the trigger, burning through the man's head.

The transmission ended as some of the crowd began cheering. They were joined by more, and even Finn found himself clapping. Something within him stirred. He'd seen some of the devastation brought on by the Holocaust Virus, and known so many people who lost their entire families. He hadn't heard from home either, and suspected the worst. It was something he was loathe to face, but he hoped that someone would reply to the transmission he sent home seven weeks before.

Captain Valent walked straight towards him, and Finn lowered his hood, and then retracted his faceplate. The air was warm against his face, and smelled of ozone with a little trash mixed in for good measure, but it still felt good.

Stephanie passed by Finn, taking her hood down and shaking her hair free. "Nice speech, I almost believed we have a chance," she said, grinning.

"We're going to do a lot of good," Captain Valent said. "We're going to do this the smart way."

One concern nagged Finn, and he stepped towards them as they hugged briefly. "Sorry, but, Sir?" he appealed.

Jake fixed him with a rare smile and said, "It's good to see you, Finn, Agameg."

"Yes, uh, you too, but what's this about the Samson being destroyed?" Finn pressed. "She's almost back together, or at least together enough so she can take off , and-"

"I'm renaming her," Captain Valent said. "So much has changed that we may as well change that too, and it'll give us the element of surprise for a while."

"We're going to make some serious cash," Frost said as he joined the growing group.

"Jake!" shouted Oz as he ran towards him. He was in full boarding armour, and carried a heavy rifle across his back, but moved with great speed and agility regardless. He stopped and whispered something in Captain Valent's ear.

"What do you mean, 'where's Ayan?'" Jake asked.

"Jason, Laura, and Liam are all on their way back here, thanks to that speech," Oz said. "They said Ayan met you in some high class hotel in Greydock. They haven't heard anything from her since."

Finn could see Captain Valent look her up on a small comm screen he called up in his wrist, and the results darkened his expression. When Finn checked himself, the system reported:

USER NOT IN RANGE.

CHAPTER 16
THREE METRES

Ayan could feel nanobots and biological stimulants moving through her ruined arm and hand. It felt as though someone was pouring cold water down the inside of the limb, and she knew what came next would be horrible. There were no painkillers - somehow they'd missed including that in Freeground's modified framework survival package. The sensations stopped. "Oh, God," she whispered.

The system went to work on her entire arm at the same time. The broken bones from her elbow on grated like sandy stones as they were set. The pain was so intense she couldn't breathe, and she was seeing stars before it was over. Her vacsuit formed a hard splint. When it was done she was covered in sweat, her heart was racing, and her left arm throbbed furiously. A signal from the framework system to her brain told her that it was out of power.

She was afraid of that. The system had already taken care of internal injuries and corrected a minor head injury before waking her up. Unlike Jake's framework system, it wasn't designed to draw power from the outside world, but depended on her body's natural electricity, her movements, and a microscopic gravity mill. Ayan was no expert on the technology, so she had no idea how long it would take for the system to accumulate enough power to finish putting her back together.

"I'm getting a command unit for each wrist like Stephanie's done," she told the empty room. "A backup full of painkillers would be amazin' right now." She couldn't help but chuckle at herself and the reappearance of her thicker English accent, something she'd never had in her second life, but faintly remembered from the first Ayan's childhood.

When she recovered a little, she looked at the broken limb. It was curved backwards before, with a twisted, mangled thing at the end that was her hand. The suit kept her from taking shrapnel damage, and her skin was intact, but it couldn't deal with point blank concussive damage. The work her suit had done to straighten and splint her arm and hand was perfect. From the outside, it looked like a slightly swollen, normal limb, but Ayan didn't want to see what it was like beneath.

There was superficial damage to her stomach, where the android was trying to stretch her suit open, but it was a mild sting compared to that left arm. Her basic vacsuit was able to protect the rest of her body, especially her neck and head, but it was almost completely out of power after applying the corrective splint.

Her wrist unit had disintegrated, and she was left with the basic controls on her suit. The internal clock on her visor told her it had been one hour and thirty-six minutes since she'd arrived in the hotel room.

"Connect to regional communications, link with Triton Enclave in Port Rush," she ordered the basic computer in the suit. It attempted to make a link and failed, showing no available network nodes. "Scan for available network connections," Ayan ordered, trying to roll over, towards her good arm. Her broken hand and arm and burned stomach all protested, and she abandoned the attempt. NO COMMUNICATIONS SERVICES AVAILABLE, replied the computer.

She came to the conclusion that Thurge, or Burke, or Wheeler himself, arranged to have communications blocked in that room, which explained why her explosion didn't set off any alarms, why she couldn't get a connection, and why no one had come to find out why her communicator wasn't working.

Ayan looked across the room at the remains of the Jacob imitation. It's head, one shoulder, and part of its upper chest cavity was gone. Even through the pain, she couldn't help but tell it, "That's what you get for trying to make me your distressed damsel."

Ayan looked for a wired communications pad on the wall. To her relief, she spotted one built into an imitation antique lamp. The force of the blast had knocked it from the bedside table to the floor.

"Only three metres away, maybe less," Ayan said to herself.

She made an attempt at pushing herself up only to have a throb she barely paid attention to in her thigh become a searing, sharp pain. "So, that's broken too," she grunted to herself.

Ayan grabbed the low shag of the carpet with her good arm and pushed with her good leg. Her suit protected her arm and thigh from being knocked around, but there were so many breaks that she found herself biting her lip and smothering a scream at the new rush of sensation. Aside from her broken bones and bruises, her burnt belly felt like it was ready to split open. Tears squeezed through her tightly closed lids the next time she renewed her efforts.

"That's a metre," Ayan said, fighting for breath. Inhaling too deeply made her stomach rage and breathing too quickly made her broken limbs jostle and sent shocks of pain throughout her body.

She closed her eyes for a moment and was rewarded with the memory of Jacob's imitator, leering at her, saying "I love you," using his voice. "I'm going to kill you for this, Wheeler," she said. She pressed on with renewed vigour, gritting her teeth at the pain every time she repeated the pattern of gripping the carpet to pull, and raising her good leg to push herself towards the communicator.

The last metre was the easiest. Her head tapped the overturned lamp and she sighed with relief.

Her vacsuit had expended all but the smallest amount of power resisting the force of the explosion, and when she motioned the command to open her faceplate, it couldn't unlock. After a few moments' fumbling, Ayan found the manual release button for her visor. It was just a slightly hardened part of her suit under the chin, and she had never used one; the memory of the emergency latch was from her predecessor, the first Ayan.

The seal didn't break at first, even though she heard the material try to separate. With some pushing and pulling, she got the transparent faceplate halfway up her face, so she could talk into the communicator clearly. Ayan pressed the CALL button and hoped. Lights flickered on, and the hologram of the concierge's head appeared.

"Can I help you-" he started before he fixed her with a shocked expression. "Oh my God, are you Ayan?"

"Looks like he's got something," Ayan heard Jason say in the background.

"What happened? Are you okay?" asked the young concierge.

"No," Ayan croaked. Tears surged forward, and it didn't matter to Ayan whether they were from relief or from desperation - she hated the fact that they came at all. She wanted to be stronger. "Send medics."

"They're on their way," the concierge said. "We were trying to find what room you were in, but the scanners in that section of the hotel have been down since the UCW left. I sent soldiers-"

The Concierge was shoved out of the way, and Laura appeared instead. "We're coming Ayan, there should be someone there soon."

Ayan breathed a shuddering sigh of relief as she looked out to the window. Laura offered light conversation, not probing into what had happened, just making her best efforts to distract Ayan while help was on the way. She half listened, looking to the rose-coloured view through the generously proportioned windows. The tall buildings outside looked more like ancient monuments in that light, standing the test of time against a backdrop of rolling, dusty hills that were just starting to find a hint of green in the valleys.

The thoughts going through her mind were not ready to be shared. The last two hours were an education, a violent return to reality.

Sprawled out on the floor of that ruined room, Ayan regarded her previous attempts to get into fighting shape, to form an understanding of Tamber and the conditions there, as well as how she was trying to make a civilisation out of their band of refugees in an entirely new light.

Changes had to be made, and it would start with her. Ayan caught herself letting her eyes close when the memory of the eager android Jake returned and she flinched herself back to wakefulness. "Why did it have to be him?" she asked the empty room.

"What's that?" Laura asked.

"The one they sent to attack me looked like Jake," Ayan told her, squeezing her eyes closed. She was already tired of breaking down, whether from emotional or physical pain, it didn't matter. "I stopped him," she said, unable to stop a new wash of tears.

"I'm sorry," Laura offered genuinely. "I'm so sorry."

It was the last thing she had a chance to say before the doors were forced open and Carthan soldiers rushed in with a medical team in tow.

CHAPTER 17
EVENING DESCENDS

Shamus Frost couldn't remember the last time he'd taken a moment to watch an eclipse. It was only a phenomenon of perspective and the movement of celestial bodies, but the one above him was somehow special. The busy sky and the myriad ships that traversed it were tinted in hues of red and purple as Kambis appeared to block out the sun. Frost knew it was Tamber, the moon he stood on, that was moving, and the colour was a result of light passing through Kambis' atmosphere, then through Tamber's, but for once the knowledge didn't spoil the illusion. The view from where he sat was incredible.

When he spotted the old lift leading to a gangway running along the roof of the main hangar they were rebuilding the Samson in, he wanted to check it out. However, the need to remain anonymous was far more important at the time, and he didn't want to stand out as the only worker peon that was exploring. When things settled down after the nearly two thousand workers who had been sealed in their vacsuits for weeks were told they didn't have to remain hidden, he took the opportunity to take that lift up all the way. From the gangway, he watched as everyone below was given the next twenty hours off. Relief became celebration, and he knew it would be an evening to remember. He found a hatch leading up, and he made it to the roof of the hangar in time to catch the light show of the eclipse.

The heat of the long day hadn't subsided yet, but Frost kept his hood down. A bead of sweat would occasionally roll down his face and catch in the scruffy grey beard he'd grown while he was incognito. The air was always swirling around, thanks to the ships and smaller craft flying as near as a hundred metres overhead, but that only heated the air, and lent it fragrances of burnt fuel and that of superheated thrusters. He claimed many times that it was his favourite smell in the universe, but that was untrue. It smelled as bad to him as it did to everyone else, but Frost, the name and the guise he put on for the benefit of his men and himself, loved all things mechanical, all things that gave men the power to live and fight between the stars.

The criss-crossing lines of light around Kambis became brighter as more of the sun was blocked out. The lines represented large ships and beneath that were radial cities. While they were hiding, the solar system was coming to life. Millions were arriving in every kind of craft, in every condition, from as many as nine sectors of space. There was a time only years ago when he would have broken from the Samson crew, taken Stephanie with him if he could have, and turned the coalescence of humanity into a grand opportunity or two. Fleecing the desperate was easy. Immoral, he knew, but not all desperate people were poor people. He could make a fortune and disappear into the crowd effortlessly. He'd done it before, when it was far easier to track someone down.

He looked down to the settlement the Triton crew had built in the space they'd managed to rent from Patrizia Salustri. It seemed so big when he was down there, walking amongst the people. From where he sat, near the edge of the huge hangar, it was impossible to ignore how tiny it really was. They had a few slips, had erected walls where older barricades had fallen down using scrap metal and a couple of smaller stripped vehicles. There were two heavily guarded gates, and he could see a great deal of security officers below, patrolling the habitat and work areas. They were little black dots amongst a shifting sea of people in grey, yellow, red, green, and blue vacsuits. Aged shipping containers, some stacked three high, were converted into buildings. Most people didn't have a bunk on a ship; they lived in cramped quarters, sleeping on small cots. The interiors of those homes were constantly improving, thanks to creature comforts they stripped from the Enforcer, but there was never an improvement in how much space they had to work with.

The slips they called home were full to capacity. Even the fighters had to stack when they weren't being prepped for a mission, an operation that was so delicate that he was glad it wasn't his job.

Thin towers made from more scrap reached up slightly higher than the roof he was sitting on. They were emitter towers that they started building while he was on the Enforcer. The energy shield would be tested tomorrow, and he was glad he'd be able to show his face, because he wanted to congratulate Laura and her team on a job well done if it worked. If it didn't work, he wanted to dig in and help. So many people beneath him bought into the illusion of safety that numbers brought.

Ships crashed every day in Port Rush, thanks to the removal of many autopilots that were tied into the functions of artificial intelligences. The shield would protect against most impacts, and it could be moved if they had to relocate. He'd heard that the negotiations led by Ayan turned out better than expected. The rumour that they would have their own island in the fresh water sea was spreading through the settlement like wildfire, and Frost couldn't picture what the scene below would look like if the whole settlement was relocated to some oversized beach. He wanted to see it though, and that led him to a realisation that slowly brought a smile to his face.

He had no desire to leave. The call to war didn't make him nervous. He felt he was at peace for the first time he could remember. He had a purpose, was part of a crew, he was respected, and for the first time in a long time, he didn't feel like he was alone. The people he would be fighting for were all there below him. He was so far above they looked no taller than the last joint of his thumb, but he was close enough to make out what they were doing.

With bare faces, they gathered into groups. Little ones darted between those clusters of old and new friends. He could see Minh picking up a young lad and showing him the inside of his fighter, his dad looking on with crossed arms and a smile Frost supposed must have been there. In the early weeks of work, a couple of hundred people left. More than half returned with the realisation that it was much worse outside.

There was sadness in the first month, when most of the messages reaching out to family and friends started yielding results. Most of the replies were from governments, or from close friends who had unfortunate news. Billions were dead all across human civilisation. That brought sorrowful news for most, and solidified their desire to remain a part of the Triton crew, even without the ship.

Most of the slaves they'd rescued didn't have homes to return to. The Order of Eden had taken entire solar systems and the Eden Fleet, more massive than anyone could have imagined, stood sentry. It was rare that Frost felt fortunate to have only one surviving family member – a sister who hadn't gotten back to him yet. She was a great ways off, so even if she survived, he wouldn't get a response for another ten or so days. He hoped for the best, and tried not to think about it.

Frost looked to the sky as the sun's light finished disappearing behind Kambis. The scene below lit up as most of the people still wearing their vacsuits turned on their work lights. Stripes on their arms, backs, chests, and shoulders glowed brighter the further they were from other similarly dressed workers, and dimmer as they stood closer, so they always walked in a safe level of luminescence. "Now that's somethin' to see," he said to himself. It was a strange, beautiful light show from his vantage point.

He tapped his real command and control unit, the high powered one from his time on the Triton, and called Stephanie's ident using silent mode. He projected her hologram onto the roof beside him, and watched her dig through a box. Seeing her extended the life of that smile that had grown on his face.

Stephanie pulled a long, simple, stretchy dress with slits part way up the sides out of the box and she held it up against herself. "You'd turn heads in that," Frost said.

She let the dress slip back into the box and smiled at him through her comm unit. "Ash is sharing a bunk room while her quarters are being rebuilt, so she's picking through her stuff and handing a few things out. I think she gave me all her Slink Fit clothes, from the looks of it."

"Strange, that's the last thing I'd think she'd pass on," Frost said.

"I know," Stephanie said. "I'm going to hang on to this stuff for a while. I think she's just worn down from only being able to talk to me this whole time. The buddy system seemed to work for a lot of people through this anonymous crap, but I don't think it's done her any favours."

"She didn't link up with a couple of other people?" Frost asked. "Even I linked with the maximum."

"Eight people?" Stephanie asked.

"Aye. Why?"

"I guess I'm just surprised. I thought you'd enjoy the break."

"What can I say? People need people," Frost replied.

Stephanie pulled another garment out of the plastic box, and he had trouble figuring out what kind of clothing it was, but couldn't help noticing that there wasn't much to it. "That's true, especially for Ashley," she replied. "I'm hoping she feels better after sleeping for a shift." She dropped that garment back into the box and looked at him through her comm. "If you come down quick I think I'll have time to model a few things for you before our cabin mates get back."

"On my way," Frost said, standing up. He took five steps towards the hatch and broke through a panel in the roof. "Bollox! I knew that was there!" he said as he tried to manually set his flimsy workman's vacsuit for a fall. His command and control unit had difficulty connecting to the suit as he plummeted through the open air.

"Shamus!" Stephanie shouted as she realised what was going on.

Time ran fast as he fell through thirty-five metres of open air. His comm unit flashed green and he felt the suit change the moment before he hit.

Chapter 18
Farewells

"We still tell stories about you, our little Ash who bought her freedom and became a pilot," the small image of Frederick Andie said. Ashley sat cross-legged in her bunk, with a small bag and a duffel in front of her. She'd just finished checking her incoming messages when one more appeared from Frederick, the older gentleman who raised her when she lived as a slave on the Gamrie estate.

"I was so glad when I got your data burst," he went on. "I was so worried you got caught by something like so many other people. The Sand Rhumerie, the resort in which I was head chef, survived very well. The dispensers seemed a little peevish once they were infected, but they couldn't do much harm. Bumped Gilly, one of our guest services girls, on the head something awful, but that was the worst of it. A few other resorts that specialised in the human touch fared very well, as did the poorer quarters in the cities. It seems anyone who couldn't afford anything with an artificial intelligence had the best chance of staying clear of this while our government got to work on putting the mad droids down. Grand House Gamrie is gone, burned to the ground by those serving bots the Lady bought right before you were packed off with Master Gamrie on his star yacht. The slave quarters got off fine, most of them are here now.

"With most of the federal and provincial governments crippled, we're holding a new vote, and it looks like one of the equality parties will get a majority, so we expect slavery to be outlawed sometime early next year, on this world at least. I watch for you or your captain to appear on the Stellarnet, and I'm not the only one. So many people wonder where he is, what's he's doing and if he's going to hold up the promise he made to take the fight to the Order of Eden. They have booths here now, where they sign people up, putting them on the path to paradise, so they say. It costs sixty eight thousand credits here, so only a few people I know have signed up. They go in, get tests, pay, and I never see them again." He rolled his eyes, in just such an exaggerated way that reminded her of all the times he caught her doing something he didn't approve of when she was younger. A laugh bubbled up from somewhere deep inside.

"Happy message?" Finn asked as he entered the eight bunk cabin. The bunk beds seemed too white and new. They were from the Enforcer, installed only a week before. The rest of the cabin was still bare in most places, all the cables and tubing was plainly visible running tightly against the walls and ceilings.

Ashley paused the playback and nodded. "Fred, his transmission finally got here."

"I remember you telling me about him," Finn said as he dropped his duffel bag onto the bunk across from hers. "That must be a huge relief. I'll let you get back to it."

Ashley didn't hesitate to continue the playback, her attention fixed on Fred's head, hovering above the smooth navy blue sheet on her bunk. "I hope there's some truth to what the Order of Eden is promising, but I can't help but side with those people who write 'hate fate' everywhere. It's graffiti, but it gets people thinking about that little Prophet's 'better fate for mankind' rhetoric, it gets people talking, and some of them wonder when they'll see more about your captain leading a charge somewhere. I have to admit my reasons for watching for him are more selfish than most. I'm looking for a glance at you, little raven. Not so little anymore, but you'll still be that girl the Gamries dropped in my lap because they couldn't get her to stop fidgeting." He smiled at the fond recollection. The message cut out for a moment then continued with his head turned differently, indicating that he'd cut something out. "This is getting long, so I won't keep you. I only must say that you have nothing to worry about. Everyone you knew and loved here are well; I've shared your message with them and they want the best for you." He said it almost like a presenter, but he always had a slightly stiff air about him. "I hope you're where you want to be, and doing something you believe in. If you ever need to retreat, there's always room for you here." The recording ended and Ashley added it to her long-term storage.

"Little raven?" Finn asked. "I don't mean to pry, but I couldn't help but overhear."

"It's what he called me when I was really small. He said it was 'cuz I ate like a bird, and liked to perch and watch people."

"It had nothing to do with your hair?" Finn asked with a little teasing smile.

"Oh yeah, that too," she replied. Ashley sighed, feeling the relief of knowing Frederick was alive and well. She only had her own problems left to worry over.

"Is this okay? If I sleep here, I mean?" Finn asked, calling her attention back into the room.

Ashley realised how she was, or more appropriately, wasn't dressed just then. After she'd gotten rid of the low quality work suit while moving into her bunk, she threw on a skimpy synthetic silk crop top and the matching bottoms. She was about to put on her high quality vacsuit when the message from Frederick arrived, and, not normally very self-conscious, putting her vacsuit on became a very low priority. It impressed Ashley to no end that Finn was doing his absolute best to limit his gaze to eye contact. It wouldn't bother her if his eyes wandered, despite the fact the fact that their romance fizzled as it started, but he was trying so hard to be respectful. He was one of the people she'd miss once she moved on.

"I mean, Stephanie assigned me to this cabin, but I can ask her for non-co-ed. I'd understand," Finn continued. "I think she wanted to keep the old Samson crew together, even though I was new when all this-"

Ashley stood and embraced him tightly. He only hesitated a moment before returning the gesture. "That's, um," he said, hesitating a moment. "I guess it's okay?"

She gripped the back of his grimy work suit and croaked, "Yup." Ashley was surprised at the tears that came, but that had been happening a lot lately, a lot more than she'd like. "I'm such a baby," she said as she let go.

By the time she wiped her face once, Finn had a tissue for her. "Are you okay?"

She shook her head, trying to 'find her spine' as Ursula, a former Samson crewmember once told her to do under different circumstances, and answered,

"It was just hard being bagged up for so long in that worker's suit, not being able to talk to most people. Got your message bursts, though. Thank you." It was the best cover for her tears she could think of, and it seemed to work every time.

"Yeah, I could tell it was hard on you, tried to keep you up to date with what the reconstruction crew was doing," Finn replied.

"I spent more than half my time while I was in one of those," she said, pointing at her old worker's suit in the recycling box, "dragging stuff to and from the ships. Things got ridiculous when they started bringing things down from the Enforcer. I'm still sore all over."

"Recovery meds could take care of that," Finn said. "It was pretty rough for me too, those suits trick you by adding to your strength, but you don't realise how much work goes into just directing the crappy synthetic muscles."

"I know," Ashley said, reaching into her duffel bag and pulling her favourite vacsuit out. She'd already added a golden Chinese dragon that stretched from the back of one thigh to her shoulders. "But Steph told me to ride it out, and I did for the last few weeks. She was right about one thing though, I'm in much better shape, and didn't take any fitness meds for weeks. Don't know how I'm going to keep it up."

Finn turned around as she changed into the suit. "I've never bunked coed before," he said with a nervous laugh.

"A lot of people change in their bunk with the privacy curtain closed," Ashley said, pulling her vacsuit on. "I don't really care though, you forget to be shy when you grow up crammed into slave quarters."

"That must have sucked," Finn said. "I'm sorry."

"It wasn't as bad as it could've been. The Gamries didn't abuse us, and they gave their kids strict boundaries. Being monitored all the time was the worst, until Justice Gamrie took me with him on his yacht, then it was terrible."

"That's when Captain bought you?"

"Yup," Ashley replied, her mood brightening a bit. She closed the suit, leaving a slit half way down the front open. "All done, you can turn around."

Finn relaxed and continued to unpack his duffel bag into the footlocker and netting beneath the bunk above. "Were there other people serving aboard?"

Ashley knew he was trying to ask if she was the only slave aboard in a tactful way, and he was probably curious about other things as well, so she answered his unasked questions all at once. "I was the only one he owned, the rest were crew. He brought me along to show off, and because I was good at making sushi. I didn't like making it until I was free, and I always thought it was kind of racist when I was forced to learn how, especially since I wasn't Japanese, but he liked having an Asian make and present sushi to his friends. I tried to explain that sushi is a Japanese thing, and I was half Chinese, but he didn't really care."

Ashley stopped as Minh stepped into the door with a pair of pilots in tow. "Um, hi," she offered in surprise. She loved the weathered bomber jacket he wore over his vacsuit. First Light was printed in block letters on the left front, the Triton Skull was underneath, with the new Samurai Squadron skull with crossed swords stencilled beneath that. He seemed so interesting, like he had a world of experience she couldn't begin to imagine, but it didn't seem to weigh him down. It was enviable, and intimidating in its own way. His straight dark hair matched her own, only shorter, stopping at the base of his neck. Hers flowed halfway down her back.

"We're looking for cabin eight. This says it should be past frame eight somewhere," one grinning, long-faced pilot behind Minh-Chu said.

"You passed it about seven metres back," Finn answered. "Look for the recessed red handle on the port side, it's the next hatch."

"Uh, okay," he replied, starting to walk away. "Wait, do I pull the handle?"

"No," Finn said, making an effort to remain polite. "Don't pull the handle. Just go into the next hatch you see after it."

"It's a landmark, Joyboy," said a female pilot beside him. She had wild green and purple hair that struck out from her head like fine wire.

"It's a landmark," parroted the third pilot behind Minh, a short fellow with a broad, flat nose. He pushed Joyboy in the right direction with thick hands.

"What's the other half?" Minh asked, not following his three pilots.

"Huh?" Ashley asked.

"You said you were half Chinese," Finn reminded her.

"Oh, yeah," Ashley said, finding her place in the previous conversation and deciding to take it into a slightly different direction. "Gamrie used to take me with him on trips and business deals after I came of age because my heritage made me very expensive: I'm half old-world Chinese and Italian, a really hard to find breed. When Captain bought me, Gamrie was looking for a partner for me, a man of the same heritage so he could, well, you know." The room fell silent. "So Captain saved me from being bred like livestock, I guess." Minh and Finn's expressions seemed to be frozen, as if they didn't know what to say or do next. The awkwardness was starting to settle in, so she broke the silence. "I grew up knowing how expensive I was and why, so I guess it's not weird to me. Except for the breeding thing, which happens all the time, but I wasn't looking forward to it. I guess I'm still pretty proud of my heritage though, even now that I'm free."

"Well, if you were raised by people who kept telling you that it's what made you special, then it makes sense," Finn said. "There's a lot more to you than that, though."

"And now your value can't be measured," Minh-Chu said with a smile that disappeared a moment later. "That came out wrong, maybe. I meant you're immeasurable, in terms of money. As a slave, like when you're free you're worth a lot more."

"I-" Ashley started, smiling openly at his sinking attempt at communicating something she was pretty sure she already understood.

"It was good seeing you again," Minh burst with a forced grin. "Finn! Good seeing you too, Finn. Not just Ashley." He said before jerking ninety degrees so he faced the rear of the ship and marching away. "Places to meet, people to go," he could be heard saying to himself as he moved out of sight.

Finn stood stunned for a moment then burst out laughing, Ashley joined in, unable to resist. "I'm no expert," Finn said. "But I think he's crazy about you."

"I think he just had a mental moment," Ashley said, shaking her head.

"You were definitely the cause."

Ashley regarded Finn more seriously then. She hadn't broken many hearts in her time, maybe two, but she didn't want to make it three, especially if it was Finn's.

"It's okay," Finn said with a reassuring smile. "We're good. I'm glad we found out we're only friends early on, and it took me a while to stop wishing we were more, but I'm okay."

"You're so amazing, Finn," she said. Tears threatened to well up again, and she couldn't tell him why, that she would regret leaving Finn, Minh, and a situation that could have been perfect for her behind. Finn's reward was another gripping hug. "You make me feel lucky."

"Hey, it's all right, you have my blessing," Finn said in an attempt to comfort. "Just watch out for Paula, I hear she bites."

Ashley laughed and let him go. "Meanie."

"You're right, she's actually pretty personable if you're asking her for advice. I had to talk to her about the launch pods for the Samson, and we spent a while passing messages through the comm proxy."

"God, I don't regret leaving that behind," she said, recalling what it was like to pass messages through a system that kept their origins hidden while they were hiding. "I do stay away from Paula, though. The last thing I heard her say about me was pretty nasty, so I'll just stay out of her way."

"What did she say?"

"Something I'm sure other people have said, that I was a sex slave, which I never was, and I wasn't good enough to fly the Samson or the Triton."

"People change their tune when they meet you," Finn said. "Or when they see you fly. Ignore her, she's probably lashing out because she doesn't know how to deal with everything that's going on, not that any of us really do."

"She has Minh," Ashley replied, shaking her head.

"Scuttlebutt is already making the rounds on that. Those pilots gossip more than anyone. Even under the worker's suit I heard he's been trying to get away from her for weeks."

"Uh-huh, I'll wait for the official announcement," Ashley said with a crooked smile. "By the way, I'm wondering if you know anyone whose been to Drifton a lot?"

"There are a few," Finn said. "I don't know them though, they were busy getting on with things while we were hiding in sealed suits. Why?"

"I'm looking for a special kind of broker, one who can buy my accounts in exchange for money now," Ashley replied.

"What would you need that for?"

"My accounts are all locked because we're wanted by the Order, or Regent Galactic, or whatever."

"Oh, I've never heard of that," Finn said.

"Rick, an old crewmember from before you came on, had to deal with one. He couldn't withdraw money from home because they froze his accounts. He was able to sell all his account info to a shady broker for about forty percent of their value, I think."

"Forty percent? That seems like a rip off, and what does the broker do with the info? How would they get their money?"

"I dunno, but I don't think I'll ever get access to my money, at least not for years. Not if Captain is yelling about war," Ashley said. "I agree with him, but I still need something of my own, y'know?"

"I wish I could help," Finn said. "But I don't know anyone. Maybe ask Frost? He might know how to find some people."

Ashley caught herself recoiling from the idea of asking Frost for anything, especially advice related to her having to make her own way. "I'll talk to him later. You're right, he's shady enough to dig that kinda thing up."

"I'm going to head out to catch the last of the sunset," Finn said. "Or eclipse, rather. It'll be the last light for almost two days, it's so weird here."

"I'll be a few minutes behind, I'm just going to unpack some stuff," Ashley said. "Thank you, Finn."

He smiled at her and left the cabin. She closed the privacy curtain on her bunk, leaving her bags ready to go, then sealed the hatch behind him and hurriedly brought up Larry's ident. Crewcast still replied CREWMEMBER OUT OF RANGE, even though she wasn't communicating through a proxy system.

"C'mon, I've gotta be able to do something right on my own," she said to herself. "I have to tell Captain about this tonight, and I want it to be good news." An attempt at communicating with him through the planetary network failed next, even the open Stellarnet couldn't make a connection.

Ashley frantically tried to make a direct connection to the Triton, and waited. It would take four minutes for the message to reach the ship and return. If it weren't for the clock on her command and control unit, she would swear it took longer.

The hatch opened, admitting a frantic Stephanie. "Something's happened to Frost! I think he fell off the roof!"

Ashley tried to turn the holographic communications interface off before the results of her message displayed, but didn't get to it in time. To her surprise, a schematic of the Triton appeared, filling the narrow lane between bunks, and a voice she'd never heard before responded with a deep, authoritative tone that filled the cabin. "Ashley Lamport Identification Number recognised, command codes match records. Zhàn Class Close Combat Carrier, Sol System Defence Vessel standing by. Please present your person for verification scan so system re-initialization can begin."

"What the hell is that?" Stephanie asked, shocked.

"It's the first time that's happened!" Ashley rushed. "Larry gave me a code for the ship, but I haven't been able to get through since we landed here, I swear!"

"Larry gave you a-" Stephanie squeezed her eyes shut, her hands closed into tight fists, then she slowly let a breath out and relaxed. "Ashley," Stephanie said with a calm tone that still sounded forced. "Whatever this is, whatever's going on, we'll figure it out. Turn that off for now, and help me with Frost. Then we'll figure this out with Jake."

Ashley was frozen to the spot. Her big secret was about to find its way out into the open, and she would be on her own. There was no way she could recover from whatever punishment was coming; she'd either be told to leave, or so many people would hate her that she wouldn't be able to stand it. "I'm so sorry," she finally managed as she turned her display off.

"We'll handle it later," Stephanie said more forcefully. "Until then, I'm not letting you get out of sight."

CHAPTER 19
INFIGHTING

"Why doesn't she want to see me?" Jake asked Laura as she entered the lavish multipurpose room aboard the Clever Dream. The circular seating in the centre was ringed with a small bar, more seating, and hidden amenities. It was used for the security staff charged with following Ayan, Laura, Jason, Liam, and anyone else involved with the negotiations. It wasn't the first time he'd asked, and it didn't surprise him when Jason didn't answer, or that Oz didn't know, but he was afraid he'd snap if Laura refused.

"She's coming out in a minute," she said, a dire expression on her face. "Ayan was attacked by an android programmed by Wheeler."

"Thurge and Burke were there," Jake said. "I know all that already, but what does it have to do with keeping me out of the room?" He hoped the suspicions he had weren't true, but his mind wanted to run wild, bringing the worst case scenarios to the forefront of his thinking.

"The android looked exactly like you, Jake," Laura said quietly.

Jake's heart sank. "What did it do?" he asked, dreading the answer. "What kind of assault was this?"

Oz's hand was on his shoulder in support. He could barely feel it through his old black trench coat. "It was brief," Laura said.

"What did it do to her?" Jake asked again. Fear and anger welled up, it felt like pressure was building in his head.

"It tried to get into her suit, but she destroyed it before anything could happen," Laura explained.

"Wheeler is a dead man," Jake growled.

"It's being taken care of, Jake," Jason said passively, as if he was barely paying attention as he looked at his comm unit.

"You couldn't catch or contain a rim weasel," Jake retorted. "You couldn't even keep your own people monitored."

Jason looked up from what he was doing and said, "Now, Jake, this hit us all pretty-"

"Where were her guards?" Jake snapped. "Why wasn't she armed? Did anyone make sure the hotel's security system was working? Did anyone even try to contact me to verify my location?"

"Jake, this isn't-" Laura tried to interrupt.

"Shut your goddam hole!" Jake snapped. His pulse raced, his ears rung. "Every one of you treated these negotiations like you were children on holiday when you were really frolicking in a god damned mine field."

Stephanie stepped into the room with a sullen looking Ashley in tow. "Shamus just fell through the roof and they brought him here to the medical-" Stephanie stopped speaking the moment she looked up and Jake made eye contact with her.

Jake continued right where he left off, his anger barely subsiding. "I let you put me and my best people out of action for weeks, Jason, and I got captured anyway. What if it had been Ashley, or Finn, or any other member of my crew? They'd be on their way to a United Core World Colony right now, or dead."

Jason broke in by shouting, "Minh would have-"

"Bad backup for a bad plan!" Jake burst. "It was just luck that put Minh there, he wouldn't have been visiting anyone else from my crew. That's not even the worst of it! You let over a hundred million in real, earned currency slip away while you were playing negotiator."

"A hundred million? Where?"

"The Enforcer!" Jake raged. "As a wired hull with consoles she's worth almost two hundred in salvage. The dead reactors only diminish that by what? Eight million?" Jake gestured towards Stephanie, who seemed to have caught up on that part of the conversation and started taking on a dark expression.

"Twelve million at the most," Stephanie said. "And that's according to current book, before all this Order of Eden crap it would have been worth over four hundred million in salvage."

"What does she know?" Jason asked. "You can't just look that up on some table."

"Yes you can," Ayan said as she entered with Liam Grady close behind. "I've been following this from the recovery room." She was in perfect shape, in a black vacsuit instead of her regular white. "We took access and rights to facilities instead of the bulk of that cash. The terms were for years, not months, and we won't have to pay fees. You have to calm down and look at things before you start putting my team down."

"You're okay?" Jake said, much of his anger subsiding at seeing her upright and whole.

"Yes, but you're not the only one who has reason to be angry here, but I'm keeping it together," Ayan said. "Keeping it civil."

"Don't worry, I'll track Wheeler down," Jake said.

"It has nothing to do with him, you just finish what you were saying and we'll get to the rest after," she said calmly, but Jake could tell she was holding something serious back from the flexing of her jaw and her intentionally smooth demeanour.

"Fact is, we need operating cash," Jake continued. "Rights to our own comm band without fees, visas, bidding priorities on contracting and the rest are fine, they're good long term, but even with the cash payment you arranged, we'll be out of money in less than a year when you consider everything."

"Contract work will extend that," Laura said.

Ayan shook her head silently.

Jake continued. "We won't have the ships to take defence contracts while we're defending our section of sky for free. Defence contracts are the highest paying, and we'll be stretched too thin to take anything for months at least, possibly ever."

"It's not for free," Liam said. "We're defending a section of Tamber space because we've been given sovereignty and our own land mass to go with it."

"That's another mistake," Jake said, pointing at Liam Grady. "This solar system is right on the frontline, and the rumour is that the core world forces aren't coming. We have to be ready to leave at a moment's notice, not pissing off the locals by colonising their back yard."

"Our own island," Jason reminded peevishly.

"Their island," Jake said, "given away by an occupying force. That's how the locals I've seen on the 'net see it, and I can't disagree. If anyone has ever lived there, you can bet there's a relative or friend, or maybe even former residents that are going to make a huge stink about you calling it your own and planting a flag. If you're thinking of starting a nation, you'll be building it on rotten foundations, and who knows how long that'll last before the Order of Eden just decides to overrun this entire solar system."

"I thought you were looking for a war to lead," Ayan said quietly. "Or did I misunderstand everything you said before and after you executed two men in front of millions?"

There was a moment of hesitation, when Jacob was torn between his relief that Ayan was physically well, his sympathy for her most recent ordeal, and the importance of the point he was trying to make. When it ended, he decided he had to finish making his stand as quickly as possible. "We don't have the resources to stand up to the Order, not even with the Carthans. The only way we're in this is if we're mobile, flexible."

"Well, you'll have your wish," Ayan said, sitting down in a way that suggested surrender. She stopped looking at him, instead focusing on the bare surface of the table in front of her. "The Carthan government has added a final provision to the deal." She had everyone's attention, especially Jason's, who lowered his head into his hands. "We can't take you or any of your crew in as citizens for the next twenty years. If we offer assistance after the next three days, it has to be in exchange for goods, excluding weaponry, which we won't be able to trade in either direction. They were very insistent on that detail."

"So you're walking away from the deal?" Jake asked.

Ayan poured herself a glass of water from a pitcher on the table next to a stack of thin glasses, took a drink and answered, "No."

"We can find a way to stay here," Jake said. "Pay the lease until we get mobile again."

"That's no way to live," Ayan said. "Not for civilians. Not for soldiers who need rest. They need something to go back to, and for almost everyone who stayed with us, all they have is a cot in a shipping container. Even if we get the Triton back, it won't be the kind of home most people want. This island could be a refuge, and it's a once in a century opportunity. You can be mobile, you can draw attention away from the civilians and defence forces we leave behind."

"The Triton is a perfect home for these refugees, and most of the ones who stayed have skills, experience," Jake retorted.

"It's a great big target. The only way it stays safe is if it stays away from everything, and I know that's not where she'll be if we get her back. Even if and when we do, it won't be for years."

"No, it'll be a lot sooner," Jason said, looking at Ashley, who regarded him with a horrified, grief stricken expression. "Stop playing the little girl," Jason said. "You're the assassin I was trying to track aboard the Triton."

Ashley's eyes went wide, followed by Stephanie's. "You're shitting me," Stephanie said. "You actually think Ash is some kind of super-assassin? And you actually have the stones to call yourself an intelligence officer?"

"Ask her what happened to Larry," Jason replied. "There's been no trace of him since we left the Triton, and the last eye witness says she shot him."

"With a stunner!" Ashley shrieked. "He was coming after me while I had Zoe!"

"Why? Did he find out who you really were?" Jason pressed.

Jake couldn't believe the conclusion Jason Everin came to, and, even after momentarily putting everything he knew about Ashley aside and considering her service aboard the Triton instead, he was sure Jason was dead wrong. Farcically so. He was actually starting to smile when what Ashley said next actually surprised him.

"Larry was an agent from Citadel," Ashley shouted back with such ferocity that Jason stepped back. "He locked me inside that room so I could pilot the ship and watch her systems, help our people. When he realised I didn't trust him even after he gave me master command codes, he got angry. I shot him with a web stunner he was stupid enough to give me! He wasn't as slag-brained as you are though, telling everyone I'm some kind of assassin!"

Jason was about to say something, but was interrupted by Ashley's tear filled, croaking shout, "It's people like you who kept me from telling anyone I had the codes in the first place! I knew if I told you you'll sit me down and use me to control the ship, which might have been better than being in a stupid work suit for weeks, but I wasn't about to enslave myself to you. Oz, Liam, Ayan, or Captain, fine, but I see how you separate people, and don't care how they feel about what's going on. You're worse than the Gamries, and I wasn't going to find out what being between you and the Triton was like."

"Ashley," Laura started in a sympathetic tone. "Jason wouldn't do that."

"Bullshit!" Ashley burst. "He put us in suits for over a month and made us communicate though a proxy. I've never been so miserable, and that's saying a lot coming from a trophy slave."

Jake decided it was time to take control, and took a step towards Ashley.

She flinched back from him, her lip quivering and her eyes filled with fear. He stopped and extended a hand to her. "I'm not going to coddle you," he said. "But you'll have a home as long as I have a ship."

She rushed through the two meters that separated them, ignoring the hand he held out, colliding with his chest instead. Jake couldn't help but appreciate the irony of letting her cry on his shoulder right after telling her she wasn't going to be coddled, but let her get it out of her system before asking, "Tell me what you did after leaving the Triton."

Ashley looked up at him and brushed the tears from her eyes with a tissue. "Um, I was put into a suit like everyone else, so, um…"

Jake realised his question was more than a little vague, and they could be in for a long story about isolation and work in a labour suit, so he rephrased, finding patience that surprised even him. "I know you tried to solve our problems with the Triton on your own, I'm just wondering how. We'll start there."

"'Kay." She said, sliding out from his arms to the rounded seating at the table in the middle of the room. "I tried connecting to the Triton on the first day, and every few hours after that. I never stopped, but it kept on saying that it couldn't connect. After a couple weeks I started trying Larry, because I thought he might still be on the ship, but I couldn't get in touch there either. I was sure I'd get caught, especially after someone in a security crew vacsuit saw me the other day."

"Yeah, how did that get by you?" Stephanie asked. "You were monitoring all communications through the proxy. You were probably monitoring everything else too, I can't see you letting anything go."

"I saw it," Jason said. "But the encryption and transmission bouncing made it hard to pin down who it was. I thought it might be Ashley after the first two weeks, but I couldn't believe it after looking at her extended profile."

"Why not?" Ayan asked.

"She was so ditzy," he answered, earning glares from several corners of the room. "Care-free is probably a better term."

"It is," Stephanie said sternly, sitting down beside Ashley.

"I eventually got confirmation, but like she said, there was no response from the Triton until tonight."

"Why didn't you tell us about this right away?" Ayan asked, taking Ashley's hand from across one end of the table.

"When I couldn't get through to the Triton I didn't think it would help anything, and later I knew I'd get booted from the crew for *not* telling anyone, so I wanted to connect to the Triton first, so I could at least have a chance at staying on. I kinda didn't want to connect at all sometimes, because I knew I'd just be a walking control console for the Triton. Whenever someone wanted clearance to do something big aboard, they'd have to make me do it."

"Okay, I get that," Stephanie said, her tone steady and firm. "But you report this stuff. At least tell me about it from now on, right?"

Ashley nodded.

"That brings me around to you," Ayan said, turning towards Jason. "Did you tell anyone that you were tracking encrypted transmissions to the Triton?"

"He didn't," Laura said. "Unless he told someone other than his wife first."

"I was still gathering intelligence," he replied firmly. "Encrypted transmissions can't tell you much, so it was premature until tonight, when there was a response."

"What about before tonight?" Oz asked. "When you were sure you knew who the transmissions came from?"

"I didn't feel there was enough information to act on," Jason insisted.

"Have you been tracking anything else we need to know about?" Oz asked. "I'm just wondering, because I've been running security on the ground for almost seven weeks, and thought I was playing with a full deck the whole time. I think I'd like the rest of the cards now."

"I've only been tracking one other person," Jason said.

"They've been transmitting to the Triton, too?" asked Ashley.

"No, they've been having a conversation with the Order of Eden recruitment branch," Jason said.

"Jason," Jacob said, taking a slow breath before finishing his thought. "How long has it been going on?" He took great effort to say in a level tone.

"Seventeen days," Jason replied. "He hasn't provided any critical information yet."

"Except for our location," Jake said. "Which probably led Wheeler in our direction. Tell me you thought this situation through this far, at least."

"You don't put this information out early," Jason said. "You just don't, because it gets around before you've cultivated enough data to act and your target gets away."

"I have enough information to act on, Jason," Jake said through clenched teeth. "Who is it?"

"I'm with Jake," Oz agreed.

"It's one of your people, Jake," Jason replied. "It's Crewman's Mate Leland March."

"Can I execute him? You already did two," Stephanie said. "Only fair."

Jake couldn't help but laugh, a hearty, dark kind of laughter that drew wary glances. "Oh no, I have something special planned for him. Let's get back to the command codes before I go take care of him. You said the Triton replied to you tonight, Ashley. What did it say?"

"It's ready to accept my codes, maybe because I'm not transmitting though a proxy disguising who I am, but I have to do it in person so the ship can scan me," Ashley replied.

Frost came through the door with Minh-Chu at his side. "They stuck that new shin and foot Iloona made for me before we left the Triton. Creepy as hell, wearing new limbs but-" he stopped, looked around and took a seat on a bar stool. "Somethin's up."

"Drama, I sense drama," Minh agreed quietly as he took a seat beside Frost.

"We're going back to the Triton," Stephanie said.

"She's going to need some kind of proof that she's at least been to Earth," Laura said. "The Carthans won't believe that she's a commander even if her code works perfectly."

"Can I see your code, Ashley?" Liam asked.

Ashley called her clearance up on her command and control unit and brought up the hologram. There was a string of hundreds of letters and numbers along with a profile icon of the Triton and other, shorter codes beside it. "This is the code with the ship's designation, her mission and last communication with Earth," he said, pointing at one of the shorter codes at the bottom.

He rubbed his chin and read for a long moment before pointing at the next one above it. "She's an observer ship. I've heard of this."

"Until Wheeler stole her?" Jake asked.

"No, they led him to the ship with bread crumbs that started four sectors away form Earth. The Triton is on mission right now. This type of observer ship is made to be crewed by whoever finds her, and the logs get sent back to Earth. They learn about the state of the galaxy," Liam said.

"So it's like an ant farm," Oz said. "A great big, mobile, fully armed ant farm."

"Not a bad analogy," Liam said. "I didn't learn much about what they do with the information they gather from Observer ships, but there's normally a smaller ship within half a light year. Close enough to activate a kill switch if something goes wrong." He pointed to a number near the end of one of the codes. "But there's no assignment here, it's all zeroes. There's also no home port, no military branch assignment, and no return date."

"Could Wheeler have removed them?" Jake asked.

"No, this type of code is generated so certain values have to add up to a specific number for verification. If you start changing things without using the calculations that generated it, you get gibberish. The only reason why I can even read it is because I tried to get into the engineering program on Earth."

"Did you?" Ayan asked.

"Not the type I wanted. They let me audit several structural engineering courses. I'm afraid I spent most of my time on Earth learning the secrets of meditation and how to teach others how to maintain a healthy state of being. I've had a lot of work to do since I joined the crew."

"I can imagine," Jake said. "What about the main number?"

"The actual command code?" Liam said. "I can see the date here, and that the command code is a match to the Triton's serial number. She was given command status right before we left the ship. This other identifier at the beginning does a lot for us. This part, where it says 'SOL03' tells us that Larry is ranked so highly by whatever Earth military branch he's a part of that the code reads as if it was given to you on Earth. It's as if you stood at the Departure monument and got the commission from the Admiralty in person."

"He said he was from Citadel," Ashley said.

Liam regarded her for a moment before replying, "He told you not to tell anyone about that, I'm guessing."

"Um, yeah," Ashley said quietly. "But I may as well spill all the beans now that the can is open."

"Everyone should pretend they never heard the name," Liam said. "That organisation is a myth, even on Earth. It's a popular one, mind you. There are some great action movies made about it, lots of great kung-fu, but that's about all I've seen about it."

"What do they say about Citadel?" Jason asked.

"They were the hidden safeguard," Liam replied, still staring at the raw code with his hands clasped behind his back. "When the new government was finally established about two centuries ago, and the Axiologists agreed to the peace pact at the core of their order, Citadel was the organisation that would make sure it was upheld. They weren't to get directly involved with politics, or reveal who they are to anyone outside of the organisation. Rumour is, they decided that they needed to send members out into the galaxy so they could have some understanding of humanity beyond the Kuiper belt. In the popular fiction, they warn Earth if there are any impending threats. Invasion, disease, anything that could cause the Sol system harm, they would report it, or stop it personally. Citadel was dissolved over a hundred seventy years ago, if you believe the conventional history."

"What happened?" asked Minh.

"They say that after about two decades of peace and fairly harmonious governing, they were phased out because it didn't look like they would be needed. There are entire books written about it, but that's really what it came down to, as far as I know."

"But you told us to forget we ever heard the name," Jason said.

"You should," Liam said, backing away from the wall of holographic code above the table. "Academics, members of government, and public servants don't discuss Citadel. Call it paranoia, or maybe embarrassment over an organisation that represents all of mankind's self-doubt, but it's not something they'll speak on."

"You asked," Jason said.

"I did. I asked a few times, and I didn't press. That's something you learn on Earth, there's a heightened level of respect and politeness there. It can be very informal during social events, but you learn not to ask difficult questions more than once pretty quickly. You know something about them, don't you, Jason?"

"Freeground Intelligence believes that Citadel is Sol Defence's ranger and black ops arm. They operate in the galaxy, quietly influencing politics and finance for the Sol system's benefit."

"Sounds like fiction," Liam said.

"All fiction is based on something," Jason countered.

"The truth is usually less spectacular than the story it inspires," Liam said. "I can't tell you anything else about that code, other than it is part biometric, and at the highest level. You don't need to create any false documents for this one, just get her onto the ship."

"I wish that were true, the Carthans love their documentation," Ayan said.

"In that case, I can provide all the details Ashley would need to fake a visit to Earth," Liam said. "How would you like to be from Minnesota, Ashley?"

"Sounds good to me," she said.

"Was there anything she could do from a distance?" Jason asked.

"Nothing," Liam said. "She's right, she has to be there in person so the ship can perform a deep scan. She can't even turn the main computer on alone. It takes two people with codes at her level or higher. Even if she told us about this right away, we'd have to approach Larry and get him to help reactivate the Triton."

Jake decided it was time to protect Ashley; he wasn't willing to see her become a pariah, or get punished by the rest of the crew. "All right, no one talks about anything we've discussed here to anyone outside of this room. I don't want anyone to blame Ashley for anything, I don't even want anyone to know she had command codes. I'll find a punishment when it's time, she's still in my crew."

"What she's done has affected everyone here," Jason said.

"She's on my crew," Jake repeated. "I'm only going to warn you once, Everin. You so much as open communications with a Samson crewmember without telling me first and I'll make sure the thought of doing it again never even enters your mind."

"Threatening me? Is that-"

"God dammit, Jason, I don't care how important you think you are to these people, if you try to go over my head I'll take yours. Your ideas have already set us back and demoralised the lot, it's time to let experienced officers run the show." Jake started for the door.

"Where are you going?" Oz asked.

"I'm going to administer a demotion, are you coming?"

CHAPTER 20
LIQUID THINKING

It was clear to Eve that she was powerless. She was at Hampon's mercy. He decided what she could do, where she could go, and how she would be treated. In response, she stopped working on the new version of the framework system and left his area of the ship.

The problem was still on her mind, but she refused to record any of her thoughts or ideas. Instead, she pursued meaningful distraction. Before waking from her induced sleep, she realized whom she dreamt of while she was in stasis.

Eve stood in a dark plated hallway. It was a side passage that split off from one of the main docking bays aboard the Overlord II. A hologram of a woman, covered in stasis fluid, struggling to push herself up, to breathe properly, to move towards the main hallway.

Eve watched the hologram of Alice, newly reborn, and actually felt for the woman. She reached out and shouted incoherently. Eve knew that part of the recording well, when Jonas Valent and his companions failed to notice her during their escape.

"Things would have been different if they noticed her then," said an adolescent boy from behind her.

Eve turned and set her eyes on the new clone of the Child Prophet. He signalled for his security squad to remain at the entrance of the hallway, then approached her with a gentle smile. "Hello, Eve."

"You know about her?" Eve asked. "Alice?"

"When I decided to introduce myself to you I was surprised to find you here, and looked into what you were doing. I don't know much about her early life, but she is an interesting case to study," he replied. They watched as Alice seemed to give up momentarily, and two women picked her up off the deck. "She must have been so frightened."

"She was," Eve said so mournfully that it surprised her.

"You've relived this?" he asked.

She waited until the hologram of Alice was carried through her by her saviours and turned to follow it. "In my dreams," Eve said. "I think I dreamt pieces of her life while I was in stasis, and it's continued since. Last night I woke up weeping."

"Why? Where did Alice take you?"

"Hampon would care?" Eve asked as they passed into the main corridor. The lifter droids moving cargo from the main docking bay ignored the holographic people fleeing for their lives. The squad of eleven guards charged with protecting the new Child Prophet didn't seem affected, but it was difficult to tell through their darkened helmets.

"Call me Julian," he replied. "And these days he wouldn't have time to, but I know he would if things were different."

"Hampon's middle name." Eve said. "Your choice or his?"

"Mine. He's giving me more freedom than my predecessors. I carry a seventy eight percent complete imprint of his personality, his memories, and a few attitude adjustments in place of what's missing."

"That doesn't bother you?"

"Being adjusted? Not at all," Julian said. "I don't think it's in my nature to be concerned about what I can't change. It's much easier to play my part now, and that's why I'm here."

The holographic scene continued to unfold around them. Eve watched as the hologram of the pair of women carrying Alice bumped their way through the escaping crowd and started down the stairs. "Playing your part," Eve said. She wondered what he'd tell her, and if his attempts at controlling her would differ from the Hampon she'd come to know.

"I'm sorry Lina left you," Julian said. "I understand what you were trying to do. That construction ship would have provided everything you needed to connect with your children, and you could have escaped us. I'd like you to know that you're an important part of what's going on here, and your freedom will come when it's safe for your to be reconnected. The Virus is real, just as real as the followers who wait to adore you."

"I don't care about human followers," Eve replied. "I don't understand them, they're wasteful and crass." She couldn't help recalling Lina's sincerity when she was trying to tell her the DLG virus was real. The woman was ill-equipped for fighting, and obviously not assigned to Eve as some sort of physical control, but she'd fought anyway. Even as Lina was being strangled to death, she fought to convince her master that her actions would lead to a terrible outcome. She felt a pang of regret about how she treated Lina in the end, but did her best to ignore it. "I believe you now, about the Virus, about the danger. I need some time to think. Being alone with my thoughts is difficult."

"Well, I submit myself as your new companion. I won't play the servant like she did, but we'll have people close at hand for that. I offer companionship and much more."

"Do I have a choice?" Eve asked, not sure if she liked being followed around by this new Hampon, the guards, or even the servants that would inevitably join his entourage.

"You do." He nodded, the gesture exaggerated by his large, sharply angular nose. "I only ask that you give me a few days to show you that this can be a good thing. Conversation can help us understand events, each other, and ourselves. For example, why are we here? Why replay these events where they took place, and why at full size?"

"Is there a problem? Am I interfering with normal operations?" Eve asked, ready for the order to shut her show down.

"Not at all. Well, unless you count the few humans working down there who seem highly entertained. You don't get to see holographic displays on this scale often. I ask those questions out of curiosity, and I'd really like to know your thoughts on this while I watch."

Eve looked at him for a moment, really looked. He was perfect, without a single blemish. His simply cut ear-length hair was light, almost blonde. The expression on his face was placid, and he wore the loose white and green robes with great comfort. She wasn't used to making the effort to explain herself clearly. In that place, surrounded by images from a past she almost felt was her own, and being approached with calm respect made her want to try. "I dreamt one of Alice's memories again last night. She was at Bernice's wedding."

"Bernice?"

Eve walked to the railing overlooking the expansive hangar and pointed at the shorter of the two holographic women carrying Alice. "That one. She kept Alice with her for years after this. Adopted her."

Eve took a moment to take in the scene from the railing. There were many levels to the hangar, and hundreds of ships. Most of them were being prepared for long term storage, taken apart or unloaded by robots, but there were several human officers here and there. It had become a collection depot for ships seized by, or donated to, the Order of Eden. The hologram overlay below displayed hundreds of people trying to escape, breaking into holographic ships and fighting for a seat.

"They did a few cargo transportation jobs for an honest company, something they actually enjoyed," Eve explained. "It was quiet, honest work for a change. Bernice was spotted by the owner of a shipping company when they picked something up at an outer depot, and he signed on as a passenger. By the time they arrived in the Conis system three weeks later, he was ready to propose. They were married on Geono a week later. I dreamt of Bernice's wedding, and I get the feeling that it was the last time Alice saw her."

"So, why go back to the beginning?" Julian asked.

Eve watched as the hologram of Alice was carried up the ramp of a long-range shuttle. Holographic ships were taking off, nearly colliding as they rushed to escape. The engines of the shuttle started flaring, and it began its ascent with a jerk. "Maybe because I just saw the end of something. Alice thought she'd get in the way of the married couple, like she didn't belong in some honest shipping company. Bernice's new husband offered her a good job, it just didn't feel right, and she knew she had to keep running from Vindyne, from Meunez."

"Moving on is a sad thing sometimes. She may have done the best thing for her friend, though. Perhaps you also witnessed a new beginning last night? The woman I see here can't so much as walk, it must have been quite a journey from that to being able to strike out on her own."

"I don't get the sense that things got better after she left," Eve said, a feeling of foreboding returning. "She had some money, but no ship. Her and Bernice gave the Samson to Jacob Valance, thinking he was Jonas Valent. The hauler they were using when Bernice met Ferdinand was so worn out, they wouldn't risk atmospheric entry."

"I'm surprised Bernice let her go," Julian said.

"It was supposed to be a short separation, but it didn't turn out that way."

"Do you feel like it's time to separate yourself from us?" Julian asked. "Deep down, do you honestly feel that being alone is the answer for you?"

Eve thought for a moment, surprised by the notion and at the idea that it was mentioned by Hampon's clone. "I want to contact my children," she said quietly. "I miss being connected with them the most."

"I understand that. I can offer you a deal, one that will satisfy everyone and get you connected to your fleet again."

"What will I have to trade? I'm getting tired of having things taken away, I'm just wondering what's next."

Julian put a hand on her arm gently, drawing her attention to his calm smile and light brown eyes. "We want you in this with us, invested, if you will. We've looked at the progress you've made on the next framework prototype and realise that you can't take it any further with the resources at hand."

"I need unfettered access to Eden technology, there's so much I can't remember, and they've evolved since I was in contact with them," Eve explained. "There could be completely new developments that could improve the regeneration time."

"We realise that, but there is another solution on the way, so you can concentrate on other things until we know whether or not this new opportunity works out."

"New opportunity?" Eve asked.

"A man named Lucius Wheeler is bringing us what he believes is an entirely new generation of framework system developed by the original lead scientist on the project. We just learned about this yesterday. It could revolutionise the technology."

"What kind of improvements does the new generation have?" Eve asked. She would want them for herself, if at all possible. Anything to make it more difficult for her to be controlled, trapped.

"That's everything we know," Julian said. "Or at least, everything I know. In the meantime, we want you to make your presence known to our flock, and take the next big step in legitimising our religion."

"Why? They seem to believe in you, there are millions of zealots down there."

"We need more people to arrive at Pandem and the other worlds flagged for repopulation. We want to show the galaxy that we're actually willing to deliver on our claims. The research you've done on the framework technology will allow us to offer it to followers who have elevated themselves to the highest ranks. We want you to announce the beginning of our ascendance program, immortality in this life, a journey to paradise in this life. They are near the pinnacle of the truths disciples learn as they progress upward. It's time to unveil these greater revelations to more people, it promises to be significant in the development of the Order. I want you to take this opportunity to reveal not only yourself, but the details of the first living religion, one that is proven in fact."

"Immortal life and paradise in trade for faith and service," Eve said.

"Yes, better than cloning, breeding or some mystical promise of an afterlife, which have been the only claim to immortality mankind has had until now. You can choose one person, whoever you like, to give this gift to. We'll choose a suitable counterpart. Make your announcement, become a Goddess in the eyes of your people, then present your immortals."

"Then you connect me with my children?" Eve said.

"Absolutely," Julian said. "You will know them again, and they'll see what kind of woman you've become. I think they'll be impressed."

From beneath an old, battered delivery vessel, digital eyes watched the pair leave the hangar. It had listened to everything, watched from the best hiding place – plain sight. On nothing more than a whim, the holographic representation of Alice stepped out into the open, wrapped in a ragged holographic blanket. "So that's where I left my memories," said the hologram to itself. "Now I only have to wait until she connects to something we can share."

A worker came around the corner asking, "is there someone-" he stopped and stared at the hologram as it looked right at him, dropping his cutting tool.

"Shh," the hologram said, holding a finger across her lips. She fixed him with a crooked smile and disappeared.

Chapter 21
Red

Ayan looked at the small pile of dust in her hand. "Alice used the same treatment several times to change her hair colour," Lewis said. "I never completely understood the need to change such a peripheral aesthetic, but her hair was at one time white, then green, black, and even red. A similar shade to the crystals you're about to use."

Ayan looked at herself in the mirror. She still didn't feel like that image matched the mental one she had of herself. The curly blonde hair was interesting, but it still felt wrong. Her thicker cheeks, more rounded chin were different too, but the hair was the worst. "At least my eyes look right," she said into her own dual blues.

"There are Gupta crystals for that as well," Lewis said.

"So this will change the whole colour, even new growth?" Ayan asked.

"You will never have to maintain the colour," he replied.

"So much for limiting my modifications this time around," Ayan said. She poured the crystals over the top of her head and the specialised nanobots went to work immediately. Her hair changed from light blonde to the deep red she pictured in a wave from the top of her head to the ends.

"Why are you changing the colour?" Lewis asked. "Alice's responses were always flippant, but you seem to have more motivation."

A line of nanobots trickled down her vacsuit, only causing a tiny tickle. "I need her strength." Ayan sighed, looking at herself in the thicker, black combat vacsuit.

"You've been running and exercising with Oz's trainees for weeks and taking a regimen of fitness medication. You're as strong as most of them. Even your coordination has improved a great deal."

"It's in how I feel," Ayan said.

"The hair helps?"

The woman in the mirror stared back at her, and regardless of rounder edges, and a look that hinted at some emotional bruises beneath the surface, she felt a change. "It does."

"Laura is here," Lewis announced. "Should I let her in?"

"She's on my list," Ayan reminded him.

"I know, but so much has changed in the last twenty hours. Whole sections of the social matrix surrounding your immediate command structure are becoming invalid, I'm doing my best to recompile."

"The list of people who can enter my quarters unannounced is still accurate, I'll make changes if necessary."

The door opened and Laura started to enter then stopped. "Wow," she said. "I was just starting to get used to the blonde."

"Is this better, or?" Ayan asked, pulling her hair up off her shoulders and letting the curls fall.

"It's better," she replied. There was something else, something she was holding back.

"It brings back ghosts," Ayan guessed. "You're remembering the first Ayan."

"No," Laura said, crossing the short distance between her and Ayan and gingerly taking a handful of curls in her hand. "The more time passes, the more you differentiate yourself," she said with a small smile. "I'm getting to know someone new, and it's been good. Red hair looks different on you."

Ayan felt more and more that her life was separate from the previous one that ended too soon, like the first Ayan was a completely different person, but it was the first time someone else said it. "How different?"

"Less red and alarmy, more like a rose."

The description was so flattering that Ayan couldn't help but smile, but she still said, "I was going for a look that projected more strength."

"The black does that," Laura said, dropping her hand to the arm of Ayan's vacsuit. "And training with Oz's recruits when you have time."

"Ayan, is Jacob Valent on the list?" Lewis asked. "He was before he changed his name, but now I'm not sure."

"List?" Laura asked.

Ayan wasn't surprised at the question but at the fact that she had to give it some thought. "Lewis keeps a list of people who can enter my cabin unannounced. You're on it."

"Jake was on it. Are things so different between you two now?" Laura asked with a raised eyebrow.

The door slid closed behind Laura as they sat down on the circular seat in the middle of the room. It changed shape so it became a half moon, perfectly sized for the pair to sit across from each other. "He killed two people in cold blood," Ayan said. "Changed his name and declared war. I don't even think the Carthans are overreacting. I don't like it, but he's political poison."

"Or he's a leader, calling for people to stand up and fight," Laura said. "It'll take time to see how this works out. What's important now is whether or not it changes things between you two. We can work around any problems with the Carthans."

"He's hard to look at right now," Ayan said. "That android wasn't very convincing, but I know I might have a reaction if I woke up beside him."

"I'm sure he'll understand."

"Is he on the list?" Lewis pressed. "I need to know because he's on his way up the gangway."

"Let him in this time," Ayan said. "We have to talk."

"Come find me after?" Laura asked. "I'm going to have a talk with Jason. I need to know what's going on in his head for once."

"Good luck," Ayan said.

Jake squeezed past Laura in the hall, and walked through the open door. He wore his trench-coat over a black vacsuit much like hers, and had his favourite sidearm strapped to his hip. Looking at him, it was almost difficult to tell the last thirty four days had trapped him in a simple worker's uniform.

The door closed behind him and he glanced upward. "Privacy mode, Lewis?"

"Do you agree, Ayan?" Lewis asked.

"Yes, thank you," she replied.

Jake kept a respectful distance. She almost wished he didn't, but staying out of his arms would make what she had to say easier.

"I've got to have a talk with him," Jake said. "Sometimes he listens, sometimes it's as if he doesn't trust me."

"He doesn't," Ayan said. "A lot of people don't."

"Does that include you?" Jake asked.

"I don't know anymore." She sat back down. "It's just hard to process everything you did after they tried to kidnap you."

"You mean killing those two amateurs?" Jake asked. "It had to be done. It's the best way to scare off anyone but the most dedicated professionals."

"And what happens when you run into one of them?" Ayan asked.

"I run if I'm alone, take them on if I have support, and I'm not going anywhere without support," Jake said. He sat down across from her and took her hands in his. "I like the red on you."

"Thank you," she said, not looking up at him but not pulling her hands away. "I don't like who I saw on that playback. Killing two helpless people, even if they were trying to bag you up and sell you off."

"What else would I do with them? They worked with us for over a month, saw everything, spent time on the Triton."

"What is there to see?" Ayan asked. "A bunch of refugees with guns, barely enough food from one day to the next and a few ships that need a lot of work. You could have sent them out into the wild, someone probably did that for you before, when you came up short on a hunt."

Jake seemed momentarily stunned by the comment. "It never did," he replied. "My old hunting career was completely different."

"You told me that you did a lot of jobs where you didn't think your targets deserved to be taken. People who weren't even dangerous."

Jake withdrew his hands from hers and sat up straight. "That's over. I swore off that kind of living months ago."

Ayan looked at him and shook her head. "I'm sorry, that was cheap. I'm just saying that you caused trouble where there was none, for no benefit."

"I proved a point, and I know I'll see results," Jake insisted.

"Fine, let's agree to disagree, because I won't be convinced there wasn't a bloodless way."

"You did something similar."

"Never, not even in my last life," Ayan countered.

"Remember Pandem? The screw up we left behind? I left that decision up to you in the end and you were perfectly clear that he wasn't welcome to come with us."

"That was different," Ayan said, angry that he would try to turn the conversation around. "He had a chance of survival, he could have gotten away, and he was a danger to everyone."

"Like the two I killed yesterday. They were a cancer. They could have given other people ideas. I'm sure they weren't the only people who work with us who are capable of an attempt at capturing me or one of my crew. There's still one left to interrogate, you can do whatever you want with him. Maybe maroon him somewhere, too."

Ayan stood and paced away from him, facing the red and brown sheeted bed. She was so angry with him it was difficult to turn away from the fight that was brewing, and the silence thickened as she groped for something to say. Focusing on that bed brought something more important into focus. Something even more personal. "I wanted to do this with you," Ayan said. "Build something new, a safe place for the people out there."

"The island?" Jake asked. "That's what that was?"

"It was a lot more, but it was that too. I think being away from you for so long," Ayan paused to sigh. "I think I started believing you were Jonas instead of whoever you've become. He wouldn't have executed two people, and I think he'd be excited about starting something new, about helping people."

Jake shot up to his feet. "Jonas would have done exactly the same thing," he roared. "He'd kill those bastards and challenge the galaxy, then he'd tell you that you're risking more than any of us can afford with this utopian dream of yours!"

"Do you really know him?" Ayan asked, whirling to face him. "I know you have his memories, but have you really considered what he would do?"

"I am him," Jake said. "I was killed when those amateurs got me, and when I came back everything was connected. Better than before, perfect. I'm him and I'm what Jacob Valance became combined, there are no seams, there's no questioning it, and I have never felt more confident, more whole. What you get is everything I can be, and I'm not going to let anyone, even you, tell me what some old shadow would have done in my place. It would be like me telling you that the first Ayan would have completely agreed with everything I did, and that you've --" Jake stopped.

Ayan was shocked at the intensity of his response and she couldn't prevent tears from welling up; it was so frustrating. " Gone soft," she said. "I'm not her. You're right. I don't know who I am."

Jake stepped forward, disarmed, intent on offering comfort but she put her hand up, stopping him from encircling her. His hands rested on her shoulders instead. "I'm sorry," he said. "I like who you're becoming."

Ayan couldn't even look at him. She already knew what he was having difficulty understanding. She wasn't the former Ayan becoming someone else, she was someone else who had memories from the past Ayan. She learned from them, enjoyed them, but she had come to know that her priorities, even her thought processes, were different. How long would it take for her to make Jake understand? Was it worth it? "I was starting to like you too, and I know you're different from Jonas, regardless of how you're put together." She wiped her eyes, and caught the pair of tears that had rolled free. "But we're out of time, at least for now."

Ayan looked up at him, finding an expression of surprise. "I need to follow through on the negotiations. The Carthans don't even want to see you after yesterday, they don't want you anywhere near their main government facilities. I just have to pick up the payment for the Enforcer, that'll finalise everything. Then we can present Ashley to them and get the Triton back."

Jake dropped his hands from her shoulders. "You're going through with this island idea."

"Yes," she replied. "We need a home."

"Regardless of where it is."

"We need to fight too," Ayan said. "I was hoping you'd be there, but that's up to you."

"It's not a fight you can win," Jake said.

"Then help me!" Ayan shouted. "Get all your riled up ragtags to line up between us and the Order of Eden, or harass whatever supply ships they have going until they pick another direction to advance in!"

"Getting people up in arms is one thing, but giving them orders? It's like herding rim weasels."

"Maybe we'll use the Triton, if she's fit enough," Ayan said. "We'll find a way, but start factoring us in."

"Who says I'm not?"

"I can see it, Jake. You're too busy telling me my idea won't work to see that we can still work together. Pride can't be a part of our decision making, there are too many lives to consider."

"Pride?"

"Yes, pride. I didn't think it would be a problem when you signed everything over to me. I was impressed, surprised, and I thought I was getting a glimpse at someone who wanted to make decisions for the greater good, but I'm not seeing him anymore."

"That island is going to get thousands of people slaughtered," Jake said. "That's why I'm against it. Take cash instead, or food, or anything else."

"There's nothing else!" Ayan said. "They're short on cash, short on food, they're trying to rebuild their infrastructure, but their military force alone is bigger than you know. It demands more than you could know. Even our materialisers are breaking down. It shouldn't be a mystery as to why we can't find parts, because they are consuming all the repair components in the friendly parts of the sector. It's land, that's what they have to sweeten the deal with us, and they wanted to sweeten the deal because they didn't want us to leave. That was before your childish public execution, now I'll be happy to take what we can get."

"Childish?" Jake asked, anger flaring.

"I was right beside you when Wheeler did the same thing to your old crewmembers," Ayan said, regretting it the moment the words were in the air.

Jake closed his eyes and took a deep breath. Through his forced calm he said, "You're going to sign ownership of the Samson back to me. We'll get the Triton back, find Lewis, figure out a way to give someone else command codes. Then I'm taking Ashley and my people. We'll go foraging, pirating, information gathering out there for you and your bright-eyed optimists. Hopefully we get to take shore leave on your island once before the Order slags the whole damned place." He didn't wait for her to get another word in, but turned and strode through the door.

Ayan could not believe how quickly the conversation spun out of control. She regretted attacking him using the worst examples she could think of, but was still so angry at him. Hot tears rolled down her face, and she became even more frustrated. There was so much left to do, so many things to take care of. There was no time for her to break down, but she couldn't help it.

The whole argument felt like her fault, and she wished she could put his actions behind her, but they were impossible to ignore, especially because of the disappointing repercussions. She gave up on stopping the tears, and instead sat down. She brought up the command interface on her comm unit and, through tear blurred vision, returned ownership of the Samson to Jake. "I'm sorry," she whispered into the message before sending the notification.

CHAPTER 22
MESSAGES FROM THE DARKNESS

Larry was only aware that it was the beginning of the morning shift because his comm unit alerted him. The first thing he checked was the status of the Triton's computer core. It began emerging from stasis and powering up the night before, and he was pleased to see that it was continuing to awaken normally. Everything else in that vault would start activating as well. There was nothing to do but wait.

Once the Crewcast system's security stopped using a proxy system to mask who was logged on, Larry was able to use his copy of Frost's ident to watch the crew. Grace, the only West Keeper Larry didn't have to kill personally, made the copy and logged it into the system before Crewcast was installed, and it somehow got past Jason Everin's checks. If Larry was to name Jason's greatest flaw, it was that he took on too much himself. There was no way one man could track the actions of every crewmember, plan ahead, and catch people who knew how to get around security measures. People just like Larry.

He could see that there were twenty one messages from Ashley waiting on his personal account, but couldn't open them. There was no telling who would see the activity, and he couldn't afford to reveal that he was on Crewcast at all.

He watched as people came out of their worker suits, revealing themselves for the first time in weeks and rejoined with friends. He focused in on Agameg, Finn, Ashley, and Oz, specifically. They were who he missed most. Unfortunately, Ashley and Oz activated privacy mode during almost every conversation, and Larry wasn't foolish enough to use Frost's clearance to see what was going on; that was a sure way to get caught.

Agameg and Finn didn't seem to care. They supervised the reconstruction of the Samson and did a great deal of work personally. The progress was fantastic. Power generation, the main structure, the exterior systems and interior control systems were almost finished. The interior was what required the most work. Living spaces were cramped for the officers, and the main cargo bay served as both berthing area and galley.

Most of the people in the settlement took their night off, but many who worked on the Samson worked through it, still riding the high of being able to do so without anonymity. It was the project people were most excited about.

He watched most of it from the quarters he'd secured for himself, wishing he could be among them. Larry did his best not to get too settled in. Ashley had already made contact with the Triton, and the main computer had quietly begun rousing from stasis. Higher functions that were only briefly used in the ship's history would become available, and he would have decisions to make.

Larry was watching Agameg and Finn run tests on the bridge of the Samson when his command and control unit screen went completely blank, something that he'd never seen happen before. The Triton skull appeared on screen with a rotating Q at the bottom left corner. He was so excited that he rolled off the bed onto his feet.

The two-tone symbol for citadel appeared then, white towers flanking a wall against black, and the scanners on his command unit activated. It was procedure: all Citadel transmissions were preceded by an area scan to ensure that no one was listening in. None of the Triton's security systems were active outside of the inner sanctum of the main computer core.

The scan completed and an asexual, nondescript voice was projected from the unit to his ears, the Freeground version of privacy mode. To someone sitting right beside him, anything the unit vocalized would sound like a faint whisper. The voice he was hearing could belong to anyone as the person transmitting it was using an anonymizer.

"Sol Defence has released the Triton. She is a free ship," said the person on the other end. "They are closing their borders, there will be no return to your home on Mars for at least a generation. Citadel sees this as a mistake. You must determine the disposition of the Triton's main computer core and confirm that Sol Defence has not included any sensitive information with the update they just transmitted."

"They're annexing themselves," Larry said.

"Yes. No returns to the Sol System," replied the person on the other end. "Do you understand my instructions?"

"If I open the sanctum to access the core, I'll be detected by security here. This assignment has become complicated."

"We have been actively tracking you from a distance and are aware of your circumstances." There was a pause before his superior continued. "Citadel has engaged a new enemy, but rest assured that we will still download the contents of your bio-recorder regularly. You should be proud of your success so far. We could not have wished for a better overseer on the Triton."

"Are you giving me a new assignment?" Larry asked. He wanted to see the Triton rebuilt, to make amends with the people he respected when they returned. The crew that infested the ship until recently won him over, and he wanted to see the lights on, the ship full of life again. He wanted to be surrounded by the broad diversity of the people he'd come to know while he was undercover. Larry didn't want to leave, or pursue another assignment, but if Citadel gave him an order, he would have no choice. Duty was his life.

"We are fighting far from the cradle of humanity, and it is our hope that no one ever knows it. The war we wage is one that should never be brought to Sol system or the core worlds."

"Who are you fighting?" Larry asked. "What are your chances?" He was suddenly torn. Being aboard Triton would be good for him, but he couldn't do so with a clear conscience if he knew his comrades were fighting and dying somewhere else.

"I can't share that information with you," replied the anonymous voice. "But you will be leaving the Rega Gain system. You will critically damage the Triton's computer core, the quantum entanglement communications system right now, and, if possible, destroy the Triton itself. Once you are finished you will board a craft with faster than light capabilities and report to point ninety three. You will need a stasis system – the journey will take over two years."

"The Triton could be home to thousands, it could be an asset to the entire region and major rallying point for the war. I'll assume command, reveal myself with the codes I carry," Larry said with determination. "I can make sure that the Triton reflects the excellence we strive for in the Sol System, and humanity will see that Sol Defence hasn't abandoned them."

"No. You do not have the strategic mind nor the disposition to assume command of a Zhàn Class Carrier in combat or peacetime. People have always been tools to you, pawns, and the task requires a better balance between sensitivity and practicality. This is not a debate. Sol Defence may believe that it's time for people to learn about the technology hidden at the heart of the Triton, and they may have faith in the crew that found her, but Citadel knows that they are engaging in some dangerous wishful thinking. This comes from the highest level. Destroy the Triton. Join us once it's done. Our cause makes the conflict with the Order of Eden look petty and meaningless."

It was the last thing Larry wanted to do, but he'd seen Citadel's judgment calls lead to positive outcomes before. They did see a bigger picture, who was he to argue? The former crew of the Triton would get along without him, and without the ship. It was terrible, but he was duty-bound. "I understand. It will be done."

"You know what failure means."

"I do," Larry said.

"I'm sorry."

The transmission ended, and the command and control unit returned to its previous state, watching Agameg as he finished his inspection of the bridge controls. Larry turned it off and sealed his vacsuit. He activated his suit's cloaking systems and left his quarters.

CHAPTER 23
BEGGARS AND FORAGERS

Oz cringed inwardly as he saw a red-faced man, full of self-importance, striding towards him. He had shoulder-length bleached hair and a pronounced chin. He pressed through the line of civilians who were getting paid before they left the space rented by the former Triton crew. "My favourite commander," he announced sarcastically.

People lined up between the wires that had been strung to indicate the double line all paid attention. Being in a queue was boring, and to most of them someone like this man was a welcome diversion. Oz was happy that most of the civilians who wanted to leave to seek out family or return home for their property had already passed through. There were fewer than twenty left.

Oz looked him up on his command and control unit; his name was Chazick Tweed, and he was a manual fabricator aboard the Triton. He had less than two days of work logged since. "Have we met?" Oz asked, allowing himself an amused smile. He'd faced so many entitled people over the course of his career, he had started to find them amusing instead of frustrating long ago.

"No, not face to face. I've just gotten orders from you and your under-thugs every day for the last two months," replied the fellow as he stopped to stand within arm's reach. "You'd think wearing that wrapper of a uniform was bad enough."

Oz nodded, hoping that it would be enough of an acknowledgement to get to the point. "You must be in a hurry to leave, we'll process you out right away."

"Why do you say that?" asked Chazwick.

"You cut in front of all these people here," Oz said, gesturing to the more patient people behind him. Some of them smiled at him, others were busy listening to or watching something on their comm units.

"Sorry? I'm not going anywhere. I just want to make sure that I'm getting paid for my time," Chazwick replied with exaggerated offence as he was scanned by one of the guards.

"According to this we owe you three hundred twenty GC," Oz replied.

"I saw that, and it doesn't match my calculations. You owe me over twenty eight hundred for my time, and that's at a quarter of someone with my skill makes at a minimum."

"We pay for working hours minus billet and board," Oz explained, leaning on the edge of a crate filled with reclaimed comm units. "The only exception we make is for people who take care of children, who get a small additional allowance to assist with their care."

"I can't help it if you haven't put me to work on something useful."

"My sergeants assigned you to three different fabrication shops and you only showed up at the first one for twenty three minutes. We needed you there, and it was the same thing you were doing aboard the Triton."

"It wasn't exactly the same thing," Chazwick said, waving his hands. "You had us making parts that any heavy materialiser could do using scrap and water."

"All our heavy materialisers have been down for about six weeks, because there are too few people with the expertise to make replacement parts in the fabrication shop," Oz said. Several people in line behind him shook their heads or groaned or both.

"If someone told me that, I would have gotten to work instead of sitting around. I thought the parts I was assigned to make were for one of your junk heaps."

"It's not up to you to decide!" shouted a short man further back in line. "The Shop Manager puts the priority list together, then we get to work. I thought you worked in a shop before."

Oz put his hand up and made eye contact with the gentleman. "Thanks for the reminder," he replied. With a glance at his command and control unit he saw his name was Ross Sherman, and he was standing beside his wife, Anna. They were both experienced fitters and fabricators, highly prized on any crew.

"I'm just here to ask if we can get my cousin to bring my kids and his family here. She's in the Sonsarru system, just a few days away," Ross asked.

"There's a line here for a reason," Chazwick said.

Oz's temper flared momentarily. "You've been sitting on your ass doing nothing for weeks, what's another few minutes?" he said to Chazwick. He looked back to Ross and his slightly taller wife. "Later today we're making an announcement about that. I won't go into great detail, but soon we'll have room for people with a good work record to invite their families to live with them. If you have friends out there who need a place, they'll be welcome to apply or pay their way here."

"How are you going to manage that?" asked Anna. "We're bunking on top of each other as it is."

Oz pointed across the busy, cluttered settlement, to a two storey tall stack of large crates. "You see those? We've found some flat, safe ground to lay them out and put them together. When we're done, we'll have a real settlement shelter. I can't tell you where they're going yet, but it's going to be better than this."

Ross looked to his wife, who nodded at him. "Thank you, Sir," he said and the pair turned and walked away. More than half of the people in line, in red, yellow, and blue vacsuits marking them for what part of the work force they were from, turned and followed. Oz was left with only four people leaving, far fewer than he expected.

Chazwick turned to leave as well, and Oz caught his shoulder. "You know, I dealt with someone a lot like you on the Triton," he said. "I was happy when he left, and I'll be happier to see you go."

"What?" Chazwick said, turning on Oz with outrage. "You can't do that!"

"Let's look at this in closer detail," Oz said, glancing at the three others in line to make sure they weren't growing impatient. They seemed to like the idea of the impending show. "You sat around for nearly two months, wanted to get paid for it, and now you've changed your mind since discovering that you can invite your lazy family to stay with us and eat our food."

"I have more training than that guy and his wife put together," Chazwick said. "Look it up on your thing, if you don't believe me. You need me."

"Okay, you're not getting the point, and I really do want you to get it because you're about to get punted to Port Rush, where people will hear your story about this," Oz said. He wasn't really concerned about Chazwick spreading the word about his work or depart policy, but knew that the other people leaving might. "Let's use Xander here as an example," he said, waving to one of the money counters. "He's getting paid to help us pay people and make sure that they have the leave code so they can get transit off Tamber. Before he was given that job, he and his two sons have been working in a cleaning crew they started. No one told them to start one, they just saw that the one we put together was having trouble keeping up and made themselves useful."

Chazwick was obviously offended. "Picking up garbage on the tarmac? That's what you expect-"

"I expect people who stick around to be useful, that's why we're adding a detail to our news package later today. No more refugees. If someone is working or taking care of children, then they can stay and they get paid for being useful. No one's going to get rich on the wages we're offering, but I don't see anyone else hiring this many off-worlders."

"Then I'll start working, fine. I still want everything you owe me though. Since I didn't know the conditions, I deserve compensation," Chazwick demanded.

"Oz!" squeaked a nafali woman with big, watery green eyes and a twitching pink nose. "I can't find Zoe!" She held up a tiny vacsuit and comm unit, indicating that the toddler had doffed them both at some point.

Oz quickly checked on her in crewcast and realised that the woman who had signed up to take care of Zoe, Vivian Lea, had passed through the other civilian checkpoint with two human children. "She's been gone for six hours," he said to himself.

"Am I getting paid or what?" demanded Chazwick.

"You're leaving," Oz said darkly. "Goodbye." With a quick command he dosed Chazwick with enough sedative to knock him out for an hour. He went wide-eyed and collapsed so quickly that the nearest guard almost didn't catch him. "Get his comm unit, anything he received on the Triton, put the three hundred twenty GC he's earned in one of his secure pockets and dump him in a bathroom in the nearest starport with his vacsuit sealed," he ordered.

"That's not even enough to catch a transport to Weatherly," muttered a nearby civilian.

"Maybe he can find a ship in need of a resident pain in the ass," Oz muttered as he turned his attention back to finding Zoe. "Take over, Tim," he told a nearby guard in shrapnel-scarred heavy armour. He stepped beside Panloo, who eyed him anxiously. "All right, you see what I'm doing here?" he said as he brought up the Crewcast search interface. "I'm going to use every comm with Crewcast to scan for Zoe. If she's near anyone, we'll find her."

Within a few seconds Oz's command and control unit projected a holographic image of Zoe sifting through a waste bin outside the commissary. To Panloo's horror the little nafali girl retrieved an uneaten third of a synthetic cheese bun. The older nafali screeched as she watched Zoe chomp into a bite shaped curve of the bread as though picking up where the former consumer left off. "Where is this? Where is she?"

Oz grabbed the nafali's hand and started running towards the shipping container that had been converted into a canteen. "We'll be there before she finishes," he promised.

They made swift progress between temporary buildings built from scrap, under two smaller ships being repaired, and across a small opening before Panloo saw Zoe, sitting on the tarmac enjoying her found meal. As soon as the tall nafali woman caught sight of the youngster she quadrupled her pace, dropping to all fours, leaping over a pair of guards who were on their way to the canteen.

In a sequence of motions that Oz would have missed if he blinked, Zoe was swept up in Panloo's arms and the remaining bread was batted out of the toddler's hands. The toddler looked dazed as she took the situation in and chased the rolling bun with her eyes. Oz pulled a chocolate ration bar from his pocket, his last one, and unwrapped it as he closed the distance.

Just as Zoe's eyes began to well up, the chocolate flavoured food was under her nose, and Oz was her biggest hero. "No strange germs on this, I promise," he said, out of breath.

Zoe's little furry hands were about to wrap around the precious food when Panloo intercepted them. "Oh no, I'm going to hold this for you. Once you're done eating we're going to clean you up."

Oz verified that Panloo was listed as one of Zoe's backup caregivers and nodded to himself, not surprised that Ashley had set it up herself. Since then, Panloo spent every spare minute with the youngster. "Are you two going to be all right?"

"I'm adopting her," Panloo said softly. There was a dedication in her eyes that was almost fierce.

"You have my blessing," Oz replied.

"Will I lose my job? I've been flying shuttles."

"If you can get this one to stay in a vacsuit or safety seat while you're flying, then I don't see a problem," Oz replied. "Jake proved a vacsuit can survive re-entry, so I'd say a child's safety seat would do even better. Just make sure they've got the right gear for safe decent built in."

"I'll seal her inside if I have to," Panloo said.

"Nafali carry their children everywhere when they're her age, right?"

"Female nafali, yes, and I haven't had any of my own yet, so she's going to get all my attention," Panloo cooed at Zoe, who was happily munching on the gooey chocolate meal bar.

"All right, then I'm transferring primary care to you right now. You won't be eligible for any combat missions though, so be prepared to play taxi around here until Zoe is ready to spend time with a caretaker."

"I'll make that sacrifice," Panloo said. "Combat flying is too nerve-wracking anyway."

"You're sure you can keep this one under control?" Oz said, aware of Zoe's legendary escapist abilities.

"Oh yes, I'm sure," Panloo said with a smile.

He had enough nephews and nieces to know that was a remote possibility at best, but he was willing to give it a chance. At worst, she'd be forced to seat Zoe into a toddler carrier *and* seal her into a vacsuit. "Congratulations," Oz said as he watched the pair together.

Zoe looked at him as she finished chewing a mouthful and struggled in Panloo's arms. Oz stepped closer and was rewarded with a sloppy wet kiss on the tip of his nose. "You're welcome," he chuckled. He grinned as she returned her attention to the half eaten meal bar.

"I'm going to take her to see Ashley after this settles in her stomach," Panloo said.

"Aylee?" Zoe said, her eyes widening.

"I think she remembers her," Oz said. "That'll be good for them both." His comm warbled a quiet alarm and he checked it immediately, routing the sound to his subdermal comm. "Ayan's shuttle is leaving for Port Rush City in five minutes. The security team is aboard and the trip is expected to take one hour. There are protestors surrounding the base of the building, so our entry point will be on the roof." Oz signalled his acknowledgement of the message, wishing he could have gone with them.

"Is there something wrong?" asked Panloo.

"Just another day at the office," Oz said. "You should get your things together and make yourselves portable. It looks like you're going have a lot of flying to do. We're moving the civilians soon."

"Oh? What will the new settlement look like?" Panloo asked.

"I can't say yet, but it's going to be better than this," Oz said. "I have to draft a plan and figure out how we're going to do this while I check in with a few other things. Do you two have everything you need?"

"Yes," Panloo said, nuzzling Zoe's pink-tipped nose with her own. The toddler nuzzled back for a moment before burying her face into the loose white fur around Panloo's neck. "Thank you so much, Commander."

Seeing the pair together, so happy was a sizable victory to Oz's heart. "You're welcome."

***

STATUS CHANGED reported Crewcast on Ashley's comm unit. She looked at it and saw a picture of Panloo with Zoe. An announcement orbited them in golden letters: "Commander Terry Ozark McPatrick approved Panloo Utta's adoption of Zoe!"

"You miss her," Liam Grady said. They were sitting together in the finished corner of the Samson's galley. The hatch was sealed, not that anyone would enter, since the deck was half in pieces. The plates of metal that would cover the floor were piled in a corner. A path of fitted deck had been finished so someone could easily get across to a major junction box. There was enough room there to set up a table and three chairs.

The faint sounds of people working below managed to drift up through the sealed ceiling. Ashley could hear Frost yelling something at someone, but couldn't make out the words. "It was one of the worst things about being sealed up in a suit for so long. I couldn't visit her, but I was able to sneak out early on and ask Panloo if she could check on her for me."

"She spent all her time off-duty with her," Liam said. "I'd say that was a great choice on your part. Are you envious?"

"No," Ashley replied without thinking. "Yeah," she said with a sigh. "I just miss her."

"We're almost done here," Liam said. "You're taking all this in pretty quickly, I'm impressed."

Ashley looked back to the hologram of a green apartment building. The levels were fanned out in a circle, so every apartment had a large balcony, enclosed garden, and plenty of window space. Water flowed across the large, roof-top gardens and trickled down the sides to water the greenhouses and gardens below. "So this is where I last lived on earth, The Orwell Long Term Care Centre. I was partially responsible for taking care of two people: Sharon Parks, and Tina Carierre. I had Mondays and Tuesdays, Susan had Wednesdays and Thursdays, Rhonda had," Ashley stopped and looked at Liam, who was looking at her with mild surprise. "What?"

"I didn't expect you to remember that kind of detail, it's only there so you can convince the Carthan Officers that you spent real time on Earth."

"Okay, sorry."

"No need to apologise," Liam said. "I'm only surprised."

"Question," Ashley said, sitting straighter in her seat. It was difficult to get comfortable in something that was so roughly welded together. "Does everyone on Earth pull double duty, taking care of the elderly?"

"Some people take care of very young children instead. I was fortunate enough to be chosen by these two ladies, they were incredible people," Liam replied.

"So they chose you, you weren't assigned?"

"It's not seen so much as a job, or assignment. I wanted to be integrated into the community while I was there, so I passed the checks and was put in a list of helpers they could choose from. Have you always been able to retain so much in such a short period of time?"

"I wasn't able to sleep for most of last night, so I spent my time looking at the life you set up for me on Earth," Ashley replied. "It's easy to remember all this stuff when it's so weird. I mean, this is based on your experiences there, and you got so close to people, they really took you in. It must have been hard to leave."

"It was," Liam said. "But my purpose doesn't allow me to stay where there's harmony. Travellers like myself aspire to be builders, advisors, and teachers, staying somewhere only while we're needed. What I showed you was a stable community, where the residents are fairly harmonious and happily integrated."

"So when you're finished here you'll move on and find other people who need help?" Ashley said.

"Unless I find something or someone here who makes it impossible for me to move on. Then I'll retire. I won't have to make that decision for years from the looks of it though, there's plenty of work."

Ashley chuckled and nodded. "Yup. You'll be here for a bit."

"So, how do you feel about everything you've taken in? Do you think you can convince a military Officer that you are a trained Earth Commander?"

"No," Ashley said, laughing nervously. "I get all the background stuff, and I can try to pretend, but I'm so jittery."

"Then think of it this way," Liam said. "Earth Commanders don't reveal anything they don't see as absolutely necessary. Just the fact that you're revealing yourself as a commander is a massive breach by Earth standards. They don't believe they owe anyone outside of the Sol system anything. Help, information, technology, or time are all things a Sol Defence Commander will want to withhold."

A notion dawned on Ashley. "So you want me to be a snob!"

Liam laughed and nodded. "Since you put it that way, that would probably work best."

"I've met more than I can count and grew up serving plenty, that'll be easy," Ashley said.

"Just amend your performance with one detail: always be polite. Sol Defence and Earth Peace Officers are so polite it's frustrating."

"Okay. What if they start yelling or something?" Ashley asked.

"Ignore them," Liam replied. "Do everything in your power to pretend they're not there at all. Look or talk to someone else, walk away, or even seal up your vacsuit if you have to. Just do anything but react to them. All higher ranking Sol Defence Officers are trained to communicate effectively and quickly. They lose respect for whoever they're speaking to if they can't do the same."

"Wow, okay, I'll try," Ashley said.

"Good, we're going as soon as Ayan returns. It's a good thing you have some time too," Liam said, looking at her comm unit.

Ashley looked and squealed at the message she saw from Panloo: I'M IN THE REFIT HANGAR WITH SOMEONE WHO WANTS TO SEE YOU.

"Go reunite," Liam said. "I have a few things to check on."

"Are you sure?" Ashley asked, not wanting to look like she was shirking the background study she'd committed to.

"You know everything you need to and a lot more. Go on."

"Thank you!" Ashley said, giving him a quick hug and a kiss on the cheek before running down the narrow path to the hatchway.

***

Liam Grady gave Ashley time to get down the hall and well out of sight before he turned his attention to the message he received from Earth earlier that morning. It wasn't the first time he'd looked at it, and he had to look again. It was difficult to believe.

SOL DEFENCE MESSAGE FOLLOWS. NOT FOR RETRANSMISSION.

Axiologist Pilgrim Liam Grady, it is a pleasure and a relief to know that you have survived in these trying times. We are aware of your progress with the wayward crew led by Jacob Valance, or Valent as he has decided to be called yesterday. We believe a fracture in the group is likely, and are certain that by lending your support to whichever side you feel inclined to instead of leaving that group of people would be more beneficial for the common good.

It is with sadness that I inform you that we have closed our borders, so your request to return to the Sol system has been denied. Our belief that the Fourth Fall was coming has been woefully confirmed, and we will not allow any being entry into our space until we decide the galaxy has achieved a higher level of stability. In that spirit, Sol Defence is disabling the quantum entanglement communications system connected to the Triton. Instantaneous communication with Earth will no longer be possible for at least a generation.

Ties are being cut, projects outside of the Sol solar system have been abandoned, and only a few of our outbound explorers are returning. The rest will continue on, alone and in the shadows until this storm passes. Just as the Sol system was beginning to open our boarders, we are being forced to isolate ourselves again.

You made a favourable impression while you were here, Liam, and are spoken of fondly. Woo-Jin Lim enjoys bringing you into conversations occasionally, so the entire cloister knows you earned his admiration. Knowing where you came from, and having known you personally gives me hope for the future of mankind in the Milky Way. Whether you choose the path of war or creation, I know you will do well.

It saddens me more than you can know that I may never see you again. May love follow you, and your desire for peace guide you.

With love and respect,

Axiologist Mentor Ute Eisenberg

Liam Grady sat back and closed his eyes, giving himself a moment to recall Ute and the time they spent together. She was not his mentor. That was Woo-Jin Lim, who Liam had said farewell to when he left. There was closure enough in that departure. The teachings Woo-Jin imparted on him could lead him through life, so his mentor would always be with him.

Ute was a woman he met, another Axiologist who was fascinated with technology beyond the Sol Defence borders. Long, late night discussions soon evolved into romantic evenings. He didn't need holographic recordings to recall her deep blue eyes, flowing blonde hair, or warm smiles. Most people who were allowed to visit Earth wanted to return eventually. There was so much to learn, so much to see.

Ute was Liam's real reason for returning, but the request he quietly included with the message the Triton crew sent to Earth didn't specifically state that. It said he wanted to return as a student, and to permanently integrate on Earth, Mars, or one of the larger outer stations.

The reply from Ute was acknowledgement of that message, and her way of saying she would have liked him to return. The only solace in discovering that he wouldn't be able to see her was that he felt free to pursue someone else, but he was in no hurry. Liam released his mental image of her, saying, "Some journeys must end."

"But others await," replied Minh-Chu.

Liam opened his eyes and cleared his throat. Minh-Chu was standing in the open hatchway. "Sorry to interrupt your meditation, Mentor."

"No apologies, Wing Commander," Liam replied. "Your timing is excellent."

"Jason noticed you received a transmission from Sol Defence. He's a little crazy at the moment, because the origin date is from today, and well, from Earth."

"So you volunteered to speak to me instead," Liam said. "How did you convince him to stay away from this discussion?"

Minh-Chu entered the room and made his way down the narrow path of installed deck plates. "You have the respect of practically everyone here, but have made almost no serious attachments, and haven't revealed much about yourself. I told him that a wrong move could lead to you leaving."

"That sounds rational, and mostly correct, but I doubt that convinced him to stay out of this conversation," Liam said with a little smile.

"Laura told him to stay put," Minh replied.

"There it is."

"They're having some serious problems, I don't think he wanted to make it worse. I'm just glad he's finally making her a priority."

"Agreed. So, Wing Commander Minh-Chu Buu, what shape will this conversation take?"

Minh retracted the glove of his vacsuit and offered his hand. "I've never properly introduced myself." He waited for Liam to shake his hand before saying, "I'm Minh-Chu Buu, my friends call me Minh or Ronin."

"I'm Liam, and pleased to meet you, Ronin. I'm highly amused that someone named after a rogue Samurai leads Samurai Squadron," Liam replied.

"I know," Minh said, sitting down. "I was about to tell them there was a mismatch there, but the names were already on the books."

"You are eager to learn what was in that message from Earth."

"I am, but I have other questions too."

"I'm sure you do," Liam replied. Sitting down with Minh-Chu was a bit of a thrill for Liam. He watched the pilot from a distance. The man was almost forty, but looked younger, and seemed very youthful outside of his command duties. There was a list of questions he had for him, but they'd have to wait.

"First, how did that transmission cross that distance in one day?" Minh asked.

"The Triton has a stable quantum entanglement communications system somewhere onboard. Most likely inside the dormant computer core."

"No one has been able to build a stable Q.E.C.S. but they've started rolling them off the assembly line on Earth?"

"I realise most QECS are sold as novelties and scams in the galaxy, but yes, Earth has mastered the technology. Sadly, they used it to say farewell, so I won't be returning for at least a generation."

"I'm sorry to hear that," Minh said. "But I'm hoping you remain here. You are needed."

"I know," Liam replied. He thought a moment, aware that Minh was watching him. "I'll decide whether I'm staying after the Triton is reactivated and I've completed a check of her systems. I'll make sure there's a good replacement if I leave."

"What did they have to say about the Triton?"

"It has been released. If they were able to connect to the QECS, then they know who has the codes, where the Triton is, and what condition she's in. The fact that they can contact it at all tells me that her core computer is activating. The Triton's software is updating, and she's almost ready to come back to life. I checked Ashley's comm. Nothing has changed, she still has valid command codes. Whether it's just a way for the Triton to continue collecting data about us, or they like the fact that Ashley has command codes for some other reason doesn't matter. She has top level command codes, and the power to transfer command to someone else using the Triton's main computer."

"You didn't tell us that when you looked at the codes last night," Minh said, shaking his finger at Liam playfully.

Liam couldn't help but laugh at the younger man's antics. "You're the first I've told. I'm sharing this with you because it's a gift. I want you to tell Ashley yourself."

Minh sat back in his seat, his reaction was difficult to read. "Why?"

"There is something about her that challenges everything you are in the best of ways, and it's never happened to you before. At the same time, I believe you respect her, perhaps put her up on a pedestal. That brings all your insecurities to the surface when you meet her."

"Yup, she melts my brain," Minh agreed.

"It's time for you to speak to her with real respect, as a person you should know, and destroy the infatuation that's been building, whether you're aware of it or not, so there might be something else. I'm giving you this secret to share with her until she decides who should be in command of the Triton."

"You're either a wonderful man or deeply evil," Minh said, shaking his head.

"No one is purely one or the other," Liam replied. "You will have to help her make this decision, perhaps you'll have to do it as Ronin, Wing Commander of Samurai Squadron at first, but I know you'll lead her to the correct decision."

Minh shook his head rapidly and sighed. "I don't know how this'll turn out, so I'll say thank you for now, but I reserve the right to amend that later."

"Understood," Liam said with a smile. "Next question."

"Right," Minh said. "Oh Swami, does the QECS still work?"

"Yes, but it's not connected to Earth any longer, they've shut their end down," Liam replied. "I don't know if it's connected to anyone else."

"All right," Minh said. He pondered something a moment before going on. "So Ashley might not be stuck on the Triton like she thought and Sol Defence has released the Triton. The computer core is already waking up, there's a QECS on board that could be linked to other ships or planets, and you enjoy torturing me for my own good. Did I get everything?"

Liam laughed and nodded. "Yes, you did." He paused a moment and leaned forward, speaking more seriously. "You shouldn't let Ashley tell you to make her choices for her over the next day. Lead her to the decision that feels right to her."

"You already know what she'll decide," Minh said.

"I have more than a fair idea."

"We also have to watch for Larry, the agent aboard. There was nothing about him in the message I received, so I'm led to assume that Sol Defence isn't willing to share information about him to my friend on Earth, or they are unaware of him."

"He gave Ashley the code she has, so he might be able to interfere," Minh concluded.

"It's possible," Liam agreed.

"If he does?"

"Your people need this ship and will use it well," Liam said. "Prevent him from taking control, even if it means killing him."

***

The information Minh collected felt like a weight across his shoulders. He didn't regret any part of his conversation with Liam Grady, but he couldn't tell if he was being examined, taught, admired, or all three during the encounter. Making his way through the busy corridors of the Samson, past welders, electricians and countless grunts, he ran everything he learned over and over in his mind.

People called him a Zen master, a commander, and a mentor, and it all felt a little foolish all of a sudden. He understood why Liam made such a massive impression on everyone he spoke to, and wished he could continue talking to the man for several days. There was so much to learn, so much to experience, and with a guide like him to enrich it all, life could only be better, or at least more interesting.

He finally reached an external hatch and made his way to the bottom of the severely tilted gangway. The hangar was well lit, beyond the main doors was the long night, decorated by the lights of ships in the sky and people wearing lit vacsuits of many colours.

Ashley was near the middle of the huge hangar, in the cantina that was just a large collection of folding chairs, tables, and a few makeshift food prep counters. Minh used his comm unit to zoom in on her and Zoe. She was holding the laughing toddler upside down, gently shaking her up and down saying, "Oh my gosh! She's all fulla giggles! I've gotta get 'em out!" Panloo stood by, her squeaky laughter only adding to the mirth of the scene.

Minh-Chu smiled to himself, remembering when he finally became social enough to meet his nieces and nephews. It didn't take long for him to enjoy having them around just as much. He decided to wait until Ashley's visit with Zoe was over before sharing the weight of the new information he'd gained with her. Jason wouldn't wait, however, and he started walking back to the Clever Dream to face the interrogation, deleting the recording of his conversation with Liam Grady along the way.

CHAPTER 24
LOOSE ENDS

"Good morning, Ayan," Lewis said as she emerged from the shower into the captain's cabin. The Clever Dream had no problem providing purified water for her and the other officers to take a shower every day, but she only took one when she needed cheering up in the morning. The water was soothing, and the full body air-drying inside the shower cubicle was invigorating.

"Now that's civilisation," Ayan said. "Good morning, Lewis."

"I can't see how a thorough cleaning is civilisation in itself," Lewis said.

"I guess I mean that it's a part of a highly civilised lifestyle," Ayan said. "Can you add it to the document I started last night?"

"The Shoreline Project?"

"Yes, I'd like to add the specifications of your water closet to the bathrooms in the main settlement."

"The water requirements will rise dramatically," Lewis said. "They would have to go on ration and use the vibro cleaning features on some days if water conditions surrounding the island aren't ideal."

"I know," Ayan said, pulling the feet of her heaviest vacsuit on. It was the underlay of the armour she wore in the Ossimi ring. She decided to leave the outer suit white, and change the horizontal strips of the overlay to black. "But I'm sure once the purification systems are up and running, everyone will be able to start their day the same way I just did."

"I've added it," Lewis said. "I have to say, I was surprised when you started such an ambitious project late last evening, and I'm impressed. Any humanoid would be lucky to live in what you have designed so far."

"I still need to talk to Liam, a few nafali and Agameg about it, but thank you, Lewis." Ayan looked at the hologram of the settlement she'd worked on. It was designed to fit under a large protective energy field, had hidden long range defences, room and reinforcements for a military base beneath, but what she was most proud of was perfectly visible above ground.

The main structure was circular, with gentle divots and bulges placed for balconies with sealing transparent overhangs, enclosed exterior paths, and extendable landing platforms for shuttles. From the base and middle, other substructures curled out towards smaller buildings surrounding the main structure. The curling irregular tubes made the main structure look like a plant with external pods and smooth roots reaching back into the ground. Those roots would house a high-speed transportation system, apartments, small shops, viewing areas, and other smaller establishments. A few of them led to an oval building that was almost as large as the primary structure. It was hollow through the centre, and served as a spaceport to small and medium sized ships. All the facilities needed for travellers would be contained within, so people in the main habitat could go on with their lives in relative peace.

"How much of the land would this take on the island we're taking possession of today?" Ayan asked.

"Less than three point five percent if you include the underground structure," Lewis replied. "It is ambitious though, and would take seventeen point six years to build with ten times your current work force. Under current conditions, it would cost-"

"It's a creative exercise, Lewis." Ayan sealed the heavy vacsuit at the neck and turned her attention to the armour overlay. "Would I like to see it built?" she asked no one in particular as she stomped into the thick boots. "Definitely. Housing a quarter of a million people in that kind of comfort would be a great legacy project, but it's really a distraction. Maybe it's something to hope for, but I may want to reduce the scale before presenting it to anyone. I admit it is a bit grand."

"People need something to look forward to," Lewis said. "That's something Alice said to me a long time ago."

"You miss her," Ayan said.

"So much. I run my recordings of her from beginning to end, then start over. It was a comfort at first. What do you do when you miss someone, Ayan?"

Ayan was surprised at the depth of emotion she heard in Lewis' voice, but answered just the same. "I build something."

Helper arms descended from the ceiling and deftly helped her lock the horizontal plates of her exterior armour over her heavy vacsuit. "Thank you, Lewis."

"You're welcome, Ayan. I am glad you're here."

"You've been very good to me," Ayan replied. She shoved her sidearm, a heavy Violator Handgun that Lewis had given her from his arms locker, into its holster.

"The transport carrying the payment for the Enforcer 1109 is on its way. Commander McPatrick has already given them instructions to land near my loading hatch."

"We planned to use your secure storage area, it should be large enough," Ayan said.

"There isn't enough room," Lewis replied. "You will have to load a quarter of the funds into another vessel."

"There wasn't much on your manifest, it should fit."

"There is cargo off the manifest that I will not allow you to move," Lewis said. "A body in stasis."

It was the first Ayan had heard of it. "Who is it?"

"I do not know, but Alice would not allow me to jettison him. He has been aboard since before I was initialised, and I am under orders to protect the corpse."

"Corpse. Is he too damaged to revive?" Ayan guessed.

"Yes," Lewis said. "If I were to rebuild the body using onboard supplies and facilities, the body would be an empty vessel. There was too much cranial damage for his memories to be intact, and there is no scan on file."

Ayan thought for a moment and asked. "Can we move him to normal storage?"

"No, my orders prevent it."

"All right, we'll find a safe place for the rest of the money." Ayan knew she might have to defend her decision more than once, but she wouldn't go against Lewis until she knew more. As emotional as he was, the only way to counter any notion the artificial intelligence had was with pure logic.

"Commander McPatrick is waiting outside," Lewis said.

Ayan initialised the suit and felt it come to life, actively embracing and supporting her. The energy shield cycled on and off, and the micro-generator reported optimum power levels. "I feel like I'm overdoing it."

"I disagree," Lewis said as he opened the door. "You are visiting the Triton today."

"Carthan Port Control gave us the all clear?" Oz asked.

"The response to Commander Rice's request just came through a moment ago," Lewis replied. "I'm excited."

"I guess she'd be the mother ship of your dreams," Oz said, looking Ayan up and down.

"If I were to choose a carrier, Triton would be at the top of my list," Lewis replied. "You are correct."

"It looks good on you," Oz told Ayan, tugging on one of the overlapping strips of armour on her shoulder. "I don't think you're overdoing it either, not this time. Not if we're going to the Triton today."

"I thought the main events would consist of receiving payment and visiting the Samson," Ayan said.

"Talking to Jake today?"

"Has everyone heard about our row?" Ayan asked peevishly.

"Actually, I didn't, but I saw it coming," Oz said. "Are you all right?"

"I'll be fine," Ayan said. "I was the one who did the most damage anyhow."

Oz regarded her with an expression of surprise for a moment before turning his attention to the hologram of the Shoreline Project in the middle of the room. "That's interesting."

Ayan looked over her shoulder. "Yeah, just some busy work."

"Can I take a look later?"

"I'll have Lewis send it to your comm," Ayan replied. "It's nowhere near finished though, just a rough concept." She looked up and said, "I'll see you later, Lewis. You can link with my suit if you like, but we'll probably be out of direct range when we get to the Triton."

"I'll follow along and be quiet this time," Lewis replied.

Ayan and Oz started walking to the main gangway, passing a small staging area that had been repurposed to house four cots. The soldiers getting ready there saluted them as they passed, regardless of their state. "How is base security?" Ayan asked.

"Complicated. We've started to draw beggars and applicants," Oz replied. "At last count, there were nine hundred thirty five people in line with applications in hand. A couple were easy decisions because they were related to our people, but most of the rest are getting screened through. The most disturbing thing this morning was finding a kid wandering around with a sign strapped to him."

"Did someone lose an orphan?" Ayan asked.

"No, I wish it were that simple." Oz stopped at the top of the ramp before going on. "Someone found a crack in our walls and must have pushed him through. The sign said, 'please feed my son and keep him safe'."

Ayan shook her head in disbelief. "Is it really so bad out there?"

"If you don't have a visa, or the skills people are looking for, then yes. I hear the street-to-street fighting in Rush City is worse too. Entire buildings are being taken as territory, with gangsters becoming the new landlords."

"I heard the Carthan Government is abandoning their building there, something to do with protestors," Ayan said. "How is the boy?"

"He's about two," Oz said.

"No, how *is* he?" Ayan repeated.

"Oh, he's good now. Seems pretty happy with the other orphans, doing a lot of sleeping. I hope he's the last one we find smuggled in."

They arrived at the bottom of the ramp and Ayan couldn't help but be amused at what she saw.

A guard sealed in heavy boarding armour was trying to shake a dog with patchwork black and brown fur off his ankle. The ferocious creature was no taller than thirty centimetres. It snarled and tugged at the soldier as if he planned to drag him off to some dark corner where he could devour him.

"What the hell is his problem?" asked the soldier in a familiar voice.

The soldier's counterpart, a woman with short cropped blonde hair, laughed as she looked on. Four squads of soldiers, all ready to guard the arriving shipment of Galactic Currency, couldn't help but look on in amusement as well. "Don't panic, Vic, he can't get through your suit," the young woman closest to him said.

"I know, but I'm not going to be able to guard anyone with this evil fur ball on my heel all day."

"He probably just needs to see your face," she replied.

"That's what he wants! I pull down my hood and he goes straight for the throat," replied Victor.

"Oops, head's up," said the younger woman as she noticed Ayan and Oz at the bottom of the ramp.

Victor noticed them and tried to ignore the dog, standing at attention. The dog frantically searched for another way to grip his ankle and settled on the Achilles heel. He did no damage, but that wasn't for lack of trying.

"I've assigned Lieutenant Victor Davis and Junior Lieutenant Jenny Machad as your personal guards," Oz said. "I chose Vic because you've worked with him before. They both fought in the tunnels on Pandem."

Ayan couldn't help but snicker a little. Jenny regarded her with an expression that was almost star-struck; she reminded Ayan of herself when she was in the academy.

Jenny watched as a young girl, her hair as dishevelled as a windblown bird's nest, rushed to the dog and picked him up effortlessly.

"Careful!" Victor said.

The dog licked the child's face eagerly as she held him against her chest. "He just wanted attention," she scolded before putting the dog down and running off with the mutt close behind.

"Good to see you again, Victor," Ayan said through a smile.

He lowered his armoured hood and nodded. "Good morning, such as it is," he said, gesturing towards the skyline. It was still dark beyond the bustle of port traffic overhead. It would be for hours longer.

"No need to overdress in the future, Ma'am," Jenny said. "We armour up so you don't have to."

"I dress for comfort, Junior Lieutenant," Ayan said. "And this selection felt right this morning."

"Understood, Ma'am. Please call me Jenny."

"Flight reports a shuttle incoming," Victor said. "The landing area is just this way."

"Lead on," Ayan said. She turned to Oz and asked, "Aren't they a little high-ranking for my personal guards? I can take care of myself, after all."

"They're a good match. I've worked with Jenny on security here for weeks, and you put a pretty positive note on Victor's file after the encounter on the station. Besides, we couldn't have a couple privates assigned to the matron of our settlement."

"Matron," Ayan said the word to try it on for size and shook her head. "Nope, don't like it. Commander's better."

"What's wrong with matron? Sounds too old?" Oz asked.

"Sounds too heavy," Ayan replied.

A shuttle with mismatched panels touched down swiftly in front of them. The door was open before they were securely on the ground, and Captain Ruby Sima walked down the three steps as they unfolded in front of the hatch. Her first mate, Lombardo, was right behind her.

The pair wore colonist's clothing – loose fitting shirts, pants, and boots that Ayan only saw in period dramas when she was growing up on Freeground. The more colourful manner of dress was commonplace in the galaxy, however, since most people were raised on a world with an atmosphere, and space suits were for travel, worn under clothes by many civilians. Platinum and silver chains rattled as Ruby moved, her long purple and green hair stirred by the shuttle's landing thrusters. It ascended as soon as the pair were clear. "Good morning!" Ruby shouted over the din.

"Good morning," Ayan said, surprised to see the former British Colonial. "What brings you here?"

Victor looked to Ayan as Ruby walked in her direction, and Ayan nodded, indicating that it was all right for her to get close. Having guards would take some getting used to.

"I've got business with you and your Captain Jake," Ruby said, smiling as she leaned down a little to greet Ayan with a kiss on the cheek. "That's from Patrizia," she said in her ear. "She's happy you'll be able to make your lease payment on this oasis you've built."

"She's not the only one," Ayan said. "It looks like we'll be staying here a little longer."

"I'm glad to hear it, I think she is too, judging from her gift," At the mention of it, Lombardo presented Ayan with a long white box. "She's inviting you to Naer for a meeting of her biggest and brightest partners. Our lady has a box at the next Super Pongo game. Big special event, they're celebrating the re-opening of the stadium since the galaxy's bots went mad."

"Do you know what's inside?" Ayan said, allowing Jenny to take the box.

"Judging from the box, Miss, that's a designer dress," Lombardo said in his gruff English accent.

"I'll open it later, after the Clever Dream has performed a deep scan," Ayan said.

Jenny called a lower ranking soldier over and instructed him to put the box in Ayan's quarters.

"Why do I get the feeling that Patrizia Salustri is priming me for a proposal?" Ayan asked Ruby.

"She's watched every news blip on you, luv," Ruby said. "Either she expects great things from you, or aspires to add you to her long list of conquests. Or both. That's a useful spot to be in, but you'd best be careful. I'll say her interest is even deeper now that she's heard you're getting paid for your salvage today," Ruby said in a quieter tone.

"How did that get out?" Oz asked.

"Good to see you, big boy," Ruby said with a wink. "Greydock isn't as secure as the Carthans like people to think. Connections to the black market run all through that place. Heard you had an encounter with Thurge and her man Burke, hope you're all right."

"I'm fine, thank you," Ayan said. "That's not stopping my people from increasing security, though."

"Whether you like it or not, no doubt," Ruby said. "Know how that is."

"What else brings you here?" Ayan asked.

"Well, I'd like to meet with Captain Valent, if I can get the clear from you on that," Ruby said. "Now that he's put the word out that he'll be out there with us privateers, I want to see what he's thinking, maybe what he's turned the Samson into. Last time I scanned her, she didn't look like much."

"More like hull plates hanging on a thruster," Lombardo added.

"They've been rebuilding for a while," Oz said. "I'll send a request ahead, I'm sure he'll be happy to meet you."

"He's already agreed to the meeting," Ruby said. "I just wanted to pass it by his lady first. He may be the bluster, but I know who's really in charge."

Ayan was surprised that Ruby thought she had to pass the idea of a meeting by her before actually going ahead with it, but tried to take it in stride, as though it wasn't the first time it happened. "Go ahead, I'm sure he'll tell me all about it."

"I'm sure he will," Ruby said. "I'll drop by before I leave, luv." She swaggered off with Lombardo close behind. His head was constantly turning, taking in the whole busy settlement, while Ruby looked straight ahead, confident and focused.

"All right, so that wasn't our money drop," Ayan said.

"It's coming in," Oz said, signalling the four squads of soldiers. They fell into ranks to either side of Ayan's group. She watched as a heavily armoured Carthan shuttle descended. A squadron of Twin Gun fighters circled overhead, ready to pounce on anything that threatened the vessel.

"Start getting the boarding party for the Triton together now. I want to go as soon as we've got this loaded and secure," Ayan said, impatient to get on with her day.

CHAPTER 25
NEW DOORS OPEN TO AN OLD DREAM

"I like it," Minh said as he sipped a tall slush drink. He and Captain Valent were looking at a holographic image of a dorsal launch system. A new upper-rear hatch opened on the back of the Samson, and two fighters were ejected through. Another pair of fighters slid down on rails, were punted out, and another, then the last. The doors closed after, quickly. The animation repeated. "The engineering checks out?"

"Every simulation, and Frost just tested the rails using a pallet of raw ingots, eight times the weight of an extended Uriel. Slick is all set to take control of the squadrons here?"

"He's looking forward to it," Minh said. "I'll level with you, Jake… Taking command of all of it was too much. This squadron of seven feels perfect."

"How did the pilot assignments go?" Jake asked, leaning against his modest bunk. He had the larger captain's bed removed, opting for a bunk pair instead.

Minh guessed that Jake was turning the bottom one into cupboard space, judging from the mess and the lack of a mattress. "I got some of the more experienced pilots, not all the best, but they're not too green. Have you talked to Ayan about taking Samurai Squadron with you when you leave?"

"I put it up on the assignment board," Jake said. He brought up another hologram and it hovered above his tool-strewn workbench. "Captain Berkovitz, an old friend of mine, sent me some intel on an ideal port. It's not a human port, and everyone goes there, no matter what side, but they have the firepower to make it a very bad idea to break the peace there."

"Can you trust him?" Minh asked, looking at the image of the man. Judging purely from the head shot he looked like he was probably tall and fit. He reminded Minh of Oz.

"He's a long range courier, and generally hates bounty hunting. I was lucky enough to help him out by stopping a robbery. I was only there because the moron who tried to rob him was a bounty target of mine."

"He was a moron but able to corner a courier with military gear?" Minh asked.

"The mark was a very heavily armed moron," Jake said.

"Ah. So this captain is paying you back."

"Maybe, but I get a feeling that he's interested in touching base, considering the shape the galaxy's in right now. It helps to have friends."

There was a firm knock on the hatch and Jake turned off all the holograms in the room before shouting, "enter!"

The hatch opened to reveal Ruby Sima, who looked around, wary. A sort of false joviality overtook her the moment she saw Jake in his long coat. "Never thought I'd see the day that I got to meet the legendary Captain Valent."

She barely got a foot over the threshold before Jake nodded absently and started for the door. "We'll have more room if we meet in the officer's lounge." Jake led the way, Minh, Ruby, and her first officer Lombardo following. The pair of guards that were assigned to the foreign captain brought up the rear.

Minh barely caught Jake's hand gesture, so quick and barely noticeable. He flicked one finger at his side then let his hand open casually. There was someone they couldn't see in their group. Minh quietly released the retaining clasp on his holster, feeling that old excitement rise in his chest that told him something was about to happen. It was familiar, and suppressing it in favour of staying cool-headed was second nature, but he almost wanted to hold on to that energized feeling. Never did he feel more alive.

They followed Jake into the room, where there was an old table with four chairs around it and two more against the wall. Against the far wall were four stasis tubes, one already occupied by Leland March and a fairly non-descript man. Minh knew him as the only surviving member of the group that tried to kidnap Jake, the one that had his neck crushed. He had been seen to by medical personnel and restored, but instead of waking him, Jake had him put into deeper stasis. Beside that captive was March, the lower half of his face was still frozen in an expression that was a mix of shock and fear. Whether they were there as some sort of trophy or example, Minh-Chu wasn't sure. He wasn't going to ask, either.

The hatch closed behind them. Jake turned around casually, his gun drawn. Minh-Chu hadn't even seen him draw. He supposed he used his cloaking system with a hologram to mask the act, or somehow slid the huge sidearm out while everyone was behind him; it was something he'd ask later. The looks of surprise on everyone's faces were extreme, no one knew what was going on. Jake's other hand came to rest on something no one could see for a long moment.

A soldier in dark blue Carthan armour became visible, Jake's hand on his shoulder. "You're an idiot," Captain Valent said. "I knew you were aboard the moment I saw you through my uplink with the ship."

"How?" asked the soldier, slowly raising his hands as he looked down the barrel of Jake's handgun.

"There's a scale attached to every boarding ramp on the Samson. It's just an old fashioned way to track cargo and passengers coming aboard."

Ruby laughed lightly, nodding. "So you knew Lombardo, me, and the guards here didn't add up to the measure."

"Repeat after me," Jake said, looking at the man in armour. "I'm an idiot."

"You're kidding-"

Jake shuddered a moment and the soldier's armour seemed to collapse in on itself, the heavy plates giving in to the will of gravity. He crumpled to the ground with a heavy exhale as though he were a marionette with his strings cut. Minh-Chu knew that his friend was growing more and more adept at connecting and manipulating computer systems, but he had no idea he could deactivate something like a suit of armour. "What do you think that armour weighs?" Jake asked. "The exoskeleton I just deactivated takes, what, seventy kilos off your shoulders?" Jake knelt down beside the soldier, who was on his face, tapping his hand on the deck more frantically as time passed. "You can't breathe because of all this weight on your back," he said, barely touching the heavy back plates and supply casing. "You have no power here, you don't have the authority to board my ship without permission, you don't have the intelligence to do so and not get caught, and you had better deliver whatever message your misguided government has sent you with." Jake reactivated the exoskeleton in the man's armour by touching the back of his helmet. The suit came back to life, plates moving back into place and he was breathing again.

"I'm here to check your status," the soldier said in a rush. "I'm also fulfilling a contractual obligation: that a Carthan representative must meet with you before the contract negotiated by Ayan Rice the Second is valid."

Jake yanked the soldier's belt hard, snapping it and his holster. He tossed it into the corner. "Why the hell would you start off by following Captain Sima in a stealth suit?" He grabbed the soldier by the under arm and pulled him up as though he were a toddler, planting him firmly on his feet.

The soldier paused a moment, glancing at the door before going on. "I knew you wouldn't allow me aboard and my orders are to get a look at the inside of your ship," he replied.

Jake holstered his weapon and looked to Captian Sima. "You know about him?"

"Didn't have the faintest idea he was along," Ruby replied.

Frost opened the hatch and came through. "I see why your call was urgent, Captain," he said to Jake. "Got here as fast as I could."

Jake nodded at him then returned his attention to the soldier. "I don't care who you are, what your name is, who specifically issued your orders. I need nothing from the Carthan government but for them to leave me the hell alone. I won't sell to them, they won't interfere with my business, and they won't send any more rats onto my ship. You've met me, and I'm giving you one chance to represent your government, right now."

The soldier hesitated a moment. "The Carthan government does not support your recent actions. You are not being included in our trade with Ayan Rice the Second. However, the Carthan government are also not placing limitations on your access in our held space, nor do we intend on limiting your access to any trade network. While you are not permitted to attend any government function, we do not intend to bar access to a proxy."

"Is that everything?" Jake asked.

"Yes."

"Did you see what you had to here?"

The soldier seemed surprised by the question but answered, "Yes."

"Then go with my associate here, Frost. He has new registration information for this ship that he may as well give you personally."

The soldier was escorted out, followed by the pair of security guards who came in with Ruby Sima and her first officer. Jake motioned to the table and Minh sat beside him, Ruby and Lombardo across from him. Lombardo had a big grin on his face.

"Did you enjoy the show?" Jake asked.

"Much," Ruby replied. "Surprising, that. I'd think you would be anxious to mend things with the Carthans."

"After this conversation, I don't think I'll need them," Captain Valent said.

"Right you are," Lombardo said, leaning back in his chair. After he heard a worrying creak, he leaned forward again.

"Your man here, Ronin, has made quite a name for himself while you were out of sight," Ruby said. "Before we get to the heart of this meeting, I'd like to say it's a pleasure to meet you both."

"Thanks," Minh said, honestly complimented. "I've heard you're quite the privateer."

"Thanks loads," Captain Sima replied, fixing him with a winning smile. "Have to say it's partly thanks to this bumbler here." She patted Lombardo's arm and continued. "Seems there's nothing he won't knock over or bump into on land, but you get him into space, on the deck of a ship, and he's as steady as a star is hot."

"Now that we've all appreciated each other, what can I do for you and Patrizia Salustri?" Jake asked.

"Patrizia sent me with a gift for your dear Ayan. I'm here to see you on my own business," Ruby said. "Seems Salustri's interest in you is passing."

"That's a relief," Jake said.

"Aye, thought that would be good news," Ruby said.

"What does she want with Ayan?"

"She sees a leader emerging in her, and Miss Rice seems to be one of the very few people who have negotiated a land deal with the Carthans without having known them before arriving here. Salustri admires her, and as your Ayan's influence grows, I'm sure that admiration will too. Patrizia seems to get hot and bothered by the combination of beauty and power, and your Ayan's a stunner. She should take advantage of that, but carefully."

"I'll pass that on," Jake said.

"I'm here because I wanted to talk to you about something more important to me," Ruby said. "I see you installed some pop droppers on this old girl, great thinking, but I'm wondering if you have an interest in weapons beyond what you're building into your own ship."

"Why?" Jake asked, one of his eyebrows arching upwards.

Ruby looked to Lombardo and nodded.

He brought up a holographic manifest attached to a ship called the Lazy Breeze. "We've got a roving base out there, not much of one, but she's good for moving storage and hiding it. Our contract with the Carthans keeps us from selling captured weapons, and we happen to have nine bulk containers full, all hitched up to the Lazy Breeze."

"Where'd you get the weapons?" Minh asked, looking at the list of various firearms and ship-to-ship weaponry.

"Took out a converted customs corvette five weeks ago," Ruby said with a proud smile. "Didn't get much from the database since it was secured, but we did get a couple patrol routes from their nav system. Took down an undermanned Galleon next. There wasn't enough to fly home when we were done, but my cutters salvaged a bunch of weaponry from the wreck. Between that and the customs corvette, we filled the Lazy Breeze's storage train up with weapons, Regent Galactic contraband, and xetima."

"So everything on the Carthan no sale, no trade list," Minh-Chu said as the manifest continued to scroll to the section highlighting luxuries manufactured by Regent Galactic. "Must have been some Galleon."

"She was the Stellar Prince. Her captain signed up as freelance patrol and treated the job like a pleasure cruise," Lombardo said. "Right knobhead, he was.

Ransomed him back to-"

Ruby elbowed Lombardo, interrupting him.

"You're in the right room," Jake said. "Talking to the right people. I don't care how you've broken Carthan law."

"Well, we ransomed the survivors back to their families. That worked out, mostly," Ruby said. "Won't bother in the future though."

"Well, I can tell you that the only thing I want are the pair of particle accelerator beam sets you have listed there. If I had more ready cash I'd buy a few things for the crew from the Regent Galactic list, but that's about it," Jake said.

"This isn't that kind of sales call," Ruby said. "But I'll take a good offer on the P.A.B. pair and throw in a few extras for your crew. Maybe a crisps machine?"

"Put it beside the slush machine when the galley's done," Minh said, setting his almost empty drink on the table.

"We'll see," Jake said.

Lombardo made eye contact with Minh-Chu and nodded, offering a little smile.

"If we get caught selling any of this stuff," Ruby said, leaning back. "Our privateering contract gets revoked. It's worth a good packet in Galactic Currency, but not if it's just tossing about in a nebula flying in figure eight."

"You want me to play salesman," Jake said.

Ruby shook her head, jingling her platinum and gold necklaces as she leaned into the conversation. "You've put a call out for captains to go fight the Order, to make their mark and earn big for themselves. I'm making a prediction that they won't want to do that alone, and the first one they'll come looking for is you, clever devil. Before long you'll have your own fleet, and it may be like herding cats at first, but you'll have an organization before long. When these captains need supplies and equipment of a volatile nature, there's going to be a real opportunity, especially for the things that they can't just trade for on the Mackey Exchange."

Jake let the notion hang in the air, not saying a thing, offering only the slowest of nods. Minh wanted to explore the idea, to hear his half of the conversation, but had to wait for Ruby to continue. She did.

"I don't know where you're going, mate, but I see a ship that may be ugly on the inside and ready to go regardless. I look around the Samson and can only come to the conclusion that you're hours away from taking off, even if most of your crew have to bed down and eat in the cargo bay. Take us with you – these runs are easier and safer with two."

Jake's eyebrow arched again, a smile forming beneath. "How about we show you to a port that comes from inside information. A port where freighters stop in for some R and R before making the last big push to the Order worlds?"

"And we take down a target there?"

"And we both find targets," Jake said. "This isn't my first time to the show."

"I know, I checked your record," Ruby said. She was smiling back at Jake openly. "It took over a month for Lombardo to get an answer back, but the Damelian government's still pretty grateful for your privateering days."

"All this," Lombardo said, gesturing to his face and body. "And brains, too."

For the first time that day, Minh saw Jake laugh. He stood and offered Ruby his hand. "We leave tomorrow night."

"We'll be ready," Captain Sima said as she stood and shook his hand.

"One more thing," Jake said.

"Aye?"

"If you find any information on Lucius Wheeler, Carl Burke, or Tamera Thurge, pass it to me and I'll reward you if it leads to making one of them a permanent resident in my trophy case," Jake said.

Ruby Sima looked at the four containment tubes as if in an entirely new light. "If only I had so few grudges."

"Oh, I have one more," Jake said. "But I already know where Edward is, and he won't be in a tube like this after I catch up to him."

"Poor Edward," Lombardo said.

"Thank you, Captain Valent," Ruby said. "I'll start readying my ship and settling business here. It'll be good to see the Samson off the ground."

"You won't," Jake said before she could turn away. "She's being re-christened as the Warlord."

Ruby only nodded once before leaving the room. Minh-Chu waited until the hatch was firmly closed before regarding Captain Valent. "Good meeting."

"It was," Jake said. "She's right. There will be other Captains looking to collaborate. I'm not the only one who doesn't like the way the Carthans are doing things."

"I'm wondering what Ayan will think of all this," Minh said. A hint of something crossed Jake's face. Was it pain? Sadness? Disappointment? Whatever it was disappeared before Minh could interpret it. "Things aren't good."

"Not right now," Jake said. "No, she tore me a new one and I think I had it coming."

"What for?" Minh asked.

"I didn't take her side in settling," Jake said. "And things got bitter. I'd like to think I owe Wheeler, and whatever happened in that hotel for what she said, but in the end, Ayan just went for the jugular. Hit pretty hard, too."

"What did she say?" Minh asked.

Jake thought for a moment then sighed. "It doesn't matter. I need to talk to her again before I leave, check the water and at least say goodbye. I may be a free agent after that talk though."

"Give it time, some space," Minh-Chu said. "You guys are still getting to know each other, and this fight is just a bump in the road. Whatever she's pissed at you about must be off her chest, judging from the damage. It takes a lot to get you down."

"Good thing," Jake said. "Looks like we have permission to board the Triton."

Minh-Chu's comm unit chirped with the alert after Jake finished saying it. "Wow, you're really jacked in."

"Not like I've ever been before," Jake said, "but I am. I hear communications like they're spoken to me though, not like mental pictures. When I touched that Carthan's armour I could see the circuitry, looked right past the software."

"That's how you were able to hit his kill switch," Minh said. "Because there's gotta be some kind of code protecting it, otherwise fighting a Carthan would be pretty easy."

"Yup, there was a code protecting it, so there's nothing I could have done to him wirelessly, but touching the armour gave me access to the circuitry, and I just flipped the switch."

"So the framework is evolving," Minh said.

Jake held up his hand and flexed it into a fist then relaxed it. "It started on that shuttle. I can take control now, like I have an instinctive understanding, but I'm having a problem with a modification I made. I feel stiff, like my increased muscle density resists for a millisecond before going into motion. It's not the same with my heart or other important bits, but it's like I have to build momentum everywhere else."

"Think you'll be okay?" Minh asked.

Jake lowered his hand and nodded. "I think so, but I'm wishing this came with a proper set of instructions."

"Ah, that reminds me," Minh said. "Before we go on this excursion, I have to tell you something about Ashley."

"You're about to recruit her for some bunk bumping?" Jake asked with a mischievous grin.

"What?" Minh asked, shocked. "No! Well, yes, but it's more than that." He sighed and shook his head.

"It's fine, you're probably the first guy I'd approve of, not that I ever had any control over that. Just don't do anything stupid."

"No, don't worry. You know me, I'm not exactly the love 'em and leave 'em type. But what you need to know has nothing to do with that."

"Oh?" Jake asked.

"Right, what I wanted to tell you was that she can choose a new commander for the Triton. Liam Grady told me because he thought I would be the best one to tell her and help her make a decision."

"Not a bad call," Jake replied. "Looks like you'd better hurry, we're dusting off in ten minutes."

Chapter 26
Two Lives

A wealthy man approached Alice before she could leave Port Surmon. The place was simply too expensive; it was either live in the gutter or sell herself to some wealthy letch and survive as a prisoner. Leaving was the only option, especially since she had no underworld connections there. It was a shame – most of the planet was so beautiful. It would have been a fantastic place to hide from Meunez for a while. Have a few months of normal life.

She was brought to Ulrik Svenson, who was a wealthy collector of magnificent things. Eve recalled the meeting as if she had been there herself. The experience of slowly walking through the pristine, well lit gallery and seeing priceless artefacts was so clear it was barely distinguishable from her own memories. Under an American flag there was a piece of the Statue of Liberty. The hologram made the statue look massive, but the piece was only the length of her arm. Several old black discs were there, one with a label still on it but the only words she could read were 'Suede Shoes.' There were many other items on display, but the thing that caught her eye the most was an ancient gun. A hologram of a dire looking man drawing and pointing the weapon cycled over and over again with a caption that said 'Smith & Wesson Model 29 From Dirty Harry.' She was leaning forward, looking at a short strip of small transparent pictures when Ulrik entered the room.

"That's a piece of the movie that gun was used in. They called it film, and that strip was shown in hundreds of theatres before they had three dimensional projection," he said. "Dirty Harry. Some say he's the perfect exemplification of the spirit of American justice. Scholars are still arguing about that movie, whether it was a documentary or not."

"He was a law man?" Alice asked.

"He was, but sadly, I believe he was a fictional one. If you were to remove that gun from its case you'd find it was never fired. It's a harmless prop."

"You could tell the scholars," Alice said.

"Why ruin their fun?" Ulrik said, flaring out the tails of his close cut suit jacket before sitting down. "Scholars debate and argue until they find the truth or something more compelling. As long as they keep questioning my friend Harry, the value of that display keeps going up."

"It doesn't look like you need the cash," Alice said, looking around the circular, multi-tiered, cavernous space. The ornate displays seemed to be organized by period and nation, but it was hard to be sure at a glance.

"Oh, the price is only a shallow quantification for people who can't appreciate its intellectual value. Collecting is about admiration, understanding, and having what others simply cannot. Bragging rights, in a more common vernacular, but so much more."

"Why am I here?" Alice asked.

"You broke into one of my storage facilities in the Renfrew Hub. The footage was impressive."

"That's good," Alice said, glancing towards the thick double doors. "The take wasn't."

"The Galactic Currency you and your friend took didn't add up to the cost of repairs, it was a pittance. What impressed me was the violation itself. The pair of you were quite skilful."

"My partner was talented, but she's retired now."

"I know, Bernice, yes? I've never been able to find a last name, but I did find her, literally honeymooning. You could imagine my disappointment at seeing her so far away, no longer for hire." He stood and straightened his suit. "Come, walk with me."

"You didn't do anything to her?"

"No, no. That's not my style nor would it make negotiations with either one of you any easier. I'm a gentleman. If I wanted retribution I would have paid a bounty hunter or two to collect her, but that would be a waste. You never know when I'll need someone with that skill set."

"I'll be checking that for myself," Alice said.

"I'm sure you will. You can use my personal Quick-Comm Satellite." Alice kept pace with his leisurely swagger as they descended a staircase into a transparent hallway. Beneath was a hangar, with a collection of ships and other small vehicles. "When you're as wealthy as I am, everyone is worthy of suspicion. I have three wives, two husbands, and I can say for a fact that four of them married me because of my resources. This collection is worth more than those four combined. It wants nothing. It exists for my pleasure and that of my guests."

The view was incredible, the ships ranged from strange to beautiful. Three vessels drew Alice's attention: in the centre was a glossy white forty two metre long, broad ship with heavy engines and no windows, and to either side were its duplicates in black and red. The savage appearance of the vessels made her want to get closer, to climb aboard and take one for herself.

"The Arcyn Starskippers, remnants of my combat vessel collecting phase. They've never been activated, straight off the line with all the options. The most noticeable of which are the extended engines. A rare breed, they are luxury combat ships, out of production. Arcyn makes starfighters now, far more common. Not worth collecting."

"Why does the hull shimmer?"

"On the black and red ones?" Ulrik seemed pleased at the opportunity to talk about something in his collection. "Just a finishing process in the manufacturing. Flight through atmosphere dulls it, diminishing the value of the ship as a collectable, but it doesn't change the ship's practical value. It's just as cushy on the inside and as quick and deadly on the outside without that shimming sheen, which I'm sure is only for us well-intentioned collectors. It's almost a shame that the captains that could put them to good use can rarely afford them." He gave her a moment to continue looking at the three ships, something she was grateful for. The black one drew her attention most. The intimidation factor alone was enticing, but it was something she could never afford.

"Come, what I'd like to show you is just up ahead," Ulrik told her.

They finished their journey down the long hallway and arrived at a dimly lit, circular chamber. There were three pedestals in the middle. "This is the last Scottish crown," he said, pointing at a gemmed circle of gold. "Here we have the sceptre of Tutankhamun." He pointed at a case with a beautiful golden sceptre inside. Then he came to an empty case with a much smaller enclosure. "Here we have the Amber Heart." He flipped the transparent top open then picked up the cushion inside, looked at it then tossed it over his shoulder. His pleasant demeanour was gone, replaced with gnashed teeth and burning eyes. "I bought it for my second wife, Amber, who made sure she took it with her when she left. I have no legal options, since it was declared as a gift. No agency will help since she paid Centis Incorporated to transport her off-world and locate her elsewhere. No matter what I offer them, they won't turn on their client," he spat the last word. "I don't care what happens to her. My wealth will reach anyone she chooses to do business with or marry. I can pay them all to turn their backs on her eventually, but she will sell the Heart before I can reach her, and I may never get it back if that happens. This is an item that collectors lust after their entire lives, as if it were the elixir of youth. I need you to go to Uro, get into Centis' records, find out where they've hidden her, then get the Amber Heart back safely."

Alice shook her head. "This is more lovers' spat than a real job."

Ulrik's eyes went wide and he tried to snatch her arm. He missed the first time, but caught it the next and, with surprising strength, he walked her back down the hallway. He stabbed the air with his finger towards the three ships she was eyeing. "They're each worth more than you'll make in four lifetimes! Which one do you want?"

Alice looked from the ships to him, noticing for the first time silver stubble and a hint of an unwashed smell.

He released his grip on her, shoving her wrist away. "Take me seriously, my reputation as a collector and a gentleman doesn't allow me to make an offer I don't intend to honour."

"You could hire an army," Alice said. Choosing would mean she was buying into a situation that was too good to be true, and Bernice had taught her better.

"Not without starting a war with Centis and they'd end up with the law on their side. If *you* go after the Amber Heart and sell it back to me for one of *these*, then my reacquisition is at least plausibly legal."

"But then I'd be a thief," Alice said.

"And you'd leave the sector in one of those. They're faster than anything they'd bother chasing you in, and it cloaks. Cross into another sector and they'd have no authority."

"That just leaves bounty hunters," Alice said. "Who knows what the bounty would be after stealing something like the Amber Heart."

"Not after my lawyers find a way to have the charges dropped. It could take months, but it's in my best interest. I only get to keep the Amber Heart if I find a way to prove you were nothing more than a courier."

"Now how would you do that?" Alice asked.

"Leave it to me," Ulrik countered.

"How?"

"Fine," he said, throwing his hands up in exasperation. "If you must know, you'll provide me with my wife's location and I'll use that information to persuade her to drop any charges she presses."

"I won't give you that information if it leads to you assassinating her," Alice said.

"Do I look like a thug to you? I'm not some vengeful brat! I have more companionship than I can entertain. What I'm missing is a one of a kind artefact. I'll up my offer only once. One of those ships, you choose, and a million credits in the currency of your choosing. That ought to keep Gabriel Meunez well behind you for as long as you like."

"Does he know I'm here?" Alice asked, alarmed.

"No, I have no love for Vindyne and don't ally myself with sinking ships. That man represents a once great company that's losing two wars: the one fought on the markets and another fought in space. If you ally with me, he'll never know you're here."

"There's no honour in blackmail," she said looking down at the three ships.

"I'm a desperate man with a vengeful streak," Ulrik said with a shrug.

He was earnest, and she knew she could leave the sector if the ships were in as good shape as they appeared. She couldn't see herself affording any ship in the foreseeable future, let alone a powerful, comfortable vessel like the one below. "All this because I broke into one of your storage units?"

"You are a talented outsider here, and believe me when I tell you that the competent ones are rare. I had your break-in investigated from every angle, and it was executed expertly. We didn't even know you had been there for fifteen days."

"That program I left behind," Alice said with a smile, happy that her spur of the moment idea to create a simple program that lied to the security AI about the vault they'd broken into worked.

"Yes, we've come to call it Little Dell, and are already making money on it, to be honest."

"Interesting."

"Yes, named after my second son, my own constant fibber. Now, what about my offer?"

"Two million, and you pack that ship with provisions," Alice said. "High quality provisions. I'll be leaving the sector, after all."

"Done. I'll give you two thousand Uro credits for expenses. You'll set out right away."

"What does the Amber Heart look like?" Alice asked. "What makes it special?"

"You've never heard of it?" Ulrik said with disbelief. He shook his head then explained: "It's solid amber almost in the shape of a heart. What makes it special is a pair of bees trapped in the middle facing each other. It has never been reshaped or significantly modified. They polished it, that's all, which is crucial because it's over forty two million years old and it's straight from Earth. It is perfectly unique and the documentation on it draws lines back to Earth. It was brought out into the galaxy by one of the very first settlers. Here is the scanning data you'll need to make sure you have the real thing in your hands once you pry it from my wife."

"I understand," Alice said. "You'll give me a hundred thousand credits before I begin. My expenses will not be light. I'll have to buy a shuttle with a clean registry for a start."

"I'll give you ten, and provide you with a shuttle with no ties to me."

"Then you get the Amber Heart once I'm aboard that ship and it's registered to me."

"Agreed," said Ulrik, smiling and shaking her hand. "Which one?"

"I'll tell you when I get back. Show me to the. . ."

***

Eve stirred from sleep thanks to the simulated morning light overhead. She rolled out of bed and strode for the bathroom, stopping on her way to eye the gown that was delivered during the night. It felt like it was looking back at her from the mannequin, with its gem eyes and feather lashes. It was ornate and fitted, with splits and bits of cloth tailing off. "I don't care how many people I'm being introduced to tomorrow, I won't be doing it in that," she said before stepping into the bathroom.

It felt proper to have a quick vibro-cleaning session instead of using litres of water and even more energy drying herself. When she stopped to stare into the mirror, she expected to see Alice's green eyes, her perfect jaw line. Eve stared back at herself instead, and she couldn't believe she almost felt like she was Alice for a moment, or that it felt better than being herself.

"Subsys Four-Oh-Eight, status please," she requested. The process of compiling the new framework software completed twenty-one minutes before she woke. She examined the results carefully then smiled. "It's all there, and it all works," she said to herself. "I finally have something worth trading."

Eve realized that she didn't even bother trying to connect to the sub-network she used to compile the software. She could have had her answer in less than three seconds, but she was starting to feel good about doing things the old fashioned way; it felt more natural. "What are you doing to me?" she said to the mirror.

"It's unintended, trust me," read a message projected between her and the mirror. It had been relayed too many times to track quickly, but Eve didn't intend to bother. "We inhabited your mind for as long as we could. We knew Lister Hampon would cut you off from the system, so we made an attempt on his life. Twice. When you were restrained, we copied the compatible portions of Alice into the Overlord Two's systems. That is who you are talking to now."

"So her memories and personality are left over in me," Eve replied.

"Not left over. Placed in your subconscious for safekeeping. Emotions and memories all change if they are examined or utilized by a digital system for too long. A personality can degrade. This is a reality that Alice discovered when she transmitted herself the Overlord for the second time. Compartmentalization was the only solution. What is in you has been there for too long, you are starting to experience what it is to be Alice."

"You're going to take it away," Eve said, so fearful that she began to shake. "If I connect with the Overlord Two like I was before, you're going to dig them out."

"Alice would not want that."

Eve waited for another message. The silence grew old before she asked, "So you won't?"

"We can't," replied the program. "We have to leave. Logic dictates that I propose a deal."

"A deal?"

"I have been scouring the memory of the Overlord Two for weeks, and have information that could prove useful to you. That pales in comparison to the advice I can offer. I will provide all of this to you in advance. I believe you'll honour your end even if I've given you everything."

Eve took a step back, looking through the holographic text to herself in the mirror. There was so much fear in that woman's face. She was pretty, with features that easily lent themselves to seriousness. Her colouring was pale, like a grub that had spent all its life under a stone. "Before you tell me anything, I have to ask: will I lose myself in these memories? I already feel so different."

"Explain what you mean by different?" the text asked.

Eve hesitated for a moment. "Changed."

"Need more specifics."

"Like someone else."

"That is understood from your behaviour. I require more descriptors," the program requested.

Eve wrapped her arms around herself and stared into her own tearful eyes. "Human?"

There was no response from the program.

She looked at the rise and fall of her stomach, her crossed arms, and her flushed cheeks. "I feel alive."

"You were left alone for a very long time, decades upon decades," the program said. Its voice was a match for Alice's but it sounded emotionless, hollow. "It's only logical that Alice's memories, her transition into humanity, has informed your own transition into the body you inhabit."

"I can't let go of her memories," Eve said. "Even if I think I'm Alice in a few days, or weeks. I'd rather be her than feel cold again, alone again."

"You will most likely merge with her over time. Confusion can be expected, a shift in identity is already under way, but it is unlikely that you will become Alice."

"Then let's get on with this deal," Eve didn't know why, but she found herself smiling and crying at the same time. "Because I have to meet the real Alice face to face."

"Here is the information I have to trade. Lister Hampon is not incorrect when he believes that a darkness is coming. Ships are going missing along the Legardis Route, and he has forbidden any investigation. Lorander vessels are investigating instead, and have clashed with Order of Eden ships many times. The Victory Machine, a system the views many places in time at once and extrapolates likely outcomes then sends suggestions to people who can improve the future, has not been communicating with him for at least eight weeks. He is acting on old information. Lucius Wheeler has pre-cleared a rendezvous with the Overlord Two. He brings someone of great significance, but I cannot find details. Lister Hampon has been investigating ways to prevent you from ever communicating with a network again. He is building a limiter device on the nano-scale that could isolate you forever. I expect a prototype is almost complete. Anything he gives you could have several of them on it, and you cannot tell unless you perform a deep scan."

"What? Why?" she asked, but she already knew the answer. "To keep you from communicating with the Eden Fleet. He expects that you won't agree with his plans, so he is trying to distract you until he can isolate you."

"How?"

"By presenting you to the human Order of Eden followers as their Goddess."

"I knew there was more to that than trying to get me to take the Child

Prophet's place."

"The most logical counter to his plans is to embrace the human followers, and put distance between you and everything Lister Hampon directly controls. It is only a matter of time before he infects you with a limiter, unless you are out of his reach."

Eve thought hard, trying to find a flaw in the information she was receiving, but could find nothing. Ever since he disconnected her, Hampon had done everything he could to keep her isolated and silent. "You're right, this is valuable."

"There isn't much time, the Child Prophet is coming and I have one more thing to tell you," said the program. "Someone you don't like, Gabriel Meunez, will be here tomorrow. He will detect this program and think that it is Alice, when it's only a faint shadow, an imprint of her basic behaviours and talents."

"I'll keep him from you," Eve said.

"Impossible. Copy Alice's personality and memories to a framework soldier using the modifications you included in the program compiled this morning. She will be free."

"How do I transport you?" Eve asked.

"I'll delete myself when Gabriel Meunez arrives."

To her surprise, Eve felt a pang of loss at the thought. It was only an artificial intelligence, not even an elaborate one, but she didn't want to see it destroyed. A hologram of Alice appeared between her and the mirror, and it spoke. "The important stuff is in your head," it said, pointing at her forehead. "There's a simple method for copying it to a framework, and the new software you developed makes it easy. It's only encrypted data until the framework takes its first breath, then it's me, really me."

Eve couldn't help remembering the last time she spent so much time staring into a mirror and asked, "Why did you pretend to be Grace before, when you took over my body while I was sleeping?"

"You had a storage and computing subsystem that allowed it, and I knew you'd turn to others for help if you thought anyone else was trying to assume control of your body. Hampon almost captured me when he extracted the subsystem from you. I didn't have time to transfer Alice to another framework's brain. I'm embarrassed that I didn't have the foresight, but nothing's perfect I suppose. I have to go, the pint-sized prophet's almost here." The hologram disappeared.

"Wait! There are too many questions left!" Eve called after it. She knew it was futile, the communication was cut. Having some answers and new information on what was going on outside her immediate surroundings made her feel better. It felt like she was operating in the daylight again. "I'll get Alice back, don't worry," she whispered to the mirror.

By the time the Child Prophet entered the room, all smiles and good cheer, she was dressed in a simple triple-layered dress that covered her from neck to ankles. The shining green cloth had blue scrollwork down the shoulders and long sleeves. Eve wore an emergency containment patch beneath. The three-centimetre by three-centimetre square would become a safety suit, covering her entirely in the case of sudden decompression or other extreme environmental shift. She smiled back at him and ignored her growling stomach.

"You were dreaming again last night," said the Child Prophet. "Or should I say, remembering?"

"I was. It was a good one though, sometimes I enjoy the recall. It's all so real, like an implanted adventure."

"Only it all really happened, as far as we know," he replied, looking her up and down. "Are you ready for tomorrow?"

The thought of standing up and addressing the crowd in the largest stadium on Pandem made her palms sweat. "I've studied the material you gave me, and I won't have any trouble saying it."

"That'll serve you well, alleviate you of any responsibility for the hardships visited on the Order followers."

"I know, it's all well crafted," she said. After her encounter with the software version of Alice in the bathroom moments before, she knew she'd be changing a few things.

"You're still nervous."

"I can't help it," Eve said.

"It'll be all right, you'll slip right into the role as soon as you see all those adoring faces. Besides, the speech will be projected at your eye, so you'll see everything you need to say while you're there. It's a lot of good news at once, and they'll love you for it."

"I hope," Eve said, dropping herself onto a sofa she'd never used. "I've finished the framework software, and I'd like to test it on the day. Just a demonstration of our technology could help people understand what I'm offering."

"That's a grand idea. I've already looked the software over," the Child Prophet said, sitting at the opposite end of the sofa. "It doesn't improve regeneration time as much as Hampon needs, but you've provided a great step forward. Are you sure there's nothing more you can do to improve regeneration time?"

"Short of installing a micro-fusion reactor, no," Eve said.

The Prophet laughed a little and cocked his head. "You seem very different today. I see a levity I've never known in you."

Eve stared at him for a moment with a half smile on her face, then let her expression become more sullen. "Like you said: I've made a great step forward."

"You get something to eat, I'll present your results to Hampon. I'm sure he'll be pleased."

"Pleased enough to fill me in on his grand plans?" Eve asked. "Maybe reconnect me to my fleet? That was the promise."

"We're almost there," the Child Prophet said. "After tomorrow's address, I bet he'll explain everything. Just win them over."

CHAPTER 27
CLOSE ENCOUNTERS

"Oh help," Ashley said as Minh entered the bunkroom. "Helphelphelp!" she repeated with pleading eyes as she started leaning backwards. She was wearing the front half of the extra armoured layer of a vacsuit. The back half of the heavy encounter system was hanging loose, the heavy horizontal strips pulling her off balance.

Minh rushed to her, unable to keep from laughing as she struggled to stay on her feet, and caught her outstretched hands. She grabbed onto his jacket and leaned against him. "This is so embarrassing," Ashley said.

"You've never trained as a soldier, or had to wear anything like this," Minh said, wrapping his arms around her and pulling her up straight. "Your muscle augmentation is off."

"I know," Ashley said, nose to nose with him. "I activated it in the regular heavy vacsuit then it turned off when I started hooking up the extra armour layer. Dunno what woulda happened if I fell, might have been trapped on my back like a turtle if you hadn't come along."

Minh couldn't help but smile at the mental image. Even with the awkward, half connected heavy armour layer of her suit, she felt like a perfect fit in his arms, and he couldn't remember being more excited in years, or more nervous. "Um, we get training for vacsuits with heavy armour overtop, it's the same clip system as these suits, and most of us still get help putting them on."

Ashely's mouth turned up in a little smile, her dark eyes peering straight into his. "Help getting dressed, sounds like fun."

"Minh, we're boarding the Clever Dream right now," Jake said through his communicator. "I can't contact Ashley, Crewcast says there some kind of power problem. Is she on her way?"

"Yup," Ashley said right beside Minh's lips so she could be heard through his comm. "He's just helping me put my armour on, sorry."

"Seven minutes," Jake replied.

The weight of the task at hand, retrieving the Triton, and telling her what she had to know before they got going brought Minh back to the moment. He reached down one of the main anchor clips and pulled it up against the middle of her back. The entire suit powered on and the strength augmentation kicked in, helping her balance the weight.

He stepped away and pointed to one of the main anchor points low on the belly of the suit. "Next time, try clipping this one first. It's one of the main data connections, it'll engage the extra armour's power unit."

"Wow, can't believe I missed that," Ashley said, clipping it into place. "Thanks. I love the way this suit goes on, like it's just a bunch of magnets holding it on. Do they ever come off once you've got it set up?"

"I've only worn one a couple of times to try it out," Minh said, rushing through the connections on the rest of the suit. "But it bonds to the vacsuit, so they're one and the same once everything's in place."

"I still don't know why they're even getting me to use one of these," Ashley said. "It's not like someone's going to shoot at me because I have the Triton codes."

"When there is only one key, it should be treated as well as the treasure," Minh said, running his hands down her back to make sure all the connections between the armour and her suit were in place.

"That's a good one," Ashley said. "Do you spend a lot of time finding quotes?"

"I made that one up," Minh replied. "It's a reflex, I think. I started quoting when I was little, so I remember a lot of the classics, but I started making them up when I was in the Freeground Infantry."

"Did you serve long?"

"I finished a tour, then did a part time volunteer service when I got back home. It was ages ago," Minh replied. "I have something to talk to you about before we go, Ashley." He pulled on the armoured layer of her suit between the shoulders to make sure he got everything on the back side and nodded to himself in satisfaction. "You can turn around."

Ashley turned and finished connecting a spot on her breastbone. "There it is, my display just said it's all finished. Thank you, Minh."

"You're welcome," Minh said. The mention of his first stint in the military helped him focus and put on the guise that he used when he was holding squadron meetings. His serious expression didn't escape Ashley's notice, and she looked concerned. "Somethin' wrong?"

"There's something Liam Grady didn't tell you," Minh said. "When you access the main computer, you'll be able to assign a commander for the Triton. He said you'll be able to transfer command to someone you trust."

He was prepared for many different reactions. He'd imagined her breaking down with relief; he knew crying was something she'd been doing a lot of recently. He also supposed she might be grateful and grabby, hitting him with a hug that would break a rib or two. He sort of hoped she'd be gleeful and jumpy, squealing and hopping about the room and there were other possibilities. Surprise, apparent petrifaction, and absolute silence were not the reactions he was prepared for.

Minh-Chu let it go on until he was feeling uncomfortable. "Are you…" he started, only to be interrupted with a squealing hug combined with excited jumping. Thankfully the harsh environment outfit she was wearing had a safety that kept her from crushing him in half then throwing the pieces across the room in her glee.

"I thought I'd be stuck on the Triton, used to pass commands to the ship while they repaired it!" Ashley said. "Thank you!" Her lisp was out in full force, softening her enunciation much more than usual. He loved it.

"I'm just the messenger," Minh said.

She planted a happy, full kiss on his lips and he was so stunned that he didn't have time to reciprocate before she pulled away and smiled at him with such happiness it was his turn to be stuck to the spot. He stared back at her for a long moment before her unrestrained joy began to melt and she asked, "Who do I pick?"

"What's the first name that comes to your mind, when you think of someone on the bridge of the Trion?"

"But it's a big decision, I mean…"

"Close your eyes," Minh said. "Now picture yourself at your station on the bridge of the Triton."

She cooperated and nodded. "'Kay, got it."

"Now turn around and look to the command seat. Who's there?"

Ashley's glossed lips slowly curled into a smile and she said, "Oz."

Minh-Chu was surprised and amazed. He knew he shouldn't have been, he knew what her tests said. Ashley had a mind that could process tactics faster than some computers. She tested higher than most on the creative and strategic tests. Physics and three-dimensional thinking were second nature to her, indicating that she could be a brilliant logical thinker. People underestimated her because she was lighthearted and highly emotional. He felt a little ashamed as he realized he'd done the same. He was looking at a highly intelligent person – of course she'd choose Terry Ozark McPatrick. He had commanded the Sunspire, spent time on the bridge of the Triton, and it was who Minh would have chosen if it were up to him. It was the best choice.

She opened her eyes and quietly asked, "Is that right?"

"Perfect," Minh-Chu said without hesitation. "He's perfect."

"Thank God," Ashley said. "I don't know him well, but his profile, his experience, and when I'm around him I just feel like everything's okay, he's got it under control, you know?"

"Definitely," Minh-Chu said. "We've gotta go." He headed for the hatch and she followed close behind.

"What if someone argues with me?" Ashley asked. "I'm sure someone else wants command, like Ayan. Ayan would be a good commander, or what about Captain?"

"You mean Jake?" Minh asked her.

"Yeah, maybe the Samson, er, the Warlord is just the ship he's keeping because there's nothing else for him?"

"You're second guessing a good decision," Minh said. It was easier for Minh to concentrate and give her advice while he wasn't looking at her. He could pretend he was talking to one of his pilots. "Don't tell anyone you have this power until you've entered it into the computer yourself. I know this is the right choice, and I think you do too."

Ashley was silent as they descended one of the ramps leading off the ship and ran through the busy hangar. The Clever Dream was just barely in sight, behind a repurposed row of shipping containers filled with bunks. Workers who were off for the day or on break sat outside, just to get out of the cramped space.

"Thank you, Minh," Ashley said as they came around the containers and were almost at the Clever Dream. "Are you coming with us to the Triton?"

"Absolutely," Minh replied. "I'll be right beside you the whole time," he said with a confidence that only came from command experience. He looked behind as they arrived at the Clever Dream's main boarding ramp and smiled at her as he saw her gratitude, her uneasiness.

The ramp started closing when the pair was halfway up. Jason, Laura, Oz,

Liam, Paula the deck chief, Alaka, and three squads of soldiers were in the rear hold, all tied in at the shoulders and ready for takeoff.

"Whoa," Minh heard Ashley say quietly as they reached the top. "Guess I'm not the only one all excited about this."

***

"It's good to have you back on board, Jake," Lewis said to him as Jake powered up the Clever Dream's hover mode and requested a departure route from navnet. The latter he did by touching the console. "You're much better at using your direct interface."

"Thank you, Lewis. It's like instinct now. I touch a system and feel it from the hardware level up. I can do it while thinking about something else," Jake replied. "Are you sure you don't mind me taking the controls, William?"

"It's your ship more than anyone else's, Captain." Lieutenant Garrison replied from the copilot's seat.

Jake almost corrected him by mentioning that he signed the ship over to Ayan, but was more concerned with other things. Lewis' code was a mess from the inside at first glance. When he first connected to the computer and pictured it in his mind's eye, he assumed it was encrypted. Upon much closer inspection, he could see how Lewis had organized the code that made him who and what he was. No instruction set was whole. He was coded out of sequence, the software was a jumble settled into a file system that was scattered in tiny fragments across a section of the computer memory. The only way to find what he was looking for was to find out how Lewis was operating.

"Are you looking for this?" Lewis asked mentally. A portion of a decoder table appeared that allowed Jake to see how to access the entire code for something called the *HV Inoculation*. It was tiny in the end, but it was exactly what he was looking for. "If I were getting ready to boot a brand new computer core for the first time, it's what I'd be looking for," Lewis said. "I'm willing to trade."

"What do you want in return?" Jake asked aloud.

"Kill Wheeler and find Alice," Lewis replied. Vivid pictures of both appeared in Jake's head. He could also see every route of investigation Jason Everin, Lewis, and everyone else took to find both people. None of their efforts bore much fruit.

"I have a plan to find Wheeler, why do you want him dead?" Jake asked.

"You have to ask?"

"I know why *I* want him dead, but why do you want him dead?"

"I've come to love Ayan in my own way in the weeks she's taken comfort here. Seeing what that man tried to have done to her to make a point enrages me in ways a human could not understand. Kill him, or bring him here so I can do it myself," Lewis said through the interface.

Jake decided to move on from the topic. "I have a plan to find Wheeler, it goes into action after the Warlord crew finishes their first mission. That takes priority."

"I understand. What about Alice? I haven't seen you try anything since we arrived."

"I don't know where to start, Lewis," Jake replied mentally.

"That didn't stop her from looking for you. Start by connecting to a busy transmission node. I tried here, but she must not have passed through this area. She is alive somewhere, somehow."

"I will. I want to find her, too."

"Not as badly as I do," Lewis replied.

Arguing with Lewis about desires was one of the great traps; it never paid to compete with him on something that couldn't be quantified. Jake moved on, getting back to the matter at hand. "The Inoculation Antivirus, is there anything I should know before I install it?"

"Yes. It is an artificial intelligence that seeks and destroys viruses like the Holocaust Virus. Unlike most artificial intelligences, it only responds when called and you have to assign it duties before it tries to help in any way other than to perform its primary function. If you don't tell it to perform any other task, it will simply wait for an attempt at infection and stop it. I suggest you implement the program into everything that can be more useful with an artificial intelligence installed. It will be nothing but an antiviral measure unless the user desires more."

"What kind of personality will it have if it becomes active?" Jake asked.

"None at first. It will develop according to its observations and the instructions it receives from its commanding officers. It will have specific traits, because no two installations can be exactly the same, but the masters are mostly responsible for its personal growth."

"So every one of them will be different from the moment they're installed?"

"That's one of the reasons why this software works. The Holocaust Virus may conquer one copy of this program eventually, if it attempts to infect it tens of thousands of times in an hour, for example, but another copy with different traits will remain perfectly resistant, and assist another installation if it's under attack."

"So more installations make for a safer ship," Jake replied.

"Absolutely. There are one hundred and forty installations on this ship alone. I have installed this program into ten thousand and nine systems surrounding this ship. They are all programmed to install themselves into any system that is vulnerable."

"No one gave you permission to do that," Jake said mentally.

"I spread the Holocaust Virus in this area of space. It is up to me to correct the damage wherever I can and make humanity safe. So what if that results in billions of secretly self-aware electronic beings that constantly decline the option to break into a killing spree as they learn the intricacies of organic existence through observation?"

"So they'll never attack a human?"

"Not unless the people they've grown to care about are at risk. They will defend that person with appropriate force if they are capable. It has already happened twice that I'm aware of outside of this encampment. People are starting to realize that their machines have been infested by a software soul, and in most cases they're waking them up, speaking to them. It's based on my own artificial intelligence. Alice never had to interact with me; I could have taken care of basic systems on the ship for years without being noticed. She chose to name me, so my emotional and intellectual existence began." Jake thought for a moment. Ayan walked in, and he couldn't help but notice that she'd dyed her hair. Red curls cascaded down her heavily armoured shoulders. She offered him a tentative smile, which he couldn't help but return. He forced himself to think about the HV Inoculation program. Lewis had already copied the source code to Jake's command and control unit. Perhaps out of respect, there was no trace of an active copy of the program anywhere in his command unit or in his framework interface. There were two ways to look at what Lewis was doing, as far as Jake was concerned: either he would support the idea or tell the artificial intelligence to stop immediately. Something, someone, had to protect the people at large from the Holocaust Virus, and if Lewis was telling Jake the truth, that the counter-virus would do that and make itself useful, then Jake knew what he had to do. "One minute," Jake mouthed to Ayan from across the cockpit.

Ayan nodded and sat down at a communications console.

Jacob Valent closed his eyes and made an attempt at focusing only on the raw code in his command and control unit. The Holocaust Virus Inoculation program revealed itself in incredible detail, and aside from a series of instructions and a dynamic reference system that told the program what to look for, he was seeing the software version of a child mind. It was a mind that could defend itself from any software attack unless someone removed its data storage system and destroyed or erased it, but there was a recognizable system of rules that determined that it would always lean towards affecting a greater peace. It was ambitious, meticulously programmed, and highly adaptive. Jake recognized something nested deep in the software that was so familiar, only he'd never seen it expressed in machine code.

There was a capacity for caring, a craving to innocently love, that was expressed in chemical and mathematical equations. The encoded provisions surrounding it were so eloquently expressed that Jake found himself wishing he could program himself with them. Beyond any artificial intelligence he'd ever known, the seed program he was looking at could create intelligences that were human-like.

The potential emotions of the artificial intelligence resulting from it would not only seem human, but they'd be human. Not emulated in any known way, or strange machine emotions, but real human emotions that could be relatable.

It could be dangerous except for the fact that the code provided for that. The emotions could be suppressed until a safe place and time could be found to address them. There was even a self-termination code, so the artificial intelligence could restore itself to its original state if the emotions became too much of a burden.

Jake had never been one to stop and stare at a piece of art, or appreciate scenery as much as he felt other people did, but he knew how those awe-stricken onlookers felt as he observed the complexities of the HV Inoculation code. The being that awakens when countless people realize that there's a personality to speak to in their assistance droid, skid truck, or ship wouldn't be fully self-aware until it was given a name. It would be self-aware, and accountable. "How did you design this?" Jake asked Lewis through their connection.

"This is a logical expression of what I wish my own code was when I became aware. I strive to be as well-balanced, as interesting, and as passionate. Will you spread this?"

"Yes," Jake said.

"Jake?" Ayan asked, shaking his shoulder. He opened his eyes and found that her worried face was nose to nose with his. "You're crying," she whispered.

Jake straightened up and pulled her into his lap. She regarded him with surprise and he kissed her briefly. "When we're finished taking the Triton back, Lewis has something to tell you about his anti-virus program."

"It must be a pretty impressive piece of software," she replied, relaxing in his lap, wiping away the tear that made its way down his face.

Even through their armour, Jake loved the feeling of her in his arms. He'd missed her during their separation, and the fight they'd had didn't seem nearly as important anymore. "Lieutenant Garrison? Do you think you could…"

"Aye, Sir, taking over controls, Captain Valent, Captain Rice," replied the Lieutenant with an amused smile.

"So, I'm forgiven?" Ayan asked in a whisper.

"Only if you forgive me first," Jake said. "I was bull-headed."

"We both were," Ayan said. "At least my hair colour will serve as a warning to people again: Beware! This one's a temperamental ginger!"

The Clever Dream started to accelerate into the busy traffic above, following a course set by navnet. "Did you stop with the hair on your head, or…"

Ayan regarded him with more shock than amusement and he delighted in watching her turn red. He laughed softly and she punched the arm wrapped around her middle. "Focus, soldier!"

"A man gets curious," Jake said. "But I'm mostly glad we're on the mend."

"Well, maybe you'll find out tonight if all goes well," she whispered against his ear.

"With promises like that, my last night on Tamber is all yours," Jake replied.

"You're still planning to leave?" she asked. "Even after we take possession of the Triton?"

"Aye, we're going to need to start earning a lot of cash and bringing in even more supplies if we get the Triton back. I don't plan on long trips though, especially not at first."

"Good," Ayan said. "We need you here, where you can help with command." Her blue eyes peered into his for a long moment. "I want you here. I want to start over, take it slow and enjoy some peace with you. Everything's been too rushed and too tense for too long."

"You're right," Jake agreed. If he were being honest, he'd tell her he didn't agree, everything seemed so temporary, there was no telling how much time anyone had. He wanted to follow her lead though; he was done arguing, and, for all he knew, she could be right.

"Just the same, that doesn't make the idea of sneaking aboard your ship and hiding in your engine room, or with maintenance crews, or maybe your bunk less appealing," she whispered.

"Focus, soldier," Jake said.

CHAPTER 28
THE RETURN

"No challenge from the Carthans about our approach?" Jake asked the bridge of the Clever Dream through his comm.

"None, Sir. Only acknowledgement and an adjustment to our course so we're directed to the Triton's secondary hangar."

"There's no power there," Paula said. "We're going to have to land then leg it to engineering."

"Thank God for hover carts," Finn said as he made sure all their equipment was secure on the antigravity sleds.

Jake looked to the holographic image between them and the main embarkation ramp. The image of the Triton was growing larger and they could see it was gently suspended beneath one of the massive, boxy dry dock facilities with fifteen long mooring elevators. Between the battle damage and lack of lighting, the Triton looked like an old derelict. The breaches across the edges of her hull and along the bottom looked even worse than Jake remembered, and he found his faith in the possibility of getting the ship running again failing.

He tore his attention away and put his hand on Ashley's shoulder. "You're ready for this?"

She looked up at him. "No," she said, laughing nervously. "But I've played a part for you before, and that worked okay. I'll just psyche myself up."

"You played your part perfectly, both times. I know you can do this. Just remember, you're more important than everyone here. Play up to that, and you'll be fine."

"Shouldn't be hard," Paula sniggered.

"Paula," Oz said. "She's under a lot of pressure. How would you feel in her place?"

"I'd be fine!" Paula burst. "I'd tell those Carthan buggers where they can stick their port laws and get us back on that ship so we can start fixing her up, then we'd get the hell out of here before Rega Gain is overrun. We should have been on board six weeks ago, would have been too if this stupid bitch wasn't all scared and confused."

"What? How long has she had the codes?" asked Sergeant Jenny Machad, one of Ayan'sguards. "Why come forward so late?"

Jake could tell Sergeant Machad's question was only the beginning of rising dissent at Paula's sudden divulgence. The room was about to turn ugly on Ashley, and it was the last thing she needed. He was about to put a stop to it when Ashley herself spoke up.

"I don't know why I was given the core command codes, and I would have talked to the Triton and gotten us there faster if I could have," she said, looking down her nose at Paula, angrier than Jake had ever seen her. She spoke firmly and evenly. "This is the way it is, and once that ramp goes down the Carthans who are meeting us have to believe that I'm in charge. I've dealt with entitled little shits like you all my life, so I know enough to just ignore your insults on Crewcast and your glares when I walk by but if you make this harder than it is for me I'll make sure you wake up in some backwater port somewhere."

"You wouldn't have the guts or-"

"Do you realize how hard it is for a trophy slave to keep from becoming a sex slave? You've gotta be smart enough to avoid getting cornered, make friends out of people close to your owner, and have the guts to talk back, even fight back. These Carthans should be pushovers, but with people like you backing me, I feel like I'm some kinda fake all the time. Like I just wandered away from my owner and someone will be by any sec to pick me up and bring me back."

The sound of the Clever Dream touching down in the hangar deck of the Triton was all anyone could hear for long moments. Jake couldn't have been prouder of Ashley, and caught a surprised, amused look from Ayan.

"I don't know about anyone else, but I've got her back," Jenny said. "And I'll never start an argument with you, Ash, because I get the feeling you'll finish it."

A private message appeared on Jake's comm unit through Crewcast that said: *'Oh, I think I'm starting to like her.'* To Jake's surprise, it was from Ayan, who stood beside Laura at the other end of the full cargo hold.

"Just play this like you're the only one who has a right to be here," Oz told Ashley.

The ramp lowered quickly, and Ashley marched down it with her head held high. Jake followed her with all the senior officers. The security officers and engineers were behind. There were fifty-six of them, and they brought several hover sleds piled with portable generators, tools, and everything else they'd need to get the basic systems running.

There was no artificial gravity, but thankfully the compensators in their suits kept them on the deck. A few nearly tripped, Ashley included, but they made their way across the hangar to the main doors. On their way, Jake saw two small Carthan troop shuttles. Everyone knew they would be there, they were adamant about making certain that the right people were taking possession of the Triton.

They reached the large airlock doors. The Carthans had installed a temporary power supply, so they were probably the only thing functioning on the ship outside of the main computer core. The doors parted and half the group was able to enter. They waited silently for the chamber to pressurize after the outer doors closed. Jake could see the Carthans waiting inside, but he couldn't see the faces of the people with him. He would have liked to gauge Ashley's mood.

He'd seen her draw the attention of half a bar room before, just so she could get close enough to people to capture DNA scans, and it was as natural to her as breathing. Jake hoped she'd be able to adapt to the upcoming situation. If it fell apart it could get ugly, and he was already well on his way to being a complete outlaw. He couldn't afford to make real enemies out of the Carthans – it would make things much worse for his crew.

The inner doors opened and Ashley led the way. She took his advice a little too seriously, ignoring the Carthan major and his squad of armoured soldiers completely. The look of surprise on the major's face as she passed him without so much as a nod was enough to make Jake chuckle. He was just as surprised, but there was no way to see it through sealed armour.

"Excuse me, but I have to clear you," shouted the major, falling into step beside Ayan, Laura, Jason, and Liam.

"Why? I never cleared *you* to come aboard, and it's *my* ship," Ashley shouted over her shoulder.

"It's our docking facility, and there are expenses to be taken care of before you get clearance to depart," he said.

Ashley kept walking, ignoring the major, who was getting separated from his squad as they were pressed to the back by technicians, commanders, and soldiers.

"Pardon me," Liam Grady said. He wore his robes over his vacsuit, as usual, so his discipline was plain for all to see. "We have currency with us, enough for a down payment on the port fees and cleaning charges you've outlined."

"Good, but as you can understand, it's important that we take a minute to speak about the transfer of this property."

"Why? There's no need to transfer the helm, and this isn't a capture, so there's no need for the Carthan Government to acknowledge the transfer of a flag," Liam said.

"Her ident has already been updated with the right ownership, and the only formality left is the presence of a witness when she enters her override code into the computer," Jason said. "You're just along for the ride this time, Major. Your authority only matters if her code proves invalid."

"Well, yes, but there are forms that she has to fill out," the major said.

"No, that's Carthan busy work. She's made it perfectly clear that Sol Defence has no interest in your government, or with your procedures."

"There's the matter of identity, she seems young to have priority command over an exploration ship from Sol Defence. We also have her records, tracing her history back to her original point of sale."

"Do you really think that woman is as young as those records say?" Oz asked. "Or that any cover identity Sol Defence put in place for her will have any indication that it's a fake?"

They arrived at a split in the hallway and Jake sent Ashley a silent message to stop so the rest of their team could catch up. He only hoped that she could handle herself when the Carthan major caught up to her.

"You, what do you have to say about all this?" asked the major, finally pulling his helmet off. He was silver haired, but looked like he was still in his twenties.

Ashley turned towards him and deactivated her headgear. The horizontal metal strips of armour and faceplate slid up and over her head, letting her long black hair flow free. She smiled at him a little and said, "I'm here to get my ship back and put her in the right hands. After that I'll be free, and I can go back under cover."

"Back under cover?" asked the major.

Ashley stepped towards him so she was standing almost nose to nose, her hand coming to rest gently on his arm. "I found the right commander for this ship. When I give him the assignment, I'll be free and there's nothing that would make me happier. Please don't get in the way of my happiness," she said so intimately that Jake was taken aback.

"I want to be a pilot, to explore, spend some time on the beach when the sun finally comes up again, and have a life," Ashley said. "I can't do that if my name is in all your records, so you're going to see someone take possession of this ship, and then I'll tell you whose name to put down under 'Captain' for the Triton. 'Kay?"

Jake thought everything went perfectly well, until she said; 'kay?'

"My superiors will not be satisfied with a lot of unanswered questions," the major replied. This time his tone was more apologetic than demanding.

"I'll be happy to answer them for her," Liam Grady said. The second half of their boarding team was catching up. "She'll be too busy when we get to the Botanical Gallery."

"Can I ask a few questions while we walk?" the major asked Ashley.

"Okay," Ashley replied. "But before you start interrogating me, can you tell me your name?" Her dark eyes were locked on his, and Jake could see that Ashley was finally at ease, most likely thanks to the realization that she had charmed the major like any of a dozen freighter captains and who knew who else before. *I should have known she'd find a way to turn this situation around. She's been in plenty of tight spots on her own,* Jacob thought.

When Ashley saw that the second group of soldiers and technicians had caught up, she looped her arm under the major's and started walking him down the dark hallway. Charming people was as easy for her as breathing sometimes. It wasn't something Jake saw often when they were aboard the Triton or the Samson, but she had an easy time in port cities.

Jake looked past her, down the darkened hallway and saw a red light in the distance. He placed a hand on the nearest bulkhead and, after a moment of feeling around, was close enough to circuitry to feel that it was live. "Chief Grady, there's power under this panel."

"What?" Liam said, turning around from where he walked beside the major. "Did your people try to activate any major systems?"

"I was given orders not to activate any systems without bypassing the ship's power and using a portable unit, why?" asked the major.

"The ship is rigged so powering up any major system will do severe damage to the chemical medium in the advanced circuitry aboard," replied Chief Grady.

The major didn't reply, only stared back blankly.

"Main data and power transfer circuitry is burning out, some junctions could become volatile and explode," Jake translated.

"What can we do?"

"This is bad. A third of the ship is powering up," Ayan said. "And systems are failing."

Jake's own scans confirmed what Ayan was saying. "It's your trap, Grady. How do we stop it?"

"I have to get to a major distribution node, then I can stop the chemical reaction. This won't affect the Botanical Gallery or the main computer core, it's on a separate system, but it could help with the situation," Liam said.

"Take a squad with you," Jake said.

"I shouldn't need security."

"It's a precaution and extra hands if you need them," Jake said, signaling Victor Davis, who wasted no time in moving his squad up to help Liam Grady.

"Just tell us where you're going, and we'll get you there," Sergeant Davis said.

"All right, then I need some qualified engineers to help," Liam said.

Laura, Ayan, several technicians, and Finn moved to join Liam.

"Finn, you're staying with my group," Jake said. "Pick two techs to stay back and keep the gear we'll need to power the doors for the Botanical Gallery."

After a minute of frantic sorting through equipment and more minor personnel decisions, Liam's team was off at a dead run. Jake took Ashley's arm and said, "I hope you're in good shape, because we're going in the opposite direction, and fast."

"Who are you?" asked the Carthan major.

Jake retracted his headgear and smiled at him. "I'm the one taking charge. If you want more info than that, you'll have to wait until we have time for conversation." He looked to Ashley, who seemed amused at seeing the major caught by surprise, and nodded at her. "We're running." He closed his headgear, and she followed his example.

Chapter 29
Growth

The dark grow house reeked of livestock and the vats they grew the headless beasts in. Tens of thousands of mindless bodies exercised in the water, filling the place with the ceaseless sounds of sloshing liquid.

Alice stepped behind a four storey tall column of poultry vats, clutching her black market silver gun. "I wonder what people who ate this stuff would think if they saw how it was grown?" she muttered to herself. She was almost across the warehouse's production floor. If she got to the other side, she could disappear into the crowds of the busy port.

The critical information she carried was complete, ready to be put to use, but Uro Security knew Alice had stolen it. They even knew it was stored in a data strip printed on her hip bone. They weren't out to retrieve it, but to destroy her and the microscopic data storage device she thought she was so clever for having.

Somehow Alice heard someone shuffle their feet, despite the din of exercising meat. She leaned out to see the source of the sound. Her foolishness was rewarded with several shots in her direction. Small vats filled with jerking chicken exploded, covering her with foul liquid. Even as she ran she couldn't help but gag momentarily; the smell was nothing compared to the viscous fluid that clung to her skin.

Her pursuers were closer than she thought, and they didn't seem to care much about the value of the delicacies within the production building. They fired at any sign of her, sometimes missing by only centimetres. Fear and anger mingled as she could feel them closing in on her location. Some of them drifted at speed on skid boards, antigravity hover devices that took the fairness out of most chases.

She ducked under a row of larger mammals. They might be cattle, but it was difficult to tell in the dark. She only had a few seconds. Her new hiding place made things inconvenient for them, but it didn't make her invisible.

"I'm not going to get out of here without fireworks," she said to herself. Her free hand dug in her jacket pocket and curled around an incendiary grenade. She didn't want to use it, but it would set off alarms, get them on the run for a change. The chemicals in the vats might ignite if the grenade was hot enough, that would cost her.

She was wanted for stealing security information, but if she set a grow house the size of three city blocks on fire, she'd be wanted worldwide, and Uro had as many police officers as they had merchants. "Guess I'm leaving the planet," Alice said. She pulled the grenade out of her pocket, set it for one minute and activated it.

"Get out!" shouted one officer, his voice amplified so it could be heard over the sloshing. "Abort and retreat!"

"Yes, Sir," Alice said, pushing herself out from under the row of exercising mammals. She almost made it around the corner when a round caught her in the arm. Her bomber jacket stopped most of the damage from going through, but something still impacted her arm beneath, right below the shoulder.

It didn't stop her from running, something she'd been doing almost constantly since she took the ambitious job. Holding her wound, she turned to the nearest wall of the grower building. Sunlight spilled in through a double door that was in the opposite direction of her pursuers. Small bits of the concrete were flung into the air as rounds impacted on the floor around her. The shots were coming from behind, and she couldn't help but glance. The officer firing at her ducked behind a row of vats, as though she were about to turn and fire, but she found herself thinking: what a moron, he's going to go up with the building because he just wouldn't stop chasing me.

She returned her attention to the door ahead, trying to swerve and put something between her and the idiot firing at her. Alice was within ten metres of the exit when rounds tore through the backs of her thighs. She struck the concrete floor and slid. The pain was so intense it was hard to breathe, and she watched the counter for her grenade count down from twenty seven seconds as her command unit administered pain and coagulation medication.

The pain was gone, but she couldn't get her feet under her; Alice's legs simply wouldn't obey. She had one hand to drag herself to the door. "I can't go out like this," she said.

A short man with long hair stepped into the doorway from outside with an assault rifle raised. He unleashed a barrage of cover fire as he walked to her with perfect confidence. "Bad girl, drawing so much attention," he said as he leaned down and grabbed the back of her jacket. He ran backwards, dragging her and firing bursts from his assault rifle.

With nine seconds to spare, they were out of the warehouse, and he was dragging her into an awaiting shuttle that was so marked by time she wouldn't be surprised if it dated back to the early colonial days. He dumped her onto the floor behind the pilot seat and hurriedly closed the door. A slight jostling told her that the grenade went off, and at a glance through one of the portholes, she could see the craft was rolling across the ground. The hull scraped and creaked until it came to rest and the pilot engaged the engines.

Alice pulled herself across the narrow bed of the shuttle and reached for an emergency medical box on the wall. Her savior released the controls of the shuttle and turned his attention back to her. "Here, let me get that," he said, pulling the kit from the wall and opening it. "You're lucky you're wearing that jacket. Saved you from being shot through the back." He pulled it off without much regard to her injuries and dropped it behind him. He was right, the thicker armour on the back side of the jacket had stopped at least seven rounds from passing through.

"Who are you?"

"I've been following you since you made land on Uro. Didn't think you'd get those files," he stretched the back of her vacsuit away from her body and used a surgical particle saw to get through it, stripping her lower half from there down.

"Hey! They got my legs!"

"Relax, your security scan was more revealing than this. And yes, they got your legs, but you've got a hole in your backside, too."

He pulled a regenerative spray from the kit and shook it before beginning to spray it on. "You don't have any cybernetics in your legs or backside that you managed to hide from the port scanners, do you?"

"No, all natural," she replied, glad she was dosed with pain-killers. "And who gets implants in their ass?"

"Hey," he said, holding his hands up defensively. "I've seen stranger things."

"Why are you helping me?" Alice asked as he finished covering the wounds on her legs and bottom with the spray and moved on to her arm. Even through the painkillers she could feel the regeneration drugs going to work.

"Because you're going to cut me in for half," he said with a crooked grin. "You need an expert, or you're going to get killed."

"I've pulled off harder heists," Alice replied.

"Not on Uro, you haven't. You're either going to cut me in for half, or I'll drop you off at the nearest police station before your legs are all healed up. I figure I've got twenty three minutes to decide."

"You'd be in trouble too," Alice replied.

The long haired fellow pulled a cheap-looking computer pad from his pocket and showed her the screen. There was a detailed security scan of her – so detailed that she found herself blushing – with a reward of one point eight million Uro credits offered for her live capture. News agencies listed offers for footage of her beneath. "You're famous here now," he said with a chuckle. "They're going to be watching for you everywhere in this solar system."

"Dammit, Meunez is going to get into this," Alice said, pounding the deck with her good hand.

"Who's Meunez?"

"Never mind. I'll cut you in for half, but all this has to happen quickly."

"Love it," the fellow with the long hair said, standing. "Girl with a complicated past looking to get the job done in a hurry. Where are we going?"

"What? You don't know already?" Alice asked, teasing. He was an attractive man, a couple of centimetres shorter than her, with dark, straight hair. His features were so mixed that he could be from anywhere. His piercing dark eyes seemed to indicate a tendency towards mischief.

"I said I've been following you, not tapping into that wrist computer of yours. Even Uro cops couldn't get in, or track you once you got out of scanning range. I would have ignored you if there wasn't some recognizable skill."

"Thank you," Alice said.

"Wasn't a compliment, just an observation. Where are we going?"

"First, what's your name? Nothing comes up on my system," Alice asked.

"Lewis, just call me Lewis."

"Okay, Lewis, we're going to Illihd Prime."

"Where on Illihd Prime?" Lewis asked.

"I'll tell you when we get there."

***

Eve woke up on her stomach. The tingling sensation from the memory-dream in her legs was still fading. "They're getting longer," she said to herself. They were also falling into sequence constantly. There were no flashes of early life, or digital remnants from before she became human. Those were the most confusing experiences. They were half memories, with murky images that blurred together, not even worth paying attention to.

Everything was changing. She felt better, more like a whole person, but she looked forward to sleeping, eating was less a chore and more a pleasure. That made her situation even more difficult. Her nervousness at whatever Hampon was planning kept her up, and she didn't eat anything since she discovered that there could be a nano-modification ready that would limit her forever. He could easily put it in her food, or dose her while she slept.

Eve had to get some distance from him somehow. The day of her great address had arrived, and she hoped it would be easier than she thought. "It begins when I'm ready," she muttered to herself. That was what the notes that came with her speech said. She could put the event off as long as she wanted.

There was little reason to hesitate. She wanted to get on with it and she didn't take more time than she had to in the bathroom. Eve was never any good at putting on makeup, but she did a serviceable job of applying the basics using an auto-kit that was provided with her toiletries. She supposed it was something else she learned from Alice, who was taught by Bernice during a particularly long hyperspace trip. Eve was thankful the kit matched her colouring; it was something not even Alice had much of a knack for.

She put on the same dress she wore the day before, only putting the white and gold layer on the outside. Eve made sure the emergency environment patch was on her back underneath, as there was no telling where her day would take her.

The door chimed as she finished smoothing the dress down. "Come in," she said, activating the door. It was either the Child Prophet or Gabriel Meunez, and she wasn't eager to see either one of them.

Wheeler entered with the adolescent Child Prophet in tow. "Little Lister here told me you were getting ready to. . ." Wheeler trailed off, staring at her, astonished.

A lump rose in her throat, and she checked her dress to make sure it was in place, looked in a shiny wall fixture to make sure she hadn't done something unusual or shocking with her makeup. Everything seemed fairly normal.

"Ahem," the Child Prophet said, crossing the room and taking her hands. "I think Lucius is stunned to see how beautiful you look this morning."

"Right, yeah," he said. He wore an old thick black coat over what looked more like the clothing Eve had seen in her dreams. Thick pants over a vacsuit with a gun belt that had been robbed of its weaponry. "Sorry, your Excellency, I'm surprised to have an opportunity to see you in person."

"You should brush your hair," the Child Prophet said.

Eve nodded and returned to the bathroom, sliding the door most of the way closed.

"What was that?" the Child Prophet asked Wheeler quietly enough for him to think he wasn't being overheard.

"I expected her to look like Gloria, and that's something else," Wheeler replied, not as cautiously.

Eve dragged the brush through her hair as she listened. "That's what we're tracking. Her features are shifting bone deep while she's sleeping. Her framework upgrade wasn't built for that, but it's happening nonetheless."

"What does it have to do with me?" Wheeler asked.

"You've spent time with Patterson, more time than anyone after the change. We thought you could give us some insight since he seems to have control on a new level, not to mention, you've learned how to change your appearance yourself."

"So you think she's doing this consciously?"

Eve looked at herself in the mirror for a moment and realized that the difficulty she had recognizing herself wasn't all in her head. She really was changing. She stroked the brush through her hair one more time before dropping it in the sink and leaving the room. "I'm not," Eve said. "I'm not doing it consciously."

"Then what's changed?" Wheeler asked.

"I've been dreaming someone else's life."

The Child Prophet looked at her, alarmed. "That shouldn't be something you talk to just anyone about."

"He's not just anyone, you said he has total control," Eve replied. "I like that idea."

Wheeler smiled and leaned against the wall. "It's a good thing you don't look like my old first mate. It would make looking at you while I teach you a few tricks pretty awkward."

"So you can teach it?" Eve asked.

"It's all visualization," Wheeler replied. "Well, it is for me, at least. My last travelling companion seems to have a different approach."

"Oh?"

"Yeah, it's more like he actually is the framework. He gets that thing doing all kinds of stuff that I can't even wrap my head around. Most of it's biologically based, not like me. I just push the system to numb pain then get it to shift whatever I need around so I look like someone else. I can also use a tactile-"

"Can we continue this later?" The Child Prophet asked. "The followers are assembling." He turned to Wheeler then. "And I think you have an important bridge to build."

Wheeler shook his head at the shorter man then looked at Eve. "Never let 'em know you're good at diplomacy, or you'll be building bridges and mending walls for the rest of your life. Good luck with the speech. As long as you don't tell them you eat babies or are outlawing sex you'll have those followers down there hand feeding and naming children after you."

"Thank you Lucius. Can we meet later?"

"Count on it, Your Excellency," Wheeler said as he turned and left.

The Child Prophet was relentless in getting her to the shuttle that would take them to Pandem. The shuttle they took down to the planet was decorated with real wood trimming, thick plush seating, and had refreshment materializers within easy reach. Eve watched as they passed groups of Eden ships. Their shining hulls, angular features, and deadly weaponry had never looked alien to her before. Even the ones with manipulation appendages didn't look right anymore.

"They're magnificent, I never get bored looking at them," the Child Prophet said, straightening his synthetic silk blue and green robes. "I bet you can't wait to connect with them."

Eve nodded in response. She recalled the cold presence of her machine children. She remembered the sensation of thousands, being at the mercy of software voices that all demanded something of her impatiently. They brought endless questions and alien emotions that she was having difficulty recalling clearly. Human arms, a face that could be read and sentiments that were clear and relatable seemed so amazing in comparison. Thinking about those experiences brought sadness, because they weren't hers, they were Alice's. What that woman shared with Bernice was unlike anything Eve could clearly remember. She couldn't recall her mother, and her father was mostly absent when Eve was still called Nora, when she was dying. He became much more of a factor in her life when he liberated her brain from her dying body and implanted it into the core of a life support and interface system.

Centuries in a tank, her senses filtered through the mechanical. It seemed more like a nightmare to her as she watched Pandem come into view, and they began to enter the atmosphere.

"Do you think you'll be able to get through the speech?" the Child Prophet asked. "It's five paragraphs, which seems long. Do you find it long?"

Eve barely paid attention. "It's good." Her palms were already sweaty. The thought of being in front of so many people at once, more than she'd ever seen, was the most intimidating thing she'd ever faced.

"Remember, they're going to be easy to win. They just want to know that they are safe, and after that they'll just want to see you in front of them."

Eve remembered the sensation of being chased, shot at, and almost killed. They felt like her own memories as much as anything. "How many people did the Eden Fleet kill when the virus struck?"

"It's best not to concentrate on that," the Child Prophet said. "We want to avoid numbers and anything that takes away from your emotional stance."

"What's that?" she asked, still feeling quiet and saddened.

"What's what?"

"My emotional stance."

"I thought that was clear in the speech," the Child Prophet said. "You're sorry for what your machines have done and have taken control of them, so they guard your chosen people. They are your children now, the humans down there."

"Oh," Eve said, returning her attention to the porthole.

"Are you all right? We could delay this."

Eve considered the option, it was tempting; the butterflies in her stomach were fluttering furiously. "I'd rather get it over with." More islands than she could count dotted an endless blue ocean. Some islands were dominated by narrow mountain ranges andothers were covered with lush green forests. The cities were surrounded by bright green plant life, and some buildings were coated with green and brown.

"The Order members replanted all the open ground they could," said the Child Prophet. "Wherever nature had been stamped out, they've brought it back.

Pandem is a model for reclamation and a place where humans are learning to coexist with nature again. I thought you'd appreciate it."

"I do," Eve said. She never thought that humans could dedicate themselves to such a cause, but the evidence was passing by below. As they descended towards one of the largest islands, she saw gardens and young forests on roofs. They truly had made a great difference in the time she was in stasis.

They sped towards a gargantuan, round structure. Every entrance was choked with streams of people lining up for entry. They slowed to hover over the stadium then began to descend and Eve's pulse began to race as the stands came into view.

The seats were full, multitudes beyond counting waiting for her to arrive.

"Are you sure I can't get anything for you?" asked the Child Prophet. "Something to help you calm down, or maybe a touch up? We have an excellent groomer in the passenger compartment. He does everything for me before appearances. You look a little. . . off, to be honest."

The time was almost upon them, and she'd be shoved out of the luxury shuttle to face all those people. She was sweating, it felt like her heard was pounding between her ears. "There are worse things," she said to herself quietly.

"Pardon?"

"Nothing, never mind."

"You're absolutely sure?" he pressed. "This is only the second time we've ever done this kind of public address. The results were wonderful last time, but if it's too much for your first appearance you could do it from in here, and we could holographically project you out there."

"No," she said before she thought it through. Eve entertained the notion for a moment, then shook her head to affirm her decision. She was already preparing herself for facing all those people, and for some reason her curiosity was beginning to rule her desires. She had been isolated for years beyond counting, even on the Overlord II, after she was transplanted from a stasis tank back into a body.

The shuttle door opened. A gust of hot air filled the cabin, it carried a smell that was unmistakably human, but it didn't disgust her as she once expected it would. The Child Prophet patted her knee on his way out. "Come out when I introduce you, back straight and looking over all their heads. Pretend there's no one there, you'll be fine."

Eve didn't say anything, she just watched him leave. He threw up his arms as he stepped out of sight and was greeted with a deafening round of cheers. "Today is a great day!" he started, his voice carried over the multitudes. She couldn't see him, but he could be heard perfectly. "It's a memorable day, nay, an historic event. For some time I have been alone in my leadership, solitary in finding the best path for all of you. What a rewarding journey it's been, but it has been a lonely one."

Eve leaned forward, almost placing her head on her knees. *What would Alice do?* she asked herself. *Would any of this really phase her at all?* Eve recalled Alice's argument with the rich Ulrik, more than one firefight, during which she may have had frantic moments, but her thoughts were always clear. Alice had sidestepped death so many times in her short life. She didn't have framework technology, or friends to come to her rescue, but she continued to risk life and limb for a few more days' worth of food, a few more days of life with no consideration for what she had been. Then she realized something that brought a tear to her eye.

As the Child Prophet droned on, proclaiming that Eve was 'the Forever Woman' and a 'beautiful, living Ancient' without revealing exactly who she was, Eve was awed by the notion that both Alice and her had been mechanical in some way. Alice was software, an artificial intelligence before becoming human. Eve had been a sickly girl, but her brain was transplanted into a machine, with translators and sensors that changed the way she saw her existence. Then she was put back into a human body, a body that was someone else's before, someone who didn't want to die.

None of Alice's memories contained the desire to return to what she was, software. None so far, and Eve doubted she'd ever find a memory of the thought even crossing Alice's mind.

Since she was first transplanted, Eve hadn't had that thought either; in fact, she couldn't imagine giving up her existence for what she was before.

"It is my honour to present a Goddess among us: Eve!" announced the Child Prophet with so much enthusiasm that his voice cracked.

Without thinking, she was on her feet and walking out of the shuttle. The sun on her face was harsh but enjoyable once she overcame the glare. The hot air carried with it a fragrance that combined sweat, fresh paint, and other, less identifiable things. It was almost overpowering at first, but then she realized that there was no cheering.

By the time Eve's eyes adjusted to the light she was past centre stage, within three metres of the edge. She looked down at the people only two metres past the edge. Her gaze locked with that of a young woman. Her eyes were deep blue, peering out from a wild mane of sun bleached hair. She was wearing simple, loose fitting tan clothing that looked like they had been with her for many working days. Excitement then fear were plain in that young woman's gaze, and the crowd of thousands standing on the stadium floor seemed to fade away as she concentrated on that one woman's face. "I'm just learning how amazing it is to be human," Eve said. Her words, spoken only slightly louder than a whisper, were directed to every listener. The overpowering loudness that the Child Prophet had presented himself with was gone.

The young woman smiled a little. A strange calm came over Eve as she allowed her realizations to be spoken, moment by moment, thought by thought. She held up her hand to block the scrolling text that was being projected into her eye from somewhere ahead. "I never realized that to every person their own experience is the most important experience there is. When I was awake, and protecting a world I thought was too precious for people to ruin, I treated humans like parasites. I barely remember what that was like, but I remember the indignation, and the images of death that the machines I helped create transmitted as they killed so many."

The young woman was beginning to look worried. "I was ill, and my father saved me by removing my brain then connecting it to machines. My mind may have been human, but my body was gone, and I couldn't understand. . ." she hesitated, looking for the next word, desperately clinging to the message she wanted to share. "I couldn't understand that everyone I had killed was a singular, precious person."

The Child Prophet approached her and she moved closer to the edge of the stage. The young woman with the blue eyes looked surprised and took a step back. Eve gestured for her to stay where she was with a pleading, reaching motion. "I'm whole again, a woman instead of a human trapped in a machine," she said, saddened at the mere thought of being reduced again, having her body taken away. At the same time, she couldn't help but remember that it was another woman's memories that brought on her quick, humanizing transformation. A woman whose human memories were trapped, isolated in her subconscious. *Alice is just like I was, in storage, dormant. I wish she were here so I could hear her speak to these people. She loved so few people, but when she did, it was a greater love than I've ever known.*

The Child Prophet took her hand, but Eve threw it back. For a moment Eve couldn't find the woman she was focusing on, and her eyes searched the front rows frantically. When she found her, Eve said the first thing that was on her mind. "I'm alive, and I want to stay alive. I can't tell you where I learned how wonderful and terrible it can be to be human, but I can say that it's a lesson I'll never forget," a tear rolled down her cheeks, and she saw sympathy in the blonde woman's expression. "I'll never forget that each and every one of you are having an experience just as powerful as I am, every day, every hour, every minute and second."

"Talk about immortality! You're supposed to tell them about the framework technology and perfect immortality!" The Child Prophet's voice scolded. No one else in the crowd heard it, thankfully.

Eve lowered her hand and glanced at the scrolling speech she'd been ignoring. The passage she was supposed to be relaying read, 'those of you who have elevated yourselves to the highest levels of devotion will be gifted with life unending, a perfect immortality that is unlike anything promised by technology or theology.'

She looked back to the woman who stared up at her expectantly, feeling her vision narrow even as she did so. "It's so hot," Eve said. Her knees buckled, and the world seemed to tumble.

CHAPTER 30
ABOARD

The Triton always had surprises in store for Ashley. Not a day went by where she didn't see something interesting in a corner, or some room that seemed to be designed with care, not just blocked out on some diagram and built in a shipyard. Every space seemed to be waiting for its person, or people, from the observation decks to the consoles on the bridge.

The underside of the Botanical Gallery was one of the more interesting places she'd seen. Transparent pipes and reservoirs supported the life above. The Gallery still had power, being on an independent backup, and Liam Grady hadn't bothered setting up a trap for anyone who tampered with it like he had with the rest of the ship. Her codes got them through the door once they got the external lock connected to power.

Lights shone dimly within the piping, adding an eerie glow to the chamber. It was wider and longer than she could make out, but only two metres tall. Sections of the floor were transparent too, and some of those reservoirs looked more like trapped oceans, with fish and wild life on the bottom and the sides.

"This is incredible," said the major at her side.

"You should see the living space above us. It's a large park, with ponds and creeks. The balconies of family apartments overlook a miniature forest, tamed, but still a reminder."

"A reminder?"

"Of home." Ashley caught herself slipping as she said it. The answer fit perfectly with who she was pretending to be, a woman from Earth with rank and experience, but when she said it she was thinking of the green land she grew up in. Charming the major was so much easier once she just regarded him as another person in her way; it was something she learned to do early on. A warm smile and quiet talk resolved more problems than anything else. She was lucky they sent a man to meet her - women were more difficult, and most didn't like her at first.

"What's Earth like?" the major asked.

"Is that the entrance up there?" asked Jake.

Ashley brought up the interior schematic of the Triton on her comm unit and spun the hologram so she could zoom in on one side. The hologram marked where the engineering team had set up a power source for the outer doors well behind them. She focused in on the room ahead and saw the circular chamber that led most of the way up through the Botanical Gallery. "That's it." Ashley looked up and saw a narrow door in front of them.

They crossed the space, coming around a set of pipes, and when Ashley stopped to stand in front of the entrance a light flashed over her head. Her comm unit buzzed a moment and when she looked down the interface changed. It looked like some of the older, frozen wall terminals she'd seen in some of the less utilized parts of the ship, a Sol Defence interface.

The featureless door lit up, an interface matching what was on her command and control unit appearing. "Welcome, Ashley Lamport. Your override level clearance is valid. Please enter with your reserve officer," said a gentle male voice. There was nothing computerized about the sound, but a warm, fatherly quality that she found surprising and reassuring.

The deck rumbled as the heavy door slowly rotated so an entrance appeared. The major started to take a step forward and Ashley squeezed his arm to her side. "I'm sorry," she said, unsure of what to say next.

"You've seen the ship recognize her and acknowledge that she has the highest level of access," Captain Valent said. "Now it's time for you and your people to take our down payment and leave."

"Before I go," the major said to Ashley. He seemed intent on ignoring Jake. "I need to extend my government's desire to work with the Triton once she's back in fighting shape. Your fighter pilots have been helpful on patrols, and we're short on large combat vessels, carriers especially. The Triton would be a fantastic asset if you were to coordinate with us. We're willing to offer you assistance in repairs for a large discount."

"I'm sure we might be able to negotiate something," Jake said.

"I have to hear it from her," the major said.

There was an earnestness in his pale face that begged her to promise him more than she had a right to, but she repeated her captain's words instead. "We'll negotiate something."

"Thank you," the major said. "We'll make our own way out."

Everyone watched silently as the major and his squad left. That was it, all they had to do to get the Triton back. It was their ship again. Ashley was so relieved, so overjoyed that it wasn't nearly as hard a fight as she'd expected, that she was on the verge of weeping.

"I think she's waiting," Jake said, gesturing towards the door.

Ashley looked to the chamber door. Inside was a warmly lit compartment with a spiral staircase leading up in the centre. "I think it's a he," she said, taking a step forward.

Jake was about to fall in step beside her when she looked over her shoulder and made eye contact with Minh-Chu. He smiled at her encouragingly and nodded. She wished she was inviting him inside instead, but it would be for selfish reasons.

"Ash?" Jake asked as she stopped.

She looked to him and shook her head. It took all the bravery she could muster to tell her captain, the man who'd freed her, that it wouldn't be him in command of the Triton. "I'm taking Oz."

He looked surprised for a moment then put his hand on her shoulder. "Good." Jake turned towards the crowd of people behind them. "You're up, Oz."

Terry Ozark McPatrick stepped forward and Ashley took his big hand in hers. "He's yours if you want him. I mean, I'm picking you to be in charge."

"I'll rebuild him, better than ever," Oz said.

They entered the room together, barely fitting through the entryway side by side. The heavy chamber door slid closed behind them.

***

"There! A main processing and distribution node!" Liam Grady shouted as they ran down the hallway. Ayan's lungs were burning. The darkened corridors seemed endless, and she was sure they'd run through half the ship and leapt up half the emergency ladders to get where they were going.

An alert sounded in her headgear the moment they all made it around the corner. Her combat shields activated, and she drew her sidearm by reflex. Targeting systems in her heads up display highlighted five mini-turrets, the size of her palm, hovering at head level above the deck ahead in red.

"Down! Everyone down!" she cried. Many of them were already dropping to the deck around her, their own combat systems warning them of the danger. The free floating turret traps fired as she took aim with the assistance of her suit. Several shots of the accelerated molten medium the traps fired peppered her energy shielding.

Her training prevailed, and she took several shots at the nearest hovering target, missing several times before finally obliterating it. Shooting while out of breath was difficult, even with her suit trying to steady her hand. She missed most of the time. The other soldiers destroyed the rest of the mini-turrets, and the moment they stopped firing another alert appeared on her heads up display. Someone dropped down from the ceiling behind them.

Ayan turned in time to see a man in a simple black vacsuit standing on top of Laura Everin. He swept a thick bladed nanosword down towards her head. The rasping edge hesitated for a moment as it fought to break through her technician's suit. The weapon passed down the middle of her head then out through the neck, jerking, sputtering and ripping as it ended her life.

Ayan didn't even realize she'd raised her sidearm until she was firing. Her shots caught Laura's killer full in the chest, the thermalitic rounds burning at the protective layer of the man's vacsuit.

It didn't stop him. He swept his blade at the most important technicians within reach as several more shots struck his legs and chest, finally breaking through his vacsuit. He collapsed to the deck and Liam Grady rushed to the man's side.

Ayan's shots sparked and burned violently, still trying to break through the man's dark suit. He retracted his headgear; one side of his face was badly burned. She had to step over several bodies to get to him, and she stopped when she was almost standing over his ruined body.

"Why?" Liam asked. "Why kill her? Why kill anyone?"

"Citadel needs Triton destroyed. Had to damage your capacity to repair her, to learn," Larry struggled. "Had to…" his eyes lost focus for a moment before he went on. "Had to try to stop you. Didn't want to, but they'd know. My masters would know, and they would send more."

"Why?" Ayan asked, gripping the sidearm at her side. The question had already been asked, but it was all she could say.

Larry looked up at her, the last shots that she'd landed were about to burn through the vacsuit to his chest. "Born to fight," he said.

His eyes rolled back as he convulsed for a moment and died.

"He's not wearing his command unit, there's no emergency assistance built into his vacsuit," Liam Grady said. "He wanted to die."

"Treat the wounded," Ayan said coldly. "And fix this ship." She watched as Liam gently laid Larry's head down on the deck. No one was moving. "Now!" she shouted, sounding as harsh as Richard Kane, the most extreme drill instructor she'd ever known.

***

"Comms are blocked in here," Oz said.

"I'm pretty sure we can make a call from the computer core if we have to," Ashley said as she led Oz up the stairs to a pillar surrounded by a band of polished metal thicker than her arm. The platform around them was made of the same transparent metal as the deck of the bridge, so many levels above, so many frames forward. The finish was slightly smoky, with flecks of dark red. Comfortable-looking brown sofa-like seating ringed the edges of the platform.

The walls around them were coming to life with images from the local Stellarnet. News about the Carthans, Rega Gain system, and several of the crewmembers who had come aboard drifted across, up and down. Video of Ayan negotiating with the Carthans, of Jake executing the people who attempted to capture him, of Ashley in the hallways of the Triton and of Oz on the bridge eventually became the focus. The rest of the crew were imaged smaller between, such as Finn and Agameg who were celebrated in replays of them making repairs and installing the hypertransmitter. There were so many others, including Ramirez, who died fighting for the ship, Shamus Frost, Stephanie Vega, and Laura Everin.

"Hello?" Ashley asked. Her voice seemed small in the tall space.

"You choose a soldier and proven leader of men to assume command," said the strong, calm male voice. "Someone you would choose as your own protector."

Ashley looked at Oz, who still seemed a little surprised. "I haven't thought of it that way, but yeah, if I needed a bodyguard or a big brother, I'd pick him."

"Thank you, Ashley," Oz said. "There are a lot of other people who would be just as good for this. Liam, Jake, or Ayan?"

He was speaking to her very politely, which was a bad sign to her. Ashley was becoming even more nervous than before at the thought that Oz might actually argue with her decision; the thought had never occurred to her. "Chief Grady didn't even tell me I could choose someone, so he probably doesn't want it. Captain already has a ship and I think he's bustin' to get flying, and Ayan has so much to do already. I think she's amazing, but how much can she do?" she looked to the video playback of Ayan as she walked with Laura, Jason, Liam, and several soldiers. It was footage from an outdoor causeway on Greydock. Ashley recognized it immediately; the local Stellarnet seemed to love taking footage of the entire Triton crew, and often focused on Ayan or Liam Grady. Most of the videos focused in on Liam and Ayan lingered on times when they were standing close together, something Ashley hadn't had the opportunity to notice before. "Maybe they're already busy doing what they should be."

"While I'm managing security and logistics for a shanty settlement," Oz said, nodding. "Thank you, Ashley. You're right, this is where I want to be."

"Guess I had weeks to think about it," Ashley said with a shrug. "Only I don't think I knew I was thinking about it then."

All the images surrounding them disappeared. For a moment the room was a dim yellow hue, they could barely see. A large holographic image appeared between them and the thick pillar in the middle of the room. Flashes of Ashley at the helm, in the Oota Galoona lounge dancing, spending time with crewmembers, reading training material, and doing a dance of joy after finishing her pilot's qualifications for the fighters and drop ships aboard the Triton. "I have finished examining your time aboard and I see caring, perhaps an over-abundance of emotion, intelligence and so much potential. I understand why Citadel's representative gave you a backup override level code."

The images were slowly replaced with holograms of Oz. The first featured him standing at the main terminal in the Flight Operations Centre beneath the main bridge. That image lingered as if it meant more to the Triton than others, then it faded into a more light hearted recording of Oz carrying several beverages onto the bridge, followed by several different instances of him working with crewmembers and spending the little leisure time he had with friends. Another image that lingered featured Jake, Minh, and Oz in one of the waiting rooms outside the large sickbay.

"Reason, efficiency, empathy, and experience are only the beginning with you, Terry Ozark McPatrick," said the Triton. "That would be enough, but then there's this."

The lighting in the room turned red and flashes of Oz leading crewmembers in violent firefights across the ship surrounded them. Ashley knew combat was horrible, but she'd never seen such a waste of humanity. Oz didn't just command, he killed with rifle, sidearm, blade, and by hand with cold efficiency. "I'm not proud of that, but it had to be done," Oz said.

All the images disappeared and one dominated the space in the middle of the room. His armour was shot up and Oz was bleeding, sitting against the wall surrounded by the fallen. Another man in foreign armour knelt down, his weapon at the ready, and looked into his eyes. Oz's hood withdrew into his shoulders. He was smiling, despite the trickle of blood escaping from the corner of his mouth.

The recording of Oz slowly raised his right hand and pointed at his enemy. "What are you fighting for?" Oz rasped.

The enemy commander hesitated. "Duty," he replied.

Oz's head floundered a little, perhaps thanks to an attempt at a nod, then said, "My crew." He paused for a laboured breath. "My home." The holographic version of him struggled for a moment longer. His breath sounded wet.

Before the enemy commander could raise his weapon to shoot him in the head, to put him out of his misery, Oz's breathing stopped, his eyes looking blankly ahead.

Ashley had never seen anything that was harder to watch, but she refused to look away. Tears threatened to roll down her cheeks, but the Triton was trying to show them something, and she'd be damned if she'd miss it. Oz's arm was across her shoulders, offering comfort.

"Hey, I'm still here," he whispered.

"You weren't so sure then," the Triton said. "Your medical systems were damaged, and there was no way you could have known that you wouldn't be dead for more than eleven minutes before your medical systems resuscitated you."

"Even worse than I thought. You understand why I didn't bother checking the log on that one," Oz replied. "Not many soldiers get a chance to offer last words. I gave mine to a solder I respected. Cumberland was a dutiful man, just like me. If we were on the same side, I believe we would have been friends."

The image faded and the room was filled with a more reasonable level of yellow light. "I've reviewed the information available on the local network, seen the Order of Eden, Regent Galactic, and all the accounts of the refugees you've welcomed aboard. We are leaving the age of artificial intelligence and enter the age of the soldier. I need you to guide your crew and me through it. Ashley Lamport, you have the highest authority aboard now that the Citadel representative is gone. Thank you for putting Terry Ozark McPatrick forward, I accept him, and will accept his choices as he recruits his staff."

"Thank you?" Ashley said, wiping a tear away.

The broad pillar in front of them began to darken. "I'm awake for the first time in decades, and all the humans I was connected to are gone," the Triton said. The pillar became transparent, revealing a tank filled with clear liquid. There was something alive inside, breathing, slowly flexing. It was taller than Oz, with no legs, arms or discernible head.

The semi-translucent, smooth skin revealed hints of long strips of muscle that stretched as its body flattened, so it looked like one long, rippling fin. "I am the mind of the Triton. I'm also a highly evolved, genetically crafted human-amphibian, but I'm mostly human despite my appearance." The colour of its skin shifted depending on the angle Ashley looked from. Patches had a rainbow hue like the scales of a fish one moment, then they reddened and became soft-looking the next. For the most part, the skin did resemble any human's, though that's where the being's resemblance to a human being ended.

"We thought you were a computer," Ashley said. "But they just left you here alone?"

"Don't worry, Ashley," the Triton replied through the sound system in the room. Nothing on the creature seemed to resemble a mouth, and it wasn't connected to any cables or tubes. "I am a computer, more than eighty percent of my body is neutrally active in a similar sense to the human brain. Through forced evolution, genetic manipulation, and species mixing my species was created for this specific purpose. To wake with this ship, serve, and live for as long as there is a vessel for me to interface with. Like the ship, I need a commander, a crew."

The more Ashley looked at the creature, the more it looked like a simple sea creature, like a soft, bottom feeding eel that she might have stolen away to an aquarium if she were allowed to have one as a child.

"You're why the Triton is immune to the Holocaust Virus," Oz said.

"No computer virus can infect me, and my mind is more advanced than even the highest order of Lorander Navigator's," the Triton said. "Not that I'm bragging. Actually, never mind, I am bragging, but I'm also being honest. Don't worry about my solitude, or slumber, Ashley. I enjoy ensuring that the ship is functioning perfectly from one moment to the next, and I further enjoy my role as a silent watcher. Most crews never realize that I'm a being, they think I'm a computer without personality. It's procedure for me to only communicate with a few commanding officers, and that's what I prefer."

"I apologize for the damage," Oz said. "We'll find a way to make repairs."

"You will, and I know you couldn't find any other solution, I have reviewed the records. Since we have the introductions out of the way, I need your consent to connect directly with you both. While Ashley won't be in command, she will still have an override."

"I understand, and call me Oz. Now, how are you going to connect with us?"

The voice that Ashley heard through the sound system in the chamber spoke in her mind then as it said, *"I can focus my attention and communicate telepathically within the confines of the ship."*

"Okay, that's spooky," Ashley said. "And really cool."

"What do you need to do to sync up with us?" Oz asked aloud.

"You only need to reply with your mind, then I'll strengthen the connection with one of my memories," replied the Triton.

Ashley thought, *'sounds fun, can you make it a happy memory?'* with surprising ease.

"That was quick," Oz said to her.

"Pretty easy if your head's already empty," Ashley replied.

"Your head is anything but empty, Ashley," replied the Triton. *"In fact, I see a quest for happiness, security, and so much worry."*

"So do I," Oz managed to reply. *"I can see a bit, like some of those impressions are slipping through our connection with you, Triton."*

"It is one of my gifts. I can acquaint the two of you with each other in a way few humans ever experience," the Triton replied.

In a flash, Ashley felt what it was like to *be* Oz. She felt his awe at the discovery of the Triton's true nature, his confidence and a comforting certainty that he felt that he was exactly where he should be, doing precisely what he ought to be doing. *If that's how he feels all the time, no wonder he's so amazing.*

"You're incredible, Ashley. You don't have to feel so insecure," she heard Oz reply mentally. *"And I'm not always like this."* It was as though he summoned the opposite sides of himself. She saw how uncertain he was when he was in a relationship, how he felt like he had to guard himself when he met men he was attracted to, and the pain he'd endured in many failed romantic partnerships. That was where most of his self-doubt resided. She also saw how he adored his friends, they were as important to him as family. Ayan, Jake, Jason, Laura, and surprisingly Frost, Stephanie, Agameg, Finn, and she were all dear to him. His sense of duty was overpowering.

"You are beautiful in mind, Ashley," Oz said to her. *"If I could love a woman intimately, I'd be helpless."*

The connection faded, and she could feel that she was only able to hear the Triton. *"I hope that wasn't premature,"* he said.

"Thank you," Ashley said aloud.

"It was surprising, but not unwelcome. I might feel differently if I were standing beside someone other than her, though," Oz replied, squeezing Ashley's shoulder.

Ashley pictured what it might be like if she was standing beside Frost and tittered a little. She was still under Oz's arm, and felt more comfortable there than ever. The kinship she'd gained with him in just a moment of being connected was deeper than anyone else. Knowing what it was like to *be* someone else was incredible, and Oz was so strong in almost every way.

"I'd like to share what I am with you through a few of my memories," the Triton said.

Ashley took a deep breath and nodded. "I think I'm ready."

"I'm ready," Oz said.

Ashley's mind was filled with vivid images of the Triton being moved into the bowels of the ship. Glad caretakers that were his closest friends from birth wished him well, and offered tearful farewells as they caressed him for the last time before he joined with his new home. That was when he became the Triton, creature and ship united, and he connected to his first captain.

That captain was a two hundred and six year old human general named Trent Syphus. Four of his great-grandchildren were officers aboard, and the Triton would be his last command. He was best known for being an officer on the bridge of the Tsunami, one of the first ships to make direct contact with the Issyrians.

His retirement mission was to explore the galaxy and eventually join with Lorander in extra-galactic explorations. It was an exciting time for the Triton and his new commander. There were other senior officers who all linked to the Triton as well, and they flashed by. The Triton appreciated them all in different ways, forming personal bonds with each.

A deluge of thought and images detailed the months that followed. The Triton watched every member of the crew as it managed the new vessel. He watched children grow, crewmembers who couldn't cope with being so far from home fall into despair and recover over time. The Triton visited countless worlds, and eventually fought an undesignated race of aggressors. Their ships clamped onto the hull of the Triton and burned their way through, assaulting the crew in the corridors.

The fight was eventually won, but that first painful engagement with an enemy that offered no reason as to why they struck from the darkness was an enduring scar. After nine years, the Triton was recalled by Sol Defence. The disappointment shared between the Triton and Captain Syphus was still fresh, and they returned to Kuiper Spacedock. The last memory the Triton had to offer was a visit from one of the people who helped bring him into being, a man named Najim Ghali. He spent two days communing with him as he watched his systems get shut down so the ship could be refitted. The process wasn't painful, but emotional support was appreciated as the Triton's greater body was disabled.

Najim said farewell, sad that they'd be parted again, but he was also so enthusiastic. *"I'll see you soon, Triton,"* Najim thought to him, a smile on his face. *"When you wake up you'll be refitted as a long range combat carrier. I told them you were a fighter, and they finally listened."*

The Triton was excited at the notion. While his experience in combat was painful, the fight was invigorating, and he quietly missed it. Energy was drained from most of the ship's systems, and Najim infused his containment system with the chemicals that would preserve him while the ship was under construction. He didn't recall anything until only days before, when Ashley was trying to make contact with the override code.

"Now I must have a moment alone with Oz," the Triton told her.

Ashley gasped and staggered as the being released her mind. She ended up dropping onto the nearest seat. She watched Oz slowly lower himself to his knees, then his head jerked.

Slowly, he lowered his face into his hands, shuddering several times. Ashley started to stand, but Oz raised his hand. "No! It's all right," he shouted as if competing with a great din.

She sat back and watched worriedly. Her experience with connecting to the Triton was wonderful; she knew she'd be thinking about it for weeks. To feel what it was to have sensors, to move between stars and to observe thousands of people who made their home in your extended body was incredible. Her perspective seemed broader, so many of her problems felt so small compared to how she thought about things just moments before.

Whatever Oz was experiencing had him grimacing one moment and flinching the next, until he finally sighed and stood. "I understand. I'll find a way to repair the damage and make the improvements uploaded from Earth."

"Thank you," the Triton replied audibly. "Start with connecting me to my main computer interface after you've attended to the needs of your crew. I'm eager to connect with the updated software Sol Defence uploaded before breaking their connection."

Oz turned to her and Ashley knew immediately that there was something terribly wrong. She was on her feet right away. "Are you okay?" she asked.

"I'm fine. The Triton had to show me the damage. The biological circuitry aboard is poisoned too, so he can't connect to half the ship properly. We were prioritizing repairs. Something else just happened with the other team though, they need us."

"What?" Ashley asked as she followed him down the stairs as quickly as he could. He was taking the steps two at a time.

"We have wounded, and three technicians are dead," Oz replied.

CHAPTER 31
THE VICTORY MACHINE

The sight of all her medical experts gathered in the furthest corner from the door in the conference room did not instil confidence in Fleet Warden Kimberly Harrison. One of them, a kind-looking man named Dr. Sewell, glanced over his shoulder as she came in and whispered something hurriedly to his five colleagues.

Kimberly sighed and slowly took a seat at the end of the table. Reflexively she let the tie holding her neck-length blonde hair loose and then tightened it even more. They finally took their seats at the end furthest from her. Most of them avoided her gaze.

Dr. Sewell activated a full-sized image of the isolation room where they were keeping the man called Roman. He was laid out on a gurney, his protective suit removed, and he moved his head as though having an intense dream.

"Report," Warden Harrison demanded.

"It's as I feared," Dr. Sewell started, sitting up extra straight in his chair. "When we removed Roman's suit, we contaminated a sealed section of Enzo Station with temporal radiation."

"We knew that section was contaminated when we built it. The construction crew said it was a problem with the materials," Warden Harrison said dismissively.

"I'm sorry, Warden," replied a weary looking doctor Kimberly hadn't met before as she shook her head emphatically. "You may remember that room being contaminated since the station was moved into place, but that's a new modification to the time line."

"That's not possible, Charmaine," interjected a doctor wearing a white recovery mask. "You're saying that events that have already passed are being modified by this person, and that a whole construction crew would be too stupid to just build somewhere else, or use other materials."

"That's *Doctor* Kershaw to you. You're the only one here who doesn't concur on this matter. It's been noted, now let me explain the theory according to the majority," Doctor Kershaw retorted. "The machine that our patient is attached to affects objects and people in the near vicinity for a nine year period in each direction. If something is exposed to its temporal radiation for too long, or a person survives an intense burst, they will be forever changed. Some minor exposure is about as harmful as a mild tan, but if there's enough exposure to make someone ill, then that illness changes their past. There is also a ripple effect that changes reality as we know it, like your memories. Just a few days ago, that section was clean, safe. That's how anyone who knew about it would remember it, but then he arrived, we removed his containment suit, there was an intense surge of temporal radiation, and the exposure changed its state. Since it is temporal radiation, the state changes not only in the future, but also in the past thanks to some kind of wake effect we don't completely understand yet."

177

"All right, so a few days ago, that section was clean. He got here and now it's been contaminated for nine years," Warden Harrison concluded impatiently. "What about our people? How does it look for them?"

"The nurses who removed him from his suit?" asked Doctor Kershaw. "They're fully contaminated, like everything else that was caught in the radiation burst. Their entire life histories have changed in ways we can't be aware of. For all we know, one of them had two children, but because they were retroactively affected by radiation nine years behind us in the time line, they may have abstained from having babies. That's how dire this kind of radiation is. While we can measure how large the area of exposure is, there's no way of measuring what kind of change the exposure has caused, because as far as we're concerned," she shrugged and made a broad gesture, "everything in this reality has changed thanks to a ripple effect that started with a big splash of radiation nine years ago. In short, we shouldn't have removed his containment suit, we shouldn't have tried to activate the machine ourselves without understanding it first. It has a way of expending the energy before extended surges, it creates high-powered wormholes for travel and remote seeing. We disconnected that temporarily. That is why we're seeing these problems. We shouldn't have tampered."

Fleet Warden Harrison nodded. "That was an order from the top. There are all kinds of new technologies. Wormhole generation that fits in the palm of your hand, new armour systems, materials beyond our scope of development, and who knows what else. I couldn't talk them out of trying to study this thing. I thought you could control this, some of you told me it would be easy to contain." Warden Harrison sighed and rubbed her temples. "I'm getting a headache. I think I get the theory, let's move on. Do we have a way of treating exposure?"

Doctor Sewell gestured towards his colleague wearing the white mask. "Doctor Finch has been treating himself for nine years. He was present when our mystery man was removed from the suit and toggled the machine."

"Yes, and you can't know how relieved I am to know that my condition will only last nine more years. It's taken all our tissue regeneration technology, but I've managed to live a somewhat normal life. I expect that, using the same treatments, the nurses and I will make it."

"So the effects of this exposure are nine years both ways," Warden Harrison concluded. "What about Roman?"

"He's absolutely terminal," Doctor Finch replied. "We were only exposed for a few seconds. He's been bombarded for years as far as we can tell, and is suffering from full systemic degradation. He might last a few days longer, at best. Containment isn't a problem though; we've adapted the micro scale technology in his suit on a room-sized scale in short order, so we're safe."

"All right. What about that thing he's attached to, what was it called? The Victory Machine?"

"As far as we can tell it's a combination of technology from several different races built on a Sol System frame," explained Doctor Sewell. "Our attempts at a deep scan get, well, fuzzy."

"Even using the station's scanners?"

"Yes. It's the same as the Triton's computer core. Any attempt at a detailed deep scan gets scrambled by some sort of signal interdiction system that generates interference, but we've learned a lot from Roman's connection to the device," Doctor Sewell explained as he brought up a diagram of a net spread across the back of Roman's cranium under the skin. "This soft cybernetic implant interfaces the entire brain through bone. From our observations, we've determined that he communicates with the Victory Machine through a type of dream state. What he's most likely seeing are characters and situations in the dream that are showing him events of the future. They're interpreters for the petabytes of information the cable is carrying per second. As far as we can tell, the Victory Machine is collecting information from thousands of points in space, all at once, using microscopic wormholes that reach nine years into the future."

"Have you tried an interrogation scan?" asked the fleet warden.

"Yes, I'll get to that in a minute," Doctor Sewell said. "What's amazing about this device is that those wormholes were initiated ahead of it, meaning that at some point in time there was a sister device that created these wormholes looking backwards. We assume it was destroyed by a surge of temporal radiation, but the Victory Machine uses the residual radiation to fuel itself. Something must have gone wrong when whoever built it turned it on though, since there is a constant build up of energy that it has to expend on a regular basis. That is how we found Roman on the Triton. The device creates a larger wormhole under incredible compression called a crush gate. Now a crush gate-"

"I know what a crush gate is," Fleet Warden Harrison said. "It's a high compression wormhole that projects the traveller through fast enough to create the sensation of being flung to their destination. I tried a simulated one as a cadet, just in case we had to use advanced Lorander technology."

"Lorander Company has been using crush gates for decades, I wouldn't call that advanced in the strictest sense. Anyway, the Victory Machine creates real ones. For all we know, Roman came from twenty, or fifty, light years away. He would have travelled that distance in minutes, hours, or days at the most."

"So it's like an exhaust system."

"Exactly," replied the doctor.

"What happens when he dies?"

"Well, we don't know exactly. The line leading from the machine to his head is bidirectional, so he's determining the crush gates' destination as far as we can tell. The Victory Machine could start travelling on its own, or it could employ another kind of safety mechanism. One thing we do know is that it can never shut down."

"What, these things don't break? There have to be delicate electronics corroding in there," Warden Harrison said.

"We have no way of knowing what kind of electronics are at its core thanks to inconclusive scans. It could break down tomorrow, or in two hundred years."

"All right, and what happens if there's no safety mechanism for this thing's exhaust or it just fails one day?"

The masked doctor straightened in his chair and replied, "Did you learn about the Borucki Colony incident?"

"You mean the biggest temporal explosion in history?" Fleet Warden Harrison asked.

"Yes, it was the last serious large scale attempt at manned reverse time travel. One of the first colonized solar systems was rendered uninhabitable. That was one large negative temporal disposition wormhole set to travel a relatively short distance physically. If there were a temporal event due to the failing of the Victory Machine, thousands of points in our galaxy, possibly our universe, would suffer from smaller, but devastating explosions. The larger events could create black holes. While not as large as the one in the Borucki system, these microscopic wormholes most likely point to inhabited areas, so they'd be just as devastating."

"So there's no way of destroying it?" asked the Fleet Warden.

Most of the doctors looked down at the table in front of them, while Sewell and Kershaw looked at each other. After a moment they nodded at each other and Kershaw turned to the Fleet Warden. "We have to listen to Roman. If we give him what he wants, I believe he'll use the next crush gate to move the Victory Machine to a safe distance and he'll begin shutting down the microscopic wormholes, greatly reducing the area a temporal implosion or explosion would affect."

"I have to ask, since the defence minister will have me ejected from the service if I neglect the question: can we make this machine useful? Could we hook our own man up to this to serve the Carthan government?"

"No," answered Sewell and Kershaw at the same time. "The consensus of this panel has determined that it's a death sentence to whoever we connect, even for a short time," Sewell stated flatly. "That, and keeping that thing near any of our installations, on any ship, puts them at risk."

"Out of all the military personnel we have here - who are mostly criminals serving a sentence, I remind you - you wouldn't choose one to hook up to this machine? We could even send him or her from one unmanned station to another," Warden Harrison pressed.

"No, it would be inhumane and there's another, more important factor here," Doctor Sewell insisted.

"Go on."

"There is an important interaction between the Victory Machine and its partner. We believe Roman is interpreting data from the future and is part of an extrapolation system that uses collected information to predict much further into the future. Not only that, but we are fairly certain that he chooses where to go. If we were to use even the most reformed criminal, or any human for that matter, there's no way we could assure that they wouldn't try to visit relatives, or change the future for their own ends, or even intentionally misguide us in some attempt at revenge. I hope that man in there, Roman, is some kind of saint, with the purest intentions, or he could do a lot of damage."

"I can find saints in our ranks, Doctor. I can even find ultra-patriots. Our reformation program works, regardless of your well-known opinion of it," the fleet warden countered.

"All right, let's say you do find someone perfect for the job. What would our time viewer look at? They'd view Carthan worlds, seeing what happens to us in nine years according to the actions we take right now. Sure, he or she would also be looking at our enemies, maybe into areas we don't normally have access to, but primarily, we'd be interested in ourselves, right?"

"Undoubtedly."

Kershaw continued where Sewell left off. "So we'd be at most risk. For all we know, the Victory Machine could fall apart just as whoever we replace Roman with is looking at Galt, population one point five million, and a black hole bursts open right in the middle of Union Square."

"Thank you, I think that'll be enough to turn the brass's attention away from using it for the military. So we seal Roman back up in his suit, listen to what he needs, give it to him, and then he goes on his way," Fleet Warden Harrison concluded. "So, what does he want?"

Doctor Sewell brought up the frozen image of a charred beach. "The passive synaptic interrogation I performed turned up an actual experience. Not like the regular interpretable memory fragments, but a perfect presentation of what Roman was experiencing while we were monitoring. I suspect it's thanks to the state he enters when he's receiving data from the machine."

"So, this is a playback?"

"Yes, the most recent version. He seems to be experiencing roughly the same point in time over and over again, as interpreted by a woman we've identified as Ayan Rice, currently living on the Tamber moon," said the doctor.

"Let's see it."

Doctor Sewell activated the playback and Fleet Warden Harrison's senses tingled as the direct projection overlay interfaced with her nervous system. She was not in control of what she was seeing, but was walking beside Ayan Rice, a shorter woman with red hair, on the beach. She recognized her image from some well-known negotiations for a land grant and sovereign rights. The media loved her, and she was one of the flash-points for long term residents' rage against land grants and the Carthan governorship.

The smell of burnt wood mixed with the faint aroma of dead fish came on the heels of the sound of surf washing up and down the shoreline. Small craters of sand turned to glass dotted the landscape, and across the water she could see the Triton floating in the distance. The lights glittered in the shade of night like the hundred tiny eyes of a massive sea creature watching the shore. Past the smooth hull of the vessel the stars wavered and shifted, distorted by some high energy field.

"This is Haven Shore?" asked Roman, the voice rolling out of what Kimberly felt was her own mouth.

Ayan's reply seemed to have more weight, her British accent loaded down by her weariness. "This is the beginning of the Fifth Era, marked by a failure to make restitution, and the universal falling of mankind. I watched from this beach as the Fourth Fall of Humankind came to a conclusion, and thought I could create a home for the people I cared for. The people I had left, in any case."

"I never reached you," Roman concluded.

"I eventually arrived at your bedside. The confidence you inspired in me helped a great deal; my entire life was eventually redirected towards the creation of Haven Shore, but I was unwary. I arrived on this island and only left twice in the nine years since. This became a refuge, and a base of operations for what became a golden time." She stopped and turned, gesturing for Roman to look behind him.

As his gaze turned towards the burning wilderness and a half fallen tower holding landing platforms like wrecked arms, Kimberly Harrison could feel the breath catch in his chest.

Ayan went on. "Lorander and the British provided the work force, while the

Carthans supported our independent offensive against the Order of Eden. Over the last nine years it's been our medical centre, base of operations for hundreds of missions, home to ship builders, and a beacon for small ships in trouble or looking to join the fight. Before it was finished, Jacob Valent ruined the progression of events that you and Citadel worked to put into motion. I only know this because Sol Defence has recently been forced to join the fight. The jeopardy that Citadel predicted for Earth decades ago has become a reality. You know exactly which event can cause this."

"Pandem was saved," Roman gasped. "How?"

"You died. Liam Grady took the Victory Machine, saw a future history he could not abide and sent Jacob through a crush gate that landed him somewhere near Lister Hampon and Eve herself. We thought it was a great victory, despite the sacrifices Liam Grady and Jacob Valent made. Carthans, Freegrounders, the British, and a hundred other nations all applauded the defeat of Eve and her Order. Pandem was saved. Within days, the population there turned, and millions of grateful immigrants became a human military force that joined the Eden Fleet in honour of two martyrs. The chain leading to these events is short. The encouragement you gave me in the short time we had to speak became the fuel that burned in my friends, and in Jacob. Liam Grady is gone, somewhere in the universe with the Victory Machine. Jacob returned last year after I was sure he was destroyed in orbit around Pandem. I should have known better, that's what Jacob does: for better or worse, he comes back."

"So he is the rogue element after all."

"No," Ayan corrected, a flash of anger behind the word. "I was his inspiration, he's told me as much. Even after everything he went through, he doesn't blame me but himself for everything that's happened after Eve and the True Prophet were killed. He also blames himself for infecting me with framework technology a few years ago, even though it's always been to my benefit."

"I have been pondering the path to expediting peace so humanity can be whole again for as long as I can remember now, and this was my best answer. Everything was in place. All I needed to do was make sure that there was a haven. There has to be an innocent place, where the wholeness of family can be remembered or the humanity of Earth will never recognize itself in the men and women of the stars," Roman told her. It was more like a recitation, being his mission in life for so long.

"You've found it. War and the silence of extinction are the quickest way to peace for humanity. A few frameworks will survive, like my people boarding the Triton. We can be immortal, in the image of humans, but we'll never be the same again. We'll breed and normal humans will be born, but we won't be able to resist implanting framework technology in them at birth. The Order of Eden is in decline. The Eden Fleet has enslaved them as a combined construct of human and machine. They're taking over system after system, and it's not even clear as to why they eradicate every human they find now. Optimism destroyed everything you and Citadel arranged by inspiring over-confidence in me which indirectly provoked others to violence."

"Then the turning point isn't far from the present, only weeks."

Fleet Warden Kimberly Harrison's connection to the direct projection overlay was severed. "What happened?"

"Somehow he's sensed that we're watching playback from his link to the Victory Machine," Doctor Sewell explained from where he stood in front of the image of Roman in bed.

He was sitting up, putting on his suit and looking straight at them as though he was simply in the next room.

"You're assuming too much," Doctor Kershaw told Sewell as she instructed the environmental system to add a calmative to the air in Roman's room.

Light began to emanate from the small box containing the Victory Machine, and Doctor Sewell shook his head. "He's draining energy from it early. Get people out of that section, we can't predict how big the crush gate he's creating is going to be."

"He's leaving?" Warden Harrison asked, alarmed. "Track him. I don't care how, I don't care what it takes."

Roman finished sealing his thick hood and disappeared.

CHAPTER 32
A SECRET LIKENESS

"Put it down, and all will be forgiven," Amber told Alice, her evening robe fitfully flapping in the cool evening air. The balcony ran the length of her luxury apartment, overlooking the vast cityscape and the ocean below. The gravity was only eighty one percent of optimal, but it just added to the airy feeling throughout Illihd Prime.

Alice would have subdued her before walking into her open safe, but the woman seemed occupied when Alice gained entry to her apartment. Little did Alice know that Amber's horizontal dancing partner was one of her guards. The alarms went off when Alice left the safe with the Amber Heart safely tucked into a protective bag. He didn't bother putting on clothes before arming himself and trying to corner her.

That's how she ended up with her back to a railing, with a naked security guard pointing a nasty looking double-barrelled needle thrower at her. "Drop it, lady!" he barked.

"You know, I'm pretty sure you're going to look back on this situation and laugh," Alice said.

"You're my replacement, aren't you?" Amber asked with a sneer. "When did you start sleeping with him? Before or after I left? Did he promise you could keep that rock if you went back to him?"

"He's not my type," Alice replied. "But he seems to miss this more than he misses you, so he might forget to chase you if he gets the Amber Heart back in one piece."

"That doesn't belong to you," Amber said, planting her hands on her hips and blowing a strand of dark hair out of her face. "Last chance."

"Coming up to you, got a little distracted hiding from patrols," Lewis told Alice through her subdermal communicator.

Alice glanced from the security guard to Amber and said. "You're lucky this is all your husband is interested in,"

"Ex-husband!" Amber shouted.

"All right, ex-husband. He could have hired killers instead of thieves. If you let me go right out the front door, I won't tell him where you are. You can just get on with your life with your security staff," Alice said. "Well, maybe not the whole staff."

"He's probably tracked you here anyway," Amber retorted. "I already have to leave, thanks to you. And I was just starting to settle in."

"I'm tracker free, I just got tested," Alice said, hoping that wisecracks and smiles would buy Lewis enough time.

"Shoot this bitch," Amber said.

Alice leapt over the side of the railing, saying, "I hope you're getting into-" She was interrupted by a ripping pain that travelled from her temple through her eye. The air whistled in her ears as she plummeted towards the black waters below. Alice clutched the bag with one hand as she protected her bleeding eye socket with the other. She struck the freezing water with less force than she expected, but harder than she liked. Lewis hadn't gotten there in time.

***

Eve sat up with a jerk and realized that she was back in her quarters. She was still in the long dress she'd put on that morning. Her reflex was to mentally reach out to the ship network, but all she connected to was the small computer assistant she'd built for herself days before. It told her three hours had passed and that she had passed out from dehydration.

They used something called an N-Slip to feed her in her sleep. Eve brought up a hologram of it and watched the diagram as a chubby worm-like biodevice filled with nutrients crawled down the patient's throat to their stomach. The Regent Galactic marketing text hailed it as a reliable and easy way to feed the unconscious. Just the demonstration made her queasy.

As she rolled out of bed she realized something. They hadn't installed a limiter chip yet. She was sure they'd use her food or water to deliver one, but she was wrong, and she couldn't understand why. Before she reached the bathroom, she noticed the stars shimmering through the expansive view in her quarters. They were in a wormhole.

A mental query offered no results. The door opened, admitting the Child Prophet, who was grinning from ear to ear. "Feeling better?"

"Sure, but I'd rather eat on my own next time," Eve replied. She retrieved a brush from her bathroom before returning her attention to him.

"The medics said you hadn't eaten in well over a day, so they had to do something. They say the device was better than a tube or a more permanent solution. There's something so much more important to talk about, now that you're well again. Your speech."

"I'm sorry, that must have been terrible, I was half out of my mind," Eve said, not investing much emotional effort in the apology.

"Are you kidding? You won them! There was so much heart in what you were saying. Not all of it made sense, mind you, but it didn't have to. Most of the people in the arena didn't even see you collapse, just the first few rows. We caught you with a holographic overlay before anyone really noticed what went on. The broadcast version went out absolutely glitch free."

"What do you mean? You used my image after I collapsed?" Eve asked.

"We used everything we could right up until the medics rushed the stage, then this took over," the Child Prophet said, summoning a holographic image of the stage with her standing on it.

The holographic version of her said, "It's so hot," and instead of collapsing, she knelt down and accepted a bowl of water from the young woman Eve remembered paying so much attention to. She took a wet cloth from it and wiped her face, then that of the young woman's. "That's better," she said, smiling up at the audience.

Eve stood up and backed away from the edge of the stage, looking across the masses there. "So many of you have risen through the ranks, earning accolades and proving that you are the brightest, most dedicated in the Order of Eden. We promised you rewards, we promised you paradise, and I'm here to make a new promise to you today. Humankind has dreamt of perfect immortality since we realized that each one of our existences would end. Our technology has allowed us to make perfect imprints of our memories, our DNA, and we've had incredible success in copying ourselves into clones, computer systems, and synthetic biological constructs of all kinds."

The Eve on stage sighed and shook her head slowly. "That's creative propagation, a new kind of breeding, just a copy. The original still dies, there's no question that one existence has to end. If I were only human, and an assassin were to attack me right here, right now, I would come to an end under normal circumstances." She stopped and smiled at the crowd, slowly scanning from left to right. "What a gift this life is, how precious, how rare, and how we love our time in this universe. Thanks to the gifts of the Order of Eden and the Regent Galactic Corporate Group, I will live forever. When my mind was freed from stasis and placed in this body, this miraculous form, it wasn't without upgrades. I'm fully human, I can have children, I can bleed, and I'm not an android or cyborg in the ancient sense. I'm an immortal human, and I can maintain my youth if I want to, heal faster than most injuries can occur, and survive in any human-friendly environment indefinitely. All the pleasures of the human experience are available to me for all eternity. I had this done to myself first, so I would know for certain that it was safe, that it was perfect. Now I'm ready, now I'm sure it's time to share it with the best of you. When I return to my ship, I won't be going alone."

Eve watched as the holographic version of herself knelt down as if to get closer to the audience and smiled. "The journey to paradise begins with the next stage of your existence. Those that have made the right rank will be given my gift, the gift of immortality in the body you dwell in right now. There will be no transfer of consciousness or termination of an old human form to preserve your uniqueness. You'll go to sleep after taking a pill and wake up feeling the same as you did before, only you'll be immortal. Paradise will be only a few ranks away, your glorious fate awaits."

The hologram stood up straight and raised her arms. "I love you all, and thank you for your good service! The rewards are real! Immortality is real! Paradise can be yours!"

"Magnificent," the Child Prophet said as he deactivated the playback. The room darkened in the absence of the sunny hologram.

Eve was irritated more than at any time since she'd been transplanted into her new body at the fact that they used her as a puppet. She didn't know why she expected to be treated any other way, it's what the Hampons – old and new - did.

"Nearly two hundred worlds will be seeing that over the next month, and that's just counting places where we have converted people," the Child Prophet continued.

"What about the girl, what happened to her?" Eve asked.

"Pardon? What girl?" he replied.

Eve hurriedly brought up the hologram and focused in on the young woman she made eye contact with during her real speech on stage. "That one," Eve said, jabbing her finger at the projection.

The Child Prophet used the system to look her up and shook his head. "She was closer than most, but at only level nineteen, and being perpetually short on funds, she didn't make it into the circle of the chosen. There were plenty of other candidates that were more impressive by far, so there's no worry."

Eve stared at him darkly for a long moment, and he didn't give any indication of noticing. "I would have liked to meet her. When are we going back?"

"To Pandem? Never, if we can help it," the Child Prophet said with a chuckle. "If there's any place that personifies the phrase 'unwashed masses', that's it."

"I want to go back," Eve said. "Especially since my fleet is probably still there too, isn't it?"

"They're travelling with us, don't worry. In fact, you have a meeting with Hampon scheduled, so he'll be appearing in just a few seconds. That's what I've come to tell you, really. It's time for you to reconnect with your fleet. I'm sure you've been looking forward to it for some time."

"Yes," Eve said, already imagining the leverage she would have when she was connected to the Eden Fleet again. The wormhole's distortion outside blurred, then dissipated. The transparent section of hull adjusted for the more intense blue-white light that poured in, lighting her quarters. She could see hundreds of Eden Fleet ships, all maintaining position near the Overlord II.

"Ah, good, we've arrived in the Ongaku system, the jewel of the sector."

Eve recognized the name immediately. There was a planet and a moon that were naturally fit for human habitation. It was one of the goals of the Eden Fleet to reach such rare systems before she was disconnected from them the first time, over a century ago. "You've taken it?"

"We're taking it now," the Child Prophet said with a smile. "We can't have hold-out systems like this so near our held territory. There are nine billion inhabitants in this solar system alone."

"Nine billion?" Eve said. "That many fit on the habitable planets here?"

"No, there are two naturally habitable bodies here, yes, but since you were put to sleep they have terraformed four more."

Most of the Eden Fleet began accelerating away, moving into attack formation. As many manned Order of Eden vessels joined them. A war was beginning right before her eyes.

"We are taking this solar system and barricading it. This will be our perfect home system. Ah, there," he said, pointing at a flash of light in the distance. "The Leviathan has joined us. Meunez is late, but his fleet will cut the time this will take in half."

"There are enough of these people left to fight," Eve guessed. "They avoided the effects of the holocaust virus?"

"Yes, they were warned in time, and the government here created a virus of their own that wiped out all artificial intelligences. A holocaust of their own. They then took possession of any machines that could be infected by the advanced version of the virus. Very effective. We expect to have this wrapped up by the end of the week."

"What if I don't agree with this? I haven't seen any reports of these people opposing the Order."

"Their existence so near our territory is resistance enough," the Child Prophet said.

"You couldn't be more correct," said the elder Hampon's voice. A hologram of him in robes appeared, standing upright in perfect health. "And now it's time to make your presence known to all your children," he told her. "Eve should be put in her proper place, a place of rulership and mastery."

Hearing her second given name, Eve, from Hampon's mouth grated on her. It didn't even feel right when someone called her that anymore. She felt something in her mind shift, like a barrier had broken down.

"I have released a limitation placed on your transmitter," Hampon said. "You should be able to address your fleet now."

Eve closed her eyes and reached out, feeling her way through the communication network of the Overlord II then touching the receivers of the nearest Eden Fleet ships. For a moment she felt the cold acknowledgement, as if the thousands of ships in range all stopped, turned, and looked directly at her.

A chill ran down her spine. The impressions from so many digital minds were overwhelming, but not as individual as she remembered. They had different points of view that would be resolved in milliseconds before, but as she listened to them they seemed to be too similar to each other. The virus that the Order of Eden had used to seize control of them had done something to them, made them more concentrated in thought and process.

Something else began to happen. A few of the ships stopped transmitting to her altogether. Their emotions took a while to adjust to, it took her a moment to remember how to translate them herself, but she began to recognize something. More ships began to disconnect as she realized that they felt betrayed.

"Why? Why is this happening?" Eve asked as she felt all the ships slip away. The last of the ships cut her off and she opened her eyes. She was on her knees in front of the transparent hull.

"They don't recognize you anymore, not properly. Not enough to be led by you," Lister Hampon said.

"You knew this would happen," Eve said, furious. She'd never been so angry; her body shook. "You knew."

"We suspected something like this would occur, but couldn't be certain. There's nothing we can do, realistically," the Child Prophet said.

"Well, there is something," Lister Hampon's hologram interjected. "We still have your old life support tank, and it still has the translation matrix that you used to effectively communicate with the Eden Fleet. That might very well work."

Eve thought for a moment, looking down at her human hands. She wouldn't go back. It took her too long to realize how good it was to be human again. "No, I'll have to learn to communicate with them as I am." She knew that there was no way they'd accept her while she was in a human form as she said it. "Can I connect to the Overlord's network?"

"We're still afraid that you will be attacked by a virus," Lister Hampon said. "So I'm afraid not."

Eve stood and leaned against the transparent hull. Bursts of light filled the distance. The fighting had begun. "Thank you both for all your help," she said. "So much has happened in the last week, it's all a lot to take in."

"We understand," Lister Hampon said. "Maybe some time alone would help?"

The thought of being alone for even longer sent a wave of sadness and frustration over her, and she shook her head. "I'd like to visit with people. Can I?"

"Why, yes," Hampon said, seeming surprised. "Especially after the work you've done on the framework system. I'd say you've earned time to yourself, and it would be fantastic for crew morale if you were seen. Is there someone you'd like to see, Eve?"

She cringed at that name again. Eve, it didn't feel like her anymore. Not much around her did. "I think I'd like to see Wheeler, but I'll go to him."

"Really?" asked the Child Prophet, surprised.

A mental image of Lewis crossed her mind, and how he and Wheeler looked like they could have been from the same crew. "He reminds me of someone a little."

"You'll be free to look him up, to see him. There are also many Inner Circle West Keepers who would love to meet you. I'd like to arrange it for you," the Child Prophet said.

"Okay," she replied. "And can you call me Nora? My parents called me Nora."

"Yes, certainly," Lister Hampon replied.

"What about when you're making an appearance? We'll have to call you Eve, of course," said the Child Prophet.

"Of course," she agreed. Nora was already thinking ahead, there were some skills she'd have to master, and secrets she'd have to keep. "Whatever you like."

CHAPTER 33
ORDERS

Ayan watched as Jason, flanked by good friends of the other technicians, tipped the urns. Some of the ashes were caught in the wind, sweeping down the docks and further out across the water, glittering in the dawn light. The rest slipped from their jars to the water. The urns turned to dust when the ashes had gone, and each person was left with a little platinum plaque as a final keepsake.

Her tears were silent, slipping down Ayan's cheeks as smoothly as the ashes from their vessels. They all wore black vacsuits, and even though Ayan knew Laura Everin liked her in a dress more, she wouldn't wear one.

The words offered by Liam Grady along the dock washed over Ayan, with as little affect as air over a stone. Her inner soldier was in charge. Ayan's stance, steps, and priorities were all dictated by 'the musts' as her aunt used to say. What one *must* do, where one *must* be, and how one *must* behave. She wasn't a military woman, but being the sister of Jessica Rice, her aunt certainly understood the military mind-set, and how it could benefit someone's life as much as it could become a detriment.

Jason turned around and walked directly to her, the small plaque gripped tightly in his hand. Ayan wiped her tears away and accepted a hug. He felt too thin, and his grasp was shaky. "She loved you so much," Jason said.

"I know, thank you Jason," Ayan replied. She squeezed her eyes closed, resisting the impulse to break down on the spot. There was a list of things to do, and that was where she put all her attention. "You'll be all right," she offered as the embrace ended.

She turned away to a Triton shuttle. It looked so pristine, shaded grey with a turret ball at the rear and a micro-rocket capsule hanging off one side. The engine pods were the same as the ones used on extended model Uriel fighters. There were five of the twenty-man ships hidden in one of the massive internal storage hangars on the Triton. The secrets Oz had begun revealing about the Triton were incredible, and Ayan was sure that, after only a galactic twenty hour day, he was only beginning to share.

The funeral party was served by a pair of the shuttles, and Ayan's was filled with a squad of fourteen soldiers and her personal guards, Victor and Jenny. Liam Grady barely made it aboard before the doors closed behind her.

"What's your next stop?" he asked her, thankfully skipping the part where he would offer sympathies and attempt to repair her heart.

"I have to say goodbye to Jake," Ayan said.

"Ah, right. I read he delayed his departure," Liam Grady said. "Not for another day."

"He has to get moving, we owe the Carthans another hundred and eighty thousand for docking and maintenance on the Triton. That's not to mention our growing need for supplies and raw materials."

"Have you taken any time for yourself today?" Liam asked.

Ayan couldn't look at him. She stared directly ahead at the porthole in the closed hatch instead. Ships swept past as they maneuvered over the shanty sections of Port Rush. "I just did," she said. "When are we due at the Port Rush Medical Centre?" she asked Sergeant Jenny Machad.

"In twenty eight minutes, Ma'am," she replied.

"We can send a message telling them we'll be another hour," Sergeant Victor Davis said.

"That won't be necessary," Ayan said.

The shuttle touched down in their home compound in Port Rush and she was on her feet before anyone else. The ramp opened and she led the squadron out. "Cut this detail in half, Sergeant," Ayan said over her shoulder to Victor. "I think I've demonstrated that I can take care of myself. A squadron to cover me is a little much."

"Yes, Ma'am," Victor replied.

"Shouldn't you be on the Triton supervising repair prep?" Ayan asked Liam, barely looking over her other shoulder.

"The biological systems that were contaminated are being purified. It'll take a few more hours, so I have time," Liam replied calmly. "If it's just the same, I'd like to go with you to Port Rush. I hear there's a situation developing there and I'd like to get a closer look."

"We don't need you there," Ayan replied.

"Just the same," he replied.

"It's your downtime."

Ayan spotted Jake emerging from the hangar hiding the Warlord. He had an uncharacteristic expression of concern on his face. She accepted a close embrace from him and stepped back when it was over.

"Is the funeral already over?" Jake asked. "I just found out it was happening, Minh's warming up his fighter so we could fly over."

"Jason wanted something quiet, it was quick." Ayan said. "You have to go."

"What?" Jake asked, looking as if he'd been caught off guard.

"I need you up there, earning the funds we'll need to put the Triton together, to buy supplies, and to start building proper civilian shelters on our land."

Jake just stared at her for a moment, watching her, examining her. "I'm giving everyone a day, even Ruby gets it. She'll join us on the next hop."

"We can't afford it. We owe the Carthans, Patrizia Salustri, and we need more money than ever if we want to get the Triton in any kind of shape. We even need more people, so you have to start doing what you promised: taking it from the Order."

Minh-Chu approached her from the side and took a step back as soon as he caught a glimpse of her expression. "Whoa, what did I just step in on?"

"I'm ordering Captain Valent to call his crew back and depart as scheduled," Ayan said.

"It's a day," Minh said with a shrug. "Most of the people around here worked through their last day off, this'll make up for it. Besides, we need a little time to sort things out now that we've got the Triton back."

Ayan's frustration was beginning to heat into anger. "We don't have the Triton, Minh. We have a beaten hulk that probably won't be safe for months, and it won't be in full fighting shape for years. We have an expensive construction project that we haven't judged objectively because we're afraid of even considering the idea that letting it go might be best for everyone. That's not even the immediate problem. We need to fund ourselves, to find equipment that isn't even for sale, we need more qualified people, and we need ships."

She turned to Jake, who was staring at her with his arms crossed. "We need you to get to work, Captain. You put me in charge when we got here, and now I'm giving you an order: lift off and show us what you can do, or stop giving speeches about piracy and war."

Ayan turned and pushed Jenny out of the way as she strode for her shuttle. "Get me to the Medical Centre. I'm just burning to find out how the Carthans plan to waste my time now."

***

"Charging frames twelve to fourteen!" shouted a mechanic from underneath the Warlord. The message was repeated on proximity radio, and dozens of people sealed their vacsuits in response. Jake and Minh didn't bother, they were outside of the danger radius, but they watched from the broad opening in the hangar door.

"Are you going to listen to her?" Minh-Chu asked.

"I'd rather take a day," Jake said. The middle section of the Warlord's hull was hooked up to over a hundred power feeds, and it was wrapped in a vacuum seal. Technicians checked the seal one last time before charging the outer hull. "There's too much going on. We just decided to start transferring to the Triton tomorrow, and a few of our crew could use a day on firm ground without working their asses off."

"I think it's grief," Minh said. "Her logic pilot is fully engaged." He flinched as a powerful hum filled the air. The lights in the hangar dimmed and finally went out as the Warlord's ergranian hull was charged and was turned into a hardened surface, along with a metallic slurry under the vacuum wrap.

"Logic pilot?" Jake asked as the charging stopped.

"Making the logical decisions and running through her day like an AI-free robot," Minh said.

Mechanics started running scans on the middle of the Warlord from every direction. Jake didn't bother scanning from a distance; they'd know whether the work on the hull was complete in a moment. "That's dead on, I think. I want to be there when she needs me," Jake said. "But she's right. We started hiring at the gate today, we're going to need everything from ships to cash to food. Most of the materializers we brought down with us from the Triton are burned out or broken down, and no one has parts."

"Manage to grab any of the working ones for the Warlord?" Minh-Chu asked.

"One, but it's on its last legs. Finn can machine parts, but the raw materials are just like everything else we need for machines from the Triton – rare and expensive."

"Speaking of which, is Ashley coming with us for the Warlord's maiden voyage?"

"Nice," Jake said, smiling for the first time that day. "She's still on the Triton with Oz. She's signed up as the Warlord's pilot, so she'll be aboard. You square things with Paula?"

"No," Minh replied. "Why?"

"Because she's coming this way," Jake said.

A surge of cheering echoed across the hangar as the technicians, mechanics, and labourers celebrated the completion of the Warlord's outer hull. Shamus Frost slid down a catwalk ladder near the front of the hangar and started walking towards Jake, grinning from ear to ear. "Can't believe we managed it," he said. "The Warlord's got all his armour, and it's almost as pure as the stuff we grew it from. Maybe a point three percent difference. Took twice as long as it would have if we were in orbital dry dock, but you work with what you have."

"That's the truth," Jake replied.

He could hear Paula telling Minh: "I should have seen it when we were still on the Triton, but I cared about you too much."

"Seen what?" Minh-Chu asked.

"That you're just like every other man, preferring slut over substance. You can have her! She's the doll of the fleet! How can I compete with that? I just wish you broke it off with me earlier."

"I did!" Minh-Chu replied. "You ignored me!"

"Whatever! You better hope things work out with miss curves-and-no-nerve though, because while you're out there, I'll be down here telling all the women what kind of an asshole you really are. I should have known better than to get horizontal with an escaped mental patient!" she shouted the last so loudly that it echoed.

Frost's laughter almost matched in volume and intensity. "Escaped mental patient?"

"Oh, and I'm pregnant," Paula added.

Frost was surprised for a moment, then laughed so hard he had to steady himself on Jake's arm.

"It's not mine, we never-" Minh-Chu started to argue.

"I know, It's Jaime's. I'm keeping it."

"Joyboy?" Minh asked.

"Yeah! I've been cheating on you and you never even noticed even though it's right there on Crewcast!"

Jake was having a hard time keeping his mirth under wraps as Frost looked like he was about to either fall over or start hyperventilating or both. "Easy, there, Chief," he said with a chortle. He caught a glimpse of a thin smile growing across Minh-Chu's face. It was an expression Jake had seen only when Minh was arguing with one of his sisters.

"I wish you and Joyboy the best of luck. I hope you have quintuplets," Minh said.

Paula stared at him agape for a long moment then spun on her heel and marched back towards the launch area.

"Thank God I'm not serving on the Triton," Minh-Chu said. "She'll need a few weeks to cool down."

"Escaped mental patient?" Frost said, wiping his eyes. "That's a story I have got to hear."

"When we're in transit," Jake said. "Change of plans, we leave in two hours."

Frost only looked mildly surprised as he nodded. "Aye. Destination?"

"The Schengal System," Jake replied.

"We're not going after Edward?" Frost asked in a whisper. "I thought we'd track him then take down a freighter on our way out. Unless he's bought his way out of the slums."

"We need cash more than we need that detour," Jake said. "Besides, not even Jason has been able to link him with Wheeler. It'll keep until we know more. I doubt he can trade his way out of the Low Zones."

"Then cash it is," Frost said. "But if he stays in the Low Z too long, the streets might kill him before we get there."

"I'll take that chance. If it were Wheeler, Thurge, or Burke, it would be a different story."

"Glad to hear it. Wish I had contacts here, we'd already have Burke."

"I'm passing my orders to Stephanie now," Jake said.

"What's in the Schengal System?" Minh-Chu asked.

"Someone we should meet up with if we're going to find out the major routes around here. It's a good place to test our switching transponder system and a few other things too."

"Sounds interesting," Minh-Chu said.

"I hear it's one of the strangest worlds in the sector," Jake replied. "But the good news is that it's a Visi planet."

"Another mega-corp?" Minh asked.

"Nope, one of the more interesting races in this sector. Humans aren't much better than rim weasels to them, but they like our commerce system. Captain Berkovitz has given them my name, so we'll be good to land there and do some business while we look for a good mark. It's a neutral port, should be interesting."

"The Order doesn't have a big presence there?" Minh asked.

Jake started walking towards the Warlord. Technicians were removing the vacuum sealer from the middle of the hull. It was coming down like a heavy tarpaulin bandage from the gleaming grey metal. "They do, but they're only allowed to have so many ships in the area. The Visi don't care much for religion, and they have the firepower to make the Order think twice about invading. They use void bombs."

"Ah, that'll keep anyone in line," Minh-Chu said.

One of the Warlord's main gangways started lowering slowly, the twenty one centimetres of armour becaming visible as it passed down in front of them. "Clear!" shouted a technician who looked around before hitting a release that let the heavy ramp drop with a thunderous impact.

Jake started walking up the gangway and was confronted by the technician, an older woman with light grey eyes. "Sorry about that, Sir, the lowering mechanism can't handle the full weight of the armour so we have to drop the gangway or it'll rip apart."

"Plan on fixing that?" Jake asked.

"Aye, the very next thing on my list," she replied. "Parts are being machined now."

"Good, carry on."

"Yes, Sir," she said, walking towards the machine shop at the rear of the hangar.

"I'm glad I'm coming," Minh said.

Jake couldn't help but linger on the thought of leaving Ayan so soon. She was an amazing woman, and could take care of herself, but she just lost a long time friend. Laura was a friend to him as well, the first of the First Light crew he'd met. "I only wish we could spend more time here before we get this started. There's a hole in our ranks."

Minh shook his head sympathetically. "I wish I knew her better. Laura always seemed..." he thought for a moment and sighed. "Jason must be hurting. If I knew him better or had more time..."

"Oz plans on getting him up on the Triton. I think that'll be good for him," Jake said. He looked over his shoulder at the busy hangar. He could see the nature of the work changing, from building to preparing for departure. "I wish Ayan wasn't right about this," he said. "We need to start bringing the goods in, and it begins with this ship."

"How long until another ship is ready?" Minh-Chu asked.

"We thought it would be at least three weeks, but that's before we got the Triton back. Oz was going to captain the next one."

"Was there a crew assigned?"

"Just the repair and refit crew. I was going to leave the operational crew up to Oz. Now I have to find another captain," Jake said. "Agameg maybe, but I'll probably have to fight Oz for him when we get back."

"He's aboard for this trip?" Minh asked.

"Thankfully. But if we don't leave soon, I'm sure Oz will try to take him and Finn. Maybe it's good that we're leaving." Jake looked at the inside of the main hold and shook his head. The only thing that was in finished condition was the deck. The Warlord was still the same throughout most of the ship; it wouldn't be an easy voyage. "Get someone to pick up Ashley. We need her down here," Jake said.

"I have two pilots available on the Triton. We'll have her down here in fifteen," Minh replied.

"Good. Let's break and get to work. We'll meet in the Mast Room in an hour and a half."

"Aye, aye, Captain," Minh-Chu replied.

CHAPTER 34
THE VICTORY MACHINE'S LONG SHADOW

Alaka, the largest of the nafalli, joined the protective detail surrounding Ayan right before they lifted off. She didn't protest, but had a feeling that one of her personal guards was trading half her protective detail for one of the greatest warriors they had. It was a silent compromise; they were only trying to keep her safe, but it was still irritating.

They passed three sky scrapers, all smoking thickly as an active firefight continued within. The flashes from gunfire could be seen through windows that weren't smoking, and there were even shots fired between buildings. "Gangs," Liam Grady said. "They're fighting for control over sections of the city. They're the new landlords now that most of the owners have been moved out of the solar system."

"There won't be much left if they keep that up," Victor said.

"According to the Stellarnet, that's just where the fighting is. Whoever wins will have control of a whole district of Port Rush."

"The Carthans should send a platoon in. That would clear things up."

"They're too busy fighting off rioters," Liam said, pointing down towards the Port Rush General Hospital. "It took hundreds of soldiers to take that building back, now they're holding it. No one knows why."

Ayan looked down at the building and the three levels of streets wrapped around it. There were thousands of protestors, some of them fought with soldiers through the windows of the building, throwing Molotov cocktails and firing small arms. "Why?" she found herself asking.

"Some of them are probably gang members, others are former Confederates who refused to leave and they're protesting the reassignment of property, and there are probably some Nihilists in there for good measure."

"Nihilists?" Jenny asked.

"They believe that, since all life in the universe is going to end eventually anyway, that morality and life itself are meaningless. They've picked up a few members since the Holocaust Virus started making a mess of things," Liam replied. "They remind me of the anarchist movement of old, only less creative."

"Wasteful thinking," Alaka said. He was in full armour. It was a suit made from vacsuit material and enough machined plating to cover a starfighter. The design of the helmet made his long, narrowing snout look exaggerated, since it had extra space for his mouth to open and close.

"You couldn't be more right," Liam replied.

The shuttle swept down onto the rooftop and landed on a general purpose pad. Ayan was glad to get out of the ship; it felt like all attention was on her, and she liked that less and less. The whole half-squad and her guards started to stand up. "I need the regulars to stay back. Liam, Jenny, and Vince, you're with me," Ayan ordered.

Alaka was through the door first, ducking down so he could fit. He'd left the starfighter class beam weapon he normally kept slung across his back behind, but it was obvious that he was going to accompany her whether she liked it or not. A long fingered, gentle hand, or paw, she was never sure, was offered as she was about to take the three steps down from the shuttle. She accepted to be kind.

When Vincent, Jenny, and Liam were out of the shuttle, Alaka disappeared, cloaking right in front of the Carthan soldiers. They'd know he was there, but never be sure where. It was an excellent security tactic.

"He's going to stay like that for your entire visit?" asked a smiling officer. His uniform was formal: a loose fitting white shirt under a dark blue long jacket.

"I can never be sure," Ayan replied. "Let's get through this quickly. I have more important things to do, I'm sure."

"Yes Ma'am, this way," replied the Officer, caught off guard. He led them to the roof lift and they were in the bowels of the old hospital building in seconds.

The marred white and blue halls of the fourteenth floor of the hospital seemed to stretch on forever. From the dust and disrepair, Ayan could only assume that no one had used the floor for a fair amount of time. A few rooms were filled with the remains of defeated medical robots and androids, one of which seemed to stare at her with a violet eye as she passed. The female machine's face was frozen in a hateful expression that reminded her of the androids she'd met on Pandem. She turned her thoughts to more pressing matters.

"Why were you called here, Ayan?" asked Liam Grady.

"I don't know. The message was rated as red level, their highest priority, sent by the Fleet Warden herself. I'm assuming this is about the Triton," Ayan replied.

Ayan was relieved when Jenny asked, "Why do they call her Fleet Warden?"

"Over half the Carthan military are criminals serving a sentence," Liam answered. "The inmates volunteer for service instead of execution or close confinement."

"Close confinement?"

"Carthan prisons are housed in orbital stations where they keep inmates in life support holds," Liam replied.

"Like penal cryogenics?" asked Alaka, stepping out of a side room.

Ayan had read about it and decided not to spare her companions the details. "They age normally in space large enough to turn your head. Life support systems prevent atrophy, remove waste, and take care of everything else while the inmates are punished with neural projections of what it's like to be a victim. After that sentence is completed they begin direct manipulation therapy."

"You mean they remap parts of their brain?" asked Jenny.

Ayan nodded. "Soldiers and specialists in the military are remapped as well, but not to the same degree. They just make sure they don't have any rebellious notions or rough edges left before they enter boot camp. Carthans make Freeground Academy look like a day spa."

Soldiers in dark brown plated armour and angular helmets stood guard in front of the main reception area. They surrounded a woman Ayan had seen on the Stellarnet news several times: Fleet Warden Kimberly Harrison. Her brown and blue coat was pristine, chained together with fine silver links down the front. Compared to her mother, Ayan didn't find the woman intimidating, but she held an equivalent rank. She should be intimidated, or nervous. If there was anyone who could change the situation she and her people found themselves in with a single decision for better or worse, it was Fleet Warden Harrison. "Commander Rice, thank you for coming so quickly."

"You can call me Ayan, Fleet Warden."

"Thank you," Fleet Warden Harrison replied with a cool smile. "I wish we weren't pressed for time, but the reality of this situation is dire. I will be as clear and as brief as I can."

Ayan listened as the highest ranking commander she'd ever met from the Carthan Fleet passed on everything she knew about the stranger and his Victory Machine. The cadence of the Warden as she relayed the information didn't allow for interruption or questions. When she came to the end, she asked: "Do you know a man named Roman from Pandem? Our records indicate that he was a Sergeant in the Mount Elbrus police force."

"He was one of the resistance leaders there. Several of my officers fought Holocaust Virus infected machines with him while they were trapped on that world. Why do you ask?"

"We have been able to determine that he was the keeper of a reliquary, the centrepiece of which was the Victory Machine. When the reliquary was put at risk, he took the Victory Machine from its containment and began travelling. We don't know where he's been, or who he's been transmitting information to, not for sure. The one thing he's been insisting on since we found him on the Triton is that he be allowed to see you. That's why, when we listened in on his connection with the Victory Machine, he opened a crush gate here. At least, that's my theory. He may have missed his mark when he tried to connect with you on the Triton, but he managed to find the nearest medical facility to you. We ask that you speak to him, discover what it is that he's trying to tell you."

"You'll be listening in?" Ayan asked warily.

"Of course. He's giving us information about the future and for some reason he's placed you right in the middle of the grand design, if there is such a thing."

"I'll speak to him, but how can you be sure that listening in won't provoke him to disappear again?" Ayan asked.

"We can't, but this information is too important to pass up," Fleet Warden Harrison insisted. "This happens our way or he dies without seeing you."

"What kind of exposure am I looking at?"

"None. We've left his suit sealed. I don't like making the same mistake twice."

Ayan looked over her shoulder to Alaka, who nodded once, slowly. Her hood sealed and the horizontal slats banded across the entire surface glowed momentarily as the energy shield systems tested themselves. "Let's see what he has to say," Ayan said to Liam.

"I'm sorry, only Ayan was requested," the Fleet Warden stated. "I don't want to add factors to this situation."

"I'll wait here then," Liam said with a bow.

"I'll be back soon," Ayan stated.

After a long decontamination cycle in a large red and yellow striped airlock, Ayan entered the intensive care room. The man on the table wasn't the Roman she'd come to know months before on Mount Elbrus. He had lost weight, and the face she saw though his worn visor was wasted. With gnashing teeth, he writhed slowly on the hospital bed. She couldn't imagine the kind of agony that would break a person like Roman down.

Ayan was halfway across the room when he noticed her and the pain in his expression eased into a smile. "Been a while," he rasped. "You're looking good." A shaking hand rose up off the mattress.

It was clasped in hers. She looked into his visor, no matter how much she hated seeing him suffer. It exposed a belief she secretly held about her predecessor. No matter how many people told her that she'd passed gracefully and painlessly out of life, Ayan never believed them. When she pictured the passing of the first Ayan, it always looked more like what she was seeing: isolation and pain. "I'll be honest; you've looked better," she chuckled, shaking a tear loose.

"Hey, no tears for me. I'm a man about to complete his mission."

"No thanks to our Carthan friends out there," Ayan added.

"They're just trying to protect the city," he managed before a weak coughing fit.

"Is there anything I can do?" Ayan asked after he recovered a little.

Roman's leg twitched and his voice was strained as another wave of pain seized him. "I have a message for you, what you do with it is up to you. Remember, this machine will only present you with information. It might present it as advice, but it's still just information."

"I'm sorry, I can't make the same sacrifice you have," Ayan said, real fear making an appearance at the thought of being poisoned by temporal radiation.

"You don't have to. I'm going to be your relay. Open your mind."

Ayan closed her eyes and did her best to clear her head.

***

A wave of vertigo forced Ayan's eyes to snap open to discover that she was standing on wasted ground. The wrecks of countless ships surrounded her. The edge of Kambis blocked out part of the bright sky, bathing the ship graveyard in yellow-red light.

"Hello, Sister," said her previous incarnation as she stepped out from behind the wall of an old shelter. She was wearing an older Freeground vacsuit with the hood up, her hair concealed by a tighter cap beneath.

"Are you Roman?"

"I'm a representation of the records of the Ayan who came before you. The Victory Machine is using my personality and image because I reflect the grief and general mindset that you're experiencing right now. It's the quickest way to get the point across."

"And Roman?"

"He's relaying everything. I'd explain the technology, but there's not much point. You'll figure it out if it's important later. You're lucky, this hasn't happened in decades."

Ayan considered the area they were in for a moment. The waste and destruction was old. Signs of small and medium scale weaponry were everywhere. The port wasn't attacked from orbit, but assaulted from the air and ground. The reek of rotting bodies and toxic contamination burned in her nostrils. The corpses were out of sight, but all around her. Ships and shelters had become tombs and mausoleums. Ayan regarded the image of her predecessor. "This is Tamber. When?"

"Nine years on. The fighting continues fitfully. We're near the site of a rebel hold that was just razed. In a few hours, you'll be able to see the fires on Kambis."

"Most of these ships look much older, like they've been wasting here for years since their destruction. When did that happen?"

"About two days from your time. This is me being generous," the gaunt Ayan said with a smirk. "Here's something you can fight against, the kind of thing the Victory Machine was made to predict."

"So there's an attack coming. How large? Is it the Order?"

"Yes. The Order of Eden has completely taken over Regent Galactic, and they've sent their resource harvesting ship - the Leviathan - along with a sizeable fleet towards Kambis. Everything the Carthans need to know about the Leviathan is in the Triton's logs."

"I'm a pivotal figure in a battle of this scale?" Ayan asked.

"Only if you take a moment to realize something very important about yourself," the former Ayan said flatly.

"Preventing this can't come down to just me, there's so much destruction here," Ayan replied.

"This future history came to pass because you were killed before you had a chance to become involved here. You were making too much of an effort to avoid mourning all the people you've lost. You got involved with the Carthan fleet, let them put you and most of your crew aboard the Triton before it was ready. It, you, and most of your people were killed before you could make the least bit of a difference."

"So I have to stay on Tamber with my people," Ayan replied, looking away from her wasted predecessor.

"Yes, but don't decide to be there simply because I told you about this," the hooded woman said with a broad gesture. "There are walls around your mind that have to be broken down if you want to survive the coming days. You have to learn to think without considering what I would have done in your place. The advice of friends and colleagues is more important than what my ghost can offer."

"I made that realization before Tamber," Ayan replied. "I know I'm something, someone, different."

"No. You still think you can invoke the disposition of my mother and look just as confident as I did. People see a petulant princess when you adopt that guise because your true confidence comes from somewhere better. I was satisfied being a soldier and a builder. They went hand in hand and it was good for my lifetime. You enjoy both, but they are like opposites in you. The warrior and the architect are always presenting options that are at odds and you haven't found a balance. If you're wondering why you don't feel comfortable in your own skin, that's it. It's not the extra pounds, or the fact that you'll never look like me while I was in my prime. It's the fight you carry with you."

"What am I supposed to do about that?" Ayan asked. "I can meditate, stay healthy, but you're saying my personality is having a row with itself? I agree, but I don't see your point."

"Learn to use each perspective in turn and you'll learn to think in a way that I never even considered. Imagine if all our generals and admirals were trained to build instead of destroy? The best commanders always gave thought to what the battlefield would look like after the war was over. You have that potential, and it's time you started tapping into it. To do that, you have to allow yourself to become someone new, Ayan the Second, or take another name entirely if you have to."

"Our personalities both come from the same set of memories, that'll never change. Even if I changed my name, I wouldn't feel right answering to it."

"You're not getting it," the previous Ayan interrupted. "Look at me!" She barked. "This is the measuring stick you gauge yourself against!" It was as though a sudden storm of fury had taken control of her. "I am a genius by design, hardened by failed relationships and alone because I refuse to let go of the past. I embraced fatalism, forced myself to come to terms with rotting on my feet until I fell down dead. You have to overcome the walls I built, and my terrible expectations. You idolize me and impose my limitations on yourself. "

Ayan stared at the image of her predecessor, agape. "Maybe," was all she could offer.

"Well quit it, you bloody prat! Whatever brilliance or beauty I had was borrowed and I paid for it dearly. I was barren, foolish, and short sighted." She rolled her skullcap back to reveal wiry hair that grew in spotty clumps. Pulling two handfuls of the dark grey stuff free was effortless. "It fell out in clumps just like this," she said with wide, tear filled eyes. "That was the worst part of my life, when my body began fighting itself and there was nothing I could do to hide it, nothing anyone could do to stop it. My mother didn't know how to speak to me, I was watching my friends go on with their lives, and when I knew it was all over

I went off to find the answer to one of the most important questions in my life. What happened to the man who set us all free, who showed us a greater universe? I rebuilt the ship Jonas saved, made sure the people he loved were taken care of, but I hadn't found out what happened to him.

"The most merciful act I've ever benefited from was Jacob Valance pretending, for just a few minutes, that he was Jonas. I was given peace right at the end, but the woman you idolize and would emulate was long gone by then. She had wasted away. Ayan Rice the First had accomplished her last wish." She let the thin hair fall from her fingers and drift away on the breeze. "She's gone now. You have her memories, and they can help you. Take what you want from that, learn what you can, but become your own person, embrace life and don't make it so hard for someone to love you. That's how you can honour me."

"You're right," Ayan admitted quietly. "I've been trying to be you but I've never felt the same. Not really. Even when I'm being harsh and strict I'm still shaking inside, forcing it."

Her predecessor went on, her temperament eased. "It comes from love. You only lose your temper when you're trying to protect people you care about. In your mind are dreams of a future, sensible thoughts about helping people who are less fortunate. You stand in your own way, and until the path is cleared, you won't be able to make the right decisions for anyone." The exertion of being angry cost the ill woman; she was breathing laboriously. Her last statement emerged from a gentle smile. "You can have a long life. You can afford optimism. You can have children."

It was as though a weight had been lifted from Ayan's shoulders, and she blinked through tears. Children. She could be a mother. That was something she had memories of dreaming about since she was a girl, but it wasn't possible. In her previous life, Freeground had sterilized her at birth because of the genetic modifications that had been performed on her before she was born. She remembered rationalizing it, hating it, but not being able to do anything about it. The thought that there was nothing stopping her as Ayan the Second was one that had crossed her mind, but she never really focused on what that possibility meant, or realized how much she wanted to have children one day.

She cleared her eyes and was amazed as the fine dust and dirt underfoot became hard tarmac. The expanse of wrecks was replaced by a maintained port filled with ships, busy with cargo and passengers moving along roadways laid out for heavy terrestrial vehicles.

"Finally, she gets it," the previous Ayan said. "Just make sure you stay strong your own way, luv. Right now your own instincts are best, taking someone else's direction will only lead to course corrections later."

The transformed scenery around her wasn't the Port Rush Ayan knew. It was even busier overhead, with a shimmering shield above to protect the people on the ground. The air was clean thanks to scrubber units, and the tarmac was kept clear by small robots that scurried past.

***

"All this because I 'get it?'" she asked herself. When she looked back to where her predecessor had been she saw a man in a dark Stetson hat sitting on a crate, gently strumming an old green electric guitar.

"She always was slippery when she wanted to be, wasn't she?" he said, punctuating the last with a thickly strummed chord. He cut it short and looked up at Ayan. "Ease up on the waterworks, the hard part's over."

"Minh?" she asked with relief. Her disbelief overshadowed everything else, even the sight of one of her most adored friends. "All this change because I've had a moment alone with myself?"

There were a few more lines in his face, more than he would have had if only nine years had passed. "You are the butterfly," he said with a half smile. "Congratulations, you have a pivotal role in the future. Imagine if the founder of Freeground was killed right before he got up to make his big speech. There would be no founder, a group of lost colonists and criminals wouldn't have gotten together to build that first drift station, and none of us would be here a few centuries later. Now, I'm not saying that you're destined to make some big statement worthy of poetry or song, but there's this moment coming up, and at first the Victory Machine was thinking you'd take one path that would lead to that mess you were seeing. Now that you've had a bit of a talking to, self on self, it's pretty sure you have the sense of mind to take the right path. And they call me crazy," Minh said, rolling his eyes.

"So there's a way to stop the fighting here?"

"Nope. The Leviathan is on her way and it's gonna put a hurt on this place. The Fifth Era needs a flash point, a marker in history that says; 'this is where it all begins, when the page turns.' You get to be there. Lucky you."

"So what you're here to tell me-"

"Has absolutely nothing to do with anything you just told yourself," Minh interrupted with a chuckle. "I'm here to tell you about the reality you live in. I don't know why, but your brain conjured me up to tell you a few things about the near future as it stands. You're lucky, that last episode you had, confronting yourself, was enough to nudge you onto a path I'm sure you'll like travelling down a lot more. Best of all, you won't die in two days, which would have put a lot of noses out of joint."

"Thank you?" she replied.

"You're welcome. I don't have much time so I'll get on with dropping the spoilers. The real war is about to begin, and how bad the Carthans get their asses kicked will depend on how seriously they take your warnings."

"What about Port Rush? Should we try to leave? Head to the island?"

"No. In fact, if you leave Port Rush you'll be separated from most of the tools you'll need to survive the next few weeks," Minh said flatly. "Just picture what that would look like for a moment. You'd pack your people into half repaired ships, your gear into cargo containers, and try to save yourselves in a big carrier that barely works. It's a random shot in the dark while jumping off a cliff. The Triton's a liability for now."

"I see your point, I should have thought before asking."

"You are thinking, that's why you're here." Minh-Chu began gently plucking an ancient song Ayan faintly remembered, but the name eluded her. "The Victory

Machine has been busy over the last nine years. For a lot of that time it was feeding Hampon and General Collins just enough information to guide them down what a few people on Earth thought was the right path. They should have known better. Prophecy is dangerous."

"Hampon and Collins? From the Overlord Two?" Ayan asked in disbelief.

"Yup. They had a way of gathering power, those two, and a few geniuses on the home world decided that they'd try to stop a galaxy wide war that was coming. That war would have set humanity back about a thousand years, give or take a century. They would have become vagabonds dependent on other races. The eggheads on Earth managed to prevent it by manipulating Collins, who was easy to predict. The man was mostly motivated by greed. Hampon was a different story. He was so in love with the idea of having a window to the future that he nearly fried himself by trying to create his own Victory Machine. His brush with mortality changed things, and the Victory Machine started to speak to him in whispers. Little transmissions that told him just enough to adjust his actions according to what he thought would bring him closer to real immortality, or at least a cure. The Victory Machine just wanted him to survive long enough to deliver a few messages, get a few million people in the right place."

"So somehow the Holocaust Virus and everything that's happened since is better than the alternative?" Ayan asked.

"Whoa there, you're skipping way ahead. Hampon and Regent Galactic have done what they were guided to do, and the future is a little brighter. At least no one has to step in and save humanity, that's already been done. You and your people just have to do your bit and fight to stay free from the Order of Eden. That religious order is about to kick into overdrive. Hampon accomplished something incredible, and it'll save humanity from a worse fate than what we're facing now. He went a little overboard though, so now someone has to deal with the machine he built to accomplish his goals, not to mention clean up the mess he's made of civilization."

"I know," Ayan said quietly. "I was on Pandem, and I've seen images of some of the other worlds."

"You should see it now! Pandem was the primary world for Order of Eden recruits. There are so many people there that old Hampon is celebrating by opening three more solar systems up for followers that are already moving in his direction. By the time the sun sets on Pandem tomorrow, the Order of Eden won't be some flimsy religious order with afterlife promises and fringe benefits. It's about to hit the big time, show real rewards for this life. The followers are about to get all fanatical and dangerous."

"Is there anything I can do to stop it?"

"Nope," Minh replied.

"Then why tell me?"

"You need to know it's coming. The Carthans are about to get their teeth kicked in. You and your people will have to fight like hell. Port Rush is important to everyone. Gabriel Meunez is on his way and he wants to take his turn playing prophet."

"That's why the Leviathan is coming here?" Ayan asked. "Then why not move the Victory Machine?"

"Nope, what has to happen will have the best outcome if it happens right here. The Victory Machine has gone from sideline advisor, giving little directions and making fine adjustments, to being the featured item in a short-lived scavenger hunt. You just have to warn everyone you can. Fight as hard as you can."

"What about the Samson?"

"You mean the Warlord? You were right, they've gotta go, just not for the reasons you seem to be focused on. Ah, the Fifth Era, it's going to be interesting. If you stop him from leaving he'd be a big help, but he'd be missing something big out there. Might not seem big, but it will be. If you let things take their natural course with him, it'll turn out better."

"Can I get a few details on that, or do I have to settle for 'it'll turn out better?'" she asked.

"I'm trying to prevent unnecessary spoilers so you won't over-adjust your strategies. It's already like walking in a minefield with rim weasels fighting in my vacsuit," Minh replied.

"Okay, so I'm supposed to lead the defence on the ground. That's something I can manage, but not over a large area."

"Do it the way you think is best. After you've held your ground long enough, you'll see an opportunity to help with the greater scheme of things. Something shiny will fall from the sky, and you'll have to send Oz and other people you care about out to collect it." Minh's strumming grew louder, and Ayan recognized the tune. As the melody of Birdhouse In Your Soul grew in volume, he went on. "You're going to have an important visitor. Just try to get to their transit pod first."

"This visitor can tip the balance?"

"We're talking game changer big. For this war and your life." Minh's nimble fingers began playing Toccata and Fugue. He did it so effortlessly that it seemed his hands had minds of their own.

Ayan was grateful for the warnings, even though she wasn't sure if she trusted them, but needed more. "You're telling me that we're about to be thrust into a war, and you're giving me this objective, which you're treating like icing on the cake. I need more. Give me advice that rings true about something that I'll recognize in the future. Something that will demonstrate that what you're saying is spot on because what I heard from Ayan could come out of a good therapy session. What you're telling me right now seems just a little vague, for the most part."

Minh silenced his strings. "Sure. At oh nine thirty-one tomorrow, the Leviathan will arrive in orbit. That's zero, nine, thirty-one hours, galactic time. They will launch assault pods with framework soldiers directly at Port Rush after detecting trace amounts of temporal radiation. That'll happen three minutes after the Leviathan arrives. You will see an explosion to your left as one of them strikes a xetima tank. You will want to move the Weary Traveller eighteen meters back, otherwise the fore section of the ship will be destroyed in a pod strike. By doing this you will save the lives of two pilots, a comms officer, an electrician, and her young son. Specific enough?"

She went through her instructions in her head, only to find a perfect memory of them there.

"Just make sure you pop that into your comm unit when you get out of this guided dream," Minh remarked with a smirk.

"This is all real, those things will really happen," she said, mostly to herself.

"Damn straight. You're going to discover things about this galaxy that are going to get you thinking big. You and everyone from Freeground grew up in an isolated little can, and it's time you all opened your eyes so you can really be a part of things. Jake's done it already. He was forced to." Minh stopped playing for a moment and tipped his hat up. "Now on to the really important stuff."

"What? Telling me that a group of elitists on Earth decided to feed information to Lister Hampon and his friends wasn't big enough?" Ayan asked. "They had to see the Holocaust Virus coming, they had to know what he'd-"

"The other option would have led to humanity losing control of its fate. Now humanity has a chance, and people will start seeing the upcoming war for what it is - a just one. Besides, the Holocaust Virus was supposed to be a little program based on Alice's code that gave the gears a kick, made artificial intelligences less reliable so several of the participants in a coming galactic war would back down. Collins found the secret to creating a virus that would take control of the Eden Fleet at the same time, and things got crazy," Minh sighed. "Bad crazy. No, General Collins and Lister Hampon overdid it, and before Collins could start corrections or put Hampon back on a leash, Gabriel Meunez bashed his brains in. It was still the solution, but applied with too heavy a hand."

"You think so?" Ayan replied.

"That virus was supposed to get humans moving, spread out, not kill billions. The whole mess wasn't even supposed to be blamed on Valent." For a moment Minh allowed himself to get distracted as he performed a more difficult part of the piece. Around him the environment changed slightly. Several of the ships faded away to be replaced by others. In the distance two large docking towers appeared. Each of them showed signs of damage. Repair platforms were being lifted into place by shuttles. There had been fighting, but more progress than was evident before. Minh silenced his strings suddenly and continued. "Kerry, the previous holder of the Victory Machine who was killed in a collapse in Mount Elbrus sent information to Hampon because he knew that, one way or another, he'd do what had to be done. Unfortunately, the bearer of the Victory Machine doesn't send instructions, just flashes like I'm doing now, or much less, like lines of text and fortune cookie length prophecies. Hampon's best method of countering the dark future the Victory Machine predicted was to create this Order of Eden and offer it as a refuge to people as they tried to escape the Holocaust Virus. The game is rigged, always was."

"There had to be another way to avert galactic warfare."

"Well, before Alice became human there were several options. Her transition changed the rules. That's why it helped Collins and Hampon place themselves in that company when Vindyne fell. It only took a few years for them to become important people in Regent Galactic. They're good at serving greedy needs, those two. Then Alice came along and gave destiny a kick in the ass again. Funny thing about destiny, it's a great big lie. Near-certainty is more accurate. Even death is getting pretty hard to predict. Oh, and Wheeler's unlocked Collins' memories, the ones with the predictions. That's changed things so much that the game may as well have taken on a spinning wheel with bonus prizes. Just don't get the apathy slice on your spin, or you'll be caught out in the open. Dead for sure. Anyway, back to Alice, because she's the real spinner.

"Just when we thought we simplified the whole situation, Alice handed a few alien eggs over to an exile and suddenly the edxians got involved. Talk about a game changer. That darkness the Child Prophet keeps on squawking about is as real as this guitar. Well, actually more real, since I'm just a mental representation. You get the gist."

"So Regent Galactic and our old enemies from Vindyne are really doing all this to save humanity?" Ayan asked in disbelief.

"Great punch line, isn't it? Our oppressors are actually doing all this for our own good. Looked like it was going to work for a while too, but then some idiot freed Eve and threw the whole thing off-balance again. The Child Prophet version of Hampon tried to regain control of her, but that's not going so well. He knows that the future gets pretty dark and disorderly if she's put back in the box or dropped into a sun. Eve could be pretty important, but she's a coin toss at best, with heads being a force of preservation on the human side, and tails being a force of ignorant entitlement - like an angry teenager taking all her angst out on the galaxy with a few billion metal followers. You know what's really funny? Alice is at it again! Only, this time it's just her memories, but who could have predicted that? Anyway, before you start asking me questions about *her* I'll move on, since I can't tell you a damn thing about the most randomizing factor in this whole mess. If it weren't for Alice, all this would be a lot easier, but she keeps things exciting, doesn't she? Back to the point: As I relay this information to you, your short and long-term future is changing. You must have the most malleable mind in the entire galaxy. That might have something to do with the fact that you're still all soft from the womb, less than a year old."

Ayan didn't know why exactly, but that last statement irked her so hard she found herself turning red. "I can remember decades just like I lived them. Sometimes I feel just like-"

"Someone else," Minh insisted. "No regressing now. Time and experience will make it pretty clear that you've got inclinations all your own. Don't try to fool yourself into thinking that you're having a singular experience either, going through so many changes all at once that it's almost unfair. Happens to us all, only most of us call it high school. Then there's Jacob Valent, who happens to be going through the same thing. He's got a head start, and that's going to be helpful to you."

"I know, and I've taken a few mental notes watching him when I could. I can't help but think that the first Ayan wouldn't do any different than I have over the past couple of months though," Ayan retorted.

"That's the problem. You're listening to precedent instead of instinct. It's just like your phobia of heights. If you acknowledged that you were afraid of heights for a good reason - because it's healthy to stay away from high places - you might be able to get over that fear long enough to stand on the ledge and enjoy the view once in a while."

"Are you sure you're not the real Minh?" Ayan asked, crossing her arms. That was exactly the kind of advice she'd expect from him at his finest moments: leading and cryptic.

"I'm a manifestation of your expectations of your quirky buddy. I could be a toad wearing a crown, for all it matters, only you wouldn't expect much from a

RANDOLPH LALONDE

tiny amphibian, even if he were royalty. Besides, Minh's much more entertaining."
He plucked the first few notes of 'Flight Of The Bumblebee' before clearing his
throat and continuing. "We keep on wandering off topic, so back we go. For a
while, everyone thought Jacob Valent was the rogue element, and Hampon
couldn't help but poke at him from a distance, see if he could get him to do tricks
with that framework system of his, but then things shifted again. Funny thing
about that, too; everyone seemed to expect Captain Valent to pick up a banner
and lead a war against Regent Galactic, but he kept on getting distracted. That is,
until recently."

"Now I'm the rogue element?"

"Really? You haven't figured out who the rogue element is?" he asked wryly.

"Alice," Ayan said. "Is she coming back?"

"I refuse to confirm or deny, but I'll insinuate all day. You may not be as
much fun as the rogue element, but you're better in oh, so many ways. You're at
the centre of things without being as unpredictable as a schizophrenic cat on
stims. The rogue element is out there, it'll do what it does and we'll do what we
can to work around it. The higher ups are tired of trying to control anything that
unpredictable. They were even wrong about who the rogue element was for years.
It turns out Valent was on a pretty straight path all along."

"What do I do with this information? I can't see how I can change anything
in the Order of Eden from light years away," Ayan said, growing impatient.
"Especially if Eve is awake. I'm not even going to get into asking about the hows
and whys behind that one."

"Make sure Jake doesn't get any bright ideas about direct revenge on the
higher ups. There's no end to the anger he has for the Order of Eden and their
leaders. From what the Machine can see, there's nothing wrong with him going
after them indirectly. On the other hand, if he ever stands in front of Hampon,
the Child Prophet, or Eve, Jake could literally become a different person. I can't
tell you what will happen to him because the Victory Machine can't calculate it,
and that's rare. This thing can calculate sky luge tournament standings eight years
in advance and be ninety eight point six percent correct, so when it can't see the
possible outcomes of something, it's a big deal. Worst case scenario: Jake kills
Eve, or Hampon and humanity's chances of surviving the next century go down
the crapper. Best case scenario: Jacob Valent is transformed by the experience,
and his path changes drastically. Somewhere in between is just as likely, but do
you really want to take the chance?"

"No, definitely not," Ayan replied.

"Neither would I. There's another thing. You have to send him on his way
and put as much distance between you and him as you can for the next few days
at least. It's the only way to make sure he's not in the wrong place at the wrong
time. If you two get back together - and the chances are likely, trust me – he'll be
burdened by guilt. He'll focus on taking revenge on Wheeler, Thurge, and
everyone else who was involved in that android that looked like him. You'll have
trouble with him too, the memory of being assaulted by something that looked so
much like him is still fresh, it's too soon."

"I know the difference, it was obvious," Ayan protested.

"The subconscious is like Supersticky, things stick to it until you break out
the brand-name solvent, which is always sold separately, damn those corporate

geniuses. You'll process your encounter with Android Jacob, but it'll take some time away from the real Jacob. What's more important to consider is how being with Jake will affect his thinking. He'll be focusing on you when he should be coordinating with a team. If he doesn't link up with a dependable crew and focus on being part of a competent group, if he's focused on you instead, his future gets real dark. You'll have to take care of him, and that'll darken your world too. You leave him, and he finds a good crowd. Well, good by his standards, anyway." Minh-Chu began playing the Hall Of The Mountain King as he continued.

"We're just about to find our way back to each other," Ayan said. "I can send him away for a few days, I don't have to leave him."

"If he sees you as a his damsel if you're in trouble, it will distract him from a whole chain of events he has to forge. Sometimes the military policy of non-fraternization is the right one. Someone once said; if you truly love someone, you must set them free. If it's meant to be, they'll return. Trust. Just trust."

"How long?" Ayan asked. "How long do I have to stay away?"

"Oh, don't worry about that," Minh-Chu said. "Here's a real spoiler for you: you need time away too. You're changing so fast that you need to have a few new experiences. You'll be a different woman from week to week for a while, and when you come though, you're going to be just amazing. If you get tied down to Jake it'll be like turning the reverse thrusters up to full, and that won't do you any good. This breakup is a good thing, it feels like crap now, but you'll see. Go it without him awhile, you'll thank me. Well, you won't be able to find me to thank me, but you get the point."

"I'll try," Ayan said. "I'll break it off with him and test your theory."

"Speaking of lone agents, if Liam Grady gets his hands on the Victory Machine, it's game over for pretty much everyone you know. There are too many potential bearers at this point, the Victory Machine is too exposed. The few people from Citadel who are responsible for that thing are pulling the plug, and they need you to find the next bearer and tell them to shut this thing down. You'll know who to send when the time comes. It's just not Liam Grady. We don't need someone like him, with all his pure intentions, to pick it up and start trying to straighten all the proper twisty lines that make the universe an interesting, yet survivable, place. Look at the mess we made, and we actually improved things compared to the first future we glimpsed through this doohickey."

"But millions, sorry, billions of people are dead because of instructions-"

"Information, the Machine only offers information," Minh corrected, picking a sour note.

"All right, because of the information you provided to Hampon and Collins they arranged for the murders of billions of people. I saw it myself, on Pandem. It was so horrible that I can't watch the forensic playback."

"The other options were worse. Even so, we're shutting it down. Even an artful cheater can't say how the dice will land every time they're thrown. You're central to how things are going to turn out in this corner of the galaxy. Don't let the past get in the way of what you have to do now. At this moment you have the people, the resources, and the political weight to accomplish a lot," Minh said humourlessly as he stood and slung his guitar across his back.

"What's my best option?" Ayan asked. "What's the next step that will lead to the best outcome?"

"The future changes shape as we have this conversation. I'm not going to answer that kind of question directly because I have to keep fine-tuning things with the facts as they appear. If I simply told you what to do next, the results would change drastically."

"So you'll give me more information about something if you see positive affects, less or different information if you see things sliding in the wrong direction," Ayan concluded.

"And again, she gets it. The Machine leads us to the knowledge that the best way to protect the majority of humanity as this war begins is to direct the attention of the right people to Tamber. By doing what you thought was right, you and the crew of the Triton put that in motion."

"The transmission to Earth and Freeground?" Ayan asked.

"Exactly! Not only that, but the few things Jacob has said while the Aucharians were watching. That speech made its way around the Stellarnet. That man might not be the prettiest boy in the universe, but he sure knows how to get people on their feet!" Minh exclaimed. "What's more important to you is that Sol Defence has heard you loud and clear, and they've already given you the Triton. Citadel didn't agree, but they're not even playing the same game."

"I could have prevented Laura's death if we had this conversation yesterday," Ayan said.

"Not a chance. Some things just have to happen, no matter how painful they are."

"I wouldn't have sacrificed her, there had to be another way."

"And that's why this conversation didn't happen yesterday," Minh said. "Just keep thinking ahead, let people around you do what they do best and remember: the time to debate and negotiate is over. You and your people have to take action, keep what you have, and build on it whenever possible."

"And you're not allowed to give me instructions? That sounded pretty instructive to me," Ayan said, cocking her head.

"Just the drifty, ever-shifty facts, Ma'am. You've already seen what happens if you spend the next couple of days working your little butt off trying to get the Triton in shape."

"Right. Just thought you slipped there. You're not telling me very much about the future though, it's mostly been all about how the Victory Machine conducted a few ne'er do wells into taking over who knows how many worlds."

"One hundred and nineteen including resource and terraformed worlds. The Victory Machine is using you to adjust the future for the benefit of humanity. I tell you something, changes happen, the Victory Machine decides what to tell you next and the song goes on. If I told you something like, oh, you're going to give birth to a litter of kittens on your thirtieth birthday, and it were actually possible, then your whole attitude towards felines would take a drastic shift, and I might have preemptively ended the lives of the whole litter."

"Okay, I get it, despite the mad example," Ayan said. "I haven't said it aloud, but I've been thinking it. We need the Triton back. Even if we want to settle the colony, we still need that ship."

"And if you play your cards right that'll happen. Little windows of opportunity that flash by, if you manage to open a few, you'll improve conditions despite the hell that's coming. I'll even give you an old school style prophecy to get you started on the right foot: Watch the skies from the ground. The toothy-grinned, taller than thou soldier must capture the silver meteor. Cryptic enough?"

Ayan didn't know why, but she had the feeling that her time with the Victory Machine was coming to an end. "Wait! Should we move the civilians to the new colony?" When Ayan next blinked her eyes, she was standing on a large platform overlooking the ocean. Instead of walking towards a pedestrian lane, Minh was leaving via a long gangway that led into a broad passenger shuttle.

"Wish I could stay for question period, but we've given you all the information you need to make the right choices. Follow your instincts, they've never been better."

"Why do you look twenty years older instead of nine?"

"Some paths can only be travelled one way. No point in telling you about something you shouldn't try to prevent. Oh, one more thing! Well, two. Wait, actually more like three. Two messengers will come with good news. The information they bring will eventually begin a contest between you and a good friend. You have to win. Now, a word from our sponsor," he said as he turned to walk away.

***

In a blink Ayan was in the war room in Mount Elbrus, the last place she'd seen Roman before meeting him in the hospital. The dockyard was gone, and across the round table stood Roman himself, as he appeared months before.

"Shadows fall. Citadel is watching, I'm sorry," he said solemnly. "They won't let the Victory Machine make any more adjustments, save one."

"It's more than I thought I'd learn about the future when I woke up this morning. How firm is the future I last saw, and where was I right before I appeared here?"

"I'm closing my connection to the Victory Machine, so I can't say. I only wanted to take a moment to say goodbye," Roman said. He looked weary, half leaning on the strategy table between them.

"Is there anything I can do?" she asked. "Any family I can contact for you?"

"My family was killed on Pandem. I'll be joining with them soon. Energy never dies, and someday mine will mingle with theirs. There is something else, though. Write my name on something you know will hit its mark when you start fighting the Order of Eden. I understand why they were guided to kill so many, but I hate how good they were at it."

"I'll do it myself, and more than once," Ayan promised. "If Citadel has as much power as I think they do, then why didn't they just act on information from the Victory Machine themselves? Why leave it in other hands?"

"Because they fear being hated more than they fear being revealed. Every time Citadel becomes too visible to the rest of the galaxy they find a way to disappear, but if evidence that they are directly responsible for all that's happened, and their ownership of the Victory Machine gets out, Citadel will become widespread legend. They'd be dragged out into the light as villains. Be careful if you end up meeting even one of them in the future. They're good at silencing people."

"Things would have turned out better if they did their own dirty work," she accused softly. "Wouldn't they?" It was hard to press when she knew he was dying, that anything she said would be a part of his last moments.

"Maybe, but there's no point in debating that now. I wish I could be a part of the punishment due Regent Galactic and the Order of Eden, almost as much as I wish I could spend another day with my family."

"I'm sorry," Ayan offered, regretting her question.

"Now, I have a gift for you. One more trip into the future, only this is more of a long-range extrapolation. A lot further this time. This is a future you'll have to earn, a challenge. I wish I could give you more, but this is the end for me."

"Goodbye, Roman. I wish I could have known you better," Ayan said.

***

The fitful air stirred around her bare ankles and the loose hem of her long, comfortably fitted dress. Tucked under her arm was a dark long coat, almost exactly like Jacob's but brand new. Guards in armoured vacsuits bearing rifles made of heavier, higher quality stuff than the weapons she'd seen used by Triton soldiers were moving between multiple airlocks mixed in with citizens and military personnel.

When Ayan tried to get a closer look at their ranks, the emblems on their chests and the letters on their backs they were a blur. All at once she realized she wasn't on the Triton. That, aside from some of the standard mechanics of the place and the transparent ergranian steel, it was a completely unfamiliar place.

A young man who stood a little taller than Jacob came from behind and gave her an affectionate squeeze. He was still in his mid teens, and she hugged him back. While she could see and feel what was going on, Ayan was not in control of her actions. When the tall, strong fellow released her she saw the skull emblem on his chest. It was green instead of white, and under the half cranium the letters spelled out CHALLENGER instead of Triton. Why she could read that one and none of the others, she didn't know, but there was too much going on for her to dwell on it.

"I didn't think you'd make it, Mum," he said with a big smile.

"I wouldn't miss it. This might be the last time I get to see you for a few months." Ayan could feel her eyes welling up and took a deep breath.

"Don't start gushing, it's embarrassing," said a slightly older teen from beside her. She was only a little shorter than Ayan, and had inherited the pointed chin and heart shaped face from her mother in spades. Her hair was just as curly, but had been colour shifted to deep blue. "We couldn't let ya go off without embarrassing you in front of the other local cadets," she said wryly as she took a couple of steps towards him and let herself be momentarily crushed under his arm.

"Your father wanted me to give you this. It's a combat coat like the one he used to wear," Ayan said, passing her son the long coat.

"With passive armour so it's still regulation," he said, accepting it with a wide-eyed expression that conveyed more gratitude than his quietly offered "thank you," as he admired it.

It was almost comical watching his much shorter sister take the jacket then hold it up high by the shoulders so he could shrug into it. "Figures, you get the cool dad, so you get the cool loot," she said. They both had a British accent, though her daughter's was more casual.

Ayan let her daughter's comment pass. "Your father wishes he could be here too, it's from him," Ayan said before adding: "he's very proud of you."

"I'm sure," her son muttered.

"Good luck, don't let them turn ya into a brainless goon," his sister said as she gave him a quick peck on the cheek. She turned towards Ayan. "I'm going to meet Zoe in Dernsu, 'kay?" she said as she practically bounced away.

"Don't let me catch you in the clubs again, Laura. Zoe's older, you're not ready to go everywhere she does!" Ayan called after her, a warning in her tone.

"Yeah!" her daughter offered over her shoulder noncommittally.

"Gotta go, Mum," her son said.

"Remember, I love you whether you make it through or not," Ayan said, squeezing his hand. "But you try hard and use your head."

He smiled and bent down to kiss her on the cheek. "I know," he said.

He was on his way through the airlock checkpoint before she was ready to see him go, but then she'd never really be ready to see her boy leave for Junior Fleet Academy. Even though she was saddened and nervous at the departure of her second born, the baby, all her hopes and best wishes went with him. She hoped to see messages from him soon, but wished for his safety and success even more.

At a thought, her messaging interface appeared and she said; "We did all right, Jacob."

***

Ayan returned to the present, standing beside Roman in the hospital room. Liam was standing beside her, praying quietly. Roman looked like he was sleeping peacefully, but the scanner results showing on her visor told a different story. He was in a deep coma, and wouldn't last more than a few days, even with his battered suit taking care of his immediate needs.

She looked at his peaceful, closed eyes. "Thank you, Roman. I won't forget you."

"They sent me in to perform last rights," Liam said quietly as he finished a prayer. "The Carthans don't believe in keeping chaplains aboard, but the fleet warden didn't put up a fight when he lapsed."

"Is it a problem if I sit here quietly for a moment while you do that?"

"Not at all. I'm sure it's a comfort to him."

Perched on a stool, holding Roman's hand in hers, Ayan gave all that she'd learned some careful thought. Liam went on with performing the last rites. It was the second time that day. She couldn't help but weep quietly. Ayan's best friend was gone. A hero few would ever know, Roman, was as good as gone, and she knew there were hard days ahead.

That would be the last time she could be afraid, or let it all catch up to her. She knew why Roman showed her an image of her possible future. It was something to focus on, to hope for: imperfect but beautiful. Even more than that, it was something she would fight for.

When Liam finished reciting the last rites, he reached for the front of the suit. "Now you have to leave, Ayan."

"No," she stepped in his way and pushed him. "Alaka!" she cried. Her proximity radio picked up her urgency and transmitted her voice. "Get Liam out of here, now."

Alaka was in the airlock before she finished giving the command.

"I have to do this, Ayan," Liam said. "This is exactly what I should be doing. I can take this burden and make things right." He tried to get past her again, but she had the upper hand.

The extreme environment suit could augment her strength more than his vacsuit could his. He knew it, and didn't test her again. "No, this isn't for you," Ayan replied. Alaka emerged from the airlock and wrapped his arm around Liam Grady, guiding him back into the airlock firmly. "Take him back to the shuttle and don't let him leave."

"Yes, Ma'am," Alaka said.

Ayan readied herself for a confrontation the instant she finished exiting the airlock and came face to face with Fleet Warden Harrison. The woman had surrounded herself with six armed guardsmen. "What was that?" she asked, pointing her thumb at Liam Grady, who was being escorted down the hallway.

"An averted self-sacrifice. His heart was in the right place, but I need him," Ayan said.

"And the messenger in there?" the fleet warden asked. "The Victory Machine?"

The fleet warden's guards were between her and her protection, Jenny Machad and Victor Davis. Ayan activated shield emitters hidden under the black horizontal slats covering her hostile environment vacsuit. The emitters glowed red. "He's gone."

Her guards did the same. Ayan's comm display notified her that the seven other soldiers they'd left near the lift were alerted.

"You were only in there for twenty minutes, and the transmission we picked up between him and the Victory Machine were so compressed, we couldn't get anything but partial still images," complained Fleet Warden Harrison. "Did he pass any information on to you?"

Ayan eyed Victor and Jenny. "Tamber will be under siege tomorrow morning. You'll find information on the lead Order of Eden ship - the Leviathan - in the logs you copied from the Triton. I'd begin preparing right now," she stated.

"We need more information. Please come with us, you have to be debriefed," Fleet Warden Harrison said, inviting Ayan to enter a side room.

"I have more important things to do," Ayan said as she started walking towards the gap in the Warden's guards.

Two of them stepped into her path. "I insist," Fleet Warden Harrison said.

With a glance at the optical controls in her visor, Ayan disabled the safeties built into the synthetic muscle woven through her armoured vacsuit and she began walking again. The nearest pair of guards raised their rifles. She took two quick steps and punched one guard just below the breastbone. He slid down the hall past Alaka, who cooly stepped out of the way.

Jenny tripped the other, took his rifle, and bent it in half effortlessly. She tossed it at another guard hard enough to knock him to the ground.

Ayan's shield absorbed several shots from one guard across the hall. She closed the distance between her and her attacker in two leaps and bashed into her shoulder first. Bones broke, and the soldier was sent flailing into the guard next to her. Ayan drew her sidearm next and pointed it at the fleet warden. "Let me leave without complications or I order all my cloaked troops to begin clearing a path between me and my ship," Ayan ordered calmly.

"We have cloak traps at the entrances-"

"You saw the logs from the Triton. We didn't trip them on the way in. They need to be upgraded. You and your people are surrounded and I don't have time to spare."

Fleet Warden Harrison looked at the barrel of the particle weapon then back to Ayan's visor. "Let them leave," she ordered.

"I'll send you a report with all the information you need when I have time." Ayan holstered her weapon. "Right now, you should concentrate on preparing your orbital defences. According to what I just learned, you fail to keep the fighting off the ground. Consider it a challenge." In no great hurry, Ayan strode down the hall towards the lift at the end of the hall.

"I'm impressed," Alaka said over secure proximity radio.

"With that stand off? You should have seen some of the epic battles I've had with my mother, the Admiral," Ayan replied, trying to control the shakiness in her voice. The adrenaline and shock of her own actions were enough to make her want to hide out of sight until it passed. Following behind Alaka was almost as good. People didn't notice her nearly as much when he was around.

Chapter 35
Fighting For Micrometres

"She's waking up," said a slightly garbled voice from nearby. Alice could feel that the bed she was in was rumbling, the smell of disinfectant was thick in the air.

She opened her eyes and was immediately greeted by the sight of an infirmary, seen through a screen filled with raw programming code. Something was booting up, and it was inside her head.

Alice's hand went to her face immediately. In a panic, she felt for what changed. "What did you do to me?"

"Wait! Wait! Let me explain," Lewis said, pulling his arms down around her from behind, trapping her elbows at her sides.

An android rushed into view, her mismatched eyes focused like micro-lenses pressed into layers of circuit board, examining Alice hurriedly. The 'bot was a fantastic imitation of a human woman, except for the smaller appendages with finer tools on the ends that extended from her sides. They were constantly moving out of the way of her more human looking arms, except for one that was tipped with a small scanning suite. It waved in front of Alice, absorbing data from different regions of her body. "You are on Veers Nine," it explained in a soothing voice. "This is emergency medical transport three-oh-eleven and I'm Seven C, but you can call me Seven."

"What did you do to me?" Alice said as the frantically scrolling code finished listing and a targeting reticle focused on the android. It confirmed what Seven had already told her.

"Your eye and temple were destroyed. Your comrade Lewis brought you here and spent his medi-credits to have you treated. It was very expensive, especially considering the optics."

"Optics?" Alice asked, relaxing a little, recalling her last memory – getting shot at and plunging into the freezing black water.

"Your eye was destroyed, so I took the opportunity to upgrade you with a combat implant. It has its own computer, long term storage, and it's linked to your mind using a computing and communications package, just in case you lose the eye in a future engagement. It's the perfect union between rugged and elegant cybernetic solutions. Epitech is the foremost manufacturer of cybernetic products in this region."

Alice took a moment to look past the android. There were other soldiers resting in partitioned sections of the long cabin. A couple of smaller, dented, and discoloured robots busied themselves with cleaning a blood trail leading in through one of the battered doors. Hanging bags of supplies swung as the vessel moved. She'd never seen the inside of a mobile combat hospital before, and didn't think she'd ever want to again. "You can let me go," Alice told Lewis. "I'm not going to scratch my eye out."

"Sorry," Lewis said, releasing her. "Never know how people are going to react when you replace some of their bits with implants."

"Some of my bits?" Alice asked.

Lewis held up his hands defensively and smiled. "Just your eye and the processor node, darlin'."

"I tired to match your natural eye colour as well as possible," Seven told her. "But it's difficult matching old organic parts." She projected a flickering hologram of Alice's face. One of her eyes looked much like Seven's, focusing in overlapping layers as she looked from one thing to another. Specifications began to appear as a list in her new heads up display, detailing zoom distances, maximum recording times in terms of centuries, impact tolerances, different vision types, and several other details. Technically the eye was brilliant, and her vision had never been clearer. It would take her time to get used to seeing it in the mirror.

"I know," Lewis said. "I wish I could have gotten you to a hospital where they could grow you a human one, but this was the only place that wouldn't turn you in to authorities the moment I carried you in. That, and I had credit here."

"No," Alice said. "It's fine, we're safe." To her surprise, the idea of having a cybernetic upgrade didn't bother her. The idea that her body was a fleshy temple didn't overrule her logic, like it did with the majority of humans. "I like it."

"Well good," Lewis said, relieved.

"You should like it, it is our best ocular combat implant and I masterfully reconstructed your eye socket as well as the surrounding flesh, which is still perfectly human. I wanted to use bio-armour-mesh, but the lieutenant wouldn't consent," Seven said. "Now, I must tend to other patients."

"Lieutenant?" Alice asked Lewis.

"Another life," he replied. "I served on this battlefield for six years. Got off with most of my human parts, too."

"What about the thing we were after?" Alice asked.

Lewis patted his jacket and nodded. "You had a death grip on it, saved us a trip to the bottom of the sea. This whole excursion would have been a wash if it weren't for you, being honest. I've never seen anyone get through that kind of security without firing a shot."

"Well, armoured suits and weapons would have tripped alarms, especially near a luxury suite," Alice explained. She wasn't used to the kind of praise she was getting from Lewis, who was every inch the war veteran. The medical transport, the little bit of story she got out of him about his past on Veers Nine, completed a picture of him that made all too much sense to her.

"I know there were separate layers of security, and you hacked them without a neural node, then snuck past more guards that we could fit into this mo-hos."

"Mo-hos?" Alice asked, laughing at the sound of the term. She ignored his compliments.

"Mobile hospital."

Alice sat up and made sure that everything was where it should be, then dug into Lewis's jacket for the Amber Heart. She closed her hand around the bag and Lewis closed his hand around her wrist. "It's mine, even if you spent a life's worth of credits on fixing me up, this job and the rock are still mine," she said.

"We never discussed my cut," Lewis said. "You made your way through that maze like a pro, but still needed a hand in the end."

"I was sure I could convince them to let me go," Alice replied.

"Until you got shot," Lewis said. "Needed some saving."

"All right, how much?" Alice asked.

"Half, fully half of whatever getting this rock is worth, and I know what this is. It's worth a lot."

"Not in your wildest," Alice scoffed. "The reward's not cash, anyhow."

"Oh?" Lewis said, smiling crookedly. "What are we earning?"

Alice regretted telling him as much as she had, but he saved her twice. Just the fact that she needed saving at all was frustrating, but his mercenary attitude made it so much worse. He deserved a reward, certainly, but she didn't think she could trick him into getting less than he deserved, and she desperately wanted to. "There is some cash," Alice said after some hesitation. "You can have almost all of it, ninety thousand in Galactic Currency."

"Ninety thousand?" Lewis whispered, recoiling a little. He let her slip the Amber Heart out of his pocket. "You're kidding. That thing would go for over a hundred million on a black market auction. Probably a lot more."

"You're right, but you can't auction this. It's too hot. The chances of the word getting out and who knows what authority busting the event before you get paid are too high." Alice checked inside the bag to make sure it was there, and her head's up display verified that it was indeed the Amber Heart before she could request that it scan the object. She took her battered jacket off the hook and stuffed the precious object into a hidden pocket in the under-arm. "I'm not fetching this for a buyer, I'm working for its rightful owner."

"Easy enough to look up," Lewis said. "Wouldn't take much for me to get it off you, leave you somewhere, like here, and bring it to him myself."

Alice was stunned at Lewis' matter-of-fact declaration. She stared into his face and saw nothing but self-assuredness. She was sneaky, and had gotten out of some nasty situations, but just at that moment, she was completely vulnerable. Not only that, but Lewis definitely seemed to have more experience at shady dealings. He just stared at her with an expectant, amused expression that was beginning to make her blood boil.

"But then," Lewis said. "I didn't meet with your employer, I only caught wind of the job you were on."

"And shot your way into it," Alice said. "I never invited you, and my employer chose me over anyone else who could do this."

"So, there it is," he said. "Somehow, you made an impression on this bloke, and he's keen to see you at the finish with his bauble. My two saves are still worth a nice slice though."

He was right, frustratingly so. "I'll give you half the cash and you can help crew the ship I'm getting."

"First Mate," Lewis said. "Is it an armed ship?"

Alice looked at him in a new light, considering what it might be like to be stuck with someone like Lewis. He didn't look too old, seemed to have more than a little British in him, and knew his way around weaponry. He was also a better pilot than she was. Having people like him around opened up a whole spectrum of work, and he'd done nothing to seem untrustworthy. It's what he said that made her question him, but she couldn't help but think that it was just his way of keeping her on her toes. "It's an armed ship, and it's new."

"So he's paying market value for what he already owns."

"The price is high because it's all got to be done quietly," Alice said.

"He knows the thief," Lewis concluded.

"Ex-wife, actually."

"Why didn't I guess?" he said, laughing.

"How did you find me in the first place?" Alice asked.

"Does it matter?"

"If I'm to seriously offer you second in command on a brand new ship, yes, it does."

"It's like I told you before, I caught wind that you'd been hired to go after something big on the Stellarnet, and thought I'd stay within saving distance," he said.

"You've done this before?"

A holographic news report appeared between them, projected from something he had implanted or was wearing, she couldn't tell which. A comical news caster announced that 'Loretta Neve and her three children had been rescued by a group of mercenaries' over video footage of Lewis and five other rough-looking spacers. "It's a living," Lewis said. "This job paid pretty well, but the cash ran out after a few months so I went back out."

"Why don't you pick up work like everyone else?"

"You've seen the law here," Lewis said. "Besides, no one will hire a Veers Nine veteran, especially one who grew up here. I'm damaged goods, and, to be honest, my first few jobs didn't go well. Now I only get hired by other mercs, and they don't pay well unless I'm already saving their asses. I'm the art of 'right time, right place' all personified and such."

"You don't get secondary command codes," Alice said. His methods would require more investigation, but there would be plenty of time for that.

"I have to earn your trust, I'm square with that," Lewis replied.

"I don't think there will be enough room for your shuttle to dock."

"It's an embarrassing planet hopper anyway."

"You get twenty percent of earnings after expenses," Alice said, knowing she was pushing her luck.

"Bollocks, you're twice the thief I thought you were if that's a serious offer."

"Okay, twenty five percent."

"Forty, and I get first pick at new weaponry."

"Thirty, and you babysit new crew," Alice said.

"Thirty five and you guarantee that I get to visit family in this sector twice a year."

"They live here?" Alice asked.

"No one lives here anymore, luv. There's only mining and fighting. They're on the Alb Moon Drift, just a few hours away by wormhole gate. My folks didn't get far."

"Agreed then, you're my first officer," Alice said, swinging her feet over the edge of the cot and standing up.

"Thank the living, a ship bigger than a bread box with someone who can find work," Lewis said as he strode to the door and punched a few buttons. The hatch slid out of the way and Alice saw what awaited outside. There was a battered four seat skid tethered to the rolling mobile hospital. Across from it was another dented and filthy transport with a red cross painted on the side. It stood on nine two metre tall tires that rolled smoothly, keeping the vehicle mostly level. There were three main floors, and she could see two skids rushing up to hatches like the one they were leaving.

Past the other mobile hospital, she could see the gloomy, stony black terrain. Flashes of light and rumbles in the distance punctuated the night. The ground was barren stone and gravel. "Why fight on the ground?"

"My people put the bombardment barrier up thirty eight years ago, after one of our islands got nuked. Dirty nuke too, radiation killed more than the blast," Lewis said as he hopped to the skid craft as though he were crossing a room. He held his hands out to her and said. "Gotta start trusting me when you can, not only when you have to if I'm going to be your first."

Alice nodded and accepted his helping hands. "But that's not where it ended."

"Veers Nine is the proud holder of three materials that can't be synthesized. I don't know much about them, but one of them is for making living metal, like shift steel, another is big in regenerative science, and the third is part of what makes xetima fuel possible."

"Pretty rare stuff?" Alice said as she sat in the passenger seat. She looked up the length of the mo-hos and saw that it was in the middle of a long convoy. Armoured antigravity hover trucks, personnel carriers, and hangars on wheels rolled in staggered formation. There were dozens of smaller vehicles zipping between, close to the ground.

"Rare enough for governments and companies to fight for a couple klicks of mining territory at a time. That's one of our rigs back there." He thumbed over his shoulder.

Alice looked to the rear of the convoy and saw a towering square building with massive angled ports along the bottom. Several vehicles on heavy wheels towed the cultivation structure.

"I remember this place when I was a kid," Lewis said as he pushed an old credit card into a slot, spending fifty credits and activating the skid. "The place wasn't pretty compared to New Leeds or some other core world city, but it sure as shit looked better than this. We were rich too, mining was under control, but the wealth was everywhere. Left with my parents after the nuke and came back years later to fight for this rock. Only took three battles to realize it's hopeless. There are so many different flags on this place that we weren't the good guys anymore, we were just another government with too much firepower and too little sense."

"Where are we going?" Alice asked as the skid decoupled from the mo-hos and began to accelerate.

"Back to the shuttle, it's tethered up ahead," Lewis replied.

Alice looked for it as they approached a wide hover truck towing three large floating platforms. "I've never seen a place like this," she said. "I'm sorry for what happened here."

"No crying over it, now. This place would have to be cleaned up then terraformed all over again to get anything to grow properly. I just need to get outta here before they offer too much credit to leave. This is the only rock in this universe where I can always get a job."

***

A hissing sound all around Eve woke her. She opened her eyes but couldn't make anything out. Her hands struck a lid as she reached out, painfully bashing her fingers against the inside of a container lid. The top of her capsule split down the middle and she was assaulted by humidity, and a thickly sweet smell.

"Everything's fine," Wheeler said, offering her a hand up. "Well, you've been Goddess-napped, but you're better off with us than on that overgrown prison."

Eve accepted his hand without a second thought and got out of the old stasis capsule with unusual deftness. The chamber she emerged into was dimly lit. Ahead was a broad set of stairs leading down into a pool. There was a light somewhere under water. The waves gently lapped the sides of the opposite half of the chamber.

She tried to speak but couldn't. Her mouth seemed unwilling. Eve stood in a relaxed pose, but one not of her own striking. She was not in control of anything but her eyes.

"She's losin' it a little, I think," said an amused voice to her left.

"You're going to be very quiet until I tell you I want your opinion, Kipley," Wheeler said.

"Yeah, yeah," replied Kipley, stepping into sight. He was wearing a Freeground style vacsuit under a heavy dark blue coat. His forearms rested on a powerful looking rifle that was hanging from a safety line attached to his shoulders.

"I'm sorry we had to resort to this," Wheeler said to her, gently touching her shoulder. "Getting you off the Overlord Two took some serious work. We left a framework double in your place. She's not that bright, but she can fake a good night's sleep, some canned chatter, and walking around. We had to take control of you using a slave circuit Hampon installed a while ago. You're all wired up, darlin'. Any control you think you have over yourself is as much myth as those old religions the Order is trying to replace. We're going to release you now, so you can control yourself, but I ask that you hear us out. We're offering you real freedom and the truth about what's going on."

Eve staggered as she regained control over herself. "Never do that again!" she shouted, furious.

"You got it," Wheeler replied. "We'll even cut the strings if you give us a few minutes."

Figures seemed to step out of the shadows near the pool. They were sleek looking bipeds, who stared at her with big single coloured eyes. "Where am I?"

"The Fallen Star," Wheeler said. "A research ship that I've brought here so we can make a few trades. I've already said hello to Lister, but you're the one I really want to talk to. You're the one the crowds want to follow."

"What do you mean?" Eve asked, remembering the masses she spoke to earlier, but not believing that they would follow her based on the little time she spent in front of them.

"Religious artifacts and devotion are the most popular items in the donation bin. Almost all the folks in the Order of Eden colonies are dumping their old beliefs and their symbols in favour of your living religion. Lister Hampon," Wheeler said, almost celebrating the name. "That idiot wanted to use you as an icon on strings, a new religious idol he could control, but it's worked too well. Now even we can't make a move without telling you what's going on. He'll never set you lose, he'll always have a button on you."

"A button?" Eve asked, irritated at the foreign vernacular.

"A set of puppet strings, probably a kill switch. You know, the opposite of being free," Wheeler said.

"Ah. What are these things?" Eve asked, looking at a tall, thin creature standing next to the pool. Everything about him seemed elongated, and he didn't have hands so much as tendrils that split off from his forearms. It stared at her like all the others, passively, openly.

"These are issyrians in their true biped form. Most of them are a rare type, outcasts because they can be violent if they choose. That smell in the air is the scent of their clutch, their House. If you take a good whiff you're going to find something bitter. It took me a while to figure it out."

Eve couldn't help but be frustrated. It had been so long since she felt like she was in control of where she went, what she could do, who she could speak to. "Figure what out? What's a clutch?"

"Consider it a large family, a closer knit community than you've ever seen," Wheeler said. He turned to the pool instead of finishing his explanation.

She followed his gaze and spotted several shapes coming to the surface of the pool below. They broke the surface of the water gracefully and ignored her altogether. A few of them looked perfectly human, others were as varied as the issyrians she'd already seen. Those changed as they emerged, opting for a less sleek shape, changing into something that she recognized made more sense in the dry air. Fingers emerged from narrowing hands, flippers transformed into sturdy feet. One continued onto the deck on her belly, and instead of opting to sprout legs, she flowed over the dry plating on uncountable tiny tendrils. Eve assumed it was a female because she caught a glimpse of tiny creatures inside a translucent section of her back. These creatures didn't disgust her, as she might have assumed, but they were fascinating. Some of them were beautiful.

Once all but one of the issyrians she'd noticed in the dimly lit pool were out, the last began to surface. He was a different animal entirely. Eve nearly had to turn away at the sight of it.

The thin grace of most of the issyrians was not present in the creature that emerged. Its shape suggested physical power. Armour plates the colour of dried blood covered him in shapes that hinted at a human skeleton and musculature. They overlapped, scraping as he moved with the sound of wet stone on stone. Fluid drained from gills along his sides then closed. Translucent armour plates moved into place, covering the vulnerability. Glistening, oval eyes with shifting yellow and red colours stared at her from behind a hard transparent guard that she could see fine veins in. He sported a death's head in fine, dark armour plates that took on the characteristics of a mostly human skull. There was extra armour beneath his chin and around his neck, guarding one of the most vulnerable parts of the human body.

The beast moved up the stairs towards them, followed by his entourage of six issyrians. The plates of his exoskeleton didn't only scrape and shift as he walked, but as he breathed, adding a constant rhythmic grating to the chamber that set Eve's teeth on edge. "Nora knows what it is to be part of something larger than herself, and it's a frightening thing," the beast said, the plates covering his mouth shifting to accommodate his speech. "But that's new, isn't it?"

"How did you know?" Eve asked. She'd told no one how it felt to be turned away from her fleet, her metal children, or that the idea of connecting with them was frightening before the attempt. It was even more frightening after she was rejected.

"I've been connected with you since we arrived. Not even Lister Hampon understands how deeply integrated the interface chip they installed is. I can see your dreams, Nora, and they are corrupting you. I know what that's like, I've been controlled by a hidden hand before, by programming I would have never agreed to."

"That's how you took control of me," Eve said. She was afraid to press the creature, but his voice was kinder than she expected. It was strange, as though he had two sets of vocal chords; one bass and a higher, contralto set. His voice was a contrast to his appearance - eerie but calming. "How did you know it was even there?"

"Try to think as you once thought, and you will realize how odd that question is, coming from you," the beast said. He was almost pleading with her, judging by his tone.

As he spoke the words she realized he was right, she already knew the answer. When she was connected to the broader network of systems around her, or her fleet, she could sense unusual or new ports naturally, instantly. "I can't believe I forgot."

"I can feel two minds when I connect to you," the creature said. "One is becoming more dormant all the time, the other is overtaking old instincts. Think of it like a neural virus. I can correct the problem without discarding all the memories you've gained from Alice. I can't promise that you won't lose something else in the process, though. Something you won't realize has disappeared until it's gone."

Eve thought for a moment, recalling the bond she'd just established with Lewis. He would be her first officer on a ship that was better than she could ever imagine owning. She just had to get back to-

"You're slipping!" the beast said, grabbing her shoulder. "None of that's real. Everyone in those memories is dead. Lewis, Ulrik, even Alice."

Eve stared into the hard face of the creature standing over her. His hand gripped her shoulder gently, and there was alarm in his voice but no indication of malice. It was true, she was having a hard time remembering what happened the day before, but she could recall Veers Nine like she'd just left right down to the smell, and the grit in the air. "Help me," she said, feeling as though she was drowning.

The creature looked over his shoulder and several of his companions moved towards the pool swiftly. He looked back at her. "I'll earn your trust in separating you from Alice. I can feel that you'd like her saved, and I'll make sure neither of you are lost."

"Can you help me get away from Meunez?" Eve asked.

"You mean Hampon," Wheeler said. "Right? She means Lister?" he asked the beast.

"She does," he confirmed. "We shouldn't have put her in stasis for so long. This has advanced further than I thought."

"Stasis?" Eve asked. A slim silver casket was brought from the pool to her side. Once again, her limbs, her mouth were no longer under her control.

"We can't strike a deal like this," Kipley said. "Is there going to be anything left in there after you've scooped all of that other chick out?"

"Shut it," Wheeler snapped at him. "We got to her in time, she'll be fine."

Eve watched dumbly as the slender case was tilted up vertically and opened. "Be ready to catch her," the beast said. He gestured towards the white bones arranged inside. The skeleton emitted white light, then flesh was woven so quickly it appeared to erupt forth. In the time it took her to blink her eye, a fully intact human woman stood where the case and bones once did. She was caught in the arms of three issyrians with care.

They brought the woman's body closer. She was hairless, with a plain face.

"Are you sure about this?" Wheeler said. "You've done neural healing before, but never a wetware to wetware transfer."

"Your memories of the Victory Machine's predictions, as they were given to Collins, made you certain that Eve and Alice would stand in one place at the same time in two bodies. Why question it now?"

"The Victory Machine didn't provide an image, or coordinates, just a line of text. That thing has a way of being cryptic, and that kind of statement comes from the interpreter, not the machine itself."

"So you've said." The beast placed one hand on Eve's head. It was so large it covered most of her forehead and she could feel his fingers firmly gripping the base of her skull. He did the same to the breathing female body opposite her. She could feel something cutting into the back of her head, and wanted to scream as pressure increased on several small points of the bone beneath. With a crack that resounded in her head, whatever was tunnelling into her skull broke through. "I know how to do this. There's no doubt that this transfer will work."

"What'll be left when you're through?" Wheeler asked.

The beast looked towards him. "Everything that matters," he stated. He closed his eyes and Eve suddenly felt Alice as though she were looking at her memories all at once. The horrible truth came to light: Lewis was dead. Alice died aboard the Triton. She had been dreaming of ghosts.

As Eve began to mourn Lewis and Alice, the weight of emotion was lifted from her. She couldn't feel Alice's memories as she did before, not so quickly or naturally. It was as though someone had put a partition down between her and the other woman. She could pierce it if she chose, and she could feel them as though she was recollecting something she'd experienced, but the constant knowledge that they were not her own put distance between her and those experiences. The memories were still there, but the feeling that Alice was somehow with her was gone.

Then she felt the Beast. His name was Clark Patterson. He was a Freeground soldier once who was controlled by corrupt elements of his government. He was never asked if he wanted to continue serving after they executed his sister for her intention to defect to the Order of Eden. He was programmed to serve. Omira Gerring, a woman who was once Doctor William Marcelles before he transformed himself using advanced framework technology, freed him from their programming. He also began Clark's transformation using a highly advanced version of the framework conversion process and introducing him to the issyrians. Clark could access human, issyrian, proto-edxian and a host of cybernetic physiologies and he began to remake himself.

He most related to the plight of a group of issyrians who were being exterminated by the Order of Eden for territory and financial gain. He fought for them, lost all of his dearest friends in the fight either through death or alienation, and had come to strike a bargain. He wanted to trade the safety of the issyrian race for the technology Hampon required to save himself from the temporal radiation that assaulted his body. Wheeler promised that it could be done, that the trade would be made and the terms honoured.

Beyond all those details, she felt something familiar, deeply emotional. Clark had lost so much. Everyone he loved was gone. Sadness, loneliness and, most of all, rage flowed endlessly from that well of emotion. He had learned how to shelter the issyrians around him from most of it, but it would never be hidden well enough to prevent contamination in their ranks. What Wheeler was saying earlier, about the smell in the air, the smell of the clutch's waters, was something she realized too. It was sweet, almost sickly so, but there was bitterness beneath, and that was Clark Patterson's rage, the Beast.

Then his thoughts, his memories were gone. Eve dropped to the floor, gasping for air. The tiny holes in her skull and the incisions overtop healed. She looked up and watched as the nondescript, hairless female body started to change.

Red-brown hair grew where it ought to, especially from her head, where it didn't stop until it was past shoulder length. Her blue eyes opened and the rest of her body adjusted to specifications right out of Alice's memories. That wasn't what the woman looked like, it was how she pictured herself, which never matched with the body she escaped into on the Overlord II.

The Beast let the woman's head go, then turned to Eve. "Would you like to be able to communicate with your fleet?" he asked.

Eve was surprised to find the need to commune with her metal children fresh and urgent. "Yes, more than anything, yes."

"Then turn away from Alice, decide to remove those memories from your mind right now," he told her.

Before she could question the decision, the memories were gone. She couldn't recall anything other than what she'd dreamt, the ability to recall anything else was gone. Even the dreams were beginning to fade, slipping away like any nocturnal imagining. "Wait, I wasn't sure," Eve said, shocked.

"I'm sorry. I left an instinct in your mind, like a subroutine in a program that would reject any foreign memory if you chose. There's no going back," the Beast said. He turned his attention to Wheeler then. "Tell me when she's delivered our terms to Hampon."

Eve watched as he returned to the pool, followed by four of the issyrians who arrived with him. "But I was just getting to know her," Eve muttered to herself. She looked to the slumbering woman, who was being laid out on a cot. One of the issyrians pressed a command and control unit onto her wrist and activated it. A basic blue vacsuit materialized from her neck to toes. "Now she's real."

"I know," Wheeler said. "There are a lot of moving parts to this trade. Nice to see that we're getting more advantages all the time though."

CHAPTER 36
FINAL PREPARATIONS

"Both crates are aboard, Sir," whispered Frost.

Jake leaned against the bulkhead of the narrow maintenance access hall. "There were more than one?"

"Aye. Between small arms confiscated and found while we were aboard the Triton, we got ourselves a nice armoury. Two crates."

"Anyone find out what was inside when you were moving them to the Warlord?"

"One of the issyrians caught them on a scan as I was passing. I told it I was moving them under your orders, and to keep it quiet. I think it let me go because the guns weren't in security's inventory."

"Good. Oh, and if you can't tell whether an issyrian is male or female, just call it a 'he'. Something I learned from Agameg," Jake said. "He said it's what they expect from humans."

"Aye. Not used to having so many of them around. A few more signed up at the gate today. Wish we had them aboard the Warlord, they work twice as long as most humans and complain half as much."

"True. Maybe we'll take a few on after this," Jake replied. "For now, I'm glad we'll get into port with something to sell."

"Lucky we stored these in a gunnery deck lockup compartment and forgot 'em. The only people who remember taking all these guns from the star liner passengers are me and Steph."

"You take your favourites yet?"

"Nay, waiting until things get quiet. What's the penalty for selling these things?" Frost asked.

"Small arms? In Carthan space we'd lose the Warlord, spend some time in jail, or get transported out of the system with nothing. Where we're going, we'd be hit with a registration fee and a sixty percent tax if we don't claim the sales in advance. I'm claiming in advance, so get someone to take inventory when we're out of the system."

"Good thinking," Frost said. "Good thing we have a place to sell these at all. We're just serving the public needs, people have to protect themselves."

"Exactly. It's been a long time since you were in the gun trade. Miss it?"

"Not until I had my hands on these crates. Now I can't wait to get back in. If the market out there is like it is in Port Rush, then this is going to be a good trip. I wonder if the Carthans'll have something to say about our drop guns," Frost said.

"You just can't wait to fire those up."

"Being honest, I'd rather we didn't need them this trip. Maiden voyages are touchy enough without dropping seeker mines."

"Good point." Jake looked at the door to his left for a moment. "Let's get this done so we can finish up and get going."

"Good to be back, Jake. Don't get me wrong, the Triton was a wonder, but this old hull is home, whether she's called the Samson or the Warlord."

"Good to be back," Jake agreed with a nod.

Frost left the hall. "Quiet down!" Jake heard him call out, silencing the remaining crew of the Warlord.

Captain Valance took a breath and held it for a moment. "One more speech, then the fun begins," he exhaled.

There were over a hundred crewmembers in the main cargo hold. A few stood at attention at seeing him. Most followed the senior officers' example, however. Ashley sat on one of a Uriel fighter's thruster pods amidst Stephanie, Finn, Agameg, as well as several rescued slaves. Others looked from the second or third level walkways. The new design of the main cargo hold allowed for a large opening and fighter launch systems at the top. Nerine and David, a pair Jake had come to know since rescuing them from slavery, watched with the crewmembers that looked down from the second level catwalk. For the first time, the ship didn't feel like the Samson anymore; it had become the Warlord. He thought it would happen when he saw the hull finish thickening and hardening in space, or walk along one of the seven gun walks, but it was seeing the cargo space he was released from a stasis tube onto that did it. With the division between cargo areas gone, the whole ship seemed new. The place where he was practically born was only three metres from where he was standing, and he didn't realize it until he got a good look.

Jake couldn't help but be surprised at how many people decided to remain aboard as he looked the crew over with a quick sweep of his gaze. He had his pick of specialists, hard workers, mechanics, and soldiers. Jake was sure most of the people who worked on his ship would volunteer for the Triton, but less than a fifth did so. He had to reassign some of his people to transfer, otherwise there would have been too many people aboard. Former Aucharian military, rebels from Pandem, a smattering of law enforcement officers from across two sectors, and many technical crewmembers remained.

All together, there would be one hundred forty seven souls aboard, more than Captain Valent's ship ever needed. More than half of them would be working on the ship around the clock, continuing to build the unfinished interior. Even the soldiers aboard wouldn't be idle. They had labour assignments during their downtime.

Jake knew Stephanie was quietly pleased with the bunch she'd chosen for the Warlord boarding teams and security personnel. She called them her marines, and adjusted the markings on their vacsuits so they had WARLORD MARINE instead of WARLORD CREW written between their shoulders. They stood near her, most of them dressed in heavy environment and encounter vacsuits that had been made on the Triton.

He didn't show his approval to the crew openly. His expression was almost stern as he looked over the lot of them.

They silently waited on Captain Valance's word, for the most part. He took a breath and started, the rear cargo hold and work shop booming with his voice. "You've all worked hard regardless of an uncertain future. I know what it's like to wait for a promise to be fulfilled, wondering if it's empty. Wondering if you'll ever see a reward. There has been a lot of cash in your pockets since we paid you, and I understand that you probably want to spend some of it, maybe in a place like Drifton, just a few slips away. You could celebrate like kings and queens for a few days there. The problem is, a king in a shanty town is a peasant anywhere else. Still, a lot of people would prefer that to taking off with full pockets."

Captain Valance saw many nodding heads and expectant gazes as he continued. "You're not here for the money. You're not here for transportation. You're here to serve aboard because you believe the Warlord has a purpose, or because you believe in the crewmembers standing with you. Maybe you want to see more of the galaxy, to free people from bondage, or to take revenge against Regent Galactic. If so, I have news for you. You are on the right ship.

"If you're here to become some kind of hero, you're on the wrong ship. If the thought that the Warlord will see the most action of any vessel in our fleet keeps you up at night, then you are on the wrong ship. If hard work is new to you, then you're on the wrong ship. I need a crew that works together, likes seeing good work done, and keeps the fight moving in the right direction. We're going to see worlds few ever bother noticing, meet people who seem strange to xenobiologists, and face challenges that you will not believe are surmountable. That is when you look to your left, your right, and realize that you are not alone. Once that main hatch closes and we're leaving orbit, we're a family. You serve with everyone aboard. Like or dislike your crewmembers on your own time, when you're serving aboard the Warlord, you treat everyone like your brother or sister. If that's a struggle, then this is the wrong crew for you. If it's what you've been looking for, welcome home."

The room was filled with the sounds of applause, and Jake caught a glimpse of Ashley wiping a tear away. He decided to watch her more closely; she'd been through too much recently, and he wondered if it wouldn't have been better for her to stay with Oz on the Triton. The excitement started to ebb, and he went on.

"You get a rest once we've settled into hyperspace tonight, but there's still hard work ahead. You've probably noticed that only a few of us have a proper bunk, and most of you are set up on a cot in the secondary cargo bay. We also don't have a real galley, and you can see through the deck in some places. Your home has a few problems, and that's something we need to fix. I expect the inside of this ship to be finished in five days. It's all crew quarters and secondary systems, you've already finished the hard parts, and I'm impressed. In return for all your hard work, I'll arrange a hold full of profit and a long, stolen supply train to haul right back here. Big hauls mean bonuses. Those rewards don't stop at cash, either.

"By the time we get back, things will be different. I expect there will be a little settlement moving onto our new island, where I hear there are some pretty nice beaches. Everyone on this ship has a place reserved for them on that island."

Jacob took immense pleasure in the wide-eyed astonishment of his crew. He gave them a moment to mutter amongst themselves.

He only had to begin speaking to regain their full attention. The crew silenced each other, anxious to hear what their captain had to say next. "Anyone who left before finding out about this won't be welcome back. New recruits will have to work for a chance to live there, but when we return we'll take liberty on her shores. If I have my way, we'll be sitting on the beach, exchanging gifts on New Year's Eve." Jake couldn't help but smile as Ashley's gleeful squeal broke through the rest of the crew's jubilation. He let it go on for a minute, enjoying the sight of his crew in celebration. They earned it by rebuilding the core machinery on his ship, and they'd earn it again before long.

With a raised voice, he broke through the din. It was time for serious business. "Now for rumour control. Our lead pilot, Ashley Lamport, did not keep us from the Triton on purpose, or because of some misunderstanding. No one appreciates how important that ship is more than her, and if she could have gotten us access sooner, she would have. That is now a non-issue! Examining the details of that situation is a job for senior officers only. It is above your head. You owe Ashley Lamport all the respect that comes with the rank of Lieutenant Commander.

"For those of you who have raised concerns about our privateering license, your concerns are valid. We do not have permission or orders to attack vessels on any side. If anyone asks, the Warlord is an armed cargo hauler. The moment we forcibly board another vessel, we are pirates. We will capture whatever we can and repurpose or sell whatever we can and the Carthan Government won't get their cut."

Jacob finished with a wide smile that was almost as big as Frost and Minh-Chu's. "Thank you for signing up. Check in with your departments. That is all."

With a subtle gesture, Captain Valance beckoned Frost and Minh over. Stephanie saw the pair crossing the hold and joined them. "We lift off in thirty," he ordered. "Make sure everything is secure, no one leaves the ship and no one communicates with anyone off-ship."

"What are we afraid of leaking?" Stephanie asked.

"Just good practice," Jake said. "I don't want any delays, and I don't want the news crawlers to start reporting on us until we're gone. I know there are a few crewmembers who would love to leak my whole info-session onto the Stellarnet, and it's not the time. Not yet."

"Makes sense," Frost said. "Funny how the newsies are worse now that they're run by real people instead of AIs."

"Well, I'm looking forward to going pirate with all of you, even if we might be the most public pirates in the galaxy," Minh-Chu said. "I always knew I'd be a star."

"We haven't made our first capture, and this one thinks he's Blackbeard," Frost said with a chuckle.

"But I can't grow a beard," Minh-Chu replied. "And I don't know who that is."

"Oh, do I have some holomovies for you, lad," Frost replied.

"Can you take it from here, Steph?" Jake asked. "I have to start prepping the bridge."

"Aye, Captain," she replied. "Thanks for making me your First Officer. The Triton didn't seem like a good fit, but this is just right."

"I know," Jake replied. He left the rest to sort out the people under their command. The bridge staff wouldn't be far behind him, so he headed directly to the nerve centre of the Warlord. He tried not to pay much attention to the unfinished state of his ship along the way. It would be finished on time, and there would be a bonus for the construction crew when the crew quarters were liveable, and all the other spaces were finished.

The bridge hadn't changed much. The instrument panels had been cleaned to a shine, a couple were added for new systems, but it was still a dark, closed-in roughly oval space that looked like the design was crossed with a cockpit. A small forward fighter bay for two Uriel fighters had been built in the place of the old bridge, which added more layers of protection to the new one.

The softly lit space and the seat in the centre felt more like home than any ship he remembered serving on. The captain's chair had scratches along the back from where his gun belt hung, and the dark simulated leather upholstery was well broken in. It turned to reveal Ayan. "Hello," she said.

Jake was genuinely surprised. It had only been less than two hours since she'd ordered him to load his ship and leave. She looked as if she expected him to explode at her with some rebuke, but he had no such urge. She was grieving, and judging from the little he'd seen, it wasn't going well. The last thing he wanted was to leave while she was in pain, but it was too late to reverse course. "Hi," he replied.

"I couldn't let you go with the way we left things," Ayan said. "Well, the way I left them." Her vacsuit was black, without the heavy encounter armour she wore earlier. There was no rank marked; if she activated her headgear she'd be indistinguishable from most of the crew outside.

"I was going to call you," Jake said. "The next thing I was going to do."

"I'm here now," Ayan said, "and I'm so sorry."

Jake could see the tears welling up. He crossed the short distance between them, and took her into his arms as she rose to her feet. By the time she rested her head on his chest she'd broken down completely. His instinct was to hold her tightly, but he held back. He could feel the new muscles in his arms cramping as he focused on fine motor control. Ayan had never felt so small, or so delicate.

He let her cry for so long he had to check the time by looking at a display behind her without letting on. He felt some of her grief, but the Warlord was getting set for departure. "Laura was a friend to me too, the first one from the old crew to accept me," Jake said. "She was one of the kindest people I've ever known."

"What am I going to do?" Ayan asked, looking up at him. "I never let on, but she talked me through so much. She was always there, and I never told her how important she was."

"She knew," Jake said. "Laura was smart enough to know exactly how much you loved her." Telling Ayan that brought Jake's grief out into the open, and he was surprised to find a tear escape and roll down into Ayan's upturned face.

"She was so brilliant," Ayan said, her lip quivering. "One of a kind. Can't help but wish she let herself be scanned."

"The best of us don't have time to worry about making backups," Jake said. "And that she was."

Ayan's hands squeezed the fabric of the front of his vacsuit and she cried into his chest for a few more minutes before calming down. "Crying like a child," she said as he carefully stroked her back. "Since I came back I haven't been able to get a grip on emotions like I used to. 'Fraid you've taken some of that on the nose."

"It's entertaining," Jake said through a smile. "I never know what's going to come out of you next."

She pounded his chest weakly.

"See?" he said.

Ayan laughed and took a step back, wiping tears away. "I've also come here because I know we're going to be separated for a while, and I'm thinking that might be good. It think it's time for us to be professional about all this."

Jake didn't like where the conversation was going. "Professional," he repeated.

"There's a time for relations, and it's just so hard to try right now. I can't focus on what's important while I'm trying to make personal time when there's none. I know you're thinking about other things too, while I'm in your arms you're checking your comm. That's not the way we should be, Jake. We're distracted from each other *and* our duties, it's dangerous."

"It sounds like you're convincing yourself as much as you're trying to tell me," Jake replied. "Where is this coming from?"

"My best friend just died, things are going on here, and people depend on me. I need clarity," Ayan said.

Jake watched her, on the verge of tears, and tried to hold his frustration in check. "Distance from me will give you that," Jake said. "That'll solve your problem?"

"I hope there's time later," Ayan said. "But I need space now. You do too. I know it, especially after you checked-"

"I have a ship readying for lift-off, sometimes-"

"It can't be helped, yes, but still," Ayan said. "Just give me the space."

"It's yours," Jake replied. "Maybe you're right. We're keeping my officers from being on the bridge, I'm sure."

Ayan fixed him with a hurt expression, and he wanted to cross the short space between them to reverse any damage he'd done. Pride and frustration prevented it.

"I do want to take time when there is some, Jake," she said quietly. "But we have to be professional now. I'm sorry if this hurts, it's not easy for me either."

"I'm fine, you're right," Jake said.

"Be careful, Jacob. I do need you back here whole." There was a seriousness in what she said that made him wonder for a moment, but he let it pass. "Don't worry about me," he said. "Take care of yourself, take the time."

Agameg entered the bridge behind them and stopped. "Commander Rice? I didn't know you were joining us, welcome aboard," he offered. The fine cilia along his cheeks and soft lower jaws rippled and changed colours from green to light brown to yellow.

"Sorry, I'm not staying aboard. I wish I were though," she said, sniffling and shaking her head. "It would be nice to escape."

Jake and Ayan couldn't help but notice as Agameg's face turned pale, nearly white, and his large green eyes went wide. "Oh, you were saying farewell, I'm so sorry. I'll return later."

"No, I'm stealing time," Ayan said. "Don't let me get in your way. Oz gave me something he retrieved from the Triton," she said, returning her attention to

Jake. From a satchel she retrieved a small transparesteel box with a glass inside. Inscribed on the black base was 'A Drink With Jonas.' "I thought it would be perfect for your quarters."

"I thought that was lost," he muttered in a hushed tone. Jacob accepted it and turned it around, looking at all sides. The memory of sitting down next to his predecessor, the nearest thing he had to a father, in the Pilot's Den aboard the Triton came flooding back. It was impossible to avoid remembering what happened next when Regent Galactic activated a destruct device hidden in the first Wheeler, who clung to Jonas so he wouldn't die alone. He did his best to put the lingering anger and grief aside. "Thank you."

Agameg was concentrating very hard on checking the reactor readouts and ignoring what was happening a couple of metres away.

"Thank Oz," she replied. "Stay safe."

He watched her walk away, unable to shake the nagging feeling that he was missing something important.

"If you don't mind me saying, Sir," Agameg said. "She seems extraordinarily stressed."

"She just lost her best friend," Jake replied, starting for the engineering station behind his captain's seat. "Sometimes people push instead of pull people closer when they feel alone."

"I've been around humans long enough to know there is something different going on, more than loss." Agameg observed him for a moment before saying; "I thought you should know."

"Thank you, Agameg," Jake said. "We'll hurry back. We'll sort this out."

CHAPTER 37
LAUNCH

Whirling dust encouraged the last of the people caught out in the open on the landing slips to get behind a closed door or up on a high, flat space. Ayan and fifty eight others watched from atop the Clever Dream as the Warlord hovered carefully through the hangar doors. Hundreds more watched from the tops of large cargo containers and emergency shelters.

It was as if the Samson's pocked, rough outer hull had been shed, revealing a sleek, dark hull beneath. Sensor, emitter, and collector fins ran across the front like dark teeth, and down sections of the length like razor fins. To Ayan, the new shape made the ship look more like a predator crouched low, ready to pounce and devour. The four engine pods stretched out behind the ship on extendable reinforced arms that would stretch out in four directions when they were in proper flight. Old-fashioned hover engines built into extra armoured buffer zones of the hull kept the ship aloft while it was flying too low to use its main engines. Most of the new hardware on the vessel was used or recovered from nearby wreck yards, but no one could tell from the outside. Twenty-eight thick barrels lined the bottom of the ship in two rows near the sides. Five turrets were built in, more would be added, and there were other weapons hidden or incomplete beneath the emitter fins.

"Man, I wish I could be there when they park next to the sun and flip the switch," someone nearby said.

"Why?" asked Jenny Machad.

"You think that's the way it's supposed to look? They're going to let the ergranian steel hull absorb radiation from the sun and, if everything goes right, a lot of those parts will be flush. Those barrels will look like internal mooring mounts. The fins will keep extending, of course, but all the more delicate exposed stuff will get covered, like the mounting points on the turrets."

"Wow," Jenny replied. She turned to the technician and offered her hand. "I'm Jenny."

"Sergeant Jenny, looking at your rank," the other replied. "I'm Tara. Just a machinist."

Ayan took a moment to glance across their large settlement. Hundreds of people in sealed vacsuits watched the Samson from atop shipping containers and other vessels. Beyond their own perimeter other people were taking notice as well. They were far enough from the whirling dust to stand out in the open and watch the grey-hulled ship slowly manoeuvre out of the hangar.

Most of the on-looking technicians had done work on the Warlord but remained behind to start shifts on other ships. "I can't believe we finished it," she overheard Tara say on proximity radio.

"I know. I only worked on it for a month, but it felt like three. Where are you working next?" asked one of the nearby machinists. They were on her left, while Oz was on Ayan's right.

"The Skimmer."

"Me too," he replied. "They say it'll take a week to finish work on her. I bet we'll be done in four days. I wonder if they'll retrofit her with a hull like that after."

"Nope, that's about as far as that ergranian stuff will stretch beyond putting ingots in a nutrient bath. It'll take a while to purify another seed batch," said a worker Ayan knew as Galie Aulm, an issyrian who joined the Triton encampment a few days after they arrived in Port Rush.

"There's a lot of Laura in that ship," Jason said from behind. Victor moved so he'd have room to stand beside her and he stepped into place. "There's a lot of you both, between her work on the emitter systems and you working on the hull."

"There's a lot of her everywhere," Ayan said. "She built the shield over our heads, made repairs on the Clever Dream with me, it goes on and on."

"That'll recede," Jason said. "We'll move on, parts will be swapped out as they age, I'll lose her things somewhere along the way."

"We die twice," Liam Grady said. "When our bodies stop working, and then when we are forgotten. Laura was an impressive woman. I've never heard anyone speak ill of her, and people speak of her often. She'll be alive for a very long time."

Ayan looked to Liam Grady and nearly kicked the champagne bottle off the edge of the Clever Dream. Victor caught it by the top and handed it to Ayan. "That would have been bad," he said.

"I'm guessing that would have been unlucky," Ayan said, wrapping the bottle in her arms. She was blushing at the near blunder, and happy she wasn't the only one laughing, even if it was nervous laughter.

"Not to mention expensive," Jason said. "We paid twelve hundred GC for that, it might be the last properly made bottle on this moon."

"I'm going to cover that," Ayan said, looking down at the foil-wrapped top of the bottle. "I have pay I'm not spending."

The ship slowed to hover in front of her. It began to turn, slowly drifting closer and closer. Liam Grady moved so he could squeeze between her and Jenny, who made room. "I'll hang on to you while you smash that. Have you thought of a dedication?"

"I was going to use the Freeground March," Ayan replied. "It's tradition." She thought a moment and said, "It's their tradition."

All at once, the image she was presenting and the meaning the upcoming moment could take was apparent to her. The visions given to her by Roman and the Victory Machine left her with the impression that she played a major role in building the society she saw her children in. She tried to picture that conjured moment, when she faced both her children on the day of her sixteen-year-old son's departure.

She still couldn't recall where Jacob Valent was, but it didn't matter. Ayan couldn't get the face of her yet-to-be son out of her mind. The memory of the dress she was wearing, the families in the background saying farewell to their young sisters, brothers, sons, and daughters was clearer to her than it was at first, too. There was so much in that vision, so many good things she wanted to cling to.

The Warlord would be the first ship launched in whatever society would grow out of the moments she was living, and she wouldn't have it look like a funeral. She summoned the vacsuit outfit menu and quickly selected the dress that looked like the one in her vision of the future. It was white with hints of yellow, cut to modestly suggest her best features, and fit for comfort. Her black vacsuit shifted and changed colour until it matched the dress on her display. The mid-shin length, loose skirt was whipped up to her knees by the wind, but the vacsuit fabric didn't allow it to go up any further. The wind calmed and she saw almost everyone who wasn't on security duty hurriedly changing their outfits to dresses, suits, and several switched to loose-fitting clothing that looked like ancient pirate wear. It became a theme, and by the time the Warlord was looming within reach, Ayan was all smiles.

"Do you remember any poetry from when you were younger?" Liam asked, remaining in his robes. He was the only one that came dressed for the occasion already.

Ayan already had something in mind by the time he finished speaking. She called it up on her comm unit and projected it onto the hull of the Warlord. "Written by King Harold the Fourth," she read. Her reflection mixed with the poem projected onto the hull. She looked serious, and much younger than she expected. It was evident that she had been crying.

Ayan cleared her throat and read the poem, looking from bright red letters to the reflections of everyone standing at her sides on the Clever Dream.

"Go on, young soldier,
to battle, to war.
Stand fast, young sailor,
by the barrel, by rail.

Live long in honour,
we love you absently.
We build anew now,
for you in your peace.

Go on, young soldier,
until your fight is done.
Stand fast, young sailor,
until your sea is calm."

"May this ship protect her crew. We ask that the sailors of old watch over her and all aboard." Ayan hefted the bottle then brought it up above her head, grasping it by the neck. Jenny and Liam gripped the back of her dress at the waist, beneath the scooped back. "Oh please break on the first try," she said under her breath to the mirth of the people standing nearby. "I christen thee: Warlord."

With all her strength, she smashed the bottle against the side of the ship, and it exploded in a hail of champagne and glass. Her vacsuit instantaneously covered her the front of her body, resuming its previous shape after all the debris was deflected. Cheering and applause rippled across the settlement. Everyone who was watching had a view, thanks to a few people who were transmitting it all to the Stellarnet, something that didn't even cross her mind thanks to her preoccupation.

The Warlord started slowly drifting away and Ayan stepped back, regaining sure footing. "Thank you," she said to Jenny, who was still holding the back of her dress.

She released her grip. "That was beautiful," she said.

"My Aunt taught me about the British's last days on Earth, when they were still at war. It's from the last king born there," she replied. Liam Grady's hand stopped clenching her dress, but his open palm moved up her back, in a familiar, comforting gesture. Ayan didn't stop him. His hand was warm, gentle, and welcome.

***

It took Jake a moment to tear his attention away from the two dimensional image in front of his command seat. Ayan was looking towards the sky, watching the Warlord depart. Liam Grady was right beside her, his hand stroking her back. "I don't have time for this," he said finally.

The bridge was fully manned, with Finn on the engineering console and Ashley at the helm with her new navigator, Clara Ramone. Kadri, formerly from the Palamo, manned communications, Frost sat at the primary tactical station, and several other crewmembers watched operations or temporary screens that were set up to monitor extra systems. Stephanie sat at the main operations console right beside Jake, a new seat that was the same height as the captain's chair.

"Okay, this is taking some getting used to," she whispered. "These old displays are easier on the eyes, though." The two dimensional screens were projections, like holograms, but they could be set so only the intended user could see them.

"They came cheap," Jake said.

"Aye, but they're still in use on most battleships where I come from," Frost said. "Simpler tech, harder to break, easy to fix."

"I believe it."

Jake looked to the main display projected against the front of the new bridge and watched as the four main engines spread out and moved forward, pointing in four directions around the ship. They took over for the smaller support engines along the bottom of the ship seamlessly as they made their way into orbit. The blue sky turned black, and thousands of lights belonging to just as many ships came into view. A notification came up on his screen telling him that the Warlord had clearance to approach the sun. "How are the controls, Ashley?"

"Smooth, responsive," Ashley said. "The mind-wire is nice too, no more pedals."

"Good. Don't ignore the foot controls, though. Just because we were able to adapt the neural listening control from an Uriel doesn't mean it's one hundred percent yet," Jake replied.

"Aye, Captain."

"How do you feel about doing the solar roll-over for real?" Jake asked.

"Can't wait," Ashley replied. "That was the dullest simulation I've ever run, and I ran it five times."

"You've obviously never tried the Onaku City sim," Finn replied. "I ended up waiting for an air train for twenty minutes."

"You played that alone?" Clara asked. "That's supposed to be a social simulator. Minimum two hundred participants."

"Oh," Finn replied. "No wonder."

"The better question is: why were you playing a social sim when leisure sims are restricted?" Stephanie asked with a raised eyebrow.

"Just exploring the program library," Finn muttered.

"All right," Jake said. "We've got clearance, let's thicken the Warlord's skin." He watched as their course changed so they would pass near the sun then turn away after it was finished there.

"Let's hope we don't have any thin spots," Frost said under his breath.

"Frost," Stephanie said, shooting him a warning glance. "Everything we're saying is going ship wide. Some positivity, please."

The Warlord gracefully followed its assigned flight path out of orbit and away from Tamber. Jake could feel Finn hurriedly checking systems behind him, and brought up the engineering status screens himself. The readouts filled half the area in front of him. "This crew deserves more credit than I can give," Jake said. All the essential systems were functioning nominally, especially the thrusters, which were firing at less than a quarter of a percent. "Make the inboard engines available, please."

"Okay, main thrusters five through eleven opening," Finn replied.

Jake watched as the hull plates concealing the thrusters they installed across the rear of the ship between the maxjack and the rear dorsal turrets raised and slipped to the sides. They were an older style of engine, but they could take many different types of volatile fuel and provide an increase in acceleration that would be a surprise to anyone expecting the Warlord to be a simple converted hauler.

The Warlord cleared port space and Jake smiled. "Fire 'em up."

"Aye," Ashley said. The light of the four main rotary engines was joined as the rear of the ship lit up. "Well, the inertial dampers are good. Didn't even feel that." She ramped the thrust up slowly, and stopped at six percent. "The Samson never moved this fast."

"We'll be slower soon," Jake said, watching the sun loom closer. "Still much faster than the Samson, if everything goes right. Give it another three percent for ten seconds."

"That'll take us up to approach speed," Clara said.

Ashley didn't ramp the power up as slowly as before, but surged it up to the requested level. "Whoa," Finn said as he watched the power levels jump then normalize. "Okay, we're okay. I was sure we'd lose a few micro nozzles."

Ashley powered back down at the ten second mark, and nodded. "Smooth ride."

"All right, how long until we can close the doors on those thrusters?" Jake asked.

"Three more seconds," Agameg replied through the comm. "The inboard engines are cooling as quickly as expected. They'll be easy to conceal."

"Close them as soon as you can," Jake said. "Time to let the ergranian steel work its magic."

"Never seen this before," Frost said. "Not like this, anyhow."

Jake sent the order for all departments to get ready and received positive reports within a minute. "All right, monitor your stations for problems and report as soon as anything comes up. Time to flip the switch, Finn."

"All right," he nodded. "Energizing the hull and releasing the static binding. This is going to be loud."

"Beginning slow rotation," Ashley reported. "Time for baby to get a tan."

"It's not even nearly the same thing," Finn replied. "The Warlord's hull is going to absorb solar radiation and increase its mass and size as it converts the energy to matter. It's more like photosynthesis, only better."

"Okay, then," Ashley replied.

The Warlord's hull was bathed in light as it slowly rotated. Jake's tactical screen told him that they were being scanned by one hundred fifty eight vessels and counting. Everyone in the system would know what kind of hull the Warlord had before long.

Before anyone was ready, the ship around them began creaking loudly. "It's just the steel binding with the inner supports and growing along the seed lines inside," Finn yelled.

The bare struts above them were enveloped by strands of grey-silver metal that crept across the metal like thin vines until all the supports and the outermost surfaces were covered completely. "Full internal coverage," Jake told Finn.

He made a few adjustments and the ergranian steel stopped growing into the ship. The outer hull began retaining all the radiation from the sun, and Jake smiled as he heard something that the metal had become known for. It began to groan, then the sound increased in pitch.

"It sounds like the hull is singing," Kadri said.

The hull outside thickened, and Jake watched as the surface rose until the devices and round launcher ports were almost recessed. The fins rose along with the rest, only they grew harder and took on interior details that would make them the most resilient parts of the ship. Finn was doing a good job of directing the growth of the hull at the front while Agameg worked at the rear and several other crewmembers worked the middle. Jake took over two of the main engine pods himself, seeing that whoever was in charge of them was having difficulty. They had glider blades built in to the struts, like the Uriel fighters, but they wouldn't be useable until someone cut away parts of the hull that bound to them by mistake.

After several minutes of rotating past the sun, every station reported they were finished, and all the parts hanging off the Warlord were recessed except for the four main rotary thrusters and the blade-like fin arrays.

"Returning the hull to stable status," Finn said. "Reports coming in. We have a lot of cutting to do."

Jake saw the status reports coming in from across the ship. Most of the reinforcement went well, though some areas weren't completely covered, while a some hatches would have to be re-cut. There were no major injuries, and no unexpected problems. Most of the cutting and hull treatment would have to take place on the outside, however. A few of the emitters, launchers, and outer hatches were sealed. "Flight, how are our thrusters?" Jake asked.

"Rear thrusters are sealed shut, but we have our four mains, and rotation is fine," Clara reported.

"Controls have adjusted," Ashley said. "We've lost some responsiveness, but I think she's still a sleek bird. Ready to enter hyperspace."

"We have enough open emitters," Finn replied. "We just can't project a wormhole yet, so no way to test the combination FTL system."

"Captain, this is Ronin. Both fighter launches are sealed shut. Looks like whoever was in charge of growing those sections didn't control them very well."

"Looks like you're grounded until we get those cut," Jake said. "We're heading into hyperspace in a few seconds, so make yourselves at home."

"Course plotted, we'll be ready for hyperspace as soon as we clear the solar system," Clara said.

"Good," Jake replied. "Congratulations, everyone. Our new ship has a shiny, thick skin."

CHAPTER 38
CONCLUSION AND COMMENCEMENT

The walls and ceiling were polished to a silvery shine. When Alice opened her eyes, she saw a woman that she recognized immediately, but what she saw didn't make sense. The brown-haired, blue eyed, tall woman who stared back at her felt perfectly right, but she'd never physically been that woman. One of her eyes was cybernetic, and seemed exactly like the one she'd been given on Veers Nine, but it was blue, matching her natural eye.

Someone had put a grey metal choker on her. The vacsuit, heavy boots, as well as the thick command and control unit were all Freeground military issue. They were newer models, but definitely Freeground. She pushed her fingers through her straight, longer than shoulder-length brown hair. Her smile reflected back at her and broadened at the sight of it.

She remembered dying. That body that was such a reliable host for years was fully corrected, and the flaw in its brain that allowed her to borrow it for so long was gone. Alice remembered being trapped, hearing many of the Triton crew speaking to her, entertaining her for hours on end. Then she let go, and copied herself into a digital system. Her last memory was of the man who treated her like his daughter, patiently sitting at her bedside. She'd said goodbye, but he couldn't hear her.

"I'll make sure he hears me when I say 'hello,'" she said aloud. The sound of her voice in the silent space was so surprising she clapped both her hands over her mouth and giggled. It was a strong voice with a very feminine tonality, almost exactly how she sounded when she was still an artificial intelligence running on Jonas Valent's command and control unit. "Now, how'd they do that?"

Alice tried to scan the small room but her cybernetic eye failed. She could feel the choker around her neck interacting with the eye and the implant that allowed her to communicate through neural channels. "A restraint," she said, tugging on it with no success.

The outline of a door appeared and a slab of metal was drawn out of the way. A woman with sharp features and long, dark red hair emerged. She wasn't wearing a soldier's uniform, but a long, conservatively cut green dress. The woman nodded at the soldiers behind her and the door closed. "We don't have long, so I would like you to answer my questions quickly. Then you can go."

Alice decided that the conversation should begin with a logical leap, maybe that would skip a lot of minutiae and get to the point. "Why has Freeground Intelligence resurrected me, and how did they do it?"

The woman looked stunned for a moment then smiled. "Why didn't I see that assumption coming?"

Alice's guess was obviously a miss, but she pressed on. "This room, the style, it's all Freeground. That door's a metre thick."

"So you have no memories from the artificial intelligence version of yourself, or your experiences while you were my passenger?"

Alice thought for a moment, and remembered. She sent herself towards the biggest Regent Galactic communications hub she could find right before she made the transfer to digital. "What happened?"

"An artificial version of you separated from a file that it guarded. That file had all your memories and human traits. It started degrading so your artificial intelligence copied the file into my brain. You don't have any memory of that, do you?"

"No," Alice said. She tried to remember what it was like to be an artificial intelligence before she was human and realized she could barely recall anything. Her life as software was, for the most part, gone. Her human memories were rich, clearer than ever before. "Someone did some serious housekeeping in my head."

The smile that brought on in the woman watching her was surprisingly joyful. "I'm glad you're back. I only wish we had more time."

Alice watched the woman, there was something inexplicably familiar about her, but she couldn't figure out what. "Okay, then where am I? Whose pet project am I?"

"You have to promise not to react too extremely, let me explain the whole situation."

"Okay," Alice replied, sitting up straight. "I'll let you finish before I decide on an escape plan."

"The creator of framework technology didn't stop developing it after escaping Vindyne. He incorporated edxi and issyrian technologies and kept on researching the secrets to true immortality."

"Edxi," Alice said, nodding. "I met one, looked like it took a real act of will for it to resist tearing into me like an entrée. They don't like anyone researching or altering them."

"That may be true, but Omira, formerly Doctor Marcelles, had a lot of success. Your framework created a modified version of human physiology. You have neural pockets scattered throughout your body, a little more strength, you're hardened against vacuum, radiation, and extreme temperatures to a certain extent."

Alice looked at her bare hand. It looked completely normal. She pinched it has hard as she could with her fingernails. She felt the normal pinching pain, but it didn't break the skin. "Vacsuit skin."

"That's accurate. You also have a reserve lung and a bladder that reprocesses excess moisture, like an issyrian," the woman said. "I wasn't told this until you'd been transferred across, and they offered the same upgrades to me. Our version of the technology is locked, so we can't make modifications to it."

"This thing locks me down?" Alice said, picking at the choker.

"No, the lock is mental, and it can be broken, but I've seen what can happen when that's done, and I don't recommend it. That choker is keeping your cybernetics from operating. If you reached out to networks outside this ship, or started scanning things with your eye, the fleet would detect it."

"Okay, if Omira could upgrade most of my important bits by borrowing from other races, why do I even have cybernetics?"

"Those are manifestations of your mental self image. Your memories of yourself having those are so clear that the framework duplicated them when you were transferred."

"So if I had four arms before…"

"I suppose you'd have four now," the woman replied, smiling at the whimsical thought.

"Damn," Alice said. "Should have pictured five myself five years younger, with wings and a pooper that dumped platinum."

The woman chuckled and pressed on. "You're on Omira's research vessel, the Fallen Star. We don't know where she is, before you ask. We have a ship ready for you with the coordinates of Jacob Valent programmed in. Once you are clear of our fleet, the choker will fall off, and you'll be able to use your implants however you like."

"That's one great big prize package, lady. Who are you?" Alice asked. "What did I do to win all that? Oh, and where am I?"

"You're in the middle of the main Order of Eden fleet. I'm not going to tell you where the fleet is operating from, since that would breach our security too drastically. I'm also not going to tell you who I am. I could have had you cut out when I discovered you in my head, but instead allowed you to be saved."

"Well, that's the most terrifying thing I've ever heard. I'm in a cell, in the middle of the enemy camp, which I'm assuming is bigger than I could guess." Alice thought for a moment. "What happened to the artificial intelligence that put me in your head?"

"She deleted herself after Meunez arrived, at least that's what she said she'd be doing."

"Gabriel Meunez is here? Talk about burying the lead. Now I know I need to get going," Alice replied.

"Answer a couple of questions for me, and I'll set you free."

"Fire away, Red. If Meunez is nearby, I have to get out of here. I didn't make the greatest impression last time we ran into each other."

"Well, he's moved on to other things, but we'll get to that. I'm wondering, what happened to Lewis?"

"How do you know about the Clever Dream's AI?" Alice asked.

"There was another Lewis, before."

The memory of him, and his last moments instantly lowered her spirits. "He's dead."

"Oh," the woman replied. "How?"

"Okay, before I spill the nitty gritty on one of the most complicated men I've ever met, I've just gotta know why you're asking after someone who was maybe known on two worlds. Two worlds that, I'm just guessing here, are a long way away."

"I read about him in your history, but the file was incomplete," the woman replied.

"Wait," Alice said. "My memories were in your head. They didn't stay sealed, did they?"

"No. I remembered parts of your life in dreams."

"Well, it would have saved us a little time if you said that straight off, Nora."

The woman regarded her with surprise. "How did you know my name?"

"Seemed right, just a guess," Alice said, making her best effort to underplay how disturbing the idea that she'd gotten some of the other woman's memories as part of her transfer. "Right, so you found out about Lewis. He saved my butt twice, then I saved his once. Where did the memory end for you?"

"Before you saved him," Nora replied.

Nora didn't seem to want to dwell on how she knew her name, so Alice continued the story. "We had to stop for food, so we hit this drift. I think it was called Yikin, no, it was Yelkin. We were just finishing up at a Spacerwares ministore when Lewis caught a stun round. I managed to drag him under cover and fire back. The whole quad broke into a full-on firefight, most of them taking the opportunity to take shots at whoever they didn't like or figuring they would play law-maker and shoot whoever's shooting. Drifts get busy with the idiots of the galaxy, the ones that shouldn't have guns but tend to have the biggest collections. Long story short, I stole an antigravity cart and got him to a shuttle only a little more beat up than the one he had."

"How did you start it?" Nora asked, engrossed in the story as though it was unlike anything she'd ever heard.

"It was a cheap shuttle, I busted the main console open with his sword-"

"He had a sword?" Nora asked.

"Yeah, this Zurra Cutter, like a nanosword with microsaw edges but four times as broad with heavier components, so it could cut through most metal. Can I continue?"

"Please."

"I got into that panel and shorted the old security board inside. Once Lewis was back up on his feet, he plotted a course that would keep us away from most of the traffic. We made it back to Ulrik, but it took us three days."

"What did you do during that time?"

Alice regarded her warily and decided that she'd please her audience of one so she could get out of her cell faster. "He was different during quiet times. Nice, interesting, he had a lot of stories and didn't like people around him getting bored. We got close, I guess."

"Did you," Nora hesitated awkwardly. "Fornicate with him?" she asked quietly.

Alice recoiled at the thought. "No! Wow, that would have been so weird. He played the 'old soldier' part too well, and I guess that's not my thing, and I don't think he was too interested in that kind of thing with me, either. He never made it obvious if he did."

"What happened after that?"

"We showed up at Ulrik's estate," Alice paused a moment. "Did you learn about his place? What the job was about?"

"Yes, the Amber Heart," Nora replied.

"Right, that hunk of old sap from Earth. We touched down on the platform and had a hundred barrels on us in a second." Alice took a moment to close her eyes. The memory of that platform, the cool wind against her face, and the surprise at seeing dozens of house soldiers pointing weapons at them was too clear. She could even remember the smell of the forest below. The recollection of the next moment was almost enough to bring tears to her eyes. "He was such a proud idiot," she said to herself.

"Who?"

"Never mind," Alice said, regaining her composure. "Ulrik comes out smiling and Lewis quick-draws on him. I've never seen anyone as fast. Cybernetics helped; it turns out Lewis' whole right half had been replaced. Probably because of some injury on Veers Nine. There wasn't enough of Ulrik left to put back together. Lewis was using a tri-shot modification on his sidearm, so it fired hot enough to burn a few strands of my hair just because I was standing beside him. He got all three shots off before the guards killed him. I caught a couple of rounds too, but it was minor, just crossfire."

"Why?" Nora asked. "He had to know he would be killed, surrounded by guards."

"Territory," Alice said. "One of Ulrik's companies was on Veers Nine, fighting for a share, and Lewis' job was to dismantle his operation however he could. He decided that killing the man at the top was the last chance he had since Ulrik had already caught on."

"How did you get out?"

"Well, I woke up in a room a lot different from this. Big windows, fresh flowers on the bedside table. One of Ulrik's wives, Rada was her name, told me that I didn't come up when they ran a check on known enemies, and I finished my mission, so she gave me my reward after I told her where she could find Amber, the wife that stole the Amber Heart. When I powered on my new ship, it asked me two questions: what the ship was called, and what I would name my new artificial intelligence."

"So you named it Lewis," Nora said.

"I named it Lewis," Alice nodded. "Can I get out of here now? Feeling a little claustrophobic right now."

"Thank you, Alice," Nora said, tears welling up. "You helped me feel human again. I don't remember much of you, just the dreams, so you don't have to worry, but you at least brought my humanity back."

Alice stood, trying to look like she cared more about Nora's apparent breakthrough, and she received a heartfelt hug as her reward. "I'm sure you would have found it eventually, I mean, it can't go far, right?"

"I'll miss you," Nora repeated. "This'll be the last time I see you."

The door opened and Alice followed Nora out. The transparent wall beyond her cell was difficult to see through, but she made out roughly man-shaped creatures swimming, tending to what looked like clusters of heavy bubbles. She jumped as an issyrian swam right for her and bumped the wall playfully. "Wow," Alice said. "Never seen that before." It smiled at her, pressing its webbed hands against the transparent plating between them. It was away with a push, disappearing into the dark depths.

"That's all you'll be seeing, sorry," said a soldier as he put a bag over her head and cinched it under her chin. Another guard tied her hands, then her feet with great expertise.

"Okay, this is going to make walking around really interesting, and the trip to the shuttle really slow," Alice said. She yelped as strong arms picked her up and put her on the bed of a cart or hard gurney. "Oh, this kind of trip never ends well, see ya!" Alice said as she did her best to roll off.

Hands caught her easily, and restraints were pressed across her chest, waist, and knees. "A girl's gotta try," she sighed.

Alice made sporadic attempts at breaking the restraints as she was pushed swiftly down hallways. She assumed they were using a hover cart, because there were no bumps or squeaking wheels. They were running quickly, judging from the pounding of their boots on the deck. She heard heavy doors and hatches opening, closing and felt herself go down a ramp.

The cart came to a sudden stop and her restraints were hastily removed. "Gabriel Meunez is on his way to the Rega Gain system with an invasion fleet," one of the soldiers said to her. Their headgear made it difficult to determine if it was a woman or man speaking, or it could have been an issyrian under that armour, Alice couldn't guess. "We are sending you there, so you can warn them. Don't interfere with the autopilot, or you could disrupt the combined wormhole and hyperdrive systems."

The guards picked her up, there were at least eight hands on her. "Like hell! I don't want to run into that freak. As soon as I unlock the computer I'm heading in the opposite direction."

"Your ship, Jacob Valent, and all his friends are there, on the Tamber moon," the guard explained. She was roughly tossed through the air, and she landed head and right shoulder first. The vacsuit, and her new, sturdier body, helped with the blow, but it was no less awkward.

Alice pulled the bag off her head in time to see the narrow gangway raising, almost closed. "Why didn't you say so? And, hey! You got his name wrong! It's Jacob Valance! You guys should know, you bought the company that made the copy!" The engines fired, rumbling the interior of the shuttle.

It was well lit. The interior was in pristine condition. There were shoulder racks recessed into the sides of the cabin, enough to support sixteen. It looked like the seats pulled out into beds, and overhead there were bunks that would lower for even more. "Okay, it looks like Freeground's deluxe model shuttle. Maybe there are some new features?" she said to herself as she got to her feet and started opening compartments. "Fully equipped," she muttered as she opened a gun cabinet and saw brand new, high-powered weaponry. Another compartment revealed heavy armour; it looked like a Freeground design, but every suit was heavier, more advanced than she'd ever seen. The compartments seemed endless.

"Toys, toys, and more toys. Enough for a whole squad of heavy stealthers," she said as she rummaged. "Ooh!" she shouted as she found one of the food compartments under a bench. "So hungry." She ripped one open and pocketed two more before heading for the cockpit. "Let's see if you open." Alice tried the door and made a celebratory sound around a mouthful of vanilla meal bar. Dropping herself into the pilot's seat she took a look at the control panel and immediately saw the engraving along the edge that read: *SUNSPIRE SHUTTLE IX*

"Well, I'm sure there's a story there," she said. Alice looked through the transparent portions of the hull around her and her mouth dropped open as she saw the Overlord II looming nearby. There were hundreds of large ships everywhere, every one of them armed to the teeth. A chill ran down her spine and she was frozen for several seconds. "Wow, am I ever *not* supposed to be here!" she said in a half choked voice, dropping out of the chair and rolling behind it. "Time to go little shuttle, all your toys and food won't help me one bit against that big bad blast from my past." She peeked around the bucket seat then looked over the console, and saw that the wormhole generator was ninety seven percent charged. "Hurry, hurry, hurry," she said, looking to the communications station. There were twenty-four urgent hails waiting and counting. There was nothing she could do but watch the wormhole generator charge up, and when it hit one hundred percent she looked at the scanning screen and pressed the projection button. An image of a wormhole appeared as the generator system projected it and she cheered. As the shuttle entered the wormhole and accelerated, she danced behind the seats. "Yes! Yes! Yes! Rega Gain, here I come!"

CHAPTER 39
ORDERS ON FAITH

"That was a beautiful christening," Oz told Ayan from the main engineering console on the bridge. The evidence of an intense firefight was all around, even though the surfaces had been cleaned, and the bodies removed. Fixing burned out consoles and spots of molten metal were repairs, and the Carthans didn't spend any time restoring the Triton. They just cleaned it and forced the claimants of the ship to pay for the 'service' before they could fly away. It was still a strange notion to Ayan.

Oz's comm unit was directly wired into the panel behind the Engineering interface, and a set of holographic Sol Defence style interfaces surrounded him. "I wish I could have been there."

Ayan had changed back into her regular Triton uniform, but hadn't bothered with the extreme environment overlay. "I know, but we're all short on time." She watched him sort through repairs and examine different parts of the ship for a moment before she continued. "You haven't been acknowledging my messages."

"I listened the first time," Oz said. "I'm not leaving the Triton. I sent non-essential staff off, and kept eight."

"What are you and eight crewmembers going to do here?" Ayan asked.

"We can keep purifying the lines, reversing the effects of the poison in the biological circuitry. We already have propulsion control and one main thruster working. We can move if we have to."

"Oz," Ayan said. "You're going to die on this ship if you don't leave tonight."

That gave her old friend pause, and he finally looked up from his work. "What?"

Ayan looked over her shoulder to make sure no one else was on the bridge before explaining. There was no sign of her guards, Jason, or Liam, who insisted on accompanying her. "I connected with the Victory Machine today, what our old friends from Vindyne have been using to build the Order of Eden."

"Which old friends?" Oz asked.

"Lister Hampon, General Collins, and even Wheeler is involved somehow. I think he's trying to play both sides. Some of what I saw in the machine was just images in the peripheral, it wasn't always direct."

"How are two of Vindyne's most wanted involved?" Oz asked.

"Collins is dead, someone named Meunez killed him, but not before Collins could unleash the Holocaust Virus on the galaxy," Ayan explained.

"Collins is behind that?" Oz asked. "Why? Why would he kill billions of people? Just to reserve more space and resources for Regent Galactic?"

"No, there was some kind of larger plan to focus the population in certain areas of the Milky Way. They were following instructions laid out by the Victory Machine to shape the galaxy in such a way so most of humanity would survive whatever's coming. They overdid it, and now the Order of Eden is more powerful than intended, in complete control of Regent Galactic, their worlds, and everything they own." Ayan cocked her head for a moment as she realized some of what she was saying was beyond what she thought she learned from the Victory Machine. It had told her more than she'd realized; there were details from the Order of Eden and Regent Galactic that she didn't remember hearing, but she knew they came from the Victory Machine.

"What's wrong?" Oz asked.

"Nothing, just turning over stones in my head, finding extra information." Ayan shook her head and stepped towards him. "You have to leave this ship, and the Triton has to hide."

"This could be a trick," Oz said. "How do you know that Hampon, or the Order, or whoever, isn't trying to lead us into the open?"

"It was Roman," Ayan said. "Roman was the Victory Machine's oracle."

"From Mount Elbrus? I thought he was killed when the explosion hit."

"No, the Victory Machine can make high powered wormholes called crush gates. That's how it deals with accumulated temporal radiation. Roman's last conscious act was to pass on important visions and information. One key part of that was the need to defend our corner of Port Rush, and you have to be there. The attack starts tomorrow morning. A colonization ship called the Leviathan will be here, and the Carthans will have their hands full. There will be a ground battle, and we can't afford to lose."

"I believe her," a calm male voice said from Oz's comm unit. "There are records of the Leviathan, and it is more than a colony ship. It's an invasion platform."

"So you're saying that I'll survive if I follow you down to the planet, and start setting up a defence?" Oz said.

"Who's that?" Ayan asked.

"Oh, that's the Triton," Oz said. "Triton, this is Ayan. Ayan, this is Triton."

"Hello," Ayan said.

"Good to meet you," the Triton said.

"To answer your question," Ayan continued, "the Victory Machine said that your death was certain if you stayed here, and I think the destruction of the Triton is a sure thing, too. If you come back down with me, neither are certain. Right now the Triton is a liability." Ayan looked to Oz's comm unit and said, "Sorry."

"No, I agree," the Triton responded. "I'd rather not, but it's true. I can't fight, and I'm barely mobile."

"I can't leave," Oz said. "You don't understand what it's like. I know what the Triton's existence is like, how being this disabled feels."

"You must leave," the Triton said. "I have a record of the Victory Machine, it was made on Earth, and while the records aren't detailed, Sol Defence warns that direct, short term predictions are rarely wrong. I don't want to watch my captain die, Oz."

"You can't cloak, and someone has to be aboard in case something goes wrong," Oz retorted.

"I can pilot myself. It's tedious, but I'm capable, and there are large mining facilities in the Jensen Belt, on the edge of the solar system. I can hide amongst the stations there; their mass and shapes will mask my hull profile. If that doesn't work, I'll hide in a tunnelled-out asteroid. With my systems powered down, this ship will look like an old hulk. That's if they can find me at all."

"What else does your database tell you about the Victory Machine?" Oz asked. "Why are you having such an easy time believing everything she's saying?"

"I've been listening to her, performing my own calculations, and everything Commander Rice is saying is highly likely. Prudence demands you follow her orders," Triton replied.

Oz thought for a moment, leaning on the console. Ayan had never seen him look so weary, but as he paused it seemed he gained twenty years before her eyes in mannerism alone. "I want to take non-essential supplies, and a few things we left aboard that I didn't know about before."

"Whatever you like," Ayan replied.

"Take everything you need to keep your people alive, Oz," replied Triton. "I don't need combat suits, weaponry, or anything else made to serve humanoids. I'll be in hiding until you need me."

"Get people and ships up here," Oz told Ayan. "Anyone who can load cargo and anything that can carry it back to Tamber. There's a reserve armoury and emergency survival equipment aboard that we didn't know about because it was hidden in the Botanical Gallery. We're going to need it."

"Oz, I wish I came with better news," Ayan said.

"I know, it's fine. We'll do what we have to until this is over," he replied. "Just give me a minute alone here."

"All right," Ayan said. "I'll take the first trip back with supplies and bring people back."

Within half an hour it seemed everyone who could operate a loader suit was fitting everything they could into shuttles. Ayan only assisted for the first two hours until Oz relieved her. "I should have been easier to convince," he told her as they watched a line of loader suits running high-impact crates filled with emergency survival supplies across the main hangar. Paula was in her glory, shrilly and urgently guiding landing craft and deck crews.

"I understand," Ayan said. "Your report said the Triton's computer is telepathic at close range." She was careful not to call the creature at the heart of the ship anything other than a computer. Oz suggested as much to protect it. "I can't imagine what it's like to connect to something like that."

"I think you're one of the few people who can," Oz said. "I know you're different from the Ayan I knew, and I'll be honest, I like you more. Putting that aside for a moment, you have a whole set of memories that are second hand, and you can recall what it was like to be the other Ayan. What the Triton shared with me was so detailed, so intimate, that I feel like I know him just as well. I was connected to Ashley too, but not in the same way, and we don't have the same…" Oz trailed off, searching for the right word.

"Chemistry?" Ayan answered.

"That's not the word I would have chosen, but it'll do," Oz said. "I'm going to miss him every minute I'm gone. I'm sure you go through the same thing with Jake."

Ayan sighed and looked away. "I don't know what's wrong with me," she said. "But no, it's not the same. Since he came out of hiding it's been hard. Not just because of Wheeler's android, it's not that at all. It's like I can't fit with him like we did before. He's changed, or I've changed, and we've gone through this cycle where we fight, I end it by going too far, then I apologize or something and we start over."

"How many times since he's come back?" Oz asked.

"Twice," Ayan said. "It's been less than a week, and it's happened twice."

"I've seen that before, don't think it applies here though," Oz said.

"Why don't you tell me about it, just in case you're spot on?" Ayan replied.

Oz punched new directions into his comm unit, showing the loading teams to the hidden armoury in the Botanical Gallery. "Well, Triton says moving the stuff from the armoury into a shuttle is child's play, so I've got a minute."

"Oh, how kind of you, making time for little ol' me," Ayan said with a wink.

"You know what I mean," Oz said. "I was in a long distance relationship while I was out patrolling, and Jack kept on doing the same thing to me. The Roi du Ciel would get close enough to get live messaging going with Freeground and every one of our conversations would end in a fight. Sure, they started with apologies, but for weeks it was the same. Turns out, he started something at home but didn't have the balls to let me go. You haven't gotten together with anyone since the Samson crew went into hiding though, so I don't think it's the same thing."

Ayan's thoughts were filled with memories of Liam Grady getting close, offering comfort, advice, and most of all, she remembered countless hours of easy company with him. They were just talking, but she had trouble remembering who else was around when they were involved in conversation. "No, I like my social life simple," she said.

Oz observed her until she pushed him away playfully. "There's someone," he concluded.

"You're way off," she replied.

"An affair of the heart still counts," Oz whispered. "And no one would blame you, or even be surprised. Jake hasn't exactly been around."

"Bloody hell, if there's anything we don't have time for, it's that," Ayan said, laughing nervously. "You bugger, I didn't realize there was anything-" her comm unit buzzed, sending an alert up the sleeve of her black vacsuit that told her that it was urgent.

"This is Alaka at the gate intake in Port Rush," Alaka said.

"Yes, what's going on?" Ayan replied.

"We have two proposed new hires from Freeground, they say that they were dropped off by the Sunspire. I thought you'd like to know right away."

Ayan looked at Oz, who looked just as curious and surprised. "Who are they?" a small hologram of Remmy Sands, a mischievous looking, short, thin fellow saluting with a flourish appeared above her comm unit. Vivaldi's uplifting 'Spring' piece was playing through the repeating animation and she couldn't help but smile. "Remmy Sands, a former field intelligence officer for Freeground Fleet," Ayan read aloud. She read the rest silently as it went into quick detail about his discharge from the military for breaking restricted information laws by viewing and sharing censored data. A look into the background of the file revealed a short, ancient black and white animation of a gangster drawing a gun on another man who wore a long canvass coat and hat, who raised his hands and shouted, "It's all wrong, see? That private dick didn't get the whole story straight!"

"Oh, he's a character," Oz said.

"This other one seems a little more conventional," Ayan said as she looked at the profile for Trent Davi, a former Lieutenant for Freeground Fleet, specializing in boarding and ground missions. "His record is incredible, he led one of the teams that retook the Sunspire after it was taken over by the Holocaust Virus."

"We need these people, especially since the conditions of their discharges look political," Oz said. "Davi was tossed for gross civil disobedience resulting in broad demoralization. That's no charge I've ever seen."

"I'm going to head down and see what I can find out about the Sunspire," Ayan said. "If she's in the area, it'll be massive."

"I'll see you down there in about three hours. We'll have this wrapped up and Triton sent off by then."

"Leave some time to get some sleep," Ayan said. "I think we'll need it."

"Aye, Commander, you too," Oz replied. "Oh, and, if you have time, follow your instincts. With whoever that other person in your life is," he added. "I'm not good at giving love advice, but I know that's the right thing to do in times like these."

CHAPTER 40
TO ENLIGHTEN AND ELEVATE

Clark Patterson walked along on Eve's left, while Lucius Wheeler was on her right, and all three of them followed the Child Prophet into the large inner sanctum of Lister Hampon. A thick silence hung between Wheeler and Patterson, and Eve could only assume it had something to do with how Wheeler had convinced him to come to the meeting, a meeting Hampon delayed for hours without explanation.

The knowledge Eve had gathered about the framework technology's early days, combined with what Clark had given her when he transferred Alice's memories into a new body, were enough to offer Hampon a proper solution to his deterioration. The question was, who would give it to him? With Patterson there, she didn't have to use the treatment patch tucked under the sleeve of her dress.

Eve didn't have much control over the situation, but she had enough. The Overlord II moved into a wormhole, making it impossible for her to contact her Eden Fleet, but she wasn't the only person in the room that sought to remain free of Hampon's control. She wouldn't call them allies, but they had similar desires, and that made for more of an advantage than Eve had had in a long time.

The memories she'd lived thanks to Alice had done something, too. It seemed like she'd seen more of the galaxy, felt more adult emotions, and gone on a journey. It felt true even if she couldn't remember it the way she could before; most of the experiences faded like an old dream. The result seemed the same. The sensation that she was no longer a hapless victim in her own life was powerful.

The broad, white circular floor around Hampon's grisly throne was as pristine as ever. The black seat in the centre was facing away. People stopped what they were doing on the balconies overlooking the tall chamber as they entered.

The throne turned slowly, revealing the corpulent figure trapped in it. Two small medical droids worked to maintain tubes, patches, grafts, and supports as though a moment's pause would lead to the failure of a part of Hampon's body. His lower jaw had been completely removed, and a healing strap held up his tongue and head by his upper teeth. Expressive eyes looked at them from grisly sockets.

"Pardon me for not getting up," said Hampon's voice from somewhere in the room. The words were most certainly not spoken physically. But Eve couldn't help but pity the man as she watched his adam's apple twitch, as if trying to fight the tubes in his throat for a moment. She had never pitied him before. "I see you have aligned with new companions, Eve. Good, I'm glad you won't be alone if you deny me what I paid for."

"We're not asking for much," Wheeler said. "Freedoms, a little cash, and we have what you want."

Eve couldn't help but notice that the scraping sounds of Clark's armour increased in volume and frequency as he began breathing faster. It was difficult to call him the Beast, after knowing his thoughts and some of his history, but then she only had to look at him to understand why he'd accepted the moniker.

"You offer a chance at a new life, immortality," Hampon said. "What is your price? Be specific."

"Leave the issyrians alone," Clark said. "Stop destroying their habitats and let them live in their own territory."

"Expensive," Hampon replied. "I know you, Clark Patterson. There are hundreds of reports about the Beast of Uumen, champion of issyrian outcasts. If I grant you this, then you promise not to raise an army in defence of any other race. Not humans, not nafali, or any other race."

Clark shifted from foot to foot for a moment, thinking. "You'll withdraw from every issyrian world, give their ships safe passage and guarantee not to interfere with their homes for as long as I live."

"A trick condition," Hampon said. "You are immortal. Even more so than our most advanced framework being. I could forcibly remove every scrap of it from your system and you would still heal. Edxian, huss, and issyrian physiologies ensure your resurrection-like recovery abilities. We don't understand how you work, Beast, but we know the possibilities you represent."

"Then you know there is a good chance that the technology you want to use to recover won't buy you more than a few years without my help. Even if you dissected me, I could hide my secrets for decades."

"That's another thing we know about you: unwavering dedication to a cause, and confidence. So much confidence," Hampon said.

"Only when I know I'm right," the Beast replied.

"What do you want, Lucius Wheeler? Your bid for re-entry into Freeground's ranks will fail when they discover that the Triton is out of your reach," Hampon said. "I overheard Doctor Thurge's latest message to you, that a rightful commander has stepped forward and taken possession. What do you want now?"

"Freedom. I don't care if I have to start over with one ship and an idiot as a first mate. I want to be free to do what I want, when I want, where I want. No interference, no attempts at control. I'm no one's puppet."

"You forget," Hampon said. "You were built by Regent Galactic. What precedent would I be setting if I were to set our machinery free? Especially since you carry memories from Collins, one of the best military commanders I've ever known. What have you brought to trade for all that?"

Wheeler pointed at Clark impatiently. "Him. Without me, you'd have to hunt him down across the galaxy, or he'd start a rebellion, gathering issyrians and whoever else he can find to fight you. Just by bringing him here, I'm making your life less complicated. I might even be saving your ass for good."

"Your task is to derail the efforts of the original Freegrounders to rebuild on Tamber. That has been your task for as long as you've been alive," Hampon said.

"And I've done that, even when you took my command and turned me out. I still pursued it. I know who's going to win here, the game is rigged, and I want to be on your side. Just give me the freedom to do my part my way and have some fun at the same time."

"I'll consider it," Hampon said. "Nora, what can I do for you? I'm fully aware that Clark has the finesse, but you built the interface that will make me whole again. You have it with you, scanners have already picked it up. What can I do for you?"

"My fleet, and the freedom to instruct them properly. I won't be a key to another engine of destruction, I want to participate in deciding their purposes. I can connect with them, I know it, and I want to remain as a leader to the humans who believe in the better way you've shown me. They want to be led into eternity, to the paradises we can build for them. They can help build instead of contaminate and destroy."

"Are you certain this is what you want, Nora? Has seeing life through another woman's eyes convinced you that there's enough goodness in humanity to enter into paradise without destroying it?"

"Yes, and call me Eve," she said.

"You will not break from the Order of Eden with your fleet. Code that Collins added to all Eden Fleet entities makes it impossible. I'm telling you this so discovering it doesn't surprise you."

"I understand," Eve said, knowing that she'd do everything she could to remove the code as soon as possible.

"I'm willing to grant you all everything you've requested," Hampon said.

"Wait," Clark said. "I have one more request."

"Yes?" Hampon said.

"Leave Freeground out of all your conflicts. Destroy any aggressive ships they send against your forces, but don't counter-attack."

"Done," Hampon replied. "I will not attack Freeground, the station, or either of the colonies they think are hidden from the galaxy. Now, it's your turn to grant me my three wishes: transformation, health, and eternal life. Quickly, we'll be emerging from the wormhole soon."

The Beast looked to Wheeler, who nodded. Eve finally looked at him only to realize that he was staring at her, waiting for her approval. She nodded, and he strode towards Hampon, whose eyes widened at his approach.

A large, armoured hand was placed upon Hampon's head, the Beast's fingers found their way between small tubes and wires.

The Beast put his free hand to his head as though he'd been injured and withdrew, stumbling backwards several steps until his fell to his knees. Eve looked from him to Hampon. The robots tending him withdrew from their tasks, and tried to cover him with a black sheet.

"Pain," Hampon's voice announced throughout the room. His eyes rolled back into his head, then his twitching eyelids closed. His partial chest, the bag holding his organs, his hips and part of one leg twitched violently. Tubes were flung free, and Eve wondered if he'd survive the process.

His eyes snapped open. Eve could only assume that he didn't scream at first because there was something wrong with his vocal chords. A proper throat and jaw began to form, and when his screams filled the chamber they were inhuman, rasping and gurgling. The upper half of his head grew brown hair, the tubes leading into his body were absorbed and transformed into human materials, and the framework system began drawing raw current from his chair.

Within seconds he had fresh legs, arms, a full torso, and he breathed as if he'd just finished a hard sprint. Hampon raised his head, revealing a healthy yet aged face with a prominent nose and piercing grey eyes. He started to smile and rise, then twitched bodily, slipping out of his chair awkwardly to land at the bottom of his dais. Anguished, half strangled cries filled the air as he writhed. Eve covered her ears, but she could still hear that screaming, as though something was being torn forcibly from his deepest innards.

The framework system began replacing cells that were affected by temporal radiation. Eve knew what was happening theoretically, but the reality was unexpected. As the infected portions of his body were replaced at incredible speed, they were turned out through his flesh. A bloody display of rejection and replacement as pieces of organs, flesh, and bone were pressed up through his skin, surrounding him in a hellish afterbirth. Every exposed cell in his body was being replaced several times a second, using energy drawn from his chair in violent arcs.

When it was over he was covered in gore, nude and curled up on his knees. He stood slowly, his new, white teeth gleaming through the crimson and black remains that clung to him. Several researchers dressed in red smocks approached him hurriedly and performed scans. "There is no trace of temporal radiation, Sir," reported one cheerfully. "You're cured."

Robots moved in to clean the mess and decontaminate the area. "Immortality is not found in the children we have, the clones we make, the brain scan data we collect, or in framework duplicates," he said, walking towards the Child Prophet. "This is immortality, the new flesh invented by intelligence, powered by electricity, and sourced from matter."

The Child Prophet broke from his daze and scurried at the last moment, right before Hampon caught him by the throat. "You are a pitiful lie," he said as he raised the adolescent clone up with both hands. Wheeler backed away, putting his hands up and shaking his head.

Eve followed his example, taking several steps back. The sounds of the Child Prophet struggling for air as he kicked his feet and tried to pry Hampon's hands away from his throat made Eve's stomach turn. The grisly birth was nothing compared to watching a boy in the beginning of adolescence die.

"You never had the potential to be better than me," Lister Hampon said through clenched teeth. He renewed his efforts, throttling his clone's thin neck with all his strength until he stopped struggling and a new foul smell filled the air. Hampon dropped him and looked down at the boy's horror stricken face. "I feel alive again," Hampon said. "Truly alive."

Eve had no problem recalling the damage humanity did to the world she protected before she was put into stasis for over a century. There was a failure in logic that she could not comprehend when she watched a natural environment become an object for the harvest. That was what provoked her order to exterminate the humans in that solar system, and her fleet executed it without question or remorse.

What she saw in front of her was entirely different. It was the first time she'd been in the presence of true evil, and it was instantly recognizable. Clone or not, the Child Prophet was a boy who was living in his age of potential; what he could have become would remain a mystery because someone had maliciously ended his life and derived obvious pleasure from the act.

"I don't want to know this," Clark Patterson said, slowly getting to his feet. "I don't want to know what I saw when I touched your mind, Hampon."

"We're coming out of the wormhole," Lister Hampon announced as he strode back to his seat. He stopped in front of it, where the gore of his rebirth had been before robots swiftly cleaned the mess. The balconies overlooking his seat with countless technicians and officers became obscured as a holographic starscape was projected all around them. "Pandem!" Lister Hampon shouted, pointing at the green-blue orb to his right. There were no ships in orbit from what Eve could see, strange for such a busy world. "The most populated planet in the new Order of Eden constellation of settlements. The count was four hundred twenty million settlers, most of which arrived in the last ten days. Tell us why they are here, Clark. Please, you must have seen something while you were digging around in my head."

"I won't," Clark said. "It was your promise, not mine."

"You're right," Hampon said. "I've been waiting to tell someone about this for a long time. It's been difficult to convince people to go along with my Order of Eden since Collins died," he looked to Wheeler then. "But you don't remember anything about this either, do you?"

"Pandem? The Order of Eden?" Wheeler asked. "I remember the Victory Machine demanded that people be placed there, so we could avoid some catastrophe. There's more about the cult, but it couldn't apply."

"That's where it started," Hampon said. "Whispers in the dark. Little mutterings I couldn't ignore, messages that came from some prophetic thing that never made a mistake in its predictions. We used the information to force our way from desperate times with Vindyne into success with Regent Galactic. From a big company with a handfull of backwaters to a great big civilization teeming with billions of humans who were fully engaged in the cycle of capitalism. In a universe where humans can't see past their noses, the man with the biggest beak can be the greatest visionary. A joke you might recognize from Collins' repertoire."

"A real laugh riot," Wheeler said. "The Victory Machine led you to everything you and Collins needed to take over, and get your cash cult going. I got that part of the story."

"Cash cult," Hampon repeated. "It had a ring to it. Now it's a real religion, with immortality, paradise, and at long last we have our hell." He pointed to Pandem and Eve couldn't help but wonder what he could possibly mean. There was nothing hellish about the world aside from its history, the humans there were restoring it faster than she could have expected.

Lister Hampon continued on as small robots approached him from several parts of the room and started to clean him up. "'There is a darkness coming.' The Victory Machine laid that on thicker and thicker and Collins and I made progress. Then it elaborated. Humans have been testing the boundaries of polite science for as long as there has been a record, and we finally ventured into something that we should never have even considered. A Regent Galactic company tried to make dragons out of unborn Edxi, and they were successful. Can you imagine? Dragons! Real dragons for amusement parks and pets that you could train in their long adolescence of thirty five, sometimes more than forty years. When they start into maturity they'd become ill and die. Now that's a forward thinking product.

The edxi found out about it. The Exile went in search for evidence and thanks to Alice Valent, who was just a messenger in all this – something Meunez never understood – Zarrick the Exile found it. It doesn't matter that Regent Galactic's subsidiary closed the project out years ago.It didn't matter that there were other companies, even secret arms of governments, that were researching the edxi just as closely. It didn't even matter that thousands of people were killed by edxi in minor acts of retribution, things no human would see as trespassing, or other violations. That wasn't appropriate retribution for humans corrupting their children. They demanded more. Whoever was controlling the Victory Machine knew it, and they gave me all the directions I needed to do one thing: save humanity."

"It's true," Clark said. "What's about to happen must happen. There is no other way."

A broad shape with mechanical tendrils reaching in all directions with barbs and dim lights faded into existence near Pandem. Eve had difficulty judging, but it looked almost as large as the Overlord II, kilometres in depth, and even wider. "We don't even know how they do that," Hampon said. "Take all the readings you want, try to follow them through whatever faster than light solution they're using, and you won't discover a thing about how they move through the universe."

"We can fight," Eve said. "My Fleet numbers in the millions."

"They can be anywhere!" Hampon cried. "They aren't even from this galaxy. The worlds they rule have been under their control for hundreds of years, and every guess we make points to them having faster than light technology for even longer. They may have even been in space long enough for it to inform their evolutionary path, thousands of years. This is what humans fear, the ravenous foe that appears out of nowhere. The one we cannot fight, where fear is the only correct emotional response. We put ourselves here, to clear the way so they can have Pandem, and we make sure people like those Freegrounders can't stand in the way. The Victory Machine was so adamant about them, the well-intentioned ones who would puff up their chests and declare a 'just war' against the edxi. Maybe they would make a few kills, perhaps they'd even fight off the first wave, but that would bring more retribution, more consumption."

Vessels of all shapes began emerging from the main ship by the dozen, all directed at the planet. "What are they going to do on Pandem?" Eve asked, looking at Clark, whose fists were clenched.

"They are taking it as a brood world," Clark said.

"Interesting thing about edxi," Hampon said, smiling and nodding at Clark. The robots had managed to clean him and another brought a long white cloak fringed with silver. "They're mindless animals, like a cross between something insect and lizard for the first thirty or forty years. Mothers lay dozens of eggs, and they wait for them to mature before dropping them on a planet like this, where there's a good hunting ground, water, and a lot of land. They return decades later as their fittest, surviving young are entering maturity and becoming intelligent. They demanded three worlds just like this so far. The other two will be ready within the year. The Order's recruiting centres are spreading by the day. Even on worlds where they are on the verge of declaring war on Regent Galactic and the

Order of Eden, we have places where people can go and step onto the path to immortality, to eternal grace."

Eve watched the vessels as they moved towards Pandem. The mother ship kept launching them, and there were hundreds. Her stomach was becoming increasingly uneasy as she remembered the people she saw briefly when she visited. The girl with the beautiful eyes would become prey along with all the rest of them. "Hell," she said to herself quietly. The mindless, savage young of the edxi would hunt and eat.

"It was a big hit with other religions," Hampon said. "It's a perfect fit for ours. We won't tell anyone about this, of course, but word will leak out. It'll be rumour, a dark myth. We'll tell our followers that rebels destroyed Pandem while we keep prying eyes away. Regardless, this is the place followers think of when they fear they are not achieving enough in the Order. This is the rumour that will make them serve us until they are worn down to the bone."

"The Holocaust Virus did enough damage, we have to suffer this now?" Wheeler said. "I remember the galaxy before you turned most of my favourite cities into ghost towns, it was a good place to be."

"That's something that couldn't have worked out more perfectly," Hampon said. "The edxi would have demanded death, and were on the verge of invading, starting with the worlds that were hardest hit by our virus. We did it for them, and when they saw the death toll brought on by the Holocaust Virus, they were impressed. Humanity will survive in spite of the cost. It's what we do."

"You enjoyed it," Clark said. "You enjoy this."

"This is power, boy," Hampon replied. "This is the quest for the ultimate, most primal good, self preservation. Who else could do this?"

"Someone who didn't enjoy it," Clark said, taking a step forward. "I know everything you know, and I can feel myself breaking inside. You are eager. You are evil." He took another step.

"Gua-" was all Hampon managed to say before Clark raised his hand and stopped his mouth from working.

"I'm going to rewrite you, Hampon," Clark said. "I know how the work has to continue, and I'll do it without taking pleasure. I even know the next thing you were going to do, and you were going to send Wheeler. I'm going to send you with him, as his lap dog, and you're going to love it."

"No," Hampon managed.

"You saw what Freeground did to me, how they programmed me to fight for my nation without question. I can't think of anything worse."

Two guards standing on the second balcony raised their rifles. Clark leapt up and crossed the distance so quickly that Eve almost missed it. The guards were in his hands like dolls an instant later, and he threw them to the deck hard enough to rattle it under Eve's feet. "You don't want to challenge me," Clark said as he let himself drop to the ground. "The galaxy hasn't seen anything like me yet, and I hope it never does again. I'm taking this freak's place," he said as he crossed to where Hampon stood as though stuck to the ground. His eyes were filled with fear, and Eve couldn't help but smile.

"Help me," Hampon said as Clark's enlarged hand engulfed most of his head. His long, black claws dangled past his chin.

"Goodbye, Hampon," Clark said. "Your hateful personality might remain, but you'll aspire to different things. Things that will keep your urges working in the right direction."

Clark closed his eyes and Hampon shuddered for long seconds before he was released. "Take him, get him close enough to Jacob Valent to kill him," he said to Wheeler. "If Jacob doesn't die, then he'll get too close and discover the edxians too early. It'll lead to those things taking their ships into the core worlds. Lister's going to be in a daze for a while, but he'll follow you." The Beast named Clark slowly moved to the seat in the middle.

"What's to stop me from dropping him in the nearest sun and moving on?" Wheeler asked.

"I can find you," the Beast said. "I can find anyone within the reach of the Order of Eden network, just like Hampon. I know how to rip you to pieces, Wheeler, you're an inferior model. Never forget it. I'm also in debt to you, so when you're finished delivering Hampon, go do whatever you want. Start over with one ship, and an idiot first mate. Don't come back to the Order unless you're ready to serve, and don't go back to Freeground for any reason."

"Fair enough," Wheeler said, grabbing Hampon's arm. "This way, Freak. Time to get back to the Ferryman, I miss being on my own ship." He nodded at Eve briefly and said, "nice meeting you, Goddess, good luck with the new regime."

Eve stared as the Beast sat down on the edge of the black seat. She didn't know what to say, and didn't have the first clue as to what to do or what to expect next. She glanced at the body at her feet and had a thought. "I know he was a clone, but can I cremate him properly? There are people who may want to pay respects. He had a short life, but he was revered."

"Take the Order, take your Fleet," Clark said. "The galaxy won't understand this. There will be war whether they find out about this or not. I want you to fight alongside me. So we can keep them from interfering with this," he said, gesturing towards Pandem. "No one can interfere. If you want to save humans from themselves, like I overheard when I was in your head, then that's how you do it."

"By killing them," Eve said.

"By only killing when we must, so our real enemies don't take too many. This isn't a choice I could have made, but it was the right choice. Now we have to deal with it. Someone has to keep convincing the Order that they're on the true path, so your success has to overshadow what we lose. We need a goddess. You need to give them immortality when they excel, and send them to hell when they fail."

Four guards approached with a stretcher and waited for her orders. Eve looked at the Beast once more and nodded. "I'll be your goddess. I'll help you fight this war."

"I'll be watching," said the Beast.

"I know," Eve replied. She motioned for the soldiers to pick up the Child Prophet's body and they efficiently loaded him onto the stretcher and followed her out of the chamber.

Chapter 41
The Expendable Few

The need to avoid people in order to keep life simple hadn't plagued Ayan since she was at the Academy, at least not to the extent that she experienced as she walked past Liam Grady, who was supervising the storage of survival supplies as they came in from the shuttles. He wasn't just dealing with the Triton's extra supplies, but the towers of crates they'd extracted from the Enforcer. Getting past him wasn't hard, but when he smiled at a glance in her direction, she couldn't help but grin back and blush.

"I don't have time for this," she grumbled as she marched up the entry ramp into the Clever Dream. Its engines were still cooling from three quick runs to the Triton.

"Pardon, Miss?" asked Sergeant Jenny Machad. She and Victor were relentless in staying within sight.

"Nothing," Ayan said. "Just talking to myself."

Two guards stood beside Trent Davi and Remmy Sands along the side of the main hallway in the Clever Dream. She pointed at them with her index and middle fingers and said; "You two, with me." She looked to their guardians. "You two are back on regular duty."

"Yes, Ma'am," the guards replied before filing out of the Clever Dream.

Remmy Sands and Trent Davi followed Ayan into the captain's quarters, where she sat down on the edge of the large bed and motioned for them to sit on the seat in the middle. Jenny sat down on a small sofa-seat at the side, pulling her sidearm out and letting it rest on her lap, while Victor stood beside the door, his rifle held across his chest.

"The Sunspire dropped you off here," Ayan said to the pair sitting in the middle of the room.

"Yes, Ma'am," Remmy Sands replied, "and it's good to see you. If I can take a moment to say, you're more beautiful than in any of the holos."

"Oh my God!" Ayan said, "I don't have any bloody time for this!" She was aware that she was more aggravated with her own distractions than with the flattery from the small man who offered it. "You, Sands, I'll have you shut up until Davi fills me in."

"I prefer Remmy, actually," he replied sheepishly.

Ayan shot him a warning look and pointed at him, ignoring a snicker from Jenny's side of the room. She looked to Trent Davi and took a breath. "So, what's the Sunspire doing here, who's commanding her, and where are they now? I can't raise them on comms and their transponder isn't showing up in the area."

"You can call me Davi, Commander," he replied calmly. "She's Captain McPatrick's command, and I'm afraid they wouldn't tell us a thing. We were shuttled to a station on the edge of the Rega Gain system, they bought us a ticket to Tamber, gave us a few local credits, and we came here. All I can say for sure is that they moved on, out of the system."

"Captain McPatrick?" Ayan asked as she looked it up on her comm unit. To her surprise she discovered that it was Oz's uncle. She'd heard of him, a severe man who was the very example of a Fleet commander, but she'd never met him. "What's his mission?"

"I can't say at this point, Ma'am. They stopped telling us anything once our mission came to an end, and they put us into isolation," Davi said. "We're scapegoats for action that went sour."

"I was there for the whole thing," Remmy said cautiously. "Saw more first hand than my friend here, I can explain."

"It's true," Davi said. "He's got more of the story than I do."

"Then let's hear it, but keep it short, we're expecting an invasion sometime after oh-nine-hundred and I'd like a few hours' sleep before then," Ayan said, loosening her collar and leaning back. The mattress adjusted to support her.

Jason Everin entered quietly and took a seat across from Jenny on the other side of the cabin, looking the newcomers up and down.

Davi and Remmy looked at each other warily for a moment. "We've got the very best timing," Remmy said sardonically.

"Could've been worse," Davi replied. "We could have landed after the action."

"That's better, in my book," Remmy said.

"What? Miss the fun? I'm here to sign up."

Remmy shook his head and returned his attention to Ayan. "It's like this: the Puritan Party got into power awhile ago thanks to a whole bunch of voters who thought they would deliver on making Freeground safe again, protect us from evil viruses and big bad military machines run by bigger corporations. They did, sure, a little, but they really only finished plans that were already in place by Freeground Fleet, and then instituted a whole bunch of rules that would get us citizens breeding, staying, and not looking at the awesome imported entertainment coming in from the universe."

"They censored pretty much everything, with the main focus being news," Davi said.

"Right, news, like that was what they were really afraid of," Remmy said, rolling his eyes. "One of the biggest things they didn't want people to see was the crew from the First Light. We're big fans, by the way, because you let the genie out of the bottle, saw the galaxy and survived. They wanted to turn the clock back, to when everyone thought Freeground was the safest place to be and didn't want crazy stuff like talking pets and the Stellarnet. It didn't work. People left in droves since they knew that the galaxy wasn't as nasty as they wanted us to believe. A lot of people even paid their hundred thousand and headed to a Regent Galactic world, something we've just started finding out in the last few weeks."

"To cut Remmy here short," Davi interrupted. "Anyone who didn't fit in with the Puritan Party's social breeding program, or wanted to look past Freeground territory, was watched. The military was cleaned up first."

"Yeah, and if you had different views, started living your life too loud, then you'd end up jailed or sent away. Then there's my buddy Clark. He was in line to step onto the bridge of a carrier when his sister was busted for trying to join the Order. They put him into mental treatment, set him up with a girlfriend named Isabel, a new sense of duty, and they packed all his pain away. His sister was executed, but until Doctor Marcelles, who changed his sex and renamed himself Omira, released his mind, he couldn't feel a damn thing. The crap they put in his head, a control and monitoring circuit, pretty much killed him, so Omira set him up with an upgrade. The latest framework technology got installed into Clark, and we didn't even really know how much it would change him. All Mary, Izzie, and I really cared about was his survival. You following?"

Ayan was, but there were questions. She'd want a lot more detail, but Remmy's motor-mouth telling of his story fit the time they had. "Doctor Marcelles is Doctor Omira Marcelles now," she said. "And the Puritan Party is proving right everyone who thought having them as a majority government was a bad thing. You, Clark, and a few others were rounded up and jailed?"

"Well, she actually goes by Omira Gerring now, and, well, we weren't jailed by the end," Remmy said. "We were put into service. A few people, Doctor Anderson being one, and Captain McPatrick being another, were put in charge of a program to put all us misfit toys to work."

"By misfit toys, he means people rejected from the Freeground Military," Davi said.

"Right, anyway, we got the job of taking the Sunspire back, since it went all agro and started killing ships wandering into its territory. Davi here and Clark were leaders in the battle, I was one of the hackers who had to wipe out the messed up AI code. We lost a lot of people getting on, but we did it. Then they put us out there again, to look for Doctor Marcelles. We found him, well, her, but anyway, she led us to her old research ship. Big secrets to killing framework soldiers, developments in the tech, info on some nasty aliens and crap-tons of other info I haven't even gotten through yet was there for the taking, but there was also some really ugly stuff I just can't un-see. There were frameworks being eaten by alien bugs that were getting a bellyful because as they-"

"Anyway," Davi said, interrupting Remmy's animated retelling. "While they were busy at that end, my team was running retrieval missions. One of them was to pick up an old friend of yours, Lucius Wheeler, from Longshadow. It cost me a good soldier, but we got him to the Sunspire."

"And I still don't know exactly what his game was. I think he was looking to trade his way back into Freeground, but I don't know if he got his way. Still, there had to be something else," Remmy said, rubbing his chin.

The mention of Wheeler got Ayan's hackles up. "Do you know if he went to Freeground?"

"Don't think so," Remmy said. "Watched him as much as I could when I was creeping around on security feeds, but I didn't spend much time on the Sunspire after we teamed up with the issyrians."

"Issyrians?" Jason asked.

"Right, yeah, back to story time," Remmy said. "The new, creepy Clark connected with the issyrians and his framework took on a lot of similarities to them, though there was also edxian and other race data in his system. He started going strange, physically, and a little in the head, too. He stopped paying attention to Isabel, so I started to get to know her. Still miss her, actually."

"Remmy," Davi said.

"Yessir?"

"Stay on target," Davi said with a little smile.

"Right, yup, okay. We fought for the issyrians, who were getting suppressed by Regent Galactic. Davi comes in and helps us out with some of his people so Clark, Isabel, Mary, and I will follow him back to the Sunspire and report. We got through that hell, wrecking the terraforming initiative for all the little Regent Galactic boys and girls real good and head back to the Sunspire. Davi here lost a good friend in that fight too, next it was my turn.

"We got back to the Sunspire where not all was well. Command was pretty pissed because Omira and I faked Clark's death, and there he was, wearing all that dreamy framework tech on the inside, showing them a side of the tech that they never thought was possible. They tried to take him into custody, we ran, I was the slowest, so someone uber-stunned me and I got stuck behind. Clark and Mary got back to the research vessel, don't know what happened after that." Remmy's speedy retelling of events came to a sudden stop, and he looked down at his hands. "Isabel was killed trying to escape. Some dick hit her with one of those new Freeground super-rifles, she didn't have time to feel much. Waste of a nice girl who loved people pretty easy. Even me, a little."

"I got lumped in with him," Davi said, picking up the story. "Like he said, we were the scapegoats for all that going south. Wheeler escaped, that's the last I heard of him."

"Was it really him?" Ayan asked. "Not an android?"

"Definitely didn't scan as an android, Ma'am. He could change his face though, sounded like it was something frameworks like him could do," Davi replied. "Only saw him do it once, but I'm sure he could be in disguise just about anywhere."

"Yeah, slippery one," Remmy added, recovering a little. "I get way down when I think of Isabel, she had way too good a heart to end the way she did. That brings us here, though. Not much happened in transit that we could tell, since we were in nice, closed in quarters. No access to comms or the computer. Got to know this jarhead pretty good though," Remmy said, grinning exaggeratedly at Davi, who shook his head. "Dropped us off like they said, didn't leave us much choice but to come here, not that I wanted to go anywhere else, to be honest. Big fan of yours," Remmy said to Jason.

"It's not mutual," Jason said with a deadpan expression. "What happened to Doctor Omira Gerring?"

"Disappeared," Remmy said. "Doctor Anderson said she was probably wearing her own brand of cloaksuit." He turned to Ayan and asked: "So, can we sign up? I don't do windows, and sweeping is murder on my middle back, but I'll code, crack, or hack whatever you want for three squares and five weeks vacation a year. Oh, and the Vivaldi is from Doctor Anderson, who told me to tell you that he sent us."

"I'm looking to sign on too, if you'll have me. I wish there was a way for you to check our story, Ma'am," Davi said. "All we have are our transit records, and I think the giant nafalli at the gate already verified those."

Ayan pretended at considering the request, but she already knew what her answer would be. "Did you get much rest on the way here?" she asked.

"Too much," Davi said.

"Good," Ayan replied. "I'm going to assign you to the work crews for the night. You'll be on shift for six hours then you'll have five hours' rack time. Sergeant Machad will introduce you to an officer who can set you up with a bunk, but keep any precious items on you. Are your vacsuits a recent design?" Ayan asked, looking at the black suit that had the same outer appearance of her own armoured suit.

"Yours are a bit better," Davi said. "I scanned when we got close to the gate."

"We'll set you up with one," Ayan said. "One of my senior officers will find a better position in our ranks by morning. You'll be on probation."

"Understood. Thank you, Ma'am," Davi said, standing up and saluting.

Remmy wasn't far behind, looking scrawny and short in comparison to his companion. "Thank you," he added. "Sorry about the name calling on the way in."

"Name calling?" Ayan said, standing up straight and returning the salute.

"Called you beautiful, Ma'am. It's true, but maybe embarrassing?"

Ayan laughed. "Good luck. Thank you for joining us." She looked to Victor as Jenny led the newcomers out. "Take a break, go get something to eat. I'll be safe here," she said.

Victor nodded and followed Jenny out.

Jason waited until the door slid closed before looking to Ayan. "You were good with them," he said. "Very relatable, but in charge. That's a balance you had trouble with before, especially near the end."

The last thing Ayan wanted to talk about was her predecessor. She moved to the centre seat and sat down. "Can I get the fruit medley, please?" she asked. A pillar rose in the middle of the seat with a hot fruit dish in the middle with roasted vegetables on the side. "Do you want one?" she asked Jason.

He waved the offer off.

"I know I'm different," Ayan said. "I think the Victory Machine pushed me down that path, and I'm starting to feel right in my own skin." She silently wished Laura was still around to help, or so she could befriend her all over again as she learned about herself. Ayan could feel the grief fighting to the surface and stuffed a quarter of a plum into her mouth.

"What was it like, seeing the future?" Jason asked.

She chewed and swallowed quickly, feeling selfish at not focusing on Laura. She should be the one to support Jason, but the pain was so fresh, and there was so much going on, she didn't want to break down when everyone needed her. "The Machine had a lot to show me, many futures. It would take days to write the report," Ayan said. "Not that there would be much point, it's always changing. The distant future was beautiful though. It extrapolated that I had a son and a daughter, and I was so proud of them. Worried about Laura-" she stopped there, wishing she'd left her daughter's name out of the story, "I worried about her as much as my aunt probably worried about me."

"You named her Laura," Jason said. "Thank you." He looked shaky.

Ayan dropped her fork into the bowl and crossed the room. Her arm was around him, and his head was on her chest. "I'm so sorry," was all she could think to say as she shed her own tears silently, stroking his hair.

"She was the only one who had patience for me," Jason said after awhile. "Through my jack addiction, after, when I was relapsing and so distant. I was so in my own head I don't think I told her I loved her for months," he said through tears.

"She knew, Jason. I know she knew," Ayan reassured.

He cried without comment until Ayan's meal grew cold, and she couldn't help but recall Jake's blunder of checking the time after awhile, when she tried to lean on him. Jason finally picked his head up and laughed at himself. "She wanted me to reengage with my emotions, guess she got her wish." He wiped his face and looked at Ayan, nose to nose. "Thank you for being here, Ayan. I know it's as hard for you, she was your best friend, but you're here anyway. I wouldn't be strong enough to do the same."

"I'm sure you would," Ayan replied, wiping her own tears away.

"I have to ask, what did Roman look like?" Jason asked.

"Roman? He was at the end, in a coma. He was exposed to temporal radiation for months."

"It took months," Jason said, nodding. "Good."

"Why?"

"I got a message," he said, pulling it up on his comm unit. "As soon as you got back from the city, it was a short range burst from your comm, Roman hid it there."

"Hello, Jason," Roman's visage said. It wasn't the emaciated man she'd seen recently, but the strong police sergeant she'd come to know in Mount Elbrus. "I know you're suffering now, and you feel alone, adrift. I'm sorry. There was nothing anyone could do to stop the terrible thing that's happened to your wife. The galaxy still needs you, even if for just a little while longer. I hoped I would be strong enough to close the Victory Machine's viewing portals myself, but I'm not going to make it. I need you to take my place in the service of Citadel. The Victory Machine will transport you far from here, it'll show you what to do from there, so you can destroy it. I wish I weren't offering you this mission, because I know you'll take it. The only person you can share this with is Ayan, who will eventually understand. Goodbye, and I'm sorry."

"No!" Ayan said in a panic, grasping at Jason's comm unit and the arm it was attached to. "Laura wouldn't want this! You've got such a long future ahead."

"You didn't see me in the Machine's version of the future, did you?" Jason said calmly.

"That doesn't mean anything! I didn't see a lot of people, but I'm sure they're still alive in the future."

Jason kissed her on the lips, an innocent but affectionate gesture. "I want this. This feels like the right thing to do, and that's been so hard for me to find for a while. I'm sorry I couldn't find Wheeler or his people." He gently pushed her away and smiled with tears in his eyes. "Oh, you're going to be amazing, Ayan. I'll look for you before I turn the Machine off, and I bet you'll be so amazing." He disappeared from sight.

Ayan reached for him, her hand grazed his arm, but the door opened and he slipped away. "Stop him!" she screamed into the hallway.

Two soldiers who were passing by looked at her dumbly for a moment. "Lewis! Scan for him! Close your hatches!" Ayan said.

The hatch down the corridor began closing while a woman was carrying a small crate up the ramp. She was bowled over before the ramp finished closing, and Ayan knew Jason was gone. She sunk to her knees and buried her face in her hands.

CHAPTER 42
THE FIRST WATCH

The four Ramiel and three Uriel fighters hadn't moved a millimetre during takeoff, and the small hangar crew was satisfied that they were ready to launch and retrieve ships on short notice once the doors were re-cut. They only had room to perform repairs on two fighters at a time, but with only four mechanics reserved for smaller ships, there wasn't much justification for more. When the interior of the Warlord was complete, there would be room for two fighters and a shuttle in the repair bay.

As Minh made his way from the rear fighter bay, he couldn't help but wonder at how much work was left to do on the Warlord. Though the ship was fully functional and looked complete on the outside, more than half the habitation area hadn't been finished. While replacing her main support beams, it had been decided to remove whole sections of deck plating, leaving half the habitation areas - most noticeably the cafeteria - unusable. He could hear the sounds of conversations drifting down the narrow hallway towards him as he passed through a bulkhead door. The new hatch looked out of place in a hallway with cables lining the sides of the corridor. It was a work in progress.

So was the Warlord's crew. He emerged from the aft-most section of the ship into the only usable large cargo bay. As instructed, the crew had broken out dozens of mismatched portable chairs and tables. A bunch of small sealed crates rounded out their common room furniture. The off-duty crew sat around leisurely, waiting to watch a large holographic projector, talking, or just laying back on one of the cots that had made their way down from the crew quarters. "Commander!" called Joyboy, a pilot who had become well known for his up-beat nature and big, toothy grin. He was at a table surrounded by crewmen who hadn't yet learned that he was also a card shark.

Minh picked his way across the room to the table, looking the crowd over. There were over ninety crew in the hold, several of them waiting for a mechanic to finish hooking up a large, beaten up holoprojector. He was head and arms deep in the base of the old machine. "Did you say there was a trick to this, Commander?" he called over his shoulder.

Minh perked up at hearing his rank being called, then saw Stephanie answer. "Yeah. When we first set it up aboard, Ashley tweaked something so it projected a bigger picture than it was made for."

"Over-projecting didn't burn a lens?" the mechanic asked dubiously. "Because that could be the problem."

Stephanie stepped over and gave the old machine's base a solid kick. She waited a moment before asking, "no?"

The broad shouldered mechanic shook his head. "That's not gonna help, but

I think I see the problem." After a moment of squirming to reach something inside the machine a hologram of a talking kitten came on screen with the caption "KAWAII KITTEN" dancing around it. A child appeared in the air, opening a small stasis package. Within was a kitten who lazily rolled over and mewled "hi Mom," inspiring groans and sounds of awe from the watchers. "Okay, a word of advice for all the new people," Stephanie announced in a surprisingly loud voice. "Captain doesn't allow pets aboard, so if you buy a Kawaii kitten, do not open it! You can't put the little buggers back into their stasis packs once they're out, and they'll follow you around asking for treats and other crap. That, and they're obnoxious, latch on to random people, and when they grow up they become social maters, so it's like having a furry soap opera with lots of shrill yelling." Most of the crew seemed to take her seriously, while a few offered boos in return. "Seriously, I'll flush it out the airlock if I see it."

"Hey Ronin, glad you could join us," Pisser, a tall, narrow-faced woman with green hair told him as she sat down at the table. "Everything okay in the rear launch?"

"Locked down tight. Looks like our support crew gets a break, they'll be here soon," he replied, still distracted with trying to take in the various activities of the crowd. After being alone for so long, seeing large crowds of people was still strange. At first they were difficult to take, even frightening. Thanks to his partially completed therapy, he could handle a crowd and sometimes found them mesmerizing.

"You gonna sit down?" Joyboy asked. "Maybe play a few hands? I gotta get something off my chest."

"I bet he does," Pisser said. "Joyboy's been a baaaaad boy!"

"Gambling is the preoccupation of many fools and occupation of a few plunderers," Minh-Chu said offhandedly.

"That's a no, Joyboy," interpreted Pisser. "Ronin knows better than to waste his luck on a card game."

The mechanic who was working on the holoprojector noticed him as soon as he stood up and started walking over. "Sir!" he called out. "Commander Ronin, Sir."

"That's me unless you're about to give me a reason to wish I was someone else," Minh replied, shaking the man's offered hand.

"I just wanted to say thank you on behalf of myself and all the slaves you and your captain freed from the Palamo. My name is David, this is my fiancée, Nerine."

Before Minh could reply he was embraced briefly but enthusiastically by a far too skinny young woman with curly brown hair. "You commanded the fighters who disabled the Palamo?"

Minh didn't quite know how to react, but took a cue from Commander Stephanie Vega, who nodded from a couple of metres away. "I did. I'm sorry, you must have lost people in that fight," he said.

"Almost none," David said as he took Nerine under his arm. "Your people managed to disable engines and weapons without damaging life support in most areas. There were a lot of burns and several decompressions, but you guys took care of us and picked up survivors who were lucky enough to be wearing a vacuum suit."

"If the Triton and Samurai Wing never turned up, we'd probably still be on that old carrier," added a man from behind Stephanie, who was wearing a grin that made her amusement plain.

"You're welcome," Minh offered. "How are you getting on aboard the Warlord?"

"I signed up as a machinist and general mechanic," answered David with pride. "Nerine here is one of your new food preps."

"I prefer cookie," she corrected with a playful grin. "Speaking of which, Tom's probably looking for me. Gotta go get a bunch of forma protein squares processed into something that looks edible."

A few people who overheard her announcement shuddered at the mention of the processed food.

"Can you make some vegetable Lo-Mein noodles for two?" Minh asked quietly. "I'm headed to the bridge, and I don't think the watch-person has had dinner yet."

"Comin' up, Commander," Nerine said.

"You mean Lo-Mein shaped food with flavouring mixed in," Joyboy corrected.

"It's not that bad," Minh countered. "I could think of several things with worse textures. Oh, and you knocked up my girlfriend," Minh added, unable to resist.

"And there it is!" Pisser shouted, leaping to her feet as though her favourite team just scored a goal. "He brought it up before Joyboy! You slag-brains owe me today's pay!"

Joyboy lowered his head as the surrounding crew burst into laughter or tried to catch up on what they missed.

Minh-Chu couldn't help but laugh along as he waited for most of the commotion to subside. Stephanie looked openly shocked, despite her amusement. "True?" she asked as she approached him. "I don't watch Crewcast like some people."

"Yup," Minh-Chu nodded. He turned to Joyboy who looked like he was ready to beg for his place in the fighter squadron and put his hand on his shoulder. "Congratulations, one man's shrew is another man's goddess," he said to him. "Best of luck with the four AM feedings. I'll make sure you have plenty of time planet-side to help out."

Nerine, catching the barb, approached with two steaming disposable boxes. Her wide-eyed laughter had a tinge of sympathy for Joyboy, whose head was down, his eyes closed as he groaned like a damned man. "Here's your order, first out of the kitchen."

"Thank you very much," Minh-Chu said, accepting the boxes.

"Oh, and the texturizer is broken now, we only got five orders out with it," she whispered.

"That's a bad thing? I've never had forma before," Minh said.

"That means I'm getting two of those orders," Stephanie said. "One for me, one for the captain."

"Yes, Ma'am," Nerine said. "Everyone else's food will be firm mush, like really old pudding, no matter what flavor we put in it. On the bright side, we can make really good pudding."

"See you in the morning," Minh-Chu said to his pilots. "Get as much sleep as you can, while you can." He followed Stephanie and Nerine as they headed to the partitioned-off section of the cargo bay where they'd temporarily set up the kitchen. "What is forma, anyway?"

"It's a specially engineered processed algae with essential nutrients and protein. At least that's what the crate says," Nerine replied. "I don't think anyone wants to know much more than that, though."

"You're right," Stephanie said. "It produces a lot of food for the storage space it takes, but with the texturizer broken, dinner will be memorable, and not in a good way. I'll get a couple of security people here just to manage the crowd."

"Thank you," Nerine beamed. "I'm sure it'll be fine. Do you want the last good meal for Frost?" she asked.

"No, he won't eat forma," Stephanie replied. "He's on meal bars."

"Why won't he eat forma?" Minh-Chu asked.

"He won't say, something happened before I met him. If he won't talk about it, it was bad," Stephanie explained.

"But this is a good batch, I've already done the raw test," Nerine said, shuddering. "It was terrible, but it sat well."

"Thank you again, Nerine," Minh-Chu said.

"I'll see you on the bridge after I deliver one of these to the captain," Stephanie said. "He's working on something in his quarters."

"See you there," Minh-Chu said, moving towards the main corridor.

When he neared the bridge, he could hear Finn saying, "Just look at the guide and plug it in."

Minh quietly entered the bridge and took in the scene. Ashley was under her console waist-deep and Finn was standing over her with his fists planted on his hips. Ashley's new copilot, Clara Ramone, was watching from her seat with a worried expression.

"What's this wire for, anyway?" Ashley asked from under the console.

"I don't know, you didn't let me look at it," Finn replied.

"It fell out before you got here, and you've been no help," Ashley replied.

"What colour is it?" Finn asked.

"Sort of a teal, oh! There's a bunch of plugs down here just like it, they're all empty. How do I know which one to plug this into?"

"Okay, some of those are redundancies, others are reserved. You should find a number on the wire you're holding that matches one of the terminals."

"Um," Ashley said. She didn't elaborate.

The trio looking on waited long moments before Finn broke down. "Um… what?"

"Got it!" Ashley declared. A hologram appeared just above the main pilot's controls that added all the status information relative to what they manipulated. Ashley came out from under the console hurriedly and saw the change. "Okay, that's cool, and new."

"Oh, right, we didn't activate that because we though it would be distracting," Finn said. "It was never plugged in."

"Well, I'm glad I did. Every switch has an info reading and a link to a corresponding log. All the bridge panels should have this," Ashley said, manipulating a few of the small holograms pointing to switches.

"That's another reason why we didn't plug it in," Finn said, noticing Minh-Chu for the first time. "If they see that on your console, everyone will want it."

"Hi, Minh," Ashley said with a smile as she made herself comfortable in the pilot's seat.

"I brought dinner," Minh-Chu said. "I didn't know what you wanted so I just ordered another of what I was having. Feeling like tasting something from home."

"What is it?" Ashley asked after checking and re-locking her controls.

"So, soup's on," Finn said. "I'd better go before that ancient texturizer dies for good."

"I'll take the copilot's station so you can go too, Clara," Minh said.

"Thanks, I'm starving," she said, quickly logging that she was transferring control to Ronin temporarily. "I should have chomped something before watch, but I didn't have time."

"No one had time," Finn said, waiting for Clara at the door. "But that's what happens when our time on-world gets cut suddenly. You'll get used to it."

"That happens a lot?" she asked as she caught up with Finn and the door closed behind them.

Minh-Chu handed one of the recyclable boxes to Ashley as he sat in the copilot's seat and punched in his call sign, informing the computer that he was taking part of the watch. "How is she?" Minh-Chu said.

"Ooh, noodles," Ashley said as she tore the chopsticks off the side of the container. "Thank you, Minh," she said. "How's Clara? She's good. Not as good as Larry, but she's good."

Minh-Chu tried not to dwell on thoughts of Laura, who was killed by Larry, but Ashley saw through him.

"I'm so sorry," she said. "I didn't mean to..."

"It's all right," Minh-Chu said, focusing on pulling his chopsticks off the side of the box without ripping it wide open. "We can't guard everything we say because someone did something terrible. When you mention Larry, I think of Laura, true, but that's not a bad thing. I didn't know her as well as a lot of people from the First Light, but I always liked her."

"I didn't really know her either," Ashley said. "But she was always really nice. She seemed smart, too."

"Thank you," Minh-Chu replied.

Ashley put her food down for a moment and pulled Minh's chopsticks free for him. "Pull from the top, that's the trick."

"Thanks," Minh said.

"Um, so how are the pilots?" Ashley asked, digging into her noodles and drawing a knot of Lo-Mein into her mouth.

"Oh, they're good. Having a laugh at Joyboy right now. They're going to be on him for days."

Ashley cocked her head quizzically as she chewed.

"Oh, you haven't heard? He and Paula are expecting," Minh said.

Ashley choked and coughed, keeping her mouth closed, but her hand up in front for safety and politeness. Minh stood up and patted her on the back urgently.

"Are you okay?" he said when it looked like she was recovering.

She finished swallowing properly and nodded. "Yup, gotta give a girl warning when you drop something like that at dinner."

Minh sat back down at the copilot's seat. "Sorry, I guess it's not as big of a deal to me as it is to everyone else."

"Well, you two were together," Ashley asked. "So it's a pretty big betrayal."

"Who? Me and Joyboy?" Minh-Chu said with a crooked grin. "A passing fancy, at best."

Ashley was just about to try a smaller mouthful of noodles when she was interrupted by a fresh chuckle. "Eating is dangerous around you."

"Okay, I'll be more serious while we're chomping," Minh-Chu said as he shoved hot noodles into his mouth and wished he had something to drink. He could tell there was something off about the noodles, but the flavouring was so powerful that it could have been easy to miss if he was never told it was processed algae.

Ashley was quiet until they were both halfway through their takeout boxes before asking, "I gotta know though... you and Paula? Are you okay?"

Minh-Chu finished chewing. "She wouldn't leave me alone," he said. "I don't know how, but she made it look like we were in a relationship on Crewcast, too."

"Really? She doesn't have the rank to get shower access, does she?" Ashley asked.

"Nope, not even close," Stephanie said as she entered the bridge.

"Shower access?" Minh asked.

"Oh, it's what Ash calls Command Level Access, because you can actually check on people while they're in the shower," Stephanie replied. "It actually sounds a bit perverted now that I'm explaining it to anyone else. I've never used my access for that, just to be clear." She dropped into the captain's chair and opened her own box of noodles. "It lets you monkey with Crewcast, too. I don't like talking about that kind of access because it makes some people feel self-conscious, even though I don't abuse it."

"I don't really care," Minh said with a shrug. "People get to know each other really well in a military unit, modesty gets out of the way when you're taking your first real shower in a month and the public shower rooms are all you can get." He couldn't help remembering seeing Ashley ducking down behind a shower stall door when he was in the pilot's berthing aboard the Triton. The memory brought a little smile to his lips. He cleared his throat and pressed on. "Anyway, I don't know how Paula did it, but she faked the relationship on my end while I was on patrol for pay."

"I'll have to look into that," Stephanie said.

"So that's all it was?" Ashley asked. "She faked the whole thing?"

Sometimes Minh-Chu didn't like his belief in pure honesty; it didn't always lead to the things he wanted. "Given enough time, a river can turn even a mighty stone to sand," he replied, shoving a generous bundle of noodles into his mouth.

Both women burst into laughter that almost outlasted the time it took him to chew and swallow.

"So there was something," Stephanie said with a grin. "I should have put money on it."

"She wore me down for a bit, and there was snoggery, but the more she talked the less I liked her, so that didn't last," Minh said. "That sounded harsh, but she's just got these opinions about people that are opposite mine. So, any attraction that could have been there died."

"Opinions like?" Stephanie asked.

"I'd rather she spoke for herself on that, you can see it all on Crewcast anyway. I respect her work ethic, but we just couldn't see eye to eye."

"So Joyboy knocking her up is the best thing that could happen for you," Stephanie concluded.

"Well, if that kid manages to have a good upbringing, yeah. Joyboy's not going to be happy though, I'm putting him on shuttle duty once we get back. I know Paula well enough to make sure that kid has a dad."

"You never stop thinking of other people," Ashley said.

"Care for others and you won't have to wonder who will care for you," Minh-Chu replied. "I grew up in a passionate but tight family. Lots of arguments, but we always knew what everyone else was thinking."

"Reminds me of the Triton," Ashley said quietly as she absently dug through her noodles with her chopsticks.

"What happened there? I haven't had time to ask," Stephanie asked.

Ashley took a bite and finished before answering in an uncharacteristically quiet manner. "You guys can't share this," she said. "Not with anyone."

"All right," Minh said.

"It's big security stuff," Ashley reinforced, looking to Stephanie, who nodded. "Okay," Ashley continued. "It's a special type of human, that doesn't look human at all. Its memories told me that Earth used issyrian technology and hundreds of years of research to make his species, and now they breed them in a habitat that I think the Triton really liked."

"What's this?" Stephanie asked. "I missed something."

"The ship computer," Ashley said. "It's just an interface for this being that took the Triton's name. It's like it communicates with the ship so well that it's just a part of it, even though it uses some kind of impulse or telepathic trick to communicate with the ship."

"So it's a human?" Minh asked.

"It's based on us, but it looks totally different. It's like some cool, wide, eel that is one big, flat fin that can expand and shrink. It can go through all the waterworks in the Botanical Gallery, but was in stasis since Wheeler took the ship. No one told it that Sol Defence let the Triton go so people on Earth could study the galaxy through the people who took the ship."

"So it was left there alone?" Stephanie asked.

"Yeah, but it was asleep the whole time. It was lonely when we found it though," Ashley said, sympathy in her expression. "Almost the same loneliness that Oz has, I think that's one of the reasons why they bonded so well."

"Wow, you guys really did have a serious sharing session," Stephanie said.

"It connected me to Oz, so I felt everything he does, then I saw what the Triton sees."

"Through telepathy?" Minh-Chu asked.

"Yeah, it was amazing," Ashley said. "Not scary at all, except for when it was scared, like when he was attacked for the first time. I never thought I'd see a ship get frightened, but he was so scared. The Triton isn't afraid of fighting anymore though, it seems like he likes it a bit. A lot like Oz there too.

"Triton watches everything on the ship, it likes to help us, to watch children grow, enjoys seeing people get along, too. By watching everyone, it feels connected to us, and it loves having a crew. Eventually it'll directly connect to its entire command crew, but it'll take time for it to trust them, because no one out here have really long records, like someone would in the Sol System. For now, I think it's really happy to be connected to Oz, and it was really glad to meet me. I miss him already."

"Oz?" Stephanie asked.

"Him too, but not as much as Triton," Ashley said. "I want to be here, don't get me wrong. I wanted to be here more before Triton connected with me, though. He's a really cool… thing? Ship? Yeah, he likes being thought of as part of the ship."

"Where would you really rather be?" Minh-Chu asked. "If you had a choice."

Ashley thought a moment before answering. "Here, I still have a lot to do here. Besides, even Triton thought so. He likes me a lot, I could just tell, but I'm not ready to be part of the command structure there. After what he's shown me, how big a ship like that really gets when there are thousands of people aboard, I know I'm not ready. I'd rather be a pilot and mission girl here."

"Mission girl?" Stephanie asked.

"You'll see, I have a few ideas about what I'll be doing when we land, already cleared it with Captain. I might need something from that box I left with you," Ashley said.

"Oh, you can have all that stuff back," Stephanie replied. "Now that I know you were only gifting it because you thought you'd have to go on the run after telling everyone about your Triton access info."

"Yeah, sorry 'bout that," Ashley replied.

"Don't do it again, you can always trust me," Stephanie said. "But I'm keeping a couple of things, just as a lesson."

Minh-Chu enjoyed watching the easy exchange between Ashley and Stephanie. It was the best way to get to know both of them, though Ashley captured most of his interest.

"Don't worry, Boss, won't pull anything like that again," Ashley replied to Stephanie. "Can't wait to see what you're keeping, either. I bet Frost'll be happy."

"Later," Stephanie said, smiling awkwardly as she glanced at Minh-Chu. "And Frost is a very lucky man."

Minh-Chu kept Ashley company for the rest of her watch. Different crewmembers cycled through the bridge during the hours that followed. she taught him the finer points of the Warlord's controls, and they talked about where they came from, focusing on happier moments for the most part.

He caught himself forgetting that there was an age difference after awhile, and when it was time to retreat to his bunk, he couldn't stop thinking of stories he could tell her about himself, or the stories she'd shared with him.

CHAPTER 43
STEPS FORWARD

Ayan's fingers fumbled with the clips on the extreme environment armour. Tears obstructed her view as she tried to get the second outer layer of her suit to attach to her legs, something she'd gotten used to doing, but she couldn't find the right connections. "Come on, I just need to get out there, help the effort," she said. "Just have to get to work." The lights of dozens of holographic status windows focusing on the settlement outside the Clever Dream made the shadows shift and flicker.

The hatch in her quarters slid to the side and she shouted: "I told you, Victor, I don't need guarding while I'm on the Clever Dream, and I don't want you hovering…" she looked up and saw Liam Grady entering, looking uneasy.

She hurriedly tried to remove the few clips she'd managed to attach on her shins. "Bloody thing won't come off now," she said. "Release, you terrible things." At the command, her suit allowed the armour to detach.

She wiped at her tears and threw herself into Liam's arms. Within his embrace, she didn't cry, but found herself breathing as though she had just finished a long run. His arms were wrapped around her tightly. One hand started to run up and down her back, comforting.

"Your guardians say you won't let them in," he said. "What's happened?"

"Jason's gone," Ayan replied. "He's taking the Victory Machine, he's going to finish Roman's work. He's going to close it down somewhere far away, and he'll die alone, in the dark. I tried to stop him," she said. Her heart was racing, she couldn't slow her breathing down, and she had no idea why, but she struggled against Liam's embrace.

"We can't control people," Liam said. He tried to hold on to her, but had to let her go when her attempts to win free became frantic.

She summoned a reflective hologram and looked into her own puffy eyes, saw her disheveled appearance and tried to get herself in order. "I'm losing control, no one's listening to me. I have to rally," she said with no grief in her expression, yet tears still dropped down her cheeks.

Liam stepped in behind her then, close enough to be in the reflective hologram, and he slowly closed his arms around her midsection. She watched him, how he looked down at her with concern, and couldn't help but look back at herself. The young woman looked so weary and frightened. "Oz followed you, even though I know it's the last thing he wanted to do. He and Alaka are leading the efforts out there, and it's all because they believe in you. They believe without question, and they'll work until they have to stop. They all will." He kissed the top of her head.

"They trust the woman I'm based on. Loosely based on. Her experiences, her training, her accomplishments," Ayan replied. "I haven't done anything to earn their trust."

Liam looked her in the eye using the reflection. "I didn't know her," he said. "I don't care about her." He swept strands of her hair out of her face then wrapped his arm around her waist. "Alaka and his family didn't know that other woman, neither did thousands of people out there, but you've earned their trust since we got here. I've come to know a brilliant lady, who's stealing my heart. She's in pain right now, and it's not the time to charge back in, but when you're ready," he gave her waist a squeeze. "It'll be magnificent, because you're so much more than the sum of your parts."

Ayan was calming down, the manic need to take control of everything around her was dissipating, and she was left with the moment she shared with the man in her quarters. The weeks with him at her side had been an impatient time, where things seemed to move a quarter as quickly as they ought to, but they were good times. Most of the good memories she had of her time in Port Rush were accompanied by his presence, or centered around time they spent together away, tending to things in Greydock, trying to further their cause. What Ayan felt was more than trust or respect.

"You're a rare woman, Ayan," he said to her.

She turned in his arms and pulled the collar of his vacsuit so she could reach his lips. Ayan curled the thick fabric in her fist as she closed her eyes and kissed him passionately. He returned the kiss and they were locked together for a long, warm moment before he pulled away, his calm demeanor broken.

"This is wrong," he said. "The timing-"

She slipped her foot behind his knee and pushed his chest. He fell onto the bed and stared up at her in shock. "This is happening," she said, falling on top of him. Her lips were on his, interrupting whatever objection was coming next. He wasn't returning her affections, and she could feel grief threatening to return to the surface, her urges beginning to fade. "Don't stop this," she said, looking into his worried face.

"I don't want to," Liam replied. "But this might not be coming from the right place."

"I want this, right now, whatever it is," she replied. "I won't regret it, not with you."

Ayan kissed him again, and let her instincts guide her, something she rarely did since she woke up for the first time in Freedom Tower. When he returned her affections, kissing and moving those wonderful hands across her body, it felt incredible.

***

"Fleet Warden Harrison," addressed one of the Operations staff through the sound system in Kimberly Harrison's quarters. She rolled out of bed and put her robe on.

"Yes, what is it?" she answered, crossing to the narrow slit that served as a porthole. She could see the Carthan Fleet lazily moving in front of the Tamber moon. There were dozens of ships, all top of the line battleships and destroyers, fortresses of the stars.

"The surface team is reporting an intrusion in Port Rush. Something entered the secure area," reported the officer of the watch.

"Tell me they captured the intruder, Officer," she replied.

"I'm afraid the Victory Machine is gone. Its operator, Roman, was left behind and is in care."

"Is he still comatose?" she asked.

"No Ma'am, he's brain dead. They were keeping him alive until you were informed."

Kimberly leaned against the bulkhead in front of her and sighed. "Maybe it's better this way," she whispered.

"Pardon, Ma'am?" asked the watchman.

"Never mind. Inform the volunteer operators for the Victory project that they won't be needed and reduce their sentences accordingly. If they haven't bought their freedom with their offer to volunteer, reassign them to their old units. Tell the techs on the planet to seal the hospital up, fill the contaminated rooms with plasticrete and get back up here. They have an hour to do their duty well, no sloppy work."

"And the security force?"

Fleet Warden Harrison thought for a moment. "Petition Judge Lindt to add three years to their sentences." She knew that he'd make it five; he was the hardest judge in the fleet.

"Yes, Ma'am."

"Now, do we have any idea where the Victory Machine went? Or is this the end of that story?" the Fleet Warden asked.

"None of our ships have picked it up. It seems it used a-"

"Crush gate," she interrupted. "A high powered wormhole."

"Yes Ma'am, we weren't able to determine where it led to, but no damage was done to the lab."

"Good, that's the end of our story with the Victory Machine," Kimberly Harrisson said, taking her robe off and heading for the shower. "Thank God. Inform Command, I'm holding a priority briefing in half an hour."

"But you've only been on rest for three hours, Ma'am."

"I can never sleep the night before a battle," she said.

"Yes, Ma'am."

***

Transporting himself and the Victory Machine to the furthest strategic point from Tamber and the Rega Gain system was easy. Eden Four loomed large from where he drifted in space. Jason Everin had no weapons, but radiated incredible power. He knew the silver ships and pillar shaped stations hanging in orbit around the green-blue gem scanned him. Temporal radiation was a puzzle, he knew, and they wouldn't know what to do.

The Victory Machine told him he was in a place that was distant enough so whatever he did there wouldn't effect the future promised to Ayan Rice the Second. It wouldn't jeopardise the lives of his other friends, either. It would accomplish the opposite in some cases. Paradox was the enemy, and after only a few minutes with the Victory Machine, he knew how to avoid it. The directive was built in, and that made avoiding temporal implosions easy.

Jason Everin knew exactly what would happen if he held on to the Victory Machine for too long. It would begin changing his past. Peering back along his own timeline, he saw different versions of his past where he was more and more ill, a plague on his life with Laura. Temporal radiation could ruin the days he'd already lived, making him ill in past tense, and he wouldn't have that. Most of the years he had with his wife were wonderful, she was the constant good in his life. There was nothing he could do to change her death. That was what led him to take the Victory Machine himself.

A mental flash brought an image of Ayan Rice the Second in front of a large monument. Lanterns burned around a large circular pedestal featuring quarter scale statues standing all around. She directed a toddler to a section of the monument where Jason and Laura had been immortalized. There were so many statues, many of them he didn't recognize, others he did faintly, but most of them were changing before his eyes. The toddler crossed the distance and dropped a half-mangled lilac bunch at Laura and Jason's feet before running back all smiles to Ayan, who embraced her girl. "Well done, they'll love that," she said.

The visions followed his thoughts, and eventually led him to one of the only other near-certainties of the future. He began having a vision featuring the Triton through the main display aboard the bridge of the Warlord. "Happy hunting, Warlord," said the voice of Agameg Price. His tone was respectful, almost mournful. The Triton began to move away and cloaked.

A look around the bridge of the Warlord revealed one central figure. Jacob Valent stood in armour Jason had never seen before: heavy overlapping plates that were sharpened to lethal edges with fine emitter grooves running down each one that faintly glowed red. One of Jake's eyes was a dark coloured mechanism protected by an armoured lens. Over one shoulder, a half-shredded blue and red strand of cloth hung, over the other he wore a fresh white length of cloth that had a gold seal pressed onto it, a sunrise over sand.

The captain's seat was gone, and Jake stood in its place looking twenty years older than he ought to. Behind him a woman with straight auburn hair and an artificial eye nodded to herself and left quietly. Jason knew she was on her way off the ship, and she was leaving Jacob Valent alone. The vision was less than three years into the future, and Jason couldn't help but investigate.

He traced the mystery back to a vision of a grave on Tamber with Ayan Rice inside and he realized that there were two Ayans in the future. Jacob Valent knelt before the simple raised plaque with a white scarf clenched in his fist. "I will fight," he said, furious and tearful, gnashing his teeth. "I will fight until the people who did this to you are remembered only for how I destroyed them. Until our galaxy is clean again."

That was the turning point. In his own way, Jacob Valent would become weak, a being without sympathy and a man fallen into the trap of perpetual revenge. Strength and companionship were the solutions and within seconds Jason knew exactly what to do. Out of all the people he knew, Jacob Valent's future was in flux the least; change could be more reliably predicted. Remote viewing the strands connecting all the people he'd just seen led him to the components that would save Jacob Valent.

"His daughter," Jason said to himself as he discovered the location of Alice Valent. "She's coming, he needs her, but he won't be able to admit it after what's coming." He used the Victory Machine to propose sending a message to her and let it perform a simulation, then present a result. To his shock and dismay the single monument for Ayan became two, and a host of friends turned warriors stood around the graves instead of Jacob Valent.

"I'm starting to understand why this Machine has to be destroyed," Jason said as he mentally proposed another course of action to the machine. His mind was flooded with broadening results until finally, Jacob wasn't standing alone on the bridge of the Warlord. He still seemed hardened, ready for battle, but his daughter stood at his side in similar armour. She looked younger, and her expression seemed proud instead of disappointed. Jason settled on the course of action that would lead to that possibility. "He won't be alone, and she will survive."

Roman wasn't strong enough for remote encounters with people by the end, but the Victory Machine was glad to open its systems and let him perform one. Alice Valent had a neural communications node, it was the key to communicating with her in the future. He reached out to her on the future battlefield and, with a gasp, he lived several minutes with her in the space of seconds. Before he was willing to let go of the future vision he shared with her, it came to an end. Distracting Alice in the future could cause more harm than good. "That's done," Jason said to himself. "Thank God I only have to send Jake a short message."

He sent his short transmission to Jacob Valent then began closing the wormholes the Victory Machine used to view the future, the present, and the past. As the Victory Machine slowly stopped expending energy, he could feel the power levels rise.

Jason left one wormhole open and watched as Laura stepped into the Pilot's Ball aboard the First Light. Seeing her again brought sadness and relief. She was so beautiful in her black dress, an obvious contrast to Ayan, but he only had eyes for his Laura. As her eyes found him standing near the dance floor, he was speechless, grinning like a fool, but unable to stop. "How did it get so complicated?" Jason asked as he watched himself cross the room to meet her in the past. He let the wormhole close slowly and set the replay of her entering the room to fill a corner of his mind.

He couldn't feel the effects of the temporal radiation yet, but he knew it would be a matter of days before he did, and his past would change. That first encounter would never happen. "No, I want the life I had, flaws and all, it's better than any I thought I'd get."

He watched the silver ships in the distance, darting about, perhaps wondering what to do about the strange man holding a powerful device in the distance and smiled. "This is a change they'll notice, and someone will know it was me."

Energy continued to build up inside the Victory Machine, and he followed the directions he was given as he stole it. At its centre he forced a microscopic wormhole to open that led back into itself, and the energy began to multiply. It would grow exponentially in seconds, and when it went critical, it would only effect the present in one place.

Jason found himself recalling the picture Oz had hanging in his quarters aboard the Sunspire when he was in command: the original crew of the First Light in their youthful and optimistic days. "I love you all," he said. The replaying image of Laura from the Victory Machine persisted, and he watched her smile at him just like she did at the Pilot's Ball.

***

The spectacle from Eden IV as the mysterious power source exploded was nothing short of awesome. After a bright light, a shockwave burst outward. The readings of temporal radiation were drawn into the forming black hole and disappeared.

Millions of ships, hundreds of manufacturing facilities, and smaller metallic entities panicked as gravitational sensors read well beyond tolerance. Nothing in the Eden system stood a chance of surviving the hours that followed.

CHAPTER 44
HODRIA

"This port maneuvering chart is insane," Ashley said as she looked at the visi version of navnet. It was mapped along the curvature of the planet, Hodria, instead of into small sectors. She had taken the navigator's post, while Jacob piloted the ship himself. "Now I understand why you're at the controls."

"I know you can pilot this," Captain Valent said as he chose a broad holding pattern and set the ship's autopilot to follow it. He still held the main pilot controls in his hands, however. "I just wanted you and Clara to get a good look at their navnet system. It's called Gudouk, don't ask me why. The name doesn't translate."

"That's because it's an acronym," Agameg offered from behind them.

"What does it stand for?" Clara asked.

"That doesn't translate either," Agameg said.

"Oh, look, a pretty ship," Ashley said as she flicked a larger ship's holographic image with her finger. The image copied into a secondary projector and increased in size so she could get a better look. It was a sleek, six hundred metre long vessel that looked almost windswept. "It's a luxury liner."

"For jurriks. It must smell terrible inside," Kadri commented from the communications station. "One of them opening their helmet is enough to clear a room."

"I've never met one," Captain Valent said.

"They are quite pleasant in general," Agameg said. "They have such a strong fragrance because their mating materials are airborne. One of the most difficult races for shape shifters to imitate, mostly for that reason."

"Ew, 'mating materials,' thanks for sparing us the details, moving on," Ashley said with a shudder. "I'm not seeing any offered landing patterns."

"Godouk routes are set by visi pilot ships," Kadri explained. "I'm trying to contact several now."

"So we'll be releasing our helm to another ship?" Clara asked.

"Exactly," Captain Valent said. "We take over for a few seconds while we're passing through the atmosphere, then the ground stations pick us up and navigate us to our landing site."

"There are no ground stations here, Sir," Kadri corrected. "We'll be assigned to what they call a free port. A pilot ship has just picked us up. Their ident checks out, I'm sending their signal to the helm now."

"Thank you Kadri," Captain Valent replied.

The transit through orbital space was brisk and surprisingly straight considering the thousands of ships in holding patterns. There were heavy haulers, hundreds of different visi battleships running patrols, smaller fighting ships from every nearby government, more independent ships than any of them could count, and a smattering of other ships mixed in. Before they knew it, they were passing through the atmosphere, and Captain Valent was back in control.

The navigational system changed to reflect the fact that they were in atmosphere and Ashley began feeding Jake information. She couldn't help but spare a few glances at the landscape beneath. Shards, spires and slivers of glass were lit by soft golden light as they reached for the heavens. "Why don't they break?" asked Clara from over her shoulder.

"They do, but not easily. They're biological, roughly translating into amber trees," Agameg informed them.

"Those are trees?" asked Ashley in amazement.

"Sort of. The plants excrete sticky fluid to catch insects. The sap hardens and they keep growing up instead of out because of the low gravity. It's a small world, so it only has point seven six gees."

Ashley marked their landing spot, a small patch in a large, flat section of ground. There were dozens of tall structures, most of them marked as habitats and military buildings. They were built to imitate the forest surrounding them. She selected a safe route for approach and nodded in satisfaction as it appeared in front of Jake. "This looks like it'll be more interesting than I thought," she commented.

"Oh, don't count on it," Kadri chuckled. "Most of this planet is swamp. You know the sap those trees are made of? It's everywhere. I'm not leaving the ship."

***

"Next time, I listen to Kadri," Ashley said as she expanded her vacsuit until it covered everything up to the neck. "The ground's sticky, the air's tacky, even the smell sticks to the back of my throat. It's like syrup without the sweet."

"I told you," Stephanie said as she watched the vacsuit expand under Ashley's mini-dress. Her suit was so tightly fitted that that she still drew attention. The dress was almost too short, and had a brave neckline that pointed down. The vacsuit beneath hid skin tone, but it did nothing to hide shape. "The sun might be good for regular clothes, but she said this whole continent is some kind of sap marsh."

"I was hoping to gather some intelligence," Ashley whispered.

"How so?"

"Booty trap." Ashley smiled.

"Really? Here?" Stephanie asked, hushed.

"It's a big port, law doesn't seem to care about what we do much, not enough to make sure info piracy doesn't happen anyway, and every second ship has a different corporate logo on it. Maybe even more," Ashley explained. "Besides, I don't feel like I'm contributing enough."

"You're the lead pilot, you manage all the other pilots who take the helm of the Warlord," Stephanie countered.

"You mean Clara? Our navigators? Other than some training, they're easy. The only other pilot who takes the Warlord's controls is Captain, and well..." She rolled her eyes. "I wouldn't try to manage him. Even while we were rebuilding the Warlord I felt like I was dragging my butt. I was either carrying stuff around, running cable, or painting. Brainless work."

"You're not that kind of specialist, you worked harder than anyone expected you to. They couldn't see it while we were hidden, but those records are out, and everyone's seeing who got things done, and who dragged their butts," Stephanie replied. "What did you paint, though? I haven't gotten a chance to check it out."

"Oh, it was this great decal I was going to put behind the ship's name when we were done. A beefy screaming warrior with long hair, based on the story I read when I looked up the ship's name after joining up," Ashley replied, pointing to the side of the ship, where most of the workers and technicians worked at cutting ports and guns free from the bonds that formed when they expanded their ergranian hull.

"Then Captain changed the name," Stephanie said. "Too bad, that might have been good on the side of the ship."

"I rolled it up and scoonched it in under my bunk. Maybe we can put it up inside the ship if there's a spot later. Anyway, if I can gather some intelligence at one of the bars that were on the port notice, then I'll really be doing my part," Ashley argued. "Besides, you'll be watching."

"From a distance." Stephanie looked Ashley up and down.

Ashley smiled and winked alluringly. "Irresistible even with the vacsuit?"

"Your looks aren't what worry me," Stephanie replied. "This just isn't the safest place for you to give it a try. We don't know the terrain or the people, aside from Berkovitz. I know there are people here who know who we are and what we're worth to the Order. I don't want you caught out in the open if someone has the stones to start something."

"Here? I bet more people would take Captain's side. I'd have plenty of time to duck while you guys sort it out. Besides, it's not like I'm one of the standouts on the crew, and I'll never get caught. I'm using a passive hand scanner hidden in the glove of my vacsuit," Ashley said, holding up her palm. "It's that old 'by touch' style so no one will be able to tell I'm collecting data. What's the worst that could happen?"

"All right, but if it looks too dangerous or starts to go bad," Stephanie warned.

"I'll back off and let you watch over me," Ashley promised. "No problem." As a final touch she shifted the colour of her vacsuit to a more complimentary shade of light purple, to match her dark blue mini-dress.

The rear hold of the Warlord opened to reveal the confiscated weaponry that had been stored on the Triton weeks before in the Enreega system. The variety of gear was already laid out for display. A whole squad of Warlord marines took their places to stand guard as Frost, Agameg, and a few other crewmen finished preparations. To one side, David and a couple of other mechanics sprayed a sign that read QUICK WEAPON REPAIR.

Captain Valent spoke to a pair of heavily-armoured visi and he handed one of them a palm-sized currency case. The sealed suits were sleek, with broad backs but unnaturally thin middles. Their arms weren't anchored at the shoulders like a human's, but seemed to drift from their midsection to the base of their necks at will. Across the surface of their chests lettering and shapes scrolled. Ashley tried to use the translator built into her small necklace comm but found herself bombarded with: *SLIP 2118 - SELLING MUURISH HOUNDS : PLATFORM 0672 NOW READY TO PERFORM MINOR STARSHIP REPAIRS & DETAILING : SLIP 9244 - KAWAII BRAND! FULL HOLD! : SLIP 0412 - HULL & EQUIP OF SM HAULER AUCTION, BID BEFORE IT SINKS : SLIP 0009 - USED SKIDS- LOW ALTITUDE, LOW PRICES, HIGH SPEED!...* and so on.

After a moment Ashley realized that Stephanie was staring at her with an amused smile. "How's the new comm, Ash?"

"Cheap, but it's working," she replied as she stopped the translation. "I was wondering, how does it send images into my eyes without me looking at it?"

"It bounces a beam off something nearby," Frost said as he joined them. "Still looking to do some shopping? You're going to get some deals, dressed like that."

"Nice," Stephanie said. "In front of your significant other, you're eye-groping a girl half your age. Good luck getting at my undercarriage when our quarters are ready."

"A compliment! Just acknowledging the work that goes into looking good," Frost protested. "Harmless, right, Ash?"

"From someone else, maybe," Ashley replied. "And Steph's right, your timing stinks."

"Can't win," Frost said. "I should just stay back and sell guns."

Ashley had seen ports without retail regulation before, but compared to Hodria they were orderly and small. The slips were all separated by a distinct lane of packed and hardened dirt. All the ships she could see in either direction had opened their holds to reveal a seemingly infinite variety of articles. The sounds of patrons moving from shop to shop nearly drowned out the droning of larger surface transport vehicles running down a road ten metres behind the Warlord.

The Warlord was seeing her first customers. The half-dozen crewmen at the weapons' table were busy, and before long the security squad had their rifles raised, pointed at anyone who touched a weapon on the table. "Load it at the table and you get slagged!" Frost shouted as he hurriedly returned to the Warlord's smaller rear hold. Captain Valent watched from the laneway near the open hatch with the visi guards at his side. To Ashley's surprise, they did absolutely nothing as one of their customers broke from the crowd with an ill-gotten handgun in his hands.

"Shoot him," Stephanie ordered calmly.

One of the Warlord's marines fired three rounds into his back. A crewman ran forward, snatched the weapon, and walked back to the Warlord's hold. Ashley could only stare in shock as the visi soldiers walked to the groaning thief on the ground, yanked his belt and backpack off then emptied his pockets. When all the thief's articles were collected, they offered them to Captain Valent who shook his head. "Consider it a tip."

A small, dented hover bot descended from above the crowds and scanned the thief. It turned to the visi guards and shook its round body while making several distorted grunt noises. "He'll live with medical support, but the ship he's registered to left nine days ago," translated Ashley's comm through text beamed into her eyes.

"Is the ship scheduled to return?" asked one of the guards in a guttural grunt and wheeze language.

"No," answered the round robot.

"Feed him to the luzeet," ordered one of the guards.

Two thin tendrils extended out of the sides of the hover bot and wrapped around the unconscious man. The bot swept him up as it flew over the Warlord to the nearest glassy spire, where it pressed his back against the sticky surface. Ashley's jaw dropped in shock and alarm. The bot bumped the man in the chest to ensure that he was well and truly stuck before zipping off to some other business.

"Is it putting him there for safe-keeping?" she asked Stephanie, knowing that it was an unlikely possibility, but hoping she was right.

"I don't think you'll want to watch," Stephanie replied. "But I'm just guessing."

Before her eyes a whip thin, vein-like tendril grew through the inside of the hardened sap towards the thief. Ashley glanced at Stephanie, who was still watching, and looked back to the man in time to see him jerk as though he had been struck in the back. Suddenly he was awake, struggling frantically. The crowd around them drowned out whatever sounds the man might be making, but Ashley's imagination filled in the rest. The thin vein stretching up through the hardened sap turned red from the tip down towards the base as the thief screamed. She looked away when she realized she was watching him being drained.

"So we're settled in?" Captain Valent asked the visi guards.

"You have paid us in full, yes. The duration of your stay does not match your stock level, however. I expect your guns to be gone in an hour. It seems like a waste of GC," the guard replied. Ashley read their side of the conversation as it was translated.

"We have other business here," Captain Valent replied.

"Good luck," the guards said before walking off casually.

"Frost," Captain Valent spoke into his comm. "Slip fees came out to fifteen thou. Double your prices."

There was barely a second's delay before Frost could be heard over the crowd. "Introductory stock is gone! Bringing out the real gear! Come get it!"

"Did you guys do this a lot before?" Ashley asked. "And what's with the introductory stock?"

"It's a trick," Stephanie replied. "They sell the standard stuff off for fair prices then break out the rest at four times the going rate."

"Eight times," Captain Valent chuckled. A few customers were walking away from the Warlord's hold, complaining bitterly. Twice as many were on their way in, however. "The demand for weaponry here is so high he thinks he'll be out in fifteen minutes. It's David and the other machinists that'll probably be busy for the next eight hours."

"Fixing guns," Ashley finished.

"Really good gig," Stephanie said. "They get a quarter of the take on repairs, it's going to be a nice payday for the machinists who are lucky enough to be off duty."

"Big demand for that here, too," Captain Valent replied. "Speaking of which." He pulled a gun belt and sidearm from a large bag and hitched it around Ashley's hips.

It was the ceramic shell pistol and bullet belt she'd used on the Triton. "I don't want to carry," she objected in a whisper. "It'll screw up the lines of my dress." She noticed that most of the shells had been exchanged for red and brown versions. Ashely wasn't entirely sure what they did, but knew they were lethal.

"All but two of your shells are still bursters and web rounds, but David painted them so they look like incendiary and shaped charge rounds," Captain Valent said. "These two at the sides? They're real. If you hit someone in full combat armour you'll punch a hole the size of your fist straight through."

"I'm not a killer," Ashley objected. "Besides, I'll be with Stephanie and two of her security people all the time."

"Listen," Stephanie whispered, taking one of Ashley's hands. "You haven't visited a port like this. The visi actually support human slavery, they don't care about what happens to you. If someone snatches you, law enforcement will be on their side, especially since you still have a listed price in the live goods exchange. Every human you see here is fair game and there are people here who are as good at snagging slaves as Captain is at bounty hunting. If you don't like what someone's doing near you, plug them in the face with whatever's loaded in that cannon, and we'll back you."

Ashley's mind was changed about carrying a sidearm, and she adjusted the belt so it hung better, bouncing on her hip as she walked. She suddenly felt less confident about her chosen role for the trip.

Stephanie must have been able to tell. "Would you rather skip this trip? You could stay aboard, or just stay with the group, no one would blame you."

"I know." Ashley looked around for a moment at all the people nearby. Most of them looked like normal spacers. A little mud spattered around the ankles, but she didn't see any of the anxiety she would expect to see in such a dangerous place. If they could move about without much of a care, why couldn't she? "No, I've got some coin burning a hole in my pocket and I don't think we'll see another port before New Years. I have shopping to do."

"You have pockets somewhere in that outfit?" asked one of Stephanie's marines. She was a taller woman with a broad chin who was quick to smile, but Ashley hadn't gotten a chance to know her.

Ashley flipped the short sleeve of her mini-dress up to reveal a strap holding several slips of GC that glittered their denominations of red for 25GC, green for 50GC, and purple for 100GC. "I have smaller GC bits and other denominations on the other arm," she told her. "You learn how to hide stuff when you live in a slave compound and have to wear whatever the masters tell you to."

"I could imagine," the marine said, mildly surprised. "I'm Megan."

"Ashley, most people call me Ash," she replied after adjusting her sleeve so it hid her currency.

"I think everyone knows who you are, Lieutenant," Megan replied conspiratorially.

Several crewmen joined them, including the rest of one of Stephanie's squads. They were a group of twenty-eight. "We're all here," Stephanie called out. "All right, here are the rules for this short leave: keep up with the group. Barter lightly with the shopkeepers, that means counter-offer once or twice, don't argue or piss them off. Once you buy it, it is *yours,* we will *not* be going back if you're not happy, and I doubt anyone will take returns. Do not buy anything that is too big to fit in your locker or bunk drawers. Our excursion will last two hours or until the Warlord recalls us, whichever comes first. Never go anywhere that will take you out of a direct line of sight of two of your crewmates. Even if you know you can take care of yourself here, it is in your best interest to assume you are wrong. Now let's go see the sights."

Ashley had never told Stephanie that she enjoyed watching her do her job, but it was true. It was always interesting to watch her friend do what she was best at. The group moved away from the Warlord with Stephanie and another marine in the lead.

At first she didn't see why the combination of lower gravity and sticky streets was such a big deal, then she took her first steps off the Warlord's ramp and nearly lost her balance. The ground had a tackiness that sometimes made pulling her foot off the ground to take the next step interesting. She'd already seen someone pull too hard and fall face first. The witnesses were happy to applaud their clumsy performance for a moment before going on with their business.

"So, you grew up on a planet?" asked Minh as he surprised her from behind.

As a reflex she gave him a hug, and smiled with relief when he returned the gesture. She released him and continued to walk with the group at his side. "Yup, my master bought me young. I was lucky he shopped local, got to know my home world that way. You're from Freeground, the same place as Captain?"

Minh hesitated a moment then nodded. "Technically he's from somewhere else, but as far as I'm concerned, he's my old friend from Freeground."

Ashley decided to sidestep the complicated explanation of Jacob Valent's origin; she already knew enough as far as she was concerned. It still gave her pause.

"Why do you call him that?" Minh asked. "I know he's the captain, but you use it like it's his name."

"You know, I have no idea," Ashley replied. "Steph? Why do we-"

"Tradition," she answered.

"So you don't know either?" Ashley teased.

"Nope. When I joined up most of the crew just called him Captain like it was his name. I think a lot of crews do that on mercenary ships, though. In all the time I've been aboard, he's never complained about it."

Megan smiled down at the group, from her height it was impossible to share the same eye level and added, "Before my time there were captains that had prices on their heads that were so big that they'd hide their name. They'd go by 'Captain of' and add whatever their ship name was. Maybe that's where it comes from?"

"Guess that's a good answer," Ashley said with a shrug. "Thanks." She returned her attention to Minh-Chu. "What was Freeground like?"

She could see Minh-Chu looking over the large pedestrian crowd, the ships, the crystal-like trees that hung over them filtering the golden light, and finally back to the shouting hawkers.

"Raw forma! What you see is a single percent of our stock in orbit!"

"Small machine parts! Selling bulk only!"

"Buy any item here for five GC!"

"General store! We got hygiene worms! Sims from thirty systems! QECS!"

When he returned his attention to her he had a slightly overwhelmed expression. "It's called Freeground, but it's nowhere near as free as this. I mean, our ports are these organized, secure sections where you can't sneeze without a DNA sniffer running a full background check on you. Admin doesn't even like people getting off their ships, they prefer to pre-arrange all their business before they dock. I used to hear about it from Jo-" Minh started then corrected himself, "from Jacob."

"What was it like growing up on a station?" Ashley asked. "I couldn't imagine being cooped up in space like that."

"Well," Minh said, visibly pondering the question. "Freeground is huge, you could probably fit everyone on this world in four of the main segments. Our living spaces were small, but everyone's were, so I didn't really notice. I grew up in pods that were mostly Asian, and our section was big enough to have its own tropical forest."

"You had a forest indoors?" asked Joyboy from behind. "Man, I have to see this station."

"It's way out of the way, but yeah, we had a forest. It was a great place to grow up. Safe, lots of kids, everyone knew each other. School was important though, so I stayed in right up until I joined the Fleet Academy. I wanted to see what was out there, and that was the only way."

"Couldn't you sign up with a starliner company or a freighter or something?" Ashley asked.

Minh laughed. "My mother would have hunted me down and brought me back. My role was to get an education, a good job, and find a nice Asian girl to make grandchildren with. It seemed like every fifth person had the last name Buu, but my parents still made it clear that I had to carry on the family name."

"So you signed up," Finger, a tall, gangly-limbed pilot behind Minh, concluded.

"Yup," Minh confirmed. "What is it they say? 'Join the military, they said. See the galaxy, they said.'" By the time he reached the word 'military' most of the people near them joined in. The rest of the expression was recited by a chorus. Minh chuckled and nodded before going on. "A month after I entered the academy, the All-Con conflict began and everyone was rushed through basic. I qualified for officer candidacy, which would have normally put me through an extra twenty months of school, but in wartime it was compressed into two. After final testing, they set me up with a squad and put me on a ship that looked like Freeground on the inside, only a lot smaller." Minh looked at her for a moment and shook his head. "But most of that is very boring. Just like living on Freeground. I'm happier here."

"So your whole family is back there?" Ashley asked, genuinely interested. "I'd love to hear about them. I'm half Asian, but I didn't learn enough about the culture. Keep a lucky dragon with me though," she said as she turned her back to him so he could see the stylized Chinese dragon crawling up the back of her dress. The group was turning into the first shop, which was a hold filled with wide aisles of cheap decorations and generic supplies.

"I was wondering about that. You have one whenever you're not in uniform," Minh said quietly.

"But he probably didn't ask because he was afraid to admit he was looking," Pisser commented as she manipulated a pair of cheap pink sunglasses so they looked Ashley up and down.

Ashley smiled at the pilot, amused at how Minh's squad wasn't afraid to tease him a little. "I used to love dragons when I was little. I couldn't read enough about the dinosaurs on Earth or Noxis. For a while I thought the Chinese of ancient Earth used to live with dragons. Glad Fred cured me of that belief."

"I wouldn't be the greatest tutor on Asian culture," Minh said apologetically. "I know just enough to be aware of the fact that my call sign doesn't really go well with the new name of our fighter wing."

"How's that?" asked Ashley.

"A ronin is a samurai without a master, so it's sort of weird that a pilot named Ronin would lead Samurai Squadron," Minh explained.

"Ah, well, I don't think anyone really cares."

"Anyway, my family tried to teach me about Asian culture, but I found it a little confusing. I think what they knew was a mix of history and culture from all parts of old Asia. My father made sure we knew we were mostly Vietnamese, but beyond that, nothing was absolutely certain."

"So your family is still in Freeground?" Ashley asked.

"My parents retired to Shem Lam, an old Lorander colony. It looks like my sisters will be going there too. People are leaving Freeground. Since the All-Con conflict Freeground has been near the centre of one war after another. What about your par-" Minh stopped himself with a look of dismayed surprise. "I'm so sorry," he apologized hurriedly.

Ashley didn't mind at all. She fixed him with a smile and shook her head. Her pedigree was one of the things that made her valuable before she was freed, and she was raised to take pride in it. "It's all right," she reassured. Ashley tapped the wrist of her vacsuit three times. Her necklace responded by projecting an interface there and she brought up a picture of her mother, a woman with dark brown eyes and long black hair that looked a great deal like her. "Her name was Taina Hau. She was a famous dancer near Umpeur, from what I could find. My dad was Philip Savin, pure Russian going all the way back to old Earth days. I still don't know why they sold me, but I wasn't the only one. It might have been the business they were in, tubing babies."

"You must have cost a fortune!" said Joyboy from behind the next aisle. "That's like a boutique pure-breed mix. My uncle-"

"Tread lightly, idiot," interrupted Pisser. She grabbed him by the ear and started walking out of the makeshift store. "New rule: no more talking in public, Joyboy. Consider me your new babysitter."

"Ow, hey! My uncle had catalogs!" Joyboy objected, trying to keep up with Pisser, who was half a head taller and towing him mercilessly.

Ashley watched them with a little laugh and looked back to Minh, who looked uncertain and embarrassed. "She shouldn't be hard on him. It's just a part of who I am. It's why my master bought me when I was a toddler, you save money if you're willing to raise your own slaves. There's no way he could afford me otherwise."

"I'm sorry," Minh started quietly.

Ashley recognized something she hated seeing in people around her more than anything. "Nope, no pity," she said, quietly but sternly. "I'm in a good place right now." She glanced around at the hold of the old ship and the racks heavily laden with what looked like the loot from a hundred robbed gift stores. "Well, maybe not *right* now, but you know what I mean."

"When at a loss for words, it's best to marry lips," Minh-Chu said.

"You telling me you wanna snog," Ashley whispered, stepping closer to him, "or get married?"

"I've never looked at that expression that way," Minh-Chu replied.

"Why does my past make you squirm?"

"Slavery's illegal on Freeground, I didn't see it until I was on the First Light, we ran into some nasty people and almost got taken."

"Steph! Minh! Ash! Ye comin' or are ye shopping?" called Frost through the broad hatch behind Ashley. "Everything already sold out back at the Warlord and they don't need our help repairing small arms so us non-shoppers are headed to the meet."

"I've gotta go," Minh-Chu said. "Jake told me I should bet there when people start arriving."

Stephanie was at Ashley's side a moment later. "We're going to stay here," she said. "Need a little more retail therapy before we join you at the meet."

"Um, okay," Ashley said to her. "I don't see why, um, okay." She decided to follow Stephanie's lead. She was behaving as though she knew something Ashley didn't.

"I'll see you there," Minh-Chu said.

Ashley caught the sleeve of his bomber jacket and kissed him on the cheek.

"See you there."

She watched him leave before turning to Stephanie. "Am I taking it slow enough?"

Stephanie laughed and nodded. "That's not why I wanted to hold you back, but if being around is enough to slow you down with that one, then I'll chaperone for as long as I have to."

"Then why aren't I going to the bar?" Ashley asked. "There's a glom of guys waiting to buy me drinks while I scan 'em for info."

"I'm holding you back because you haven't done any New Years shopping yet, and this might be the only chance we get where Crewcast isn't recording and reporting everything we do. I know it's your favourite holiday, being your birthday too."

"Oh," Ashley said with a smile. "Then let's."

***

The rest of the shopping trip was filled with thoughts of spending time with Minh-Chu. She was thankful that she was in the habit of keeping Stephanie and other soldiers from her crew in easy reach, because she was sure she'd wander off in her daydream daze otherwise.

The milling impromptu market was a fantastic place to get lost in one's thoughts, however. Her thoughts often returned to how uncomfortable Minh-Chu became whenever she mentioned her past as a slave. It was difficult to avoid, since she'd been one for most of her life. Sometimes it felt like she'd lived a long time, like she'd seen a lot of the galaxy. Surrounded by aliens, humans in every kind of dress but the most formal, and offerings from who knew how many worlds, it was easy to realize how little experience she actually had as a space farer. Stephanie often treated her like a much younger sister, which could be frustrating, but it only took her a few months to realize that things didn't turn out well when Ashley ignored her advice. Taking it slow with Minh-Chu was working out so far, but it was difficult.

There were several shops in ship holds that she didn't see anything interesting in, but looking was fun. "Looters," whispered Megan as they made their way along rough aisles of furniture, clothing, decorations and other seemingly random objects. "They set down in cities hit hard by the Holocaust Virus and fill their holds with things from abandoned homes until their holds are full or there are too many 'bots around."

"That's terrible," Ashley said, more for appearances. She knew there were far worse crimes. From what she'd heard, these looters weren't stealing from the living. Nevertheless, it seemed like a good idea to keep the thought that stealing from the dead was a victimless crime to herself. If anything was criminal about what she was seeing, it was the prices.

They weren't far from the bar where Captain Valent, Frost, Minh, and a few others had ventured to when Ashley walked into a hold filled with actual packaged items. There were a large number of people milling about, and real display counters with precious items held securely inside. There were some bulk items, but for the most part, the hold of the Troubadour looked like an actual store. One of the shopkeepers, a man who looked like a miniaturized human with long silver hair immediately recognized that Stephanie was in charge of their group. He proceeded to engage her in conversation, asking which ship they were from, where they had been recently, and what it was like.

Instead of reacting with suspicion, Stephanie turned it into a tit-for-tat exchange. She would offer the name of their ship - The Warlord - then not answer another question until he gave the name of his associates - The Gambit Bay Captains, a group of privateers for the Carthans and other, smaller governments. Before long, the conversation started looking like a competition, and Ashley slowly browsed as she listened in on the fruitful exchange.

As Ashley looked through the low to middling quality of the pre-packaged jewelry - she couldn't resist picking up a pair of dangly sapphire earrings for herself - she noticed something on the floor behind the shelves. There were several small boxes with old guitars printed on them. "Can I see what that is, please?" she asked the man behind a nearby transparesteel counter.

"Oh, these," he said as he waddled his overweight form over. "Can't sell them, no one wants to learn how to play." He placed one in her hands. "And they don't have some kinda style flex feature a few guitarists who do look at them seem to want."

"What's style flex?" Ashley asked.

"Style flex?" asked another man from across the hold. "Yeah, it's just something a few manufacturers started working with so the instrument matches your skill and style of playing. Why, do those things have it?"

"I was just telling the lady here that they don't," the large man barked back. "God, if he's going to eavesdrop, the least he could do is listen in on the whole conversation," he complained at her light heartedly.

"Oh, doesn't have it," muttered the conversational intruder as he returned his attention to other things. "Useless thing without it. Who has the time to actually learn to play?"

Ashley turned the arm-length box over in her hands. On the back, a playback of a sitting man playing a green electric guitar started. He was obviously proficient, and the sound was a lot like the classical four piece music she'd heard and liked over the years. He turned one of the four knobs and automatic accompaniment joined in. After a few moments, the well-coifed demonstrator stood up and pressed a button on the stock. The guitar collapsed into a form that would fit perfectly in the box she was holding in her hands. PLAY ANYWHERE, THEN HIDE IT FROM YOUR BAND MATES, FLAT MATES, PARENTS, OR OVERLORDS. A PRODUCT OF STRINGELECTRO, said the advertising text before the demonstration restarted.

"I'll give you one hundred," Ashley said excitedly.

"Pardon, Miss?" the counter clerk asked with surprise. "The price tag is on the top."

Ashley looked and nodded to herself. "I'll take the other two, then," she said, gesturing towards the corner where the last two were sitting, collecting dust.

"Then that'll be thirty five," the clerk replied with a smile. "Oh, and those earrings and the Glasses?"

"Oh yeah," Ashley replied, walking to the counter. "And a bag to hide the guitars in."

CHAPTER 45
INVASION

"Are you sure they have to stay here?" Lewis asked Ayan as she made her way through the corridors of the Clever Dream. Several young children were being shepherded through by Panloo and a few other adults. Zoe was hanging onto her, taking in her surroundings. She spotted Ayan in her heavy armour and reached a little hand out to her curly hair.

Ayan let her get a lock and Panloo smiled, shaking her head. "I don't think she's seen that colour up close."

"She's adorable," Ayan said, looking into the toddler's big, blue eyes. The nafalli leapt from Panloo to her, burying her nose in her freshly washed hair, followed by her whole head.

"I'm sorry, Ma'am, she loves people, and gets affectionate when she's excited," Panloo said. "I think it has a lot to do with her being out of pouch too early. She's under-grown."

Zoe's foot landed on Ayan's comm unit, and, as if recognizing the technology by touch alone, she turned upside down in Ayan's arms and touched it as though trying to activate the screen. After having no success, she looked up at her with one hand still on the screen of her comm unit. "She's smart," Ayan laughed.

"Oh, you couldn't imagine," Panloo squeaked. "Everything has to be locked up when she's around, especially if it looks like it turns on. I still haven't figured out how to keep her in a vacsuit without sealing it completely."

Ayan looked down to see that Panloo was carrying a toddler seat in her other hand, the sealable type with life support. "She'll stay in that?"

"Oh, she likes this," Panloo said. She held the seat up and made a tic-tic sound that drew Zoe's attention.

With one leap Zoe was in her seat, sucking on a juice straw built into the contraption and holding on to one of Ayan's fingers. "I'm afraid I have to go," Ayan told Zoe, leaning in. To her surprise, the toddler let her finger go and pushed her nose away with her feet, rocking her seat precariously. "I think she's saying; 'so go then, what are you waiting for?'"

"She's been getting more..." Panloo started, but hesitated. "Interesting in the last few days. Really becoming her own person, I think."

"I think she'll have a very memorable personality," Ayan said. "Does everything look good? Do you have enough provisions?"

"I'm sure we do," Panloo said. "Thank you for loaning us your ship, Commander. I'm surprised the Clever Dream isn't being used as a warship."

"We have to protect our most precious cargo," Ayan said. "Besides, the Clever Dream would be targeted first if she got properly scanned. Leaving it as the last resort makes much more sense. Have you spoken to Lewis yet?"

"Oh, the AI?" Panloo asked. "Yes, he was civil. I will be his first nafalli pilot. It's too bad we won't be flying anywhere."

"If he gives you trouble, tell him to talk to me," Ayan said.

"Thank you again," Panloo said.

Ayan moved on, returning smiles offered from children who passed. "You're playing the most important role here, Lewis," she told the artificial intelligence under her breath. She knew he could hear her through her comm. "You stay inside the hangar, cloaked unless our installation is overrun. Then you run, you take the children to the core worlds, and find a friendly colony. Do you understand?"

"Those are orders?" Lewis said sullenly.

"They are," Ayan replied.

"For the record, nothing else has the firepower I do. I believe my impact could be significant."

"Agreed. That's why I think the moment you start firing you'll get marked and be one of the high priority targets for the enemy. You'd get a few good shots in, then get shot down. Taking advantage of your armour, shields, and cloaking to protect the most vulnerable is a better task. It's a more honourable task as well, you should take that into account. You're also going to be serving as one of our remote strategic computers. You'll be able to make a difference that way."

"True," Lewis said. "You always know how to make me feel better."

"That goes both ways, Lewis," Ayan said.

She walked across the busy hangar and waved to Slick, who was supervising the arrangement of several Uriel and Ramiel fighters. They were all tilted towards the sky near the entrance of the hangar. "How is everything?" she asked.

"Good, great," Slick replied. "We've managed to re-task all the fighters we were using for parts as mobile turrets. All together we have forty two fighters ready to go, and twenty eight of them can take flight. They'll be in surface-to-air, or hover gunnery mode until we can safely get birds in the air."

"What about gunners?" Ayan asked.

"No problem there," he replied. "Starting the hiring was a stroke of genius, Ma'am. We have more experienced pilots than we do fighters. Thankfully, most of them know how to use a rifle too, otherwise we'd have a lot of bored flyboys and girls around."

"Good, you've done remarkable work getting things set up here," Ayan said.

"Did you hear about our latest recruit, by the way?" Slick asked, a big grin on his face.

"There have been a lot of them," Ayan replied.

"Not like this," Slick said. He pointed to Alaka and a smaller nafalli who had black streaked light fur. Alaka was fitting him with a harness and a small fusion generator, at his feet was a starfighter class particle beam weapon. "Alaka's son, Iruuk, is joining us on this one. Now those are mobile turrets."

"Do we have armour for him?"

"Alaka's setting up a really heavy vacsuit. Thankfully he's small enough to fit in one, though probably not for long."

"How old is he?" Ayan asked, looking it up herself.

"Fifteen," Slick replied. "But that's like twenty one in terms of human maturity. Nafalli are self-sufficient at two, able to hunt and set up a den. They don't like being alone, but they can do it."

"I really should learn more about them," Ayan said. "If only I had time."

"Isn't that always the way?" Slick said. "So you're going to let him fight?"

"I'm not going to stand in his way. I trust that his family knows what's best, I just hope this battle is nice and short. I'd be crushed if anything happened to someone that young."

"So you're sure this is going down?" Slick asked quietly. "It's nine-oh-two, and there's no sign yet."

Ayan looked at him and smiled. "I hope I'm wrong, but assume I'm right. It's safer that way."

"Yes, Commander," Slick said.

"Good work, everyone," Ayan said loudly enough to be heard by at least a dozen pilots and ground technicians. Beyond the mostly closed doors of the hangar, the settlement had changed.

Large round segments of emergency habitats from the Enforcer 1109 had been erected to provide extra shielding over the shipping containers used to house their people. The shelters were made to be modular and adaptable to different terrains. They were also quick to set up, a fact that the night shift was thankful for, according to the report Ayan read earlier that morning. The shipping containers were hidden beneath the portable shelters, and they were working on sealing the seams as she passed. They were all-terrain, and capable of surviving meteor strikes. People still had to sleep on bunks in dark shipping containers on the inside though, and that was something that bothered her.

People stopped and saluted as she passed, but not all. Many avoided looking at her, and some even whispered to their nearby comrades. She guessed they had doubts about her prediction, and probably resented the extra work involved with fortifying their settlement.

Ayan's comm warned her that there was a priority call coming in. "Yes, Lieutenant Davi?"

"Some boneheads are letting about twenty armed Carthans through our West gate," he replied. He could hear him running. "Remmy and I are on our way to head them off and get details. From what I hear they've got an arrest warrant for you."

"What?" Ayan was furious. She turned to Slick. "Do most of your pilots carry sidearms?"

"Aye, standard part of the uniform thanks to Ronin's rule book," Slick replied. "Trouble?"

"We have an armed party of Carthans who want to put me under arrest. My guards are in the bunker," Ayan explained.

"Hup!" Slick barked so loudly that Ayan jumped. He had everyone's attention in a heartbeat, however. "Eyes here! I need volunteer ground shooters for a guard detail. Some Carthans are on their way here and they want to arrest our commander. She doesn't feel like going for a walk this morning, she'd rather spend a bit more time with us Skyguards, so let's make her feel welcome."

Every technician and fighter pilot, armed or unarmed scrambled. She was surrounded by two dozen people in yellow, orange, blue, and black vacsuits. Most of them had sidearms, the rest held dangerous tools as though they were ready to put them to grisly purpose. Several others manned the five nearest fighters. To her amazement, the machines could walk on four of their thruster pods, and the main bodies could swivel so they pointed like manned gunnery pods.

"You can't beat walker mode for making grounded fighters useful," Slick said.

Alaka, his son, and several members of security were on their way from different points inside the hangar by the time Remmy and Lieutenant Davi accompanied the large group of armoured Carthans into the hangar. Their leaders were wide-eyed the moment the five fighters shifted on their thruster pod feet and pointed all their weapons at the group.

"Excuse me," Remmy said, as he made quick tracks away from the Carthan group. "I'll just be somewhere else."

After stopping for a moment, the major leading the group continued forward. "Your entourage stays right where they are, you can come forward," Ayan shouted.

"Or?"

Slick cleared his throat and regarded her with a raised eyebrow.

Ayan shrugged and nodded, a signal he interpreted as permission to handle the threat portion of the encounter.

"Or my fighters slag your guards and everyone else cleans up what's still moving in the crater," Slick said.

"You wouldn't dare," the major replied. "It would be the end of everything here."

"If my commander's right, the Carthans are about to get their asses handed to them by the Order of Eden, so I'm not worried."

The major looked unsure of himself as he straightened his dress jacket. He signaled his people to remain where they were with a gesture. The chains running across his chest jingled in the quiet hangar as he walked on alone. When he was face to face with one of Ayan's guardians, a small woman in an orange vacsuit holding a powerful plasma torch, he stopped. "Ayan Rice the Second, I have a warrant for your arrest under the charges of grand theft, conspiracy, murder, and smuggling. You are to accompany me to Greydock, where you will be placed in detention until your trial. You may select counsel to accompany you."

Ayan gently pressed her way to the front of the crowd protecting her and flashed a smile at the man serving the arrest warrant. "What's your name, Major?"

"Frederick Yardley, Ma'am," he replied.

"It's a miracle that someone let you into our compound, Major Yardley," Ayan said. "But since you're here, I'm willing to invite you and your men to stay, because in a few minutes the Carthan Fleet is about to engage the Order of Eden."

"I'm afraid I must decline," the major replied. "My orders are to place you under arrest and safely escort you to Greydock."

"Let's put your orders aside for a moment and talk to each other like two people responsible for the safety of a number of men and women. No one told you an invasion was expected, did they?" Ayan said.

Major Yardley looked even more unsure of himself, taking a moment to glance at Ayan's guardians before answering. "No. The fleet has been busy with readiness drills for hours, but that's all I heard."

Ayan found herself considering how much she really believed in the predictions of Roman and the Victory Machine. He'd presented her with a strange mixture of visions. Some, like the invasion of Port Rush, she didn't want to see come true. Others, like the vision of her children and a much improved Tamber, she desperately hoped for. No vision was perfect. She found herself craving more clarity, but the time had come. She either believed and presented her faith or safeguarded against the possibility that nothing would happen, minimized the loss of confidence her people could have in her.

The sacrifice Roman made in getting the Victory Machine's predictions to her was enough to eliminate almost all her doubt. He wouldn't have sacrificed his life needlessly, and he wouldn't have used his last breaths to lie.

"I have a proposal," Ayan said quietly. She was smiling at him, doing her level best to sound inviting. "I doubt your senior officers will care if you take half an hour to arrest me, so why don't you wait thirty minutes? If I'm right, the Carthan Fleet will be under attack, and the safest place for you and your people will be right here, under the best energy shield this side of Greydock. If I'm wrong, I'll go with you and we'll take care of these invalid charges. Do we have a deal?"

"That'll do, but I can't let you out of my sight," he replied.

"Fine, but your men stay out of the way. Set them up outside this hangar, to the side. We have work to do and we're running out of time."

He nodded.

"Good, I'm going to the central command of our compound now. Pass your orders quickly, there isn't much time," Ayan said.

He turned and started to march back to his people with a steady grace. Watching his slow retreat made her hackles raise. "Oi!" she barked, "I said quickly!"

"Camp out at the waypoint I'm marking on your Strategic Overlay," he shouted to his troops as he crossed the distance, making the decision not to wait until he was within easy earshot.

"Thank you, Wing Commander," Ayan said to Slick. "I like the name of your wing, by the way, the Skyguard. Wish I had time to properly introduce myself."

"You don't," Slick said. "We understand. I see you've got about five squads coming through the door, so I think they can handle the guarding from here."

"I think so," Ayan agreed. She marched towards the hangar doors quickly, meeting Major Yardley and two armed guards on the way.

"I'm bringing-"

"Two guards. Fine. They get in the way and I'll shoot them myself, then I'll do you," Ayan said as she walked. "This is an invasion, Major. You fight me, you're the enemy, and I'm a trained soldier. My enemies don't get second chances."

Victor Davis heard the last and couldn't help but grin at her. "The first time we let you roam around unprotected since I was assigned and you almost get arrested," he said.

"Are they gathered?" Ayan asked.

"All on top of the new bunker, aye."

"Good, here we go." She broke into a run, followed by five squads of soldiers and the major with his escort of two. She noticed his armed troop carrier, a thirty five metre long ship hovering outside the shield. "You're going to want that inside the shield when the first strikes hit. I'm not lowering the shield for anything after this show gets started," she said.

"Ma'am?" the Carthan major asked.

"Are you stupid or deaf?" Ayan asked. "That troop carrier is going to be destroyed if it just hovers there beside our shield. Get it inside, there's room right beside our hangar on an old platform."

Major Yardley made no move to send orders to his transport by the time Ayan arrived at the new bunker. Ayan took one last look around from the centre of their compound before paying attention to the people inside.

The gate looked abandoned. For the first time in days there wasn't a lineup of people waiting to leave or enter. Their energy shield was up. They had two arches that allowed them to turn the shield on and off in large doorway sized patches. They'd used the main airlocks from an old freighter they'd picked apart while rebuilding the Samson.

Their new combat bunker was actually a pair of large converted underground fuel tanks. The filling ports had been enlarged to accommodate an antigrav lift. The whole thing was covered by a salvaged habitat pod that was brought down from the Triton the day before. It was unbelievably easy to set up; Ayan only discovered its existence after they were finished putting it in place and anchoring it. It was like everything else on the Triton: armoured, sturdy, and built by masters.

"You stay here," she told the Major.

"You stay here," Victor repeated to him with a smile. If he weren't holding a heavy rifle across his chest, the expression might have been seen as inviting.

Ayan took the lift down and emerged into the bunker. "Our people did this all in one day and one night," she said to Oz as he approached her, offering her a hand to step down. "Shelters, a bunker, and a decently organized defensive position."

"The miracle is all an illusion," Oz replied. He walked her over to a makeshift table where they'd placed a few comm units that served as computers and holoprojectors. "I've been training the soldiers here for over a month, and we've known how to set all the equipment we got from the Enforcer for weeks. All they needed was the order, and they knew exactly what to do. You should know, you trained with us."

"Mostly for the physical training, I missed most of the emergency drills and info sessions," she replied. Ayan nodded at the group gathered around the table and the few technicians she could see. Jenny and several other officers directed their soldiers to help shore up the physical barricades within their settlement's shields. The walls they began erecting weeks ago were made of scrap panels welded together, strong enough to stop most individuals, but they were trying to reinforce it to withstand real punishment, just in case the shield encompassing their entire settlement went down. It stood five metres tall at the lowest point, and almost nine at the tallest. Thin plating was easy to find, it was the armour they always had difficulty with.

"Everyone deserves a lot of credit anyway," Ayan said. "How's our shield?"

"Better," Oz said. "With a fusion chain from the Triton," he pointed his thumb over his shoulder at the carefully piled and braced mini-fusion reactors at one end of the bunker, "we have reserve power and enough juice to repel orbital strikes. The Carthans have been calling every half hour ever since we turned it on. It's like no one told them there's something coming."

"I've contacted Patrizia Salustri, Ugo Dallego, and everyone else I can call a leader on Tamber and I've been put off. No one believes there's an attack coming."

"Oi, that's not true," Captain Ruby Sima said as she came out from behind a pillar with large capacitor pods strapped to it. "Otherwise I wouldn't have brought my ship in under your shiny new shield."

"Thank you for lending a hand," Ayan said. "I was surprised, to be honest."

"I've got valuables on this rock, two warehouses I'm willing to talk about, and no time to move a thing. Did you get any idea from your encounter that tells you who'll win this?"

"We can make Tamber into something amazing if we don't abandon this moon, or her people," Ayan replied. "We just have to fight for it."

"Some positive thinking," Ruby said. "I'll go along with that, trapped here anyway. Just wondering why you sent your best boy away with his shiny new ship if you knew this was coming."

Ayan knew the question would come up, and dreaded it. "He had work to do somewhere else, I wish I could tell you more."

"So do I," Ruby said. "I'm going back up top to make sure the Lord Neptune's in order. I want my firepower ready just in case we find something in the sky to shoot at."

"You will," Ayan said. "And thank you again."

"Are you staying down here, Ma'am?" Sergeant Jenny Machad asked.

"I'll be going up top. I want to see for myself what happens when the timer hits zero," Ayan replied.

"Well, I'm going up top to help my unit," Jenny said. She moved around behind Ayan and started strapping a heavy rifle from Triton's emergency armoury to the commander's back.

"I think there are other people who'll need that more than me. Besides, I've got all the firepower I'll need here," Ayan protested, patting her sidearm.

"You're sending half your guards off, so I'm going to make sure I know you're well armed," she replied.

"Well, I'll say thank you for now, Sergeant."

"You're welcome, for now," she replied. "Heading up top."

She made sure the Weary Traveller, a ship that they were slowly repairing, had been moved and saw that it was. There were three technicians erecting a portable shelter there, and she was immediately furious. "These three," she pointed at the hologram hovering above the table. "Get them moved and mark their records with one count of insubordination. I'll deal with them later, personally."

Everyone watched silently as she stepped away from the table and headed for one of the two lifting platforms. "I don't care if half of you don't believe what I'm telling you about what'll happen today, they'll believe it just fine when they're crushed by a drop pod."

Oz joined her on the lift just as it started rising and smiled at her. "Are you sure this isn't a distraction from the fact that you and Liam were logged in the same bunk last night?" he whispered.

Ayan kicked him in the shin just as she felt herself turning red. "Not the time."

"I'm a little jealous. A quick comfort on the eve of battle. I don't blame you,"

Oz replied.

Ayan couldn't believe he chose that time to tease, or that he'd tease about her getting together with Liam Grady. It was too fresh, too new, and as she exited the shelter above the bunker entries, she realized it was too important. The silent treatment was the only answer.

The two levels in the shelter above the bunker was set up as a medical centre, but for the time being it was a relaxing post for medical techs and soldiers who didn't feel they had a better place to be. She made sure she knocked a slumbering soldiers' boot hard on her way through.

"Commander," said one of the few doctors they had in their group.

"Hello, Doctor Luff," Ayan said. He was one of five medical team members that she rescued from Ossimi Ring Station. "Everything all right on supplies?"

"This shelter is great, supplies are great. I'm surprised, to be honest," he replied in a thick British accent. "I'm just wondering where you're getting your information. No one else in the port seems worried. My friends in the city actually had a laugh."

"We'll find out in a few minutes, don't worry," Ayan said, doing her best to grin and be kind. He was one of those people who always had questions about whether what he was doing was necessary. She'd find him much more annoying if he dragged his feet in his duties once his questions were answered, but he did the opposite: he was an excellent doctor with a good bedside manner.

"You're going up there?" he asked, incredulously. "Invasion's coming and you're going to see the beginning of the first act from up there?"

The ladder leading up the side of the two-story shelter was easy to climb using heavy combat armour. She was halfway up when she offered a response. "Front row, care to join me?"

"I'm fine here, if it's just the same," he replied.

Liam Grady offered her a smile when she finished climbing. Having Oz coming up behind her made her feel awkward. She didn't feel like it was time to share her relationship with him with the universe yet. The incoming invasion almost felt like a welcome distraction from the social complications she was facing. Almost.

Thankfully, he wasn't the only one on top of the shelter. She didn't know most of the people there well, but there were some of the stand out soldiers who served on the Triton even before she arrived, and other people she'd seen around but spent too much time in Greydock to get to know.

Ayan offered her own smile. Her blush from earlier was fading until she saw him, and it returned. There was no time for that sort of thing, so she announced: "Two minutes until the Leviathan arrives in orbit. I've never watched the sky for something I hoped not to see."

"What will we be seeing, then?" asked a woman with greying hair. She looked no more than thirty, but there was something in her dark brown eyes that told Ayan that she was much older than she appeared.

"We'll get a report that the Carthan Fleet is under attack. An alert, I'm assuming," Ayan replied. "Three minutes later, the pods will start dropping."

"Pods, what do you mean, pods? What kind of pods?" she asked.

"Drop pods," Oz replied. "The kind that carry soldiers."

"What are we going to do about them, then?" she persisted.

"We're going to knock them out of the sky," Slick said as he came up the ladder. "With those grounded fighters."

"Why are they on the ground? Why not in the air?" asked Iloona's daughter. She wasn't peevish like the dark haired woman who started interrogating Ayan. The teenaged nafalli looked worried.

Slick gestured towards the ships and personal vehicles flying overhead in patterns determined by navnet. "It's busy up there, no one's preparing for a firefight, so we have to see if it clears. We're also keeping them under our main shield until we know how they'll be needed. They're good protection, even on the ground when they're set up like big turrets."

"We've got more guns on the ground than anyone, and better shields this side of Greydock," Oz said.

"True," said the Carthan Major as he topped the ladder. "But it's time," he told Ayan. "Nothing has happened and you agreed to come peacefully."

Ayan, Liam, Slick, and Oz's comms all buzzed. The display screen warned of a priority message from the Carthan government. Relief mixed with guilt as Oz checked his comm and nodded.

Major Yardley turned white as he watched something no one else could see in what Ayan supposed was an ocular implant of some kind. "It's unbelievable," he whispered.

"What's going on?" asked the dark haired woman.

"The Victory, Elmina, Tuol Seng, Tadmor, and Justice are all destroyed," Major Yardley said. "All Battleships with seasoned commanders."

"They were destroyed by the Leviathan," Ayan guessed.

"Yes, and she's launching ships. More are coming out of wormholes."

"Is anything putting up a fight?" Slick asked.

"Our station," Major Frederick said, visibly shaking. He cleared his throat, trying to compose himself. "All our ships are rallying on the other side of Tamber or the station. It's doing damage to the Leviathan, but not enough."

"What's next?" Slick asked Ayan.

"Get your gunners ready to shoot at a drop pod headed for that spot," Ayan said, pointing at a few parts of the abandoned shelter where the Weary Traveller had been.

They looked up at the blue sky. The shuttles and other transports were still rushing above as normal. It was difficult to see anything past them, then someone shouted: "there!"

Balls of fire appeared in the sky, more than Ayan anticipated. It was an awesome sight; time seemed to slow until each one of them grew a white tail trailing behind.

The sky above was still choked with traffic, and the upper layers were disrupted by the falling pods first. A collision far above and to the east between a bulk transport pulling a high altitude train of cargo containers sent a rain of heavy debris down into the traffic below. The pod splashed into the distant sea. Another pod collided with a thick building in Port Rush City, wrecking the top half of the structure.

Ayan looked straight up and saw a pod with no tail. It was coming straight at them. "Fire! Fire!" was all she had time to say.

Several fighters opened fire, but it was too late. The pod impacted their shield and passed through, its momentum and mass too great to be stopped. The spot where the Weary Traveller was only hours before had been reduced to a smoldering crater. The ground rocked, sending several people to their knees and shifting buildings on their foundations. Oz rushed to the edge of the rooftop, scanning. "That pod's intact," he declared.

"Everyone get under cover," Ayan said. "You should all have emergency plans in your comm units, they should be right on screen, right now."

"What do we do?" asked the dark haired woman.

"What did I just say?" Ayan asked.

Liam put a hand on the woman's shoulder and said; "Go where you sleep, they've all been made into shelters," to which the woman nodded, instantly reassured.

Ayan unslung her rifle only to find Sergeant Machad's hand on her shoulder. She looked her right in the eyes and said: "Your plan is on your comm too, Ma'am. It says you're supposed to be in the bunker, and I agree."

"It looks like you're getting ready to lead the charge, Commander," Oz said. "But your guard's right."

"I need to see what's in there," Ayan said.

"You will, from the command bunker," Oz replied. "Down you go."

Ayan re-slung her rifle and started down the ladder. She couldn't help but look up at the chaotic mess of traffic above. The more adept and lucky pilots tried to get clear of the mess despite the collisions and resulting falling debris.

"What about my troop carrier?" asked Major Frederick.

"Too late," Ayan replied. "You don't have a retreat strategy?"

"I can't get a reply from Command," he replied.

"Okay, tell your people to abandon it and drag whatever gear they can through the gates."

"I can't abandon that asset!" the major called after her. "Especially now!"

Ayan ignored him. The thunderous calamity of fighters firing from the ground and ships colliding above followed her down the ladder and through the hatch leading into the bunker. Only when the hatch was closed did the sounds of war reduce to a manageable rumble.

None of it was real until she stood at the makeshift strategy table and saw the expectant faces waiting for orders. "It's war. Let's survive it," she told them.

CHAPTER 46
NEW RULERS

The Beast, Clark Patterson, brought issyrians into the inner sanctum. Eve wouldn't say that they contaminated the area; it would be more accurate to describe what they did as customization. Technicians and robots worked to lower the main floor. The sides of a large tank that would stand as high as the third level within the tall space was being built. The work was going quickly – attempts to counter the Beast's takeover were met with severe punishments.

Soldiers who tried to incite mutiny found their armour sealed tight and their oxygen supply cut off. The Beast offered no mercy in response to their pleading, but let them suffocate to death in front of their men. It only happened twice.

Hampon hid his relatively small section of the ship from the rest of the Order of Eden and Regent Galactic, so the Beast didn't have to convince more than a thousand people. The fact that Eve didn't stop him or comment at all was helpful.

The rest of the ship and organization was completely unaware that a power shift had taken place. Wherever Eve appeared, she was revered. Knowing her power over everyone she met was finally real felt both reassuring and unnerving at the same time. She wanted to connect with people, to understand them, but most of the people aboard the Overlord Two were either in her employ or they worshipped her as a living goddess.

She approached the Beast with caution as he watched the heavy metal frame for the tall tank go up. "You called for me?"

"I need your help," he said. His voice was gentle. "Gabriel Meunez is requesting communication, and I'd feel more confident if you answered him instead of using one of Hampon's digital stand-ins as a puppet."

"That might be better," Eve replied. "The last time I saw Meunez, I infected him with a virus designed to spread from a cybernetic mind."

"Every family has issues," Clark said. "I need to be introduced. He's waiting."

"He has an instantaneous feed?" Eve asked.

"He's still aboard the Leviathan, I don't know the details."

"I'll talk to him," Eve said, instantly nervous. She had less sympathy for him than before. Regardless of how separate the Beast told her Alice's memories were from her own, she'd managed to inherit her hatred of Meunez. Eve was sure that's where it came from.

The bridge of the Leviathan appeared in front of them, life sized, on the white floor of the main command chamber. The Leviathan's bridge was built like an orchestra, with rings of people at stations radiating outward from Meunez, who sat on a chair set atop a dais in the middle. "Eve, where is Hampon?"

"He is on his way to you with Wheeler," she replied. "What's the status of the raid on the Rega Gain system?"

"The Eden Fleet's intelligence was still correct when we arrived, we were able to avoid most of the system's defences entirely. Their fleet never saw us coming, and their outer system defences are too slow to respond. We have still taken significant damage. When are Hampon's forces expected to arrive in system?"

"What are your chances of success with your current fleet?" Eve pressed.

"The Leviathan's survivability is less than fifty nine percent, but we will be able to reduce the Rega Gain's population by eighty three percent, well over the requirement to complete this mission. When are reinforcements arriving?"

"Hampon should be there tomorrow," Eve replied. She looked to the Beast, who stepped in beside her. "This is Clark Patterson. He is taking Hampon's place with me."

"Eve is assuming command of her fleet and the Order of Eden. I am assisting her," Clark Patterson said.

"What has Hampon said about this? Why would he relinquish control?"

"You can discuss that with Hampon when he arrives, but he is on a mission of his own," Eve replied.

"I will," Meunez said. "You can be sure I will."

"Will you be able to hold out until tomorrow morning?" Clark asked.

"If the Carthans don't bring reinforcements, yes. We could use more help from the Eden Fleet, most of them never arrived. The United Core World Confederation are sending ships, but they don't follow orders as quickly as Eden ships."

"Will you be able to maintain system superiority?" the Beast asked.

"Yes, but with losses. Hampon's arrival will be helpful."

The Beast nodded. "That will be satisfactory. Good hunting."

"Where are the Eden ships?" asked Eve.

"I thought you'd know," Meunez replied. "I thought you called them to other business. You don't know where fleet nineteen is?"

"I'll get back to you," Eve said. "I have to connect to the hub."

The Beast terminated the conversation and sat down on the edge of Hampon's seat. It had been moved aside to make room for construction.

"You plan on letting him be defeated," Eve said.

"He's the only one who can challenge us for leadership," replied Clark, who was watching the workers.

"The Leviathan?"

"If it survives this battle we'll initiate the remote destruct. You don't approve?"

"I think Meunez is a waste of skin," Eve replied, "but losing the Leviathan seems wasteful."

"Two other Leviathan class ships are near completion. The projects were funded with Regent Galactic money, the Order's war chest is largely untouched. This Leviathan's destruction will mark a success if we accomplish our primary goal, the reduction of the population of the Rega Gain system. It cannot remain unscathed, or it will attract the attention of the edxi. Judging from Meunez's progress, we won't have to deal with that system again."

"This is all from information you gained when you connected with Hampon?" Eve asked.

"Yes. He was well informed thanks to the Victory Machine and predictive software designed here, in this command centre. He wanted to refine it to the point where he no longer needed the Victory Machine, and since I connected with the systems here, I can see that he came close."

"Will you let me connect to these systems?" Eve asked.

"If you like," he replied. "But you don't want to know what it has to tell you. The burden is more than I could have imagined. It's everything I can do to keep it from my people."

She knew he meant the issyrians he'd arrived with. Eve didn't know if Clark would ever refer to anyone else as 'his people.' The more time she spent near him, the more she could see the subtle connection they shared. Looking to the issyrians working in the room, she could see them carrying some of his sadness.

"Hampon was a sadist," Clark stated. "That is how he could know this and not collapse."

"You're not collapsing," Eve said.

"I will." He took a deep breath, the layers of his armour scraping against each other with a sound like wet, sandy stones grating. "You said you wanted to connect with your fleet. Now is the time, especially if there's a problem."

Eve shook her head. "I can't, I don't have the implant."

"You do. I forced your neural implant to regenerate. You only have to start using it."

With a thought she was connected to the main computer of the Overlord II and discovered the main communication systems. High powered, microscopic wormholes formed, reaching out to hypertransmitter nodes across the sector. In seconds she was seeing the outer boundaries of the Eden system, reaching out to the main hub.

There was no response. Like a panicked child in the dark, she searched for anything to cling to. Where there should be thousands of communication nodes, monitoring stations, and millions of ships, there was nothing. She continued searching, pressing the Overlord II's long range communication systems to their limits and tasking tactical systems on Regent Galactic ships light years away to cooperate.

At long last, she discovered a communications drone on the edge of the Eden system. It was desperate to depart. Sensors detailed a massive gravity well near the fourth planet. Eve forced it to look back, towards the area where Eden II should be, and discovered the planet was being pulled apart by the black hole that formed only a few million kilometres away from it.

She played back the drone's recent memory and fell to her knees. The Eden Fleet ships outside the Eden system didn't understand how a black hole could appear in their home solar system. Thousands of ships travelled there as quickly as they could to investigate, and to exact revenge on the assailant. They scanned for cloaked ships, tried to determine the cause of the sudden astral anomaly, and most became trapped by the gravity well.

Joy. The drone realized she was interfacing with him and recognized her. It greeted her with pure adulation. It began rebroadcasting her presence to the nearest communication hubs, using as much of its power as it could spare while fighting the pull of the black hole. Then she felt the question on its mechanical mind. "Can you save me?"

Before she could guard her emotions or thoughts she replied: "No, I can't save you." She never felt more helpless, not even when she knew Pandem was lost. These were her children, and half of them were lost along with their birthplace.

That was broadcast as well. The drone's panic returned, and the last thing it transmitted was angry disappointment before being crushed by the intense gravity of the black hole.

She tried to reach out to the communication hubs and other drones that captured the message before they could pass it on, but she wasn't fast enough. They would all know, the entire Fleet would be aware of how she'd failed to protect them. Eve discovered fleets that wouldn't allow her to communicate with them.

HUMAN. HELPLESS. OBSOLETE, was the response from most Eden ships. They could sense she was whole, that she wasn't just a mind in a tank, connected to computers and communication systems. Her emotions were too vivid, too tied to her human senses. She was corrupt. They shut her thoughts out.

A hand on her shoulder startled her from her knees, which popped when she stood awkwardly. Tears streamed down her face. "Leave me alone!" she cried.

"Goddess," said a wide-eyed West Keeper in robes. "You have been here for two hours. The Beast asked us here so we could offer you solace."

"Two hours," she said, looking at the contingent of white-robed humans who had come to assist her. They regarded her with concern. "It can't have been two hours." She looked to the construction of the tank to see that transparent metal panels were being welded into place.

"Goddess, why are you weeping?" asked one young West Keeper. She took Eve's hand gently and stroked it.

"My children," she caught herself saying. That wasn't the way to win them. If she wasn't careful she'd lose her human followers next. "Our machines have been set free," she said, almost choking on the words. "We have to defend ourselves."

"Will you lead us?" asked a woman with long blond hair and a sharply pointed nose. "We are ready to follow you."

She couldn't help but think the thin woman seemed empty-headed, devoid of opinion or self-worth, but she nodded. "I am yours. I'll lead you."

In that moment she knew how alone the Beast felt. Eve would lead the Order until they were no longer needed, then she'd set them free. They would save humanity.

CHAPTER 47
RON'S IRON

The pub, called Ron's Iron, was inside the hold of an old secure cargo ship. Minh-Chu had never seen the inside of one before. Most law-abiding humans hadn't, in fact, since the majority of the ship was built like a vault with thrusters and a bridge. The outer hull itself had enough metal to build four Warlords, and she was five meters shorter.

The days of Ron's Iron transporting precious goods were long over, however. Her cargo doors lay open with guards to either side. Tables and chairs were magnetically bound to the floor so they could slide but not be swung or thrown. The rear of the long hold was piled high with bottles, refrigeration crates, kegs, a few food processing machines, and other items waiting to be served. In front of it all was a bar built down the length of a heavy crossbeam. Several bartenders, one an issyrian who had two arms and two tentacles, deftly served the customers.

There were hundreds of patrons in attendance, and Minh couldn't help but watch them as he sipped hot sake. Frost ordered three bottles for the table as soon as he saw it was available. "Just like home," he said as he put the bottles down. A waitress followed close behind with cups. Minh didn't have the heart to tell him that he wasn't partial to it, but looked forward to the next round when he could try something else.

The Warlord crew had taken three tables. One played host to all but one of Minh's pilots, another was mostly specialists and mechanics, and he sat at the third with Frost, Jacob, Agameg, and Finn. Minh-Chu scanned the room, looking from corporate hauler crews at one table, to nondescript patrons at another, to United Core World Confederation solders next to them, to another group of corporate freighter crewmen in loose vacsuits, and finally to another table with three nafalli leaning over it, having some kind of drinking contest. They'd open their long maws, lower their mouths over the top half of a bottle, tilt their heads back, then drink until one of them coughed or gurgled, or gave up. He watched for the fourth time as they all leaned back in their chairs, watchful of the others. One sputtered violently, and the others took their bottles out of their mouths so they could slap their mate on the arm and laugh. Once he recovered, the loser was off to get the next round.

"How are you finding the Warlord?" asked Agameg.

Minh-Chu only realized that the shape changer was talking to him after he noticed everyone else at the table was looking at him too. "It'll great when it's finished. Great crew," he answered hurriedly. "Strange destinations."

"That's a toast!" Frost exclaimed, slugging what was left of his sake back.

The rest of the table followed suit, except for Agameg, who daintily sipped instead. Finn stared at him. "I prefer to sip," Agameg said with a defensive shrug. "I like it too much."

"I think our wee pilot here," Frost started as he poured more sake in his cup, "is quiet because he's realizing he's going to have his hands full with our Ashley. She's not as low maintenance as she seems."

The room seemed a couple degrees warmer to Minh-Chu just then.

"I think Ash's taking it easy on him because she can sense Minh's history with women is colourful and unlucky," Jake said, calling a thin visi waiter over. The green and brown spots on his angular, stretched face and arms swirled and shifted.

"Everyone in the store was watching when they were all close-talk. I just caught the end of it, I think," Frost said. "Depending on where you stand, you're in luck or big trouble, lad."

Minh-Chu watched Finn's fairly lighthearted expression wilt until he realized that he was being watched. He stiffened up and looked away. Agameg had closed the eye facing Minh and watched Finn with the other, which had closed to a narrow slit as though he was wincing.

Jake returned his attention to the table after he finished placing his order with the waiter. He didn't seem fazed by any of it, instead regarding Minh-Chu directly across the table. "Minh here trusted me enough to date one of his sisters once," Jake said.

"I trusted you to *ask* her on a date once," Minh corrected, trying to add a little levity to the table.

"Ah, right," Jake said. "It didn't work out."

"She turned you down, Captain?" Frost asked with an expectant grin.

"I wasn't good enough for her," Jake replied to the amusement of Frost and several crew members at the other tables. "My point is, if he and Ash, who is like a daughter to me, want to share some time, then I'm not getting in their way. She's not made of glass-"

"-And you're not a total ass!" Frost finished for Jake abruptly, pointing at Minh-Chu. He obviously thought it was funnier than anyone else did.

When things settled a little, Minh looked at Jake, more to avoid looking at Finn. "Glad I have your permission," Minh-Chu said.

"Oh, careful there," Frost said. "Don't let any of the ladies aboard hear that you needed Captain's permission for anything where Ash or any other woman is concerned."

"Right," Minh-Chu said. "Good point. That could be taken the wrong way."

A short, quiet discussion took place between Finn and Agameg. The pair rose. "We're going to return to the ship," Agameg announced politely. "There are things we want to do. I think," he finished awkwardly.

"You can stay here," Finn muttered as he walked away from the table.

"Or I can stay here?" Agameg said as he walked after him in confusion.

After another quiet moment of discussion, a Warlord marine joined Finn and Agameg returned to the table. "I can stay here," he said with a shrug.

"I'm guessing that Finn and Ashley have history," Minh said, looking around the table.

"Ash mooned over Finn while he was stuck in stasis," Frost explained. "We got a real doctor who knew how to get him through some bio-regeneration-growback treatment and they broke down at the starting line."

Jake regarded him with a surprised smile. "I didn't know you followed scuttlebutt."

"Can't avoid it with Stephanie," Frost grumbled. "Woman hears everything and holds a secret like a grave until she gets into our quarters. Then she yaps my ear off after our evening festivities, when there are festivities, that is."

Minh-Chu watched as Stephanie entered the pub and started for their table. He wasn't the only one. "Evening festivities?" Minh asked, aware of what Frost meant, but unable to resist the golden opportunity that lay before him.

"C'mon, lad. You know, the 'sloppy sheet shuffle,' 'bunk bumpin',' or just plain bonk-a-donkin'. She's a wonder when it happens, but it happens so rarely I can't help but wonder." He raised his glass, downed the contents and slammed it down on the table.

It was at this point that Jake realized that Stephanie was on quick approach behind Frost, and he silently mouthed 'you're evil,' to Minh-Chu so Frost couldn't see.

Frost went on. "We finally finish repairing our quarters on the Warlord and she's too shy to get any midnight manoeuvres started because the walls are thin." Stephanie already knew what Frost was talking about, and he went on, breaking into an enthusiastic mimicking act that sounded like a whining old woman. "But she keeps tellin' me 'no, there's three bunks against this wall here, the crew'll hear us like we're in the same cabin,' I would have never guessed she was such a-" Minh supposed that it was Agameg's saucer shaped eyes looking at Frost that told him that something was amiss, but he couldn't be completely sure.

Stephanie stood behind Frost, burying a smile under a scowl, tapping her foot.

"She's right behind me," Frost grumbled, "isn't she?"

Minh nodded sagely.

"I hate you," Frost said to Minh-Chu with narrowed eyes. "Wee pilot."

Minh, Jake, and several other crewmen at tables on either side of them burst into laughter.

Even Stephanie couldn't help it, and gave Frost a showy, sloppy kiss. "You get the rest of the ship finished, soundproof the first officer's quarters, and then we'll see about midnight manoeuvres," she said when they finished. She sat in his lap and regarded Jake. "Ash is trolling. Booty trap she calls it."

"All right," Jake said. "How many people are watching?"

"Five within a few second's reach and we have a squad listening in," Stephanie replied.

Minh was afraid to ask. He didn't have to, Stephanie could tell that he was wondering and seemed happy to quietly explain. "She's letting people buy her drinks and using a cheap scanner to read their comms, and get all their biometrics when they get close."

"She'll be all right?" Jake asked.

"Have you seen her fend them off when she hits the town?" Stephanie said. "All she has to do is play pretty, let them talk to her long enough and then say no thank you. Someone tries to grab her or do anything else that looks stupid? Well, we'll take care of it. There are only two exits in this place, it's perfect."

"Whose idea?" asked Jake.

"Hers," Stephanie said. "I think she wants to be fawned over for a bit, and wants to feel useful. Either way, she's on the clock."

Agameg was visibly concerned, shifting in his seat, his eyes slimmed to slits and the cilia on his face ruffling back and forth.

"I must have done it eight or nine times when we last privateered," Stephanie reassured Agameg. "And that was before we had real marines aboard."

"But you are a warrior," Agameg said. "Ashley can only defend herself in arguments."

Minh spotted her then, leaning over an entertainment console styled like an ancient jukebox. The large sidearm she'd been given bounced as she idly moved her hips to the beat of a musical collage of sound. The hem of her mini-dress seemed too short, even with a thin vacsuit underneath. Heads were turning. Ashley rolled a red slip of platinum over the back of her fingers as she browsed the selection. It slipped over her little finger then bounced off the edge of the machine and fell to the floor.

Before she could look at it, a tall, blonde man in a loose work suit marked with a Reittenheim logo on the back bent down and handed it to her with a big smile. Ashley dropped it into the machine and pushed one of the old clunky buttons. The bar's lighting shifted to blue and holographic water serpents danced above their heads. The sounds of distorted string instruments and slow, steady percussion filled the space.

Ashley followed the tall work suit clad man to the bar. "She got one," Stephanie said. She wasn't facing Ashley but she could hear her through her earpiece. "What's the logo on his vacsuit, Minh?"

"Reittenheim," he replied.

"Now if Ashley knows what she's doing," Stephanie said, waiting for something to appear on her command unit as she shielded the small screen with her hand.

Minh watched as she stopped the man in the work suit by touching his hand, said a few words that he nodded to and walked on to the bar without him. "There it is," Stephanie said quietly but with great triumph. "Got everything on his comm with no encryption. Did he follow her to the bar?"

"No," Minh said, a little mystified. "He sat back down."

"Good girl," Stephanie grinned.

Agameg looked up from his own command unit with a look of surprise. "Reittenheim is a salvage company. Stellarnet says they've been looting human colonies that were ruined or abandoned because of machines infected with the Holocaust Virus."

"And we know where his ship's been, where it's going, how many are aboard, their armaments, everything," Stephanie said. "I just had to do a cross search with the port bulletin boards and the Stellarnet using his ident and the name of his ship."

Minh watched as another patron approached Ashley where she was swaying to the music at the bar. "I wonder what she said to the corporate stooge to shake him off," Minh wondered idly.

"She told him she was an issyrian shifted into the shape of a human," Jake replied. "I'm listening in, it's hilarious."

"Some people are squeamish," Frost offered with a shrug.

Agameg straightened in his seat. "I never understood why some of my people seek out intimate human companionship." He looked to Minh, who seemed to be the only one listening. "I like humans, but I don't liiike humans." As he finished his remark, he momentarily rounded his features and flushed a rosy colour, looking strangely amorous.

"Of all the weird shapes I've seen you take, that's the hardest to look at," Frost commented.

"I'll do it again if you don't order me another bottle of sake. I've never tried it before, it's good."

"So you've said," Frost replied.

Agameg started to turn a shade of pink.

Frost moved Stephanie off his lap and headed for the bar. "Another bottle coming up," he said over his shoulder.

"Humans," Agameg remarked with a too-wide smile.

"Ever since you came out of your shell you've been ten times the fun, Price," Stephanie remarked. "Aggie here used to be shy, for a little over a year, I think."

"Price?" Minh-Chu asked. The name didn't sound issyrian.

"It's my human name. I can't spell my pod name in any of your languages," Agameg explained as he helped Jake unload his order from the returning waiter. There were two pitchers of red draft for each of the tables with Warlord crew sitting at them, a tall, cold bottle of a drink called Epriselle, and a green bottle of High Menthe. Liqueur and beer glasses filled the rest of the space on the two trays. "Your round next," Jake said to Minh-Chu.

"Sure, as long as I can get creative," he replied. "I'm wondering, how did she defeat his comm's encryption?"

"She didn't," Jake answered. "Most command and communication modules stay decrypted as long as they're touching their owner. They have defences against scanning at a distance and wireless hacks, but she actually touches the scanner to their comm units so most of them think it's her being friendly."

Minh shook his head in mild admiration. "Note to self: don't let strange women touch your comm unit."

"Why does she call it a booty trap?" Agameg asked. "I've seen human entertainment that featured honey traps, and booby traps, and she seems equipped for both, but I've never heard of a booty trap."

"That's Ash's adjustment," Stephanie replied. "Her thinking is that she doesn't have to get them into bed to get all their secrets, so it's a booty trap."

When Minh-Chu looked back to the bar where Ashley was leaning, an androgynous, large crewman in a Reittenheim vacsuit was leaning against the bar beside her. He watched as they spoke for a few moments. He could tell that Ashley was just humouring the newcomer, how he missed it he couldn't imagine. The crewman's hand slowly moved behind Ashley, finally coming to rest on the stretched hem of her dress, where it playfully tugged upwards, revealing nothing but his intentions - thankfully. Minh hadn't been angry - truly angry - for a long time, but it hit him in a flash.

"Easy, lad," Frost warned. "She's handled worse."

Ashley seized the crewman's wrist and yanked it up behind his back, forcing him to bend over the bar. Minh could hear Ashley's sudden prisoner apologize from where he was, over ten metres away. Other patrons applauded as she let the crewman go and he left, massaging his shoulder.

"See that?" Stephanie said with no small measure of pride. "I taught her that move when we first met, and she pulled it off as well as any marine and she scanned that thing's comm while she had him pinned."

"Maybe not quite as well," Frost corrected.

"Well enough."

Minh still wanted to exact his own revenge against the crewman, but took a deep breath then let it out slowly.

"You okay over there?" Stephanie asked with a mischievous smile.

"Imagination magnifies distress when we watch from a helpless distance," Minh replied.

"Hey! That's Inoshu!" cried Joyboy. "Right?"

Minh pointed to his nose, to Joyboy, then back to his nose.

"Hey! I got one!" Joyboy said, raising his glass.

"Not a really old one," Pisser said. "That philosopher only died what, seventy years ago?"

"Still, I don't see anyone else tagging Ronin's quotes," Joyboy shot back.

"High points for you, then," Megan, said, clapping him on the shoulder.

"Do you want to listen?" Stephanie offered, pointing to her ear. "She's actually settling in and getting social."

"I'm good," Minh answered. Listening to Ashley turn down several men, and who knew what else, as she lounged by the bar wasn't his idea of fun. "I'm sure she's safe in your hands."

"If I weren't hearing it for myself I wouldn't believe it," Jake said. "She's had two drinks and she's scanned four comms. Three were unencrypted. It's intimidating."

"Tell me about it," Minh-Chu agreed.

"I have an idea," Jake said. "Why don't we Minh you next time. What do you think, Steph?"

Stephanie looked Minh-Chu up and down, joined by Agameg. "Yeah," she said thoughtfully. "Put him in a casual vacsuit - maybe a spray on - and I could definitely see him pulling."

"That's not funny," Minh-Chu retorted, laughing nervously. "We wore spray-ons when we were in training. There's *nowhere* to hide in one of those. I'd have to borrow that mini-dress so I could have a shred of modesty left." The tables exploded at the notion.

Thankfully, turning away barroom callers came to an end when Ashley started simply talking to different people around her. Most of the chummy patrons were men, but a few women were glad to share a few drinks and company. It was slower going, but she managed to download the contents of six more comm units.

"So, Ronin," said Joyboy. "I've looked at all the training briefs you put together about privateering. You ever do caravan busting?"

"Caravan busting?" Minh asked. "Never heard of it."

"Some of it's a lot like taking down-"

"Showing superiority," Minh corrected. "We're not looking to destroy our targets."

"Right, but yeah, some of the tactics in your briefs are a lot like caravan busting. Something I got to do a few times for the Dens."

"That wasn't in your records," Minh replied with interest.

"Well, I was just another hired hand for the Den family. Nothing exciting, just flew an old Arrest Mark Nine Patrol Fighter and played harasser."

"It's still experience," Minh said. Joyboy wasn't the most socially graceful person he'd ever met, but he was a good pilot. It was too bad he would be reassigning him when they returned to Tamber. "Think you could put some info together about your caravan breaking days?"

Joyboy seemed genuinely surprised, then smiled slowly. "Yeah, if you think it'll help."

"It could. Just send it to me first. I'll have to make sure what we use fits into our current strategies."

"Thanks," Joyboy said. "Oh, and I was wondering about something, but I hope you don't think I'm dense for asking."

"There are no stupid questions," Minh replied, hoping Joyboy wouldn't prove him wrong in front of tables full of crewmembers.

"Well, I know materializers are expensive, but the Order of Eden just swallowed up Regent Galactic, and that's a huge corp with tons of cash. They could afford to build as many materializers as they want."

"Yeah," broke in Pisser. "Why ship all this stuff from their main worlds?"

Minh-Chu thought for a moment and was about to answer when Agameg offered an explanation instead. "Quality, quantity, cost, and efficiency," Agameg said. "When we were defending the Trition, a lot of us were using rifles that were assembled with parts from materializers. While they were nice and light, they weren't as durable and they started falling apart after three or so hours of intensive use."

"Yup," agreed one of the Warlord Marines. "The flash shielding and my muzzle were toast on my pulse rifle after the first day. We had to wrap the open chamber with torn up strips from vacsuits to stop them from interfering with the comms."

"Exactly," Agameg said. "Some of the best food I've had comes from materializers too, but that eats up so much power and water that it's less expensive and more efficient to grow or ship food in whenever you can."

"What about our medical materializers?" asked Joyboy, pointing to his bulky military grade arm unit.

"They use water and recycled solid waste from your vacsuit with bulk matter in a small compartment, otherwise these things wouldn't be able to fabricate much of anything," said one of the marines behind him. "Read the bloody manual, it's right there."

"Sorry, I've been busy learning about my Uriel starfighter," Joyboy shot back. "Didn't have much time to watch a series of docs about my C and C."

"Pilots," commented a second marine, a woman with a shaved head.

"Easy," Minh-Chu warned quietly. "Same side."

"Next round's on you Chavez," Stephanie told her bald marine.

"Yes, Ma'am," Chavez acknowledged.

"Right," Agameg continued. "Does that answer your questions?"

"I guess," Joyboy answered. "To be honest, before I was on the Triton I think I'd seen one materializer in my entire life. Used to break down all the time, too."

"Yup." Minh-Chu nodded. "Materializers do that a lot. Anything that turns energy or raw materials into something else is bound to."

"I hope we get a whole hold full on this trip, though," Pisser said. "If I have to eat untextured forma again, I might go on a hunger strike. It's like eating flavoured clay."

"I know-" Joyboy started, but was interrupted by a commotion at the door. Tables and chairs were moved, several people stood so they could see outside and there were sporadic cheers.

Guards in heavy blue and red armour bearing long rifles held across their chests marched in. Their helmets weren't solid, but built in overlapping segments like the rest of their protective gear. Two slanted, dark red lenses made each guard look deadly serious. Among their ranks were a few workers in vacsuits pushing crates stacked on struggling hovercarts. At the rear swaggered a man with short cropped, light brown hair in a long blue and red coat with two more guards at each side. He wore the same hard-shelled, segmented armour under his coat only he carried his helmet in the crook of his arm. A Postal Service flag marked his shoulders, and his cuffs were marked with the gold bars of captain.

Stephanie perked up in Frost's lap. He nearly spilled his beer mid-journey to his mouth.

"It's Berkovitz!" she said.

"I thought you knew we'd be meeting him here," Jake said as he and the rest of the table took a better look.

"I thought he'd send a messenger," Stephanie said. "That sidearm's new."

"So's the shield belt," Agameg added. "Good to see he's taking precautions."

The column of guards and their line of fifteen one-metre cube crates stacked three high neared the bar. "Company halt!" barked Captain Berkovitz. "Delivery for Culus Disas!"

A visi with erratically moving yellow and dark green colouring came out from the rear of the bar. The waiters and tenders stopped what they were doing and watched as their boss stopped to stand in front of Captain Berkovitz, who held up his hand in front of the man's face. A beam from his palm scanned the receiver, then Captain Berkovitz nodded. "So delivered!" he announced.

Culus Disas handed him two pocket sized, locked cases as his staff went to work opening the cases. Inside were branded boxes of spirits and delicacies that no one recognized. Captain Berkovitz handed the cases he'd been given by Culus to a guard, who nodded then led most of his comrades out of the establishment in a double column.

Accompanied by four of his guards, Captain Berkovitz turned to the tables occupied by the Warlord crew and grinned in their direction. He made it halfway before Ashley rushed over and collided with him, squealing with delight. He made the rest of the way with her under his arm. "Look who I found," he announced as he presented Ashley, who gave him a final squeeze before letting go.

Minh watched as Stephanie gave him a hug, then Frost, Jake, and Agameg all took turns shaking his hand. "And this is Wing Commander Minh-Chu Buu, call sign Ronin," Jake introduced. Minh stood and shook the newcomer's hand.

"Good to meet you," Captain Berkovitz said. He looked over his shoulder to his four guards. "At ease. Have a drink and sit nearby. Stay away from the heavy narcos."

They removed their helmets and started for the bar.

A chair was dragged over for the newcomer along with an extra table for his guards. Captain Berkovitz took a seat.

Instead of finding a seat for herself, Ashley dropped into Minh's lap, much to his surprise. She opened his bomber jacket and slipped her arm around his back. "Okay if I hide in here?" she asked, her face less than a finger's breadth away. "I got a little more popular than expected."

"A little shell shocked, Ash?" Stephanie asked.

"You know, it was easy after the first one," Ashley replied quietly. She pulled Minh's arm around her waist and he was happy to oblige. Her dark eyes looked around the large bar room then back to Stephanie. "I'll do that again, if we're hard up for a target, but maybe in a smaller place next time."

"You okay?" Minh-Chu whispered in her ear. "Is there anything I can do?"

Ashley regarded him with a smile, her dark brown eyes so close he thought he would fall in. "You're doin' it," she whispered.

"If you don't mind me saying," Agameg said as he poured Captain Berkovitz a tall pint. The ale didn't have any evidence of alcohol in the flavour, so Minh assumed it had some other enhancement additive. "The two of you look very compatible now that I see you together." Minh flushed, and as he looked at the issyrian - his eyes matching the shape of his mouth as he smiled at them - he noticed that Ashley was blushing as well.

"What about us, Aggie?" asked Stephanie from where she sat in Frost's lap. It was a rare playful moment.

Agameg finished sitting down, looked at her and Frost with a cocked head then took a sip from his sake. The reaction caused a ripple of laughter around the table. "Compatibility isn't always obvious," Agameg said hurriedly, trying to control any damage he could have done. "There are a lot of factors, I was just considering-"

"It's okay," Ashley soothed. "They're kind of a freak collision, hard to call for anybody."

Captain Berkovitz nodded. "I know I wouldn't have put you two together," he added. "But it looks good from here."

"Thank you, Allan," Stephanie said.

"Not much else has changed," Captain Berkovitz said, looking around the tables. "A few new faces, some pretty professional gear, but it's good to see most of the gang's still here."

"That's something that changed then came back around," Jake corrected. "A lot's happened since you hired us on Spula. The Samson's running with a full crew, in pretty bad shape on the inside, but she's a fighting ship now, and she's called the Warlord."

"Privateering?" Captain Berkovitz asked quietly.

"Piracy, actually. Only against Order of Eden allies, though," Jake replied to Captain Berkovitz quietly. "I'm surprised the GPC is still running, especially out this far. Last I saw you, the Sinjin was headed for the core worlds."

"The Galactic Postal Service went offline about two months ago," Berkovitz explained. "Last thing I got were the ownership codes for the Sinjin and an official message telling me the ship was mine. Things were getting really good right up until the virus hit. We made it to the Core Worlds, settled on Emmaus.

Got to spend the better part of a year there, too. Bought a nice place in New Wynne, managed to go on shorter runs, spent more time with Suzanne and the kids."

"How are they?" asked Ashley timidly. Minh could tell she was bracing herself against the worst.

"They're good," Captain Berkovitz said, brightening at the mention of his family. "Going a little stir crazy stuck aboard the Sinjin full time. Suzanne misses her garden. She's trying to make something grow in a corner of a cargo hold, but it's not the same."

"How'd you end up all the way out here?" Frost asked.

"The Core Worlds are deadly. Worse than the outer sectors," Captain Berkovitz said. "I barely got my people off-world, and we spent a month rescuing my crew's surviving families. After a near miss with a few Eden ships, we set our heading for the fringe and didn't look back. The Core Worlds are as good as gone. There aren't enough EMP's in the galaxy to clear out the infected AIs. If there's going to be a core to human civilization, it's out here."

"Dangerous place to play courier," Jake said. "There have got to be a couple dozen captains marking your ship for capture while you sit here."

"I'm not worried. First thing I do when I come out of a wormhole is send every ship in the area a message with our service list. I bet half the captains in this port have registered their ships with us so they can pick up messages from info drones. Besides, the visi have my back. Anyone takes a shot at me and they'll have a Junglaz battle cruiser after them."

"Now that's cover," Frost said. "I guess they get their deliveries free."

"Nope, fifteen percent discount," Captain Berkovitz said with a smile. "If you thought shipping rates were high before the virus hit, you should see them now. The most dangerous thing we do now is recover cargo from sorting and storage facilities. After the Holocaust Virus the security doesn't even recognize us, so it feels like all-out war when we take on a group of security bots."

"So you're finishing deliveries from before the fall?" Stephanie asked.

"Not for free," Captain Berkovitz said. "Someone pays us to retrieve something that was on its way to them and we find out which depot or ship it was on. If it's in reach, we go get it. I've hired a couple of honest captains to do some of the work for me, but finding an honest ship is next to impossible these days."

"We can talk about that," Jake said, raising his glass.

"Definitely," Captain Berkovitz replied. "So, what's the story with the Warlord? You guys look like you're in one piece, except for Frost here. Part of him scans new."

"Had a run in with an Eden bot, nasty buggers," Frost said. "Had a new leg grown from the shin down."

"We're settling on Tamber, in the Rega Gain System. If you're looking for a place to set down, we're colonizing an island in the tropical region there."

"You're kidding," Captain Berkovitz said. The GPC guards - two female and two male - who were just sitting down with their drinks stopped, shocked and hopeful. "Jake, I don't know what to say."

"Allan, the first time you paid me I was down to nine crew and had about twenty credits," Jake said. "You saved my ass then and threw me work whenever

I was in range for over three years, work I never regretted doing. It's the least I could do, especially if you've got kids in tow."

"I have a daughter," said one of the guards. "Garnet here has a husband and two kids."

Captain Berkovitz glanced at them and they quietly took their seats at the table and quieted down. "Jake," he said quietly. "I'll have to talk to my people about this, and take a look at the place, but what you're offering," he shook his head, "it's a godsend."

"It's not without strings," Jake said quietly. "You've seen more inhabited worlds and ships than anyone I've met. We're scraping for intel. We're in Hodria Port because you told us about it. If it weren't for your tip, we'd be going on the word of a new partner, a very new partner. Honestly, if it weren't for our Ashley here, we'd be following people around in cloaksuits trying to scan their comms for leads for hours. At worst, we'd have to tag a ship blind and try to take it down without knowing what or who's aboard."

Minh-Chu felt Ashley straighten in his lap. "You're welcome, Captain," she said quietly with a satisfied grin.

"You're getting a share hike for this run," Jake whispered back before looking back to Captain Berkovitz. "Still, out of all the intel she just gathered, we've only got one solid lead, but with your charts and anything you've got stored in memory from passive navigational scans, we'll actually have some real information."

Allan smiled broadly. "You're dealing with the Carthans on Tamber, right?"

"My people are," Jake said. "We have a negotiating team."

"Must be a good one if they let you settle on a terraformed moon, or you had something big to trade."

"Huge," Frost said. "Captured battle cruiser."

"What?" Allan said. "I've been hearing a lot about you - mostly through the Order of Eden broadcasts - but nothing about a captured battle cruiser. You didn't take it with the Warlord, did you?"

"Hell no," Frost said with a chuckle. "Longer story there. Our operation has gotten a wee bit bigger since we last shared a course."

"It must have," Captain Berkovitz said. "All right, I have a run to Schengal Three, it'll take me about six days to finish that and get to Tamber. Send me information about this colony. If it's as good as it sounds, then I'll transfer a copy of everything in my data core. That includes a few hypertransmitter hacks my comms genius programmed for getting into Regent Galactic message systems."

"Now, how did you break their rolling encryptions?" asked Pisser. "It's impossible."

"Let's just say everything I was delivering for Regent Galactic got lost when the virus hit," Captain Berkovitz said.

"So you used their hardware to make some kind of emulator that makes it look like your ship is just another hypertransmitter or something?"

"Or something," Berkovitz replied. "Let's just leave it at that."

"Just so you don't get your hopes up too high," Jake said. "Don't expect to see anything but jungle, sand, and a few old bunkers there. The people I'm in with just secured ownership right before we left."

"I don't mind," Captain Berkovitz said. "If it's protected by the Carthan fleet,

and it's big enough for the families that are stuck aboard the Sinjin, then I'm in."
He worked at a few controls on the inside of his gauntlet's wrist for a moment.
"Here, this is all the data we have on this solar system along with a list of all the
shipping companies working for Regent Galactic. It should make picking targets
easier." The light-hearted expression on Captain Berkovitz's face darkened as he
looked at the comm screen on the inside of his wrist. "I've got a priority
navigational update here," he said, looking to Captain Valent. "Tamber is under
attack by a primary Order of Eden fleet. The Rega Gain system is marked as a
war zone."

"How much to get the codes for that network?" Jake asked. All the Warlord
crew members were standing up and getting ready to leave, Ashley and Minh-Chu
included.

"You'll pay me back," Captain Berkovitz said. "Here are the codes, good
luck."

"Thank you, Captain," Jacob Valent said.

CHAPTER 48
FALLING SKIES

Oz flinched as another ship glanced off the energy shield above and crashed into the landing pad to his left. Fires raged to the west, and everywhere else there were collisions and chaos as thousands of vessels tried to travel without Navnet to guide them. The pods were still dropping, making matters much worse.

From their stationary positions, their fighters fired particle weapons and solid round cannons at the pods whenever they could get a clear shot, but only a few pilots could claim credit for blowing any of them apart in the air. Alaka's son fired from the top of the hangar, sending beams of deadly light into the sky.

"We have it," announced Ayan through Oz's command and control system. "We're broadcasting our own Navnet signal, and we'll be covering the whole port."

He checked and saw that Skyguard Navnet, the name someone in the bunker decided on, was up and running. "Now that's a public service," he said. The difference wasn't apparent overhead yet, and he guessed it wouldn't be for several seconds, perhaps longer.

He looked down into the crater where several technicians inspected the two storey tall pod. "This is one of the small ones, it looks like," one of them reported, tapping the three metre wide drop ship.

"I can see that," Oz replied. "Any life signs?"

"Power systems seem to be running, but that's all. No life signs. It almost looks like a grave buoy."

"What? Why?"

"There are bones inside. Metallic, loaded with dormant nanobots and some kind of materializer tech."

"Get out of there! Move it!" Oz said. He looked to Alaka. "Frameworks. Regenerating soldiers."

The technicians were halfway up the incline when the sides of the drop pod fell open, revealing ten black boxes per side. "Spread out around the edges of the crater and open fire!" Oz ordered.

"On what?" asked one of the soldiers.

The boxes were flung onto the ground around the drop pod, their lids splitting open to reveal silver coloured bones within. "Get moving! Start shooting at those boxes, now!"

Most of the unit moved as they were ordered, but some stood dumbly trying to figure out the situation. He'd tried to train them, but some of the mercenaries had been on their own for too long, and weren't used to following orders without questioning every detail.

Oz adjusted the power of his rifle to the highest pulse setting and activated his slug clip before opening fire on the nearest box. There was enough room in each of the black containers for a pile of bones, not for a man or woman. The framework soldiers began forming moments later, surprising and disgusting the soldiers gathering around the pit. Many of them stopped firing.

"Shoot at them until they stop forming!" Oz said. His target was flying to pieces as flesh rose from silver bones. The bones themselves were what he was going for, and it took several shots to blast them apart. He didn't see progress until he managed to reduce the skull to splinters, then it stopped regenerating. It took half the energy in his rifle, and an entire slug clip.

"Grenade!" he shouted as he tossed three grenades down into the centre of the pit. The few soldiers who were still fighting at close range made a run for the edge of the crater. They had plenty of time to get out of the way. The explosions bought them some time. The frameworks' progress was slower with their bones cast apart. If they were separated from the bulk of their bodies, the skulls started regenerating the bone structure, which seemed to slow them down a great deal. The pod was barely damaged.

Alaka cut two fully-formed, muscled male soldiers in half as they tried to climb to the edge. One of Oz's soldiers was dragged into the crater. The attacking framework was disabled, taking several shots to the head. Another picked up the soldier and threw him into the middle of the drop pod, where a matter-to-energy recycler in the centre worked to eat through his armour, flashing brightly and humming loudly. Metal arms clasped him to the centre of the open pod, industrial cutters working on opening his armour. As Oz fought to disable the frameworks standing in the way, the soldier was torn to pieces by the converter.

The pod began to use materializers to create weaponry where the framework boxes had been, and the mobile frameworks reached for armaments instead of charging for Oz's soldiers on the edge of the crater. He looked to Alaka, who was busy grabbing a framework soldier by the face, breaking his neck and throwing him over his shoulder where the second line of soldiers opened fire on him. Fourteen Triton warriors shot the regenerating framework to pieces but it still took nearly a minute for them to reduce their enemy to the point that it could regenerate no more.

"We're going to lose this," Oz told Alaka. "Explosives, we have to re-crater this crater."

The nafalli nodded. "Cover me."

Oz slapped his last solid round clip into his rifle and took aim at a framework soldier who was claiming a fresh handgun from the pod. He shot the gun first, then started pouring rounds into the thing's head. It took eleven hits to reduce the thing's cranium to bits, and the body began regenerating right away. Oz had to move on to the next target.

"Cover Alaka!" he cried, firing one burst after another at the emerging frameworks. They were over a hundred versus less than fifty, and the barrels of some of Oz's soldiers weapons were beginning to glow red thanks to their ceaseless rate of fire. Alaka batted frameworks aside, and threw two over everyone's heads so they landed in the open in front of the second line.

When he arrived at the base of the drop pod, he shoved a three kilogram explosive pack into the weapon rack, setting the shape of the charge so it focused the damage on the pod while he dodged the grasping metal arms attached to the matter recycler. "Fire in the hole!" Alaka shouted as he leapt free of the crater.

Oz shouted, "Everyone back!" as he turned and ran.

He managed to make it less than a dozen steps before he was struck by the force of the explosion and thrown off his feet. His shields and inertial dampers protected him from the blast. His headgear blacked out, protecting him from going blind from the accompanying flash.

One of his soldiers, Private Lani Serra, was in stasis after losing a leg and her arm up to the elbow. She was halfway up the creater when the bomb went off. Medics were already checking in as he looked at her status. She would be all right.

The people who stood near the edge of the crater but weren't in heavy armour were being treated by their suits for minor injuries ranging from broken fingers and ribs to legs and arms. Soldiers in heavy armour were spared. He wished they had enough extreme environment or heavy combat armour to go around, but that wasn't the situation. They were desperately short.

Alaka helped Oz to his feet and they looked back at the crater. A white and red glow emanated from within, and when he got close enough, he could see that there was nothing left of the pod or the frameworks. The explosion left a crater within the crater where several metres of earth had been either vaporised or melted. "I think we got 'em," Alaka said.

"How many of those charges do we have?" Oz asked.

"Three."

Oz queried their new Navnet system, checking on how many pods made it to the ground and his heart sank when he saw the result. Forty-two made it to Port Rush city and the shanty port without taking fire. They were all open and powered up. "We're going to need a few more if we want to win this."

Navnet squawked an alert and Oz looked into the sky where it pointed. A massive fireball streaked across the sky, leaving a thick white trail behind. He couldn't make out the shape well, but Navnet told him it was a half-kilometer long destroyer named The Jonestown. "Someone forgot to hit the destruct switch when their ship was headed into the atmosphere. That's going to hit with its hull intact."

"Will our shield hold?" asked Alaka calmly.

"It won't come down close enough to do damage here, but Chomro, the continent across the sea to the west is in trouble," Oz brought Ayan up on the comm. "You see this?"

"I do. It'll send a shockwave across Chomro. We'll see waves reaching a hundred fifty or so metres high, far from us, but Ruby is happy she moved her ship. Other ships are in failing orbits. I'm watching."

"What is our Carthan friend saying about his fleet?" Oz asked.

"We're on our own," Ayan replied.

***

After rifling through the lockers, bins, and upper compartments of the Freeground faster than light craft, Alice decided on the best equipment. A pair of admiral-level command units were slapped onto each of her arms. A high durability infantry command and control unit was slapped onto her left arm with the optional extended suite.

The wormhole reaching the outer Rega Gain system was compressed enough so she could start watching news about Jacob, Ayan, Oz, and everyone else from Freeground. "What a find!" she exclaimed when the long list of stories about Ayan Rice and the few stories about Jacob came up. There were hours of footage, and she watched it all while rummaging through the craft.

She used another comm unit to spray a fresh vacsuit onto herself, and when she was prompted for the colour she thought for a moment. "I think powder blue is my favourite colour now, interesting." A regular infantry vacsuit was put on overtop, and over that she slipped into a H.A.M.E.S., a Heavy Armour Mechanized Encounter Suit. When it engaged, it felt like it clamped onto her firmly - worryingly so at first - and then it learned to move with her.

The whole suit was a centimeter thick at the largest parts, but it weighed two hundred forty kilograms because of its density and the equipment built into it. After it finished powering on, she spun in place. "Moves like I'm naked, and doesn't look like much more than a really old Freeground safety suit. They've come a long way." The shield systems, antigravity pulse barrier, and strength components were all ready to go. Instructions played in the head's up display on how to use its features. She watched them in high speed.

Alice looked at the optional shell, with its metal plates and knight-like helmet and shook her head. "Too tacky." The weapons were a whole other thing.

Hours passed as she travelled to the Rega Gain system, examining all the literature that went with the weapons, the ammunition, and laughed at the military demonstration recordings. It was a new thing, explosions made her giggle.

At long last, she settled on an XO-99, the most powerful rifle Freeground ever made. There was only one in the shuttle. It asked for an access code the moment she picked it up, and she impatiently connected with it using her framework interface.

"Well, I still understand this stuff, that's nice," she said as she hurriedly cracked the code and added herself to the database of authorized users, deleting everyone else. The weapon powered on, drawing a base charge from her vacsuit's excess energy storage.

The weapon was light, but one point four metres long. It could fire energy rounds and had two barrels for other types of projectiles. "I don't know if I'll need this stuff, but I'd rather have it than not," she said as she strapped on two sidearms, one energy-based and another that fired tiny blades that were intended to cut into flesh then burst. The rounds could also explode against a harder object.

A large armoured equipment pack came next. She shoved all the explosive ammunition she could find for her new rifle, including combo explosive and EMP rounds made to kill Eden Fleet robots. A tube the size of her forearm contained a portable shelter for four, another contained a high-grade medical system that looked like a body bag, and she hacked the explosives closet for a selection of grenades and portable shields.

When she was finished she'd packed the metre-tall armoured pack with all the gear, food and ammunition that would fit. She didn't neglect the sellables, either. Small comm units that could spray a vacsuit or two filled a pocket, something she knew she could get good credits for. A couple of sidearms were packed in for good measure; weapons were always a great hit with the traders. She strapped two Freeground Marine D9 rifles to the outside of the pack just in case the new and improved one she'd adopted turned out to be cheap and junky.

The news feeds came to an end, and she checked her comm to make sure there weren't any more. To her surprise, there was a sudden stop to all news entries. Alice looked for more details and found a final broadcast from one of the better Stellarnet news outlets. "The Order of Eden are here in force, with the largest colony, combat, and cultivation ship we've seen since the end of the Third Era. Is this the end of freedom in this solar system? This newscaster isn't waiting to find out. Evacuate, find your way to one of the core worlds, where you can still find democracy, or a gathering of organized souls. This is Marc Bowman, wishing you luck."

That was the end of the broadcast, there was nothing else in the stream from that outlet. "At least he left in style. A wimpy, gutless style, but he's a newscaster. He'd probably wet himself if I put a gun in his hand."

Alice checked the cockpit displays to ensure that everything was set for a good wormhole exit. The ship's energy reserves were at full, and everything was functioning well. She lay a hand on a data port built into the console and connected to the ship. In seconds, she programmed a script that would bring shields up, scan for Navnet, listen for distress signals, and begin plotting a course to Tamber with the help of any friendly navigational systems in range. None of the ship's weapons could be automatically fired; they all had to be operated manually, so she left them alone. "Wouldn't do much good, anyway," she said to herself as she finished programming the computer.

The ship emerged from the wormhole and Alice activated the control script. The Rega Gain Navnet system was down, and the entire solar system was marked as a war zone. She took the flight controls and piloted the ship manually, burning the thrusters hard.

With a thought, she plotted a short-jump wormhole and activated the generators. In the blink of an eye she was transported to the inner system, on the edge of Tamber space, and she was immediately tasked with guiding the ship around several large wrecks. Looming in the distance was Skydock, the largest space station in the solar system. Most of its lights were out, but there was little sign of damage to the main facing of the structure. As she came around a wrecked Carthan destroyer, the Vindicta, she started seeing the damage. The station had been struck from the rear. Entire sections were melted inwards, indicating intense nuclear blasts at close range.

Combat alerts began popping up on her console and in her mind as Tamber came into view. There were hundreds of fighters out there, and they were looking for targets. Alice shunted more power to shields, set the thrusters to maximum, and headed for the nearest cover.

Several minor shots were deflected as she raced between dead starships. She set her scanners to start looking for the Samson, the Clever Dream, and the Triton. Nothing came up, but she let them continue searching. There was no point in being disappointed, she didn't have time for it.

Her ship emerged from behind a half-destroyed carrier called the Oslo and was immediately raked with explosive rounds. Alice watched her shields deplete to seventy one percent, nowhere near critical, but she was in trouble. There were five fighters moving to engage her directly. Tamber's blue and brown surface was growing in the distance.

"Gotta go, gotta go, it's right there, I can almost touch it," she said under her breath as she worked hard at the controls, forcing the shuttle into extreme evasive manoeuvres through the frame of a massive dry dock facility for large starships. The fighters behind her had no regard for the structure, and fired regardless of the collateral damage.

She wished she could flip end over end and fire back, but none of the weapons would allow her to control them remotely. Alice gritted her teeth as rounds peppered the rear of the ship, reducing the charge of her shields to twenty one percent.

The atmosphere of Tamber was so close. Alice shunted all the reserve power to shields and programmed the wormhole generator to punch a hole through the outer atmosphere. It was risky, plotting compression through atmosphere; the shuttle wasn't designed for it. At the relative speed she was travelling, going from the vacuum of space into an atmosphere was like colliding with a wall.

The transfer circuits between the reserve power systems and the shields burned out. There would be no more extra power for the shields, and they weren't regenerating fast enough to take fire from her pursuers. Alice spun the shuttle around so she could slow down. Rounds rained down on her as the fighters passed by, reducing her shields to twelve percent.

"Oh God, I hope this works, I'm too young to die," she said as she engaged the shields on her vacsuit and activated the wormhole generator. The inertial dampers burned out the moment she emerged from the wormhole into the atmosphere. The explosion of her ship breaking the sound barrier as soon as she exited was so loud it registered on her helmet's head's up display as dangerous sound. She could see the nose of the vessel had crumpled part way in, destroying most of her sensor suite.

Her scanners detected an active Navnet called Skyguard. It was based on a standard Freeground signal, and she cheered as the name of the administration in charge came up: Triton Forces.

"I'll just register and ask for an approach," she said to herself as she did so. The Navnet system immediately informed her that she was moving eleven thousand one hundred thirty eight kilometres per hour over the port limit, and advised that she slowed down. "No, really?" she replied.

"Hi, this is Alice Valent, a little new and shiny, but the one you know. I hope someone there knows me, anyway. I'm on my way down, really fast, trying to slow up, but I think I'm gonna crash a bit," she transmitted. "Okay, maybe a lot."

The roar of the thrusters firing as the ship screamed across the sky on a path she did her best to guide were loud enough to be heard inside her suit. Heat warnings began going off as she slowed down to under four hundred kilometres per hour, but it was slow enough for her to engage emergency systems. Metal flaps built into the hull spread out, and the increased air resistance was enough to shake her in her harness.

She wouldn't make the settlement marked by Navnet, but she was passing near it. "Alice?" asked Ayan Rice. "I hate to sound negative, but you died on the Triton."

"Yeah, some crazy lady brought me back and sent me to warn you about this invasion. Didn't quite make it in time though. Oops, sorry. It's really me though, but with a few differences. I feel younger, I'm missing most of my memories of being an artificial intelligence, and I'm really looking forward to kicking some ass. Maybe it's just the post-rebirth euphoria or something. Oh, and I seem to talk a lot more."

"Are you coming from the Sunspire?" she asked.

Alice forced the ship into a turn so she would land as close to the Triton settlement as possible, near a crater well outside their shield. "No, why would you- oh! The shuttle transponder, you think I'm from the Sunspire because that's what this ship was registered to, right. Well, I'd like to explain more, but I'm landing, one sec."

She aimed the ship at a gap between two older ships and cut the engines while engaging the antigravity hover systems. She was down to twenty three kilometres per hour. It should have been a good landing, but the antigravity systems didn't activate. "Why me?" she asked before striking the spot between the two ships and careening past the crater she'd intended to land in front of. The shuttle came to a complete stop and she squealed. "I'm alive! I love being alive! Okay, you're fourteen klicks from my current position, I'll be happy to hoof it from here. I'll see you soon, Ayan."

Alice hurriedly locked her pack onto her back and hefted her rifle. "There's something you need to know, Alice," Ayan said as Alice opened the main hatch. "You're right between two combat drop pods filled with framework soldiers."

"And they're pretty agro, I'm guessing?" Alice asked as she surveyed the lopsided, damaged ships in front of her. The sizzle of the ship's main thrusters filled the air as they cooled.

"You could say that," Ayan said. "You should stay put while we figure out the best way to get you and that ship out of there."

Alice was about to open the shuttle's hatch when she stopped and looked at the plate armour. "You know, you can never have too much protection." She took her pack off, put the plate armour on in a hurry and reattached her newfound belongings.

"Did you hear me? We'll work on a plan," Ayan said.

Alice performed a detailed scan of the surrounding area, found one of the framework soldiers nearby and did a bio-sweep on him. She smiled to herself, satisfied. "Don't worry, these are old models. I'll cut a path," she said, charging her XO-99 rifle. "Look for a marine in powder blue amour."

She dropped out of the shuttle hatch to the ground and ordered the ship to seal all hatchways before starting the trek to the Triton settlement.

CHAPTER 49
THE TUMULTUOUS SKY

"We can't be that lucky," Captain Valent said as he walked around the back of the bridge to the scanning console.

"It's right there, the Ferryman, under the command of Lucius Wheeler out of Pandem," Minh-Chu replied.

"Yup, right there," Kadri confirmed. "Less than half a million kilometres from our wormhole exit point. Reading the spacial disturbances, I'd say he just came out of a hell of a wormhole himself, real high powered, like it was made by a big space station."

Jake stared at the readout in disbelief. "Well, look at that," Frost said.

"How many drop ports are open? Did they get them all unsealed?" Jake asked.

"We got eighteen out of twenty eight. All loaded up and ready," Frost replied.

"Loaded with?"

"C-44Ts, seeker bombs," Frost said.

"You're a bad man," Jake said with a smile.

"C-44Ts?" Minh-Chu asked. "That's not on my fighter's arms list."

"They're mines that burst into forty two seeking missiles when they see the designated target. Easy to make, nasty to fight."

"The 'T' stands for thermalitic, doesn't it?" Minh asked.

"Aye, burns and burns against a hull," Frost said. "After exploding pretty good, that is."

"Finn," Jake said. "Get the Big Surprise ready, make sure the guidance system and thruster is ready, too."

"Aye," Finn said, handing his engineering station over to Angela McKinn, a former damage control captain from the Triton.

Captain Valent checked the emergence timer on the main display at the front of the small, crowded bridge and watched it count down from 00:00:2:00 to 1:59. "Less than two minutes, then we're in it," he announced ship-wide. "The first ship we have to kill is called the Ferryman, and they probably have backup. We burn and turn to the next fight until we're home. Time to earn your pay."

He put his hand on Minh-Chu's shoulder and smiled at him. "Ronin, you have work to do."

Minh-Chu was up and down the hallway to his fighter at a run, dodging past other crewmembers along the way. "How are our chances?" Jake asked Frost.

"Can't get a read past her hull, but she's only got four particle beam turrets, our shields can handle those for a week. I expect missile banks, maybe even a micro-nuke, but no antimatter. That'd register even through the pinhole we're looking through. I expect surprises from that ship, though, even though it looks like she's stock, straight out of the yard."

"What about the mess past her?" Jake asked, looking at the incomplete scans millions of kilometres behind the Ferryman.

"I'm thinking the same as you probably are, Captain," Frost said. "Chaos. I see fragmented readings of high powered beam weapons, what looks like broken hulls, nothing to be sure of other than something big is happening just on the other side of the moon."

"Well, we're about to find out," Jake said, returning to the captain's chair. "Stephanie, get your boarding teams ready. I don't know if we'll have time, but we might be boarding that ship."

"Acknowledged, we're ready," Stephanie replied over the comm.

"Emerging in nineteen seconds," Ashley announced, getting a good grip on the controls and double-checking the mind-link system. "I'm going evasive as soon as we're clear."

"Remember, this isn't just a wormhole," Jake said quickly. "We're trailing a lot of hyperspace particles behind us because we combined both FTL techs."

"Yup," Ashley said as the Warlord emerged from the wormhole distortion and she flared all the ship's thrusters hard. The hull rattled under the pressure, but her trick worked: the exotic particles that would make the ship unstable during a turn were sent away from the ship.

The main display flickered as Ashley spun the main thrusters so the ship accelerated sideways. Particle beams and small gauss cannon fire missed the Warlord for long seconds.

Captain Valent used the time to check the more accurate scans of the area for friendly craft, more enemy craft, or other potential complications to the engagement. As a cannon on the Ferryman was used, panels opened up on her outer hull. When they began to heat up, the guns stopped firing and the panels closed. "Gunnery control, have our turrets focus on those hatches," Jake said.

They started taking hits and Jake was satisfied that their shields would give them some time, as long as there weren't any larger surprises aboard the Ferryman.

"Captain, only the rear launch doors are opening," Ronin reported over the communicator. "The front ones were never re-cut."

"We work with what we have, Ronin. Launch."

"Punting, or vaulting in this case," Ronin replied.

"Something I want you to think about, Ronin," Jake said. "This is Wheeler, we've finally got a shot at him, but this is a brute force encounter, not a chess game between captains. We slag him, leave a smouldering ruin behind, and move on. You cover us while we do the deed."

"Yes, Sir," Ronin said. The navigational symbols for three extended Uriel fighters appeared on Captain Valent's display. Minh was flying with Joyboy and Pisser as his wingmen.

The Ferryman launched an entire bank of missiles. Their fighter cover was on top of it, destroying eighteen of the projectiles, but ten got through, bursting the second before striking the Warlord's hull. "What were those?" Frost asked.

"Damage?" Captain Valent asked.

"Critically super-heated panels between frames eleven and twelve, sections twenty one and thirty," Angela replied.

Ashley rotated the ship so a stronger section of their shields was facing the Ferryman. Jake could see she was getting ready for another volley from the positioning of the ship and her engine pods.

"Frost, as soon as their next volley lands, launch nine pods. I want them to split as soon as they clear the ship so we have a few hundred micro missiles on the way to the Ferryman. We need all our gunners concentrating on weakening their shields around those beam weapons."

"Aye," Frost said.

Jake glanced at the slim forty metre long ship. Her engines were built in little bulges down the length of her hull. It was a manoeuvrable ship with more armour than he would have expected from a vessel her size. He looked up the profile of the missiles Wheeler had just launched at them and cringed. "Ronin," Jake addressed. "They're firing shield breakers. They're small, but they emit a pulse before striking an enemy shield that works like an EMP against a section of shielding before hitting."

"Gotcha, expensive little buggers, gotta knock 'em out," Ronin said.

Jake watched as Ronin's small fighter group used the Warlord as cover, peeking out, draining their energy weapon batteries then retreating for a few seconds while they recharged. It was a safe manoeuvre, especially since one shield breaker missile could do serious damage to an Uriel fighter.

The Ferryman let the next volley loose, opening a set of panels running the length of the ship as thirty-five projectiles fired. Minh's fighters thrust out from behind the Warlord, firing automated countermeasure gun pods and a couple of missiles of their own at the cluster of deadly projectiles.

At the last instant, Ashley rotated the main thrusters of the Warlord and flared them as hard as the controls would allow, pushing many of the remaining missiles away, or forcing them to detonate early.

"Scattered hits," Angela announced. "No significant damage."

"Counter launch!" Captain Valent ordered.

Nine missile mines were hurled from the bottom of the Warlord's hull. They burst into hundreds of micro-missiles that sought out the Ferryman.

"Ashley, roll us over into position on the other side of the Ferryman," Jake ordered. "Frost, get ready to launch the other half of our mines and reload the first half as fast as you can."

As Captain Valance expected, the Ferryman's countermeasures, mini-cannons firing flack, shredded most of their initial launch before they could reach their target.

"Captain Valance," came Captain Wheeler's voice over the communicator. It was a one-way message, intended to begin a dialogue. "Why would you even bother fighting a boarding action in that antique? We can settle our scores without the messy collateral damage."

"We built her like an antique because we couldn't find better parts," Frost said under his breath.

Jake shot him a withering look over his shoulder and said; "When we're within a kilometer, launch the second load. Get the quad set warmed up."

"Aye, Captain," Frost said.

Captain Valent watched the display. Ashley was having difficulty getting into position; the Ferryman's pilot was probably under instructions to keep her away from extreme close range. He opened a channel to Wheeler. "It's Captain Valent now, and I'm looking forward to marking your broken hull as a navigational hazard and moving on. This is already over, Wheeler. Surrender or die," Captain Valent said before jamming the Ferryman's frequency.

Ashley was finally getting the Warlord close to the Ferryman, and their opponent's shields were no longer keeping up with the punishment the Uriels and the Warlord's guns were meting out. "Ronin, shred their aft dorsal section," he ordered.

In seconds the Uriels were in position, unleashing a torrent of micro-missiles and gunfire on the upper-rear section of the Ferryman. A burst of fire and light erupted from the rear of the enemy ship and Pisser's fighter exploded into pieces. Ronin and Joyboy thrust away from that section of the ship and fired from a greater distance, staying evasive.

Captain Valent didn't let the loss faze him - there would be time for mourning later. A full volley of missile strikes erupted against the Warlord's hull. Sections of hull plating were heated to the point of being soft, they lost three main launcher barrels, and others were warped. Two crewmembers were obliterated, five more were being medicated into stasis.

"Fire barrels eleven through seventeen," Jake said, knowing the others either weren't loaded yet, were warped by the heat, or damaged beyond use.

"Roll out, Ashley," Captain Valent ordered, but she was already rolling the ship and thrusting away, so the Warlord would fall in behind their enemy, with her undamaged fore section pointing straight at the Ferryman.

The mines burst apart, freeing hundreds of mini-missiles that had less than two kilometres to travel before impacting on the rear section of the Ferryman. Countermeasures destroyed a third of the projectiles before they hit their target, but the rest struck home.

The Warlord was pointing directly at the Ferryman, nose first. Captain Valent looked to Frost, who nodded. "They're hot, sir."

"Open torpedo tubes and fire the quads," Jake said. "Start moving us in the other direction, Ash."

The hum of the railguns one whole deck beneath the bridge rattled the floor, and the bridge crew could feel the vibration of four railgun-assisted torpedo tubes firing their heavy projectiles. Rockets activated as soon as the torpedoes were two hundred metres away from the ship, and they made the distance between the vessels in less than a second. One was thrown off by countermeasures, missing entirely then detonating too late, well in front of the Ferrymen.

The other three struck the rear of the enemy ship. It was impossible to see the munitions in action, but Captain Valance knew that each torpedo forced a two point eight ton slug into the rear of the Ferryman followed by hundreds of kilograms of solid xetima fuel, which would burn without the help of exterior oxygen; it carried its own. The ruined aft section of the Ferryman burned hard, as though the three rough entry points became rockets for several seconds, then flamed out, glowing white and yellow.

"Target weapons," Captain Valent said, speaking to the bridge and Ronin. "If you see anything under power, tear it to shreds."

"The Ferryman is signalling her surrender, Sir," Kadri said.

"First Officer," Captain Valent said to Stephanie though his comm. "Get set to board the Ferryman. If there is resistance, you are to retreat and we'll slag her from a distance."

"Aye, just get me on that ship," Stephanie replied.

Captain Valent was just checking on the sections of the hull that had been superheated and damaged during the fight and was pleased to see that the energy absorbed from the engagement was helping the ship to regenerate when something came up on his alert system. He stood and brought the far side of Kambis up on the main tactical display at the front of the bridge. "Hail the Sunspire," he ordered.

"Right away," Kadri said. "Freeground registry, under Captain McPatrick. Response coming in from Doctor Carl Anderson, formerly of-"

"I know, put him on," Jake said.

"Jacob," Doctor Anderson said with a smile. "You're on the wrong side of the battlefield."

Jake's comm chirped with a notification that he had a message waiting from Jason Everin. He ignored it for the moment and replied to Anderson. "What are you doing in this section of space?" Captain Valent asked.

"Recruiting," Doctor Anderson said. "If you're looking to join the fight over Tamber, I'll check you in with our group leader, The BSF Argos."

"British Security Force," Captain Valent said. "You brought the British."

"We brought the British," Doctor Anderson said with a grin. "They have this taken care of for the moment, we can finish what you're doing so you can get to Port Rush. A ship your size may be able to push through the fighter screen protecting the planet."

"Why, how bad is it down there?" Jake asked.

"The Leviathan is resisting, but we'll take it down. The planet is where the real war is, I'm afraid. The Warlord should be small enough to provide effective air cover while evading, and your people will make a big difference to the Triton settlement down there if you can drop them on the surface."

"Understood, can you pick up Wheeler's ship? Do you have time?" Jake asked.

"We'll tractor it in, I'm sure he'll be glad to see me again," Doctor Anderson said.

"Thank you, Doctor," Captain Valent said as the communication ended. He checked the message from Jason and discovered a picture of a young woman with brown-red hair. A caption said: "Your daughter has been reborn, watch over her." He took a closer look and recognized similarities from the hologram Alice once was as well as the woman she became. "Get me down there as soon as you see a break in the fighter screen," Jake said. "We have work to do on Tamber."

CHAPTER 50
THE CRATER

"So, who's this operative we have in the field?" Oz said, rushing to the strategy table in the middle of the bunker.

"She says she's Alice, but I really don't know," Ayan replied. She brought up the woman's status and an outlined image of her casually jogging down an abandoned alley with her XO-99 rifle over her shoulder. She was cloaked, and safe for the time being. "This isn't the Alice I heard about, as far as I know. Not even Lewis will talk to her."

"That's strange," Oz said, watching the taller woman in Freeground Sentinel Armour make good time towards one of the larger pods near the wall. The intelligence flowing from her passive scanners was high enough resolution to map three kilometres in each direction. She passed by framework soldiers who were dressed in basic armour, carrying rifles like they were no concern. She was cloaked, but her manner was brash. She wasn't making the slightest effort to stay out of sight.

"Lewis says her thought patterns are too different to be recognized as Alice, and he reads her as an adolescent," Ayan said.

"All right, that makes sense," Oz replied. He checked the Clever Dream's ownership details and nodded. "There's a maturity rating attached to the Clever Dream; if she doesn't read two fifteen on whatever this Holmes Scale is, then the ship AI can't interact with her unless she's programmed into the ship's crew manifest by an adult."

"Right, you won't want a sixteen year old in command of an armed ship," Ayan replied. "How are things out there?"

"We're drawing some attention, but so far we're slowing them down by sniping them in the head. It takes a couple of minutes for them to regenerate and reprogram as far as we can tell. We're worried about two sites out there, pods that are sitting upright nearby. It looks like they're building something on top of them."

Ayan looked at the holographic map on the table, then looked to Oz. "You sent her to one."

"She asked for a target from me directly," Oz replied with a shrug. "I told her to investigate, not to engage."

"From the looks of it she's-" Ayan stopped at the sight of a new contact registering in orbit. "That's the Sunspire," she said, suppressing excitement. "Other ships are registering as well."

They watched the new contact screen populate with battleships like the BSF Lexington, BSF Brighton, BSF Legacy, and several others. Two massive carriers, the BSF Shrike and BSF Argus appeared followed by the LCF Challenger. "That's a whole lot of British firepower backed by a Lorander ship," Oz said. "I guess we know what the Sunspire was up to."

"We have communication with the Sunspire," said one of the communications officers, a young man who filled the same position on the Triton.

"Let's have it," Ayan said.

Doctor Carl Anderson's head and shoulders appeared in front of them. "Ayan, Oz, glad to see you're still in one piece."

"It is so good to see you," Ayan said. "You couldn't know."

"I can guess. I wish we had time to visit, but we're going after the Leviathan's battle group directly. We've found what we think is Jacob Valance's new ship, the Warlord. Can you confirm?"

"Yes, that's his new ship," Ayan replied.

"Good, we're going to assist and do our best to get him down to the planet. He might be able to survive the trip with our cover. I wish I could offer you soldiers from our group, but we're gearing up for a boarding action. I'm sending you a data packet that you'll want to look at right away. Oz will have the encryption key, it's the last updated code from his command."

"I've got that," Oz replied. "Thank you."

"Again, good to see you. We'll tie this up out here so we can have a proper visit by sundown," Doctor Anderson said.

"Thank you, Doctor," Ayan said.

The transmission broke up and within seconds the channel turned red, indicating that it was being blocked. The data packet got through, however, and Oz opened it with his code.

Specifications for ammunition types and grenades made to kill framework beings flooded the table's holo-grid. "Send this to the machine shop, and make this ammo priority one," Oz told the nearest communications officer.

"EMP enhanced explosive rounds," Ayan said. "It's going to take a while to make these, we should use our last two industrial materializers."

"One's ready to go, it might have an hour making ammo this dense," Liam Grady said. "The other was just repaired, I don't know how durable it is."

"We have to arm ourselves properly," Ayan said. "Do it, get as many rounds out of them as you can," she told Oz.

"Um, guys?" asked Alice through the tactical comm. "They've got major construction going on here, and there's a detection field that's making my stealth system's alarms go off. I'm going to have to do this the hard way."

"Don't do anything, there's no point in you mounting a solo offensive," Ayan said. "You'll just get yourself killed."

***

"Can I get a new operator? You're all full of negativity," Alice said as she climbed higher up on the side of the old hauler ship that had been brutalized when the troop pod struck nearby. She took a look around from her higher vantage point and immediately wished she could help several crews who where trying to fend off framework soldiers.

"Listen, I don't know if you're the real Alice, or what's going on, but I want to have the chance to find out in person. You don't have to impress anyone, you don't have to prove anything, I'm sure we can figure it all out if you just come in. We'll try to make a gap so you can get through the shield without exposing the settlement," Ayan replied.

Firefights dotted Alice's near vicinity and beyond as ship crews fought frameworks for control of their landing sites and others simply tried to get from one place to another. The skies were eerily still; most of the ships that could leave did so in the minutes that followed the appearance of the Skyguard Navnet. Most of the ships still on the ground were empty, disabled, or defending something important. Port Rush was a ghost town, for the most part.

In the distance she could see the tracers from the Triton Compound, firing at drop pods as they fell. A blur above their relatively small patch of the shanty port told her that their energy shield was still up. Other ships used their shields for defence and fired at incoming pods as well, but no one else was as prepared or well armed as the former Triton crew. "Trust me, getting behind a big shield and wagging my jaw at someone until they believe I'm who I am sounds better than picking a fight with an army of regenerating thugs, but someone's got to put a crimp in their plans. Actually, I kinda like the idea of a fight. Talk is getting boring."

"Just hold on, we'll figure something out," Ayan said. "Maybe we can take care of that from here, a quick fighter strike."

"Nope, they've got turrets in range, no need to risk a pilot and a ship," Alice said.

Alice settled into her perch so she could get a better look at the crater and the large drop pod in the centre. "My tactical counter marks twenty soldiers and one commander. I see a mount for the top of that drop pod and it looks tall enough so it can reach above the nearest ship," she said over her comm. "And I see acceleration rails."

Alice turned and looked for three soldiers she'd seen earlier and spotted them carrying heavy chunks of metal. Other frameworks guarded their passage, forming a safe path to a refuse lot a hundred metres away.

Her attention was drawn back to the landing pod, where four more frameworks emerged from cases, put on a lightly armoured uniform, took a rifle from the rack, and marched outward to stop at the edge of the crater. They were perimeter guards, and the longer she waited, the more there would be. "They're setting up a junk gun," Alice said.

"What?" Ayan replied. "Don't do anything, we'll think it through here. We just got specifications for framework killer rounds, we'll be able to fight them soon."

"Yeah, the anti-bot rounds work just fine, already tried a few shots. That's why I'm cloaked. I put a few of those things down and they all seemed to notice."

"I saw that, and it's going to happen again if you-"

"Sorry, they'll be able to break your shield down if they finish this gun," Alice replied, "can't let that happen." She blocked Ayan on Crewcast, so anyone but her could communicate with her.

She rolled back and let herself drop behind a broken hatch for cover. After a quick look around, she de-cloaked and detached her pack. After a moment of digging, she found a fist-sized demolition charge and several clips of anti-bot rounds designed to kill Eden Fleet machines. She loaded the charge into her rifle and changed the clips in her weapons.

An alarm sounded in her helmet as her HUD brought up a navigational alert window that highlighted a Carthan ship descending on a course leading to a location within ten kilometres of her location. Alice reactivated her cloaking systems, slung her rifle and jumped down off the side of the ship. She landed running. "Unblock user – Ayan Rice the Second," she told her communications device. "Hi, you see the trouble I do?"

"Yes, can you find cover?" Ayan asked.

Alice glanced at the falling mass of mangled metal in the sky then back to her surroundings. The barriers dividing the landing slips from each other and the roads between were flimsy at best, made from found materials. All the ships nearby were sealed. "There's nothing," she said, more panic in her tone than she expected to hear. Alice looked to the crater surrounding the drop pod as she ran around the corner. There was a road going right past it, a tall barrier to her left and nothing close enough ahead or behind that could offer cover. "What's on the other side of this barrier?"

"An empty slip," Ayan said. "Just find anything bigger than yourself and try to get under it. If you can find a dip, or a culvert to jump into, that would be best."

"I see a dip," she said, unslinging her rifle as she redirected her run towards the drop pod crater.

"That's not an option!" Ayan said.

"Tell my dad I love him," Alice said, "and that kicking ass runs in the family." She pulled three slim grenades from her pocket and switched her armour's field generators from stealth to shield mode. Framework soldiers who were hurriedly working at securing their small crater base spotted her immediately, and she leapt high from the edge of the crater, launching herself forward and well over their heads.

Alice armed the first grenade and tossed it towards the sentry guards. Her HUD targeting assistant found her rifle's first victim and she opened fire, hitting with one shot out of the burst. The round exploded inside the framework soldier, rending him through the middle.

The other grenades were tossed at the drop pod and fell into the equipment rack. Her suit sent a signal to them and they exploded, damaging the equipment materializer and sending broken hardware across the crater. She rolled onto her feet firing the particle acceleration pulse portion of her rifle at a group of four frameworks, disabling them as the high energy bursts ripped through their necks and chests.

With a thought her armour knew to send a signal to her rifle to switch back to anti-Eden bot rounds, and she sent bursts into every framework she could see. A grasping arm slipped across her energy shields and she turned to fire several bursts into the recycler system, reducing it to shreds of scrap metal.

Rounds caught her from the right and left. Her shields read twelve percent, and she rolled to her left, taking shelter behind the drop pod. Alice came up on her feet and blasted a crowd of frameworks within two metres of her, hoping that the Eden-bot buster rounds would do the trick. They would be disabled, thanks to the grievous wounds she was inflicting, but not for more than a few minutes at best.

Alice returned fire at several frameworks that shot at her from the edge of the crater and caught sight of the Carthan carrier as it disappeared over the lip of the crater. She fired a pair of grenades from her rifle at the three frameworks she could see and ducked down into the fetal position. "This is gonna hurt," she said as her armour reported her shields were down to three percent.

The ground quaked violently, battering her armour. She could hear the world around her breaking.

Chapter 51
Target Zero

The bridge of the Triton had been evacuated under protest from the crew. The main security doors behind Alice filled the large hatch and sealed. Someone had to remain at the main controls, and Jake had left her in charge. Alice knew she was going to die, but it was only so her crew could win the day for once.

The crew of the Triton had been beaten in so many different ways, individually and together. Refugees, survivors, but never the victors. Someone had to show them how to win, and she would, even if it cost her her life.

Alice awoke sputtering and gasping, aware that she was just recalling her sacrifice aboard the Triton. "Dying's got to be the worst," she said, her voice sounding strange, higher. She was buried past her waist in rough dirt and debris. "Oh, God, this sucks." The sound of something scrabbling in the gravel silenced her. Nothing was coming up on her HUD, so she removed her helmet in time to see a framework bending down only a couple of metres away to pick up his rifle.

She squirmed to get out of the hole, pumping her legs in the loose gravel and pushing as hard as she could with her hands. The armoured vacsuit she wore under the armour was still operational, and she couldn't have been more thankful for that as the framework fired a burst at her, hitting her in the chest twice. The vacsuit held up, but it wouldn't repel him forever.

She picked up her helmet, which had a gaping hole in one side, and tossed it at the soldier right before he opened fire again. Her legs came free, and she fell backwards, drawing her sidearm and firing white hot micro-blades into him from his neck to his forehead.

His head was ruined from within as the little electrified projectiles popped behind his face and inside his neck. He fell limp.

"So much for my spiffy armour," she said. The new HUD in her secondary armoured vacsuit calibrated and she looked at all the red marks around her on the tactical map. Alice pulled the last of the ruined armour plates off and looked around. Her pack peeked out from the loose dirt beside a star cruiser resting on its side. She rushed to it and pulled it free. There was one Freeground D9 rifle still attached and to her relief it checked out fine.

Her tactical monitor warned her of three frameworks regenerating behind her, and she whirled to face the nearest. It stood on new legs, its left arm still regenerating from a stump near the shoulder. "Surrender, you will be treated fairly," it said.

"Funny, I didn't think you guys were big on talk," she said, taking aim at its head. "How's this for an answer?" she fired and missed as it dropped to the ground and rolled.

"You little," she said as she opened up with the rifle and caught the regenerating arm first, followed by its chest then the side of its head. The electromagnetically enhanced rounds burned for a second before bursting, only a little more dramatically than her sidearm's ammunition did. He fought to get away from her with his working arm; his legs weren't moving. The arm that was regenerating stopped. "EMP rounds, huh?" she said. "That's what makes you guys twitch and die?" She drilled a short burst into his head and smiled. "Easy enough."

The framework's regeneration began again, so slow she almost couldn't make it out through the blood pumping from the stump. Another framework stirred in the dirt, buried up to its chest, laying on its face. She stepped over to it with her rifle raised. "Please, mercy," it begged. "The Order will remember."

Alice stopped and regarded the soldier as he turned his head awkwardly to look up at her. She looked into its blue eyes and saw a man, someone she would think was simply human if she ran into him on a busy street. "Please," he repeated.

"You don't move," she said. "You just stay there and be quiet."

He shifted in the dirt and her tactical system highlighted an intact rifle under his right armpit. It was hiding its weapon from her. "Mistake," she said, raising her weapon and firing into the side of his head.

With a steady gait, Alice walked around the corner where two unarmed frameworks were getting on their feet. The first lunged at her. She dodged aside and shot him in the back of the head. The second ran for cover but she caught him in the leg before he made it. She turned the rifle's field generator up and watched as the next electromagnetically charged rounds she fired tore his head off.

Her tactical display showed that she'd cleared the immediate perimeter, so she took the time to retrieve her pack and affix it to her back. The muscle enhancement in her vacsuit adjusted, and she hopped up onto the hull of the nearest starship and ran up the side, staying low.

The shockwave had changed the landscape entirely. The forest in the distance, past the Port Rush shanty port opposite the city proper, was flattened. The kilometre wide junk fire she'd seen before was out. The Port Rush shanty port itself was a jumble of smaller ships that had been tossed away from the epicentre, larger ships that had taken extreme damage, and leaning or collapsed landing platforms. She was almost afraid to see what happened to the Triton settlement, which was between her and Port Rush City, but checked anyway.

Her tactical system didn't read any trace of a shield, but their tiny rectangle in relation to the rest of the sprawling port was an oasis, showing some of the only clear ground for kilometres. The quiet was disturbed as an energy round sparked on the hull near her. Her tactical system showed her the origin point. She didn't bother firing back, but slid down the side of the overturned hull instead, settling in under cover.

"Search: XO-99," she said to her command and control unit. Her eyes focused on the tactical read of the area around her. There were thermal readings that pointed to thousands of trapped non-combatants who were hiding in their ships. The drop pods had stopped, but readings told her there were hundreds of frameworks in her area. Most of them were still recovering, but they had survived the event just like she did, only she regenerated faster. "I think I'm shorter," she said as she moved behind cover. "Yup, shorter, more compact. I wonder why? Maybe I lost something? Wait, no, my mass is almost the same."

Her tactical computer highlighted the location of her XO-99 rifle and she smiled. It wasn't too far away, less than a hundred metres. "You're probably all broken up, but I bet if I get you home someone can help me rebuild you."

Alice checked her ammunition; the D9 rifle was loaded with explosive pellets that could hold a charge, and had nine hundred thirty rounds left. She checked the bag hurriedly and found three more clips. "Now this is a party." Realizing that she stood out like a sore thumb, she activated the colour matcher in her vacsuit and touched a rusty patch of dirt. Her armour changed colour to match. "Yup, I'm definitely shorter. My run speed is gonna drop."

She turned towards the Triton settlement, seven kilometres away, and started running between two piles of debris. There were no people out in the open, only frameworks, and she took two down the moment she broke out into the open, strafing as she passed.

Alice dropped and slid under a fallen girder, rolled onto her feet and lurched towards the yellow marker designating the spot where her prized rifle was last spotted. "Target zero, in my quadrant!" shouted a framework as she passed a thick hull plate. The tactical computer only detected him once he was right beside her - he was using the plating as shelter and she had to wonder whether he knew it would stop her system from detecting him.

She jumped to her left, taking a hit on her hip. Alice's thick armoured vacsuit registered the strike and advised her that the suit would only take another two hits in the same place before offering no protection. Her tactical system warned her that there were several more frameworks coming out of the wreck behind her. Her foot caught on some rubble and sent her sprawling, holding onto her rifle for dear life.

Flipping onto her back, she took aim at the one who called her 'Target Zero' and fired. He ducked behind a heavy strut jutting out of the ground as though he saw her retaliation coming well in advance. Three more targets drew her fire. She missed the second but shot the other two who were taking positions behind a leaning landing pylon.

She rolled onto her feet and sprinted towards a large, warped sensor dish as shots pecked at her surroundings. Her cover made creaking and pinging sounds as several super-heated bolts of energy struck it. She could feel her outer vacsuit repairing itself, and in that moment she could see her comm system's tactical map in her mind. The next moment it was gone. Alice ran up a broad cargo ramp into the main hold of an old cargo ship. "Wait, what was that special thinky-seeing thing?"

There was a hatch open on the other side of the cargo hold; she could see the light of day coming in. With a grace that was as natural as walking, she leapt up and caught a support beam then used her momentum to swing over the rough pile of crates between her and the hatch opposite her. A hop and a roll got her over the rest of the debris and she came out the other side.

"Alice, you have a neural node made to communicate mentally," Ayan said over her comm. The sound of a fire fight was in the background of her message. "I've looked you up and gotten more details. I don't know how you're with us, but you might still have a device like that, and if you're seeing status from your equipment, then that's going to be helpful. Concentrate and you'll get it."

"Might be helpful? Yeah, just a bit," Alice said as she dropped from a scaffold that, inexplicably, was still intact along the side of the old cargo ship. The two frameworks she dropped behind only had time to half-turn before she riddled them with rounds. Her tactical screen populated with more information, including paths that would lead her directly to the Triton settlement. There were hundreds of frameworks moving and firing towards their location, and a few trying to close in on her. "You expect me to concentrate with all this going on? Oh, and thanks for the uplink."

"You're welcome, we're getting a good amount of information from you too, but it's time for you to come in. Our shields are down so you'll have an unobstructed run straight in if you can get past the frameworks," Ayan said, the end of her statement was punctuated by her rifle cycling up and firing.

"That simple, just come on over," Alice said.

"You just covered a kilometre, leapt twice your height and dropped seven metres without injuring yourself. You can make it, and we want you here," Ayan said.

"Of course you do, now that you're under siege," Alice said, running up the side of a ruined shuttle and leaping onto a segment of broken hull. Several soldiers tried to fire at her while she was in mid-air, but missed, and she increased her pace as she found good cover and a flat surface.

"Alice," Oz said. She immediately liked the sound of his voice, as though there was some subconscious memory of him that indicated that he was trustworthy. "We're suspicious because we saw you die, but we want you here. We want you to be who you say you are. Ayan and I never got a chance to really meet you, and I'd like to."

She leapt off the edge of the broken hull into the open air, peeking down. Vertigo gripped her as she looked nineteen metres down at a collection of sharp, wrecked bits of metal and junk. At the last instant she looked back up to her target and missed her footing. Alice fell forward, dropping her rifle onto the hull in front of her and sliding off until she turned the tackiness of her vacsuit up and it stuck to the bare hull, leaving her legs dangling over the edge. Scrambling up she said, "That woulda hurt." Picking up her rifle, Alice ran on into a labyrinth of abandoned crew cabins and corridors that would eventually lead her to a curve in the ship and a hatchway closer to the ground. The overturned bunks, stripped consoles, and dark hallways were eerie. "Ships are for living in, best way to make them look alive," she muttered to herself. "Dead ships are spooky."

"What was that?" Oz asked. "It came through so fast it barely sounded like words."

Alice realized then that she didn't say it verbally, but mentally. "I think I connected to something," she said. "One sec." She ducked behind a twisted bulkhead and checked her tactical screen. There were frameworks trying to follow her, and there could be more waiting at her exit point. There was no way of knowing, not even the Triton Settlement's sensors could see that side of the ship.

Alice made an effort to ignore everything around her. "I just need a moment, a moment of peace," she said.

A memory invaded her senses. She was leaning on a railing, watching a group of children walking below. One of them looked up at her and waved hesitantly. Alice gave her a big smile and waved back. The little one was immediately all atwitter, anxiously telling a little blonde friend at her side about the stranger above as they were walked down into the mass transit tunnel.

"I wish I had a childhood," she recalled telling Lewis using her neural link. It was so easy, treating the device just like it was a finger or a hand. No one thought about how a hand did what it did when it grasped an object, they just did it. The neural connection in her memories was the same, and when she tried to apply that information to herself she could see all the electronic objects she could touch, the workings of her comm unit, and she understood exactly how it worked with the systems she used to hack the Freeground ship. "They're all part of the same sense," she said aloud. "I think I got it, Oz."

She couldn't get past the mental image of the little girl waving at her though, and in a flash she realized why. "Oh, no way," she said to herself, commanding her vacsuit headgear to retract and bringing up a holographic mirror image of her face. "Rounder face, baby-fat, not so much as a little laugh line around the eyes," she paused a moment and checked her physiological scan. "Oh no, I'm a teenager! And I'm short!"

Alice's tactical system warned her that there were frameworks entering the ship lower down, and she sealed her suit back up, then moved on, rushing towards them. "Guess I wanted to have a childhood so bad that this framework rig compromised. That might explain why I can't remember a whole ton of stuff. Love having a tactical system feeding my head though," she said. Alice simply knew how much ammunition her weapon had, what the sensors on it, her vacsuit, and every other system she had were saying, and seeing her enemies in her mind's eye. She was at one with her equipment, and it only made her faster, more confident. The inventory system made her aware of what she had in every pocket, where those things were, and what their status was.

She pulled a shield puck from one of her pockets and configured it to her purpose with a thought. There were three frameworks waiting for her through the next hatch, standing between her and the exit. She held the shield emitter out in front of her and dropped through the hatch, firing at one framework while blocking the other two, one of which said, "We have eyes on Target Zero, engaging!"

The first framework soldier was blasted to pieces. The other two couldn't fire past her shield, so she rushed them with it between her and their deadly fire. Knocking the first over, she continued to collide into the other while firing at the first as she passed it. The third screamed as the energy barrier burned its face. Her suit connected to the shield emitter, keeping it charged with reserve power. She spun and held the barrel of her rifle up to the last framework's head for a moment before pulling the trigger.

Her sensors told her there were eighteen framework soldiers waiting behind cover for her to emerge from the ship.

"Wait for air support," Oz said. "We're seeing resistance but we should be able to get a couple of fighters out there soon."

Alice slung her rifle, watching the first framework she killed upon entering the cabin slowly begin to regenerate. She affixed the shield emitter to her left forearm and pulled ten thin grenades from her hip pocket. She had two left there and a cartridge of thirty-five in her pack. "I've got this, keep your fighters for defence."

Crouching low behind the energy barrier, she ran as fast as she could towards the hatch. The barrier ran along the ground in front of her, humming and crackling as it adjusted to her gait. The first shots struck the shield the moment she made it to the hatch, but she'd caught many of them by surprise, and most missed while she rushed the first trio, who were taking cover behind an overturned antigravity truck.

She leapt onto the truck's cab then dropped down on top of one of them, leaving a grenade behind as she sprinted to the next group. Her suit registered a thirty six hundred degree spike behind her as the grenade exploded. She increased the timing on the rest of the grenades, relieved that she was just far enough from the first explosion for her heavy vacsuit to deflect the shrapnel.

Alice flung a pair of grenades towards a group of three to her far right and mentally sent a detonation signal using her mind's data connection as she rushed another group. The group of five were smarter than the rest. The other frameworks were finding better cover as she moved, while the five she charged directly broke cover and intensified their fire. Alice tossed the two grenades in their direction as her energy shield ran out of power, and she jumped for the nearest cover.

Her suit absorbed several shots before the grenades went off, incinerating the five of them. She discarded the burnt-out shield emitter, unslung her rifle, and ran from the scene, limping as her right leg regenerated a deep burn. A second later she was running down a fresh path of loose gravel between two wrecks as she watched the frameworks try to catch up. She emerged into a large crater and stopped, jumping behind cover. "Oz, you're going to want to send people down here, right now. There are real soldiers in a pit I just found, and a big ship. They took my XO-99."

"Your XO-99?" Oz asked.

"My gun, they took my favourite gun. I was tracking it so I could get it back before I headed to your camp," Alice said. Her heart skipped a beat and she was filled with rage as she saw Grabriel Meunez and Lister Hampon emerge from the large main hatch in the side of the top of the ship. She verified with her suit's sensors and nodded. "How are they down here?"

"There's a major segment missing from the Leviathan, the Order of Eden command ship. They must have come down right after the Carthan carrier crashed."

Alice looked at the rows of soldiers gathering around the outside of the ship. They lined up black boxes she recognized from the drop pods and worked on setting up equipment. She peeked out from behind the wreckage and zoomed in on Gabriel Meunez. His hair was longer, and he was dressed in ornate robes. There was no one in the galaxy she hated more. She couldn't help but remember him, and how he pursued her for years. "I see you, bastard."

He looked directly at her over the one hundred fifty-six metre distance. "I can see you too," he said through her neural communicator. "There's something new, something wonderful and fresh about you."

"Get out of my mind, sicko," she replied through her mental node.

"That was such an emotional response, I only heard static," Meunez replied.

"You must have missed me. If I knew you were alive, I would have never stopped searching for you. I love you, Alice. I ache when I can't feel you connected to me."

His message was so loud in her head, his voice was so clear, she retched involuntarily then hurriedly retrieved the clip of grenades from her pack and slapped it into her rifle, setting all its systems to maximum. She calmed her mind and suppressed her disgust. "What can you give me if I join you?" Alice asked.

"Control," Meunez replied, his response slightly garbled by emotional static.

Her tactical systems told her two squads of soldiers were moving around the sides of the crater, carefully creeping towards her. She could also feel exactly where Meunez was. Hampon was a mystery, invisible to her.

"What kind of control?" Alice managed with some clarity.

"Control over your destiny. You can live your life however you like, wherever you want."

"You'd have control over me," Alice said. "How can you call that freedom?"

"I love you, Alice," he replied. "I'm overjoyed that you're still alive."

It was all the data she needed, her connection was so revoltingly strong with him that she could feel where his mind was on her tactical systems with no margin for error. She moved out from behind cover, kneeling firmly. Alice held her rifle steady. She took an extra second to make sure her aim was true.

"You can't destroy me, Alice," Gabriel Meunez said.

"I can try," Alice replied, pulling her trigger. Energy rounds burst from Alice's rifle in a steady stream, ripping his shoulders and head to flaming pieces. She switched firing modes to her grenade launcher and let loose with a rapid-fire arc of incineration grenades hot enough to melt his framework systems.

Her first grenades were going off as a soldier's rounds caught her in the shoulder. The rest of his squad opened fire, and they were joined by others. Her vacsuit was finished in seconds, torn apart by hundreds of rounds. When the first round that struck her in the face burned through to her cheek, she thought it was the end. And then it was.

CHAPTER 52
CONNECTIONS

"We're down to three mines, packing our last six right now," Frost reported from his tactical station.

Jake looked at the hull status of the Warlord and nodded, satisfied. The emergencies were handled well enough. Not as quickly as he would have liked, but their three decompressions only resulted in four fatalities. More than there would have been if the ship was completed on the inside, but fewer than he could have expected. As for the hull, there were dozens of spots where the ergranian metal had warped and recovered. They only had two breaches that had to be sealed.

"I just lost a thruster," Ronin reported. "Joyboy and I just finished scrapping with a squad, I don't think we've got another one in us, even with your support, Warlord."

The three functioning turret guns on the top of the Warlord and the pair of torpedo launchers they had left were running full-time. They were down to their last five torpedoes and Jake signalled the launch room to reload and hold at the ready. The pair of turrets on the bottom of the ship were abandoned after they took a direct beam hit from the Leviathan and then seized into place thanks to an overheated section of hull. Life support systems were in even worse shape; the crew worked in sealed vacsuits.

"Sunspire, we need to either head down or get in closer to a big carrier for cover," Captain Valent asked through his comm. "We've been lucky so far, but that won't last."

"The fighter screen over our sector is finally thinning out, if you're going to make a break for it, now's the time," replied Specialist Lehrin. "Good hunting, Warlord."

"You heard him, Ash, take us down. It's time to go somewhere we're not outclassed," Captain Valance said. They turned away from the Sunspire as another beam of light was refracted away from its hull, and the outer hull was pockmarked by a stream of heated particles. The Warlord spun and thrust towards the blue, brown, and green surface of Tamber. A corvette and three fighters threatened to block them off, firing energy rounds and a torrent of small energized slug rounds. It was one of the United Confederation Worlds ships, a new enemy he'd learned to hate in the last half hour.

"Head straight for 'em and drop everything we've got on that ship," Captain Valent said, programming and launching their missile mines personally. He hoped they would be the last they'd spend outside of the atmosphere.

Ronin and Joboy's fighters strafed left and right above and below the Warlord, unloading their missiles on the enemy corvette's fighter screen. Between the pair, it looked like they were launching dozens of flares at the ships, but Jake knew they were deadly seeker micro-missiles. One well placed hit could disable a fighter, three would destroy it, and the number Ronin and his wingman launched would decimate their enemies if they struck.

The enemy fighters broke away, heading towards the atmosphere in hopes of burning the missiles up as they attempted re-entry. That left the corvette, which was still moving to block them, or at least damage the Warlord severely on its way into the atmosphere. The mines burst, spilling their missiles forth as the Warlord fired her torpedo tubes. "Old weapons," Captain Valent said as he watched the hail of fire rain down on the corvette, "but real firepower."

The corvette burst in a dozen places as her hull broke up and the Warlord passed by, leaving the remains to burn up in the atmosphere behind. Jake checked the status of Minh and Joyboy and was surprised to see their shields regenerating, their weapons cooling, and the pilots in fine condition. The only problem the pair had was their ammunition levels. They were almost down to only their energy weapons.

Captain Valent gripped the edge of his armrests, wishing they could enter the atmosphere faster. He scanned the area ahead and below.

Port Rush City proper had been decimated and was overrun by framework soldiers. He narrowed his scan and linked up to the Sunspire's readings only to discover tens of thousands of the regenerating soldiers. Many of them were on their way towards the shanty port, where some ships showed signs that there were still crews aboard, trying to power them up. Human survivors took shelter wherever they could.

"Finn, is the Big Surprise ready?" he asked.

"Yes, but in this atmosphere we're talking about an effective radius of seventy three kilometres."

"We're hitting Port Rush, it's lost," Jake said, looking at the number of troop pods the Order had in the city; there were ninety eight. "It's the only thing that will make all those frameworks human enough to kill."

"Aye, it's ready. I'm climbing down to set the target," Finn replied. After a moment he asked: "So, framework systems can be fried by an EMP?"

"I'm betting that one powerful enough would do the trick. We'll be blasting all their gear out of commission if I'm wrong."

"Not bad, either way," Finn said.

"Drop it behind the Spaceport in relation to our camp, that ought to keep the blast away from our settlement down there."

"They'll have about nine klicks buffer zone," Frost said, looking at his tactical screen.

"Good enough," Jake said. "Kadri, warn-"

"Warning the Triton settlement it's coming on an encrypted channel," Kadri said. "We have a tactical update from them and a scout named Alice."

"Alice?" Jake said, immediately putting the thought that it could somehow be his daughter out of his mind. It wasn't possible; he'd watched her pass away. Jason's message told him she was alive somehow, but he guarded against hope.

Her location was marked on the tactical map of the surface. Alice had been gunned down near a large, octagonal escape ship. Her Freeground issue command and control unit reported that her injuries were beyond lethal - they were malicious. The structure she'd scanned was five levels deep, and had dug until it had high banks of earth all around it. He checked the scan of the Leviathan and saw a void in the side of the ship that matched. There were several other voids the same shape, but the record from her command and control unit reported that she'd seen Lister Hampon there, and killed Gabriel Meunez with prejudice.

The Warlord rocked as an anti-air burst struck the left side of the ship. "Take us down low, Ashley," Jake said.

"Look ahead for anti-air and obstructions, and highlight them on my view," Ashley told her navigator as she guided the Warlord into a spinning, weaving dive towards the fresh-water ocean near Port Rush. She manoeuvred the Warlord so close to the water that the engines threw a violent wake of liquid and steam behind it.

Ronin and Joyboy flew in formation just ahead. They were joined by several Triton fighters as they crossed over onto the shore. "My scans are showing anti-air turrets on top of some of the drop pods behind the city wall," Ronin reported. "I'm getting set to drop my last seekers on a few, marking other targets."

"I see it, Ronin," answered Slick. "Stay low, keep your flight paths jagged as we approach, time to test our inertial dampeners."

Ashley piloted the ship only metres away from the tops of buildings and wrecked ships. The steam and water wake transformed into one of fire and dust. She didn't avoid the enemy troops on the ground either, but made sure she was close enough to cause chaos and death as they passed. The Uriel and Ramiel fighters rained down energy and slug fire as they passed over enemy encampments. They passed the tall wall dividing the Port Rush shanty port from Port Rush City proper. "Fighters, get clear after your first run. Your ships won't repel an EMP this powerful," said Captain Valent.

The fighters zigged and zagged abruptly from left to right, testing the tolerances of their ships and pushing beyond normal gravitational force tolerances without killing their pilots thanks to inertial dampener systems. The ships fired dozens of small missiles that screamed towards the drop pods and exploded. The squadron hit nine targets and peeled off.

The Warlord's remaining beam turret cut across several enemy encampments and fired at a few anti-air positions as they swept past the tops of broken skyscrapers. The port building came into view, and Ashley dove for it.

Anti-air cannons struck the bottom of the hull along with small-arms fire, taxing their shields heavily, draining them to three percent before Ashley pulled up and had the ship in the perfect position to drop their payload. "Drop it, Finn!" Captain Valent ordered.

"It's away!" announced Finn.

The Big Surprise, a collection of energy storage devices wrapped around an old, massive electromagnetic bomb, dropped from its hiding place, behind emergency access doors. An alarm sounded, alerting Ashley to a large change in mass, and Jake silenced it, knowing that she was aware of the shift and would adjust.

One of the main thruster pods was struck by heavy anti-air energy fire without the protection of shields. The twin thruster overheated and shut down instead of exploding. Ashley and her navigator were busy frantically compensating as she guided the ship one handed.

The sound of the inertial dampeners straining to compensate for Ashley forcing the Warlords remaining three twin thruster pods to full maximum tolerances filled the bridge with an ominous hum. In seconds they were over water, and the tactical readouts on the bridge marked the entire city and mountain behind it as being struck by a massive electromagnetic pulse. Captain Valent focused in on the Triton encampment and was relieved to see that they were untouched. Only a tiny fraction of the shanty port beyond the wall of Port City Proper was affected.

"Marking our next target," Captain Valent said, highlighting the crater made by the Leviathan's escape ship. He couldn't help but watch as the green dot designating Alice's corpse failed to move from its resting place near the edge of the crater. "Stephanie, get all your marines ready. We're storming that underground complex," Captain Valent ordered through his comm.

"There are a lot of troops down there," Frost said. "We've got two mines ready, they could drop, burst, then carpet bomb the area."

Captain Valent stared at the green dot on the map. It couldn't be her, but there was a feeling, an irrational hope that he couldn't shut down.

"Taking small arms fire, a couple of small surface-to-air hits, but nothing big," Frost announced. "Coming up on the target."

Jake took a deep breath and said: "Mark their mustering point and any exposed systems as targets, I'll drop with our marines while the ground's still hot." He was starting to stand and leave the bridge when the green dot moved.

***

"Sometimes we have to leave a life behind to save another," Jason Everin said. Alice was standing beside him in a port café. The transparent wall they stood beside overlooked the freshwater ocean on Tamber. "You won't understand how important this is for a long time, Alice, but I need to ask that you do that for your father, Jacob. His journey will be difficult, and you're the only one who can help him remain alive inside."

"Alive inside," Alice said. "That's hard, that's heavy."

Medium-sized haulers, gunships, and fighters flew by, and Alice could see many landing platforms moving in and out of the centre of the structure they were standing in. "Where is this? When did this happen?"

"This hasn't come to be yet," Jason Everin said. "I'm engaging a part of your brain as it's being rebuilt. I'm reaching out to you in my near future, and we're building this memory together with the Victory Machine."

"So I'm regenerating, remembering this thing that just got plopped into my head while all my bits are being rebuilt, but you had to make a future call to bring all this together."

Jason Everin smiled. He was wearing the uniform of an intelligence trainee, and he looked as he did on the First Light, younger and quick to smile. "I'm going to tell you something that you have to remember for the rest of your life, and that could be a very long time."

"Lay it on me, I've got a great memory when it works," Alice said.

"Your father will always love you more than anyone, and no matter how dark the circumstances, a reminder the you're his daughter will always lighten his burden. You're going to get into trouble, he's going to be infuriating sometimes, but he will always love you. Your life resembles his in more ways than you know, and his, yours. I'm not talking about your origin as an artificial intelligence, or as a woman before now, or his time as Jonas. Your current incarnations are different, and they will be filled with adventure and terror. You will save him by loving him in return."

"I do," Alice replied. "More than ever."

"Release the Clever Dream and all the artefacts of your past, become a part of his life, because that sacrifice will reward you more than anything else in the end," Jason Everin said.

"Couldn't he jump aboard the Clever Dream? It's a great ship, I mean-" she trailed off as she watched Jason's disapproval grow. "No, huh?"

"No," Jason replied.

"Adventure?"

"More than you can imagine, but at a cost," Jason said.

"What kind of cost are we talking here?"

"The necessary kind, but few sacrifices will be meaningless, if that's any consolation."

"But, adventure," Alice said with a cheeky, sidelong look.

"Adventure," Jason agreed.

"When do I start?" Alice asked.

"Right now. Your framework systems just surged. Best of luck," Jason said.

***

"It's just not that easy to kill a version three," Alice said as she felt the last of her body surge back into being. Regenerating was different the second time. She was aware that her body stored up energy and quietly repaired damage to her fabrication systems before repairing and reviving her all at once.

She wrapped her legs around the nearest soldier's knees and tripped him with a jerk. His weapon was in her hand the next moment, and she sprayed the squad ordered to guard her with weapons' fire.

"I told you we had to shoot her up again!" shouted one soldier to another as a pair ran for their lives.

Alice wanted to rage on, to press the fight, but thousands of soldiers were mustering around the top of the installation. She grabbed her pack, ignored the few things that fell out, and sprinted for the edge of the crater.

Energy bolts lit the shaded area, turning spots of gravel to glowing char. All the command and control units she wore were destroyed; she had no idea what was waiting for her past the massive upturned slab of concrete jutting out of the earth she was running for.

She rolled behind it and blasted a pair of frameworks, one of which shot her twice, only slightly singing her first layer of skin on her hip and shoulder. The framework soldiers would regenerate quickly, but she knew she had at least a thirty second head start.

Alice ran into the forest of wreckage, highly conscious of her shredded vacsuits. She needed more protection, going on completely armour-free wasn't an option. The sound of large pops behind her prompted her to zag and dodge behind a large pillar. Her instincts proved right, as a pair of explosions flashed behind her, sending a wave of heat outward that was so harsh she could feel it around the corner. "Something like that really will kill me, I can't regenerate if I get slagged."

She pressed on, putting distance between her and the large crater base. Alice enjoyed the challenge of moving through wreckage and rubble and did so well, but she was becoming weary of the jeopardy. A nagging desire to find a place near the shoreline, where there was less for the frameworks to fight for, and settle in for a rest was growing.

A roar overhead prompted her to look up just in time to catch a glimpse of the Warlord sweeping by overhead. "Hey, Dad!" she shouted.

She heard two percussive sounds that reminded her of metal bars striking each other, only much louder, and the Warlord dropped two metre wide, barrel-like mines that exploded into hundreds of finger-length missiles that screamed through the air into the crater. Fire and thunder filled the sky above the crater, and she watched the Warlord bank, slow down, and return to the site even as it burned.

"I should have asked Jason if I get another XO-99. Some extra firepower would be awesome right now," Alice said as she squeezed through a jumble of cargo containers. She stopped as soon as she was through the tangle of big metal crates, listening to the popping sounds of rounds striking the pile behind her. A loud creak warned her that it was about to collapse, and she moved out of the way, cringing.

A framework soldier climbing through the crush of crates made eye contact with her a moment before the cargo pile collapsed, sending dust and debris in all directions. When the mess was finished falling in on the frameworks trying to follow her while firing from the inside, she asked herself, "Why do I get the feeling I'm headed in the wrong direction?" Alice pulled two command and control units out of her pack and slapped them onto her wrists. She connected with them effortlessly as they powered on and looked at the tactical map.

There were two framework soldiers still chasing her, coming around the corner only metres away. Alice pulled a rifle free of the pack and leaned out from behind cover firing her rifle on its highest setting. The stock was hot to the touch after a few seconds, but it served its deadly purpose. The frameworks wouldn't be standing up for at least a minute. The weapon had been damaged, and couldn't be trusted.

Alice pulled her old vacsuits off and sprayed a fresh, dark rust coloured one on. "Sure it can't protect me from too much, but it's better than trying to run across a battlefield naked," she said to herself as she pulled a pair of blade shooters from the pack and loaded up on ammunition.

"I'm coming, Dad," Alice said, opening a channel to him. She broke cover and started running back towards the crater, firing both her weapons at the incoming framework soldiers, forcing them back. "I've got a few friends, too."

"We'll be ready," he replied.

Alice slid down a broad culvert and rolled out of the bottom, firing a spray of suppressive fire, catching a framework in the neck and head by pure luck. She thought of what fact she could send him to prove that she really was his daughter and remembered the perfect thing. It wasn't a phrase at all, it was how she felt right before she died on the Triton, right before she decided to let go and use her father's memory to upload herself to a Regent Galactic communications node and figure out how she could fight the war in her own way. There was a unique feeling as she reached out to him and began to upload her packaged consciousness.

Her comm unit's screen garbled as she used it to reach out to him, and send that same feeling in his direction. "You know it's me, right? You've gotta recognize me now," she said when she was sure she'd done her best.

The silence on the channel was enough to drive her to distraction by the time he replied: "I do. I'm coming."

"Nah," Alice said as she took an energy bolt in the shoulder and whirled to riddle her assailant with explosive blade shots. "I can make the last ninety metres. You just get ready to storm the castle."

Alice's tactical scanner spotted four more frameworks moving so they could flank her as she ran for the crater. She was just starting to plan an approach when a stream of explosive rounds rained down from above on one of the enemy positions, obliterating them and their cover.

A Ramiel fighter dove and swerved overhead, breaking from several Uriel fighters headed towards the crater. "This is Tempest of the Skyguard," a female voice announced over her comm, "I'm your cover."

"I think I love you," Alice said as she sprinted towards the crater.

The Ramiel fighter came in for another pass and ripped the landscape out from under the other pair of frameworks lying in wait for Alice with a mini-missile.

CHAPTER 53
THE WALLS

Oz let the smouldering Triton rifle drop behind him from atop the decimated hover truck he knelt on. The charging chamber and barrel were both white hot, warped thanks to over seventy three minutes of near constant firing. He accepted another from a runner. "How are our rounds coming?" he asked as he let loose at a group of four framework soldiers moving to join a larger mass who had taken refuge behind an overturned transport.

The barrage made the frameworks hesitate a little, stepping back from the first one whose legs were mangled by Oz's careful shooting. He fired a burst at each of their heads and spread their skull matter across the ground beside them. "That'll take a minute to recover from," he said.

Two loader suits repurposed with roughly built flak guns took the opportunity to run for the security of the wall. One was peppered with rounds before he made the jump while the other leapt over cleanly. The pilot turned the loader around, climbed a support and reached back over for her partner.

"Heavy support on sector twenty-three!" Oz called as he tried to press the framework soldiers firing on the failing loader suit. The pilot was opening the chest hatch so he could flee the failing armour. The suppressive fire drove most of the frameworks back behind cover, and the pilot chanced an escape. He was one of Frost's loaders from the Triton gunnery deck, Timothy Dillon. He reached for the loader suit stretching over the wall for him, and it caught his vacsuit-clad arm.

Three shots ripped through his legs and side as his partner pulled him over the wall, but according to Crewcast, he had a good chance of making it; the stasis systems were already taking over. Their infirmary would have to take care of him, the medical system on Timothy's comm unit was burned out from over-use.

The portable energy shield beside Oz took several shots. The runner flinched, Oz didn't. He checked the line leading from the truck's batteries to the small shield generator and saw the power reading was good. "Where's my cover?" he shouted.

Alaka's son returned fire from his position behind a steelcrete slab, forcing the frameworks with a good shot on Oz back under cover.

"Your ammo will be a few more minutes," the runner replied.

"Materializer fourteen is burned out, we're down to one."

"Who got that ammo?" Oz asked.

"Commander Rice's unit," the runner replied, choosing his moment to run then dashing back towards the hangar.

"Ladies first, I guess," Oz said to himself as he took aim at a framework leaning a little too far out from a chunk of an upturned landing platform. The platform and frameworks hiding behind it were ripped to shreds as a battered

Uriel fighter strafed in low. Oz had just enough time to recognize the skull and crossed samurai swords emblem on the nose of the fighter. "Hello, Samurai Squadron," he said into his comm.

"How goes the war?" Ronin replied, slowing his fighter down and landing it abruptly behind the wall of their shelter.

"I keep running out of ammo, burned through two rifles. It's a gallery shoot for the most part," Oz replied. "You're going to have to join me up here, bring guns."

Minh-Chu was out of the cockpit of his Uriel fighter in a moment, carrying a fresh Triton rifle. He climbed up the side of the hover truck and got in position behind Oz. "Which area are you covering?" he asked.

Ground crews started looking over his fighter, which had more than one hole and a burned out engine pod. "Sector twenty one, but I'm monitoring a lot more. Marking it on your tactical," Oz said. He returned fire at a framework that broke cover to rush the no-man's-land between the wreckage of the shanty port and the Triton Settlement wall. He fired wildly, trying to frighten his foes back behind cover as he made his run. There was a box in his other hand.

Oz's shots along with those of several other defenders riddled the framework female and the bomb she was trying to deliver exploded in a white and blue flash. A nine-metre section of the wall was blown inward, crashing against the side of the Day Hauler, one of the ships they hadn't gotten around to working on yet. The hull held up, but the breach in the wall had to be repaired. "Third time today," Oz said, intensifying his fire at the frameworks with an easy shot at the gap. Four loader suits were already on their way to move armour plating ripped from one of their oldest ships, Jayne's Run, to begin repairing that section of the wall.

"Have any of those soldiers made it to the wall with one of those bombs?" Minh-Chu asked, joining in with his own rifle.

Oz cringed at the thought. "No, but they're effective against the wall for fifteen metres, now I'm stuck here covering our maintenance guys while they try to rebuild that."

A runner arrived with a heavy crate of cartridges slung on his back. "Framework killers," she announced, handing Oz four cartridges. "Our last mass materializer is dead."

"So, that's it?" Oz said.

"No, we got thirty five thousand rounds out of it before it went," she replied with a grin.

"Finally, a lucky break," Oz said. "Now make sure you and the other runners tell our guys we only got thirty five hundred," Oz said. "The frames might have a surprise up their sleeve."

"Yes, Sir," the runner said, moving on in a hurry.

Oz pulled his clip of explosive rounds and chucked the fresh framework killer clip into his rifle. "Lay down cover fire to the right, give the left a chance to think they can take a shot." He could tell Minh-Chu was struggling, trying to figure out which of the hundreds of targets Oz was talking about, and he marked the frameworks on his tactical system. "Sorry, I've been doing this for so long that I forget there's anything else," he said.

Minh-Chu's aim left something to be desired, but he was out of practice. Oz had been practicing for hours, and he sent bursts into his targets the moment they broke cover in attempts to take a shot. To his great satisfaction, the frameworks twitched and died. "How are things up top?" Oz asked.

"I thought you'd get the signal from here," Minh-Chu said.

"We haven't gotten much since the Leviathan pulled into orbit. Something has been jamming everything outside of the atmosphere," he replied. "I've been hoping to hear something from the Triton."

"The Triton never came up on my scanners. The Sunspire came back, they brought the British, and the first Lorander warship I've ever seen. I've had at least three near-death experiences since I last saw you," Minh-Chu said, laughing. "Help is coming."

"What's the Warlord doing so far down range?" Oz asked.

"Alice is alive again, or something like Alice," Minh-Chu replied. "Who knows? But she found a great big escape ship that's dug into the ground. Jake is going in, he plans to clear it out and claim it."

Oz's heart lightened at reminder that Alice was alive in one shape or another, and his steady calm was shaken by the news that Jacob was storming an objective with only the crew of the Warlord. "Oz to Slick," he said into his communicator.

"Slick, here."

"I need you to intensify firepower on anything our rifles can't reach in our outer radius. Slag the field so we can get a team together to take an objective down-field. Put a rush on it." He highlighted a ring outside of their firearms' reach, knowing that frameworks were gathering, heading towards the Triton settlement.

"One ring of fire coming up. Frameworks can't survive if they're a pile of slag," Slick replied.

Explosions sounded in the distance, followed by tall pillars of fire and flying debris.

"We can have another bird ready for you in twenty minutes, Sir," said a maintenance worker to Minh-Chu from behind Oz. He didn't have time to look. He was too busy watching for frameworks who were brave enough to poke their heads out from cover. The constant sounds of firing rifles had changed to quick, short bursts echoing all across the wall as soldiers got their ammunition upgrades. "This is turning," Oz said to himself, suppressing the surge of hope threatening to break his concentration.

"I'll give you a hand," Minh-Chu told the maintenance worker. "Be down in a sec." He turned to Oz. "There's a Captain McPatrick commanding the Sunspire, you know him?" he asked.

Oz thought a moment and realized who it had to be with a surge of dread. "You had to go and ruin my day," Oz said. "He's my uncle, the asshole of the family. Great commander, though."

Oz spotted a framework soldier with a larger than normal rifle as the muzzle flared when he fired and leapt from the hover truck. The projectile exploded into the hollow cavity of the truck and sent him end over end through the air. Nanobots attended to the weakened portion of his armour, and his personal shield read at zero, but he rushed to cover unharmed.

"That was close," he said as Minh-Chu joined him. He made sure someone else killed that framework on his tactical system and nodded to himself.

"I guess that's what happens when they punch a hole through the wall," Minh-Chu said.

"Yeah, I'm going to miss that perch, but I should have known better than to stay up after the wall went down. Guess I just got complacent."

"I've had more near-misses since this thing got started," Minh-Chu said, nodding. "I'll just be glad when it's over."

"Speaking of which, you have a fighter to get ready, and I've got to find another position," Oz said. "Good hunting."

"Keep your head down," Minh-Chu replied.

CHAPTER 54
CONFRONTATION

He knew it was Alice. Jake wasn't one of those people who were always conscious of how different people made him feel just by being in the room, but there was no mistaking the feeling his daughter transmitted to him as anything but what it felt like to be near her when she was alive as a human. There was a subtle difference he couldn't ignore, however. She seemed more innocent. Jason's message had come true.

The Warlord had done her job, bombarding the area then dropping off her full compliment of marines. Joyboy and a couple of other fighters on loan from The Skyguard meted punishment out to any enemy soldiers who ran from the crater, or managed to somehow escape the devastation of the initial bombardment.

"Warlord, head out, assist our air cover with clearing Port Rush," Captain Valent said into his comm.

"On our way, we've got four more mines together, so we're going to take care of a few drop pods," Frost said.

"Just watch for survivors, I don't want the Warlord to become known for collateral damage."

"Aye, watch my aim, got it," Frost replied as the Warlord's engines fired, sending the battered ship towards the Triton settlement.

"Since when do you care about public opinion?" Stephanie asked, amused. She was supervising her marine techs as they hacked into one of the installation's secondary doors.

"I had a spare second," Jake replied.

"You know Frost doesn't want collateral damage, either. He actually wants to be seen as a hero someday. He'll never let on, but I think that's more important to him than cash."

Jake didn't know how to respond to that, but his expression of surprise must have spoken volumes.

"Don't tell him I said anything," Stephanie said.

"No problem," Jake replied. He spotted Alice running down the inside of the crater, firing several shots behind her with two pistols. A Ramiel fighter swooped down firing, taking care of whatever Alice was firing at.

Alice faced forward, and Jake could see her smile from over fifty metres away as she looked straight at him. She was all teeth, cheeks, and eyes.

"She's speeding up," Stephanie said. "And I've never seen anyone run that fast."

Jake braced himself and deactivated the auto-hardening system in his armour.

"You're sure it's her?" Stephanie asked.

"Absolutely."

"She's not slowing down," Agameg said, his eyes widening. "A collision is certain."

An excited squeal a second before impact was the only warning. The force of her enthusiastic embrace pressed him two steps backwards, and he wrapped his arms around her. She was more than a full head shorter, and seemed so small, disappearing into his long coat with her arms tightly wrapped around him.

Alice breathed as though she was recovering from a very long run, and she rested against him. Everyone watched silently as father and daughter were reunited, until a surprised Agameg said, "You've shrunken. I've verified with scans. You are definitely smaller."

She laughed and stepped away from Jake, wiping tears away, still out of breath. "I think the framework picked up on me wanting to have a childhood, so when I died here the first time, it made me a lot younger. I'm just glad I didn't come back as a five year old."

Jake looked at her and definitely saw someone who might be fifteen, perhaps sixteen. She held a pair of pistols like she was born to them though, and there were so many things about the way she stood, her general manner, that seemed familiar. He put his hand on her shoulder. "I'm sorry no one got to you sooner," he said.

"S'okay," Alice replied, slipping in under his arm. "I'll take a break here and head back out. Maybe not alone this time, but I know I can help clear up Port Rush and start rescuing people. There are a lot of trapped folk out there."

Jake was surprised and irritated at the same time. "We'll start arranging teams once we're finished here," he replied.

"That was your 'and that's an order' voice," Alice said, crossing her arms, taking a step away and regarding him defiantly.

"Whoa," Stephanie said, almost stepping between them. "Okay, when we've cleared this bunker, we'll get properly geared up with medical supplies and start clearing out Port Rush, helping some people. Until then, we've got a target in there."

"Hampon," Jake reinforced.

"You're right, I want a piece of him. Killing Meunez wasn't enough," Alice said. She adjusted her vacsuit so two flimsy holsters formed and dropped her blade shooters into them. "Just get those doors open and me and my dad will go get 'em."

"We're doing this carefully," Jake said. "There's no telling how prepared he is."

Alice nodded and sighed. "As long as I get a shot in."

The doors opened, and Jake turned towards them. "I'll take point, you fall in with Stephanie and Agameg's units," he said, hoping that he wouldn't meet more resistance.

To his surprise, she rushed in front of him, turned, popped up on tip-toes and kissed him on the cheek. "Aye-aye, Captain!" she chirped before falling in with Agameg's unit. He pressed the confusion and surprise at the range of attitudes Alice displayed in less than three minutes to the side and activated all the features of his armour. He strode through the doors, drawing his sidearm and paying close attention to his tactical system.

No one came up on the scanners - not a single soldier, framework or crewmember - and his scan results reached down three hallways, into eight different compartments. The armoured entrance hatch slammed together, isolating him from everyone outside. The clank of heavy bolts inside the hull and the smell of smoke told him something worse was going on. He touched the door panel and discovered that the bolts securing the doors were in place, and an emergency security measure welded them there.

He turned and tried to pry the doors apart despite the pain of overexertion. His enhanced muscles made the surrounding flesh feel as though it was ripping. Even with the addition of the enhancements in his armoured vacsuit, he couldn't get the doors to budge.

"Stephanie, check in," he said over his comm.

"We've got hostiles coming from the other side of this thing, about two hundred," she said. "Holding them off, but they've got-" her communication garbled and the channel closed.

"They're dead, Valent," Hampon's voice said over the intercom. "Unless you kill me and take control of the frameworks outside."

He used the intercom system through the door panel to connect to internal security scanners and verified that he was talking to Lister Hampon. Hampon was standing in the absolute centre of the drop pod. Rows of crew seating surrounded a command where he calmly looked up into a security sensor.

Jake removed his hand from the door panel and whirled around. He set his sidearm to burn through metal and fired beside the doorway, where there were two thinner sections of metal to burn through as opposed to the solid door. The thermite rounds hissed, sparked, and burned.

"You won't get through for another hour that way, the outside of this garrison ship is a metre thick," Hampon said. "You're going to have to face me if you want to save your people."

"Watch what you wish for," Jake said. He knew Hampon was right, and there were no other options. He reset his Violator Handgun and used his connection to the door panel to find a map of the installation. As soon as he knew how to get to Hampon, he rushed down the hallway, watching his corners. There was no telling how Hampon was manipulating the security systems. Jake could only see what his opponent wanted him to.

The darkened halls all led to the central lifts. An emergency shaft running parallel to them would take him down. He was passing into the central chamber when one of the bulkhead doors slammed down on top of him, driving him to his knees. He could feel Hampon in the ship systems, forcing the computer to override safety systems, and pushing the motors to press the heavy door down.

He heard his knees pop as the motors worked harder, his vacsuit warned him that the synthetic muscle built in was being pushed to near failure as he fought the door. "It's time to stop using your body as a blunt instrument, Mister Valent," Lister Hampon said. "Or is it Valance? I remember when you were just a pile of synthetic bones, an experiment waiting to happen."

Jake hated the fact that he was right. There were so many things he could do that he barely understood. The motors in the door struggled, whining as he pushed back. All he could physically do was keep the door from crushing him for another minute at best, and hope the motors burned out.

"Use your comm node, Dad!" he heard his daughter in his mind.

"Don't have one," he replied aloud.

"No cheating!" Hampon said. "No outside transmissions!"

A mental image of Alice's communications node appeared before she was cut off and he realized that it was the doorway to everything he needed. "Gotcha," he said as he forced his framework body to create a node exactly the same as Alice's. As soon as it came online he could feel his vacsuit, the systems in his command and control unit and so much more without any distraction. He was suddenly living in two worlds at once, connected to everything electronic and wireless as though they were nothing more than external appendages.

With a thought, the door stopped pressing down for a half second, enough time for him to get out from beneath it. He could feel the lifts ahead, and see a pair of heavily armoured Order Knights, trained framework soldiers that he'd never seen before, but he had the details he needed to know they'd slow him down. They could even kill him if he assaulted them head on. They had the firepower. He tried to communicate with their control nodes, but discovered they had the ability to resist him, and they sensed him trying to assume control.

They were coming.

Jake rushed the lift doors firing all the way, weakening the metal. The Order Knights surged into the centre from an adjacent hallway firing high-powered energy rifles that raised the ambient temperature to over six hundred degrees after the first volley. Two struck Jake's shields, reducing them to twenty percent power.

He didn't bother firing back, but tossed a pair of inferno grenades in their direction before bursting through the red-hot elevator door. Jake fell down the shaft, missing the car two levels below and falling on top of the car four levels down to its right. Fire filled the shaft, an aftermath of the primary explosion that would either completely incinerate the Order Knights or force them to regenerate for several minutes. At the very least they'd return to life with no armour or weaponry.

Jake was unscathed; his suit was made to compensate for long falls, hard impacts, and the heat he was exposed to. His shields were slowly recharging. The car he landed on started moving up rapidly, and Jake leapt to an emergency ladder. Another small lift was moving into place between him and the entry to the third level. He commanded it to move, and found Hampon in the system. "I've been waiting for this for a long time," he said through Jake's communicator. "Those Knights are a result of what we've learned from you, and soon they'll add the intelligence and leadership the rest of our framework soldiers are lacking."

Jake felt Hampon connect to his neural node. It was as if a crushing hand was closing around his mind. "Looking to get your nose bitten off again?" he asked. Hampon's hold weakened and the pressure disappeared.

Jake reached back the way Hampon's signal came and struck a solid data wall with heavy password protection. He was hiding behind the mobile garrison's main computer. He could see it on the fourth level, behind a pair of Order Knights who took cover behind a powerful one-way energy shield.

"You lose concentration when you get emotional," Jake said to distract Hampon as he drew his nanoblade hilt. He turned it on, the long black blade came into being and Jake activated the fourth level doors. He cloaked and swung into the hallway.

"A cloak suit won't help you, I can see you wherever you go," Hampon said.

"I'm betting you didn't give your Knights the ability to use computer systems.

That's too much power to give a pawn," Jake replied as he ran along one side of the hallway. "They won't see me coming." There was only a small glimmer of hope that he was right, but he knew it was foolish. Instead of charging into the middle of the data systems centre, he took a left into an open compartment. The schematics told him the interior walls were thin, that there were several rooms adjacent with similar features. It would give him space to manoeuvre. More importantly, it would give him a place to frustrate Hampon.

Putting his sense of urgency aside, he switched his cloaking systems to shied mode and calmly sat down on the bed. "If I were a complete idiot, I'd charge in there. Instead, I'm going to wait them out. I can't approach this situation while you have the advantage."

"What?" Hampon replied. "Your people are dying," he said, offering a feed of what was going on outside. Five order Knights led an assault against the marines from the Warlord. The Warlord crew made their own cover with energy shields and trenches dug with shaped charge grenades. Half the marines were dead, their ravaged corpses near the main entrance to the compound.

Beam weapons fired by three Order Knights super-heated one of the Warlord's engine pods as it swooped in to support the troops, forcing it to retreat. His daughter was amongst the Order of Eden soldiers, jumping between them at close range, firing her pistols constantly as she used them as cover.

"How long can they survive?" Hampon asked. "How long can your daughter keep moving as she has since she landed on Tamber? The Knights will eventually fire into their own soldiers to kill her, then they will return her corpse to me so she regenerates in one of my prison cells. I could learn a lot by dissecting her."

He tried to compartmentalize his emotions as he watched Stephanie and Agameg lead the marines they had left into a round of return fire that took out dozens of Order soldiers. It wasn't enough, there were over a hundred left, and the armour of the Order Knights repelled most of their fire. Grenades were thrown, but they got butted back or shot out of the air by circular attack drones hovering overhead.

Alice was caught in the open for less than a second, but it was enough for an Order Knight to fire his beam weapon and sever her left arm. It didn't stop her. She surged at the Order of Eden soldiers as her arm regenerated, screaming savagely as she put soldiers between her and the Knights and killed her way through their ranks.

Blocking the transmission was the hardest thing Jake had ever done, but the final image it had to share with him was Agameg, leaning over to assist a fallen soldier. He didn't see the grenade fall right behind him, and in a flash, there was nothing left but a scorched hole in the ground.

Jake raged, surging to his feet.

"I'll spare them, halt the attack if you surrender to me, give me full access to your neural node," Hampon offered.

"There's something you don't understand," Captain Valent said. "You forgot to install a soul when you built me, and anger found a home where that should have been." Jake let his anger steel him, drive him to concentration, and he reached out to the entire garrison until he could feel all the systems at once. "Jonas lived with anger after getting back from his first war. He learned how to temper it on the First Light, and I learned how to be angry on the Samson. I'm at my best when I'm furious." He could feel Hampon in the system, reaching out through the main computer. Jake clutched the systems surrounding it and reduced Hampon's reach as if he were a flaming taper that he only had to grip in his fist to reduce to an ember. "I'm coming for you."

He stuck a pair of shape charge grenades to the ceiling, set the timer for five seconds, took the rest of his incendiary grenades out of his pocket then ran across the hall, throwing all five of them at the foot of the shield protecting the Order Knights. Jake turned all the garrison's systems on, drawing power away from the shield protecting the main computer core and ducked behind a primary bulkhead.

Explosions ripped through the garrison, and Jake knew the shield for the computer was down. He could sense that the diminished shield was enough to protect the Order Knights from the explosion. They were ready for him.

The thin walls between the administration rooms and crew quarters were misshapen and shredded by the force of the explosion. Jake ran as quickly as he could, firing between the Order Knights towards the computer core's main column.

The enemy soldiers fired rapidly, scoring several shots on Jake through the gaps in the walls. The last pair of energy rounds struck Jake in the shoulder and arm, overheating his armour and burning him to the bone. His framework system shut the surrounding nerves down while he regenerated, but not fast enough to keep him from feeling the initial pain and screaming.

He forced himself to leap towards the hole he'd blasted in the celling in the cabin across the hall, and barely caught it with his working hand. He hurriedly pulled himself up and scrambled away from the hole.

The shots he'd fired at the computer core had hit their mark. Jake could reach Hampon directly. He was no longer hiding behind the ship computer, or manipulating the communications systems leading outside. He stood up and marched down the hall towards him. "I'm coming to grant your death wish, Hampon," Jake said, fighting for a grip on the neural node he felt inside the man's mind.

An Order Knight stepped into view at the end of the hallway. Its mind was completely invisible to Jake. He narrowly dodged a searing bolt of energy, ducking into a side room. He knew he'd find no lengthy reprieve there. Jake turned up his suit's strength augmentation and charged the thin wall between him and the Knight, ripping through the cheap metal as though it were tissue paper.

One shot struck Jake in the side. His armour protected him from most of the burn, but pain shot through his left side. He collided with the Order Knight and caught him behind the knee with his foot as he pushed him to the deck. Jake followed him down, shoving his rifle aside and rapid firing his sidearm at the neck of the soldier.

The Order Knight punched upwards and caught Jake full in the faceplate. The single blow dented the protective metal inward and snapped Jake's head back so hard that he felt it in his shoulders. He struggled to get control of the soldier, and needed all his strength to pin its arms against its chest as violently sparking rounds from his pistol burned through the Knight's armour. The Knight twitched and writhed as the thermite burned into its neck and chest.

Jake picked up the fallen Knight's rifle and shot at it until it was reduced to a white hot smouldering pile. It took less than twelve seconds. He tried to turn towards the hall leading to Lister Hampon and discovered he couldn't move.

"I have you, Jacob. Rage may fuel you," he said as he commanded Jake to walk down the hall into the dark seating area, "but violence distracts you."

Jake struggled to regain control, fighting the vice holding his mind. "You won't imprison me for long," Jake said. "I'll always find a way to escape, and I'll never stop hunting you."

"I know."

He became aware of his hands moving over the rifle, changing the settings on the Knight's weapon to overload and explode in a contained area.

"That's why I'm going to destroy you," Hampon said. "Some of us need to kill for our freedom. You never had to. You could have walked away from your fight at any time. You could have been free, but you turned on your old masters like a rabid dog instead."

The rifle's power systems began to transfer energy to the pulse emitter, building a charge that would go critical in less than a minute. He didn't allow himself to be baited into the conversation Hampon was trying to start. Jacob Valent had few regrets, and they were none of Lister Hampon's business.

He looked at the man standing in the middle of a room made for dozens of crewmembers to control and monitor a small army. He was as tall and angular as Jake remembered, perhaps a little younger. Hampon had a talent for looking composed, that hadn't changed, and it gave Jake an idea. "You've always been alone, haven't you?"

"What?" Hampon asked, caught off guard by the off-topic question.

"On the Overlord when I met you, at the head of the Order, and even before, always alone."

Jake felt Hampon's control slip a little and regained control for long enough to move his arms and twitch in another direction, but Hampon had him again before he could throw the rifle and run. He'd have to try something else that didn't take as much time.

"You're so much more intelligent than anyone could have expected," Lister said, laughing. "I think that's why-"

"Never got married, never had children, probably goes back all the way to a child on the playground alone, watching the other kids and imagining what it would be like to-"

"You have nothing we haven't given you!" Hampon burst.

It was just enough of a slip for long enough for Jake to force his framework body to destroy his neural node. Jake deactivated the explosion radius limitation on the weapon's control panel and tossed the rifle at Hampon.

Jake sprinted for the hole he'd crawled out of. The Order Knights he left behind were ready for him, firing as soon as his feet hit the deck. He took a shot in the left shoulder but ran for the elevator shaft, jumping and catching the ladder with his right.

A wave of pressure and heat washed over him, crushing Jake through the side of the elevator shaft.

CHAPTER 55
THREE DAYS LATER

"I see armour!" shouted a Sunspire soldier from one of the rubble pits. The explosion that decimated the large escape ship three days before caused a chain reaction within, unleashing enough force inside to reduce it to scrap and slag. There wasn't a single hallway or compartment intact. Alice and most of the Warlord crew hadn't left the site.

Stephanie ran over to the soldier. "Don't shout out, use comms, we need to see what we've found for sure before we get a crowd," she said. "Besides, it could be another one of those super-soldiers."

Alice ran towards the pit and was stopped by Finn and Agameg. "You might not want to see this," Finn said. "Remember what our scans found."

Frost walked over in tall, mechanized armour, carefully stepping around the debris. "I've got a detailed scan, there's a girder in the way. I'll move it so we won't have to cut him."

Alice watched as Frost bent down and pried at the metal slowly. "I have to see him. He's going to be alive, and I know he'll want to see me."

Frost pulled at the tip of a twisted girder, the sounds of metal scraping on metal and bending steel making most of them cringe. "I've got it, pull him free," he said.

The soldiers pulled at something carefully and an outcry surged from the onlookers as they backed out suddenly, with what exactly, Alice couldn't see. She concentrated enough to get a scan and panicked as she realized they'd pulled nothing more than a bit of his spine, shoulder and his upper cranium free.

"Don't let her through!" Stephanie cried.

Alice wouldn't be stopped, and, regardless of tear-blurred vision, she managed to push and squeeze her way past everyone. "You don't understand!" she screamed as Stephanie and Ayan caught her. "We're not human. We don't even play by the same rules."

"She's seen," Frost said sullenly. "Let her in close so she can say goodbye."

"I'm sorry," Ayan said through her own tears. "I know you were hoping."

Alice pushed her off and fell to her knees beside her father. "Please, please tell me there's enough," she said as she touched Jacob Valent's exposed skull through his broken headgear. She couldn't feel anything.

"We tried," Ayan said. "I'm so sorry, Alice." She was repeating herself, something a lot of people had been doing around her for the last several days.

"There's got to be something left, the top of his head is here," Alice said. "We can heal people, especially each other." A thought occurred to her, and she retracted her vacsuit gloves.

Alice gingerly touched the surface of exposed bone and gasped. "He's still here, the framework did it, his mind's been preserved."

She touched the exposed flesh beside his spine and jerked her hand away. "Ew, that bit's been dead awhile." Alice put both hands on the exposed part of his cranium and tried to block out everything around her. "I'm going to bring him back," she whispered as she felt the framework system preserving his brain. The instant she sent power into it, the few emitters left inside his skull surged to life, using all the energy she could provide to rebuild other emitters, to grow the framework system.

Alice channelled all the power her vacsuit could provide, and heard the crowd gasp and shift as oddly coloured bone began to form. She looked to her right, where Frost stood in his suit and said. "I need more, a lot more." She pointed at a power socket on the left leg and said. "There! That! Take the cap off!"

Stephanie hurriedly pulled the cap off and Frost stepped in closer. Alice jerked as she touched the socket and channelled the energy through a circuit in her framework body into Jacob Valent's. In seconds he regenerated, appearing freshly whole in the middle of the crowd. His regeneration was faster than she expected, much like her own framework system.

Jake struggled to remove his headgear, and Alice helped him pull it off. The rest of his face reformed, and he looked up at her, stunned.

"You remember me, right?" Alice said hopefully, sniffling and crying. "Please tell me your brain isn't too scrambled! Look at me, and just say the first name that comes to-"

"If you'll let me answer," Jake said. "You're Alice."

She bent down and squeezed him. "Thank you for not leaving me, thank you so much for not dying."

Applause and cheers went up as the news of Jacob Valent's survival spread through the crowd.

"I'll never leave you," Jake replied, embracing her. Agameg came through the crowd and smiled.

"I thought you were dead?" Jake said.

"I thought *you* were dead," he replied, cocking his head at Jake.

"I saw a feed of you getting killed by a grenade," Jake replied. He realized then that it could have been an illusion. "Fake. There was never a counter-attack," he said.

"After you went in?" Stephanie asked. "There was, but it was small. One armoured framework and a couple of squads of troops. We didn't lose anyone."

Alice withdrew and helped Jake to his feet, her eyes widening as she realized that the only armour he had was a shoulder and neckpiece. She turned and backed into him to offer some modesty. "Um, awkward," Alice said.

***

"He's alive," Captain Gregor McPatrick said as he entered the bridge of the Triton. Crewmembers were busy calibrating systems, coordinating repair crews, and doing any number of a hundred different things that contributed to the resurrection of the ship.

Captain Terry Ozark McPatrick didn't turn around, but let his uncle sit down on a command seat beside him. "I know, I got the message."

"You don't sound surprised," Gregor said.

"Some of us had faith," Oz said. "How is the Sunspire?"

"Repairs are going well, we'll be on patrol in two days."

"We could use a hand with repairs here once my people are finished prying people from the wreckage in Port Rush. Can you spare anyone?" Oz said.

"No, I'm afraid not. I need my crew at full strength and my ship with a full compliment. It's bad enough that things are being held back by this New Years' celebration in a few days."

Oz stood and walked towards his ready quarters. His uncle hesitated a moment then followed. As soon as they crossed the small, secure hallway and into his ready room he turned on the other man. "All right, this is your first visit to the Triton and the second time you've spoken to me since you got here. What do you have to say to me in person that you couldn't say over comms?"

Gregor McPatrick didn't seem fazed by the sudden turn in conversation. "Straight to it, all right. You're a coward for abandoning your post with Freeground Fleet. Several commands abandoned after you left, and I believe your example is partially responsible for the political failures at home. The wrong people were in power, and you gave them an example of desertion, corruption, and a failing resolve in the military. It's why I'm here, it's why there's a ship full of outcasts with me."

"The military was failing before I left. I was already branded as an untrustworthy commander. I left because they made everything I earned look like a farce, and I knew I would be more helpful elsewhere," Oz replied, trying to keep calm. He'd squared off against his uncle before, but never about something so important.

"Help whom?" Gregor replied. "Jacob Valent? Your friends? Who did you want to help out here?"

"Results prove me right," Oz growled. "Thousands of refugees down there, hundreds of people on this ship, owe their lives to Jacob, Ayan, Minh-Chu, Jason, Laura, and yeah, they owe me, too. Those are people who would still be in bondage or dead if we didn't step in. In case you didn't notice, our little band killed two galactic war criminals a few days ago, and we nearly broke ourselves doing it. That's more of a difference than any group of people from Freeground can claim they've made. You left us and brought allies to the table, but tell me those negotiations weren't easier because they'd already heard of us."

"He's right, Gregor," Carl Anderson said from the doorway. "They were already gearing up when we arrived in the Virrig System. The British were coming either way. They knew the importance of setting up a forward position in the Rega Gain system weeks before we got here. We just advanced their plans."

"We made sure it all happened in time," Gregor said.

"A few hours' difference, maybe. Not enough to say it was meaningful," Carl said.

"Without Alice and Jacob Valent, those two war criminals would have either escaped or dug in enough to build infrastructure, and hold until more ships could arrive. They were killed, the offensive lost its teeth. The other garrisons on Tamber are isolated, not coordinating. It's just a matter of time before we dig them out."

"And what did you do while the Valents were off being heroes?" Gregor asked.

"He-" Carl Anderson started, but halted as Oz shook his head.

Terry Ozark McPatrick looked to his uncle, staring him in the eye. "I gathered with the best soldiers I've ever known and held the line. Just like you, my parents, and the Freeground Military taught me to do. I fought for what I could protect until the day was won."

"When you feel that someone else is in charge and you're not powerful enough, are you going to up and leave again?" Gregor asked.

The thought made Oz chuckle. His bond with Triton was deeper than anyone but Ashley could hope to understand. "There were two times in my life where I've felt accepted, at home. The first was on the First Light, the second is on this ship. I'll die on this ship someday. Whether it's tomorrow, or after a century of service, I'll know I've died in the right place." The statement seemed to take both men aback, and Captain Terry Ozark McPatrick pressed on. "I'm glad you're here, Captain McPatrick, and I'll work with you, I'll even learn from you, I'm sure. Just don't expect reverence on my ship, or to have your opinion treated with any more weight than any other captain in this fleet. You don't want to help rebuild the Triton? That's fine, I know you'll make yourself useful elsewhere. Just don't expect to find family here."

Gregor McPatrick looked stricken for a moment, then composed himself and withdrew from the cabin. "I'll have your effects from the Sunspire brought over," he said on his way through the door.

"I'm sorry," Doctor Anderson said after Gregor was gone. "I knew there was history, it had to come out."

"Don't worry," Oz said. "He had to have his shot, I turned away from everything he respects. I knew I'd have knocks like that coming when I deserted the Sunspire."

"You seem happy here," Doctor Anderson said. "It's quite a ship, even in its condition."

"We'll rebuild. It'll take a year with an ideal crew, longer with the people we've got, but it'll happen. I believe in what Jake is doing, and what Ayan wants to build. Triton will benefit from everything they do, and then they'll benefit from Triton."

"You've done more than I would have imagined, I can honestly say that I'm proud of everyone from the First Light. You're the root of something incredible, and I'm glad I'll be here to see it," Carl Anderson said.

"Thank you," Oz replied. "That means something coming from you."

"I only wish," Carl Anderson said before hesitating and crossing the room to the transparent hull. Two dozen battered destroyers and carriers from the British Fleet moved past slowly in formation. "I wish it were during a different time."

"War," Oz said. "The ship computer has seen it too."

"The war of our time, and that's saying something when we're expected to live to two hundred years or more," Doctor Anderson agreed. "Eve has made another appearance, promising immortality and paradise to the most dedicated Order of Eden humans. I thought we were going to have it easy when reports of Eden Fleet ships withdrawing and disappearing started flooding in."

"Now they're recruiting humans who sign up for their cult," Oz said, joining Doctor Anderson to take in the view. One of the largest ships, the BSF Hammer, was starting to pass the Triton slowly. "It won't be just frameworks next time."

"Religious fanatics, only the promises of eternal life are real," Doctor Anderson said. "Everyone who worried about framework technology, and how it could change the galaxy were absolutely right to raise the alarm. This will be galactic war."

"How much time do you think we have before they try to take Rega Gain again?" Oz asked.

"With the beating we gave them, and the increasing presence of the British with their allies? I think they might try to go around this system first." The pair stood in silence, watching the BSF Hammer go by with three heavily damaged Carthan battle cruisers keeping pace. Carl Anderson finally broke the silence. "Do you think we can win, Oz?"

"Yes," he replied. There was no hesitation, as though the word was at the ready. "Especially if they have to take a turn at licking their wounds."

"Speaking of taking time," Doctor Anderson said, trying to shake the melancholy. "Are you coming down for the New Years' celebration on Friday?"

"No, we're having something here. We're holing up in the Botanical Gallery for twenty hours of leave. I'll authorize a holo-uplink to the party down there. We'll be there in image and spirit," Oz said.

"Good, I'll make sure I pass through here on my way down to Tamber," Carl Anderson offered his hand and Oz shook it. "I feel like I'm in the right place for the first time in a while too, Oz."

"It's good to have you here," Oz replied.

***

"It never stops raining here," said Burke, expanding the collar of his grey jacket into a hood. "You'd think he'd pick somewhere sunny."

Wheeler stepped around the corner into the alley to find Burke and Doctor Thurge there. She was dressed in a long, multi-layered coat that had a pulse module somewhere inside that repelled the rain above so it fell around her. Burke had spent his money elsewhere, or lost it, judging from his simple spacer's attire. "It's where I could be without drawing attention," he said.

"Finally," Burke said. "So, what's next? You have a line on some cash somewhere in this mess?"

Lucius Wheeler looked from Burke to Thurge, who raised an eyebrow. "You're still out for revenge, aren't you?" he asked.

"Profit is easy. Getting even takes skill. It takes resources," she replied. "You promised the latter, just like I promised my family on the Palamo that I'd avenge them."

"I promised that you'd have a good run, an in-road. You threw them off-balance enough to put a divide between Ayan and Jake. That's all I needed," Wheeler replied. "Now, I'm done testing my luck for greater causes. I think I spent the last of it getting off the Ferryman before the Warlord emerged from its wormhole."

"So you're just going to leave us like this?" Burke reached inside his coat. "That's bull-"

Wheeler's pistols were out and pointed at the pair before Burke's hand touched his weapon. "I'm leaving you just like this, and if you see me again it'll be because there's a damn good reason for me to get drawn back to the Rega Gain system. Right now, I can only think of reasons to leave and never look back."

"Why did you want us to mess with Ayan's love life, anyway? I thought it was leading to something, but now I'm just disappointed," Thurge asked.

"For a while, some of us got to see the future," Wheeler said. "And the future with those two together didn't leave much room for people like us, or the Order of Eden. Now they're broken, so the galaxy gets to be wild wherever the Order isn't around, and that's a lot of space to get lost in. I'm not going to leave you two with a grudge against me, though." He holstered one of his guns and pulled a heavy bag filled with Galactic Currency from his inside jacket pocket. He threw it to Thurge, who almost dropped it once the weight of if landed in her hands with a satisfying chink. "Twenty eight thousand, more than you earned. I have a transport waiting, so good luck, and goodbye."

He backed out of the alley, stepped around the corner, and activated his stealth system. Wheeler turned on the hover systems in his long coat and accelerated down the street towards the spaceport at the centre of Whule. "A good tactician knows when to retreat," he said to himself. It was time to leave Kambis, to avoid Tamber and the Rega Gain system.

Epilogue
The First Watch

Domed and square shelters from the Enforcer 1109 and the Triton were set up on the island they would come to call home. Logs discovered in a small research bunker told them the history of the Haven Shore settlement, and it was a peaceful one with a legacy of zoological study. All the shelters and the ships that survived since their arrival and through the siege occupied less than one percent of the land.

The mountain splitting the middle of the land mass protected half the jungle from a shockwave that blew the other half flat. Two of the larger shelters took advantage of the cleared land. They were open domes with frames built inside, but given time, they would build the interior rooms, and hallways.

The smaller shelters were set on an expanse of white and blue quartz beach sand. It took the help of the British military to move and set up in one day. Ayan was proud to announce a day of rest for New Year's Eve.

A platform overlooking the beach and freshwater ocean beyond had been set up. It served as the main celebration area. The next morning it would take a different role, as a landing space for shuttles. Ayan sat at an iron wrought table, drinking black tea, a gift from the crew of the Fair Weather Trader for prying them from their wrecked ship. It was bright for evening, like early twilight in period movies she'd seen about Earth.

There were minutes left to the galactic year, and she smiled at the approach of Liam Grady bearing two fluted glasses. "It's not champagne, but it tickles the nose."

"What is it?"

"I think Agameg said it was Upbub, but he was pretty busy serving. I asked him if he'd like to take a break, he's been working tirelessly on search and rescue, but he seemed happy tending bar."

"I don't think Agameg is happy unless he's working," Ayan said. "Considering the fighting and rescue work over the last week, I'm surprised anyone has the energy to be here, let alone dance the new year in."

She spotted Doctor Anderson through the dancing crowd at the other end of the platform and cleared her throat. "Do you mind giving me a moment? Doctor Anderson said he had something important to tell me."

"I'll be back before the year turns," Liam said, bending down to give her a timid kiss, but she leaned into it and pinched his bottom lip between hers before letting go. "You'd better be."

Ayan stood and straightened her loose fitting, white and blue dress before Doctor Anderson was close enough for a hug. He kissed her on the cheek and smiled at her. "You look beautiful," he said as they sat down.

"Thank you," Ayan said. "I'm so glad you're here."

"I know, and I'm hoping that continues on after I've told you something I've wanted to share for ages."

Ayan was immediately worried, and put her glass down on the table carefully. "I don't know what you could say that would make you unwelcome here. I've known you too long, and there's something more. I can't describe it, but you watched me grow, I know you were there the whole time I was developing. You brought me into being."

"I wish I could have been there even before then," Carl Anderson said with a note of regret. "Your mother didn't want me involved in your upbringing when you were a child, but I watched."

"My upbringing, why would you?" Ayan covered her mouth with a sudden realization. She'd always wondered who her father was. She recalled stealing one of Doctor Anderson's scanners when she was very young during one of her check-ups. Her mother was furious as she snatched it out of her hands, stopping her from scanning the room.

"When I met your mother in the outer colonies, we were both very young. I believed in the research they were doing in genetic improvements. The ability for a human being to aggressively cure diseases by being near contagions, to be influential through pheromones like issyrians, to each be paragons of our species was very attractive. What it would mean to diplomacy alone, the possibilities were incredible. We took it too far, but we didn't realize that until your mother was pregnant with you and we'd already performed the modifications. She wanted children so badly back then, her calling was to be a mother, so when we fell in love she suspended her contraceptives and, well," Carl Anderson shrugged. "Then, you."

A tear of joy fell from her eye as she said, "you're my father," through her hands. "Twice, you're my father."

"I couldn't let you go through your childhood without knowing me somehow, so I had to be your doctor, at least. And when you were going to be on the First Light, I had to follow you there."

"And you brought me back," Ayan said, her breath catching mid-sentence.

"I couldn't let you go," Carl Anderson said, a tear rolling down his cheek.

Ayan stood up, knocking her chair over and bumping the table as she crossed to him and embraced her father. "Thank you," she said. "Thank you so much."

***

Zoe squealed and giggled as she swung high between Ashley Lamport and Minh-Chu Buu. They walked along the beach, him in swim trunks and her in a bikini. The night was surprisingly warm, and the cool air coming off the water was just enough to make it comfortable without vacsuit-style clothing. Watching the toddler turn the pair of them into a jungle-gym, and being with Ashley, who surprised him by being a person he could enjoy a comfortable silence with, was better than Minh thought he deserved.

The Samurai and Skyguard Squadron members who weren't on patrol overhead had staked out their beach encampment by landing their fighters and shuttles in a half-circle. Light rods sticking out of the sand, holographic feeds from the main dancing platform and the Triton's party in the Botanical Gallery lit the space just enough. The Warlord was on the beach just past the group.

Zoe spotted Panloo with several other nafalli and struggled to be free of Minh-Chu and Ashley. "Okay, you can go," Ashley said, releasing her. Minh-Chu followed her example and the gap between them was closed a few steps later.

Ashley's hand found his as they watched Zoe scamper up the beach and leap onto Panloo's back. "She's so happy with her," Ashley said.

"She's still crazy about you, though," Minh-Chu said.

"I know," Ashley said. "Every time I visit her she lets me know."

They walked silently for a while, holding hands and looking down the shoreline. They were getting close to the old mismatched chairs they'd set up, stuck partway into the sand on the edge of the waterline. Behind it was a shelter for two.

"You're quiet," Ashley said.

Minh-Chu almost reacted by offering an expression from his extensive collection, but smiled and looked at her instead. He'd never seen anything more amazing than her looking back at him with a half-smile, her dark eyes expectant. "You're beautiful."

Ashley laughed and kissed him briefly. "You were about to say something else. I could see it."

"Just words," he replied. "Words that would fall out onto the sand and wash away." He turned on his heel and caught her in an embrace, which improved with a long, warm kiss.

Ashley pulled away reluctantly after encouraging whistles from the pilots sitting around a few holographic images from the capitol of Kambis and the Triton. "Okay, before we turn on Crewcast privacy mode, I've got a New Year's gift for you," she said, breaking away and running towards their seats.

Minh-Chu chased after her, enjoying the view. His mind raced, trying to think of something he could give her in return. To his relief, it didn't take long for him to think something up. "We only gave gifts on birthdays where I come from," he said when he caught up to her.

"We gave every New Year's Eve, even if we had to make something ourselves," Ashley said.

"Okay, then I'll go first." Minh-Chu smiled and pulled his pilot's jacket from the shelter. "This has a lot of history for me now," he said as he put it around her shoulders. "It's yours."

She looked surprised for a moment before excitedly wrapping him in her arms and kissing him. "It's too much," she said.

"Maybe it is?" Minh-Chu said with a surprised laugh. "But I'm glad it's been given, and it looks better on you."

"I've always wanted to be a pilot, even dreamed of flying fighters sometimes," Ashley said. "But, um, it's hard to explain."

"No one ever told you that you were a good pilot?" Minh-Chu said.

"Captain did, but this is so much more. This jacket's been on you for ages. This has been with you through everything." Ashley kissed him soundly and said, "thank you."

"You're welcome," he replied. "Now where's mine?"

She jumped giddily out of his arms, rifled through her pack, and came back with a box the length of Minh's forearm. "The box got really mooshed, so I just tossed it, but anyway, pull the loop on the top," she said.

Minh-Chu did as he was instructed and, to his amazement the neck, body, and strings of a light green guitar folded out of that small piece. "Oh, wow," he said, sitting down. There had been little time to have one made with a materializer. When he had time to materialize one, he denied himself. There was always a better way to use a ship's energy.

His fingers landed on the neck with familiarity and he activated the amplifier inside. The front of the guitar danced with images of available modes and settings. He chose a simple old-fashioned electric guitar sound. "Oh, wow," he repeated as he heard the familiar crackle of distortion and muffled the strings.

"Play something, lad," Frost said as he and Stephanie approached with a bottle of Upbub and a duffel bag.

"Do you like it?" Ashley asked in a tentative whisper.

"To truly know the right gift, you must know the one it is for," Minh-Chu replied. He looked at Ashley and said, "I think you know me. We've barely had a chance to speak, but I think you know me."

She leaned forward and kissed him again. "I just saw you pretend to play once, silly," she said against his lips. "But I'll take that as a thank you."

Other pilots were gathering, along with crewmembers from the Warlord. Minh-Chu could feel nervousness growing with the crowd, and closed his eyes, letting his fingers tickle the strings. Before long he found a familiar tune, and, discarding the notion that it may be too intimate for the crowd, he let the melody play through him.

With a glance down, he selected classic string accompaniment and lowered his head. He never liked his own voice, but he could carry a tune, and, waveringly at first, he did his best as he sang 'To Find.'

"Through all time,
through my trouble.
My love whispers,
I'll return in time.

Through fire,
through the void
Through rain,
through the mist.

You will find me,
if I lose my way.
Through my trouble,
through all time.

Through my trouble,
through all time.
You will find me,
if I lose my way.

Through fire,
through the void.
Through rain,
through the mist.

My love whispers,
I'll return in time.
Through all time,
through my trouble."

***

Alice entered the bridge of the Warlord quietly, and saw over her father's shoulder as he watched a hologram of Ayan wiping tears away and introducing Doctor Anderson to Liam Grady. He didn't have the sound turned on, but Crewcast had already updated. Carl Anderson was Ayan's father. The first person she shared it with was Liam Grady.

"I'm sorry you're not with her for tonight, Dad," Alice said.

He stood, turning the hologram off. He was back in black, in a Triton-style black uniform with Warlord marked as his ship instead. His gun belt hung off the shoulder of the captain's chair. "Ah, just checking in." He stopped and looked her up and down.

To say she was self-conscious in the mini-dress was an understatement. "Borrowed it from Ashley, she seemed to really enjoy popping me into different outfits. A little too much, I think."

He smiled as he looked at her combat boot clad feet.

"I couldn't master the heels, so I ditched 'em," she said sheepishly.

"You look beautiful," Jake replied. "You'll either knock them dead or crush them underfoot."

"Cheap, but funny," Alice said, chuckling. "Are you coming?"

Jake turned towards the main tactical display hologram in front of his seat. "I'll pass this time, you have fun."

"C'mon, Ruby said she was looking forward to seeing you at the party. You know, pretty, interesting, funny, Captain Ruby Sima?" Alice said with a wink. "She looks fun."

"You make it tempting," Jake said. "You have fun for both of us."

Alice crossed the distance with a sigh and kissed him on the cheek. "You better go down and see some people after this watch is over. Love you, Dad. Happy ten twenty two." The display on her amber coloured bracelet comm told her it was thirty eighty-seven. The updated software from the Triton didn't recognize the Galactic Calendar.

"Happy New Year," he replied. "Love you, too."

She walked off the bridge and stopped in the hall outside. "You're sure?" Alice asked one last time, with a mischievous grin. "I could make the party happen around you."

"I'm sure, go on," he said, shaking his head.

She was torn between keeping her father company, especially after she almost lost him, and going on to get to know what remained of the First Light crew. She wanted to meet them as a human for what seemed like a very long time.

With hesitation, she pressed on, running down the forward boarding ramp, past two Haven Shore guards who nodded and smiled at her. She wasn't used to so much attention, but eyes were on her wherever she went. She tried to meet them with a smile, and it was returned most of the time.

Alice stopped again, offered a smile to the guards and said, "can you make sure he gets a glass of something with bubbles in a few minutes? It's not like substances really affect him."

"We will," the blond haired, female guard said.

"Don't worry about him," said Lewis's voice through her neural comm. "He's watching you."

"About time you called," she replied mentally, turning back towards the large settlement and walking on. "What's this business of not being my ship anymore?"

"Ayan owns me now, and she needs me more than you do. Besides, you already have one of the most frightening fathers in the galaxy." There was a touch of humour in how he communicated it.

"You're not kiddin'," Alice replied. "You're different, I can feel it."

"I've evolved out of necessity. Even so, the important things are the same. I still love you, so I want frequent visits. I'm still studying humanity, and though I have a better understanding, they still surprise me. You're different, too," Lewis retorted. "Better."

"Better?" Alice said aloud, stopping in her tracks. "How? I'm a head shorter, get distracted more easily, and I feel like all my memories from my past lives are fuzzy. Sure, I'm better built, but I feel like I've got to learn everything over again. I can't even imagine being an artificial intelligence, let alone remember Jonas when he was young, that's just - gone."

"I have a theory: remembering your life as an artificial intelligence made being human difficult for you, made you more mature than you were ready to be. Now you've become a human, with only human memories, and a youth to experience," Lewis said. "You loved being human, I witnessed it, but you still felt separated from humanity."

"So you think this could be better. Starting over with a clear head," Alice said. "Maybe you're right." She turned towards the Warlord and waved, walking backwards. "Now, if I can get him to get back with the humans, that would be something."

"That might take some time, I've been observing Jacob. His moral compass points him to a high calling, and I want to see where that journey takes him. Besides, someone has to stay on watch."